MW01088954

Rogue TRADER

THE OMNIBUS

More Warhammer 40,000 from Black Library

DARK IMPERIUM
Guy Haley

LEGACY OF THE WULFEN
Robbie MacNiven and David Annandale

AZRAEL
Gav Thorpe

THE DEVASTATION OF BAAL
Guy Haley

THE TALON OF HORUS
Aaron Dembski-Bowden

CADIA STANDS
Justin D Hill

THE HORUSIAN WARS: RESURRECTION
John French

SISTERS OF BATTLE: THE OMNIBUS
James Swallow

THE EYE OF MEDUSA
David Guymer

FARSIGHT: CRISIS OF FAITH
Phil Kelly

RISE OF THE YNNARI: GHOST WARRIOR
Gav Thorpe

I AM SLAUGHTER
Dan Abnett

HORUS RISING
Dan Abnett

WARHAMMER 40,000

Rogue TRADER

THE OMNIBUS

ANDY HOARE

A BLACK LIBRARY PUBLICATION

Rogue Star first published in 2006.
Star of Damocles first published in 2007.
Savage Scars first published in 2011.
'Cold Trade' first published in 2013.
'Ambition Knows No Bounds' first published in 2010.
This edition published in Great Britain in 2018 by
Black Library,
Games Workshop Ltd.,
Willow Road,
Nottingham, NG7 2WS, UK.

10 9 8 7 6 5 4 3 2 1

Produced by Games Workshop in Nottingham.
Cover illustration by Imaginary Friends Studios.

Rogue Trader: The Omnibus © Copyright Games Workshop Limited 2018. Rogue Trader: The Omnibus, GW, Games Workshop, Black Library, The Horus Heresy, The Horus Heresy Eye logo, Space Marine, 40K, Warhammer, Warhammer 40,000, the 'Aquila' Double-headed Eagle logo, and all associated logos, illustrations, images, names, creatures, races, vehicles, locations, weapons, characters, and the distinctive likenesses thereof, are either ® or TM, and/or © Games Workshop Limited, variably registered around the world.
All Rights Reserved.

A CIP record for this book is available from the British Library.

ISBN 13: 978 1 78496 681 2

No part of this publication may be reproduced, stored in a retrieval system, or transmitted in any form or by any means, electronic, mechanical, photocopying, recording or otherwise, without the prior permission of the publishers.

This is a work of fiction. All the characters and events portrayed in this book are fictional, and any resemblance to real people or incidents is purely coincidental.

See Black Library on the internet at

blacklibrary.com

Find out more about Games Workshop and the world of Warhammer 40,000 at

games-workshop.com

Printed and bound by CPI Group (UK) Ltd, Croydon, CR0 4YY

It is the 41st millennium. For more than a hundred centuries the Emperor has sat immobile on the Golden Throne of Earth. He is the Master of Mankind by the will of the gods, and master of a million worlds by the might of His inexhaustible armies. He is a rotting carcass writhing invisibly with power from the Dark Age of Technology. He is the Carrion Lord of the Imperium for whom a thousand souls are sacrificed every day, so that He may never truly die.

Yet even in His deathless state, the Emperor continues His eternal vigilance. Mighty battlefleets cross the daemon-infested miasma of the warp, the only route between distant stars, their way lit by the Astronomican, the psychic manifestation of the Emperor's will. Vast armies give battle in His name on uncounted worlds. Greatest amongst His soldiers are the Adeptus Astartes, the Space Marines, bioengineered super-warriors. Their comrades in arms are legion: the Astra Militarum and countless planetary defence forces, the ever-vigilant Inquisition and the tech-priests of the Adeptus Mechanicus to name only a few. But for all their multitudes, they are barely enough to hold off the ever-present threat from aliens, heretics, mutants – and worse.

To be a man in such times is to be one amongst untold billions. It is to live in the cruellest and most bloody regime imaginable. These are the tales of those times. Forget the power of technology and science, for so much has been forgotten, never to be re-learned. Forget the promise of progress and understanding, for in the grim dark future there is only war. There is no peace amongst the stars, only an eternity of carnage and slaughter, and the laughter of thirsting gods.

CONTENTS

ROGUE STAR

CHAPTER 1

'Helm, seven degrees pitch to starboard! Number three's misbehaving again. Deal with it.'

Lucian Gerrit, rogue trader, turned his back on Raldi, his helmsman and resumed his vigil at the bridge viewing port. His vessel, the heavy cruiser *Oceanid,* felt cold to him. The after-effect, he knew, of so long a voyage through the empyrean to reach this far-flung system at the very border of the Emperor's domains.

A jarring shudder ran through the deck plate, felt in the bones more than heard.

'If you can't compensate for a grizzling plasma drive, Mister Raldi, I can always disconnect one of the waste ingestion servitors and see if it's capable of making a better show of it than you appear to be. Do I make myself clear?'

If the helmsman answered, Lucian wasn't in the mood to hear. Though a ship to be proud of, the *Oceanid* was long past her prime. Even in a space-faring culture in which vessels remained in service for centuries, even millennia, she was old. Her homeport, Ariadne Halo, had fallen to alien attack in Lucian's great, great grandfather's time. All her sister ships were distant memories. She was the last of a long line. Much like Lucian himself, in fact.

Where once a deck crew of dozens had attended to their stations in the crew pit, now half of Lucian's crew were hard-wired servitors, each mumbling an impenetrable catechism of the Machine-God. Vacant-eyed and drooling, each monitored a single aspect of the vessel's running. Vessels such as the *Oceanid* relied on their like, for many tasks were beyond the abilities of a man to perform. Yet, over the years, the availability and quality of competent crewmen had diminished to such an extent that Lucian was forced to rely on servitors. Though essential in many roles, the hideous machine-corpse custodians were no substitute for a man when it came to obeying orders in a crisis. Each knew only its allotted purpose, and would remain tethered uncaring to its station even were it to burst into flames.

Raldi, one of the men of flesh and blood, rather than carrion and oil, onboard the *Oceanid*, called out. 'Sir, we're beginning our run on the rendezvous point. Provided we don't pick up any ionisation we should be within hailing range.'

'Well enough, helm. Keep her even.'

Once more, Lucian took in the view beyond the armoured port. The nameless star, recorded merely as QX-445-2 on the star charts, cast its wan light, barely illuminating a thick corona of misty stellar dust. Somewhere within that befogged region lay Lucian's destination, the system's only inhabited world: Mundus Chasmata.

Before making planetfall on that forgotten backwater of a port, however, Lucian had first to gather about him his flotilla. The cruisers *Rosetta* and *Fairlight* were due to enter range at any moment, but any number of fates could have befallen them whilst traversing the unreal dimension known as the warp. The least of such fates was delay; the worst was too terrible to ponder.

'Surveyor return at three twenty by nine sir!' called a junior rating.

Lucian strode to his command throne and sat, reclining in the worn leather seat from which generations of his predecessors had directed the fortunes of the dynasty.

'Punch it up.'

A servitor, its eye sockets replaced by data ports from which bundles of cable snaked and writhed, bobbed its head once in response. Half its cranium was replaced by cybernetic implants, the right side of its brain, associated with creativity and emotion, having been cut away, deemed unnecessary by its creators. At an unheard command, the bridge lights dimmed and a revolving green globe of light, criss-crossed by motes of static, sprang into being before the command throne.

Grainy points of light resolved themselves into distinct features. At the hologram's centre sat the *Oceanid*, all around her banks of pale green and jade stellar dust clouds. Deep within one such bank the position of Mundus Chasmata was indicated by a crosshair, her moons dancing around her. To the *Oceanid*'s stern, an indistinct smear indicated the distant return.

'All engines to idle. Fore thrusters to best speed. Thirty-second burn on my mark.'

Lucian's words were relayed through the deck crew to the entire ship. Within seconds, the omnipresent rumble of the *Oceanid*'s engines changed pitch, deepening to a subsonic drone as sweating engineering crews nursed them to idle.

'Mark.'

A mournful siren pealed throughout the vessel, echoing down dark and dingy companionways. The mighty banks of retro thrusters mounted either side of the armoured prow coughed into life. The titanic force of the deceleration caused Lucian's head to pitch forward. Raldi barely won his fight to remain standing.

'Station nine! Why aren't the compensators on line?'

The servitor at station nine, the position responsible for monitoring the *Oceanid*'s gravitic generators, opened its mouth and squealed a response in garbled machine language. The engine pitch deepened and the bridge lights flickered before Lucian felt the gravity field fluctuate, compensating for the deceleration.

'Better,' growled Lucian.

The retro thrusters ended their burn, and with the main plasma drives idling, the *Oceanid* was eerily quiet. Previously unheard, the groaning and creaking of the ship's metal skeleton was now plainly audible.

'Station keeping please, helm,' ordered Lucian, and stood once more, hands clasped behind his back. Now the vessel was still, the hologram grew clearer. Where a single, garbled return had indicated the presence of another ship, or ships, that blob now resolved itself into five, then four, then two distinct points. Hard machine language yammered from the baroque grilles around the base of the projector, and in a moment, a stream of text flowed beside each of the two points. The noise ended at the same instant the text froze. The word '*Rosetta*' flashed next to the lead return; '*Fairlight*' next to the second.

Lucian released a breath that no one other than himself would have known he was holding. Though the last leg of their voyage had been upon a relatively safe course, warp travel between systems was rarely without incident. That both vessels had evidently arrived simultaneously was testament to the skills of their Navigators, for time within the warp bore little or no relation to that within the physical universe. Every mariner, from the most veteran of ships' masters to the lowliest rating, was well versed in the tales of ships setting out, to arrive at their destination mere weeks later yet having aged decades. Other tales told of vessels that had arrived many centuries late, having spent mere days within the warp, while others still told of vessels arriving before having even set out. The life of a space mariner was one filled with superstition and ritual: they clung with nigh religious fervour to anything that might belay such bad luck.

'Station three, open a channel to *Rosetta*.'

The servitor at the communications station croaked a vaguely human-sounding response, and angry static flooded the bridge address system. Machine noise broke through the static, a random staccato that would establish a secure communications channel synchronised with the systems of the other vessel. A second series of harsh bleeps cut in, the two streams flooding the bridge with arrhythmic machine nonsense. The servitor at station three turned a brass dial, and the two code streams converged until they burbled and gargled in synchronisation.

'*...id.* Repeat, this is *Rosetta* hailing *Oceanid*. Holding station at primary rendezvous point, awaiting your response. Repeat, this is–'

'Glad you could make it, Korvane,' Lucian addressed his son, the master of the *Rosetta*, 'I trust your journey was a pleasant one?'

A moment's delay hinted at the still vast distance between the ships, before Korvane's voice broke through the static.

'Yes, Father. No major problems to report. The new loading crew gave us some trouble as we translated, but once they realised they weren't going home, they relented. Otherwise, a very smooth journey.'

'Good. You know how much is hanging on this mission. Any more problems, you know what to do, out.'

'Station three. Give me a channel to *Fairlight*.'

The connection established; a new voice cut through the ever-present static and whine of the long-range communication channel. It was that of Brielle, Lucian's daughter, and captain of the *Fairlight*.

'*Fairlight*, receiving. Go ahead, Father.'

'Anything to report, Brielle?'

There was a pause as the transmission beamed across a million kilometres of space, and then the simple reply, 'No, Father. The voyage was pleasantly uneventful.'

'Good.' Addressing both ships, Lucian said, 'You both know how important the coming negotiations are, so I want this to go without a hitch. We begin our final approach as planned. Form up in echelon to starboard, fifty kilometres separation for the run, down to one on my mark as we close. We have to make this look good. Brielle, follow your brother in as we practised. Do you both understand?'

His son replied immediately in the affirmative, but Lucian felt his daughter's terse reply took longer than the communications lag would account for.

The channel closed, Lucian left Raldi with orders to proceed on their course inbound to Mundus Chasmata. Leaving the bridge, he made for his cabin. He passed down ill-lit passageways that had once shone with light reflected from polished brass fittings. In his youth, smartly attired junior officers had hurried along these very companionways, eager to fulfil the captain's orders; but all that had changed.

For millennia, the Arcadius Dynasty, of which Lucian was the latest scion, had penetrated the darkness of the Eastern Rim. His ancestor, the great Lord Arcadius Maxim Gerrit, had earned the favour of none other than the High Lords of the Administratum. His leadership during the Easthead Nebula Crusade was rewarded with a charter to explore and exploit the black spaces on the star charts, to bring the light of the Emperor to the benighted worlds beyond the borders of the Imperium. It was well known that the charter was intended to remove the Lord Arcadius from the circles of power that orbited the High Lords of Terra, lest his successes afford him ambitions incompatible with those of the Administratum, but Maxim was ever a pragmatic man, and established a dynasty that would flourish for the next three thousand years.

The dynasty had hit hard times. Its traditional area of operation beyond the eastern spiral arm had rapidly become untenable. Lucian was in the business of trading, of exploitation, yet where once virgin worlds awaited his vessels, only barren, lifeless planets were to be found. Something was out there, feeding on regions that the Arcadius Dynasty depended upon for its very future.

Reaching his cabin, Lucian heaved open the heavy bulkhead door that would have been attended by a young rating, once. He entered and crossed to an ornately carved, wooden cabinet. Opening its exquisite hatch, he withdrew a small glass and a bottle of thick, golden liquid. He poured himself a shot and knocked it back in one motion. Lucian had little time for the affectations of high society, amongst which amasec was the drink of the so-called connoisseur. Rogue traders, being a unique breed, followed their own heading, and the Arcadius suffered pretension poorly. The coming negotiations would test Lucian's skills and, he knew, his patience, to the limit.

After pouring a second shot of asuave, Lucian crossed to his wardrobe. The coming talks would call not only for diplomatic and trading skills, but also for a display of status. At his approach, a hunch-backed and calliper-limbed servitor glided silently from the shadows, and a baroque-framed mirror as tall as Lucian rose from its hidden recess in the deck. Lucian shrugged off his outer jacket and lifted his chin. The servitor lifted a polished, deep crimson gorget edged with burnished gold, fitting it around Lucian's neck and fastening it across his back. Next, a heavy breastplate was attached, followed by the accompanying back armour. With the addition of similarly burnished leg, arm and shoulder guards, Lucian soon stood arrayed in his ancestral finery.

He regarded himself in the mirror. He was tall at over six feet, powerfully built and heavy set. His face showed age, but few ever guessed his years. As was ever the case with those who spent a lifetime traversing the space lanes, Lucian counted two ages. His objective age, that counted by the ever-constant universe was something approaching half a millennia. His subjective age, the years he actually noted the passing of, was one fifth that. Still, he appeared no older than half a century, for despite the downturn in his fortunes, he had access to surgical treatments about which the common subjects of the Imperium could only dream. Regular juvenat courses held back the years and maintained strength, ensuring that he would guide his dynasty through another century at least, so long as the Arcadius survived the next decade.

His familial armour donned, Lucian nodded as the servitor bowed and lifted before him a delicately carved, wooden case. Lucian would allow none other to handle the contents. Not even his children, until their inheritance granted them that right.

As he laid his hand upon the lid of the case, cunningly wrought gene locks confirmed his identity with a rapid pinprick. Had they detected the blood of anyone other than a son or daughter of his line, deadly poisons would, even now, be surging through his system, cutting synapses and paralysing nerves.

With the lifting of the lid, the stasis field within the case deactivated. He lifted the first of the contents: a medal in the form of a shining star, its surface inlaid with the rarest of precious metals. It was The Ward of Cadia; granted to his grandfather, in recognition of the aid he had leant halting an incursion through the Cadian Gate.

He affixed the gleaming medal to his breastplate and, reaching once more within the box, withdrew a green disc inlaid with golden filigree. The Order of Voss, awarded to his father by the tech-priests of that great forge world in thanks for his aiding their Titan Legions in defence against ork attack.

Next, was a medal of very different design and manufacture, presented to Lucian himself by the White Scars Chapter of the Adeptus Astartes, in recognition for his assistance in the purging of the xenos presence beneath the tunnel world of Arat. It was a hand-carved representation of a snarling, bestial face, a stylised lightning flash bisecting its features.

Half a dozen more gleaming tokens of mighty deeds followed, each afforded their place upon his armour with utmost honour and reverence until but one remained.

Lucian's hand slowed as he reached once more into the case. Even he was given pause by the significance of the last item. Whispering a prayer, he reached within and brought out the pride of his dynasty. Only the Charter of Trade and the banner presented to the dynasty by the Senatorum Imperialis could equal this medal in worth. Awarded to Maxim Gerrit by the High Lords of Terra themselves, for his display of epic leadership as well as personal courage at the height of the Eastlight Nebula Crusade, Lucian lifted the winged medal of the Order of Ollanius Pius. Bearing the golden face of an angelic youth, laurel leaves arrayed across his noble brow, the medal represented the very highest honour a mortal man could earn in the service of the Imperium. Intricate scrollwork beneath the beatific visage bore an inscription:

'Amid the weeping and the woe,
Accursed Daemon remain and rot,
I know thee filthy as thou art,
I know.'

The words sent a shiver up Lucian's spine, for they spoke of things few men were allowed to know, but his position at the head of his dynasty granted him knowledge that the authorities had few means of barring from him. For most, daemons were the terrifying creatures of nightmares. Real, most certainly, but kept at bay by prayer and the eternal vigilance of the God-Emperor of Mankind. For the likes of Lucian Gerrit, they were the denizens of the empyrean, for vessels such as his must intrude into their realm when travelling between the stars.

The medals affixed to Lucian's crowded breastplate, the servitor appeared once more. It bore a mighty cloak of luxurious fur. The snarling head of a beast of terrible aspect was mounted upon his right shoulder, its huge fore-claws draped across his back and over his left shoulder.

Lastly, he opened an armoured hatch upon the wall. He brought out an antique leather belt. Attached to it was a pair of ornate holsters. The first held a heavy, blunt-nosed pistol, a plasma weapon created for his line by the famed master artificer Ernst Heckler, impossibly intricate devotional text carved upon its every surface.

Lucian lifted the weapon, activating it with the press of a stud and savouring the rapidly rising, near ultrasonic whine that indicated that the weapon's war spirit was content. The second weapon was of unknown manufacture, a pistol-sized device of pure crystal. Violet and blue lights danced within as he hefted it. He knew not who or what had constructed the bizarre weapon, but on many occasions had had cause to thank their skill. The weapon unleashed a blinding ray that interfered with its target's brain functions, reducing him to a gibbering imbecile in seconds; very useful in some of the places Lucian had visited.

He then slid onto his fingers a series of rings, each a cunningly wrought, miniature laser weapon. With luck, such weapons would not be required, but few authorities in the galaxy, short of an Inquisitor Lord or Space Marine Chapter Master, would presume to demand a rogue trader divest himself of his arms. Given the dynasty's standing, he would expect that even they would do so politely.

He regarded himself in the mirror one last time, before striding from the cabin. He would take to his command throne and guide the *Oceanid*, and with her, the Arcadius Dynasty, to a bright, new future.

The rogue trader flotilla slid through banks of pale green stellar dust, flashes of lightning illuminating them from deep within. Such regions were the stuff of space mariners' superstitions, for they awoke primal notions, the fear of the unknown, and of 'things' lurking in the mist. The vessels navigated by dead reckoning alone, for their augur banks were useless amidst the thick cloud. It was all too easy to become jittery, reflected Lucian, for the surveyor reported all manner of weird returns. Ghostlights they were often called, for they would appear solid and real one moment, only to fade to nothing the next.

Communications too, were troublesome in such a region. Where the cloud thinned, short range, line of sight transmission was possible, but psychic communication was by far more efficient, except that the vessel's telepath was near incapacitated at present: burnt-out, Lucian suspected. The guild had so far been unwilling to replace him, a sore point that would need addressing once the current crisis was resolved.

Lucian watched as the cloud thinned, the system's star penetrating the green murk. The dust parted, and the *Oceanid* glided clear, gases swirling at her passing. The view from the bridge was suddenly one of clear space, Mundus Chasmata visible as a black disc eclipsing its star.

Lucian stood, savouring the moment as he prepared to hail

Mundus Chasmata's outer defence monitor. He glanced at the surveyor, certain in the knowledge that his son and daughter would be ordering their vessels into formation astern of his own. Two returns indicated they were. Behind them, however, four more returns flashed an angry red. They were set upon a headlong dive towards the *Rosetta* as she emerged from the cloud, their course indicating but one possible motive: attack!

'General quarters!' bellowed Lucian as he took to the command throne. Sirens wailed and the bridge lights flickered off, to be replaced an instant later by the red glow of the emergency lights employed during battle. Lucian wondered how the hell raiders had found his flotilla in deep space. Were they betrayed so soon? He would have to deal with them first, and worry about the details later.

'Helm, on my mark, all engines to ten per cent, new heading thirty to starboard. Comms, give me a channel to my fleet.'

The address system chimed to indicate the channel was open. Korvane's voice burst forth. '...ur of them one fifty to port, contact in nine. I could do with some help here.'

'Do as I say, both of you. On my signal, Korvane, power up and come about to forty-five degrees to starboard. Brielle, maintain your current speed and come about to forty-five to your port. Do you both understand?'

Both Korvane and Brielle indicated they understood their father's instructions. He glanced down at the surveyor screen, paused, and calmly ordered: 'Mark!'

The compensators cut in an instant late, as the *Oceanid* decelerated. Raldi simultaneously veered the ship to starboard. The surveyor tracked the *Rosetta* as she increased her speed, crossing the *Fairlight*'s bow with the four raiders in pursuit. Viewed from the bridge, the manoeuvre was a stately affair, but Lucian knew, a potentially deadly one.

The graceful manoeuvre brought the *Oceanid* to the attackers' eight o'clock, and the *Fairlight* to their four.

'Starboard battery aft! Open fire on lead target!'

Below decks, the mighty weapons bank locked onto its target: the fast-moving raider closing in on the position the *Rosetta* had occupied minutes before. The master of the smaller vessel evidently saw his coming fate, but a moment too late. The battery erupted in blinding fire, launching huge, high-explosive projectiles across the gulf of space.

Lucian watched on the surveyor screen as the raider pitched to starboard, a last desperate attempt to avoid the *Oceanid*'s wrath. It failed, as Lucian had seen it would. The salvo struck the smaller vessel amidships, robbing it of forward momentum with such violence that it split into two, its entire prow tumbling forwards whilst its drive section sheered off at forty-five degrees. Even at this distance, the spectacle was impressive, as the plasma core at the heart of the engine cluster went critical, creating a second sun for a moment.

Lucian winced as the explosion flooded his bridge with harsh white light, the viewing port dimming a moment later to compensate. When his vision had cleared, he looked out once more to see the *Fairlight* opening fire upon the second raider, but this vessel recovered far more quickly than its recently deceased comrade had, evading its former prey with ease.

A veteran of a hundred such skirmishes, Lucian read the raiders' manoeuvres with practiced ease. His redeployment had caught them at the moment they had anticipated easy victory, but their captains were not fools. Even now, they were rallying, recovering from the shock of their prey's counter-attack. They were coming about for a second attack run. Lucian performed a mental calculation: three raider frigates, probably up-gunned, certainly up-armoured, and therefore slower and less manoeuvrable than would ordinarily be the case; and his own vessels: a heavy cruiser and two light cruisers. Under normal circumstances, his small flotilla would have little to fear, but all three of the rogue trader vessels were running at reduced capacity, the sad result of the dynasty's deteriorating fortunes. Now of all times, he could not afford damage to his precious vessels.

His decision reached, Lucian addressed his offspring.

'Korvane, Brielle, as much as I'd savour the opportunity to smear these motherless bastards across space, we have more important matters to attend to. You both set course for the Mundus Chasmata primary at best speed. I'll lead them on to the outer platform. Do you understand?'

Korvane was first to answer. 'Aye, Father, I agree. We are best served reaching Chasmata intact.'

'Brielle?'

'Father, we can take them here. I'll hold back and draw them onto your guns. It should only take a single–'

'You will not!' shouted Lucian, surging to his feet at his daughter's defiance. 'You will set course for Mundus Chasmata Primary as ordered! Do I make myself clear?'

His daughter did not reply, but Lucian had his answer as he saw the *Fairlight* move to come around as per his instructions. Grunting, he sat once more.

Lucian waited until he was satisfied that both Korvane and Brielle were following his orders, before addressing his bridge.

'On my signal, power down to ten per cent, and burn port retros at full for fifteen.' Raldi turned his head and opened his mouth as if to speak, but decided against protesting upon meeting Lucian's glare.

The *Oceanid* shuddered violently as the portside retro thrusters ignited, forestalling the vessel's forward motion and slowly bringing her to starboard. The first of the raiders passed, overtaking Lucian's cruiser before its own captain had time to react. Lucian knew that it would have to enter a long, wide arc in order to circle back: it was out of the fight for some time at least.

The second raider did react to the *Oceanid*'s ungainly manoeuvre, but its captain had evidently misread Lucian's intentions. Rather than compensating for the course change with a similar move, this raider veered to port, the master fearing perhaps that the heavy cruiser sought to entrap him as she had his erstwhile compatriot. The ill-judged reaction cost the raider vessel dear, for she too would be out of the fight while she came about to intersect the *Oceanid*'s course.

The last raider altered her course, finding herself bearing down on the wallowing *Oceanid*. Its forward weapons batteries opened fire, catching the *Oceanid* a glancing blow across the dorsal shields.

'Station six! How are we holding?' Station six was manned not by a servitor, but by a man, though the rating sported so many cybernetic implants that the external difference was minimal. Lucian reasoned that the shields were generally only needed in an emergency, and had learned through bitter experience that an Emperor-fearing man reacted to orders far better than a servitor under such circumstances, benefiting as he did from a sense of self-preservation that the servitor lacked.

'Nothing she can't handle sir, though the feedback caused some casualties in coil chamber beta.'

Lucian wasted no time in mourning the press-ganged scum that toiled in the depths of his vessel. Most would have been executed long ago had not their sentences been commuted to his service.

'Well enough six. Helm, come about to three nine three and all ahead full! Go!'

The *Oceanid* shook as the full power of her plasma reactor was fed to her drive systems. She soon outdistanced the first two raiders to pass her, and only the third remained, though closing, astern.

Lucian activated the holograph, focusing on an area of space only a few thousand kilometres ahead. He saw what he was looking for.

'Helm, we're coming up on Chasmata's outer defence platform. At five hundred, yaw thirty so she passes us to port at around fifty.'

A shudder travelled up the length of the vessel, as the raider dogging her stern unleashed a second volley. Lucian looked up, meeting the eye of the man at station six.

'Holding, sir, for now.'

'Good. Comms, signal the platform. Let them know who we are. Now would be a bad time for a misunderstanding.'

As the *Oceanid* ploughed on, the defence platform came into view off the port bow. Though not much larger than the rogue trader vessel, the platform bristled with weaponry, from lance batteries to torpedo tubes. The comms servitor had evidently succeeded in transmitting the correct signal. Had it not, those batteries of fearsome destruction would have been opening fire on the *Oceanid*.

Instead, they opened fire on the raider. The captain of the raiding frigate was so intent upon his prey that he could not have seen his death approaching. It came quickly, in the form of a mighty broadside, macro cannon shells obliterating the smaller vessel in the blink of an eye.

Lucian glanced down at the surveyor to see the rapidly fading debris field spread across the screen. The last two raiders, visible as indistinct returns at the screen's edge, turned tail and bolted.

'Get me a drink,' he ordered no one in particular.

Mundus Chasmata's primary orbital dock filled the bridge viewing port. The three vessels had formed up as they closed on the planet, presenting a stately procession worthy of the Arcadius Dynasty. Lucian had awaited the customary picket escort any rogue trader would expect from the port authorities of such a world, but had been mildly surprised and not a little put out when none had appeared.

As the ships closed on the vast, slab-sided orbital dock, its aged condition became apparent. Lucian had visited many such installations, often in a similar state of disrepair, but he thought this one appeared somehow more dilapidated than normal. The armoured skin of the multiple, interconnected domes was pockmarked by centuries of micrometeorite impacts, and entire sections had evidently fallen into disuse. One docking limb appeared entirely open to space, its hatches hanging as if creaking in a non-existent wind.

Not only was the absence of an escort notable, but Lucian's practiced eye took in every detail of the dock and its environs. All six docking limbs were devoid of craft. No freighters, no system defence boats, no tankers, troop transports or ships of any type were tethered to the station's multiple docking points. No service craft or tugs went about the endless maintenance tasks any other station would demand. No shuttles transported goods and passengers back and forth between the dock and the surface.

This far out on the borders of the Imperium's space, Lucian would have expected some degree of neglect, but not so much, he reflected with growing unease, that the locals would not be sent into a frenzy of activity at a pirate attack so close to their capital.

As the *Oceanid* came alongside the station, Raldi expertly guiding the heavy cruiser to within a mere twenty metres of the allotted docking arm, mighty docking clamps reached out to grasp her. The metallic clang echoed through the vessel as cursing crew chiefs harangued press-ganged crews to make her fast. The *Oceanid* became a hive of activity as Lucian prepared to go ashore. The talks would have to wait; his flotilla had been attacked. A fine welcome to the Eastern Rim, he thought.

CHAPTER TWO

The airlock portal swung open, acrid gases venting from corroded grilles with an angry hiss. Lucian stepped through, and set foot upon the Mundus Chasmata orbital primary. The hall ran the length of the docking limb, airlocks identical to that he had just exited situated at regular points along its length. The occasional longshoreman went about his business, but where Lucian would expect to be confronted with heaving crowds of dockers, an eerie quiet was all he found.

The deck below his feet was rusted and uneven, and heavy chains dripping with toxic run-off swung, unused, from the high, vaulted ceiling. His footsteps echoed the length of the hall, and the lighting flickered erratically. The stink of sewage and pollution assaulted him. He had smelled worse, he reflected, but not outside of the grave-mires of Quillik V.

A high-pressure hiss and a tortured, metallic squeal sounded from the far end of the hall. As banks of gases cleared, Lucian caught sight of him. Although outwardly his father's son, Korvane carried himself entirely differently, his mannerisms those of his mother's people: studied and reserved, haughty and cold.

'Father,' Korvane bowed stiffly at Lucian's approach. 'I greet you with glad heart.'

Ignoring the formality of Korvane's greeting, Lucian embraced his son in a vigorous bear hug, causing the younger man to stumble as his feet were lifted from the deck. He had not set eyes upon either of his children in long months.

'Glad heart indeed. Are you well?'

'I am well, Father. I spent the bulk of the last leg studying the archives. Chasmata's ruling class has a fascinating range of ceremonies. We would do well to remain on our guard around these people.'

'Huh,' Lucian grunted. 'You're new to this business son, so I'll give you the benefit of the doubt. I've engaged in talks with men and with abominations, and there's only two ways of dealing with either. You take control of proceedings, blustering your way through as if it's all second nature, or, you keep your eyes open and your mouth shut until the moment comes to take control. How do you think your grandfather got past the Cambro Huthans? How do think old Abad sidestepped the Argent Protocol, or the Hyburian Interdiction?'

Korvane nodded, though he looked far from convinced.

'That's how business gets done out here son, and don't you forget it.' Lucian turned as he heard a second airlock vent its noxious gases into the hall. A figure emerged out of the clouds.

Where Korvane outwardly resembled his father, but mirrored his mother in comportment, Lucian's daughter Brielle was the exact opposite. Although not tall, Brielle carried herself with a confidence bordering on aggression. Her features were brooding and dusky, and she wore her black and purple-dyed hair in the complex braids of her mother's people: the highborn clans of the feral world of Chogoris. Her features were her mother's, but Brielle's manners were akin to Lucian's, for she radiated the same air of professionalism that a rogue trader depended upon to prosper in their hostile world.

However much Lucian loved his daughter, a gulf existed between them. The elder of his offspring, Brielle had been raised to assume the leadership of the Arcadius Dynasty one day. Yet, with times so hard, Lucian had entered into his marriage of convenience with Korvane's mother. It was a business deal; one he had entered as he would any other transaction. Korvane's mother gained the status that marriage into a rogue trader dynasty afforded, and the Arcadius, through Korvane, would, upon her passing come into a substantial inheritance and thus secure their future.

Although the Arcadius would ultimately be saved from slow extinction, Brielle had been robbed of her claim to the leadership of the dynasty. The terms of the marriage demanded that the first male child of the union would inherit both his mother and father's titles, and so Brielle had been passed over in favour of her stepbrother. The two barely spoke, and when they did, it was inevitably in words of remonstration. When angered, Brielle had the temper of her mother's people as well as their looks, and combined with Lucian's directness, tension between the siblings bubbled constantly below the surface.

'Brielle, I'm so glad to see you,' Lucian said. She responded by placing a cold kiss upon his cheek, but showed no sign of familial affection.

Realising that he would get little more from his daughter, Lucian determined to continue regardless. He had a dynasty to save, and no amount of childish sibling petulance would stand in his way.

But before the trio set off for the surface, Lucian intended to pay a visit to the harbour master. Someone would answer for the attack on his vessels, in the supposedly secure inner reaches of an Imperial system.

'What on Sacred Terra do you mean "outside your purview"?'

Lucian, flanked by his offspring, dominated the cramped office of the harbour master of the Mundus Chasmata Orbital – the space station through which all traffic to and from the world's surface had to pass. He loomed over the adept's wide desk, sweeping aside rolled parchments and toppling a stack of cargo manifests. They had arrived unannounced, Lucian pushing his way contemptuously past the attendant who had attempted to inform him that the master would not be receiving callers for another three years at best. If he wanted to expedite the process, the functionary had spluttered, Lucian would need to complete an Application of Extraordinary Exception, in triplicate.

Lucian had insisted, quite forcibly, that the lackey contact his superiors on the surface, before confronting the harbour master himself.

'Our system monitor boat is currently, er, out of system. That you recklessly drew your attacker onto the defence platform's guns is not my responsibility. That platform has not been required to fire its weapons in three centuries, sir. The expended ordnance will be replenished at your expense.'

'Wait a moment.' Lucian was losing patience with the harbour master. 'That my ships were attacked in your system is not your fault, because your system defence boat was not present, defending its system? If I understand correctly, you expect recompense for the shells fired by your system defence platform? Shells fired whilst performing its sacred duty of defending its system?'

'Sir, I suggest you familiarise yourself with the terms of the Pax Chasmatus, chapter seventy-nine, verse one hundred and thirty–'

'Emperor's balls! I've heard eldar make more sense than you! Give me clearance to make planetfall before I do something you might regret.'

'I'm afraid, sir, that I cannot do that. As I said, it is outside my purview. The dictates of the Pax Chasmatus state that you must await the next shuttle. You may not travel to the surface in your own vehicle.'

Suspecting he would not care for the answer, Lucian asked, 'And when is the next shuttle scheduled to arrive?'

'Three months from now. The waiting chamber is located on level Gamma Twelve, Sector Nine, past the containment chambers, on the left.'

Lucian's right hand moved to the holster at his left hip, that holding the, non-lethal, neural disruptor. He thought better of the act, however. His hand moved instead to the, highly lethal, plasma pistol held in the holster at his right hip. Before his hand reached the holster, a metallic chime sounded from a brass grille set into the harbour master's desk.

Cautiously, the man reached across to open the channel. 'Adept Telsi?' He cleared his throat with a nervous cough. 'Go ahead.'

A tinny voice squawked from the grille. It was the harbour master's functionary, and he had received a reply from the message Lucian had insisted he deliver. The hint of a smile appeared at the edge of his mouth.

'I take it the shuttle's schedule is not quite as inflexible as it may at first have appeared?' He leant over the desk once more, making an exaggerated show of tidying the paper strewn across it.

The harbour master bristled at the sight of the rogue trader interfering with his paperwork, but held on to his composure. 'Yes sir, bay Alpha Six, three hours. The waiting chamber is–'

'Past the containment chambers, on the left,' Lucian growled, before turning on the spot and sweeping out of the harbour master's office. Brielle winked at the man and turned to follow her father. Korvane snorted contemptuously and followed them both out.

The descent from orbit took only thirty minutes, and soon the shuttle was screaming through the night skies of Mundus Chasmata. Lucian looked out through the armoured porthole, seeing the distant horizon lit smoky violet in a predawn glow. The shuttle was shabby and ill-maintained. The three rogue traders had been forced to share its sparse passenger compartment with a handful of menials and petty administrators; second assistant-under-deputy clerks, he judged, no doubt returning to the surface following their long, tedious and mind-numbingly boring work rotations aboard the orbital.

As the shuttle crossed the world's terminator line, the landscape below became visible. Although a world of myriad terrain types, from high altitude, sub-zero polar oxide wastes to inland seas of stinking ammonia, the predominant feature of Mundus Chasmata was the deep scars gouged out of its crust in its distant pre-history. These formed kilometres-long, kilometres-deep gullies, although most were little more than a few dozen metres across.

'Wouldn't want to get marooned here,' said Brielle, her statement echoing Lucian's thoughts unerringly. Even if you survived a crash, he knew, you'd never make it to civilisation. The densely packed chasms would claim anyone foolish enough to attempt crossing them.

Korvane had been poring over a data-slate, which he now handed to his father. Across its monochrome green and black screen scrolled reams of data. Every detail from average rainfall to import/export figures was covered. Lucian called up a summary.

The world of Mundus Chasmata was colonised, the data-slate reported, at an unrecorded date prior to the thirty-third millennium. That hardly surprised Lucian, for most such civilisations he had visited predated the Imperium of Man by many thousands of years, although few records preserved any more details than the name of a founding dynasty. The world's population was just over the one billion mark, a figure consistent with many similar worlds. Lucian had visited agri-worlds farmed by machines whose human populations were counted in the hundreds, and hive worlds where billions crowded into kilometres-high spires. The Imperium was nothing if not diverse.

The system's location at the borders of human space put it at risk of alien predation, and this far out it could count little on aid arriving in time to save it in the event of attack. Aside from the irregular visits of lone Imperial Navy vessels on long-ranged patrol, Mundus Chasmata could look only to itself for defence. One in ten adults were therefore required to serve in the world's Planetary Defence Force, an institution that had, on four recorded occasions in the last three centuries provided troops for the Imperial Guard.

More text streamed across the data-slate's screen. Mundus Chasmata vied with its neighbour Arris Epsilon, located at the opposite extreme of the Timbra subsector, for what little trade the region would support. The planets of this lonely area were, by necessity it appeared, largely self-sufficient. They had little contact with the Imperium, and little to offer it in terms of resources. That was what made the planet's ruler's offer too promising to pass up.

A hereditary noble class, purporting to have its roots in the world's founding, ruled Mundus Chasmata, the Luneberg family, headed by the present Imperial Commander, Culpepper Luneberg the Twenty-ninth, lording over their world as a private fiefdom. Indeed, so long as they paid the Imperium its tithes once in every generation, that was exactly what it was. Mundus Chasmata appeared to be the perfect place to do business of the type that the Imperium at large might not look upon too kindly.

As the shuttle banked over Chasmata Capitalis, the world's first city and its seat of government, dawn broke. The light was the colour of honeyed gold and high clouds of deep red scudded across the sky.

The city sat at the centre of a wide, flat plain; Lucian had seen similar sights, and hazarded an informed, if unsubstantiated guess that it was the very spot at which the world's first colonists had made planetfall. If so, its original construction might have proceeded along prescribed lines, Chasmata Capitalis subsequently sprawling in all directions, as many such cities were wont to do two or three generations after their founding. Lucian caught a glimpse of distant hydroponics domes at the city's outer edge, although the shuttle changed course before he could examine the curiosity further.

The shuttle's final approach brought it low over what appeared to form the city's merchant quarter. Rendered the colour of tarnished gold by the light of Chasmata's star, Lucian identified the buildings as representative of the Late Declivitous style, a typically ornate school of architecture seen across the quadrant and beyond. The streets were tightly packed together, ground vehicles visibly competing with the pedestrians who crowded their markets and bazaars. Atop the tallest buildings nested mighty defence laser batteries, although it took Lucian only a moment to decide that they were inert and neglected: a sorry state of affairs indeed, inviting to Lucian's mind pirate, or alien attack.

At the last, the shuttle screamed in over the city to circle its main landing field. Its thrusters kicked and bucked as they arrested the transport's momentum, the pilot easing it down to the armoured landing platform with only a slight jarring. Lucian stood from his grav-couch as the ramp at the end of the passenger bay lowered. It hit the landing pad's surface with a metallic crash, the world's air flooding into the cabin. Lucian stood at the top of the ramp, flanked by his offspring. A cloaked figure at the head of a column of heavily armoured soldiers waited at its base.

Lucian stepped out to the top of the ramp. He saw that the landing pad was one of several dozen, raised high above the city upon ancient stilts. Beyond these, he could see the ancient city, its buildings clustered together haphazardly, and in the middle distance the great bulk of the Imperial Commander's palace.

'My Lord Arcadius,' spoke a figure at the base of the ramp, the mouth barely visible beneath the hood. 'In the name of my master, I bid you welcome to our world.'

Having gained his bearings, Lucian strode down the ramp, the scant seconds it took him to reach its base used to the full. He took in the scene before him. The figure that welcomed him appeared to be some flunky, for he wore simple functionary's robes, adorned with little in the way of frivolous ornamentation; unlike the troopers arrayed in two long lines behind him. These were, no doubt, the household guard, for their sturdy carapace armour, probably imported at great expense, marked them above the common Planetary Defence Force conscripts. White armour, edged with gold, shone hazily in the thick morning light. Tall, white feathers were attached to the helm of each, and reflective visors covered any hint of facial expression. The troopers bore long-barrelled rifles; a glance at the stock revealed to Lucian a power pack of unfamiliar manufacture, although he judged the weapons to be some form of ceremonial hunting rifle. Very pretty, and very expensive, Lucian thought, but not a whole lot of use in a real fight.

With a thud, Lucian's heavy boot heel made contact with the platform's armoured surface. He stood before the functionary and addressed him in the voice he liked to use to impress the locals.

'Please convey to your master my thanks for his hospitality. I greet you in the name of the Arcadius.'

The rogue traders had been led from the landing platform, through the merchants' quarter and to the outer reaches of the vastness of the governor's palace, accompanied all the while by ranks of marching household guard. The palace itself must have been one of the oldest structures in the city – indeed, on the world – for its every surface was layered with strata of dust. Heraldic banners made tattered and threadbare by the passing of millennia lined its long passages. Electro-lumen flickered and guttered in the high, vaulted ceilings, where vat-grown cyber cherubs capered in and out of the shadows. Parchments and prayer strips were affixed to every surface by great gobbets of sealing wax; endless votives imploring the God-Emperor for His mercy and blessings.

As the group neared the centre of the palace, the character of the place changed. The atmosphere became thicker, somehow heavy, as if made sluggish by the weight of ages. Incense cloyed at the nostrils, but the scent failed to mask the fact that the exact same substance had been burned, day in and day out, for uncounted centuries. The high ceilings were waxy with its build-up. Statuettes and gargoyles crowded point-arched recesses, gold leaf skin peeling from their every surface. Cables snaked across walls and along floors, laid reverently, but with little in the way of art or understanding. Small scrips attached to terminus points indicated the identity of the technician, and the date he had attended to his labour. Many such cables had been laid many centuries in the past, and when severed had had more prayer seals applied, so that the most damaged formed riotous, fluttering garlands draped across the walls.

As the group came upon the regions of the inner palace, a flock of servo-skulls joined them. The actual skulls of the most favoured of the Imperium's servants, these were preserved after death and implanted with all manner of machine devices, in order for the previous owner to go on serving his master long after his passing. A rudimentary machine spirit guided each, causing it to hover at shoulder height upon tiny anti-grav generators. The lead servo-skull was fitted with a heavy bronze bell, which it visibly laboured to hold aloft whilst it veered from left to right, its ringing preceding the rogue traders as they progressed down the dusty corridors. Another sported a large, mechanical eye that clicked and whirred as its lenses adjusted, hovering right at Lucian's shoulder and evidently recording or examining him for some unknowable purpose. Another had attached to it a set of miniature, crab-like pincers, with which it dived to grab tiny, perhaps imagined, impediments to the group's progress, whilst the last appeared to sniff at the rogue traders through its bony cavity of a nose.

Finally, the procession reached the atrium of the inner hall. The mighty brass doors that led into the governor's audience chamber dominated this area, their tops lost ten metres or more above in the incense-bound shadows of the vaulted ceilings. Scenes from legend were carved in bas-relief upon the doors' surfaces. The Emperor stood astride a globe, his sword arcing to hack at the neck of a writhing serpent. Lucian had viewed many such scenes on his journeys, but they never failed to move him: the sight of the most holy of men to have lived, sacrificing all, that mankind might survive in a universe set upon nothing less than his destruction. Lucian was a rogue trader; he well knew the meaning of this.

As the last of the household guard formed up in parade ground precision at either side of the trio, the functionary addressed the rogue traders.

'Are you ready my lords?'

Lucian turned to each of his offspring, Korvane indicating his eagerness for the coming proceedings with a bow of his head, Brielle hers with a wry smile.

'Well enough.' Lucian inclined his head to the degree required by protocol, indicating to the functionary that the rogue traders were ready to meet with the Imperial Commander of Mundus Chasmata.

The functionary activated a mechanical device hidden in the depths of his cavernous sleeves. An instant later, mighty pistons at either side of the portal strained until the forces required to haul open the vast doors were achieved. Clouds of choking dust billowed at the doors' passing, a signal to Lucian that they had not been opened in some considerable time. A sure message, Lucian noted, that the group passing through was to be received in honour.

The doors swung fully open, and Lucian and his children saw for the first time the audience chamber of Culpepper Luneberg the Twenty-ninth, Imperial Commander, upon the soil of his own world second in authority only to the High Lords of Terra themselves.

The group found itself stepping out onto a landing, an expansive space to the top of a vast flight of stairs. These swept down many hundreds of steps to a wide floor, and beyond that another raised area appeared to house Luneberg's, currently empty, throne. The entire area was enclosed in a chamber several times taller than it was wide, and vast pillars of stone supported a roof that was entirely lost to the eye in shadow and incense haze. Every surface was caked in pealing, tarnished gold leaf, dust of countless centuries built up in drifts and tumbling in powdery falls from recesses. Gossamer webs, presumably those of spiders, or some local equivalent, stretched from one leering gargoyle to the next, the light of hovering electro lumens twinkling where it reflected off the thin, silken strands.

Lucian strode to the top of the stairs, taking a moment to cast his glance around the vast space. The hovering lights swarmed the chamber, their flight describing random patterns across the space and creating bubbles of flickering yellow light within the gloom. The floor at the bottom of the steps appeared crowded with figures, although Lucian could make out scant details from his position.

So far, little of what Lucian had seen surprised him in any way. Being a rogue trader, he and his kind occupied a unique position within the upper echelons of the Imperium. Unlike the teeming billions of Imperial subjects crowding the million and more domains of the Emperor's rule, rogue traders had cause to escape the worlds of their birth and go forth to visit others. Most worlds in the Imperium were largely self-sufficient, or at most inter-dependent with others in the immediate region.

It was only the most privileged who would ever leave his world, unless he was conscripted into the Imperial Guard and sent to fight some far-away war, never to return home again. Rogue traders carried their Charter of Trade as a badge of office, with it gaining entrance to places others would be executed for visiting. Lucian had participated in the ritual currently playing out on scores of occasions. The places and the people differed, as did the grandeur of the surroundings, but whether mud hut, rad-shelter, chapel-city or xenos-nest, the pattern was invariably a familiar one.

Half way down the flight of stairs, Lucian was able to discern some details of the milling crowds at its base. The courtiers, for Lucian could now make out that these people were at the least minor nobility, wore elaborate costumes of the most rare of materials, but the fabrics were faded and tattered, as tarnished with age as the architecture all around. At his approach, periwigs turned, small clouds of powder or dust, Lucian was unsure which, puffing around the nobles' heads and causing them to cough demurely. The women wore their hair in elaborate steeples, but rogue strands lent them a bedraggled appearance quite at odds with the pomp and ceremony of the event.

Approaching the bottom of the stairs, Lucian could now examine in closer detail the nearer of the courtiers. Many wore exquisite jewellery, tiny gems that twinkled and cycled through all the colours of the spectrum. Lucian supposed they may be some locally manufactured curio, but had an inkling they were procured off-world, for Chasmata was not known for the manufacture of such fine jewellery; had it been so, he would have known. Many sported bracelets and necklaces fashioned from some unfamiliar resin or ceramic; again, unlikely to be of local pedigree. He examined the faces even closer. Both men and women appeared bored, as if the proceedings unfolding around them were in some manner tiresome. Was this some highborn affectation? Lucian had certainly encountered those who feigned haughty disinterest in the goings-on around them, but rarely in an entire crowd of people. He sought to make eye contact with those closest. A nearby man turned away from his gaze as soon as he met it. A woman fluttered spidery eyelashes before turning pointedly to engage her neighbour.

As Lucian and his offspring stepped on to the wide, polished floor, the functionary still following a polite distance behind, the crowd of milling courtiers slowly parted, creating, as if by coincidence, a clear route to the podium housing Luneberg's throne. Definitely affectation, Lucian decided; these people were evidently masters of highly refined, and completely manufactured disinterest. Though they showed no outward interest in the rogue traders, Lucian saw that their movements betrayed exquisite and, no doubt highly choreographed ritual.

Heads turning away at their passing, the trio approached the high throne, and stood before it, as a hush descended upon the chamber.

The robed functionary stepped forward, ascending a short flight of stairs at the side of the podium. He pulled back his hood, and turned to address the chamber at large.

'My lords!' his voice rang out loudly, picked up, Lucian guessed, by the servo-skulls orbiting the podium, and amplified by speakers lost amongst the statuary. 'All will heed the coming of our liege, Imperial Commander Culpepper Luneberg the Twenty-Ninth!'

At these words, every perfumed hairpiece in the chamber turned towards the podium. Previously vacant faces showed sudden, near rapturous attention. The shadows at one side of the raised area stirred, and Lucian received his first glimpse of the Imperial Commander of Mundus Chasmata: the man with whom he had come to do business, the man on whom the survival, for the next decade at least, of the Arcadius might depend.

A massive figure stepped from the shadows. Culpepper Luneberg the Twenty-Ninth was almost as wide as he was tall, and radiated a palpable aura of authority.

'Culpepper Luneberg, Lord of Mundus Chasmata and the three Dominions!'

Lucian took the measure of the man who ruled this world. As large as he was, Lucian judged it was not all the fat of the idle rich.

'Culpepper Luneberg, Commander-in-Chief of the Legions Chasmata!'

He wore a uniform of exquisite cut. Gold braids edged his heavy, long, black velvet coat, its high collars fluted behind his bald head.

'Culpepper Luneberg, twenty-ninth in the most noble line of Harrid!'

He wore more medals than Lucian did, and the epaulettes upon his broad shoulders made plain that he held the highest possible military rank.

'Culpepper Luneberg, Son of Boniface the Just.'

As Luneberg approached his throne, every step in time with the recital of his status, a cavalcade of followers emerged from the shadows behind him.

'Culpepper Luneberg, Deliverer of the Outer Nine!'

A line of women, courtesans Lucian saw immediately, followed in the Imperial Commander's wake. Each wore little more than an elaborate, tall, teetering white hairpiece, their bodies accented by the same multi-spectral jewels sported in far more modest quantities by the courtiers.

'Culpepper Luneberg, Scourge of the outcast Janykho!'

Luneberg reached his throne, and lowered himself into it with a grace that belied his bulk. His harem arranged itself languidly at his feet, each courtesan reclining with an expression of studied disinterest that made the courtiers' appear positively amateurish. So distant were their expressions that Lucian briefly entertained the notion that they might be drugged, or perhaps even lobotomised; it certainly would not be the first time he had encountered such.

Silence descended once more. Although mere seconds in duration, the interval seemed to last an eternity. Eyes open, mouth shut, Lucian reminded himself, and was rewarded for his patience as, for a second time, the functionary addressed the chamber.

'My lords!' The crowd's attention switched to the functionary once more. Luneberg, who had thus far paid no visible attention to the proceedings, turned his head and nodded subtly to the functionary. 'I present to you, the Lord Arcadius, Lucian Gerrit!'

Every head in the chamber turned towards Lucian, sudden fascination writ large across each face. It was as if the crowd had noticed them for the first time. Men bowed in salute; women pouted behind quivering fans. The transition was quite startling, and Lucian struggled to retain his composure lest the slightest hint of surprise cross his face and insult his host.

Luneberg turned from his functionary to look directly at Lucian. His courtesans, suddenly attentive, leaned forwards, dark, predatory eyes and parted lips betraying no-doubt feigned attraction.

Luneberg spread his arms wide. 'Let the talks begin!'

CHAPTER THREE

'Archeotech? You're sure?'

Luneberg had led the rogue traders straight to his private audience chamber, displaying a haste to dive into negotiations verging on what Lucian considered impolitic. Furthermore, Lucian noted straight away that the Imperial Commander appeared unwilling to trust even the slightest detail of the talks to a chancellor or attendant. So be it, Lucian had thought; we'll do things his way.

Lucian leaned forwards in his seat, his elbows resting on the ancient wood of the table. Across from him, a gaggle of powdered flunkies crowded around to attend their master as he held court. Luneberg waved off a fussing servant.

'Quite sure. My agents located the source whilst pursuing privateers in the employ of a troublesome neighbour. I have since entered into an arrangement with the... locals, and opened up a trade route.'

Lucian's interest was piqued. So, Luneberg had come into a supply of ancient technological artefacts pre-dating the Imperium. Known as archeotech, Lucian knew, as only a man of his station could, that such items were the remnants of the first wave of human colonisation of the galaxy, leftovers from a golden age long lost to the men of the forty-first millennium, and valuable beyond measure or imagination, even his.

He glanced towards Korvane, and then Brielle, glad to see that both were keeping a straight face, before continuing.

'So you have a supply–' Lucian said, 'but you need a broker; someone with the contacts to turn that supply into demand.'

Luneberg lifted a wide, balloon-shaped glass and took a hefty swig of what Lucian saw was imported amasec of middling pedigree. 'Quite so, my dear Lucian. I offer you exclusive brokerage. Name your rate.'

Now it was Lucian's turn to feign indifference. Behind his neutral facade his mind raced, calculating a thousand and more possibilities; a steady supply of archeotech that he and he alone could sell on to those who had an interest in such things. It was in total contravention of the laws of the Imperium of course, but Lucian was a rogue trader, and to all intents and purposes above such constraints. On many occasions that an Arcadius had conquered a new world, certain items of 'specialist' interest had found their way back to the Imperium. Many and varied were those who would pay extremely well for pre-Imperium or xenos artefacts, ranging from the arcane researchers of the Adeptus Mechanicus to the highborn dilettantes for their private collections. Such an enterprise might save the Arcadius from short-term bankruptcy, keeping them afloat until Korvane came into his inheritance.

'Thirty-three per cent, to be reviewed after the first shipment; I collect.'

Luneberg placed his glass on the table before him, his movements calculated and deliberate. He made a show of studying the vessel for a moment before replying. 'Twenty-five, and you don't.'

Lucian had known that the Imperial Commander would never accept his opening offer, but was curious as to how he would react to Lucian collecting the artefacts himself. Would he try to protect his source, did he trust Lucian enough to factor it into the deal?

'Thirty. I collect.' Lucian heard Korvane cough at this. His son was no doubt trying, in his way, to warn him against pushing Luneberg too far. Korvane knew as well as Lucian how threatened the dynasty's fortunes were.

'I see you for a man who trusts only his own skill, Gerrit, and I can sympathise entirely. The burden of command of a world of the Imperium is perhaps not so different to your own position as head of your dynasty.' If Luneberg was trying to get a reaction out of him he would fail, thought Lucian, although, despite himself, he felt his hackles rise.

Luneberg leant forward, locking eyes with Lucian. 'Twenty, and you may collect. That's my final offer.'

Lucian held the Imperial Commander's gaze, acutely aware that his son was squirming with discomfort at the deal on the table. 'To be reviewed upon the first collection.'

Luneberg raised his glass. 'To be reviewed upon the first collection.'

'That's it, Father?' Korvane almost stumbled as he ran to keep up with Lucian as he strode to the waiting shuttle. 'That's the negotiations over?'

Lucian halted, turning to face his son in one fluid movement. 'Over? No son, that's just the beginning. Even now, we're deep in negotiations. What you just saw were only the opening moves. Luneberg's up to something. I know that, and he knows I know that. Depending on what we bring back from the first run, that's when we really start doing business.'

'That's why you refused to be drawn on us collecting the goods?' Korvane asked as Brielle caught up with him and her father.

'Correct. So long as he's open to reviewing the deal after the first run, I don't care what margin we make at this point. I need to ascertain exactly what we're dealing with before we make any commitments. Luneberg knows that too, so he's letting us do things on our terms for the time being.'

Korvane considered this, while Brielle asked, 'Does he know what he really has, with this so-called archeotech?'

Glad that at least one of his offspring was paying attention, Lucian said, 'I suspect not. Most likely that's for us to worry about. If we find he's on to something good, he'll know that by our negotiating stance.'

Brielle nodded, her face thoughtful as a gentle wind stirred her long black braids. For an instant, Lucian was reminded of her mother. He dismissed the image as soon as it appeared in his mind.

As the breeze built, the three boarded their shuttle, to return to the orbital and their vessels. Lucian hesitated for a moment, however, before raising the ramp, compelled to cast a glance behind him at the brooding form of Culpepper Luneberg's vast palace as it dominated the jumbled skyline of Chasmata Capitalis. He was struck by the notion that all was not well on the Eastern Rim, and that events might soon get interesting. Not for the first time in his long life, Lucian savoured the thought that few led as remarkable a life as that of a rogue trader.

He slapped the ramp control, and stalked from the portal as the shuttle lifted off.

Lucian reclined in his command throne as he studied the star maps of the surrounding region of space. The flotilla had exited the warp, its Navigators maintaining formation with such skill that within half a day, all three vessels were inbound to the world upon which they were to obtain Luneberg's archeotech – Sigma Q-77.

The Q-77 system lay upon the very shores of an area of space referred to as the Damocles Gulf. Fifty thousand light years from Sacred Terra, the region had barely been surveyed, even ten thousand years into the Age of the Imperium. Many systems along the outer edge of the eastern spiral arm were isolated and inward-looking, wracked with self-interest and paranoia, as fearful of attracting the notice of the Administratum – the Imperium's impossibly vast bureaucracy – as they were of hostile alien attention.

Lucian considered such a mindset perfectly appropriate for the teeming, planet-bound masses. The common man had no business with space travel, Lucian held, and it was certainly true that a great many worlds within the Imperium kept their subjects in ignorance as to its nature. Some populations were so efficiently ruled that the common man had no inkling that the Imperium existed beyond his own, planet-bound horizons. Rogue traders however, had an Emperor-given right, indeed, a responsibility to pierce the outer dark, shining the light of civilisation into the vast, uncharted reaches of space, and, inevitably, to amass power and wealth beyond measure along the way.

The region into which Lucian and his flotilla travelled was one rarely visited by the agents of the Imperium. Few had any business this far out, except for outbound Explorator fleets and rogue traders such as he. Those that did pass beyond the Imperium's borders rarely returned, for horrors beyond imagining lurked about the ancient stars at the very galaxy's edge. The archives of the Arcadius were full to overflowing with accounts of contact with creatures the like of which the preachers of the Imperial Creed denounced as utter blasphemies. Yet Lucian's ancestors had always returned triumphant from such encounters, their cargo holds groaning with booty. Some had conquered through war, others through trade. To the Arcadius, each was but one side of the same coin. Lucian yearned for such days again, and held on to the precious notion that his fortunes would soon improve.

Yet, out here, such dreams rang hollow, thought Lucian, as he cast his gaze through the forward viewing port. There was something about the region that left a chill in the soul, a deep-seated impression that something was... somehow wrong. The stellar cluster that contained Luneberg's world, as well as the domains of several dozen other Imperial Commanders bordered the gulf on its coreward side. Then, to the galactic east, nothing, for light years – not even the most insignificant of nebulae. It was as if the galaxy itself shunned the depths of the gulf, only the light of the stars on its far side daring to cross it. Those stars were densely packed, but never surveyed, according to the archives of the Arcadius, although that did not mean an Explorator fleet had not passed through at some time in the past millennia. The records of the Imperium were simply too vast, too sprawling, too incomplete to record all such information.

'Entering upper orbit sir,' called the helmsman, snapping Lucian out of his reflections.

As the *Oceanid* came about, entering her station-keeping orbit in as stately a manner as the most grand of Imperial Navy battleships, the world of Sigma Q-77 climbed into view. The archives spoke little of the Q-77 system, and Luneberg had provided most of the data that Lucian was expected to rely upon. That meant Lucian would not rely upon it – not yet at least. The records stated it was a barren, lifeless world, with an atmosphere only barely capable of supporting human life. What business life had needed Q-77 to support there, Lucian could not tell. From orbit, he could see that airborne particles choked the skies of Q-77, swept along in kilometres-high streams. The dust storms raging across the surface were so dense that not a scrap of land was visible, not even the landing zone, and that was apparently sited in the area least affected by the foul atmospheric conditions.

'Operations?' Lucian called over to an officer stationed in the crew pit. The old man, Rantakha, had served three generations of the Arcadius, and looked, to Lucian's eyes, more like one of the servitors each year. He looked up from the cogitator bank into which he had been entering a long stream of data. 'Have my shuttle readied and coordinate a flight plan with the *Rosetta* and the *Fairlight*. I'll be there shortly.'

Rantakha saluted smartly, and Lucian heard him efficiently issuing his orders to his operations crew as he strode off the deck.

Passing his cabin, Lucian walked down the central companionway of his vessel. Though not as vast as a Navy ship, the *Oceanid* had once been home to several thousand souls, but the soulless automatons that were servitors served increasingly more and more functions, and the numbers of honest, flesh and blood men in his service decreased in direct proportion. Human crew carried out many more; crew press-ganged upon a number of worlds, of which the Arcadius held the ancestral rite to take its cut of the varied flotsam and jetsam that washed up there. As Lucian approached his destination, he was given cause to curse the fate that had filled his beloved ship with men such as these.

Approaching the shuttle bay amidships, Lucian turned first to enter the battery - that part of the vessel set aside to store the many thousands of tonnes of highly destructive ordnance used by its mighty weapons. The battery was situated in the very heart of the *Oceanid*. It was surrounded by many metres of adamantium, the strongest, most resilient material known to man. Lucian's father had frequently regaled him with the story that should the *Oceanid* be destroyed, her battery would survive intact, to drift endlessly in space until devoured by a void beast, or ensnared by the inexorable pull of a black hole. Lucian had believed him at the time, and even now, standing in front of the battery's armoured portal, it was not such an easy tale to dismiss out of hand.

A gene-lock guarded the portal, ensuring that no one other than Lucian, the master of ordnance and his trusted under-officers could gain access to it. Lucian inserted his hand into a waiting recess, as far as his wrist, palm up. He felt the sharp prick of the needle that was siphoning off a tiny sample of his blood. A moment later, a chime sounded and the armoured portals rumbled open amidst a burst of steam and flashing red beacons.

Lucian entered the battery. Within, vast racks of ordnance receded several hundred metres down the very spine of the ship, darkness swallowing all but the closest. Clunking servitors, three times larger than those serving on the bridge, prowled the rows; only their heads and upper torso betrayed a human origin, for pistons and power couplings had replaced much of their bodies, enabling them to heft the mighty shells onto waiting gurneys. These paid Lucian no heed as he took a candle – part votive, part light source – from a waiting alcove, and lit it, the better to navigate down a row of plasma coil fuses. He entered an arched nook.

Within was housed Lucian's personal armoury. The Arcadius had amassed, over the generations, the weapons to equip a small army, and had in fact done so several times in their history. The weapons and equipment housed within the battery, however, were of an entirely different nature. They were rare in the extreme, and in many cases, devastating beyond compare with any weapons in the Imperium's arsenal. Many were the creations of the most celebrated of weaponsmiths, others were of unknown heritage, some perhaps even pre-dating the Imperium itself. Still more were of obvious alien manufacture, such as the disruptor Lucian wore at his belt, and these were the most jealously guarded of all.

At the end of the long racks of exotic weapons, suits of armour stood motionless. They were painted in the hereditary colours of the Arcadius: deep red edged with gold, yet each was very different in design. Some were old, their lovingly repainted shells pitted with scars won in countless glorious battles. Others were covered in spidery script, litanies of protection against the enemies of mankind. Several suits were lightweight, designed for situations when a degree of protection could be sacrificed in exchange for additional mobility. Others were heavy and cumbersome, rivalling the Terminator armour worn by the elite of the Adeptus Astartes, so heavy were their armoured plates.

Once more, a tale from childhood came unbidden to Lucian's mind. The story told of an ancestor who had fallen in battle, against the eldar if he recalled correctly; but this ancient Arcadius had not died, though his wounds were indeed grievous. According to the tale, the tech-priests of the Adeptus Mechanicus had borne him away, to attend to him in their machine temple, to minister to his body and, they had promised, make him one with the Omnissiah – the Machine-God. His followers had awaited his return for many days and nights, praying that the tech-priests might restore his body to at least a semblance of its former vitality. Finally, having almost given up hope, the retainers were astounded when a hulking machine, twice the height of a man, emerged from the temple, its metal skin painted deep red and gold. Understanding dawned upon them only slowly, but when the metal beast addressed them through loud hailers mounted upon its armour, they heard the barest remnants of the voice of their master. His broken body was forever encased within a dreadnought, an honour usually reserved exclusively for the mightiest of Space Marines. Lucian's ancestor had led his dynasty for many decades to come. He had forged his place in the history of the Imperium, leading many more conquests against the benighted worlds of the eastern rim.

In his darker moments, Lucian feared such days might never return to his line.

Sighing, Lucian selected a suit of armour. He anticipated no trouble on Sigma Q-77, yet as head of the Arcadius, he was expected, by centuries of tradition, to wear the hereditary symbol of his rank. A suit of power armour would suffice, one Lucian had worn many times, one whose war spirit knew him as well as he knew it. The individual parts of the armour were cumbersome, yet Lucian dressed himself, preferring the additional effort to the intrusion of a servitor or rating aiding him. As he pulled on the armoured gloves, flexing them to awaken the machine impulses, Lucian reflected on the suit's vintage. It had come into the dynasty during the time of Mathan Gerrit, known for his xenocidal crusade against the burgeoning Reek Exclaves, and still bore the scar from the encounter that killed its first owner. Lucian drew strength from the fact that he wore a suit in which an ancestor had met a violent death, knowing that, although Mathan sat at the right hand of the Emperor, some trace of his famously indomitable will remained, forever dwelling within his battle armour.

With his pistols at his belt, and his armour fully powered up, Lucian felt a familiar strength return to him. The armour was too heavy for a normal man to bear, relying instead on a complex array of fibre bundles to move its weight in response to its wearer's movements. Lucian found the effect emboldening, lending him strength and confidence as he strode out from the armoury, making his way along the central companionway towards the shuttle hangar.

The shuttle idled upon the armoured deck, the under-lighting of the deck lights lending it a threatening aspect amidst the shadowed, cavernous bay. Fat cables snaked all around the shuttle as its systems were made ready for the coming flight, its reactor primed and its machine spirit fully awakened. A pair of heavy servitors and a power lifter plodded heavy-footed around the ship, loading external fuel tanks and cargo pods. The rear portion of the shuttle consisted of a modular component that could be swapped out, depending upon the nature of the shuttle's mission. This component was configured to transport Lucian himself and a small amount of cargo, and it awaited him in its lowered position, its open front accessible below the blunt prow and swept wings of the ship. He knew that both his children's shuttles would be configured in a like manner, and whilst he would have liked to have made the planetfall with one or both of them, they needed to maximise the amount of cargo they could carry back to the waiting vessels.

The pilot, Oria Kayle, stood waiting beneath the shuttle's wings. A tall man in his thirties, Kayle was the latest of a long line that had served the Arcadius faithfully for many centuries. Lucian's father had awarded the Orias the status of freeman for his part in saving the *Oceanid* from alien infiltration during the De-Norm Extermination. Oria's father had accepted the promotion in status, yet remained to serve the Arcadius, pledging his line willingly and proudly to voluntary service. Lucian was grateful he had, for the Kayles bred pilots without compare.

Kayle threw a smart salute as Lucian approached, the bundle of cables hanging loose from the left side of his forehead shaking as he did so.

'Is she ready, Oria?' Lucian cast a professional eye over the shuttle, seeing for himself in an instant that she was.

'Yes my lord. All preparations are complete. Our flight plan is registered and we can launch as soon as you give the order.'

'It'll be a rough drop. You're sure she's up to it?' Lucian harboured no doubts regarding his pilot's skill or the preparations invested in the shuttle, but knew the risks of the landing they were about to undertake. The atmospheric conditions were appalling, and the data on the landing zone incomplete.

'My lord, if your order is to land upon the surface of Sigma Q-77, then this will happen. I pledge it upon my family's honour. You have my word.'

Lucian nodded. He needed no more; for he knew the pilot's word was as good as his own. 'What are we hanging about here for then?' He smiled. 'Let's go.'

The storm-wracked skies of Sigma Q-77 filled the porthole at Lucian's side, the view shaking violently as the shuttle hurtled through the thin, upper atmosphere. Although compensated for by the shuttle's systems, the violence of the drop was notable. Lucian could feel the heat building up, his power armour's own mechanisms fighting to counter it.

Kayle's voice sounded in Lucian's ear, carried by the ships intercom yet crackling and distorted as if transmitted across light years of space. 'Passing through the ionosphere now, my lord. There appears to have been some recent solar activity, so I expect some plasma damage. Nothing we can't handle though. The Emperor protects.'

'The Emperor protects,' Lucian echoed. The shuttle bucked violently, throwing Lucian's head against the padded seatback. The shaking increased and the temperature rose noticeably. The upper atmosphere of Sigma Q-77 now completely filled the port, and Lucian could make out the patterns of the raging storm clouds, angry white, violet and grey. Mighty energy discharges arced across the skies, back lighting banks of clouds many hundreds of kilometres across.

The clouds loomed, and rose impossibly fast to swallow the shuttle. The viewing port was swamped, the clouds so dense that only the strobing lightning was visible. The shaking increased still further, made violent and jarring by the additional friction generated as the shuttle screamed through the high clouds.

Kayle's voice sounded once more. 'My lord, we're approaching a rough–' He was cut off as the shuttle lurched upwards, only to plummet what felt to Lucian like several kilometres in the span of mere seconds. This was shaping up to be a rough drop, thought Lucian, perhaps as rough as the Kalpurnican Interface. He gritted his teeth against a second lurch, and a further plunge that exceeded even the first.

Except this second drop in altitude brought the shuttle out below the cloud layer, and Lucian was afforded a view of the surface of Sigma Q-77. Under raging skies, a ground the colour of rust rushed up to meet them. Kayle adjusted the shuttle's vector, bringing them in on a slow, rounded dive that shed velocity startlingly fast. The shaking and vibrating abated, leaving the shuttle buffeted by high altitude winds, but otherwise unmolested.

Lucian loosened the harness that had kept him secure during the worst of the drop, and activated the intercom. 'My compliments, Oria, how are we looking?'

Lucian could hear the relief as Kayle responded, the channel now clear of distortion. 'My thanks, my lord. That was... testing. No appreciable damage, but the vessel's war spirit is much displeased with its handling as we crossed into the troposphere. I fear I may be required to make contrition upon our return, my lord.'

Lucian grinned wryly at Kayle's understatement. He knew the pilot would be ministering to the shuttle's machine spirit for many long hours upon their return, seeking its forgiveness for its mistreatment.

'Do what you must, Oria, but first get us back safely.'

'Aye, sir, we approach the landing site now.'

'Well enough, Mister Kayle. Bring us down.'

The meteorospex readout informed Lucian that the atmosphere outside the shuttle was, as Luneberg's information had stated, breathable. It contained a high level of airborne hydrocarbons however, and Lucian took the precaution of inserting miniaturised filtration plugs into the back of his throat. These would allow him to breathe even if the atmosphere became dangerously toxic, although they would be of no use should oxygen levels drop below a breathable threshold.

Checking his auspex was operational and the coordinates for the meeting with Luneberg's contact locked in, Lucian activated the lock. The seal broke, and the ramp lowered, oxide dust blowing into the small compartment before the ramp was fully lowered.

The surface of Sigma Q-77 was every bit as inviting as it had appeared from orbit, and far above, deep purple and grey clouds trailed across the sky, livid violet lightning arcing between them. The ground was barren and cratered, deep oxide red, yet cast a ghostly hue by the lightning. A cold wind howled, its touch chilling Lucian's face and its shrieking filling his ears.

Although hostile, the terrain barely registered with Lucian, for he had visited scores of worlds in his career, many far, far stranger and more inhospitable than Sigma Q-77. Over the millennia, the Arcadius had developed a sixth sense when it came to new worlds, an intuitive skill passed down from father to son, demonstrated rather than taught, felt rather than reasoned.

Every world had a feel. Whether you landed first upon arid equatorial desert, tropical island chain or frozen tundra, Lucian knew that each world had its own character, quite apart and distinct from mere terrain or weather. Some Lucian had visited felt welcoming, fecund, and ripe for exploitation. Others were instantly hostile, as if aware that the coming of strangers would change its fate forever. Lucian had read accounts of worlds that his ancestors swore blind manifested an actual, malefic intelligence, rejecting their presence with every asset at its disposal, from weather to flora and fauna.

Lucian paused before stepping out onto the dusty ground. The feel of this world immediately struck him: it felt... it felt wrong.

Rounding an outcropping of rock worn into a twisted archway by aeons of erosion, Lucian saw that Korvane and Brielle had arrived at the rendezvous point ahead of him. He was glad, for the planet had about it a deathly air, and every moment he had spent trudging through the dust towards the meeting point had seen him grow steadily more ill at ease.

Korvane was standing, scanning the horizon through magnoculars, while his sister sat on a rock some distance from him, her discomfort obvious. Both wore armoured bodysuits in the colours of the Arcadius, although neither was as ornate as that he himself wore as head of the family.

Brielle looked up, hearing her father's footsteps crunching towards them. She stood as Korvane turned and saw Lucian too.

The three having exchanged greetings, Lucian asked his offspring, 'What do you make of this world?'

Korvane answered first, consulting his data-slate as he spoke. 'I'm surprised that Lord Luneberg's agents encountered natives here, Father. The archives make no mention of a colony here, and I can't imagine it harbouring autochthonic forms unless–'

Brielle interrupted her brother. 'That's not the point.' She visibly shivered as she looked out across the windblown expanses. Lucian felt the same chill, and it wasn't caused by the temperature.

Lucian addressed his daughter. 'What is it then Brielle?'

'I can't tell, Father, but something isn't right. There's something in the wind: echoes of something old.'

Lucian held his daughter's gaze until she looked away, her dark eyes cast down. A thought formed in his mind, and fled before he could grasp it, as Korvane interjected. 'Well, nothing's showing up on the auspex, so I think it's safe to move off.'

Brielle looked askance at Lucian before turning and stalking off. Lucian clapped his son on the shoulder. 'Let's go son, and keep a weather eye out.' Korvane raised his auspex, but Lucian pushed it down again. 'An eye.' He pointed at his own. 'Trust your own senses, son.' As Brielle clearly trusted hers, Lucian thought.

Lucian and his offspring trudged across a barren, lifeless landscape, the wind steadily increasing until the dust it carried became so dense that visibility was reduced to ten metres and less. Twisted rock structures loomed from the dust, silhouetted as angry lightning illuminated the surroundings, and reminding Lucian of rearing slasher beasts. His feeling of discomfort had steadily increased as they had marched towards the site at which they would meet Luneberg's contact. He wondered about his daughter's reaction to her surroundings. Where he perceived the nature of the world as a spiritual chill, Brielle clearly interpreted it in an entirely different manner, speaking of voices whispering at the edge of hearing. Korvane, on the other hand, apparently felt nothing. He was either commendably steady of nerve, or stunningly insensate – Lucian could not, as yet, tell which. Either way, the boy was fated to inherit the mantle of the Arcadius, and Lucian would ensure that he did.

Lightning strobed, and thunder crashed an instant later. Korvane turned and shouted over the rising storm. 'Half a kilometre to go, Father, the meeting point is–'

Before Lucian's son could finish the sentence, a dark shape detached itself from a nearby rock formation, dropping the three metres or so in the blink of an eye. Lucian saw this, but had no time to shout a warning before Korvane was bowled to the ground amidst a blur of thrashing alien appendages. Lucian drew his plasma pistol and charged forwards, reaching Korvane as his son thrust out his legs with enough force to propel the beast from him, its many-legged form crashing into the rock spire from which it had attacked. Having hit the rock, the creature dropped to the ground and tensed, ready to leap once more.

Lucian had never seen its like, for it appeared unnatural in physiology. A lumpy and misshaped body, a metre in diameter, sat at the centre of at least a dozen long, multi-jointed legs, each ending in a cluster of razor-sharp talons. A clutch of eyes scanned the scene before it, each focusing on a different target. In an instant, the beast focused its attentions on Brielle, who had arrived at the scene a moment after her father. It leapt through the air, propelling itself with a force that would surely decapitate anyone standing before it.

Brielle sidestepped the beast, allowing it to pass scant inches from her face. She raised her right hand and dropped to a kneeling position in one fluid motion. The beast hit the ground at the base of another rock spire and made to scuttle up it. A jet of blinding fame spouted from a miniature weapon on Brielle's wrist, leaping through the air to strike the rock. The flame splashed across the spot that the beast occupied at the instant it launched itself clear, yet it howled with ultrasonic rage as the jet caught it a glancing blow across its torso. A screaming, flaming comet of flailing claws, the creature arced through the air once more. It landed beside Korvane, who rolled aside as Lucian was finally able to draw a bead on it with his plasma pistol.

'Korvane, roll left!' Lucian yelled, seeing that the beast would be upon his son in an instant if he did not intervene.

Korvane's armour had taken the brunt of the beast's attack on him, but he was stunned nonetheless. Despite this, he obeyed his father's order without question, flinging himself bodily against the rock spire.

Lucian fired, a ball of blinding plasma erupting from his pistol, to strike the flaming, squealing beast. The plasma bolt struck the creature's torso, causing it to explode in an eruption of smoking gore and razor-sharp limbs. One such limb, tipped with diamond-hard chitin, was propelled through the air to score a deep scar across Lucian's shoulder armour, causing him to give brief, but heartfelt thanks to the suit's war spirit.

Lucian lowered his smoking weapon, its vents shedding excess heat in hazy waves. He looked to Korvane, only to see that his son's eyes had focused upon something behind his shoulder.

Slowly, Lucian turned. Behind him stood a tall figure, features entirely concealed amidst long, flowing robes. How long had it stood there, he thought – had it been waiting the whole time, to see whether or not they would win out against the beast's attack?

A whispery voice emanated from the depths of the figure's hood. 'You are, I take it, the servants of the esteemed Lord Culpepper?'

Wind howling outside, Lucian stood at the centre of a large cavern of obviously artificial construction, beside him Korvane, his wounds hastily dressed, and Brielle. Before him stood Luneberg's contact, and behind the tall, spindly figure, a pile of crates stacked to the cavern's roof.

Having appeared at the site of the alien beast's attack, the tall figure had spoken only to confirm Lucian's identity, apparently caring little for the fact that, as Lucian had explained, the rogue traders were not servants, but partners of Luneberg. Lucian had discerned what he took for a chuckle at this information, and the contact had merely stalked off into the storm with a gesture indicating that Lucian and his offspring should follow.

As Lucian had followed the figure, his feeling of discomfort had increased. The storm had closed in, until visibility was reduced to scant metres; they had nearly lost the contact several times, but always found him waiting patiently just around the next turn. They had been led along twisting pathways of rock spires, down which the wind echoed and wailed, only serving to increase Lucian's unease.

A glance at Brielle told Lucian that his daughter felt likewise, for her brow was furrowed and her eyes steely. Korvane, by contrast, appeared well at ease. Lucian knew that he took the situation for a formal contact between trading parties, and would proceed along such lines until fate determined otherwise. At moments like this, Lucian thought, Korvane had the right idea.

In short order, they had arrived at the entrance to the cave in which they now stood. Entering, Lucian had been greeted by the sight of the crates piled high. The contact now crossed to the nearest and activated a control set in its side. The crate floated up half a metre, to hover at waist height. Lucian concealed his surprise, for anti-gravitic technology was rare within the Imperium, and generally confined to small applications such as those generators found within servo-skulls or to far larger uses in starship construction. Lucian had never seen it manifested in such a utilitarian manner as to raise a simple cargo crate.

The robed figure activated a second control stud, and the crate's top lifted open with a slight hiss of escaping, pressurised air. A wisp of vapour rose and dissipated, as the contact reached into the crate to withdraw a metallic cylinder, which he proffered to Lucian as he bowed. Lucian took the object, his gaze lingering on the tall figure for a moment before he examined it.

The object was heavy and solid, with no obvious function that Lucian could discern. One end appeared to house some form of terminus, though just what type of machine it would interface with was beyond even Lucian. Turning the object over in his hands, Lucian saw that the other end was adorned with some form of script. Lucian's heart missed a beat, yet he remained dispassionate, handing the object back to the contact.

'Luneberg will be pleased.' Lucian addressed the figure. 'I am happy to take delivery of these items.'

'Archeotech my arse!'

The three rogue traders stood at the ramp of Brielle's shuttle, the crates ready to load. Having ascertained the true nature of the items they had taken possession of, Lucian had instructed his children to activate the anti-grav motors in each crate, and had taken leave of Luneberg's contact in as hasty a manner as he could without it appearing so. The three now stood ready to load the crates onto Brielle's shuttle, which was larger than Lucian's or Korvane's.

Brielle laid a hand on a nearby crate, and asked her father: 'What then?'

'Whatever's in these crates is not of pre-Imperium manufacture. In fact, I can't believe Luneberg would think these could be anything other than xenos artefacts.'

Korvane broke in. 'So he lied?'

Brielle replied, 'Or he has no idea.'

'More likely,' Lucian said, 'he knows far more than he's letting on. He may not be aware of exactly who, or what, he's doing business with, but he knows it goes way beyond the pale of what the Administratum considers acceptable behaviour for an Imperial Commander. That's why he needs us. We're rogue traders. We can go places he cannot, meet contacts he cannot. Do deals he cannot.'

'Deals with xenos,' Brielle said.

CHAPTER FOUR

Brielle waited until her shuttle had cleared Sigma Q-77's outer atmosphere, before freeing herself from the grav-couch harness. The small cabin was crowded with the alien cargo crates. She crossed to the nearest, perching herself on its edge and running a fingertip along the invisible seam around its top. She had guessed immediately that the so-called 'archeotech' was in fact xenos in origin; in fact, she had had her suspicions the moment Luneberg's contact had appeared. Although her father had not remarked upon it, for his own unknowable reasons, she had immediately taken the tall figure for something other than human. That wasn't to say, however, that it was entirely alien, for humanity was a truly diverse species, with stabilised mutant strains common, particularly far from the Imperium's centres of power.

Brielle had served at her father's side since childhood, and, far more so than her stepbrother, had been faced with aliens before. She had conversed with the eldar of the Steel Eye Reavers, stood before the haunting Chanters of Miras, and had even caught a glimpse, as few humans ever had and lived, of the near-extinct khrave. Korvane had achieved none of this, having studied the intrigues of high court at his mother's side whilst Brielle travelled the stars with her father. While Korvane's childhood had been a time of cloistered study and training, Brielle had learned the ways of her mother's people and her father's both, simultaneously drawing strength from the traditions of Chogoris and the Arcadius.

As she traced the crate's alien lines, her touch reached the control stud set into its side. She hopped off the crate's top before pressing the stud down. She knew she should not do so. Her father would disapprove. She did so anyway.

The previously invisible seam parted, and the lid rose with a gentle hiss. As the vapour cleared, she looked within. A polyhedral object lay inside, a thin sheen of frost glistening briefly before dispersing. A thrill coursed through her as she considered that merely to possess such an item was, for the vast majority of humans, to invite the wrath of the Imperium's highest authorities. Yet Brielle had learned from her father's example that such laws did not apply to such as her.

To the common subject of the Imperium of Man, the xenos was a ghastly, slavering beast gnawing at the borders of human space, waiting in ambush amongst the stars to entrap, enslave or devour those foolish enough to leave the security of their own world. In fact, most humans had no inkling as to the existence of alien races, beyond the few names that ranting preachers berated them with. They knew of orks, the barbarous green-skinned and utterly war-like beasts that made war on the Imperium in ever-increasing invasions, but they had no idea as to the orks' true nature. Brielle had visited the wastes of Gommoragh and seen first hand what they could do to a world. They may also have heard of the eldar, a race that was often held up as the ultimate warning against intemperance and self-serving profligacy. Such tales repelled most people, although others were strangely attracted to them. Such was the nature of humanity.

She reached into the case, a thrill of danger passing through her. This was dangerous, she knew, foolish in the extreme, for the case might contain anything from toxic chemicals to a lethal weapon. She felt the cold of its unseen stabilisation systems, but hesitated for only a heartbeat before laying her hand upon the cold metal of the object she found within. She lifted it clear, holding it up before her face. Its many surfaces were constructed of some form of dull, hard metal, and each facet housed a single, hemispherical bulge of a deep, green, jewel-like material. Its purpose was entirely hidden, and no control devices of any sort were apparent. Brielle turned the object around in her hand, holding it higher to catch the light of the cabin's illumination. The shallowest of seams were etched across its surfaces, tracing a delicate lattice, yet still she could discern no way in which the object might be activated or utilised. She brought the object close to her face and peered right into the glassy depths of one of the green bulges.

She gasped, almost dropping the object as a shiver ran through her. Just for an instant, as she looked within the jewel, she had the distinct and unpleasant sensation that something had peered right back out at her.

The intercom buzzed, a voice announcing, 'Mistress. We are beginning our approach on the *Fairlight*.'

Delicately, Brielle replaced the xenos device in its crate, the bracing moulding itself around the object's bulk. She activated the control stud, and the lid slid back on silent runners, sealing itself against the outside world, its seam disappearing.

Brielle looked across at her grav-couch, but decided against crossing to it. She would travel in the cockpit. It may be less well appointed, she thought, but from there she could view her cruiser, the *Fairlight* as they approached. It was as well to savour the trappings of power every now and then.

There was a heavy bulkhead door at the fore of the cabin, which Brielle hauled open, passing down a short companionway to the cabin. Her pilot turned in greeting as she appeared behind him, his hard-wired cybernetics restricting the movement to his neck and upper torso.

'Mistress, we dock in four point seven minutes,' Goanna the pilot said.

'Good. I think I'll watch,' Brielle said as she climbed into the unoccupied co-pilot's position.

'Yes, mistress,' he said, before turning back to focus his entire attention on his task. If the man felt any discomfort at his mistress's presence, he hid it well. Brielle had trouble reading old Goanna at the best of times, for, over the decades he had served the Arcadius, he had become increasingly at one with his vessel, and had been fitted with ever more cybernetic interfaces and ports, allowing him to commune more closely with its machine spirit. At times, she suspected that he was in the grip of some form of religious ecstasy, such as the saints of the scriptures were wont to enter when at one with the spirit of the Emperor. Several years back, he had requested he be allowed to take permanent station at the shuttle's controls, and Brielle had granted him his wish. Since then, he had led the existence of a servitor, yet he was no lobotomised, mind-scrubbed mono-tasker. He was a valued servant of her dynasty, and he honoured his mistress with his sacrifice in her service.

Brielle reclined in the grav-couch, strapping herself in as they began their approach on the *Fairlight*. At first, her vessel was not visible, for it was lost in the shadow of Sigma Q-77. Then, as Goanna adjusted the shuttle's course, a small constellation rose into view, the tightly arranged running lights of her ship, the only sign of the cruiser that was visible against the inky black of space.

A series of red lights flickered and strobed across Goanna's controls, but he spoke without sparing them a glance. 'Four minutes, mistress.'

The shuttle's manoeuvring jets fired, the controlled blasts rumbling through the small cabin. Expertly, and with little in the way of physical manipulation, Goanna nursed the shuttle around onto a heading that would bring it into perfect interception with the *Fairlight*'s shuttle bay. Brielle reflected with silent respect just how deeply her pilot now communed with his vessel, suspecting that the pairing was by now permanent.

The manoeuvring complete, Goanna gently fed power to the main drives. The shuttle moved forwards again, and the *Fairlight* loomed out of the gloom. Smaller than the *Oceanid* by a quarter of a length, the vessel was a classic of the Bakkan shipwrights' art, her prow long and elegant and her swept fins affording her the aspect of a sleek, predatory sea creature. Her hull was the colour of slate, making her harder yet to make out against the inky black of space, yet the fins, mounted vertically on either side of the prow sported the colours of the Arcadius – deep red, with golden chevrons, a device that even the most haughty of rogue traders knew, and had once at least, respected.

A line of dancing red lights indicated the landing bay, although Brielle knew Goanna had no need of their guidance. He brought the shuttle in on a graceful course, the heavy, armoured landing bay portal lifting only as the shuttle closed to the last fifty metres. Brielle glanced to her side, watching her pilot as he went about his work. She looked up only as the bright, cavernous bay swallowed the shuttle, the docking arms reaching out to secure her as the portal closed behind, and atmosphere was pumped back into the vast space.

Brielle made her way along low-lit companionways lined with ancient, polished wood panels. Much like the *Oceanid*, the *Fairlight* ran at a reduced crew level, the bulk of her ratings drawn from press-ganged scum given the choice between execution and service. Specialised servitors, who were greatly valued for their specific expertise, carried out much of the work, but Brielle shared her father's view that the family had become too reliant upon them. Only a fraction of the *Fairlight*'s crew was made up of free men, and these formed the officer cadre aboard ship. They were the only members of her crew with whom Brielle had regular contact.

Having disembarked from her shuttle, Brielle had ordered the cargo of alien artefacts to be transferred to the most secure of the *Fairlight*'s holds. She had stood watch as hulking heavy grade servitors had carried each crate away in piston-driven, mechanical arms. She had decided against informing the sweating crew that each crate had an anti-gravi drive fitted, evidently designed to allow its effortless handling. She knew the almost literally brainless servitors could be trusted, but knew better than to tempt the press-ganged crew with such potentially valuable knowledge.

She had only set off for her bridge once she was sure the cargo was safely stowed away, watching as the hold was sealed, and applying her personal cipher to the lock. Now, she brooded as she strode the nigh-deserted companionways, considering the state of the deal with Luneberg.

The Imperial Commander had explicitly stated to her father that the items to which he had gained access were archeotech. Such items were far from common, but they were within the area of expertise of the Arcadius, and should have proved simple enough to trade for a handsome profit. However, the artefacts had proved to be not pre-Imperium human in origin, but something else entirely. They were, Brielle was certain beyond a shadow of a doubt, alien. In many ways, the Arcadius were the perfect choice of business partner for such a deal, yet Brielle was troubled that Luneberg had determined to conceal the true nature of the items from them. As she had stated to her father, Brielle was of the opinion that Luneberg was not the canny player he pretended to be. The more she pondered on it, the more she came to believe that Luneberg was dealing with powers beyond his ken, that he needed the Arcadius far more than he had let on, far more, perhaps, than they needed him.

Yet, her father had pinned a huge amount on the success of this venture. With Korvane not due to inherit his mother's fortune for potentially many years to come, her father had used every contact he had to scour the Eastern Rim for some opportunity, some deal that would see the Arcadius through the next decade or so. The result had been the deal with Luneberg, yet Brielle was becoming ever more uncomfortable with it.

Were she the next in line to the lordship of the Arcadius, as she had been raised to be, she would have been able to challenge her father on the issue, forcing him to hear her concerns. Since Korvane had entered the family however, she had lost her father's ear on such matters. She had been raised to lead a rogue trader dynasty, and now she was compelled to remain in the shadows, to watch as others set that dynasty on a course she considered at best ill advised.

In the beginning, she had attempted to raise the issue with Korvane, swallowing her pride and hoping to appeal to him as a sister. Yet he had rejected her advice, for he was raised in the ways of the high courts, and perceived only weakness in her humility. He had repeated, word for word, their father's view. From that point onward, she had resolved to follow her mother's teachings on such matters. If those around her were blind to their folly, and that folly was likely to doom them all, then she would keep her own counsel, working to resolve matters in her own way.

She reached the bridge, and entered her cipher into the reader at the door. It chimed, and she hauled on the heavy wheel, applying her scant weight to the door and pushing her way through. She entered her bridge, a large, richly appointed chamber lined with the same wood panelling that adorned all of the *Fairlight*'s main companionways. Wide, curved deck-to-ceiling viewing ports dominated three sides, baroque brasswork framing each as if it were a work of art. The bridge crew's stations were arranged in aisles, all facing towards the forward viewing port.

Brielle's command throne sat atop a raised dais at the rear of the bridge, from which the captain had a fine view of her crew at work, and of the immediate area of space. She mounted the steps to the dais, and as she reached its top, a face descended from the shadows above it. A hard-wired servitor, little more than head, upper torso and arms, and anchored to the ceiling by writhing metallic tubing, it held in its emaciated arms a data-slate, which it proffered to Brielle.

She took the data-slate without acknowledgement, and the servitor rose once more, to disappear into the depths of gloom above the command throne. She sat, reclining in her throne, its shape reminding her that, despite the family politics, she was mistress of a rogue trader vessel. She had at her command several thousand souls and banks of mighty weapons, with which she could take her will to the stars.

She stretched, cat-like, and planted her feet upon a command console in a manner she knew her father would have found most unbecoming for a rogue trader. She grinned as she thought how her mother would have approved.

She lifted the data-slate, reading off its title. It contained a communiqué from the *Fairlight*'s Navigator, Adept Sagis. Brielle had never met the Navigator face to face, for he occupied a sealed blister mounted just fore of the *Fairlight*'s drive section, its armoured viewing ports affording the Navigator a panoramic view of space. It wasn't the space of the real universe that the Navigator gazed out upon, however, it was the realm of pure spiritual energy that was the warp, for the vessel would be lost, adrift upon the Sea of Souls were it to attempt warp travel without a Navigator.

As a child, Brielle had once asked her father about the Navigators, but had found him unwilling to discuss the matter in any detail, merely telling her that the Navigator families made warp travel possible, and that the Imperium would be no more than a disparate collection of isolated worlds without them. Only when she had come of age, and commanded her own vessel had she discovered at least a part of the truth of the matter. The Navigators were an impossibly ancient arm of humanity, one that had arisen on Old Terra at the time of the Emperor's rise to power. They were masters of an extraordinary gift, in that they could see into the warp, reading its currents, and thereby guide a vessel safely through it.

Such a gift came at a price, however, for it was rooted in the genes, and therefore subject to the vagaries of breeding. In order to keep their blood lines clean, and their abilities intact, the Navigator families were forced to control their breeding, selecting matches between Navigator clans that would result in 'pure' offspring. Even with such selective controls in place, the Navigators were shockingly prone to mutation, an affliction that, Brielle had gleaned, was wont to worsen with age. The most powerful of Navigators enjoyed a prodigious lifespan, but many grew increasingly mutated as their years advanced. Brielle had discovered that when this occurred, a Navigator who remained in service would retire to his chamber, hiding himself away from all but his peers, with whom he had scant contact, to serve in isolation.

Sagis's clan, the Locarno, had entered into partnership with the Arcadius before the dynasty had received its Charter of Trade, and the details of the affiliation were unknown to Brielle, although she suspected that her father knew the truth of it. She had guessed that old Sagis had become too mutated to leave his blister, although he had served with the skill and dedication for which his clan were renowned, despite this.

Absentmindedly, for the affair with Luneberg's xenos artefacts gnawed at her mind, Brielle read the communiqué. Transient conditions in the warp had been favourable for most of the journey to Mundus Chasmata, but had worsened the closer to the Damocles Gulf they had travelled. Sagis described the region as permeated with a tangible stain, an after-image of great spiritual turmoil and upheaval. The gulf itself was an area Sagis counselled vehemently against attempting to cross, for warp conditions were such that any vessel attempting to do so might be pulled violently off-course, or lost entirely to the raging tides of the empyrean.

Something in Sagis's words reminded Brielle of the voices she had half-heard, whispering just below the wind upon the surface of Sigma Q-77. It was as if he was describing a small part of the same phenomenon she had experienced, although in entirely different and subjective terms. The notion hit her that something had occurred in the region, something of stellar scale, something entirely alien and wrong. The fact that Luneberg had sent the rogue traders to the very edge of the afflicted region, to recover alien artefacts, filled Brielle with suspicion. She felt the spirit of her mother's people fill her – if Luneberg's actions brought woe to her family, Luneberg would pay. Brielle would see to that.

A harsh chime cut through Brielle's reverie, and she held the data-slate out to one side, the servitor descending once more to take it from her. 'Go ahead.'

A moment later, her father's voice boomed from the speaker grilles mounted above the command throne. 'Korvane, Brielle, we have what we came for. We'll rendezvous at the prearranged point in Luneberg's system. My Navigator informs me it's a twenty-day voyage, subjective, although he tells me that he and Sagis both have concerns about the tides in the warp, so I want formation kept as tight as possible. The chances are we'll arrive together, but I don't want to take any chances on any unwelcome guests waiting for us at the other end. They knew exactly where to expect us last time. I don't want us to be caught off guard again. Is that understood?'

Korvane answered before Brielle. He always did. 'Understood, Father.'

'Brielle,' Brielle's father addressed her. 'Is the cargo safe?'

'It is safe, Father. It's stowed in number three stasis. Nothing can happen to it in there.'

'Good. Now, I wish you both a dull and uneventful journey. The Emperor protects.'

'The Emperor protects,' Brielle heard Korvane repeat.

'The Emperor protects.'

Brielle watched from her command throne as the distant form of the *Oceanid* broke formation, moving to a safe distance from which she would commence her dive into the warp. Such a manoeuvre was inherently dangerous, and in populated systems was subject to a plethora of ordinances, each designed to minimise the impact of any mishap on nearby vessels, or even worlds. Brielle had heard all manner of grisly tales of catastrophic warp drive malfunction, and had even witnessed the aftermath of one, at the world of Radina V. There, a bulk carrier had mistimed its translation, sheering off the gravity pull of Radina V's third moon. The carrier was caught in a slingshot as it dived in to the warp, pulled in too many dimensions by forces impossible to comprehend. The vessel had broken up, and been smeared across space in a debris field that engulfed the moon and part of Radina itself with fallout. It wasn't the sort of fallout that could be scrubbed by decontamination teams. It was spiritual fallout, the residue of the three thousand souls lost in the disaster, and it afflicted the minds of every man, woman and child upon the moon's surface, and several hundred thousand more upon Radina V. They were driven insane within hours, their souls touched by the warp as it leaked through the three thousand tiny warp portals created at the instant of the carrier's destruction.

The rogue traders had delivered an Ordo Hereticus strike force to Radina V, and Brielle had watched from orbit as the Emperor's mercy had been delivered to hundreds of thousands of afflicted subjects. An entire continent had been burned clean of the unclean stain of the warp, those driven beyond the limit of sanity by its touch delivered by cleansing flame.

Radina V was found to be the fault of the carrier's master, who had ordered the vessel to enter the warp too close to the world's gravity well. Although the official investigation had levelled no criticism upon the vessel's Navigator, Brielle's father had voiced the opinion that the fault lay chiefly with him, because it was his responsibility to override any order that would compromise the safety of the ship. However, the Navigator families were one of the Imperium's most powerful institutions and no blame would ever be levelled upon them.

Brielle had few concerns that such an incident might occur with the Navigators of the Locarno clan guiding the fleet. As the *Oceanid* accelerated away, Brielle knew that her father would be making his vessel ready for translation to the warp, while the *Oceanid*'s Navigator entered a deep trance, in which he would guide the vessel through the unpredictable Sea of Souls. The *Oceanid* now far beyond visible range, Brielle watched as Korvane's vessel manoeuvred onto a similar heading, a course designed to ensure all three vessels remained in as coherent a formation within the warp as was possible.

Brielle reached to her left and pulled back a heavy lever, half a dozen pict-slates descending from the ceiling to surround her.

Static buzzed from the screens, before each resolved into a different rendition of the immediate area of space. Across one screen scrolled entirely abstract columns of numerical data, while another represented the *Fairlight*'s environs in a riot of machine-sight gradations. Brielle had acquired the knack of reading all simultaneously, for her bridge lacked the rare, three-dimensional holograph of the *Oceanid*. She noted how the *Oceanid*'s number three drive bled wispy clouds of superheated plasma through its emergency venting, a symptom of the neglect of the fleet's vessels brought about by the dynasty's misfortunes.

Moving at incredible velocity, the *Oceanid* began her dive. The screens erupted in activity, the machine devices attempting to describe that which should not even be possible. Brielle saw that the *Oceanid*'s Geller Field was raised, creating a delicate bubble of real space around her, within which she would find shelter from the raging energies of the warp. Just before the *Oceanid* passed beyond the furthest extent of the *Fairlight*'s augurs, Brielle caught the dazzling explosion of metaphysical energies as the ship dived into the warp. Each warp drive and each Navigator interacted with the warp in a unique manner, meaning that no two dives were identical. The sight, rendered across half a dozen pict-slates in as many different forms, was something quite beautiful, and quite terrible to behold. The *Oceanid*'s passing forcibly ripped a gash in the intangible fabric of the universe, bleeding the raw stuff of the warp, for an instant. Yet, even as questing tentacles of something unreal seeped forth, the scar was healed, the laws of the universe reasserting themselves once more.

A moment later, a familiar wave of sickness passed over Brielle and was gone: the spiritual wake of the *Oceanid*'s warp jump.

Seeing that Korvane's vessel was moving into position for its own dive, Brielle checked that her ship was prepared for its jump, and then addressed her bridge crew.

'We make warp in three minutes. All hands to station.'

At her words, the bridge became a hive of activity. Although her crew was well versed in the manoeuvre, making a warp jump was never taken lightly, at least not by any crew that wanted to make it safely back to port. Chanting filled the bridge, and a line of lay priests emerged from the chapel to the rear, blessed incense billowing around them as they anointed the *Fairlight*'s systems with holy unguents. These would ward off the evil intentions of the denizens of the warp and ensure the vessel's safe passage.

Next, a deck officer passed quickly from one station to the next, ensuring that each rating and servitor was secured to his seat. This was not for their own safety, but for that of the vessel, for it had been known for the weak to be driven to insanity at the moment of entry into the warp, and to run amok upon a ship's bridge, killing all within reach. Brielle knew that it had happened to a member of her father's bridge crew long before she was born, the man killing three of his fellows with his teeth alone, before her father had put a data-spike through his head. Such enflamed passions at the moment of the jump were, according to space-lore, the result of the call of the warp-bound daemon, and to heed its lies was to invite the loss of every soul on the ship. Thus, every precaution possible was taken against it.

A message from Navigator Sagis scrolled across a data-slate. He confirmed that he was ready to enter his warp trance, and wished Brielle the Emperor's blessings. The words of a prayer began scrolling across the screen, 'We pray for those lost in the warp...' and Brielle knew that it would loop over, repeatedly, until Sagis was awakened, and the *Fairlight* was once again safe in the real universe.

She reclined in her command throne as she felt the deep growl of the *Fairlight*'s warp drive steadily build. A build up of psychic power, felt deep in the soul, accompanyed the subsonic noise. Every spacefarer felt it differently, but to Brielle it was a keen longing for home, or to be anywhere other than where they were about to go.

As the last of the crew assumed their stations, the deck officer strapping himself into his own chair last, the *Fairlight* began her dive. As her forward velocity increased exponentially, the air pressure on the bridge rose and a violent shaking set in. Brielle saw from a nearby pict that the *Rosetta* had completed her dive, and quickly scanned the surrounding area one last time.

The order to dive perched on her lips, Brielle stalled. Despite the screen's jarring vibrations, she could make out a huge return less than forty thousand kilometres off the *Fairlight*'s port bow. She punched a comm channel, connecting her straight through to her Navigator.

'Sagis... you see it?'

She forced down a rising sense of panic, praying that her Navigator had not yet fully entered his trance, but realising that they were inexorably committed to the warp jump. The Navigator's reply scrolled across a data-slate.

++I see it ma'am. I shall attempt to compensate for its mass and proximity. The Emperor protect us all.++

Brielle's mind raced. The other ship had emerged from nowhere, and she could read that its gravitic signature was well in excess of its class. Her breath caught in her throat as she realised with a start that it was clearly alien in origin. It did not appear to be intent upon any hostile action, but its mere appearance at such a crucial point in the *Fairlight*'s jump had put Brielle's ship in incredible danger. She saw that she had but one option. She must trust to her Navigator's skill, for to pull out of the dive might tear her ship apart.

Gripping the arms of her command throne, Brielle issued her order. 'Jump!'

CHAPTER FIVE

Korvane stood upon the shuttle pad at Chasmata Capitalis, his father's back facing him. The golden orb of Chasmata's star was just beginning its slow descent, sinking below the distant, jagged horizon, silhouetting the master of Arcadius against the dusky sky.

'We cannot wait for her, father. If we keep Luneberg hanging on he might take exception and cancel the deal.'

'Without her, there is no deal. Most of the artefacts are aboard the *Fairlight*.'

Where the hell was she? Lucian looked up into the rapidly darkening skies of Mundus Chasmata, as if he would see his daughter's shuttle descending through the dark clouds. He knew that could not be of course, for there appeared to be only a single shuttle operating the surface to orbit route, and the Chasmatans forbade travellers descending in their own vessels.

'She must have mistimed her jump. She'll ruin the whole thing if she's late.'

'Hmm.' Lucian turned to face his son. 'We have two choices: beg that scat-hound Luneberg to wait until Brielle arrives with her cargo, or bluff our way through. If we let him know she's been delayed, he'll sense weakness and the whole deal will go ahead on his, not our, terms. We can certainly delay for a short time – even Luneberg knows ships don't travel through the empyrean in perfect formation. If we proceed as if everything's fine, we'll earn Brielle time to catch up.'

'Do you think she'll arrive at all, Father?'

Lucian bristled at his son's words. He had faith that his daughter was safe, but he had been concerned enough to seek the counsel of the *Oceanid*'s Navigator.

'I've consulted Adept Baru. He informs me that conditions became rough immediately following our translation, but he felt confident that Sagis and the vessel he navigated had come to no harm.'

Baru had actually said more than that, but Lucian was far from keen to repeat his words. The Navigator had stated that, had the *Fairlight* come to harm within the warp, he would have known immediately. The beasts that dwell within the Sea of Souls would have howled with such desire at the prospect of devouring a Navigator that every one of his kind in the sector would have felt their brother's soul-death.

'So we continue with the talks as if nothing was awry. Understood?'

'Understood, Father.'

'I trust your mission was successful my dear Lucian? The... goods were transported without incident?'

Culpepper Luneberg sprawled upon his throne, a courtesan leaning languidly at each shoulder. Lucian stood before him, his son at his side. The vast throne room was empty, silent and eerie, swallowing up the small group in its deep gloom. Luneberg had summoned the rogue traders to his court the instant that they had landed; typical, Lucian thought, of the man's manners.

'It was most successful, my lord.' Lucian would remain polite on the exterior, but inside he found himself feeling more irritated by Luneberg each time they met. The man presumed himself to be Lucian's superior, and addressed him as such. Did he not know that the Arcadius held a mandate as weighty as that of any Imperial Commander? By their Charter of Trade, granted by the authority of the High Lords of Terra, the Arcadius had the right to demand any service they required from the likes of Luneberg when going about their business. It was only at times such as these, when not directly pursuing that business, that Lucian was compelled to be polite to those he considered the petty nobility of a backwater world that had not once, in all the recorded annals of the Imperium's long, wartorn history, contributed anything of any worth to the race of men.

'I'm so glad to hear it. You must join my court in a celebratory feast, this evening.'

'We'd be delighted,' he demurred, whilst thinking: she'll never be here in time, we're skewed.

A courtesan put cherry-red lips to Luneberg's ear, whispering softly to him. Luneberg went to shoo her away, but looked at Lucian as he listened to her muffled words. She regarded Lucian smugly as Luneberg addressed him.

'All three of you will be joining us of course?'

Utterly skewed. 'Of course, my lord, my family and myself will be honoured.'

'Good. My factor will take care of our business.' Luneberg's ever-present functionary bowed to Lucian.

He hadn't noted the man's presence before it was mentioned.

'I have arranged,' the man now said, 'to have our cargo lighters convey the goods directly from your ships. They are docking with the *Rosetta*, even now, and we only require your authority to complete the transfer.

'Understood,' Lucian replied to the man, noting that, only now, when it suited them, were the Chasmatans capable of displaying a degree of efficiency.

Lucian bowed as Luneberg stood, the courtesans arranging themselves demurely around the Imperial Commander as he did so. With the slightest of reciprocal nods, the Imperial Commander left, leaving Lucian distractedly wondering what the hell had become of his daughter, and the cargo she carried.

Brielle stood in the centre of her cargo hold, opened crates scattered around her feet.

The chamber's stasis field had failed during the jump, and once the *Fairlight* was back in the real universe, in the Chasmata system and safely inbound to Chasmata itself, Brielle had come to inspect the damage. Several of the crates had fallen open, and what she had found within the first few had driven her to open them all.

Weapons, the crates contained weapons. The Arcadius had been reduced to gunrunners. Seeing that each item was unique, Brielle had immediately realised that the shipment represented a collection of samples. It was nothing more than that.

Brielle simmered as she hefted a long rifle. It was something approaching two metres in length, but was almost too easy to lift. Its business end housed a metallic sphere that rotated in three dimensions, allowing, Brielle guessed, for its smooth handling. She braced the weapon at her shoulder, marvelling at the way its bulk rotated around the gyroscopic sphere, and closed one eye. As she drew a bead on a non-existent target, a small box rose from the body of the weapon. She started, pulling her head sharply away, but saw that the box housed some form of sighting device. She placed her eye to it, cautiously peering through. On the tiny screen within, blocky alien text flowed around a central crosshair, picking out all manner of objects within the hold.

Brielle could not read the text, but she knew such a weapon far surpassed the vast majority of those of human manufacture. Granted, those such as the mighty Adeptus Astartes had access to equivalent technologies, but what might Luneberg want with them? She could draw only one conclusion. Luneberg meant to make war – but on whom?

As far as Brielle was concerned, Luneberg had dishonoured the Arcadius gravely. He had made them petty smugglers, and her father had failed to see it coming. She felt her rage boil to the surface as she remembered how Korvane had simpered, certain in his view that what he saw as a respectable joint venture with the Imperial Commander would bring both parties profit and honour. She expected more of her father, but would he listen to her if she warned him? Should she try now? Most likely, he would accuse her of meddling in matters outside of her concern. Better to bide her time, she decided, before contacting her father.

She kicked an open crate, hard. This whole deal was rapidly spiralling out of control, and she seemed to be the only one with any idea just how badly.

Lucian, in his stateroom, stood before a mirror that magnified his image threefold, studying his reflection. His reflection glared straight back at him, his discomfort and annoyance writ large on his face. He wore the finest familial regalia, armour, medals, cloak and all, intent as he was upon distracting Luneberg from Brielle's absence.

Whilst his son had been called away to deal with the business of authorising the cargo transfer from the *Rosetta*, Lucian had contacted the *Oceanid*, speaking to the vessel's Navigator once more. Adept Baru had restated his earlier opinion that the *Fairlight* had not been lost upon the tides of the warp, and had appeared confident that Brielle had not been greatly delayed. Lucian was tense nonetheless, for a Navigator was, in his experience generally pleased enough with a window of several weeks, so long as no harm came to his vessel. Baru was undoubtedly a cut above the average Navigator, if such a thing was possible; yet Lucian still felt his grasp on events outside of his navigation blister was vague at best.

Not for the first time during this venture, Lucian regarded the medals crowded across his chest. Each meant so much, yet might be rendered meaningless should the dynasty fail. So much relied upon the deal with Luneberg, and so much had already been invested in simply voyaging to the Eastern Rim, that Lucian could see precious little of a future for the Arcadius should the deal fail.

He was reminded of the tale his father had told him of old Abad Gerrit, the great Arcadius who had pacified the Scallarn Cluster. According to his father, Abad had risked much to raise an army, entirely at his own expense, with which to take back the dozen worlds of the cluster from the yoke of ork enslavement. He had purchased scores of troop transports to carry his newly risen armies, and hired on innumerable auxiliary vessels and crews to service his conquest fleet.

The pacification attempts of just the first world of the cluster had faced fierce resistance, and had taken three decades to complete. By then, Lucian's father had told him, old Abad was all but stripped of resources, his fleet down to half a dozen vessels and his armies a mere fraction of their former strength. However, Abad had a trick up his sleeve. He had used all his contacts and influence to reinstate the former ruler of that single liberated world, presenting to him a free, if somewhat wartorn domain. The newly installed leader had bankrolled the remainder of the re-conquest, the rulership of each liberated world going to those of his choosing, while Abad was rewarded greatly for his services.

Lucian's father had insisted that there was a lesson in Abad's tale. Lucian had always thought the only real lesson to be gleaned was that Abad was an old, mercenary bastard with the scruples of an eldar. Perhaps, he now pondered, Abad had been onto something.

A rap at the apartment door interrupted Lucian's chain of thought.

'Enter!'

The huge, gilded portal swung inwards, a white-robed servant bowing deeply as he entered.

'My lord, my master requests the company of the Arcadius this night.'

No point stalling, Lucian thought. With a final glance at his reflection, he strode from the chamber, and Korvane joined him as he returned from his business with the cargo transfer. The servant closed the great doors at his passing.

Brielle planted her hands on her hips and took a deep breath. For the second time, she found herself standing in the small office of the harbour master of the Chasmata Primary Orbital, although on this occasion she, and not her father, would be the one to deal with him. She was really going to give the fool a piece of her mind.

'Please ma'am, you must understand. I cannot authorise a shuttle to the surface without a counter-signed declaration amounting to a level epsilon exception. You do not hold such a declaration.'

'Listen to me you space-damned rimfluke. If you can't organise a shuttle, I'm simply going to take my own. Do you understand me?'

The pale-faced harbour master bristled still further, gathering up a pile of nearby papers, presumably some ingrained nervous reaction to being balled out by the angry daughter of a powerful (as far as he was concerned at least) rogue trader lord.

'I'm afraid, that is simply out of the question. Three hundred and nine ordinances expressly forbid it. Should you attempt an unauthorised interface the Chasmata System Levy is required to shoot you down before you even break orbit.'

'Really, and how will they do that?'

'How will they–?'

'How will your system defence force stop me, when it has no vessels?'

'My lady, that is entirely academic. The point is that they are empowered and required to do so. That in itself should be sufficient reason.'

Culpepper Luneberg's banquet hall was like no venue Lucian had ever visited, although he did not allow his impressions to show upon his face. As with the majority of the palace he had thus far seen, the hall was vast in extent. Yet, conversely, it felt claustrophobic, for Lucian and his son moved through small havens of light cast by hovering lumens, beyond which impenetrable darkness swallowed all. He caught glimpses of an impossibly high, vaulted ceiling, bats or cyber-cherubs – it was too gloomy to tell which – capering amongst rope-thick cobwebs. The chamber was incongruously narrow, barely wide enough in fact to accommodate the table that ran from one shadowed end to the other.

The table also grabbed Lucian's attention. Amongst elaborate candelabras from which trails of molten wax overflowed, was laid a veritable riot of gastronomic excess. Every manner of plate, dish, pot, tray, container and multi-tiered service held every manner of foodstuff, from cauldrons of bubbling, weirdly coloured liquids to the elaborately dressed, roasted carcasses of alien beasts the like of which not even Lucian had seen before. The aroma of all this assaulted Lucian's nose, causing his body a moment of doubt as it decided whether to order his stomach to wretch or his mouth to water.

An impossibly elaborate array of cutlery, drinking vessels and plates, each manufactured from the most exquisite of materials and decorated by the most skilled of artisans, made up each place setting, leaving barely a square inch of the vast table's surface uncluttered. Tall-backed chairs finished the place settings, a servant hovering behind each one, ready to wait upon the diner's merest whim.

One such attendant, a hunched and wizened old man, stepped forward, bowing deeply to Lucian. Lucian waited whilst the man struggled to heave the heavy chair from its place at the table. Lucian saw that Korvane was now entering the dining hall, being offered a seat several places down from him. The servant finished manoeuvring the seat into position, and Lucian nodded his gratitude to him, before taking his place at the table.

He also noted that a seat several places down from Korvane remained empty. He assumed this was intended for Brielle, and hoped that it was sufficiently far removed from wherever Luneberg would be seated so as not to announce her absence too loudly.

More guests filed into the narrow hall, passing down either side of the table. Lucian could barely make out those at its furthest extent, for the far end was shrouded in shadow, but those seats flanking his own were soon occupied. The other guests were evidently the great and the good of Mundus Chasmata's ruling class, each diner's rank communicated not by insignia, but by the sheer amount of portable wealth on display.

To Lucian's left sat a man of indeterminate age, both his eyes replaced by gaudy, jewelled prosthetics, each pulsing as they cycled through the spectrum. He wore a white periwig and a long coat of the finest gold thread, and, to Lucian's mind, sat at the centre of an intense cloud of cloying perfume. Lucian nodded politely to the man, taking the opportunity to study the lenses that replaced his eyes. They were of the same type so strategically sported by Luneberg's harem, although the courtesans wore them upon fine golden chains that did little to hide their non-existent modesty. These were far larger, but obviously of the same type. Lucian was now sure they were of xenos manufacture, but tucked the suspicion to the back of his mind, until such time as it would prove useful to act upon it.

An elderly woman with the tallest hair Lucian had ever seen took the seat to his right. He nodded to her too, causing her to lift a pair of intricate lenses mounted upon a delicate, bone handle to her eyes. She peered back at him, the lenses whirring and her eyes magnified disturbingly. The woman let out a high pitched, nasal sound before turning away from him. Lucian saw then what was coming: introductions.

Every culture had its own manner of introducing strangers into its midst, and Lucian had found that, the more refined the culture in question the more involved, and often ridiculous the details of those introductions. The spectacle in the throne room had told Lucian an enormous amount about Luneberg and his court, and he had noted that he appeared not to exist until he was introduced to the court members. There, he had been introduced to the court as a whole by Luneberg's functionary, telling Lucian that in this particular culture it was customary for the lower ranked members to do the introducing, to the higher ranked. Lucian had seen, and partaken of several hundred variations on such a custom, and knew that the best way to avoid insulting one's host was to remain attentive, yet silent, until addressed.

Soon, every seat was taken, except of course for Brielle's, and the one immediately opposite Lucian. This was clearly Luneberg's, for it was twice the width of the others, and the delicacies piled before it yet more exquisite. Luneberg's functionary appeared from the shadows, and stood beside his master's empty seat.

Every head at the table turned to the functionary, a reverent silence descending. In a moment, only the hissing of candles was audible.

'My lords, ladies and gentlemen, please stand for the Lord and Master of Mundus Chasmata. Lord Culpepper Luneberg the Twenty-Ninth!'

Lucian stood only a fraction of a second after the other diners, following their lead in giving polite applause as Luneberg entered the dining hall. The Imperial Commander was flanked not by his harem but by a gaggle of scraping servants, each intent upon attending to a single aspect of their master's wellbeing. Lucian saw that these were Luneberg's body servants; each with a task no doubt ranging from cutting up their master's food and drink, to tasting it.

Luneberg reached his seat, his servants fussing around him. One lifted a massive goblet, sampling a tiny portion of the deep red liquid within. The man made to take a second taste, just to be sure, Lucian thought, before Luneberg grabbed it from him.

Luneberg raised the goblet, golden candlelight glinting from its finely engraved surfaces. The servant stationed behind Lucian's seat appeared, proffering a goblet of the same type that Luneberg raised, although somewhat smaller.

'My dear and loyal subjects, I welcome you to my table. Let us feast!'

A resounding chorus of affirmation filled the dining hall, echoing from the high ceiling. Luneberg drained his goblet in one motion. An instant later, the guests did likewise, waiting for Luneberg to lower his bulk into his seat before sitting themselves.

'Now then,' said Luneberg, looking across at Lucian. Lucian met his gaze, noting how it flitted for an instant to Brielle's empty seat. 'Our esteemed Arcadius finds himself at a disadvantage, and I myself remiss as a host. Naal?' Luneberg's functionary, seated next to his master, nodded, and stood.

Lucian had noted how this Naal appeared to fulfil the role of advisor or chancellor to the Imperial Commander, and was curious as to how much power he really held. Lucian had met with men who held title over worlds, over entire systems, who nonetheless devolved power to their advisors, to their military chiefs, to their favourite mistresses or, in one memorable case, to a favoured pet ptera-squirrel. He knew that Luneberg was no fool, but determined to gain the measure of his inner circle.

Naal bowed deeply, first to his master, and then to the diners as a whole. His hood was back, revealing him to be a man perhaps in his thirties, with High Gothic script tattooed across his left cheek and the elaborate coat of arms of Luneberg's dynasty, the Harrid, upon his forehead.

Naal turned to his left, clearing his throat before addressing the man seated there, 'My lord, I introduce to you the Lord Arcadius, Lucian Gerrit, rogue trader.' The grandee, a stolid man formally attired in what was, very obviously, a military uniform denoting the highest rank, nodded impassively to Lucian. 'My Lord Gerrit, High Colonel Hugost Trevelyan-Constance the Third, General Officer Commanding the Legions Chasmatus.'

By the man's uniform, Lucian deduced that the general staff of the Mundus Chasmata Planetary Defence Force thought very highly of themselves. Lucian had dined with Lords Militant who wore finery that was far more restrained. He was the type of man, Lucian thought, who would use every political trick in the book to avoid service in the Imperium's armies, preferring instead to remain on his own world, lording it up over his small military kingdom.

Naal turned his attention to a man three seats down from Lucian, repeating his earlier introduction of the rogue trader. 'My Lord Voltemoth, Supreme High Comptroller to the House of Luneberg.' The man was wizened and ascetic, one eye, his nose and an ear replaced by cybernetic implants that no doubt facilitated his role within Luneberg's bureaucracy.

Voltemoth regarded Lucian down his mighty, hawk like nose, his bushy grey eyebrows creasing as he appeared to Lucian to consider whether or not acknowledging the rogue trader was an efficient use of his time. He evidently decided some acknowledgement was in fact required, crossing his hands across his chest in the sign of the aquila.

A third introduction followed, this time to the fellow sitting on Lucian's left. 'The Lord Procreator General, Theodulf Raffenswine.' Lucian stifled a cough. Had Naal really just introduced the man as what he thought he had? He remained impassive, bowing politely as Raffenswine nodded back, his jewel-like cybernetic eyes twinkling.

Lucian's estimation of the court of Luneberg was being refined with each introduction. The Imperial Commander appeared to have surrounded himself with the effete and the ineffectual: highborn autocrats, all, to Lucian's practiced eye, lords and masters of their small world, yet ultimately, entirely subservient to the will of their overlord. It appeared to Lucian that either Luneberg, or perhaps some ancestor who had instigated such a system, had concocted a very good way of controlling his world's ruling class.

Another introduction interrupted Lucian's chain of thought. 'My Lady, Madam Clarimonde Vulviniam-Clancy.' Lucian was unsure whether that was the woman's rank or her name, but bowed politely to her nonetheless. She nodded back, her tall hairpiece threatening to topple as she did so.

A round of introductions to diners of apparently lesser rank followed, Naal passing over each with increasing brevity, until, finally, Lucian was introduced to every guest he could at least see, for the far ends of the table were still obscured in gloom. Lucian had noted throughout the introductions that at no point had even the lowest-ranked diner been introduced to him; it was always the other way around. He pondered whether this was an intentional, conscious snub on Luneberg's part, or a more generalised condescension towards outsiders manifested in the court's customs.

Luneberg snapped his fingers, and Naal bent at the waist to attend his words. From his position, Lucian could not hear the exchange, but it resulted in Naal standing straight once more, and clapping his hands together once.

A tangible sense of anticipation swept the hall. The shadows behind Naal stirred, and a procession of servants appeared, each holding a silver dish covered by a tall dome. The train snaked around the table, until a servant stood at the right side of each diner. At some unspoken command, each servant bent forward and lifted the heavy dome, holding forth the silver plate for the diners' inspection.

The guests let out a collective gasp, part thrill, part horror. Lucian studied their faces. Each diner bore an expression that sat somewhere between rapture and pain, while Luneberg regarded Lucian intently, seeking, Lucian deduced, any sign of uncertainty that might be turned to the Imperial Commander's advantage.

Luneberg spread his arms wide and addressed the table. 'My loyal friends, we have the honour of the presence of a great guest, and it is my intention to honour him and his kin in return by serving the very finest of delicacies! My agents, at prodigious expense to myself, and extreme personal danger to themselves, have procured from the distant world of Catachan,' – a murmur of appreciation – 'the most exquisite dish in the quadrant: The Catachan face eater!'

The servant at Lucian's side proffered him the plate. Lucian looked down. Upon it was a colourless, shapeless slab of twitching muscle.

The servant waited for a response. When none was immediately forthcoming, he addressed Lucian. 'Is the creature to my lord's satisfaction?'

Lucian nodded to the servant, who covered the dish once more, and withdrew. He swallowed hard; these people were utterly, irredeemably, mad.

Brielle seethed as Goanna brought the shuttle down upon the landing pad at Chasmata Capitalis. She had foregone the Chasmatans' planetary shuttle, boarding her own and ordering her pilot to breach the non-existent blockade. The journey to the capital had taken less than an hour, but she had fallen into a deep brooding during the flight, during which she had come to the conclusion that her father and her stepbrother must be stopped from dragging the dynasty into oblivion. She knew they would not listen to her warnings, so she had determined to impress her will in any way she was able.

She unbuckled her safety harness, and was out of her seat before the shuttle had finished touching down. She struck the ramp release, striking it a second time when it failed to engage. The shuttle safely down and the lockouts disengaged, her third strike caused the ramp to lower, and she stormed down it, into the cold evening air of Mundus Chasmata.

'My lady, I must ask that you halt immediately!'

A squad of Luneberg's household guard stood blocking Brielle's path from the pad, their white armour ghostly in the dim light of the dusk. She stopped, and stood before them, looking them over mockingly.

'Which of you clones is in charge?'

A white and gold-armoured trooper, wearing armour as white and gold as the others, stepped forward.

'I am, of course. Ma'am, you do not have clearance to land.'

'Oh dear, silly me, I seem to have done so anyway. What do you propose to do about it?'

'You must obtain the proper retroactive clearance.'

'Fine, I'll do that. I was on my way to an audience with the Imperial Commander anyway. He is empowered to grant me a retroactive landing permit I suppose?'

The trooper's mouth opened and closed for a moment, before he came to an obvious decision. 'Yes ma'am, I suggest you do so.'

Brielle was already pushing through the squad, her course now clear in her mind.

In what felt like entirely too short a time, the dish had returned. Lucian had spent the intervening period engaged in meaningless small talk with those on either side of him. The man introduced as the 'Procreator General' was, despite Lucian's initial misgivings, a likeable enough fellow, despite the fact that conversation with him was somewhat awkward because eye contact was not made with human eyes but with his multi-spectral, artificial ones. Lucian had been mildly curious as to Raffenswine's position within the ruling elite, but had thought twice about broaching the subject, knowing that many cultures found such topics vulgar. Lucian suspected this might be literally true in the Procreator General's case.

The elderly woman to Lucian's right turned out to be one of

the most unpleasant individuals Lucian had ever had the misfortune of meeting, and he had in his time spoken with some highly unpleasant beings. Though she feigned an air of disinterest in her surroundings, she reminded Lucian of a haemonculus of the xenos eldar that he had once had cause to meet. She shared the eldar's apparent distain for other beings, clearly being of the opinion that all such lower creatures were a simple waste of flesh. Lucian was quite pleased when the Catachan face eater was placed before him.

Luneberg tapped his goblet twice with a silver spoon, the diners immediately hanging on his coming words. 'My friends, our finest chefs have prepared for us a dish of supreme delicacy. You have all seen with your own eyes that the creatures were in good condition, if necessarily sedated when presented to you. They have now received the tender mercies of our kitchens, and await your pleasure. Enjoy!'

The servant lifted the dome covering the dish, placing the face eater on the table in front of Lucian. He looked around at the other diners, seeing that every one was nodding in appreciation, yet none seemed willing to eat first.

'My dear Lucian,' Luneberg called from across the table, 'I trust such a dish is nothing exotic to one such as you.' Every diner in the hall looked up at him, pleased, he judged, by the distraction.

Lucian saw immediately that Luneberg sought to test him. Fine, he thought, better men than him had tried. 'I have eaten many such dishes, my dear Culpepper,' Lucian said, using Luneberg's forename deliberately, weighing up the risk in terms of breaching etiquette, 'though never so exquisitely prepared as this variant.'

An appreciative murmur emanated from several nearby diners. Lucian had the distinct impression that they were enjoying the spectacle.

'Well,' Luneberg leaned back in his seat, 'you will have to demonstrate the correct manner in which such a dish is consumed. We are but a frontier world, and the ways of high court are slow to reach us.'

Now Lucian knew Luneberg was upping his game. What did the Imperial Commander have to gain from doing so? Did he seek some pretext under which to take offence at Lucian's deportment? Wars had certainly been fought over such trivial matters as which direction the svort was passed after dinner, so such a motive was certainly not out of the question.

'Certainly.' Lucian looked down at the dish before him. The fleshy, translucent meat of the Catachan face eater lay on a bed of delicate green shoots. Lucian knew a little about the creature's habits, and knew, full well, how it had come by its name. When first offered for the diners' inspection the creatures were very much alive, though as Luneberg had stated, sedated enough to stop them from launching themselves at the guests. The creature spasmed, indicating to Lucian that he was expected to eat it alive. Fine, he thought, he'd eaten far more repulsive, though less dangerous creatures before, and would do so again were it to aid the survival of his dynasty.

That thought in mind, Lucian reached for an eating implement, judging expertly which of the score of utensils at his placing was set aside for the task at hand. He chose what he took for the filleting knife, guessing that he would need to make an incision that would incapacitate, as opposed to awaken, the deadly creature.

He raised the knife as a, literally, deadly silence gripped the hall. The face eater twitched once more. In one fluid motion, Lucian sank the knife into the part of its flesh that had moved, slicing away a thin morsel of still-convulsing muscle and popping it into his mouth. He chewed, as a polite round of compliments rippled through the diners.

'Well, I must say, that's one way of going about it. I prefer to wallop the blighters with a mallet myself!'

The diners let out a nervous titter, picking up the miniature hammers set amongst the cutlery, and tapping the food upon their dishes nervously. Lucian chuckled inwardly as he saw that, in many cases this just served to make the food angry. Lucian noted, however, that Raffenswine, seated next to him, was eating the dish as Lucian had, and within minutes half the diners in the hall were doing the same.

'You've made quite an impression upon my court, my dear Lucian,' said Luneberg. 'I hope the meat is to your taste?'

Lucian nodded. 'Yes my lord. The dish is quite exquisite,' he lied. In fact, it was quite tasteless. He saw immediately that Luneberg had served such a dangerous dish not for its taste, but for its entertainment value. Clearly, some form of ennui had descended upon the court, driving it to ever more contrived distractions, from its hyper-cultured mores to its culinary eccentricities.

The entrée consumed, Naal had ordered the main course to be served. Lucian had scant chance to discover what manner of dish this might be, however, before a commotion at the far end of the hall caught his attention.

He looked around the table, catching Korvane's eye. His son appeared pained, yet none of the diners appeared to have noticed. Looking closer, Lucian saw that the other guests appeared to be concentrating especially hard upon their neighbours, heads nodding eagerly in determined agreement with the most insignificant of statements.

As the commotion grew louder, the diners turned their heads away from the direction from which it emanated, assiduously ignoring its source. Lucian heard a raised voice, and knew, an instant before she appeared, that it belonged to his daughter.

Relief flooded through him, for his daughter was safe. As she stepped from the shadows, exasperated servants trailing behind her, he made to stand to greet her. Before he could however, Korvane coughed, drawing his attention to his son. With the slightest of motions, Korvane shook his head, and indicated Luneberg, who was staring, red-faced, into his goblet. The Imperial Commander's servants were in some distress, for they appeared not to know where to look, so obvious was their master's displeasure.

Brielle walked straight past him, and then past Korvane, and sat, before the attendant servant had the chance to pull out her seat for her. She swung her legs up onto the table, and crossed them, resting them on its edge. The movement caused priceless crystal goblets to tumble and smash upon the stone floor, and the crimson liquid within spilled across the table's surface. She reached across the table and lifted a crystal decanter, pouring herself a glass of its contents.

Lucian stared straight at his daughter, unable to fathom her behaviour. The room was now utterly silent; every head turned discreetly away from Brielle, yet, every eye glued to her.

She lifted the glass to her lips.

Luneberg surged to his feet. His servants scattered in all

directions and priceless goblets toppled, spilling their contents across the table.

'Lucian!'

Lucian stood, guessing what was coming next.

'Lucian, this is a travesty! Take her away this instant!'

Lucian did not say a word. He merely walked over to his daughter and proffered her his arm. She took it demurely, and together, they walked, heads held high, from Luneberg's dining hall.

CHAPTER SIX

'What by Vandire's hole is wrong with you, girl?'

Brielle remained silent. She would weather the storm of her father's wrath. Only once she had afforded him the opportunity to fully vent his spleen would she be able to act. He had remained silent all the way from Luneberg's dining hall back to the stateroom, but Brielle had sensed his boiling, inner rage from the moment they had left the chamber. He had not said a word, even to Korvane, who had caught up with them having made his apologies to Luneberg, until the door of the suite had closed behind them.

'You know how much is hanging on this mission, and yet you stroll into Luneberg's court with absolutely no concern for etiquette. Have I taught you nothing?'

Brielle bristled at that, for she held dear the memories of the lessons learned at her father's side, before Korvane had arrived. She remained impassive regardless, determined that any damage done would not be caused by her, despite the fact that her father was quite correct. Her actions had been contrary to all she knew of courtly etiquette, and deliberately so.

'If I didn't know better, I might have thought you'd done it–'

'Father?' Korvane broke in, calm in the face of his father's wrath. Easy enough for him, thought Brielle, for it was not directed at him. In fact, Brielle thought, he probably sought to turn it to his own advantage.

'What?' Her father held Brielle's gaze for a couple of seconds before turning to face her stepbrother.

'Father, I think we need to plan what to do next. I've been

studying the Chasmatans' traditions, and there's precedent to suggest they might have grounds to cancel any contract we might have entered into.'

Lucian took a deep breath, before addressing both his children. 'Korvane, Brielle, you both need to understand something about the nature of our deal with Luneberg. As I explained after the initial talks, this is not the type of contract recognised by high law and enforceable in the courts. This is not simple trade. This isn't even a transaction, and Luneberg is neither our partner nor our customer. He wanted something from us, and as much as he needed us at the beginning, we're as good as competitors in the long run.'

Brielle fought hard to hold her tongue, for as much as she agreed with her father's assessment, she felt even more strongly that he should never have entered into the venture in the first place.

'Luneberg needed us in order to gauge whether or not he was on to something good. The fact that we signed up, and have returned here, tells him he is,' Lucian said.

'But still,' Korvane spoke up, 'he needs us to move the goods on. Without us, he's surely just sitting on worthless merchandise.'

Brielle thought back to the cargo still sitting in her hold. She knew it was far from worthless. She had seen it for what it was – a mere sample of goods to be provided in the future. She would keep this information to herself though, and only reveal at a time most suited to her own ends. Her deliberate behaviour at the dining hall would pay dividends in the long run, but had left her stock low in the short term.

'I need to speak to Luneberg,' said Lucian. 'Try to patch things up and find out what he really wants from us. I know I can turn this to our profit, but I need both of you,' he looked straight at Brielle, 'both of you behind me. We are, in case you have forgotten, Arcadius.'

Brielle nodded, a vision of contrition, and her father visibly calmed. 'Korvane and I will get back to Luneberg. You,' he squeezed her hand, 'stay out of trouble.'

Only once her father and stepbrother had left the suite did Brielle allow herself a wry grin. She had succeeded in complicating the deal to the point where it might collapse entirely, but was unsure exactly where to go from there. When she had discovered the nature of the items in her hold, she had intended merely to steer her father away from the deal, souring it to the extent that it would collapse largely of its own accord. She thought of this as entirely unselfish, but had come to realise that her father, and certainly her stepbrother, would hardly see it that way.

If she was to be damned, she thought, she would be damned for good reason. If she succeeded in ruining the deal with Luneberg, she would need to make some kind of power play against her stepbrother, for he would never forgive her, even if her father did. That made Korvane a long-term enemy, and now, Brielle realised, was the best time to deal with him.

Brielle crossed to the tall, glass doors that formed one wall of the stateroom, hauling them open upon corroded runners. She stepped out onto the high gallery, and looked out on a panoramic view of Luneberg's capital city. The sun was almost set, the last of its rays turning the sky a deep bronze, and casting the air in a thick, golden haze. The city sprawled for many kilometres in every direction, distant, craggy mountains just visible on the horizon. Below her, the palace grounds were arrayed. She noted how these appeared overgrown and untended, not like the lovingly maintained ornamental gardens she would have expected to grace Luneberg's estates. Beyond the grounds, the merchants' quarter spread as far as the distant warehouses at the city's edge, its street markets alive with activity even at this late hour.

Brielle felt a sudden urge to be free of the shackles of responsibility, if only for a short time. Luneberg's court was a claustrophobic and stale environment, and little advantage was to be had skulking in the dusty guest suites. She looked out at the city, and then back towards the door of the apartment. She came to her decision.

While her father and stepbrother wasted time with Luneberg and his pet fops, Brielle would go out into his domain. She knew not what she might find, but she reasoned it had to be better than what she had here.

The household guards made no attempt to challenge Brielle as she strode through the main gates. They resolutely ignored her in fact, staring straight ahead, out into the city streets beyond. She reasoned that their task was to challenge those attempting to enter the palace. Her thus far limited experience with the Chasmatans' bureaucracy suggested that their vigilance did not extend to those attempting to leave. An interesting observation, and one that might prove worth remembering, she thought.

The city streets outside the palace were narrow and old, the buildings overlooking them of pre-Imperial vintage, blocky and pre-fabricated to some long-lost pattern. Brielle stood outside the gates, looking first left, and then right down the empty thoroughfare. She knew the mercantile quarter lay to the east, and so turned left, headed for the junction at the end of the street.

Reaching the junction, she noticed how the further from the palace she travelled, the more people were out on the streets. She saw no signs of law enforcement, which on most of the Imperium's more populous worlds was conspicuous, and proactive in keeping the subjects in line. Here, the enforcers were conspicuous by their absence. Was the populace so well behaved as to make enforcement unnecessary? She doubted that, for she knew that rebellion and heresy lay just below the surface on every world of the Imperium. Not a single world, least of all sacred Terra itself, was untouched by war, and most such conflicts were internal in nature, even when triggered by external factors.

Though rogue traders populated a rarefied world beyond the norms, if such a thing could even be said to exist, of human society, they only existed in reference to that society. While they conquered the stars and commanded vast private fleets and armies, they did so ultimately for the benefit of mankind as a whole. They could only bring the rule of law to the stars if they knew that rule would be upheld once established. To Brielle and her kind, the law was something that applied to others, but it was vital nonetheless. The thought that worlds such as Mundus Chasmata might fail in their God-Emperor-given duty to uphold the Pax Imperialis was, to Brielle, unsettling in the extreme. She checked the miniature weapons worn as jewellery on her fingers, just to be certain that she could enforce her own authority, should she need to.

Following no particular course, she rounded a corner. Yet more people were about their business as the day drew to a close. She walked casually, so as not to draw attention to herself. No doubt, many would mark her as a stranger, yet Brielle had learned from her father that it often paid to keep a low profile in such surroundings.

She studied the men and women travelling up and down the streets. There was something about them, something also evident in Luneberg's court, which made her cautious. She knew her father had noted it too, though she doubted the less worldly Korvane had. There was a tiredness about the people, and the place in which they lived, as if they had simply lost interest in their own lives. Why should this be, Brielle asked herself? Many of the Imperium's subjects lived their lives in hardship and toil, or in constant threat from marauding enemies. These people suffered no such circumstances; their world was prosperous and in no immediate danger of invasion. Perhaps that was the problem, Brielle thought. Perhaps the people of Mundus Chasmata had grown lazy and complacent without the crucible of war and poverty to unite them against an ultimately hostile universe.

Brielle saw that she was approaching the merchants' quarter, the streets ahead lined with covered market stalls and thronged with strolling people.

A gruff voice interrupted her thoughts. She looked down, to see a man slumped against a doorway, looking up at her. He had addressed her, though she had not caught his slurred words.

The man repeated himself, and she realised he was not merely slurring his words, but speaking a heavily accented, local dialect, as opposed to the High Gothic spoken by rogue traders and by Luneberg's aristocratic court.

'You realise that upon any civilised world of the Imperium you would be shot on the spot for begging thus?' she said, more a statement than a question. She made to walk away, leaving the man lying in his own filth, before noting that, although heavily soiled, the clothes he wore were of a very fine cut and material. Looking closer, she saw that this was no derelict beggar, but a gentleman of some means.

The man spat what Brielle could only take for a stream of particularly insulting local invective. She could decipher only one word in ten, and that related to an improbable biological function she was not prepared to undertake.

She shook her head, deciding to waste no more of her time on the man. She carried on towards the busy market place, leaving the local in a pool of his own making.

The street upon which the market was being held evidently marked the border of the merchant quarter, for Brielle could see crowds of shoppers filling the streets beyond. She came to the first stall, looking between the shoulders of the customers before it. Nothing of particular interest, merely locally made eating vessels. She moved on to the next, pushing into the ever more dense crowd.

The next stall stocked all manner of spices, a variety of pungent aromas greeting her as she approached. Wide-brimmed pots and smaller, stoppered bottles contained all manner of brightly coloured powdered substances, small parchment scrips detailing the source of the contents. Brielle read the hand-written label on a small, glass container holding a bright, blue substance. Extract of legfish proboscis, it read. Brielle let out a small snort of amusement.

'Would madam care to sample some snout powder?' The stallholder appeared at Brielle's side, clutching her arm obsequiously.

She stiffened, mildly insulted by his approach to selling, and snatched her arm away from his grasp. 'No. She would not.' She stalked off, hearing the seller chuckling to himself behind her back.

Crossing the street, Brielle noticed that the sun had entirely gone down, lights coming on all around the market. Like those in Luneberg's throne room, these were free-floating, supported by some manner of artificial, anti-gravity generator. She studied one, her interest piqued, for such technology was comparatively rare on most worlds of the Imperium, and she had certainly never seen it utilised for mere street lighting. A couple dressed in merchants' finery walked beneath the floating light, and Brielle watched as it followed after them at a short distance, before they entered the pool of light cast by another. At that point the second floating light took over, the first gently floating until it came upon another pedestrian in apparent need of illumination.

She looked around at the faces of the people in the street. None of them appeared to acknowledge the presence of the floating lumens. She studied the upper storeys of the overhanging buildings, noting, as she thought she would, that older street furniture adorned their faces, static, conventional street lights rusting away unnoticed and unlit.

Feigning an air of nonchalant disinterest quite at odds with what was going through her mind, Brielle approached another stall. This one offered a staggering variety of small, decorated vials, each containing a miniscule quantity of oily liquid. The stallholder, a robed woman whose face was almost entirely shrouded, addressed her in heavily accented, but understandable Low Gothic. 'Looking for something special my dear?'

Brielle looked down her nose at the woman, but curiosity temporarily got the better of her. 'Yes. Yes, I might be.'

'I thought so.' The woman gave Brielle a quick appraisal, and then reached in amongst the mass of containers, picking out a small, unassuming bottle. 'This,' the woman gently lifted the stopper from the tiny bottle, 'is what you want, I think.'

The stallholder lifted the bottle to Brielle's nose. She hesitated for an instant, and then gently inhaled. A scent like none she had ever experienced struck her. Blood rushed to her head, and the sound of her heart pounding filled her ears. Her eyes watered and her knees trembled, before the sensation quickly passed and the world came back into focus before her.

'Good, no?'

Brielle could only nod.

'You should see what it does when you drink it.'

Wandering deeper into the city streets, Brielle came upon a wide, open plaza. Here the crowds thinned, until she stood alone, gazing at crumbling statuary. She looked up at the night sky, noticing, as any spacefarer would, that the stars appeared absent on what was an otherwise clear, cloudless night. Puzzled, she looked around, realising with mild surprise that the patch of sky she had, by chance, looked up into was not sky at all, but a vast, black silhouette against the night.

The silhouette described an impossibly tall tower, a cluster of spires at its summit piercing the night sky. This must be the city's cathedral, Brielle realised, finding herself drawn towards it.

As she crossed the empty square, she became increasingly aware of her isolation. Not a single soul was to be seen anywhere near the cathedral. The feeling grew more intense as she crossed the square, and she could not help casting a glance over her shoulder as she neared the vast structure. The crowds appeared a very great distance away. She turned back towards the cathedral, craning her neck to look up at its bulk.

It was dark. No lights shone from what should have been, literally, a shining beacon of faith. Such buildings were to be found on every major world of the Imperium, many hosting one in every city. Her discomfort deepened as she reflected on how such a centre of spiritual authority should have been heaving with activity. Officers of the Imperial Creed, worshippers, penitents, petitioners, pilgrims; the cathedral should have been crowded with people, but it was silent.

Brielle approached the vast steps, at the top of which stood mighty doors of cast bronze. She began to climb, her unease growing with each step she took. She reached the top and studied the doors. The weakest of flickering candlelight shone through the gap at the base, and for the briefest of moments, something approaching hope pulled at her.

A small hatch was set into the vast doors, and she tested its handle. It swung inward, its hinges groaning so loudly that she winced as she heard the noise echo back from the depths of the cathedral. She stepped through, to be greeted with inky blackness.

After a few moments, her eyes adjusted to the darkness, and Brielle could discern her immediate surroundings. Wan candlelight flickered and guttered by the door, but beyond it, she could scarcely see. Yet she felt the vast, cold emptiness of the cathedral, sensing the huge space that seemed to swallow her up, body and soul.

She took a step forwards, coughing as dust billowed up from the floor, disturbed by her tread. How long had the cathedral stood abandoned, and why? Such a question was beyond her experience, for although she had faced all manner of alien monstrosities, she had never had to deal with such heresy upon a loyal world of the Imperium. How could a civilised world exist beyond the constraints of faith?

She started forwards into the darkness, her eyes adjusting further as she moved away from the circle of light cast by the flickering candles. She began to discern other, tiny pinpricks of light against the all-encompassing veil of darkness.

She closed in on one such candle, finding it guttering and hissing, almost entirely spent. As the small flame flickered and died, a chill swept through her body. An involuntary gasp escaping her lips, she turned, and saw a terribly misshapen face looming towards her from the darkness.

Brielle dived to her left, a bulky form moving through the space she had just vacated. She froze, ready to defend herself against attack, but none came. Instead, a second flame ignited, lighting the form and revealing it to belong to a decrepit mono-task servitor. She saw that the flame emanated from a nozzle that replaced the servitor's right hand.

She watched as the servitor replaced the dying candle from a stock carried in a large sack strung around its shoulder, lighting the replacement by way of its own flame. Its task complete, Brielle expected the mono-task to shuffle off, but before it did, it lingered a moment. She watched in silence; she could have sworn it mumbled a quiet prayer as it gazed into the newly lit flame. Then it did shuffle off, its sack of replacement candles dragging at its feet.

Brielle waited until she could hear the servitor no longer, determined to continue. Cautiously, for despite the trail of renewed candles left in the servitor's wake, the cathedral was still dim and the dust thick. She followed a cloistered walkway, statues of ancient saints ensconced along its walls, until she reached the entrance to what she knew would be the cathedral's inner sanctum. She stood before the entrance, and hauled upon the brass doors. They gave only slowly, the grating of metal on stone painfully loud in the vast emptiness.

The doors open enough to allow her passage, Brielle stepped through. She was greeted by a vast, hexagonal space, many times taller than it was wide. Massive columns supported an intricately worked glass ceiling. Through the glass, shafts of silvered moonlight beamed straight down, illuminating the altar at the centre of the chamber.

Brielle stepped forwards, her head tilted up. She stepped into the light. Looking down at the altar, she turned her head sharply as the moonlight glinted from a metal statuette set upon it. She waited for the retinal burn to fade, before cautiously looking upon the altar once more. The statue represented a martyr she did not recognise, although the stylised tears running down its face were a common enough motif. She looked around, seeing that the cathedral must have fallen into disuse many years ago. The tears of unnamed saints had not kept the flock faithful, she mused, a bitterness rising unbidden within her. As incredible as it was to her, she saw that the Imperial Creed had simply faded away, as forgotten to the people of Mundus Chasmata, as was their world to the Imperium. Such a thing ran contrary to everything she had been brought up to believe. Yet she stood in the very centre of an abandoned and forgotten cathedral, the people given over to their own selfish follies and affectations.

Verses from the Creed ran through Brielle's mind, clashing and contradicting where once they had soothed. Unfamiliar teachings stabbed at her, until she realised that she was hearing not her own, inner voice, but distant words echoing through the night outside the cathedral.

Holding her breath so that she could hear well enough to determine the voice's direction, Brielle stepped out of the shaft of moonlight cascading from above. She ghosted down dusty, cobweb-strewn corridors, the voice growing louder all the while. After several minutes, she came upon a small portal, and stepped through it. She was in the plaza once more, on the opposite side of the cathedral to where she had entered, and she could clearly hear the voice, across the square from her. A crowd clustered on the plaza's edge, the voice clearly audible. Now that she was in the open, Brielle could hear that the voice was an angry one, that of a preacher haranguing a crowd. She looked behind her at the vast, empty cathedral, curious as to why such an expression of faith would be manifested outside of the institution of the Creed.

She started towards the crowd, the words of the speaker becoming clearer.

'And there shall be a great apocalypse! A great war whose might and clamour shall dwarf all the wars that have come before.'

The familiar verse drifted towards her, and she instinctively raised her hands to her chest to make the sign of the aquila, but something made her hesitate. Some deeply hidden doubt rose to the surface, a feeling of tension that only increased as she neared the crowd.

'We bring upon ourselves the doom of all that was and all that is!'

Reaching the nearest of the crowd, Brielle stood upon the tips of her toes in order to see over the shoulders of those before her. She caught a glimpse of the preacher, and was surprised to see that he appeared not to be a robed priest, but a trader or a merchant.

'We the masses huddle in our hovels, unaware of the war fought on our account.'

Brielle did not recognise this segment, although there were so many thousands of variations of the books of the Creed that that alone did not concern her.

'How long shall the masses toil in silence? How long must we labour in ignorance?'

A chorus of agreement swept the crowd. Yet their reaction was not one of anger or of fervour, but of curiosity. Brielle studied the faces of those nearest her. Each man and woman appeared to listen intently, as if a spectator at a theatrical performance. Small quips and witticisms abounded, ripples of applause sounding at what the crowd perceived as particularly well-constructed verses.

She raised herself up once more, intent upon a closer look at the speaker.

'What is our fate, if not to adapt, to evolve?'

After each verse, the speaker leant forward, studying the crowd as if reading their reaction. He caught Brielle's eye, and delivered his next line straight to her.

'Are we not uncounted individuals, striving for a common purpose? Why must they deny us our fate? Who are they to control and direct from afar, when we know ourselves as they never can?'

The man's words struck a chord deep within Brielle's heart, yet she knew he trod a path at odds with the teachings of the Imperial Creed, and he did so openly, in the shadow of an abandoned cathedral.

'The old ways hold no meaning for us!' He was pointing straight at Brielle. 'Only we can avert doomsday, and only then by uniting for the good of all!'

The old ways have no meaning. Brielle was shocked to hear such words spoken on a world of the Imperium, yet she found they spoke to her more than a thousand sermons of the type she had grown up with. The people here listened, and considered the speaker's words, they did not make hollow and meaningless responses learned by rote but never truly understood. She was beginning to understand the apparent ennui evinced in the behaviour of Luneberg's court. Perhaps they were not simply bored, casting around for distraction as she had assumed. Perhaps they were simply free of the constraints that bound so many worlds of the Imperium.

Yet, what remained once obedience and faith were stripped away? How deep did the teachings of this man, and his like, cut? Brielle could sympathise with a wish to be rid of the shackles of rule, after all, she was a rogue trader and existed outside of such laws, but still she held on to a core of faith in the Emperor. The boundaries of that faith were being redefined as she listened, but she also knew that nothing the speaker could ever say would make her reject the God-Emperor of Mankind. Nothing would change her belief in Him.

'Change is the only constant!' the man bellowed, bowing to his audience before departing with a flourish. The crowd cheered, mightily impressed at such a witty turn of phrase.

'The wise adapt,' Brielle whispered, standing in silence as the crowd broke up around her.

Brielle had found herself wandering aimlessly along the city's streets, the crowds thinning as the night drew on. She headed in the vague direction of Luneberg's palace, yet she cared little to return to the company of her father and her stepbrother. Her wanderings brought her back through the centre of the merchants' quarter, were she slowed, idly looking for some distraction that would delay her return to the palace.

This part of the city remained busy. Commerce, it appeared, never slept. Merchants in their gaudy dress paraded the streets, ostentatious in their displays of personal wealth. The sounds of drunken merriment emanated from the establishments that crowded the streets, signs above each announcing their specialised venality.

Brielle was in no mood for shallow vices. She wandered on, until she heard the rumble of shouting and yelling from an entrance ahead. Reaching it, a sign above the door declared that it was an auction house, and by the sound emanating from within, she had no doubt that a sale was in progress, even at such a late hour.

She entered, a pair of burly guards letting her pass without question, and followed the sound of the shouting up a wide set of stairs, a threadbare, though once elaborate carpet running its length. At the top of the stairs, an archway of crumbling stone led to a gallery, through which Brielle could see crowds of people up on their feet, waving their hands in some agitation.

She stepped through the archway, and pushed past the rear ranks of the crowd.

'Sold to the representative of the Drefus Cartel!' A wave of disappointed jeering swept the crowd, and several men, wealthy merchants by their dress, threw papers to the floor, cursing colourfully. Brielle looked to the front of the hall, and saw that she stood upon one gallery of many, arranged around a central pit. The auctioneer sat on a podium, opposite, and appeared to have a large speaker grille for a mouth and a periwig that trailed almost to the floor.

The auctioneer waved chubby hands, his distorted, artificial voice shouting, 'Order please gentlemen, order!' through his speaker-mouth.

A modicum of calm filled the hall, the merchants chattering excitedly nonetheless. 'Our next sale is an exquisite example of out-rim xenocana.'

An attendant stepped out onto the floor of the pit, and a hush descended over the crowd as he held aloft a white staff capped with an elaborate array of multi-faceted jewels and fluted panels. The attendant circled the pit, the staff held high for the closest of the bidders to examine.

'This fine item comes to us from many light years away, and many brave men perished to capture it. It was once the staff of office of the Terror of the Trident Nebula, who wielded it against the orks of the Chrazhgkek tribe.' The crowd cooed in awe at this, although Brielle had to struggle to stifle a laugh. As much as she was amused at the blatantly fraudulent description, she was even more surprised to witness such an artefact, whether or not it was genuine, on view and for sale on a world of the Imperium. She sighed, beginning to enjoy the freedoms she was witnessing around her.

'What am I bid for this fine, rare item?'

A comically overweight merchant, half of his bulk spilling over the gallery's railing, threw his hand in the air. The bidding was on. Brielle watched in wry fascination, her incredulity growing as the bidding increased. She noted that the bidders tendered trade bonds, promissory notes she guessed, that tied them to a common, local market. Such tender would be meaningless outside of Mundus Chasmata, and appeared a deliberate policy to ensure that the trade did not attract the attention of outside authorities.

As the bidding reached its finale, so the bidders became more unruly. Brielle realised that up to this point, she had not seen the Chasmatans exhibit much in the way of emotion beyond studied disinterest. She wondered whether the acquisition of xenos artefacts, even ones that were likely to be fakes, was merely a new distraction that temporarily sated their apparent languor. The auction reached its conclusion, and the auctioneer hammered his gavel, the crowd erupting once more into bedlam.

Except that one person stood quite still, and Brielle felt his gaze upon her before turning to see him looking in her direction from the next gallery. A moment later, the robed figure nodded, and ducked into the crowd. Brielle froze, her father's advice coming to mind: when in doubt, eyes open, mouth closed.

A minute or two later, and just as the crowd was beginning to quieten, the robed man appeared at Brielle's side, as she had suspected he would. She turned to face him as he pulled down his hood, to reveal a shaved head, and a square-jawed face, flowing Gothic script tattooed across the cheeks and a heraldic device upon the forehead.

'Naal?' Brielle asked.

The man bowed, a smile creasing his sombre face. 'Indeed my lady. It is an honour to be remembered.'

'Not at all,' Brielle demurred, wincing as the auctioneer bellowed the details of the next item to be sold, the crowd exploding into raucous chaos once more.

Naal indicated the archway with a sweeping arm. 'Shall we?'

She nodded, and walked by his side out of the gallery. 'If you don't mind my asking, madam, do you wish to be escorted back to the palace, or might I be permitted to show you the real sights of Chasmata Capitalis?'

'The real sights?' Brielle liked the sound of that. 'Why not?'

* * *

Swirling, discordant rhythms filled the hall, driving howling cadences into Brielle's skull as she reclined upon a low couch of exquisite brocade. The highborn elite of Mundus Chasmata passed the night away on similar seats, all around. Gossamer drapes suspended from low, carved archways afforded the courtiers a ghostly aspect, their features obscured behind the rich, diaphanous fabric.

Naal had led Brielle through the back alleys and side streets of the capital's old town, in amongst the ancestral piles of the landed ruling class. They had made small talk along the way, Naal revealing himself to be something other than the subservient functionary he had appeared at court. Brielle had found herself intrigued, yet was wily enough not to let her guard down. She would see what this hidden side of Chasmatan society had to offer, and whether she might find profit there.

The establishment to which Naal had led her was low and sprawling, gloomy yet intimate. At first, it appeared to be some private, aristocratic bordello, although Brielle soon saw that it was something more than that. Small groups of nobles and wealthy merchants huddled in alcoves, some focused upon intent discussion, others observing the other patrons. This was a place, Brielle quickly realised, to see and be seen in. Only an idle-rich, highborn ruling class such as this could sustain such a place, for it evidently relied upon the sort of mutually assured discretion that only an entrenched, nigh incestuous ruling class could maintain.

Heads had turned as Brielle and Naal had entered, ducking low through the arched doorway and holding aside silken drapes as they passed. Cushions were scattered across the stone floor, and low candles provided scant illumination by which to navigate the scene. Naal had led Brielle to an arched alcove, and bade her sit amongst a group of what were evidently high-ranking courtiers. Then he had pardoned himself, departing to find drinks, and leaving her to observe the scene.

Occupying the alcove alongside her, the courtiers wore clothes of the most exquisite cut, although Brielle saw that here, as in Luneberg's court, the fabric was aged and worn, as if the wearer had lost the means, or the will, to maintain or replace it. On the other hand, perhaps the men and women had simply lost interest in their appearance, merely sporting the trappings of wealth and status, whilst evincing little concern for its substance. The courtiers, both men and women, wore powdered wigs and prodigious amounts of make-up, and whispered conspiratorially, the men smirking whilst the women giggled behind fluttering fans. Brielle caught them casting furtive glances her way, more low laughter emanating each time; she sighed, finding such behaviour foolish.

'My apologies for leaving you, Brielle.' Naal had returned, and placed a crystal decanter on the low table in the centre of the alcove before lowering himself onto the plush seat beside her. He produced a pair of balloon glasses, and poured a small amount of the syrupy liquid from the decanter into each, before handing one to Brielle.

She raised the glass, inhaling the rich aroma. Although no connoisseur of fine spirits, she knew enough of such things to tell from the thick, woody scent that this was a liquor of the finest quality. She sipped, the complex, powerful flavours washing over her.

Naal was speaking, but Brielle's attention was distracted, as the area at the centre of the room filled with sudden activity. A group of servants, previously unseen, was clearing the floor of cushions and tying back drapes, creating a small, open area, into which a tall figure attired in a scarlet robe stepped. The figure bowed to the onlookers, who, like Brielle, craned their necks to see what would happen next.

'My friends,' the man announced, 'we have for your edification this night, a guest of the utmost singularity. I present to you, the virtuoso!'

A chorus of gasps and fluttering fans filled the room, and the already low lighting dimmed even more, leaving just the central space bathed in a soft glow. The robed figure retired to the shadows, and an indistinct form glided on from the opposite side. Brielle had expected some exotic dance or song, and shifted her body around on the couch to gain a better view of what promised to be something else entirely.

It most certainly was something else. A sphere of glass, less than a metre in diameter, floated into the light in the open area. Brielle lifted herself on her arms, exhilaration flooding her. Something moved within the sphere, something dark: something... alive.

'It is perfectly safe, my lady. Have no fear,' said Naal.

'I don't,' said Brielle, turning her head sharply towards him, uncaring of the irritation in her tone. 'I'm curious. Where is it from?'

'Please excuse me, I meant no offence. We know not from where the creature hails, exactly, but it is one of several of its type to have come into contact with our merchants working the eastern domains. It has, as you will see, a very special talent.'

Brielle turned back, all her attention focused on the sphere. It bobbed a metre or two above the floor for a moment, and then began to spin slowly. A deep, bass note droned at the edge of hearing, vibrating through the spectators' bodies, and something quite amazing took place.

Every loose item in the room levitated a metre into the air. Brielle sat bolt upright, her knees drawn up under her chin. She looked back at Naal, who was chuckling to himself quietly. He leaned forward, plucked Brielle's balloon glass from the air, and handed it back to her. She hesitated, and took the glass from him.

The air of the room was now crowded with levitating objects, ranging from other drinking vessels, to loosened hairpins, coins, ornate fans and all manner of personal effects. The courtiers clapped demurely, some retrieving objects as Naal had, while others seemed quite delighted to see their possessions floating away; and this they did, the items gently gravitating to the centre of the room, where they began a slow orbit around the glass sphere, which Brielle could barely make out once it had pulled in all the objects.

The bass hum deepened still further, the low tables rattling as vibrations passed through them. A woman opposite giggled, but Brielle caught the nervous glances that she cast around her, and clearly heard the edge of delirium in her laugh. Brielle could see that most of the idle aristocrats had enjoyed this spectacle before, but those that hadn't were clearly uncomfortable and unsure as to what might happen next.

As well they might be, thought Brielle, who knew full well that the xenos was not to be made sport of. One with such powers as those on display might conceivably cause enormous loss of life if it happened to turn on its... captors? Masters? Partners? What was the relationship between the man who had announced the show, and the alien itself?

The bass drone dropped a tone further, hovering at the very limit of human hearing. There it stayed for several minutes, building slowly in tone, an air of tension, or expectation growing with it.

A sudden electric pulse burst outwards from the sphere, causing the woman opposite Brielle to gasp in shock. The myriad objects orbiting the sphere increased their speed, and the bass tone took on a rhythm, modulated, Brielle discerned, by the speed and bulk of those objects.

The smaller items swung out, orbiting the sphere at a greater distance. As their course changed, a high-pitched counter-rhythm grew, the movements of glinting hairpins generating sharp, darting notes at the upper edge of hearing.

The larger items orbiting the sphere then closed in to it, their course slow and graceful. The bass note altered its pulsing to match the movements of slowly tumbling balloon glasses, their syrupy contents sloshing, yet never quite escaping.

The remaining items each took up a complex orbit, some remaining constant in speed and course whilst others moved into figure of eight formations, some orbiting each other while others moved in relation to the sphere. As each object moved into its unique position in the dance, a corresponding rhythm manifested itself.

Several hundred objects of varying sizes spun in perfect, dazzling formation around the room, the spectators utterly entranced. Brielle glanced sidelong at the woman sitting opposite, not surprised to see that she had ceased her coy display of shock, and was now staring with open-mouthed rapture at the sight before her.

Brielle quite lost track of time as the display continued, the complex, interwoven movements and their corresponding rhythms building to an explosive crescendo. At the last, the rhythms synchronised, locked in perfect union for a fleeting,moment in time. The objects froze, hanging motionless in the air. The music ceased, the softest of echoes fading to the edge of perception, and then evaporating into nothing. The objects gently sank to the floor, the force holding them releasing its grasp.

Brielle turned to Naal, surprised to note that a tear ran down her cheek. As her senses returned, she wiped her eyes and shook her head to clear it. She watched the glass sphere bob for a moment, catching fleeting movement within, and then it retired once more to the shadows.

Those around the room were slowly awakening too, looking around as if roused from a deep sleep. Murmurs of appreciation swept the room, and in a brief moment drinks were being called for and raucous laughter rising.

Naal took Brielle's glass from her, and she allowed him to refill it before accepting it back. She sipped, looking around the room. Diaphanous voiles muffled the sounds of merriment and cast bodies in silhouette, but it was clear to Brielle that the festivities had now taken on a keener edge. The woman opposite, who had evinced such shock at the appearance of the virtuoso, had apparently cast off her elaborate outfit and was straddling her neighbour's lap.

Brielle took another sip of her liqueur. The remainder of the night passed in a haze.

CHAPTER SEVEN

Lucian paced the floor before Luneberg's empty throne, while Korvane stood restlessly nearby. The hour was late and the vast hall was abandoned. Lucian's footsteps echoed in the darkness, the only other sound the fluttering of artificial wings high above. Cyber-cherubs; Lucian hated the damn things. Vat-grown pets for shallow-minded men.

'This might be our last chance, Korvane, so you leave the talking to me. You will wait while I engage the Imperial Commander. Do you understand?' Lucian addressed his son, the only other human in the hall.

'I understand, Father.' His son hid his disappointment well, thought Lucian. 'What do you have planned?'

Lucian resumed his pacing, addressing his words as much to the looming shadows as to Korvane. 'Planned? You can't make plans when you're dealing with this sort.' Lucian was rapidly going off this entire deal, but was determined to salvage some semblance of profit, even if it did mean bringing himself down to what he saw as Luneberg's level.

'I'm going to find out once and for all what he wants from us. Make him reveal his cards, one way or another.'

'Father, if you push him, he'll take offence. The Chasmatans' rules of etiquette are quite specific on the subject.'

'Take offence?' Lucian threw his head back and laughed a single, barking report. The sound echoed into the shadowy eaves, setting off a commotion amongst the creatures roosting there. 'He might well take offence. If that's the only way then that's how we play this.'

'Father, please. Please keep your voice down.' Korvane made an obvious show of looking around the darkness, before lowering his voice. 'There'll be monitoring devices planted all over the palace.'

Lucian regarded his son. He had a lot to learn. 'Of course there are. It's all part of the game,' Lucian said, looking up towards the dark ceiling once more. He sidestepped smartly as a well-aimed dollop of cherub dung dropped, landing with a wet splatter on the flagstone floor. He chuckled, aware of the note of appreciation in his own voice. 'All part of the game.'

'Father?' he looked up at the tone in Korvane's voice. Korvane nodded towards the shadows, and a figure emerged, crossing to the pool of light in front of the throne, to stand before Lucian and Korvane.

'Gerrit.'

Lucian recognised the man who addressed him as the High Colonel, Trevelyan-Constance, who had been introduced to him at the meal as the head of the Legions Chasmata. The man was a model of military deportment, tall and stiff, his shoulders wide with gaudy epaulettes.

'I understand you go before my Lord Luneberg presently.' The colonel stood a few centimetres taller than Lucian did, and although he appeared far older, he looked down his hawk-like nose, as if sizing him up.

'That is correct my dear high colonel,' said Lucian, studying the man for any reaction or offence he might display at the familiarity. By the warp, thought Lucian, in some twisted way I'm starting to enjoy these people's games. 'I trust all is well with the Imperial Commander?'

The colonel made no response other than a slight rising of the right eyebrow. 'Oh yes, quite well, quite well indeed. He will be able to receive you presently. In the meantime, as my lord's chief advisor in matters of war, I wish to consult with you, regarding the wider military situation in the region.'

This took Lucian aback. He had judged Trevelyan-Constance to be a lackey, albeit one with a particularly impressive uniform, so what was he after? Was he acting above his station? A flutter of wings in the shadows above reminded Lucian that their conversation was unlikely to be private, and if anyone understood that, it would be the head of the Mundus Chasmata military.

The colonel shot a furtive glance overhead, and lowered his voice. 'You must understand, Gerrit, the last time we received an official delegation of any standing from the Adeptus Terra was over three decades ago, and that was the first in half a century. Don't misunderstand me, Mundus Chasmata is as loyal a world as any, but we are a great distance from the major trade routes. You yourself know this better than I do. I merely ask: what of the wars against the xenos?'

'Well.' Lucian's mind raced as he sought to filter the half-truths he was sure he was hearing, from the lies he guessed interlaced them. 'There is, as you know, no peace amongst the stars. Ultima Segmentum faces many threats, not the least of which is the Kurtoum Uprising. You will have heard of the great victory won at Orman VII?' Lucian asked this by way of a test. By no standards was Orman VII a great victory.

The high colonel failed. 'Yes, yes indeed, and what of the ork menace?'

Lucian considered for a moment before answering. What if the high colonel knew he was being tested? Was he that bright? He would find out. 'The Arch-arsonist grows more cunning with each passing cycle, although I doubt he will threaten your borders for some time to come.'

'My intelligence would tend to agree, Gerrit, but it is good to hear it confirmed.'

Confirmed my arse, thought Lucian. The empire of the self-titled ork warlord, the Arch-arsonist of Charadon, was located on the western extreme of Ultima Segmentum, over thirty thousand light years away. Many other ork domains offered far greater, though less impressively named, threats.

'And what of...' the high colonel hesitated for a moment, 'the Imperial Navy?'

Now things are getting interesting, Lucian thought to himself. He's definitely up to something, but what is he really asking?

'The Navy is, as ever, fighting a war on many fronts, against myriad foes. Yet, by the grace of the Emperor, it yet prevails.'

The high colonel bowed, making the sign of aquila as he did so. 'I am gratified to hear that is the case, sir. We hear too little of such things this far out. What, may I ask, is the state of the Navy's operation in the Timbra sub, and the whole Ring?'

Lucian knew that the Ring was the local name for a group of stars at the heart of the Borealis Cluster, the appendage of the great Eastern Spiral arm in which Mundus Chasmata was located. The high colonel, Luneberg's chief military advisor, was asking him for information regarding Naval operations in the area surrounding his own world. These people really were isolated.

'Well.' Lucian decided to tell Trevelyan-Constance the truth in this matter, for he could scarcely believe the question was anything other than a test, delivered in the same manner that he himself had attempted to test the high colonel, only a moment earlier. 'The last Navy vessel we encountered was the battleship *Lord Cathek*, three days out of Al Adhara, and she was heading for the Kleist colony. The route we took to Mundus Chasmata was not one along which regular Naval patrols are made, unless the Navy has a reason to do so.'

This last was Lucian's own little test, a subtle way of goading some reaction from the high colonel.

He got none, or Trevelyan-Constance hid it well if he did react. 'Quite, quite, and Al Adhara is how many light years distant would you say?'

The high colonel was truly isolated if he genuinely had no knowledge of Al Adhara, the largest Naval way point for three sectors. Once again, the thought that Trevelyan-Constance might be testing him crossed Lucian's mind. He resolved to himself that, no matter how tempted, he would not fall foul of mistaking this man for the ignoramus he gave every impression of being.

'Given a good run at the eastern tail, seven. If not, the next best route adds up to nigh on ten, if you're prepared to risk the Straits of Kephus.'

The high colonel appeared to think upon this information, mulling it over as if it was confirmation of a long-held suspicion rather than solid fact. Then he visibly shook himself out of the reverie he had entered, and stood straight, tugging at the waist of his uniform jacket in an exaggerated display of trimness.

'Well, Gerrit, I thank you for your time, a most fruitful discussion. You must forgive me for detaining you, for I am quite sure my Lord Culpepper must be waiting. Please, follow me.'

The high colonel bowed and indicated Lucian should precede

him up the steps to the podium. Korvane bowed to the high colonel, and nodded to his father, remaining where he was as Lucian had instructed. Trevelyan-Constance led Lucian through the side door through which he had appeared, and into the corridors of the private quarters beyond. If the throne room and the passages leading to it appeared neglected and dust-strewn, these were somehow worse.

A palpable atmosphere of abandonment pervaded the lonely ways. It was not that they were in any worse condition, but that the impression of decay was more apparent the more sumptuous that which decayed had once been. Statuettes of once stunning beauty graced gloomy alcoves along the passage, their peeling or cracked surfaces even more obvious because of the quality of their original craftsmanship.

In minutes, they reached what was obviously the antechamber to Luneberg's private quarters. A white-clad household guard stood on either side of the metal doorway, the white feathers mounted upon their helmets bent against the archway above. A glance told Lucian that similarly attired guards had stood watch here for countless centuries, for above each trooper, a small area of the low, stone ceiling was worn smooth where the feathers touched. The high colonel nodded to the guard standing on the right, and he silently sub-vocalised into the communicator mounted at his throat.

A moment passed, and the guard nodded back to Trevelyan-Constance. The high colonel placed a hand on the iron portal, and leaned his weight against it until it slowly swung upon massive hinges.

Passing through the arched doorway, Lucian was greeted with a sight that suggested all the decayed finery he had thus far witnessed was but a tiny portion of the whole, sad truth. Luneberg's private chambers were dark and gloomy, quite in line with the remainder of his palace, yet the effect here was multiplied one hundred-fold. Every surface of every wall was crammed with priceless artefacts, from far and wide in time and distance. A sword that Lucian estimated to be of second era Ultramar in origin, possibly even dating to the time of the great primarch Guilliman himself, was mounted on one wall, its once gleaming blade encrusted with centuries, even millennia of dust and grime.

Beside the blade stood a tall xenos beast, stuffed, badly, Lucian noted, and preserved for all time as testament to the skill of the hunter that had brought it down. Lucian had no inkling from where the beast might have come, but was sure it was not from Mundus Chasmata, and neither was the hunter from Luneberg's world.

Lucian stepped forward, looking around for a sign of his host. He saw none, so resumed his perusal of the bizarre display. If Luneberg intended to keep him waiting, he would happily participate in his little game.

A mighty banner stood nearby, tattered and scorched by chemical burns, and leant against a wall where it appeared to have rested for many centuries. A stylised flameburst surrounded a circular field, the numeral '11/5' still visible. Lucian did not recognise the unit. How could he, for it was but one body amongst millions that had served the Emperor. Served and died for, by the state of the banner, for its bearer must surely have suffered similar wounds to his charge.

A painting, barely visible amongst the shadows, hung beside the banner. Lucian stepped closer, and saw that a layer of fine, grey dust obscured the surface of the work. He gently blew on it, revealing the portrait of a brightly armoured man, his noble chin held high and laurel leaves gracing his haughty brow. Another arrogant backwater lord, thought Lucian, feeling nothing but disdain for the watered down bloodline that ruled this pointless world.

'My dear Lucian!' Luneberg emerged from the shadows at the other end of the room. 'I see you've found great uncle Nappiermor. Impressive looking man, don't you think?'

Lucian suppressed a grimace at being caught unawares, looking sideways at the high colonel, who made a great show of ignoring the Imperial Commander.

'Quite so, my lord. Was he close?'

'Close? My no, the family hated him. Heard he preferred the company of filthy mutants to honest men. Ones with extra... bits... if you know what I mean.'

Lucian remained stoically impassive, before allowing the slightest of grins to touch the corner of his mouth. Luneburg's powdered face split in a mighty smile in return, which soon transformed into side-splitting laughter. Evidently, Luneberg was a great fan of wit, his own, at least.

Mopping his sweating brow with a dainty kerchief, Luneberg finally, and with some effort, reined in his hilarity. 'I do hope the high colonel hasn't bored you too much?'

Lucian smiled politely, not allowing himself to be baited. When he failed to reply, Luneberg huffed, pocketing his kerchief with a flourish. Lucian was struck once more, as he had been upon first meeting the Imperial Commander, by the apparent contradiction between foppish buffoon and physical presence. Luneberg might present such an air, but there was much more to him, lurking just below the surface. Lucian was reminded, as he had been on each occasion they had met, that he must always be upon his guard around Luneberg.

'Anyway,' Luneberg continued. 'will you join me for a stroll in the royal gardens?'

'Certainly,' Lucian replied, 'I would be happy to do so.'

Luneberg turned, but halted, as he appeared to remember that Trevelyan-Constance was still present. 'Your counsel will not be required, colonel.' Lucian could hardly fail to catch the icy tone of the command, and wondered if it was for show or if indeed the Imperial Commander really felt such evident disdain for his chief military attaché.

Whether or not the high colonel himself was concerned was impossible for Lucian to tell, for he simply clicked his heels smartly, bowed and turned on the spot, departing smartly and leaving Lucian and Luneberg alone.

Lucian was the first to speak. 'You mentioned your gardens?' Luneberg had apparently been considering something else entirely, for Lucian's words evidently broke his chain of thought.

'What? Yes, the gardens. Please, do follow me my dear Lucian.'

Lucian watched Luneberg's back for a moment as the Imperial Commander walked off towards a portal at the far end of the trophy-strewn chamber. He shook his head, the realisation that Luneberg was not entirely stable beginning to settle there. Pushing the notion aside, he followed after.

'Do tell me,' Luneberg asked Lucian as they stepped out into the royal gardens, 'about the Arcadius dynasty.'

Lucian looked around him while gathering his thoughts. The royal gardens were not as he would have expected. Instead of the meticulously maintained flora appropriate to the setting, the gardens were overgrown and untended. Twisting, alien weeds pushed their way through cracks in marble paving, and creepers sporting wickedly sharp thorns writhed across the path, around fine statuary, choking the remaining life from ornamental trees. The sun had long since set, but small lumens bobbed along the path a few steps ahead of Luneberg, ensuring that his way was always lit. The overall impression was one of neglect and decay, far from the impression a man such as Luneberg would ordinarily seek to give a visitor.

'Where to start,' Lucian said, buying himself time. 'We are but one dynasty amongst many granted a Charter of Trade to exploit and to expand the frontiers of the Emperor's domains. We have done so for many centuries, not without success.'

'Oh come now,' replied Luneberg, not turning his head as he walked slowly along the dark, overgrown path. 'Such false modesty is unbecoming. Tell me of the world in which you live.'

As had Trevelyan-Constance before him, Luneberg appeared now to be seeking information regarding the wider Imperium, of the vast galaxy beyond the borders of his own small fiefdom.

'The world in which I live?' said Lucian, following Luneberg's lead in not taking his attention from the path ahead. 'My world is one of contrasts. A rogue trader moves in many circles, from the very highest, to the very lowest.' At present, he felt himself moving in one of the latter, but refrained from imbuing his words with such a notion, so as not to cause Luneberg undue insult.

Luneberg nodded, clearly of the opinion that his own company qualified as one of those highest circles. 'Do go on Lucian. Have you, for example, much in the way of contact with the Imperial Court?'

Lucian saw little harm in replying honestly, for Luneberg was clearly a man obsessed with status. 'I have, though infrequently, for my calling takes me far from Terra. Nonetheless, I like to maintain contact with the Senatorum, and visit in person whenever possible.'

Luneberg appeared to consider this, nodding to himself slowly. He halted, his hand raised to his chin as he looked out, into the dark, overgrown expanse of the royal gardens. 'Tell me of Terra, would you Lucian?'

Lucian now detected the slightest hint of mania in Luneberg's words. He determined to tread even more cautiously than he had intended, for there was evidently something more to Luneberg's line of questioning than was apparent.

He stopped beside Luneberg, looking out into the same darkness, yet not seeing what held the Imperial Commander's attention. 'To set foot upon sacred Terra is to tread the very same ground as was once walked by the Emperor.' Lucian made the sign of the aquila. A sidelong glance told him that Luneberg did not. He continued. 'The very air of Terra is holy, laced with the scent of incense burned many centuries, millennia, before. Each time I have returned, I have been restored, for my calling takes me far from the light of the Emperor.'

Lucian turned to regard Luneberg, and saw that he had dipped his head. The Imperial Commander spoke, his words ever so slightly slurred. 'That light at times seems like barely a guttering candle to us, so distant are we from its source.'

Lucian felt his hackles rise. 'Sir, you must not speak thus.'

'Do you judge me heretic, Lucian?' Still Luneberg's head was lowered, his words muted.

'I do not.'

'Then what?'

Lucian took a deep breath before answering, tasting decay upon the stale air. 'I have travelled further into the darkness than you can imagine, Luneberg. You believe your world estranged from Holy Terra? I have walked upon worlds in the sway of such beasts as would curdle your blood, and I have never felt that the Emperor did not walk beside me.'

Luneberg's head rose, and he turned to face Lucian. 'Tell me of them.'

'Them?' Lucian was confused for a moment as to the Imperial Commander's meaning, caught off balance by the manic gleam in the other man's eyes.

'Yes, of them! What beasts? What worlds? Tell me of them!'

'I may not speak of them sir. It is forbidden.'

'By the Administratum? You fear the Priesthood of Terra?'

'By the Inquisition, my lord. I fear the Ordo Xenos.'

By Luneberg's reaction to their mention, Lucian was gratified to see that the Imperial Commander had knowledge of one of the Imperium's institutions at least. Luneberg visibly trembled at Lucian's words, displaying a healthy fear for the agents of the Imperium's highest powers, those whose task it was to hunt down the vile alien, and those who would consort with them, and issue due punishment.

Now Luneberg turned towards Lucian. 'But you are a rogue trader. You have no cause to fear the Ordo Xenos, surely?'

'I am a rogue trader, as you say, and you are indeed correct in that the power vested in me by the High Lords of Terra grants me certain... advantages. That does not put me outside of the power of the Inquisition however. One in my position must tread a fine line. Fortunately, we often do so beyond the sight of those who might object.'

'I see. I believe we are much alike then, you and I.' Luneberg was now staring into the darkness once more, his voice subdued as before.

'How so?' asked Lucian, looking into the darkness too, and once again failing to see anything there.

'I am an Imperial Commander, and my power too is passed down from the High Lords. Where your charter compels you to discover and exploit many new worlds, mine compels me to hold onto just one, by whatever means I deem necessary.'

Lucian considered the other man's words, aware that they contained undertones not clear to him. He considered his next words cautiously, before asking, 'Is your rule here disputed?'

With a sudden motion, Luneberg ploughed forwards before turning to Lucian, a shadow amongst the darkness. 'Disputed?' he shouted, a very definite edge of mania edging his words. 'Certainly it is disputed.'

Lucian had not expected to hear this, but pressed on, asking, 'Who disputes your right to rule here?'

'How little you know of our corner of the Imperium my dear Lucian,' Luneberg called back, a wry giggle entering his voice.

Lucian was tiring of Luneberg's nonsense, but was acutely aware of just how much hung upon the deal between them. He needed this madman, and he just hoped Luneberg needed him an equal amount. He resolved to push on, intent upon getting to the truth of the matter.

Lucian repeated his question. 'Who disputes your right to rule here?'

Luneberg turned and resumed his stroll along the overgrown pathway. Lucian strode to catch up, and looked sideways at him as they walked. 'In truth, no man disputes my rule. Not as such.'

'Not as such?'

'I find myself, my world, in a war, a long and bitter, war.'

Lucian stopped, risking offence by gripping Luneberg's arm. 'I see no sign of a war here. Tell me straight!'

Luneberg giggled once more, and explained. 'Not that sort of war, my dear Lucian, not that sort. The war in which I find myself engaged is one you yourself should understand!'

At last, Lucian began to feel he was getting somewhere, although he knew that Luneberg's cooperation was tenuous. 'Enlighten me, if you would.'

Luneberg let out a deep, exaggerated sigh, as if about to launch into a prolonged explanation for the benefit of an ignorant child. 'Trade war, Lucian, trade war.'

Another piece in the puzzle slotted into place, and Lucian looked around with fresh eyes. The decay that ran so deep through Mundus Chasmata suddenly began to make sense, as did Luneberg's apparent willingness to enter into a potentially dangerous deal with a rogue trader with whom he had had no previous contact. Still, Lucian knew there was more, some underlying stain upon the people of Luneberg's world.

Lucian pressed on. 'A trade war with whom?'

'Lucian, you may know much of the breadth of the Imperium, but I suspect your knowledge lacks something in the way of depth.'

Lucian did not take offence at the statement, for he knew it to be true, at least in part. A rogue trader might travel from one end of the galaxy to the other, visiting hundreds of worlds along the way, but he knew a world had far more to it than a space port, a trade mission, or a governor's mansion.

Luneberg continued. 'My line has ruled this world, this system, and indeed three other nearby, uninhabited, systems, for longer than the archives record. There are documents in our library that reference the granting of that rule, and it is known that the Administratum has formally ratified our authority at least three times in the last seven centuries. In fact, they do so less formally each time they accept our tithe, each time a regiment is raised for the Guard.'

Lucian nodded, feeling that he knew where this was heading, but saying nothing that might distract the other man from his explanation.

'I may rule in the name of Terra, Lucian, but there are other rules by which we must live. Our neighbours have long sought to enforce their own laws, seeking to dominate what little trade exists in this region and extend their own power. The Administratum can do little or nothing to stop this. Were another world to launch an actual assault upon Mundus Chasmata, it is likely Terra would not hear of it for decades or even centuries. The Navy has other foes to battle; so long as it was quick and clean, and tithes were uninterrupted, no one would care, or comment. Or even notice.'

'So,' ventured Lucian, 'others would take advantage of your great distance from the centres of Imperial power, extending their own influence by means of low level lawlessness and fiscal malpractice?'

Luneberg chuckled once more; that edge of mania still very much evident. 'Others? Yes, you might say that, but mostly that bastard, Droon.' Luneberg's voice altered in tone as he voiced the name of, Lucian guessed, the individual he held responsible for his world's misfortunes.

'Droon?'

'Droon!' Luneberg shouted, as the pair reached an ornamental gallery that afforded a moonlit view of a great expanse of decayed, formal gardens. The Imperial Commander leant his weight against the stone railing, small chunks of loose masonry tumbling away to the weed-choked lawn below. 'Droon. He rules Arris Epsilon. It's a stinking hole just about...' Luneberg looked up into the night sky, and pointed towards one end of a deep purple band that spanned the entire vista, '...there, at the end of the Borealis Ring.'

Lucian followed Luneberg's gesture, just able to make out the star towards which the other man pointed. 'Arris Epsilon. I know it from the local star charts, but have not had cause to visit it.'

'Visit Arris Epsilon?' Luneberg laughed, 'Believe me Lucian, you would not wish to do so.'

'Why not?'

'I told you didn't I? It's a stinking hole. Its people are boastful and arrogant, and entirely self-serving. No dignity.'

Suspecting he knew the answer, Lucian asked, 'You have visited then?'

Luneberg let out another laugh, this one more akin to a bark than any sound a man, particularly an Imperial Commander, should make. 'Have I visited Arris Epsilon? My dear Lucian, you really are downright ignorant about some things aren't you?' Indeed, thought Lucian, knowing the answer. 'I most certainly have not. I am proud to say that I have never had the misfortune of visiting Arris Epsilon, or any other world beyond my own domains. Of that fact I am immensely proud.'

Lucian sighed inwardly. The notion that a man might not have had cause to leave his own world was fine with him, but that an Imperial Commander might follow the same tenet was somewhat outside his experience.

Luneberg went on. 'I am entirely proud to state too that not one of my line has ever, since records began, had cause to leave Mundus Chasmata. It is my firmly held belief that since my unnamed predecessor stepped off the colony vessel that carried him from Terra however many millennia passed, no descendent of his has had cause to leave.' Luneberg turned towards Lucian, his chest puffed out with pride, but mania clearly gleaming in his eyes. 'What do you think of that?'

Utterly mad, was what Lucian thought, but he kept his opinion to himself. This man and his people are as scared of the greater Imperium as they are of the myriad external forces that would assail them. As scared, he realised, of men as of aliens. He looked into Luneberg's eyes, and saw that fear embedded deep within. Fear, Lucian knew, made men unpredictable, even dangerous.

Certainly, it made them the worst type of business partner.

'I think, I think you have given me much upon which to ponder, Luneberg.'

'But you will join me? Will you aid me against that bastard Droon? Your ships, you have the means.'

Not if the High Lords ordered me to, in person, thought Lucian, backing away from the other man.

'Not that it matters,' Luneberg pressed on. 'I have the means now, thanks to you! I've got other friends you know, friends who'll help me, even if you won't. Such pretty toys... you could be my contact, my voice. You could speak for me Lucian! You could bring to me all they offer!'

As Luneberg disintegrated into a fit of manic giggling and muttering, Lucian made his excuses and left. The Imperial Commander appeared not to notice Lucian's departure, for he was addressing a rant to the floating lumen bobbing above his head.

Lucian listened for a moment, his gorge rising at Luneberg's half-garbled words, before leaving the dark garden. Luneberg's mad laughter echoed behind. He would rejoin Korvane and head back to their suite.

Lucian had some serious thinking to do.

CHAPTER EIGHT

Consciousness came to Brielle only slowly, and she was far from sure it was welcome. She opened her eyes nonetheless, blinking several times until her vision came into focus. She lay upon some unfeasibly comfortable fabric, and above her, floated a number of the small, globelike lumens that she vaguely recalled seeing the previous evening. They were evidently set to give off only a low illumination, the light they emitted soft and warm. She studied them for a moment, watching as they bobbed silently in the air.

She was content to lie still, for the moment, waiting for the moment of clarity that she knew was coming, when she would recall exactly where she was and have to do something about it.

She moved her head a fraction to the left, seeking to gain a better view of her surroundings. The lumen closest to her brightened and homed in towards her, causing her a moment of mild shock, before the notion that the device was no threat appeared in her mind. Where that thought had emanated she was unsure, although she felt confident that it was connected to the, as yet, unremembered events of the previous evening.

She sat up, gently, for her head was still far from clear. She recognised the chamber in which she had spent the night, the memory of the bizarre alien... entertainer (?) coming back to her. She paused to recall the incredible display she had witnessed, shaking her head in bewilderment.

She turned to scan her surroundings more fully, blinking at the shaft of harsh sunlight flooding in through the grilles of an arched window behind her. All around the low chamber were scattered plump cushions and crumpled furs. The recumbent forms of dozing nobles were arrayed amongst them, although she could not see Naal anywhere. Somehow, that fact neither surprised nor disturbed her. Empty bottles, glasses and vials were abandoned close by each body, and she looked closer at those nearest, seeing how the elaborately applied make-up and powder, on both men and women, now appeared so soiled, and even ugly. One man, who had the previous evening, appeared to Brielle a handsome and charming individual, looked by the wan morning light an ineffectual, painted fop, his make-up smeared half across his face and half across the rump of the woman upon whose body he slept.

The woman, Brielle noticed, was draped in fine chains, hundreds of small jewels dangling from them. Each jewel was lit from within by a slowly pulsing light, lending the woman's skin a multihued aspect that appeared quite sickly and unnatural in the light of day. Brielle had a sudden flash of recall, a vision of those same chains spinning, the light merging into blurred streaks as their owner danced.

She was unsure whether the vision was a memory or a dream. She leant over, reaching out an arm, cautiously, towards the woman, and taking one of the tiny jewels between her forefinger and thumb. She pulled gently until the chain gave way, slipping from the woman's thigh. As Brielle lifted the jewel to examine it, it took on a deep, green hue, reminding her of something she had seen before.

Something she had seen in the hold of her vessel returning from Q-77. The alien device she had examined had glowed with the exact same green, inner light. This woman was wearing items of jewellery obviously of alien manufacture, yet somehow this realisation neither surprised nor outraged Brielle. This entire world, she realised, was enamoured of the exotic, enamoured, quite literally, of the alien.

The woman groaned softly in her sleep, rolling languidly onto her side. The man sleeping next to her grumbled in response, forced to reposition his head lest it roll from its resting place. Brielle froze, for some unknown reason not wishing to awaken any of the sleeping nobles. By the number of empty glass vials beside them, she doubted they would wake for some time. The couple's dozing having resumed, Brielle let out a breath, and looked around for the clothes that she had, evidently, discarded at some unremembered point during the previous evening.

Stepping over the dozing forms of the guards, Brielle left the establishment. She could only imagine it was some private bordello, reserved for the use of the idle and decadent rich. She stood in the wan morning light, blinking against the glare, unsure of her location in relation to Luneberg's palace. Fractured details of the previous evening came to her, unbidden. She recalled having met Luneberg's functionary, Naal, at a trading house in the merchants' quarter. Thinking of Naal, she recalled snatches of conversation, made blurred and incoherent by the evening's excesses. No matter; it would come to her in time, when her head had eventually cleared.

Standing in the centre of the narrow, empty street, Brielle turned slowly around, her head pitched upwards towards the morning sky. She realised she had no clue in which direction the palace lay, and so continued slowly revolving until instinct, or folly, told her which direction to walk in. East, she decided, and set off.

The street down which she walked was by all appearances rarely travelled, at this time of the day at least, for although it contained the detritus of any city the size of Chasmata Capitalis, it was deserted of Luneberg's subjects. Reaching a junction, Brielle looked around, growing increasingly aware of the fact that few, if in fact any, people were out and about. The thought struck her that perhaps all of the citizens of this world were as pampered and idle as the nobles with whom she had passed the night. Could it really be that an entire society could function thus? What of the workers and the indentured serfs? What of the ever-present and largely invisible underclasses upon which most worlds relied? Did they lie abed too, dozing in a drug-induced haze upon the soft bellies of their lovers?

She considered this notion, blinking against the sunlight as a floating lumen hovered slowly by, its light no longer required as the day began. She studied it quizzically, wondering who performed the myriad duties she, in her own life, had always taken for granted as being carried out by others. She considered the hundreds of crew serving upon the *Fairlight*, the thousands serving under her father in the flotilla as a whole. Many were the scions of families indentured to the Arcadius generations previously; others were press-ganged at those ports where the dynasty was granted the right to recruit. Still more were even less willing, convicted of petty crimes, death sentences commuted to service aboard Navy or merchant vessels. Others were servitors, lobotomised creatures, part man, mostly machine, and despite being consecrated by the officers of the Creed, and highly valued, unthinking things of cold flesh. What if, she wondered, as she avoided a pile of stinking rubbish on the ground, what if all those hundreds and thousands of men, women and machines were offered the choice of whether or not they would serve? Would they continue to serve, for the good of all, or would their own selfish desires win out, as they appeared to here upon Mundus Chasmata?

The thought occurred to her that the people of this world, or the ruling classes at least, were weak and foolish, yet there was undeniably an underlying hint of coherent dogma in their apparently mindless hedonism. Snatches of conversation from the previous night came to her once more, a vision of Naal's face as he expounded upon the nature of life upon Mundus Chasmata. She shook her head, mildly frustrated with herself for having such trouble recalling the details of what was clearly an evening of some importance.

Wandering down an avenue lined with closed up drinking dens and establishments of no doubt ill repute, Brielle at last caught sight of Luneberg's palace, tall, gilded spires silhouetted against the sunrise. She realised with a stab of apprehension that she must soon face up to her actions, and make her play once and for all, but what was it she needed to achieve? She forced herself to focus on the situation at hand, to address the task that she must now undertake.

If she really was to take a hand in the future of the dynasty, she must do so now, she pondered. The deal with Luneberg was against the interests of the Arcadius, of that much she was sure, and she was growing increasingly confident in her belief that it was she, and not Korvane, who should be preparing to take over the dynasty, and who should have their father's ear until doing so. Hadn't Naal told her as much? He had, she realised, another small part of the previous evening coming back to her in a flash. She had spoken at some length with Luneberg's functionary, and he had shared, even fostered, her opinion that Korvane was weak.

If she wished to usurp her stepbrother's position, she would need to take a hand in the immediate, short-term fortunes of the Arcadius. She would need to undermine him to such an extent that he would never be able to recover his influence. Perhaps she should go further, she thought. In fact, hadn't Naal said that she should?

She halted, suddenly shocked by her own train of thought. Had she really discussed such things with a stranger? She realised she had, and much more besides. She recalled Naal promising to lend her aid. All she need do, she remembered him saying, was to give him the word, when she judged that the time was right.

Her mind set upon a confrontation with Korvane, Brielle turned her thoughts to her father's ongoing talks with the Imperial Commander, Luneberg. Part of her was still furious that Luneberg had attempted to turn the Arcadius into lowly gunrunners. Yet, she was no longer so disposed towards undermining the deal entirely. Her perspective had shifted, and she now considered herself in a far more favourable position. She had made powerful friends, Naal being a far more influential man than she had supposed, at first. With his aid, she might redefine the terms of the deal entirely; if she could convince her father that Naal and his associates offered a greater opportunity than did the Imperial Commander.

Associates? She started walking once more, but slower, her footsteps less sure. Her frustration grew more intense as she tried to remember the details of her conversation with Naal. He had made it clear, she was sure, that he had some power over Luneberg, and could influence him to change the terms of the deal, so long as it had not yet been finalised. She realised that this implied she must act soon, sooner than she might like, sooner perhaps than she was ready for.

She quickened her pace as she reached a resolution. It was clear to her that she must stymie the talks, ensuring that her father and Luneberg did not reach a final conclusion that would lead to the Arcadius submitting entirely to his service, and destroying themselves in the process. Korvane, she knew, would attempt to block her in this, and so she must time her intervention carefully, since it would inevitably lead to a confrontation with him. She knew that she must manage all this without falling so completely out of favour with her father that he would never again place his trust in her, or consider her a worthy inheritor of his mantle.

She briefly wished for the oblivion of the previous night, or even the relative simplicity of ship-to-ship combat.

Brielle swept into the apartment, to find Korvane waiting for her, a typically supercilious expression on his face. 'Where is he?' she demanded, slamming the door behind her and striding into the chamber. She was not in the mood for formalities.

'I'd ask where you have been, but I can see it's not a subject for polite conversation,' Korvane rejoined.

Little fool, thought Brielle, her hackles rising. 'This isn't the Court of Nankirk, Korvane, and you have no right to judge me. Where is Father?'

Korvane visibly bristled at Brielle's mention of his mother's court. 'It certainly is not,' he said, making a show of surveying his surroundings, 'and neither is it the annual tribal gathering.' He made a further show of looking her up and down, exaggerated disgust on his smirking face. 'Although you certainly appear to have attended it.'

Hatred flared in Brielle. She had always known that Korvane considered himself vastly superior to her in more ways than the order of inheritance. He had cast a slur upon the culture from which her mother came, that of the feral world of Chogoris. The world formed a large part of her own identity, despite not having been afforded much time amongst her mother's people.

Brielle stepped towards her brother, barely resisting the urge to forcibly remove the smug expression he wore across his stupid face. 'I'll ask you once more and then I won't be quite so polite,' she snarled. 'Where is Father?'

Korvane stood his ground, but indicated, with a nod, the door to the private conference room. 'He's in closed session with Luneberg. You'll have to wait until they have concluded business.'

Damn them, she thought, they're in there now, closing the deal. She would have to take drastic action and worry about the fallout later.

'Get out of my way,' Brielle said as she pushed past her brother.

She caught him off balance and he stumbled to one side before catching himself and spinning round. He grabbed her at the elbow.

'I'm not going to let you mess this up, Brielle, so don't even think it. Don't get involved in matters that are beyond you.'

Brielle snapped. Without thinking, she lashed out, feeling her fist strike her stepbrother's face and something brittle break beneath the impact. Korvane cried out and stumbled backwards, affording her a clear path to the door. She forged on, flinging the door wide without pause for thought.

Beyond, a wooden, oval table dominated the wide conference room, the back wall made entirely of glass, with a mighty eagle, symbol of the Imperium, mounted upon its outer face. Luneberg sat at the far side of the table, courtesans arranged demurely around him. Seated at either side were a dozen or so hooded scribes, feathered quills scratching across dry parchment in unison.

Her father sat, alone, on the other side of the table, his back towards her.

Luneberg had been speaking, but stopped as she entered, his mouth flapping in outrage. The quills halted too, and the scribes looked up, their faces barely visible beneath the deep hoods they wore. The courtesans whispered furtively, covering mouths with bejewelled hands.

'Father,' she said, suddenly unsure what to do.

Her father's head turned, and he looked straight at her, confusion in his eyes. 'Brielle, what are you doing here?'

'I need to speak to you, Father, we need to–'

The door behind Brielle flew open even further, slamming against the wall with a crash. Korvane burst through it, blood pouring from his ruined nose. 'Father, don't listen to her, she's gone mad! She's trying to ruin everything!'

Brielle's father opened his mouth to speak, but Luneberg pre-empted him, bellowing in rage, 'What, by all that is holy, is the meaning of this?' He turned on Lucian, pointing a finger at him. 'This upstart girl has interrupted us twice, Gerrit, twice she has perpetrated such breaches of protocol as would ordinarily earn a flogging. Well, I tell you this, you may have sought to wriggle out of our deal,' Brielle's mouth fell open at this, 'but I am inclined to throw you all in my dungeons!'

'Wriggle out of the deal'?

Brielle looked to her father, who was addressing Luneberg.

'My lord,' said Lucian, 'please forgive my daughter. I will speak with her presently, but please, may we conclude matters?'

'"Conclude matters"? If by that you mean will I allow you to run out on me without a shred of compensation, then absolutely not. You will find the terms of our original contract quite specific in this regard.'

'"Specific"?' Lucian surged to his feet. 'We had no such deal Luneberg. We can leave whenever we please!'

'How little you know of life, you who consider yourself so well-travelled. I require neither contract nor treaty Lucian, for I am master of this world and may do as I choose. I deem you beholden to me and you may not back out of our arrangement. Not without substantial penalty.'

'You're mad,' said Brielle, interrupting Luneberg's tirade. Every head in the chamber turned towards her, a stunned silence descending.

Luneberg stood, straightening out his uniform as he did so. 'Lucian, you will punish your daughter, or I will. If you refuse to, I will have every one of you arrested. Do you understand?'

Lucian stood facing the other man across the wide table. He leant forward. 'I will not punish my daughter, Luneberg, for she speaks the truth,'

The collective intake of breath from around the chamber would have sounded comical were it not for the tension of the situation. Brielle watched as her father's knuckles turned white, a sure sign, she knew, of his anger.

'Then you are condemned by your own words. Naal, have them arrested.'

Brielle had not seen Naal standing behind his master, but was grateful for his presence, as he stepped forwards. Their eyes met, and she recalled the promise he had made the previous night. She had only to indicate she needed, and wanted his help, and it would be hers. She nodded, the slightest movement, so that only he would see. He did likewise.

Though he appeared not to be armed with any form of projectile weapon, as would have been the case whenever paying court to such as Luneberg, Lucian now proved he was most certainly not unarmed. In that brief moment, Lucian raised his arm, the concealed digital weapon he always carried upon his right hand ring finger pointed straight across the table, at the Imperial Commander. 'You will allow us to withdraw to our vessel and to leave in peace.'

'You will never leave here, Gerrit,' Luneberg replied. Brielle could only assume that the man had never before had the business end of a digital weapon pointed at him. She chuckled inwardly as she saw that the weapon her father pointed was one that would not kill, but would instead have a far more interesting effect upon the target's nervous system. Luneberg, Brielle realised, had entirely failed to grasp the gravity of the situation.

'I had a feeling that would be your answer,' said Lucian. 'These talks are at an end.'

He fired the tiny weapon, a blinding white stream of light arcing across the space between the two men and striking Luneberg square between the eyes. The Imperial Commander stood transfixed as actinic lightning played around his head, before losing control of his bowels, explosively, and collapsing to the floor. There he lay, wailing and puking like a newborn, while his harem recoiled in horror.

Pandemonium descended. Before she could react, Brielle felt her hand caught by her father's as he ran past her, pulling her after him as he rapidly left the room. Korvane, blood streaming from his nose, caught them up in the corridor outside, and the three were soon racing down the claustrophobic passageways, unable to speak, because they were desperate to get a head start over their pursuers.

Her father in the lead and her stepbrother behind, Brielle raced down the dark corridors of Luneberg's palace. Clouds of dust billowed at their passing and candles guttered, making the way hard to discern. There were no lumens in sight.

'To the left, Father!' Brielle heard Korvane shout from behind, looking ahead in time to see her father veer off down a side corridor. 'I remember this area from our first visit. This is an access corridor used by servants.'

Lucian was leaning against the wall, catching his breath. Brielle did likewise, for although the flight had not been long, it had been sudden and she was in no fit state for such exertions. 'Well done my son,' said Lucian, clapping a hand on Korvane's shoulder. He took another deep breath and looked across at Brielle, holding the contact for a few seconds. 'Whatever that was about will have to wait,' he said, turning away before Brielle could answer. She felt the situation slipping rapidly from her control, and could see no immediate way of regaining it.

'Which way, Korvane?' Lucian asked, pushing himself from the wall once more.

'I think we continue on this corridor until it meets the main spine again. Then we need to work out how to get past the guards, to Brielle's shuttle.'

Assuming I'll let you on my shuttle, you pompous idiot, Brielle thought, staring daggers into her stepbrother's back as they moved off, her father leading the way.

An angry shout sounded from behind, the deafeningly loud report of a large-calibre handgun following a moment later. The household guard had finally got its act together, and was closing with each passing minute.

'Right! Right!' shouted Korvane as the three closed on another junction. They had been fleeing for what Brielle judged was no more than fifteen minutes, yet it felt like hours.

'How far to the gate?' she heard her father shout, flinching as another shot was fired somewhere behind them. So far, they had been fortunate, for the guards had not taken proper aim before shooting. She prayed that remained the case.

'I think it's the next passage on the left,' Korvane called.

'No!' Brielle interjected before she could stop herself. 'No, it's the next right.'

The three slowed, Lucian ducking back while Korvane peered around the next corner. 'Which is it?'

'The left,' Korvane repeated, at the same moment Brielle said, 'The right,' her tone now assured. 'I remember from last night. I passed this way on my way out into the city.'

Korvane sneered, but her father only nodded. 'You're sure?'

She was. 'I'm sure.'

Brielle signalled silence, edging around a corner. 'It's here. Only two guards. We can take them.'

'We cannot "take them",' said Korvane, 'we've committed grave enough crimes already without adding murder to the list.'

'We may have no choice, my son,' Lucian said, moving next to Brielle for a view of the corridor down which she was looking. As if to punctuate his words, more shouts sounded from behind. The household guards were closing. Brielle realised they would need to make a decision here and now.

'We do it now, Father, or we fight both groups.'

Lucian patted Brielle's shoulder before turning to Korvane. 'Brielle is right, Korvane. Are you ready?'

Korvane sighed, over dramatically, Brielle thought, and drew his power sword. He checked the charge, disengaged the safety, and said, 'As ready as can be.'

'Good,' said Lucian. 'We don't have time for subtleties, so let's keep this simple. We need to get as close as possible and take them down before they know we're on them, understood?'

Brielle sighed with impatience and frustration. She stepped around the bend and simply ran towards the guards. As she did so, she saw the expression of shock on her father's face, but she kept going nonetheless. She knew they had no time to sneak up on the guards at the portal, but she knew something else too, a fact of which her father and her stepbrother were entirely ignorant.

She ran on down the corridor, her vision filled by the back of the nearest guard. As she had noted the previous evening upon taking her leave of the palace, its guards stood watch against strangers attempting to gain entry. They expressed no interest whatsoever in events within the palace.

That was their undoing. As Brielle closed on the first guard, she made a fist, raising her arm and bringing it down in a wide swing across the back of the guard's head. The rings on her fingers made for brutal weapons, and she bit back the feeling of revulsion that welled within her as she felt the man's skull crack beneath her attack. In some detached part of her mind, she consoled herself that the guard would live, given half-decent medical attention.

Brielle's attack had taken only a second, but the other guard was already reacting. He turned as the momentum of her charge propelled her past him, shock and surprise writ large upon his face. Brielle came to a halt and spun to face the man, the realisation that she may have taken on more than she could handle dawning as he advanced upon her.

'Brielle, duck!'

Brielle threw herself to the floor.

A high-pitched whine filled the corridor, followed an instant later by the screaming report of an energy weapon discharging at close quarters – another of her father's hidden, digital weapons, she guessed. The roiling bolt raced the length of the corridor, its light blinding in the enclosed space, before slamming into the guard's left shoulder.

The man's shoulder disintegrated, leaving nothing to attach his left arm to his body. The catastrophic wound was cauterised before the blackened arm flopped to the floor, to be followed a moment later by the rest of the guard.

Brielle looked into his fading eyes as life left them, the part of her that had rejoiced that the other man was not fatally hurt now strangely silent.

'Damn!' she shouted. 'I had him. You didn't need to kill him!'

Lucian reached Brielle, offering her a hand to stand up. The hand, she noted, that bore a lethal array of hidden weaponry. 'Believe me, Brielle, if I could have avoided it I would have. When it comes down to it, you mean substantially more to me than he did.'

'But...' she said as her father helped her to her feet. 'Of course, I'm sorry.'

'You should be, but we can save that for later. Now let's get to the shuttle before we lose our lead.'

At last, thought Brielle, as the three charged up the tread boards to the shuttle pad. They had, after what seemed like hours, but no doubt was less than one, reached the spaceport. Having dealt with the guards, the remainder of their flight had been swift, and no one, thankfully, had challenged them.

As they gained the top of the ramp, she saw her shuttle standing proud where she had left it, silhouetted against the honey-golden sky of Mundus Chasmata. She had harboured a nagging doubt throughout the chase to the landing pad that Luneberg might have had it tampered with.

'Is everything in order?' Lucian called to Brielle from the steps behind. He was covering the rear, one ring-festooned hand raised as Korvane came in beside her.

'It is,' she called back, hardly able to believe it herself. They would make it after all.

'Don't be so sure,' said Korvane, pointing across the pad to a figure standing at its far edge, its features invisible against the glow of the sky. Brielle followed his gesture, raising her hand to her eyes to shade them from the glare.

'A friend of yours?' asked Lucian, arriving at his daughter's side.

She looked closer, realising that her father was correct. 'Yes, yes I think so.'

'In that case move it, girl!' said Lucian, and started towards Brielle's shuttle, Korvane following close behind. She hesitated a moment longer, her gaze lingering on the hooded face of the figure. It was Naal, she had no doubt, fulfilling her request for aid.

She ran after her father and stepbrother.

CHAPTER NINE

'Full charge, all drives! Prepare to make way with all haste.'

Sirens wailed and the lights changed to flashing, deep red, as Korvane leant forward in his command throne, the bridge of the *Rosetta* a riot of activity below him. 'I want all weapons batteries operational within fifteen minutes.'

The bridge filled with shouts of 'Aye sir', junior officers, deck crew and dozens of servitors going about the business of getting the *Rosetta* under way and clear of the space station – the Chasmata Orbital. Korvane, his father and his stepsister had raced from the surface aboard Brielle's shuttle, each rendezvousing with their own vessel. No one had pursued them; a fact that Korvane put down to the laxity of Mundus Chasmata's security forces. Furthermore, they had gambled that the staff of the orbital would be lax in their security and would not to attempt to intercept them. To Korvane's huge relief, such had been the case.

The cargo lighters dispatched, what seemed days before, to offload the goods collected at Q-77, had still to complete their task, but had fled for the orbital as Korvane had ordered the *Rosetta* to general quarters. He gave them no more thought, because getting clear of the orbital was likely to require all of his attention.

'Disengage, all points,' Korvane ordered.

A deck officer stationed nearby looked up from his console, concern written across his face. 'Sir, the umbilicals aren't made fast, we'll lose–'

'I said, Mister Taviss, "disengage all points". Do so now or I will order you left behind.'

The man nodded, before speaking into a fluted horn at his station. He gave the order. The rogue traders had no time to waste in the protracted process of breaking dock; his father had made it clear to Korvane that they should disengage with all haste, regardless of the consequences. A shudder rumbled through the vessel, her bow thrusters awakening. Any moment, they would clear their throats, and the *Rosetta* would move slowly sideways, clearing the orbital's docking arm.

'Thruster burn in thirty seconds, sir,' called the helmsman, and a brass-rimmed clock face mounted above the forward viewing port began to count down the seconds.

Korvane watched the clock's hand as it moved, knowing that even now men on the lower decks would be racing for the safety of the inner chambers. Not all would make it, some would suffocate as the outer chambers depressurised, and a few would be sucked out into space through the unsecured outer portals, as the umbilicals were ripped away from their mountings.

He gave them no more thought. The clock hand reached 30.

The port bow thrusters coughed into life, their power staggering as they laboured to move the vast bulk of the cruiser. For what seemed an age the *Rosetta* wallowed, unmoving despite the vast energies unleashed. Then, inexorably, the scene outside the viewing port shifted, the docking arm receding as the *Rosetta* slid gracefully to starboard. Once moving, her speed increased, and a moment later a terrible grinding sound travelled along her decks, the unsecured umbilicals, and by the sound of it, several mounting plates, being ripped free.

A moment later and the helmsman called, 'We're free sir, full speed ahead?'

'Full speed ahead, Mister Ellik. Form us up on the *Oceanid*.'

'Sir,' the *Rosetta*'s Master of Ordnance called, 'augurs are detecting a power surge from the orbital! I believe it is–'

Before the officer could finish his report, a blinding flash filled the forward viewing port. Korvane held his breath, but the impact he expected did not materialise.

'Report!' bellowed Korvane, suddenly filled with anger at the thought of someone daring to fire upon his vessel.

The Master of Ordnance bent over his console, his hands working a multitude of dials and levers, his screens filled with scrolling gibberish. 'The cogitators can't identify sir. It was extremely high powered, but left no etheric wake.'

Deciding not to risk a second volley, Korvane ordered, 'Shields to full capacity. Helm, get us moving right now, at full speed. I want to put some distance between us and that orbital.'

Once more, the bridge filled with shouts of "aye sir", as the crew hurried about its tasks. Korvane scanned the viewing screens crowded around his command throne, seeking any clue as to the type of weapon the orbital had employed, if indeed it was a weapon at all.

'Sir, a second power surge!'

This time Korvane glanced across at his screens as the surge spiked, reams of machine code language screaming indecipherable warnings.

A second flash, but this time accompanied by the unmistakable sensation of the *Rosetta*'s shields absorbing an impact. The bridge lights flickered and dimmed as every last kilojoule of available power was diverted to the screaming shield generators. A patch of space, a section of the field projected in front of the vessel, glowed white-hot at the point where the weapon had struck.

Fear stabbed cold in Korvane's chest. What by the Emperor, had the orbital just fired at them? Whatever type of weapon it was, it had, a quick scan of the cogitator screens told him, stripped the *Rosetta*'s shield arrays to less than half of their capacity.

'Helm,' Korvane shouted. 'Use every unit of power not required for the shields to get us out of range of that weapon, now!'

'Aye sir,' called back the helmsman, sweating at his wheel and labouring on a mighty lever, feeding as much power to the main drives as he dared.

'Shields?'

A servitor at the shield control station turned its head towards him, spitting a ream of parchment roll from its rictus mouth. A nearby rating passed the paper to Korvane. A cursory scan confirmed what he had feared. The shield arrays were severely damaged; he doubted they could take a second impact.'

'Sir?' the Master of Ordnance called. 'The cogitators observed the second discharge in full. They have formulated an analysis. The weapon fired some form of hyper-velocity projectile. It was solid, not energy based. Our shields absorbed its force, but are not configured to convert such high-velocity particle impacts.

Korvane's mind raced. He knew nothing of such weapons, for the majority of human vessels used either high explosive projectiles or energy-based laser weapons. He knew the other space faring races fielded a wide range of exotic weapon types, but with the exception of those of the eldar such weapons were rarely of undue threat.

He looked once more to the banks of nearby screens, seeking some clue as to the actions of the *Oceanid* and the *Fairlight*. He quickly saw that his father's vessel had disengaged and was manoeuvring away from the orbital. Beyond, his stepsister's vessel had yet to separate fully from the docking arm.

The monotone voice of the servitor at the comms station intoned, 'Incoming ship-to-ship transmission. Source: *Oceanid*.'

Korvane stood. 'Patch it through.'

Angry static filled the air, interspersed with random clicks and pops.

'Korvane, Brielle?' His father's voice cut through the static.

'Here, Father,' he replied, hearing his stepsister do likewise after a short delay.

'Listen carefully both of you. I'm transmitting jump coordinates.' A glance at his screens told Korvane they were being received. 'We scatter here, and make the jump as soon as we're clear. Understood?'

Korvane scanned the coordinates scrolling across his screens. They indicated the destination as the nearest inhabited system, Arris Epsilon. They gave an outbound jump point only two astronomical units out.

'Father, are you're sure it's safe?' he asked.

A small delay was followed by his father's reply, 'No, but my augurs are showing that we're not just up against the orbital. Check near space tracking.'

Korvane called up the long-range augur returns. 'What the...?'

He stared for a moment as a group of signal returns appeared at the extent of his augur range.

'I don't know who they are Korvane, but I'm not prepared to sit here and find out the hard way. We jump as soon as we're clear.'

'Understood,' replied Korvane.

'Good luck, the pair of you,' he heard his father say, before a howl of feedback screamed from the speaker grilles, and then silence.

The Master of Ordnance spoke up, 'Sir, another surge.'

'All hands,' Korvane called, preparing himself for the catastrophic damage he knew was about to be done to his vessel, 'brace for impact.'

None came.

He looked to the bank of screens, seeing that it was not the *Rosetta* that had been the target of this attack, but the *Oceanid*. Having manoeuvred his vessel away from the docking arm, his father had not ordered her away, but had come around to engage the station in a deadly broadside.

Cataclysmic energies played across the *Oceanid*'s dying shields, secondary fires raging across her port as atmosphere bled into space. Korvane stood from his command throne and crossed to another viewing port, from which he could make out the epic confrontation unfolding only a few hundred metres distant.

He watched in awe as fire blossomed across the *Oceanid*'s side, the discharge of her port weapons batteries unleashing a fearsome broadside at extreme short range. The orbital station was wreathed in fire as the devastating attack struck home, and several docking arms sheared off as explosions gutted the central core.

Yet the station was far from dead, despite the terrible damage done by the *Oceanid*'s broadside. Korvane winced as another, blinding flash indicated that the station's deadly projectile weapon was still operational. Though the projectile itself was invisible, he saw its passing etched upon the smoke and fire billowing into space from both the *Oceanid* and the station. It struck his father's ship a glancing blow to a dorsal augur array, the structure shearing off and spinning into space.

Stunned by the ferocity of the battle raging before him, it took Korvane a moment to realise that he was hearing his father's voice addressing him over the communications system.

'...peat, get moving the pair of you, now! Good luck.'

Korvane opened an intercom channel to Adept Mykelo, his Navigator. 'Awaiting your order adept. You have the vessel.'

A pause, before the adept replied. 'This is against my better judgement sir, but given the circumstances I shall undertake the manoeuvre. Pray for us all.'

Korvane closed the channel and leant back in his command throne, watching as the bridge crew made the final preparations for the emergency warp jump. This was the second time the vessel and her crew had undergone a warp jump recently, and it appeared as if Mykelo would reject Korvane's order. It was entirely within his rights as a Navigator to do so, Korvane knew, for any and all matters relating to a vessel's passage through the warp were entirely the province of its Navigator, by ancient decree. Mykelo had considered the situation, realising that they had little choice if they were to avoid a confrontation with the unknown vessels, which were bearing down on them with obviously hostile intent.

A mournful peal sounded from the ship's address system, the signal that a warp jump was imminent. Korvane knew somehow that this would be a bad one, although he had no idea in what way. He had heard the tales.

The signal ended and all of the lights on the bridge died. Korvane could hear his own pulse thundering in his ears, and he gripped the arms of the command throne all the tighter.

A distant sound became audible, an atonal drone, building in volume to the scream of a billion, billion souls adrift upon an ocean of pain and chaos. Korvane's own voice added to the terrible din, as did that of every man and woman onboard the *Rosetta*. They were joined together in a terrible communion, sharing the damnation of the denizens of the abyss.

Then there was silence.

Korvane opened his eyes, and then vomited. The bridge lights flickered back to life, one by one. He heard coughing and moaning from the bridge crew. Having painfully voided the contents of his stomach, Korvane looked around his bridge, breathing heavily as he fought to make some sense of what had just occurred.

Something had gone terribly wrong, that much was clear. His crew was scattered around the bridge, or slumped over consoles, groaning or silent, unconscious, insensible, or worse. Only the servitors appeared to have escaped unharmed. The Master of Ordnance sat up and looked towards Korvane with madness in his eyes.

Korvane saw with a start that the man's hair was now entirely white, while it had been merely grey-shot before the jump. Utter shock threatened to overwhelm him, and he strove to maintain control of his faculties in the face of what had happened.

'We pray for those lost in the warp,' Korvane mumbled, the words of the spacefarers' prayer coming unbidden to his lips. The prayer gave him some comfort, and he felt himself calming. He glanced at the banks of screens surrounding his command throne. All were dead.

Realising that he would need to take visible control of the situation, Korvane stood, shakily at first. A junior officer appeared nearby, offering aid, which he waved away.

'Bridge crew, listen to me. I need a full situation report and I need it now.' He straightened as he spoke, feeling confidence return as he played the role for which he was born and raised – that of leader. 'Then I need to know where the hell we are.'

'Aye sir,' came the mumbled replies from the crew. Men straightened themselves out, smoothing creased uniforms as they returned to their stations. Within minutes, the bridge bore some resemblance to its normal state – men, and mostly servitors, going about their business. Yet still the screens were dead.

He turned to the junior officer hovering nearby. 'Find out if Adept Mykelo is in need of help.' The man nodded and hurried away.

Korvane crossed to the forward viewing port. Looking out, he was confronted with unfamiliar constellations, but at least, he thought, it was space out there, and not somewhere else. He shook the thought off and studied the view; a nearby star glowed white through the halo of a comet's debris, yet he had no clue if it was Arris Epsilon, or an entirely different system.

The rating appeared at his side once more. 'Report,' he ordered.

'Sir, we're being hailed.'

Leaving the question of the Navigator's state to one side, Korvane asked, 'The *Oceanid*?' He doubted, even as he asked, that either of the other two rogue trader vessels would be nearby.

'I cannot tell, sir.'

'Why can't you tell, lieutenant?'

'Sir, the comms systems appear to have sustained some damage. We have crews working on getting them fully operational. We have short-ranged hailing, but little else.'

'Fine.' Korvane felt at a major disadvantage with his ship's systems running under capacity, but he would have to make the best of the situation. 'Open a channel, and contact Mykelo.'

'Aye sir,' the officer said, before ordering the servitor at the comms station to patch through the transmission.

'...vessel. Repeat. Activate identification transponders immediately or be fired upon. You have entered sovereign space and we will fire if you do not identify yourself. Repeat–'

Korvane cleared his throat, before announcing, 'This is the rogue trader vessel *Rosetta*, of the Arcadius. I am Korvane Gerrit of the Arcadius, son of Lucian, heritor of the Arcadius. To whom do I speak?'

The channel burbled and whistled for a second or two, before the reply came back, '*Rosetta*, this is Epsilon system defence boat *Gamma Secondus*. You will lock onto our signal and follow us in. Then you will be ferried to the surface, is that understood?

Korvane sighed. He was intensely relieved that they had reached their intended destination of Arris Epsilon. With many of the ship's augur systems still incapacitated he had no clue as to whether his father and stepsister had yet arrived. That, to his mind, put him in a position of authority.

Perhaps, at Arris Epsilon, he could repair some of the damage his stepsister had done at Mundus Chasmata.

'Do as they instruct,' he ordered the helmsman, before retiring to his quarters to prepare to board the other vessel.

'Arris Epsilon, my lord.'

Korvane looked through the shuttle's cockpit port as the small ship swept through the upper atmosphere of Arris Epsilon: vast, bioluminescent clouds glowed acid yellow and jade green, casting the landscape far below in an actinic, murky half-light.

He nodded to the captain of the security cutter, his mind engaged by conflicting distractions: the need to plan for the coming meeting with this world's leaders, and the need to gather as much information on this world as possible. The view, which was really quite stunning, was another distraction.

Spotting the smudge of what he assumed was a distant conurbation, Korvane turned to the captain, 'How far to your capital?'

The man bowed his head as he communed with the shuttle's machine spirit, his soul intermingling with that of the machine via the consecrated mind impulse cables threaded from the back of his head to the ports behind him.

The captain raised his head, 'Thirty-seven point five.' Korvane raised his eyebrows, holding the man's eye. 'Local,' he finished, Korvane nodding.

Korvane settled back in his seat, deciding to use the time wisely. He had gathered, from what little conversation had taken place between the security cutter's crew and himself, that an Imperial Commander named Zachary Droon ruled Arris Epsilon. His ancestral seat lay in a range of mountains that bisected the world's main landmass, his capital named Arralow City.

Beyond that, Korvane had scarcely gleaned anything, for the Epsilon security personnel were tight lipped, even for the natives of such a backwater world. It wasn't that they had a problem communicating, for their Low Gothic was uncommonly coherent. They simply didn't communicate very much.

Korvane sighed, inwardly, for to do so out loud would be, to him, an unforgivable rudeness. He looked once more out of the cockpit's port, his eyes tracing the patterns in the vast cloud formations. Many hundreds of kilometres tall, they formed pillars that connected the various strata of Arris Epsilon's atmosphere. The incredibly complex convection currents within each supported entire worlds of microscopic life, or so the captain had informed him. Apparently, it was the only subject on which he was capable of holding forth.

Korvane's mind wandered, casting back to the warp jump from Mundus Chasmata. Before leaving his vessel to board the security cutter, Korvane had ensured that he knew about his Navigator's condition. The adept had been able to speak to him only briefly, but had communicated to him the enormity of what had transpired during the jump. Korvane knew that the adept was talking down to him, speaking in layman's terms, but he had been chilled to the bone by the Navigator's report. The *Rosetta*, Mykelo had croaked through parched lips, had been struck a glancing blow by... something... in the warp. He knew not what, but likened the event to a small boat cast adrift upon a raging ocean, only to be caught by the passing of a mighty leviathan. The... leviathan... might have been entirely ignorant as the tiny vessel was dashed by its fins, caught in its wake, swept across the ocean, and cast up on unknown shores.

It was only thanks to the skill of Adept Mykelo that, so Korvane gathered, the *Rosetta* had escaped the thing's embrace, the Navigator dumping the vessel back into real space. By some bizarre chance, perhaps because they were, literally, caught up on the leviathan's back, they had emerged on the outskirts of the system for which they had been making.

Mykelo had cautioned Korvane against welcoming such an event, however, warning him that the cost might have been higher than any could imagine. Mykelo had shivered as he had explained just how fortunate they had been not to have been swept up entirely, to be carried across space and time to the very ends of the universe.

He shook his head, attempting to clear the memory of those terrible seconds within the warp. At least, it had appeared mere seconds, but it might have been minutes, hours or weeks. He might have been locked in his soul scream for decades, his mortal mind only able to comprehend the smallest portion of damnation.

Korvane shook his head again, focusing on the view outside the shuttle in an effort to shed the cold that had descended upon his soul. The vast cloudbanks were receding, and an impossibly tall mountain chain that stretched from one horizon to the other dominated the view. He saw that the line marked the world's current terminator line, the darkness of rapidly descending night all that was visible beyond.

The shuttle swept on, banking to gain height over the rising mountains below. The copper green rocks soon rose to meet them, and Korvane saw that the shuttle was following the meandering course of a valley many dozens of kilometres deep, the bottom of which was wreathed in pulsating silver mist.

Following the course of the valley, Korvane saw that it came to a head amid the mountains above. The shuttle rose, following the valley to its termination in the mountain's crags. More of the silver, inwardly glowing mist wreathed this tallest of mountains, but Korvane soon made out the unmistakable pattern described by racing landing lights.

The shuttle throttled back, bleeding velocity as the pilot brought it expertly in through the coiling mist. It settled upon its landing gear, the captain throwing a bank of switches and disengaging its engines.

Korvane realised as they touched down upon the surface of Arris Epsilon that the future of the Arcadius Dynasty might rest entirely in his hands.

He grinned.

Arralow City, seat of power of Imperial Commander Zachary Droon, was an ancient stone structure, perched precariously atop the highest peak of the mountain range. The chain stretched from the eastern to the western horizons, forming a mighty, jagged and unbroken spine. The valley along which the cutter had approached ran to the south, receding from view as it descended to the mist-wreathed flats below. An immense plain stretched to the north, the bioluminescent cloud formations dancing across its endless surface.

Korvane saw all this as he stood on the windswept landing pad, awaiting the approach of a ceremonial guard. He felt a mild, but pleasant surprise that such had been ordered, for he had given no advance warning of his visit and was not known to the Imperial Commander. It was a good sign, he judged, going by his experience of dealing in matters of courtly etiquette.

He stood in polite silence, flanked by the captain and first mate of the cutter. The shock of the exit from the warp was clearing, and he was struck by the unusual scent upon the air, a vaguely noxious combination of chemical sharpness and decay. He realised that it must be some by-product of the exotic eco-system at play within the clouds, and guessed that the natives were entirely unaware of it. He stifled a cough, and determined not to mention it.

The ceremonial procession approached, Korvane able to make out the details of the guards' uniforms and weapons. They offered a jarring contrast to Luneberg's household guard, who had worn uniforms of stark white with tall feathers at their brows. These wore rough spun, un-dyed cloth, and carried simple, sturdy lasguns in place of the overly ornate and entirely impractical long rifles that Luneberg's men had carried.

The procession reached the edge of the landing pad, and an

officer, barely distinguishable to Korvane from the other guards, stepped forwards and bowed.

'I welcome you, Lord Gerrit of the Arcadius, to the world of Arris Epsilon. My master, the Imperial Commander Lord Droon bids you attend him.'

Korvane was struck by the clarity of the man's Low Gothic, just as he had been by that of the cutter's captain. It was most unusual, in his experience, to find a dialect this far out on the Eastern Rim that was so understandable. So clear was it, in fact that Korvane guessed it was a derivation of High Gothic rather than one of the hybrid dialects used on most worlds. All this passed through his mind in the span of time it took the officer to speak, Korvane's expert instincts gleaning potentially valuable information from every aspect of his situation.

'I gladly do so,' he replied, bowing ever so slightly at the waist and reading the other man's reaction all the while. Seeing the other bow yet lower told him that his conventions were correct when it came to acknowledging comparative social ranking.

The officer turned, his squad doing likewise in perfect unison. Korvane stepped forwards, and the guards marched off as he passed them. He found himself walking along a tall, thin access-way crossing a vast gulf to a rocky spire several hundred metres away. He glanced over the rail-less edge, glad that the ground was not visible, the mist bubbling away far below.

Looking ahead, Korvane saw the bulk of what he took to be Imperial Commander Zachary Droon's palace, perched upon the highest peak of mountain towards which the walkway led. It consisted of a multitude of peaked turrets, verandas and galleries, each connected, he guessed, by a honeycomb of tunnels cut into the rock of the mountain.

The walkway terminated in a tall, thin portal in the rock, flanked on either side by long, fluttering pennants. The doors opened on well-oiled hinges, swinging inwards to reveal a brightly lit passage leading into the mountain.

The procession passed through the portal, following the passage cut through the raw stone for a hundred metres or so, to a second set of tall, thin doors. The guards now changed formation, forming a perfect line behind Korvane. At some unheard signal, the doors swung open and a bright light burst forth, briefly dazzling Korvane.

He was so determined to avoid causing offence that he stepped forwards, regardless that his vision had yet to clear. As his sight adjusted to the brightness, Korvane saw that he stood in the centre of a wide, tall space cut into the side of the mountain. The world's sun entirely filled the view beyond the cave's mouth, its centre the brightest white, its halo a serene jade. Silhouetted against the sun, Korvane could just make out a tall form, which stepped towards him.

The silhouette resolved in Korvane's vision, forming into a tall, thin-faced man, his hair receding, wearing a long robe of plain linen. This was Zachary Droon, judged Korvane, an ascetic, by his appearance, although Korvane recalled the numerous times his father had warned him against acting on first impressions.

'Welcome to my court, Lord Gerrit.' Droon made an expansive motion with his long, thin arms. Korvane followed the gesture, noting the courtiers arrayed upon either side, dressed in the same, simple garb as their master. 'We so seldom receive guests, and when we do, we are never found wanting as hosts. You arrived unannounced, Lord Gerrit?'

Korvane caught the inference immediately – Droon was sizing him up, while simultaneously hedging his bets lest Korvane prove to be a potential ally, or a potential threat. The Imperial Commander appeared to have accepted that Korvane was, as he had identified himself, a rogue trader, for which Korvane was grateful. He guessed that Droon was prepared to believe him, for now, but would require a more solid indication at some point in the not too distant future.

'Yes my Lord Droon, for which I beg your forgiveness.' A little contrition was hardly inappropriate at this juncture, Korvane thought. Evidently, Droon thought the same thing, for he nodded sagely at Korvane's reply. 'A mishap whilst traversing the empyrean brought us to your domains in this manner, although we were bound for Arris Epsilon in any case.'

Droon's eyebrows rose. 'Really? We expected no such visit. Please, do go on.'

Korvane felt hot prickles rise at his neck, for Droon appeared more inclined to press his guest for an explanation than would ordinarily be politic. He went on, 'No, my lord, and again, I must ask your forbearance. My vessel and two others were fleeing an attack at a nearby system. In our haste to escape, we determined that this was the safest destination.'

Upon hearing this, the Imperial Commander turned his head to one side, considering, Korvane guessed, the likelihood of Korvane's story.

'Your attackers were... raiders? Pirates?'

'No, my lord, unfortunately not, we were engaged in a trade negotiation upon Mundus Chasmata–'

'Luneberg?' Droon interjected, his previously blank expression suddenly one of anger.

'Indeed, my lord.'

'What cause did he have to attack your vessels? What was the nature of your negotiations?' Droon's manner had shifted, from one of detached civility to something bordering on hostility.

Korvane thought quickly, judging that Droon's reaction was caused by some underlying enmity towards the Imperial Commander of Mundus Chasmata. 'The talks were to ascertain the profitability of opening up a permanent trade route between Chasmata and a number of coreward mercantile concerns,' a minor lie, but Korvane was ill disposed towards revealing the true nature of the deal. 'The confrontation was caused when Luneberg attempted to forcibly impose unfavourable terms.'

'Luneberg attacked you because you refused to accede to his authority?'

Korvane hesitated before answering, aware that his reply might shape events to come in ways that he could not yet predict. 'Yes, my lord,' he said, 'I believe the Lord Luneberg is not entirely–'

'Sane?' Interjected Droon. 'You're saying that Culpepper Luneberg is dangerously unstable and unfit to rule his world?'

Korvane had said no such thing, although he certainly held that opinion. Before he could answer, however, Droon cut in.

'Well, you'd be absolutely correct. Luneberg is a sinful waste of skin, and you can consider yourself fortunate to have escaped his clutches. He's been attempting to make deals with the likes of you for many years. I've had my suspicions for some time, but

I believe you have confirmed them. The man has cracked. He's on the verge of taking his world, and this entire sector, to the brink of rebellion.'

Oh God-Emperor preserve us all, Korvane thought, another mad Imperial Commander.

'Lord Gerrit?'

Korvane forced himself to return his attention to the Imperial Commander.

'Lord Gerrit, I need your help.'

Once more, Korvane's mind raced. Had he really escaped the clutches of one madman, only to flee right into those of another? He would not allow it. The Arcadius stood on the brink, and he would ensure their survival.

'You need my help?'

'Indeed. You are, as you say, a rogue trader of some means. I am but a humble Imperial Commander, my own means limited. I have been aware for many years that Luneberg's madness has driven this entire region into the grip of recidivism, and I believe he is on the verge of entirely forsaking his oaths to Terra.'

'You believe Luneberg is a rebel?'

'Indeed I do, Lord Gerrit, indeed I do. His policies, and those of many generations of his line prior to him, have plunged this sector into isolation from Terra. He believes himself above the Pax Imperialis. We must bring him into line, or there will be a terrible price to pay. For us all'

Korvane's instincts sensed an opening. 'I see, and how may I be of assistance in averting such a disaster?'

Droon bowed, turning as he did so and indicating with another expansive sweep of his long arms an archway, beyond which a side chamber was visible. 'Please, let us retire to discuss the details.'

'You realise,' said Zachary Droon, 'that your name will be spoken in awe by generations to come.'

Korvane stood beside Droon, atop a craggy promontory, watching as the legions of the Epsilon Planetary Defence Force marched by in perfect formation. They filed onto two waiting transports, which would take them to orbit. From there they would be packed onto the *Rosetta*, and, Korvane hoped, and had promised, onto the *Oceanid* and the *Fairlight*, as soon as they arrived.

'You flatter me, my Lord Droon,' Korvane replied, not taking his eyes from the spectacle below. 'I wish only to serve.'

Droon chuckled at this, but did Korvane the kindness of not commenting further. The two had come to a deal. A far better deal, Korvane believed, than his father had attempted to enter into with that madman Luneberg. He was sure that he had secured the immediate future of the Arcadius, by pledging the three vessels to aid Droon in his righteous war against the recidivist Luneberg. To start with, all they need do was transport Droon's Planetary Defence Force troops to Mundus Chasmata, where they would launch a devastating and entirely unforeseen assault on Luneberg's centres of power. The world would fall in short order, of that Korvane was positive, and the Arcadius would reap the rewards of their loyal service to the forces of law and order.

Korvane smiled to himself as he watched the troops parading by. His day had finally arrived. His father would cede control to him, and force his bitch of a stepsister to tow the line or leave.

Oh yes, he thought, his time was coming.

CHAPTER TEN

The *Oceanid*'s warp drive howled a plaintive wail, disturbingly human in tone, as the vessel crashed through the non-existent barrier between the real world and the empyrean. Lucian opened his eyes, mouthing a prayer to the almighty God-Emperor, a prayer of thanks that his vessel was delivered once more to the physical universe.

The warp drive continued its screaming, the terrible, soul-wrenching sound audible even on the *Oceanid*'s bridge, hundreds of metres fore of the drive section. Lucian knew it indicated that something had come very close to going incredibly wrong whilst they were within the warp, but knew better than to dwell on what disaster might have been close to befalling his vessel. Instead, he resolved to seek his Navigator's counsel on the matter as soon as the adept had been given time to recover from the voyage.

Lucian looked to the head of his bridge, seeing nothing of note or out of the ordinary through the wide viewing port that dominated it, 'Helm, situation report if you will.'

Helmsman Raldi consulted the constellation of blinking lights, glass dials and scrolling readouts clustered around his station before replying.

'We're within point five A.U.s of the marker, sir.'

'Stress points?'

'Yes sir, several. I couldn't say for sure, but I think that jump might have taken its toll.'

'My thoughts too, Mister Raldi. Station ten?' A rating at one of the deck stations stood to attention. 'Do we have a reference?'

Though he was unsure as to its nature, Lucian's experience told him that all was not well with the warp jump. He was relieved in the extreme that the *Oceanid* was in more or less the correct position; she was where she should be. Next, he needed to ascertain that his vessel was when she should be. The warp was capable of playing some extreme and cruel tricks with relative time, particularly when conditions within it were rough.

The rating bent over his station, feverishly working the dials and levers, before turning back to Lucian. 'Astrographicus indicates we have arrived ahead of schedule sir. Transient conditions within the warp, I would surmise.'

'Early?' Doubt gripped Lucian's heart. 'How early?'

'Only point zero five sir, we're–'

'Good,' interrupted Lucian. It was a fact that the warp did odd things to time and space and his ilk had to live with that. The consequences of some particularly extreme distortions however were scarcely worth considering.

'Station three. Scan for the *Fairlight* and *Rosetta*.'

The servitor hard-wired to the instruments at station three gave forth its electronic contralto, a disturbing mixture of human and machine generated sound. This continued for several minutes, Lucian feeling more unsettled as time dragged on.

'Holo,' he ordered, the holograph display resolving before him. At first grainy and blurred, the image became more detailed as the augurs gathered more and more information on the area of space immediately surrounding the *Oceanid*. Lucian cursed as one third of the image remained empty – the result of losing a scanner tower in the confrontation with the Chasmata orbital.

'Station three, no luck?'

The servitor at the communications station ceased its machine gibberish, shaking its head in a motion that Lucian might have taken for sadness in a fully human crewman.

'Well enough.' If the *Oceanid*'s jump had been affected by adverse conditions within the warp, it stood to reason that the other vessels might have been too. However, given the circumstances of the jump, Lucian was determined to be sure.

'Mister Raldi?' The helmsman turned. 'I'm going to speak with Master Karisan. You have the bridge.'

'Aye sir,' Lucian heard the helmsman reply as he stalked from the bridge. If conventional, machine-guided communications could offer no clue, perhaps the ship's astropath might have more luck, he thought.

The astropath's chamber was situated amidships, on the lowest deck. Lucian's journey took him through an area of his vessel that had taken damage during the skirmish with the Chasmata orbital, and he was forced to double back on himself several times to avoid areas made inaccessible. Work gangs and H-grade servitors packed the gloomy companionways, their junior officers working them around the clock to get the damage repaired, or at least contained.

As Lucian walked, he cast his mind back over the confrontation, and subsequent emergency jump into warp space. He could feel a pattern emerging, fragments of an overall picture that was not yet ready to reveal itself to him. Luneberg had concealed the true nature of the deal he had sought to negotiate; that much was obvious. Lucian suspected that the Imperial Commander had sought to tie him down on some point of contract, but that, for some reason or other he had changed his mind. Brielle had certainly had some part to play in that, for she had apparently sabotaged the talks quite deliberately. He would find out why, when he found out where she was.

He recalled the flight from Luneberg's palace. The man had truly cracked when Brielle had burst in on their final negotiations, and the rogue traders had only barely escaped with their lives. When the orbital had opened fire on them with a weapon that Lucian knew was of alien origin, things had begun to make more sense to him. The weapon, what Lucian took to be some manner of ultra-high velocity mass driver, took its toll on the *Oceanid*, although she had suffered far worse in her time. The question that begged to be answered, was just where Luneberg had acquired the weapon. He had all but admitted that, at the very least, his world was estranged from the mainstream of the Imperium. Lucian suspected that the Imperial Commander had wavered on the threshold of heresy for some time, and the fact that he had obtained, and used, xenos weaponry suggested that he had decided to take that final step.

As he waited for a plodding cargo-servitor to pass, Lucian

wondered who Luneberg's allies might be, and on what part he had expected Lucian to fulfil in the venture. Lucian cast his mind over the archives he could recall of this region, but he could not think of a single xenos race that might have entered into such an arrangement. Indeed, he knew of no xenos this side of the Damocles Gulf that had anything like the level of technology exhibited by the orbital's weaponry: a previously untracked eldar craftworld, perhaps? He would be surprised in the extreme if a man such as Luneberg had extracted anything out of the enigmatic and unfathomable race, for they were notoriously self-interested and only dealt with others if they were likely to benefit most from the arrangement. Perhaps, thought Lucian, there were other races out there, in the dense and barely charted regions beyond the gulf.

Looking up from his thoughts, Lucian realised that he had reached his destination: the chamber of Master Karisan. He extended his hand to knock on the frame, but withdrew it as the door was pulled open from within, and he was greeted by a musty, incense-laden scent.

'My master, please enter,' said a voice from within the dimly lit chamber.

Lucian stepped through, into the domain of the flotilla's astropath. The man was ancient, having served a long series of vessels for many decades. He was long past his prime, in Lucian's opinion, and he rarely called upon his services unless it was vital. He had resolved to seek a replacement when he was able, but the guild had thus far been unwilling to retire Master Karisan. Lucian suspected that they wanted the ancient telepath out of way, and it would take a substantial disbursement to change their minds. It was just one more unwelcome reminder of the failing power of the dynasty.

The chamber was wide and low, taking the form of a blister upon the *Oceanid*'s underbelly. One entire wall was a mighty viewing port, beyond which the vessel's underside and the blackness of starry space were visible. The room was cramped, but not for want of available space. Instead, every surface was crammed with what Lucian took for junk. Long-burned candles, crumpled parchment, dry, dead things and other unidentifiable rubbish littered the place. Master Karisan appeared entirely at home in this environment, for his own appearance was equally dishevelled. A halo of wispy unkempt grey hair framed his craggy face, from which his empty eye sockets stared blankly, his eyes having been burned away by the rite of Soul Binding. He wore a soiled robe of what was, once, lustrous dark green velvet. The telepath bowed as Lucian entered.

'You have need of my services, my master?'

'I do, Master Karisan,' although I wish I didn't, thought Lucian.

'Quite so,' said Karisan. 'Please, be seated.'

It took Lucian a moment to determine exactly where Karisan expected him to sit, before the telepath indicated a soiled cushion in the centre of the rubbish-strewn floor. He sat, disturbing something living as he did so, which scuttled off into a dark corner.

'Rats,' said Karisan. 'They are ever attracted to the lower decks.'

Lucian suppressed the thought that the vermin were also attracted to chambers full of stinking rubbish.

'Master Karisan, I need you to attempt to reach the *Rosetta* or the *Fairlight*. I fear they may be–'

'Adrift?' Karisan cut in.

Irritation flared in Lucian at the man's interruption.

'Or delayed, displaced. You know what might occur within the warp, Master Karisan.'

The other man let out a high-pitched giggle, 'Oh yes my lord, well do I know what awaits within the Sea of Souls. Well do I know.' The telepath reached up and clutched a dried fetish from where it dangled on a leather thong. He sniffed it, and rubbed it along his cheek with a delicacy that Lucian found quite disturbing to witness.

'I am asking you, Master Karisan, to do what you can to contact them. Are you able to do so?'

'Able? Yes my master, I am able.' The telepath cast about him to clear a space on the floor, and then drew his legs up under him into a crossed-legged pose. 'Willing, you might say, yes? The object of our search might yet be beyond our reach, traversing, as you say, the empyrean. Never mind, for even there, they will be known to us.'

Lucian had witnessed several rites of astropathic communication in his time. No two had ever been the same, but he knew better than to interrupt the man, and so settled back to await the result.

Master Karisan began to mutter under his breath, the words just about audible, but entirely unintelligible to Lucian. The man's breathing deepened, and he appeared to enter the opening phase of some form of trance. The muttering became more guttural, and Karisan's head rolled back. At the same moment, the temperature in the chamber dropped sharply, a creeping sensation passing over Lucian's scalp. The shadows in the gloomy chamber drew in, and Lucian felt the unmistakable notion that something hostile lurked within them, looking out, straight at him.

'They cannot hurt you, master,' muttered Karisan, Lucian forcing himself to keep his eyes on the other man, and not to fall to the instinct to look behind himself.

The temperature fell still further, a thin skein of ice creeping across the viewing port, obscuring the view of space beyond. Karisan groaned, opening his mouth a number of times, as if attempting, but unable to speak.

Then he burst out, 'They are there!' The telepath's head rolled back to its normal position, and he looked straight at Lucian through empty eye sockets. 'They are not where you feared my master, or at least, your son is not.'

'Explain.'

'The warp is calm now, but it was wracked as we crossed it. The *Rosetta* is certainly not within the empyrean, of that I am certain, although I cannot speak so surely of the *Fairlight*. I sense that the *Rosetta* is nearer, in real space, in the here and now. I shall seek her out.'

Karisan sank into his trance once more, much quicker this time. He muttered what sounded to Lucian like nothing more than nonsense. The temperature dropped still further, and Lucian caught the fleeting scent of something sharp and acidic.

'Voices!' Karisan called, a childlike, wondrous expression appearing on his wizened old face. 'Many voices... my brothers. The ether is alive with them!'

'Alive with what, Master Karisan? Explain!'

Karisan leant forward and took Lucian's elbows in his gnarled old hands, shaking him. 'Alive with the Song of the Ever-Choir, my master. It's quite beautiful. I have not heard it sung so eloquently in many years, and never at all this far out on the Rim.'

Lucian fought to keep control of his rising temper. Karisan was rapidly becoming a liability; that much was clear. He had been for some time in fact. Lucian took a deep breath nonetheless, determined that he would not lose control, not yet at least, not until he was in a position to negotiate with the guild for a replacement astropath.

'Karisan,' now Lucian leaned forwards, trying as hard as he could to engage the man in meaningful conversation. 'Karisan, listen to me. I need to know what, by Saint Katherine's holy arse, you are going on–'

'Astropathic messages my master! The ether is alive with them. They are so–'

'From whom, Karisan?' asked Lucian, a dreadful idea already forming in his mind. 'From whom?'

'From everyone, my master!' Now Karisan began to laugh, a genuinely gleeful sound, not the manic laughter of a madman that he had voiced earlier. 'I shall add my call to theirs.'

'From everyone?' Lucian was prepared to strike the astropath, despite the severe censure from the guild that such an act would earn him when it was discovered. 'What are they saying Karisan? Tell me this and I shall leave you to add your voice to your fellows.'

Karisan leaned in towards Lucian, normality, even sanity, apparently returning once more. 'The voices belong to my brother and sister astropaths, my master, and the song they sing is of such beauty because they all sing the same message. Every astropath for ten, twenty, thirty light years sings the same message.'

Lucian nodded his encouragement, determined not to interrupt the man now that he was finally making some sense.

'They sing words of freedom!'

Lucian sat back, rocked to his core by the news. They sang of freedom – a relative notion in the Imperium of Man, he knew, and invariably one much closer to heresy, recidivism or revolt. Every world within anything up to thirty light years, that might be dozens, scores even of civilised systems, each with a population of many millions. How? Who could have instigated such a thing? More to the point, he realised, who could have coordinated it? The logistics of the treachery were truly staggering, the possibilities stretching out before Lucian as he struggled to imagine them.

His reverie was broken by a new sound, that of Karisan chanting. It was not the insane muttering that he had voiced as he had entered his trance, but something entirely different. The temperature in the room began to rise once more, the frost filming the viewing port melting in the space of scant seconds, to run in rivulets and to collect at the base. Lucian stood, and picked his way across the junk strewn chamber. He left without pausing to look behind, certain that the astropath would now be useless for some time to come. He had in fact been useless for some time past, but Lucian had had no choice other than to tolerate him and his strange ways.

Ducking through the portal to the corridor beyond, Lucian was surprised to find a junior deck officer standing to attention, and awaiting his emergence with obvious discomfort. Lucian knew immediately that something was wrong.

'What? What is it?' Lucian glanced at the man's epaulettes, 'second lieutenant?'

'Sir... sir, your presence is needed on the bridge immediately.' The young man was quite obviously in some distress and had run from the bridge to Karisan's chamber, his voice competing with the need to draw breath.

'What is it man? Calm down and tell me.'

'The... the augurs, sir, they've detected...'

'Detected what, lieutenant?'

'Detected a... a fleet, sir. A massive fleet, inbound on our position.'

Lucian stood on the deck of his bridge, the holograph rotating before him. The static-laced, green-lit representation of surrounding space was incomplete, flickering in and out of focus, but despite this, he could clearly make out the augur returns of a number of capital-scale vessels as they closed on Arris Epsilon.

'Times three, magnify.' The holo blurred out of focus for a moment, before resolving into a tighter view of the incoming fleet. Lucian studied the vessels, reams of text scrolling next to each, as the *Oceanid*'s cogitator banks struggled to analyse what scant data the augurs could provide.

At least seven vessels, all of unknown pattern. All, Lucian judged, of unknown origin. They were alien, he was certain of that, but where had they come from? He knew of no alien civilisation within one hundred light years capable of putting to space at all, let alone in such obviously spaceworthy vessels. He was a rogue trader, and it was his business to know such things, hence he had ordered his vessel onto silent running, augurs restricted to passive mode only, lest the xenos detect their questing spirits.

'Systems?'

The operations officer at station four turned, replying, 'All steady sir. She's displacing less than ten per cent. Not a bad turn for an old girl.'

Lucian allowed himself a slight grin at the operations chief's obvious affection for the *Oceanid*. He shared his appraisal that the old vessel was maintaining herself well. She had not been required to run on such a low level of operation for years, decades even, Lucian realised, and her continued existence may now rely on her being able to do so.

Turning back to the holograph, Lucian watched as the xenos fleet moved into a high orbit over Arris Epsilon, the augur returns breaking up against the background of the planet. He didn't know for sure whether his son was on the world, or whether Korvane's vessel orbited it, perhaps wallowing in the darkness of the far side, but he offered up a silent prayer to the Emperor that he would be afforded some warning of their coming, that he would have time to go to ground before he was discovered.

Realising there was nothing he could do from his current position, Lucian came to the decision that it would be better for all if the *Oceanid* retired to the Arris system's outer reaches, where he would run less risk of detection, and from where he could await the arrival of his daughter. Only then might they be able to plan their next move.

He turned to sit on his command throne, and a harsh electronic siren wail screamed through the bridge address system, before it cut out jarringly. Lucian turned, instantly, knowing that something was afoot.

'Station four?'

The servitor at the communications station squealed machine nonsense as its implanted appendages worked the dials and levers across its console. Indicators lit, telling Lucian that the servitor had isolated and intercepted a wide band broadcast from nearby. A moment later a voice rang out across the bridge, the signal perfectly clear, the words flawless High Gothic.

'We come as allies to the Domains of Arris, and invoke the friendship of comrades in arms. This world, as per previous concords, is declared a protectorate. Your warriors are granted the honour of service to the Fire Caste. Your messengers and pilots will soar under the wings of the Air Caste. Your scientists will gain learning and purpose under the supervision of the Earth Caste. Your leaders and merchants will learn words of wisdom and mutual profit under the tutelage of the Water Caste; and all will endeavour towards the ultimate Greater Good, under the guidance of the Blessed Ones: under the protection of the tau empire.'

Lucian stood, stunned. Not at the fact that an alien race was seeking to gain influence over a human world, that much he had seen before. No, it was the scale of what he was witnessing. This was mass betrayal.

Karisan had reported that dozens of systems for light years around were declaring their independence from the Imperium of Man. Here, he knew that he saw the instigators of that treachery. Alien fleets, no doubt closing in on dozens of worlds, declaring that the planets were under their control, and, presumably, being welcomed with open arms by the treacherous leaders of those worlds.

He spat on the cold, metal deck. Someone would pay for this, he promised.

CHAPTER ELEVEN

'You see the Mark IIIs of Five Corps?' Imperial Commander Droon asked Korvane, turning from the railing to look back at his guest, lowering the magnoculars as he did so. 'Nine entire brigades, a thousand battle tanks: the pride of the Arris Defence Force!'

Korvane looked through his own magnoculars, following the expansive gesture that Droon made towards the valley floor below. He was stunned by the enormity of the procession unfolding below, although he was humble enough to realise that it was not for his benefit; it was long in the planning, that much was clear, and Korvane waited patiently for its ultimate purpose to be revealed.

Many thousands of troops having paraded by, a column of mighty armoured vehicles cruised past, ten vehicles wide and a hundred deep, command tanks with their characteristic antennae leading each. The vehicles were a spotless, factory-applied 'Codex' grey, each bearing not a vehicle, platoon or company designation, but a multi-digit serial number. Korvane was not a man of a military background, but he knew these vehicles must have been produced with some haste. A thought occurred to him.

'My lord,' he addressed Droon, who was back at the gallery railing enjoying the spectacle unfolding below. 'My lord, my fleet's vessels will be hard pressed to berth the infantry and their equipment. I am unsure how we will accommodate the armoured units.'

'Oh, don't worry about that, Korvane. The fact that your ships will be capable of transporting the troops and light units is service enough. The tank companies will follow the initial drop. With them we shall overrun any of Luneberg's dogs that dare stand against us. I'll grind the bastards beneath our tracks; show them the folly of starting a war with Arris Epsilon.'

Korvane listened as he watched the last of the tank companies grind past, followed by an entire recon regiment of gangling light walkers, each of which swivelled and dipped its cockpit in salute to Lord Droon as they passed. Droon had, on several occasions, hinted at some ongoing and bitter enmity between the worlds of Mundus Chasmata and Arris Epsilon, although Korvane knew better than to press him for details. High court etiquette demanded that such matters were only divulged at the discretion of the host, and it appeared to him that the mores by which Droon lived were similar enough to those he himself observed for that to be the case here.

As the walkers stalked past, their pilots saluting smartly from open cabs, the throaty growl of yet more armoured vehicles filled the air once more, although this sound was noticeably quieter than that of the battle tanks.

'Ah! See here, Gerrit,' Droon nodded his head towards a column of armoured transports snaking its way across the valley floor, 'the First Hussars, in their new vehicles no less.'

Korvane looked as instructed, and saw the vehicles. 'Chimeras?' he asked, easily recognising the ubiquitous personnel carrier, utilised by security forces, Planetary Defence units and the Imperial Guard the galaxy over. In fact, several dozen languished in the *Rosetta*'s hold, adorned in the deep red and burnished gold livery of the Arcadius, but unused for several decades.

'Chimeras, yes, most certainly, but of a pattern I doubt you will have encountered before.' Korvane could not help but note the pride evident in Droon's voice, and considered it politic, even expected, to press him further.

'How so my lord? My knowledge of military vehicles is somewhat lacking.'

Droon chuckled, welcoming the opening to expound on the merits of his forces. 'This pattern is drawn from a rarely used template, one that only we of Arris Epsilon may utilise. I am told that their power cores are entirely unique, in that they are motivated not by fossil fuel, but by some manner of cold atomic reaction.'

Korvane looked straight at the Imperial Commander, whose eyes were fixed firmly on the vehicles below. As a rogue trader, he knew that such a thing was indeed rare, and much sought after across the Imperium. Technology, he knew, was a dark art more akin to archaeology, and it was unusual for a new device to be uncovered and utilised. If Droon's people had access to some unexploited technological resource, then the possibilities for trade and exploitation were potentially staggering.

Droon was addressing Korvane once more, pointing towards the lead vehicle. It appeared to be some command variant, for in place of an enclosed passenger compartment and forward turret, the entire rear of the vehicle was open. A group of men stood within that section, their uniforms marking them out as high-ranking officers, although even these were plain in comparison to those worn by the lowest ranked troopers in Culpepper Luneberg's household guard. However, it was not the officers' uniforms that Droon was indicating, but a banner one of them held.

'The standard of the First Hussars,' Droon announced, his tone indicating that the banner carried particular significance.

Korvane turned a dial on the side of his magnoculars, increasing the magnification, which allowed him to make out the banner. It was a simple standard, far simpler in fact than many that Korvane had seen. Having walked the approach to the Eternity Gate on Sacred Terra, the long avenue lined with countless thousands of banners bearing witness to ten thousand years of total war, Korvane could not help but feel distinctly unimpressed by the decidedly plain standard of the First Hussars.

'You see the honours listed upon the standard?' Droon asked, Korvane squinting to make out the details on the fluttering banner. 'Each is a victory over our pernicious enemies; but the last honour has yet to be won.'

Korvane saw that at the bottom of the banner's face a scroll devoid of text awaited the embroidery that the others shared. Each listed the title and date of some noteworthy battle in the history of the First Hussars, probably, Korvane realised, in the history of Arris Epsilon itself.

'That honour will be won now, Korvane, do you see?'

'Indeed, my lord,' Korvane answered, reading off the list of battles. Each one, he realised, had been fought against the forces of

Mundus Chasmata, and each had been given a grandiose title such as the 'Siege of the Three Dominions' or the 'Relief of the Outer Nine.' Korvane cast his mind back to the introduction given to his family and himself when they first went before Imperial Commander Culpepper Luneberg. The titles given to the ruler of Mundus Chasmata matched those mentioned on the Standard of the First, although each was presented in a decidedly different light.

'You see, Korvane, that the attack we launch is far from some petty border clash.' Korvane said nothing, conscious that Droon was on the verge of communicating something of great import. 'Epsilon and Mundus Chasmata have been locked in ongoing disputes for centuries, millennia perhaps – it is hard to say exactly when things started to get... unpleasant.'

'Your records are incomplete on the subject?' Korvane asked, knowing that many historical archives were missing great swathes of information, so long and fractured was the history of the Imperium.

'Incomplete? Oh no, Korvane, not incomplete.' Droon watched the passing personnel carriers wistfully, the standard of the First receding into the distance. 'Our histories are very specific on the matter of the grievances between our two worlds; each has been recorded in great detail. It is more a case of tracking the escalation, for each time Epsilon's forces have laid a debt of honour to rest, those of Mundus Chasmata have retaliated once more, and so the debt is renewed.'

'I understand,' said Korvane, beginning to appreciate the nature of the conflict between the two worlds and their ruling dynasties. He let Droon continue his explanation.

'You see, Korvane, this region has long been settled by mankind, but has never attained the status of those sectors closer to the centres of power. The Timbra Subsector, and the entire Borealis Ring lie at the furthest extent of Ultima Segmentum. We look to the Segment Fortress at Kar Duniash for aid in times of strife, yet we would do as well to petition Terra herself for help, for both are so distant that we would be long in our graves before any arrived. Thus, we may look only to ourselves, or to third parties, such as you, when times are hard.'

The growling of the engines of armoured vehicles filled the valley floor once more. Korvane knew that the regiment of self-propelled artillery crawling by were called basilisks.

Droon was forced to raise his voice over the roar. 'And that, Korvane, is the reason for all this!' The Imperial Commander spread his arms wide, the gesture encompassing the vast parade and the entire valley floor. 'You see,' Droon shouted, 'Luneberg's forebears owe my own a debt of honour, and the interest has grown quite considerably.'

'What debt my lord?' Korvane asked, his own voice raised.

'The debt of ages, Korvane. You see, many, many generations past, my own ancestors and those of Luneberg entered into a partnership. They formed the core of a trade consortium that they intended would in time grow to encompass all the worlds of the subsector, and eventually, they hoped, bring prosperity to the entire Eastern Rim.'

'A noble ambition,' Korvane replied, seeing the sense in the region's worlds uniting in a common purpose.

'The intentions of my own ancestors were indeed noble, but this was sadly not so in the case of Luneberg's. It appears that, several years after the cartel was established, they decided to renegotiate its terms. You see, Mundus Chasmata and Arris Epsilon had established a profitable partnership, and were on the verge of bringing other worlds in the subsector into talks. However, Luneberg's forebears wished to dominate the emerging bloc, and displayed no qualms in reneging on the terms of the cartel's creation. They wished to cut us out, Korvane, and to establish themselves as the pre-eminent power in the Timbra subsector. You yourself have seen this propensity to dishonour, have you not Korvane?'

Korvane thought back to the talks between his father and the Imperial Governor of Mundus Chasmata, realising that indeed, Luneberg appeared to believe he had some Emperor-granted right to change the terms of the agreement upon a whim. 'Indeed, my lord, I have seen it, and it helps to explain some of what Luneberg was attempting to gain from dealing with the Arcadius.'

'Yes, he was almost certainly attempting to revive the ambitions of his forebears, to establish himself as a new power. However, I have good reason to believe he planned to do so not to build unification of trade interests, but for entirely selfish reasons. I believe Luneberg sees himself as superior to his neighbours, and wishes to establish direct power over the entire region. The man is a traitor and a bastard, the latest in a long, long line of traitorous bastards.'

Korvane nodded, raising his magnoculars once more, and looking down towards the valley floor. He saw that the last of the Arris Epsilon Planetary Defence Force was filing by, ranks upon ranks of troopers, each bearing aloft a pennant sporting the crest of the House of Droon – an eagle's wing upon a golden circle, against a black field. Droon had good cause to launch a pre-emptive strike against his neighbour, for Luneberg was clearly mad, and more than likely to drag the entire region into madness with him.

'And so, Korvane, I have taken steps to curtail his ambitions, here, and now.' Droon looked to the sky as he spoke. 'You see, we do not have our own fleet, such is the hardship imposed upon us by Luneberg's self-interest, but I have initiated a plan in which yours will play a leading role.'

Korvane followed the Imperial Commander's gaze, craning his neck to look up into the sky.

Droon continued, 'Your coming here was unexpected, but fits my plan well.' He turned as he stared up into the sky. 'Your fleet will transport my troops, while theirs...' Droon pointed into the sky, 'will utterly destroy Luneberg's puny system defence force.'

Korvane followed Droon's gesture, blinking against the glare and initially unable to see just what it was he was pointing at.

'After they have bombed his cities from orbit, my armies will land. Thanks to you Korvane, this will not be a mere raid. It will be a full-scale invasion.'

Korvane's vision adjusted to the glare as he squinted into the bright sky. A dark spot appeared, swooping out of the sun's coronal halo. It separated into a number of smaller forms, moving at speed and in perfect formation. They grew in size as they approached, and within less than a minute, Korvane could see that they were vessels.

'My lord?' he said, looking to Droon for some explanation of this new development. The Imperial Commander merely chuckled, not taking his eyes off the incoming ships.

Korvane gathered his thoughts, forcing himself to adopt an outward calm that he did not entirely feel within. As he watched, he saw that there were five vessels inbound on their own position, each somewhat larger than the shuttles the Arcadius made use of for interface operations.

The ships were wide and flat, with the distinct appearance of some bizarre sea creature. A wide, curved delta wing bristled with weapons turrets, a double hammerhead shape forming the prow. Korvane saw instantly that these vessels were of undoubted xenos origin, for no human ship he had ever seen moved so smoothly through the air, or, he realised with a shock, so quietly, for the vessels made barely a sound as they swept in.

'They are quite beautiful, in their way, are they not, Korvane?' Droon asked, still not taking his gaze away from the sight of the alien vessels' approach.

Korvane had seen alien ships before, been onboard them in fact, and spoken with their masters, but nonetheless, he could not identify the origins of these vessels. 'Indeed, my lord. Might I ask–'

'Who they are?' Droon now turned to face Korvane. 'They are my new allies, or more accurately, they are mercenaries, willing to fight for our cause against the likes of Luneberg.'

They were better equipped than any mercenary company Korvane had ever encountered, but at least that put them in Droon's employ, he thought, which might serve to keep them under control. 'And their origin?' he asked.

'The galactic east, so I am told, beyond the Ring,' Droon said, his tone dismissive.

'Across the Gulf?' Korvane asked, unsure from Droon's answer whether the Imperial Commander was being evasive, or was merely ignorant of the issue.

'I could not say with any certainty, Korvane, and I would scarcely expect them to divulge the location of their world. I do not care from where they come, merely that their service will enable me, us, once and for all, to curtail Luneberg's treacherous ambitions. Do you condemn me, Korvane?'

'Of course not, my lord,' Korvane answered. Droon evidently felt some unease with the fact that he was forced to employ hireling xenos to prosecute his war, but Korvane was the scion of a rogue trader dynasty, and above such concerns. 'I merely ask out of curiosity, for I like to know with whom I deal.'

'Commendable, I'm sure,' replied Droon. 'Few men would understand the plight we on the Eastern Rim must face. Few would understand the means we must go to in order to defend ourselves from those who covet what little we have. Ah! Look, they land.'

The five alien vessels had completed their approach run, and now lingered in almost complete silence over the valley floor. Korvane saw that they hovered over the only area of ground not occupied by the precisely arrayed defence force units. As he watched, the air beneath each shimmered, the tell-tale indication, Korvane knew, of powerful gravity drives in action. They would have to be powerful, he thought, to hold aloft the bulk of these craft.

In a single, perfectly synchronous manoeuvre, the five vessels descended the last one hundred metres, landing gear deploying from the belly of each at the last possible moment, and settled on the ground with barely a sound.

A silence settled upon the scene, Korvane sensing Droon's anticipation, and the defence troopers' unease at their proximity to the alien vessels. Turret-mounted weapons atop each of the craft swivelled, sweeping the area around the vessels, but thankfully not lingering on any one target. As seconds stretched into minutes and no other activity was evident, Korvane envisaged the slaughter that would ensue if violence were to erupt between the five vessels and the ranks of troopers, tanks and artillery arrayed on the valley floor. The damage wreaked upon each would be terrible, he saw, although he could not say with any confidence which side would come off the worst.

Finally, a large section of the underbelly of each ship detached, descending slowly on what appeared to be pneumatic arms. The wide, rectangular platforms of all five vessels simultaneously touched the ground. From the gallery, Korvane could barely see whether any passengers rode on the platforms, but a moment later, he saw a number of disc-shaped objects glide out from under each vessel, spreading out and forming a perimeter around each.

The discs were around a metre in diameter, and coloured a pale, off-green, insignia in the form of red stripes adorning their panels. Some form of antenna protruded from the discs' upper face, and a single lens was mounted in an underslung, armoured housing.

The discs hovered several metres above the ground, another indication, Korvane saw, that this race, whoever they were, had attained a level of mastery of the anti-gravitic arts surpassing those of mankind. Although the discs bore no obvious weaponry, their proximity to the troops was causing obvious tension, and Korvane noted how the NCOs issued growling threats to their men to remain steady and to show no sign of disorder or dissension.

The discs having taken station around each vessel, Korvane saw, through the sights of his magnoculars, that the elevator platforms did indeed carry passengers. A procession set out from the nearest vessel. The first figure to come into view as it emerged from beneath the vessels was more or less man sized, thin, and sporting long, flowing robes of a fine, silvery material.

'Ah! He has come, as they said he would,' exclaimed Droon, some relief evident upon his face. Korvane remained silent; he would no doubt discover what concerns Droon had had in due course.

As the tall figure stepped forwards, more emerged behind it. These were of an entirely different build, and it took Korvane a moment to ascertain that in all likelihood they were some form of motivated armour or light vehicles, for they were tall and square, with what could only be weaponry mounted upon each arm. Behind these, more figures emerged. They were more like the first, although shorter and broader of shoulder, each helmeted and bearing a long, slender rifle. Warriors, no doubt, thought Korvane, an honour guard for the first figure.

Korvane looked towards the other alien vessels and saw more warriors, tall, armoured forms as well as those on foot, marching out from beneath each vehicle. Once arrayed, he could see that each vessel had disgorged something in the region of fifty warriors. Except the process was evidently not yet complete, for now a huge ramp lowered from the rear of each vessel, and before it had even touched the ground, a number of armoured vehicles disembarked, each borne aloft upon shimmering anti-grav fields, and each sporting what appeared to be quite fearsome weapons mounted on smoothly rotating turrets.

At the last, the hovering vehicles moved into formation with the ranks of alien infantry. Each of the five formations appeared to Korvane as large as a company of the Arris Epsilon Planetary

Defence Force, though granted far greater firepower thanks to their armoured gunships. The tall alien, his silver robes flowing elegantly in the gentle breeze, stood at the head of the formation. Behind them were the low, wide vessels in which they had arrived, and to either side and behind were arrayed the endless ranks of Droon's own forces. From the gallery upon which he stood, the sight was nothing short of spectacular, thought Korvane. Standing beside him, Droon appeared almost drunk with the vision of power below him, evidently relishing the opportunity afforded to him finally to end the ancestral war with Mundus Chasmata.

Droon turned to Korvane. 'Come, Korvane, and meet the tau.'

Korvane stood in the centre of the apartment given over to his use, donning his formal attire, for he was expected at the Imperial Commander's court in mere minutes. There he would be introduced to the aliens that Droon referred to as mercenaries.

Could they really be mercenaries? Korvane had come into contact with all manner of hired guns and sell-swords in his career, and they had ranged from highly professional outfits to near-brigands, but they had never, in his experience at least, taken a form such as these aliens.

It was not the fact that the mercenaries were aliens that bothered him, for he had spoken the truth when he had told Droon that it did not concern him. It was more that this particular race appeared possessed of a high level of technology, and combined with the fact that Droon appeared ignorant of their origin, Korvane was far from sure that they would be as cooperative or as trustworthy as Droon had stated.

Although nervous, he resolved to hold off judging them, but to remain cautious and on his guard nonetheless. These aliens were, he judged, well organised and possessed of highly advanced technology. They might prove a threat to more than the Timbra Subsector, he thought. They might prove a threat to the Imperium.

As he buttoned the gold brocade across the armoured breast of his formal jacket, Korvane's thoughts turned to what course of action his father might take in such circumstances. No doubt, he would brazen his way through, Korvane thought, keeping his cards characteristically close to his chest throughout, before somehow coming out on top. Having been brought up in the rarefied atmosphere of high court, Korvane found such an approach deeply irksome, despite the fact that it was more often than not successful.

Successful in the short term, Korvane thought, but not in the longer term; the future of the Arcadius Dynasty, now, more than ever, looked grim. Granted, his father commanded a flotilla of cruisers and owned other, sizable interests on a string of worlds between the Eastern Rim and Terra, but for how long? If the dynasty could not be maintained those interests would be sold off one by one, until, at the end, just the three of them remained, commanding a flotilla of crewless vessels, their holds empty and their reactors cold.

This expedition had been intended to secure the dynasty's future, until the point, no doubt still many years off, when Korvane would come into the inheritance guaranteed as part of the terms of marriage between his mother and his father. But his mother, Emperor bless her shrivelled soul, had, thanks to countless rejuve courses, lived two centuries already, and appeared likely to live for another two at least. Korvane had already reached the conclusion that only he could ultimately save the Arcadius, and here and now, he knew that to be truer than ever.

As he fastened his belt, hefting the sanctified falchion gifted him by his great uncle, the Hierarch of Terrabellum Nine, Korvane determined that whatever came of this encounter with the aliens, he would ensure that, by his actions the fortunes of the Arcadius would be revived, for all time.

A knock sounded at the apartment door, and Korvane knew it was time to pay court. This, he thought, smiling to himself, was what he was born and raised to do.

The door to Droon's audience chamber swung open, and Korvane stepped through into the cavernous space carved into the mountainside. The chamber thronged with courtiers and the setting sun, visible through the open cave mouth, cast the scene in a deep, jade light.

'Ah! Korvane, step forward and meet our new associates!'

The head of every courtier in the chamber turned towards

Korvane. Droon addressed him from his throne at the cave mouth, and beside him stood the tall alien who had led the procession from the xenos vessels. The alien took a step forwards, and paused before Korvane.

The figure was slightly taller than an average man, his spindly arms and legs engulfed in the flowing robes of shimmering, silver fabric. His face was visible beneath a wide, flat hat, and that face was without a nose and dominated by black, almond shaped eyes. The skin was a pale, bluish grey, and the mouth wide, flat and expressionless. Korvane noted a vertical slit in the centre of the forehead, only barely discernible beneath the wide hat – an olfactory organ perhaps, or something more exotic, thought Korvane.

The figure stood before Korvane and made a slight bow. Korvane's courtly upbringing told him instantly that here was a being skilled in the political arts. This was no commander of mercenaries, thought Korvane, but some manner of ambassador or diplomat. This might be an alien, but some things varied little between races.

'I present,' Droon announced, 'Korvane Gerrit of the Arcadius, trader and master of the Arcadius fleet.'

Korvane remained silent, aware of his part in the unfolding ceremony. Droon had introduced Korvane to the alien, in all likelihood indicating that the Imperial Commander at least considered the alien of higher rank than Korvane. He would let that slide, for now at least.

Then, his voice booming with evident pride, Droon introduced the alien, 'Por'o'Sar, envoy of the tau.'

Korvane dipped his head in greeting, waiting to see whether the alien would address him directly, or whether Droon would speak on his behalf.

'Master Gerrit,' the alien said in flawless, smooth High Gothic, surprising Korvane with the clarity of his speech. 'I am honoured to meet you. Lord Droon tells me you are a trader of some means. I hope we can make our relationship profitable to all.'

With practiced ease, Korvane covered his surprise that the alien spoke the High Gothic tongue so perfectly, replying, 'That is so, and I share your hope.'

'Good!' Droon clapped his hands once and stood from his throne, descending the steps to stand beside Korvane and the alien. 'I believe then, we can all go into this venture boldly, with common purpose.'

'Indeed,' replied the alien. 'The forces of the tau stand beside you, ready to aid you in casting off the shackles of oppression. You agree to the price for our aid?'

Korvane felt a sudden dread at the alien's tone, and looked to Droon as the Imperial Commander gave his answer. 'I agree to your price, Por'o'Sar.'

Korvane felt the urge to interrupt, to demand to know what Droon had agreed to pay in return for the services of these aliens. His courtly training asserted itself however, and he maintained his outward calm, despite the rising doubts he felt within.

'Good,' the alien said. 'Then I, Por'o'Sar, Envoy of the Council of the Highest, Nexus of the Third Sun, Voice of Kari'La, pledge to you, Droon, of Arris Epsilon, called Epsil'ye'Kal, the friendship and alliance of the tau, in this time of adversity.' The alien produced from his voluminous robes a pendant, a round icon of a substance unfamiliar to Korvane. Droon lowered his head as the envoy lifted the pendant over it.

'And by your words and your deeds, do you pledge your world and your people, for now and for all time, to the service of the tau empire?'

The court filled with a deafening silence. Korvane fought to remain outwardly unmoved, despite the fact that grand treason was unfolding before him, the likes of which he had never before witnessed. He realised that he too was right at the heart of it, his immediate future, as well as that of the Arcadius, entirely reliant on what occurred here, today.

'I do so pledge,' replied Droon, the alien lowering the pendant over his head. The former Imperial Commander raised his head once more and looked around him, the expression in his eyes suggesting that he was viewing his court and his subjects with entirely new eyes.

He looked directly at Korvane. 'Today, history is written. No longer will Arris Epsilon – Epsil'ye'Kal,' the alien nodded slowly, 'live as some long-forgotten orphan, at the mercy of a hostile universe and an uncaring Imperium. No. This day, we take our place alongside our friends the tau, with whose aid we shall settle our debt of honour with Mundus Chasmata, for all time.'

Mercenaries indeed, thought Korvane, the price for whose service was the casting off of ten thousand-year old vows. Droon had bought the service of the tau at a terrible, unthinkable price: secession from the Imperium of Man. The Imperium would hear of this, Korvane knew, no matter that it might take years for retribution to come. Come it would, of that he was sure, for the wages of such treachery could only ever be death.

However, that might not occur for some time, Korvane realised, so what of the here and the now? His agreement with Droon still stood, despite the fact that Droon himself had changed loyalties. Can I really aid this man and his xenos allies... masters... in his attack on Mundus Chasmata? he wondered. Can I afford not to?

The brief ceremony complete, Droon and the alien envoy now turned towards him as one, the Imperial Commander addressing him. 'Korvane, you will join us, and pledge the service of the Arcadius to the,' he looked to the alien, and then back at Korvane, 'to the greater good?'

Damn them, thought Korvane. They don't just want my help in the attack on Chasmata. They want me to revoke my loyalty to the Imperium.

CHAPTER TWELVE

'All stop!' Lucian ordered, his bridge a hive of activity as servitors responded to orders and human bridge crew relayed them to the other decks.

'All stop, aye,' called back Helmsman Raldi, 'holding station at one, one ten.'

'Well enough, helm,' responded Lucian, leaning forwards in his command throne. 'I want total surprise, or so help me I'll void every last one of you out of the sub-space crapper. Clear?'

Those of the deck crew capable of comprehending Lucian's threat nodded, Lucian heartened to see the terror writ across their faces. Good, he thought. I mean it, too.

Lucian studied the holograph, a green glow against the red of general quarters. The *Oceanid* had shadowed the alien vessels as they closed on Arris Epsilon, Lucian ordering the distance kept to a maximum lest their prey detect their presence. He now watched as they disgorged a number of landers to the surface. He had been faced with a stark choice, although there was only a single possible course of action. While Brielle was evidently yet to arrive in system, Korvane was down there now, he knew, stuck in the middle of an alien invasion. Well, he wasn't prepared to let these alien swine take an Imperial world from under his nose, not while one of his own was down there at least.

'One hundred kilometres,' called the helmsman.

Lucian leaned forwards still more, intent upon the formation of the alien vessels. He looked for any sign that they might have detected the *Oceanid*'s presence, any sign at all that he might have revealed his hand too soon.

Still, the alien vessels wallowed in orbit, more interested, Lucian guessed, in what was going on down below than what was coming at them from behind. He'd never fall for such a trick, Lucian thought, not since that privateer attack at Krysla VII, at least.

'Comms, is everything set?' Lucian addressed the servitor at station three, receiving a garbled burst of machine noise, accompanied by a stiff nod. 'Good, stand by.'

'Seventy-five,' called the helmsman, a note of tension creeping into his voice.

'Hold steady.' Lucian replied, referring as much to the vessel's course as the helmsman's nerves.

The range counter on the holograph counted down, and there was still no response from the alien fleet.

'Fifty kilometres.'

'Good.' Lucian stood, adjusting the holster at his belt. 'Full power to secondary arrays.'

The red lighting dimmed for a moment as the secondary communications array bled off the power it needed to go from cold to fully ready in mere seconds. Lucian kept his eyes on the holograph, knowing that the aliens would pick up the power surge at any moment.

'Station three, open a–' the green holographic icons representing the alien vessels suddenly shifted, breaking formation as Lucian had known they would.

'Twenty-five,' called the helmsman.

'Station three, open it now!'

The bridge filled with howling static as the servitor at the communications station opened a broadcast on all channels on which the secondary array was capable of transmitting. This had better work, thought Lucian.

'Alien fleet,' he said, knowing that his words would be flooding the ether across every conceivable frequency. 'Alien fleet, this is the *Oceanid*, flagship of the Arcadius Grand Fleet. Please respond immediately.'

The bridge address system howled with feedback as the communications servitor adjusted the gain, sweeping the channels for any sign of a response. Lucian had hoped to get as close as possible to Arris Epsilon before announcing his presence, looking to gain any advantage possible over the aliens. He strained to filter out the random noise flooding the bridge, looking for any sign of an intelligible response. Of course, even if the aliens could, and did respond, there was no guarantee they would be able to communicate with one another. No matter, he thought, for that was why he had been so careful to gain the upper hand. If they could not or would not talk, he would settle things the old-fashioned way.

A high-pitched wail burst forth, modulated by an arrhythmic pulse. The communications servitor opened its mouth and gave out a squeal, turning its head and looking straight at Lucian, almost accusingly, as it did so. The pulse continued for ten seconds or so, before the channel went completely silent, and a clear voice cut through.

'*Oceanid*,' the voice said in perfectly enunciated High Gothic. 'This is the Water Caste starship *Vior'la'Gal'Leath'Shas'el*. Please state your intentions.'

Lucian stepped from his command throne, towards the forward viewing port. The distance between the *Oceanid* and the alien vessels was too great to afford visual recognition, but Lucian looked towards the area of space where he knew the aliens' position lay as he replied.

'Alien vessel, my intentions depend entirely upon your own. Please stand down and allow me to approach.'

As he awaited an answer, Lucian looked sidelong at Raldi. The helmsman mouthed 'twenty-five' back at him.

At their current speed, Lucian would expect the alien vessels to be visible in the next few minutes. Then, and only then, he would be able to gauge the relative odds.

'*Oceanid*, it is not in our nature to seek meaningless confrontation. You may approach, but be warned, our vessels are heavily armed, and will fire if threatened.'

Lucian chuckled to himself before replying, 'Understood. Stand by.'

Indicating to the communications station with a finger drawn across his throat that the channel should be closed, Lucian turned back to the holograph. As the range shortened, the seven vessels took on more detail, the *Oceanid*'s cogitation banks providing details of size, mass and approximate power levels. The minutes passed, Lucian absorbing the data presented in the readouts. He looked to make an estimate of the alien vessels' capabilities relative to the *Oceanid*'s, but the cogitators simply could not discern enough data, never having encountered this race, or their vessels, before.

'Coming up on ten kilometres, sir,' called Helmsman Raldi, Lucian looking to the viewing port once more.

The yellow-green globe of Arris Epsilon dominated the view, but Lucian could just make out the glittering constellation of lights that he knew to be the alien fleet. The seven vessels had dispersed their formation, entering a pattern from which they could afford one another mutual support were things to get ugly. It was no surprise to Lucian when he saw that the vessel that had answered his transmission, the '*Vior'la* something-or-other', had taken position at the centre of the formation.

I would have done the same thing in their place, thought Lucian, his suspicions that he was not facing idiots confirmed.

Drawing closer to the alien fleet, the *Oceanid* passed the first of the alien vessels. He studied it as it slid silently by to starboard, its long, blocky form filling the smaller portholes as it passed. It was large, Lucian saw, of greater length than his own vessel, that much was immediately evident. It took the form of a long, central spine with a large drive section at the rear. Part way along the spine were mounted large, square structures, looking to Lucian like some form of modular cargo space, and at the fore a large prow featured what appeared to be a command tower bristling with antennae. Of most interest to Lucian were the long, rectangular barrelled weapons protruding from mountings just below the curved prow. These he had seen before.

Although few, Lucian judged these weapons capable of inflicting severe damage upon his vessel. In his judgement, the *Oceanid* could certainly take on several of these alien ships at once, and provided she got a good broadside on them could, in all likelihood, put them out of the fight. What Lucian took for cargo bays appeared to have been fitted at the expense of heavier or more numerous weapons batteries, and he guessed that other, up-gunned configurations existed.

Although larger than a manmade cruiser, Lucian judged these vessels of equivalent capability. Well, he thought, he'd taken on plenty of cruiser-sized enemies, and left blazing hulks dead in space behind him. If it came to it now, he'd do so again.

'Ordnance,' Lucian called to the servitor at station two. 'I want all batteries made ready, but keep the ports closed until I give the order.' The servitor gave a mechanical buzz in acknowledgement, its multiple, implanted appendages moving across the fire control console as it relayed Lucian's orders to the waiting weapons crews.

Another of the alien vessels was now by on the port side and Lucian noted that this one was configured in the same manner as the first. Emperor willing, he thought, all seven vessels would be of a similar, or even identical class.

'Closing on target,' called the helmsman, Lucian seeing that the vessel with which he had communicated now loomed in the centre of the viewing port. He grinned, admitting to himself that he lived for moments such as these, despite the seriousness of the situation.

'Well enough, helm. Bring her alongside and reduce to station keeping.' The alien flagship, for that was what Lucian took it to be, was prow on to the *Oceanid*, its fore-mounted weapons batteries facing towards Lucian's vessel, but evidently not, yet, tracking her. The *Oceanid*'s drives growled as the helmsman reduced the ship's velocity, a rattling vibration running through the deck as the alien vessel loomed to starboard.

'Number three again?' said Lucian in response to the juddering, grating sound. The helmsman nodded, though he did not turn to make eye contact with his master. 'Keep an eye on her Mister Raldi. If she misbehaves now we'll all be walking home.'

'Aye sir,' replied the helmsman, his right hand pulling back on a lever, coaxing power from the misbehaving drive, while the other kept the helm steady.

'Any second... there we are Mister Raldi, station keeping if you will.'

The *Oceanid* slowed to a near dead stop as she came alongside the alien vessel, the starboard portholes entirely filled with its slab-sided bulk. Lucian clasped his hands behind his back as he cleared his throat and then nodded to the communications servitor.

'Alien vessel, this is *Oceanid*. Please acknowledge this signal.'

'*Oceanid, Vior'la'Gal'Leath'Shas'el* acknowledges. Please state your business.'

'My business,' Lucian smirked ever so slightly as he spoke, 'is to receive your immediate and unconditional surrender, in the name of the Arcadius Grand Fleet and the Emperor of Man.' He turned and nodded to the servitor at the ordnance station, who activated the controls that would raise the weapons ports on the *Oceanid*'s flanks. He shoved to the back of his mind any doubts that the aliens would not fall for his bluff, counting on them not being able to take the risk that, as he had implied, his was the lead vessel of an incoming, and yet to be detected, fleet.

'*Oceanid*, please confirm your last transmission,' the reply came from the alien vessel. 'Did you state that you expected to receive our surrender?'

Lucian's smirk now turned into a dirty grin. He really did enjoy his work too much sometimes, he thought. 'That is correct,' he replied. 'I expect you to heave to, power down and prepare for boarding.' Lucian glanced across at the holograph, seeing that the outermost of the alien vessels were coming around, as he had expected they would.

'Do you surrender?' he asked.

A momentary delay, and then the terse reply, 'No, *Oceanid*, we do not surrender.'

'I had a feeling,' replied Lucian, crossing to his command throne and sitting, 'that you would say that.'

'Fire!'

The *Oceanid*'s starboard weapons banks opened fire as one, their mighty roar filling the ship, their report vibrating through the decks.

'Hard to starboard, Mister Raldi, cross the T,' ordered Lucian without even looking to see what, if any damage the broadside had inflicted upon the alien vessel.

'Aye sir,' called back the helmsman, hauling on the wheel as he brought the *Oceanid* around.

'Damage?' called Lucian.

'Significant, sir,' the officer at the operations station called back in reply. Lucian glanced at the banks of screens all around his command throne, seeing that, indeed, the sucker punch of a broadside had inflicted fearsome damage upon the alien. The other vessel was listing to its port, thick, oily smoke billowing from its mid-section, flickering plasma fire lighting the clouds from within.

'Ordnance, prepare a second volley.'

Lucian watched as the view from the forward viewing port showed the alien ship's drives to starboard. Wait, he steadied himself, sensing a kill if he timed the volley exactly right.

'Lined up sir!' Raldi called, struggling with the mighty wheel of the helm.

'Thank you, Mister Raldi,' replied Lucian, waiting one, two, three seconds more before ordering. 'Starboard batteries, fire!'

The *Oceanid* was once more filled with the mighty roar of the cannons' discharge. This time, Lucian watched the other ship as the broadside slammed into its rear section. A handful of the projectiles exploded prematurely as they were swallowed in the superheated wake of the vessel's vast engines, but the majority struck the superstructure, smashing through the metres-thick armoured engine casings and exploding deep within.

For a moment, the two vessels continued to glide past one another, the *Oceanid* having crossed the T and carried on past. Then, as Lucian watched, the alien ship's drive section was rent asunder as a mighty split appeared along its length, blinding white, atomic fire lancing out of the crack. A second later the entire drive section came away from the spine connecting it to the bulk of the vessel, jettisoned, Lucian judged, by the ship's captain in a last ditch effort to save his crew.

The effort was wasted, though, for the damage to the drive section was such that it entered a critical chain reaction before it could entirely separate, disappearing as it was swallowed in a rapidly expanding ball of the purest, most blinding white light. Lucian turned his head away as the viewing port dimmed to compensate for the blast, bracing himself against the blast's wave front that buffeted his vessel less than a second later. He was shocked, for a moment, at the violence of the alien vessel's death.

He glanced at the holograph, which was still recovering from the interference created by the vessel's demise. The outer ships were completing their manoeuvre, and he quickly chose his next victim, reading off its coordinates to the helmsman.

'What next, sir?' called Raldi. 'They're closing on us!'

'Now,' Lucian called back, 'we make for the *Rosetta* and pray that Korvane has the good sense to take advantage of the little distraction we've just created, and gets back to his ship.'

'And then, sir?'

'Then it's just a small matter of fighting our way clear.'

'Of all six alien ships, sir?'

'Stop asking awkward questions and do your job, Mister Raldi. All power, on previous heading, if you please.'

Lucian leant back in his command throne, inwardly still quite shocked at the manner of the death of the alien ship. Despite the power of its primary weapons batteries, its class was evidently incapable of withstanding a couple of good broadsides. He knew, however, that the scales would soon be evened, as the other alien ships were inbound and scarcely likely to allow him to get as close to them as he had to their flagship.

'Four minutes, sir,' said the helmsman, Lucian seeing from the holograph that the alien vessel onto which he had locked was coming around, attempting to bring its forward weapons batteries to bear on his ship.

'This is going to sting,' Lucian said, addressing no one in particular. 'Shields to full, helm, bring us in on our port. Port weapons, stand by.'

The *Oceanid* lined up its prey, the gulf between the two vessels closing rapidly. At ten kilometres, the alien ship opened fire, its forward weapons flashing as they threw hyper-velocity projectiles across the void.

The first volley went wide, thanks to the fact that the *Oceanid* was prow on to the other ship, but mere seconds later it unleashed a second, this one far more accurate, and deadly.

Lucian felt the *Oceanid* stagger beneath him as the enemy weapons hit home, blasting great chunks out of her armoured prow. The bridge was plunged into almost total darkness, lit only by the strobe of a third volley fired by the closing ship.

This volley struck the port superstructure a glancing blow, an entire fin tearing itself free of the hull and spinning crazily into space. A series of secondary explosions sounded through the deck, and Lucian judged that these were the forward conversion plants. We can survive without them, he told himself, if we can survive this.

'Helm! Full retros, ten second burn. Cut mains to fifty per cent,' Lucian ordered, as the distance between the two vessels passed the one kilometre mark. He knew he would get only one salvo in against this enemy, and even that might be bought at too high a price. He would not sit idly by and abandon his son to an alien invasion of Arris Epsilon, however; he would do all he could to afford Korvane the opportunity to escape.

The *Oceanid* shuddered once more, the retro thrusters struggling to arrest her forward momentum. As the bridge lights sputtered back to life, Lucian saw from the read-outs that the alien vessel's second volley had damaged one of the thrusters, and felt his ship veering to port under the uneven thrust.

'Compensate; plus fifty to the starboard primary, plus twenty to the secondary,' he ordered the helm, feeling the *Oceanid* coming back on course.

No sooner was his ship brought back under control than the two vessels were right on top of each other, and as the alien cruiser passed to starboard, Lucian roared, 'Open fire! All port batteries!'

The range was not so great, and the angle, nowhere near as good as the broadside on the first alien nonetheless, the volley was a good one. The mighty cannon spat death across the void, macro-shells crossing the gulf between the two vessels in seconds. The alien vessel had been preparing a fourth shot when the *Oceanid*'s broadside hit, its forward batteries caught in the process of turning to track and acquire their target.

Half of the broadside merely glanced, or missed the target entirely, but the other half struck home. The alien vessel's shields were smashed asunder, barely registering on Lucian's read-outs. The macro-shells impacted at an apparently weak point between two of the modules slung under the ship's spine, dislodging a protruding section of superstructure, which crashed into the forward of the modules. As Lucian watched, the module exploded violently, secondary explosions blossoming forwards to engulf the lower portion of the vessel's prow. At the last, the three remaining modules ejected, spinning off into space as the crippled vessel disengaged, evidently seeking to put as much space between itself and the *Oceanid* as possible, in as short a time as it could.

Lucian laughed out loud for the joy of it all, scarcely able to believe that he had seen off a second alien vessel in one day.

'Who was it once said you never feel more alive than when someone's just shot at you and missed?' he asked no one in particular, revelling in the familiar feeling of victory. He looked to the holograph for the next target.

'Sir,' called the helmsman. 'Shall I adjust?'

'What?' Lucian asked, looking to the holograph in search of whatever Raldi was talking about. 'I see nothing. What is it?'

'Forty-five high to port, sir, inbound.'

Lucian saw that the area of space to which Raldi referred was invisible to the augurs and black on the holograph, and would remain so until the augur arrays were repaired, following the damage done to them in the flight from Mundus Chasmata. He surged to his feet and crossed to the viewing port, immediately seeing what his helmsman was talking about.

'Damn,' he said.

A fleet of capital ships, all Imperial in design, was closing in on the *Oceanid*'s position. Lucian immediately saw from their heading that they were far from friendly. In fact, he knew immediately who they belonged to.

'Gerrit!' The communications array burst into angry, hissing life. 'Gerrit, this is Imperial Commander Culpepper Luneberg. I order you to kill your engines and surrender now. Do so and I shall show you mercy.'

'Keep your mercy,' growled Lucian, turning to the servitor at station three. 'Comms, open a channel to Korvane, wherever he is, right now.'

He sat once more, his mind racing with the possibilities. He had faced tough odds when it was just the alien vessels he had to fight through, to link up with the *Rosetta*, but now he faced Luneberg's fleet too, things looked decidedly grim. Yet still, he would not abandon his son.

'Helm, best speed for the *Rosetta*, by the fastest route, if you will.' Lucian ordered.

'Through the–?' Helmsman Raldi started to reply.

'Centre of Luneberg's fleet, yes, if that is the fastest route.' Lucian interjected. 'Shields to full, main drives to full; all secondary systems to stand by.'

Once again, servitors worked their consoles while the few men in the deck crew hurried to ensure that Lucian's orders were enacted. In times such as these, it was evident that the servitors were more efficient in the prosecution of their tasks, yet he still mourned for an age when the *Oceanid* was crewed by men and women of courage and soul.

Lucian watched the read-outs and dials as they reported the *Oceanid*'s main drives building to full power. The shields too were drawing as much power as their mighty generatoria could provide, the myriad of non-critical systems across the vessel powering down for the duration. Lucian hoped they would have the opportunity to power up again.

He studied the nature and deployment of Luneberg's vessels. Although still some distance away, he judged that they were not large ships, most about the size of an escort. Two, however, were of greater mass, Lucian estimating them equivalent to light cruiser scale. Ordinarily, the *Oceanid*, being equivalent to a heavy cruiser would have little trouble seeing them off, but in her current condition, and with the aliens in the fight too, he was not quite so confident. Nevertheless, he had set himself on this course of action, and he would see it through.

Studying the positions of Luneberg's ships, Lucian saw that they must be under the Imperial Commander's personal command, for they were deployed in such a way as to follow behind the lead cruiser, providing a dense escort, yet ill-prepared to provide one another with any effective fire support. He grinned, seeing in Luneberg's deployment a means of gaining some, much needed, advantage.

'Helm, set your intersect at plus nine, seventeen to port.'

Helmsman Raldi hesitated as he calculated the course, and then replied, 'Right through the middle of them, sir?'

Lucian saw the hint of a grin touch Raldi's lips as he turned to confirm the order, replying, 'Aye helm, right through the middle. We'll scatter them to the solar winds.'

Lucian leant back in his command throne, gripping the arms as he felt the *Oceanid*'s drives reach the peak of their potential output. A glance at the data-screens around the throne and suspended from the ceiling above him told Lucian that his ship would pass through Luneberg's fleet at exactly the point he intended. Furthermore, the manoeuvre would carry them through to link up with the *Rosetta*, all going well.

Lucian counted down the distance between the *Oceanid* and Luneberg's fleet, his gaze fixed on the point in space less than half a kilometre to port of the vessel that he judged to be Luneberg's flagship. 'Trim point two five to port, Mister Raldi,' he ordered, reducing the distance at which the two ships would pass to an absurd two hundred and fifty metres. Closer even than old Jeliko strafing the traitor grand cruiser at the Battle of Van Goethe's Rapidity, he guessed, although his ancestor did end his career by ramming an ork ship, so maybe he wouldn't beat his record quite yet.

After a minute, he noted how the vessels of Luneberg's fleet reacted to his bearing straight at them. At first, the smaller escorts began to move away, but then returned to their previous headings. If only we could listen in on Luneberg's command channel, Lucian thought. No doubt, the Imperial Commander was turning the ether blue with his orders to his escorts to protect his flagship from the *Oceanid*'s mad course.

The range reduced still further, and in no time at all the *Oceanid* was bearing in on Luneberg's fleet. The enemy vessels fully within visual range, Lucian saw that the smaller vessels were, as he had estimated, escorts. They were of a class he had only rarely seen, being more common amongst system and subsector reserve fleets of the southern reaches. They were old by any accounting, and ill-suited to even the smallest of fleet actions. They were better suited to convoy duties, where they would act as a reasonable deterrent to opportunistic raiders, who would be unlikely to risk even a single salvo from their prow torpedoes.

Speaking of torpedoes, Lucian knew that only the *Rosetta* carried such a weapon, the arsenals of the other two rogue trader vessels having years ago exhausted the last of their stocks and their replacement unlikely in the current situation. A single torpedo might cost as much as a light cruiser, and so Lucian had placed his son under the strictest instructions only to fire their last one under his direct orders. It had become something of an irony that the most valuable heirloom his son possessed was a weapon he dared not use.

Another minute passed, and Lucian saw that the escorts were turning from the *Oceanid*'s path once again, their captains evidently developing some sense of self-preservation, or perhaps serious but temporary communications problems. As he had hoped it would, the Chasmatan fleet scattered, almost in slow motion, before him, each escort choosing its own heading. Lucian leant forwards in his command throne as he studied the enemy movements, judging each captain's skill from the manner in which he handled his ship. Two of the escorts came perilously close to one another as they veered desperately to starboard, causing Lucian to bark out a harsh laugh as he judged the enemy captains' skill only slightly higher than those of a drunken ork.

At the last, the *Oceanid* closed in on the lead cruiser, gliding past it so close that the discharge of its manoeuvring thrusters sprayed across her bow as the other vessel sought to steer out of her path. The sight of Luneberg's flagship filled the portside viewers. She was so close that Lucian could read the vessel's name painted in fifty foot tall letters along her prow. The *Borealis Defensor*, Lucian read, judging the title typical of the ego of its master.

As the *Oceanid* completed her manoeuvre, Luneberg's fleet was scattered, its constituent vessels spread over an area of space up to twenty kilometres across, and each on an entirely different heading. It would take even a skilled admiral some time to consolidate his force, thought Lucian, and he was damn sure that Luneberg was anything other than that.

He watched on the flickering holograph as the Chasmatan fleet attempted, in vain, to knot itself into something resembling order. If only he had been travelling at a speed at which he could have unleashed a broadside. As much as he would have savoured the opportunity to damage Luneberg's flagship, that had not been the objective of his manoeuvre. Instead, he had hoped only to buy time for his son.

The enemy fleet did not redeploy in the manner he had expected it to. He had been certain it would be forced to spend some considerable time bringing its vessels around and regaining its previous formation, before powering after him towards the *Rosetta*; but that was not what they appeared to be doing.

Lucian watched intently as the escorts closed in once more on the two cruisers. Although ragged and ungraceful, the fleet soon regained some semblance of order, continuing on its previous course.

Lucian reached forwards and turned a dial on the plinth of the holograph, the static-filled, grainy projection above it blurring, before regaining focus, having zoomed out several dozen kilometres.

Lucian saw immediately the course on which the Chasmatan fleet was engaged. Luneberg was taking his ships against the alien vessels, which had formed up on one another and were likewise homing in on the other ships.

He could scarcely believe his luck. His enemies were going to pummel each other to the warp while he made good his escape!

The two fleets closed on one another with stately elegance, and Lucian felt tempted to pour himself a drink as Luneberg's force manoeuvred for what the Imperial Commander obviously intended to be a fearsome exchange of fire. Would the aliens really allow themselves to be drawn into such a position for a third time? Amazingly, it appeared to Lucian that the xenos vessels were indeed heading for another pasting, although he noted that this time they clustered together for mutual defence. He ran the coming action through his mind, estimating that the two cruisers of Luneberg's fleet would have the better of a broadside, if they could pull one off, although they would pay a high price as the aliens converged their fire in retaliation.

That, however, would have to wait, Lucian realised, as the servitor at the communications station had evidently been successful in opening a channel to Korvane.

'...ahead *Oceanid*,' Korvane's voice sounded amidst a riot of static laden interference. 'This is Korvane.'

'Korvane?' replied Lucian, filled with a sudden relief at the sound of his son's voice. 'Korvane, what's your situation?'

'Father,' Korvane's voice came back, made distorted and tinny by interference on the channel. 'I am inbound to the *Rosetta*, e.t.a. ten minutes.'

'Good to hear Korvane,' replied Lucian, realising that his delaying attack against the aliens had indeed bought his son the time to make a dash for the *Rosetta* aboard his shuttle. 'I take it you evaded the invasion forces?'

'Invasion forces?' Korvane's reply came back. 'Father, I don't think you–'

'That'll have to wait, Korvane,' cut in Lucian. 'For now we need to concentrate on not getting involved, in finding Brielle and getting clear of this–'

'No, Father,' cut in Korvane, Lucian realising instantly that something must be severely amiss for his son to speak in such a manner. 'We are involved.'

Despite the howling feedback and static flooding the communications channel, Lucian picked up on his son's tone instantly, and he didn't like it one bit. 'Explain,' he said.

There was a moment's delay as only angry static answered Lucian, and then Korvane's voice came back. 'We are involved. The *Rosetta* arrived unexpectedly early at Arris Epsilon, Father, and in your absence I made contact with Imperial Commander Zachary Droon.'

'And?'

'And, I told him of Luneberg's treacherous actions at the talks, and Droon told me of the ongoing conflict between the two worlds.'

'It's just a bush war, Korvane, nothing we need get involved with.'

'Yes, Father, but he asked me for help, and he offered to pay quite a considerable–'

'You've signed us over to some border princeling?' Lucian felt his gorge rise, and fought to keep his temper in check despite the fact that he was quite sure he knew what his son's answer would be.

'I have pledged Droon our aid in ending the war against Luneberg.'

Lucian stood, anger flaring within him. 'You may not have noticed, Korvane, but it appears that Luneberg has the same idea.' Why the hell couldn't Korvane have kept out of it? he thought, trying, despite himself, not to condemn his son for his actions.

'Aye, Father, so I see, but I have negotiated a highly favourable deal, one that will recoup the losses incurred thus far. With the aid of the tau we will–'

'The aliens, I take it?' Lucian interrupted his son.

'Yes, the aliens. I had no choice, but the deal may recoup our losses.'

Lucian knew Korvane referred to the collapsed deal with Luneberg, as if that was the fault of anyone other than the mad Imperial Commander. He sighed, knowing that his son was, if nothing else, an expert in such matters, and would have the deal sewn up so tight that he would have little choice other than to honour it. Well, he thought, looking to the holograph where he saw the two fleets about to clash, looks like we're sticking around for the fight.

'Right then,' announced Lucian, decided upon his course. 'Listen, Korvane, I am the Arcadius; not you, not Brielle, and not some squabbling petty noble. I say how our fortunes are made or lost. I say how we live or how we die. Do I make myself clear?'

Lucian listened for Korvane's response, which came after a short delay. 'Father, I understand, but I had no–'

'You will do as I say or I will denounce your claim!' Lucian bellowed, determined now more than ever to rein in his son's good intentions. Good intentions never got anyone anywhere, not in the galaxy in which he lived.

'Now listen,' Lucian said, feeling a measure of calm returning now that he had put Korvane in his place. 'This is how we're going to get the hell out of this mess you've negotiated us all into.'

The *Fairlight* burst out of the Immaterium, Brielle immediately scanning the surrounding space for signs of her father or her stepbrother. She found them straight away, as she had expected to do, but she was somewhat shocked to see two entire fleets of vessels, apparently closing in on one another, as well.

'What the hell has he got us into now?' she asked herself, deciding immediately that something must have gone terribly wrong. She activated the data-slates surrounding her command throne, a dozen and more screens lowering from the shadows above. The screens sputtered to life, the *Fairlight*'s cogitator banks pumping reams upon reams of data across them. With practiced ease, she separated out the superfluous information, homing in on that which she needed.

The *Oceanid* and the *Rosetta*, her father's vessel closing fast on her stepbrother's, which appeared at anchor. One hundred and ten kilometres from their position, two fleets. One human, Luneberg's, she knew, and one not. She smiled.

Reaching up to adjust the data-slates' settings, Brielle homed in on the other two rogue trader vessels, picking up a signal from–

'Brielle?' The communication grilles set in the back of her command throne burst into life, causing her to jump in shock. She spat a spacer's curse, before answering sweetly.

'Father, this is Brielle, what's happening? Are you alright?'

'Yes, Brielle, now listen, as I won't repeat myself.' He wasted no time in pleasantries, she thought, typical of him to get straight to the point. '*Rosetta* and *Fairlight* are to converge on my position and follow my orders to the letter. You will not deviate from the course I give you, and you will not fire upon any targets until I order you to do so. Do I make myself completely clear?'

For a moment, Brielle was speechless. What the hell was his problem? 'Father,' she replied. 'I am perfectly–'

'Do I make myself completely clear?' her father repeated, his tone angry and brooking no argument.

'Completely,' she said, slamming her fist down on the console and closing the channel. How the hell could he speak to her like that? Who the hell did he think she was? Had Korvane poisoned him against her to such an extent that this was how it would be from here on out?

Well, she thought, her stepbrother had had his day. She'd already seen to that.

CHAPTER THIRTEEN

Lucian stood in the centre of his bridge, studying the flickering image projected into the air by the holograph. The green globe was incomplete, almost half of the space invisible to him thanks to a damaged near-space augur array. Three groups of icons dominated the remainder, the one representing the *Oceanid* sitting dead centre, the movements of the others relayed relative to her position.

Some one hundred kilometres to the *Oceanid*'s fore, two of the groups of icons danced, reams of data scrolling next to each. The larger of the groups represented the alien vessels, and there were five of these. Lucian noted, with a professional's appreciation, the formation that the alien ships had assumed, their weapons' fields of fire overlapping in such a manner as to make approach from any angle other than directly to stern all but suicidal.

In contrast to the aliens' deployment, the other group displayed only disarray. Lucian sneered as he regarded its arrangement, one cruiser and a dozen or so smaller escorts clustered around the vessel that he knew to be Imperial Commander Culpepper Luneberg's flagship. It was typical of the man's flawed character that he should deny his captains the benefit of a mutually supportive fire plan, instead concentrating solely on his own protection. He sought to destroy his enemy, the forces of the Imperial Commander Zachary Droon, but was evidently determined to minimise any risk to his own, personal safety. Well, thought Lucian, space battles were no respecters of safety, personal or otherwise.

The alien fleet and that of Imperial Commander Luneberg were currently engaged in the opening moves of what Lucian was quite sure would prove to be the last battle for one of them. Luneberg's forces had sought to engage their foe, but had been evaded now on several passes. The aliens would fight, of that Lucian was certain, but they had been hurt by his own broadsides, and would do so only on their own terms. The ballet continued: the humans unable to close on their target, and the aliens thus far unwilling to be closed upon.

The last group of icons visible in the holograph's globe of light represented his own, small flotilla. The *Oceanid* was a capable heavy cruiser, despite the damage she had suffered in recent engagements. Ten kilometres to the *Oceanid*'s port side lay the *Rosetta,* the cruiser captained by Lucian's son, Korvane, who, only minutes before, had returned by shuttle from the surface of the world below. Inbound on their position, a mere fifteen kilometres distant, was the third and last of Lucian's fleet, the cruiser, *Fairlight,* captained by his daughter, Brielle.

Lucian folded his arms as he considered his position, prowling around the holograph, seeking to examine the situation, literally, from every possible angle. He had been pitched into this battle by the actions of his son, who had negotiated an alliance with Imperial Commander Zachary Droon. The only problem was, he had destroyed one of the aliens' vessels and crippled another before his son had informed him that these aliens were, by dint of the agreement brokered by his son, allies. The life of a rogue trader was never a simple one.

'*Fairlight,*' Lucian said, the servitor at the *Oceanid*'s communications station patching him through to the bridge of his daughter's ship.

'Go ahead, Father,' came the response. Lucian noted instantly that his daughter sounded even more uptight than normal. He had no time to worry about her state of mind however.

'*Rosetta.*' The servitor opened the channel to the bridge of Korvane's ship.

Lucian reached down to the console at the base of the holograph and depressed a control stud. 'I am transmitting the approach plan to you both. You will note your positions within that plan. Do you receive and understand?'

He waited, affording his son and his daughter the time to relay the headings to their respective helmsmen. A minute later, his son was the first to respond.

'Understood, Father.' Lucian was pleased to note that his son offered no further response. Perhaps he was suitably chastised following their earlier confrontation on the subject of Korvane's negotiating the alliance with Droon in his father's absence.

He waited a minute more, before asking, 'Brielle? Are you clear as to your role?'

'I am clear, Father,' came the response, after a delay that Lucian knew was calculated to communicate Brielle's displeasure.

Just like her mother, he thought, allowing himself a wry grin at his daughter's wilful behaviour.

'Well enough,' he said. 'You both have your orders. Good hunting, and good luck.'

'Good hunting,' Korvane echoed, followed a moment later by his stepsister. Lucian took his seat at the command throne, taking a deep breath before issuing his order, 'Helm, time to get under way.'

'Aye, sir,' responded Helmsman Raldi, saluting his captain before turning and leaning his weight to the mighty wheel.

Lucian looked to the holograph, seeing that his son's vessel was manoeuvring into her allotted position. A couple of minutes later and the *Rosetta* was in position. He watched the *Fairlight*, his studied eye seeing instantly, and without recourse to his instruments that his daughter's ship was out of station by at least a kilometre.

He sighed. 'Brielle,' he said, the communications servitor patching him through the ship-to-ship array instantaneously.

'Go ahead,' the clipped reply came back.

'Brielle, you're out of position. Close up on the *Rosetta*, now.'

A delay was followed by, 'Yes, Father, I will. I'm simply picking up some flare. I can ride it out, but I don't want to risk the compensators, not now.'

Lucian sighed for a second time. He had never been able to tell for sure whether his daughter was simply being evasive or whether she was outright lying. Another characteristic she had inherited from her mother and her people. It certainly wasn't passed down from his own side of the family.

'Well enough, Brielle. Just make sure you've shaken it by two point five. Understood?'

'Understood, Father,' the reply came back.

He smiled to himself. Brielle never could do things the simple way.

'Ship to fleet,' Lucian called to the communications servitor. It nodded an instant later to indicate that he was speaking to both ships. 'Korvane, Brielle. We begin our approach run now.' He nodded to the helmsman, who hauled on the huge, floor-mounted lever, feeding power to the main drives. The deck vibrated as engines roared into life, although thankfully they showed no sign of trouble from the misbehaving drive unit.

'We find ourselves on the same side as these aliens, the tau as Korvane calls them. Now,' Lucian continued speaking so as to forestall his son's inevitable interjection, 'this could prove troublesome, given that not a couple of hours ago I personally sent several thousand of them to the depths of the seven hells. Despite that, I did so for entirely plausible reasons, but I feel that the remaining vessels may not share our newfound friendship. Therefore, if we are to honour the obligations entered into on our behalf, we are forced to take a somewhat unusual approach. This then, is my plan. We must draw the tau onto the guns of Luneberg's fleet.'

He sat back, knowing what was coming next. It came.

'Father!' Korvane's voice came back, Lucian's son's anger obvious, even over the static-filled and distorted ship-to-ship channel. 'Father, I negotiated our agreement in good faith, and even though you disapprove, we are honour bound to abide by it. The tau might be aliens, but they are Droon's allies, and we cannot be responsible for their demise.'

Lucian grinned. By the Emperor, he really had spawned a couple of humourless whelps.

'Korvane, I am not asking you to do so. Just follow your orders and shut the hell up,' he said, slamming his palm down and cutting the channel. He chuckled, imagining his son's spluttering indignation at his words. He would have some explaining to do, later.

That would have to wait, however, as the three rogue trader vessels were closing on their target, a point of space just over three hundred kilometres ahead of Luneberg's fleet.

'Hard to starboard, if you would, Mister Raldi,' Lucian ordered, his helmsman, who hauled on the wheel in response, bringing the

Oceanid around on a new heading perpendicular to the Chasmatan vessels. 'Trim mains to twenty.'

He sat back and studied the holograph, for Luneberg's fleet was too far distant to see with the naked eye. He forced his breathing to a slow rate, not prepared to admit even to himself that he might be anything other than entirely confident that Luneberg would take the bait. One, two, three, he counted the minutes, looking for any sign of a change in course.

He saw it. Luneberg's flagship began a long slow turn, intended, Lucian saw instantly, to intersect his current position, which it would do in something approaching ten minutes. He smiled. Imperial Commanders should restrict themselves to commanding Imperial worlds, he thought, for they clearly hadn't got the faintest clue how to command a fleet.

'Thirty to port, Mister Raldi,' ordered Lucian, his helmsman bringing the *Oceanid* around upon the new course. 'Open them up.'

The *Oceanid* thundered forwards, Lucian seeing from the holograph that the *Rosetta* and the *Fairlight* were maintaining formation, although his daughter's vessel was still out of position, if not excessively. He let it pass.

He looked to the range counter on the holograph, seeing that it was rapidly counting down to the point of, what he knew was no return. In only a few minutes, the tau fleet would be within visual range.

Lucian felt an itch on the back of his neck and looked to the projection, seeing that Luneberg's fleet had completed its arc and was now pursuing the rogue trader ships, maintaining a range of eighty kilometres and closing.

'Trim mains by ten,' he ordered the helm, watching as the Chasmatan fleet closed even further. This was a game of cat and mouse on a grand scale, and by the Emperor, he loved it. 'Forty to starboard if you please.'

The *Oceanid* began a graceful turn, Lucian watching the holo as the Chasmatans followed hard on his fleet's tail. What they did not appear to be paying attention to, as Lucian had counted on them not doing, was the position of the alien fleet.

Lucian let out an exultant whoop as the *Oceanid* and her attending ships swept across the fore of the tau vessels' formation. He watched, as they came into visual range, his gaze fixed on their prow-mounted turrets, which turned wildly, seeking to acquire the *Oceanid* in their sights. They failed; as Lucian had gambled they would, the three rogue trader cruisers passing out of the most deadly portion of the aliens' field of fire before a single shot could be fired.

As his ship powered away from the tau fleet, he saw the flash Lucian had hoped and prayed would follow his passing. It was, he knew without even looking to the holograph, the aliens opening fire with their prow-mounted weapons, directly at Luneberg's vessels as they crossed the T with their fleet. Lucian knew that the ships of both fleets were configured in such a manner that such a formation should prove mutually destructive.

He knew he had been correct as he watched a number of the icons representing Luneberg's escorts fall out of formation. Reams of data scrolled by each, Lucian seeing that the damage wrought upon the smaller ships was such that they would be left dead in space, if their crew were lucky.

Meanwhile, however, the two cruisers of Luneberg's fleet had reached the optimum point at which to open fire, and did so at exactly the moment the Admiralty Staff textbooks told their captains they should. Lucian watched, his breath caught in his throat, as the moment of truth finally arrived.

Nothing happened.

Lucian slammed both palms down on the arms of his command throne, his laughter filling the bridge. 'I knew it!'

Brielle smiled demurely to herself as she realised the trick her father had just pulled. He had, she saw, gambled that Luneberg's vessels were outfitted with weapons provided to them by the tau, as the orbital station at Mundus Chasmata had been. Furthermore, he had surmised, again correctly, that the tau weapons would not fire upon their own, leaving Luneberg's vessels suddenly helpless at the crucial point in their confrontation.

He was a wily old bastard; she had to give him that, but he hadn't foreseen this. She tapped a code into the communications readout beside her command throne.

'This,' she said aloud, hitting the key labelled 'Transmit,' 'is for the greater good.'

Lucian watched from the starboard viewing port as explosions blossomed across the lengths of Luneberg's two cruisers. He had seen that the Borialis Defensor was equipped with xenos-supplied weapons when he had passed her earlier, and realised instantly that these were the same, high velocity projectile weapons that had been unleashed against him by the Chasmatan orbital. He had gambled upon their not firing on their own, but something else entirely was occurring here.

A dozen points of rapidly expanding orange studded the length of both enemy vessels, the exact locations, he knew, of the alien weaponry. Luneberg had sought to play them all – the rogue traders and the tau both – for suckers, but appeared to have been played himself.

The *Borealis Defensor* listed to port, her captain, Lucian guessed, attempting desperately to manoeuvre his vessel out of the alien ships' kill zone. The other cruiser responded by opening up her engines, the enormous power building inexorably to propel her forwards and away from danger.

Neither vessel had even the slightest chance of escape, however, for they were firmly trapped within the aliens' most deadly fire arc. The multiple, prow-mounted turrets on each of the five vessels turned as one, tracking the nameless cruiser as she attempted in vain to pull away. The muzzle of each spat blue fire, the hyper-velocity projectiles propelled across space in the blink of an eye.

The cruiser was struck to starboard, amidships, a line of explosions blossoming across its spine. Even larger explosions appeared on the vessel's port flank, the projectiles having passed entirely through its vast bulk.

Lucian stood speechless, too stunned even to order his helmsman to steer away from the almost tragically uneven battle. Violet plasma geysered from the cruiser's exit wounds, lending it the appearance of some gargantuan sea creature bleeding its guts into the churning ocean. A series of secondary explosions spread within the dying vessel, and its ravaged midsection bowed as fires danced along its length, fed white-hot by the ship's rapidly escaping air.

The fate of the first cruiser sealed, the tau vessels turned their attention to the *Borealis Defensor*.

'Hard to port, full power to mains!' Lucian snapped out of his trance as the blazing wreck of the first cruiser drifted from his view. With the aliens intent on Luneberg's flagship, he saw only one way of ending this in anything like a favourable position.

'Comms!' he shouted, the interference-laden ship-to-ship channel bursting to life. '*Fairlight*, *Rosetta*, this is *Oceanid*!'

'Go ahead, Father, I read you,' came back Brielle's reply.

Then silence.

'Korvane?' Lucian said, looking across to the communications servitor. 'Korvane, do you read me?'

The only answer was the angry howl of the open communications channel.

The *Rosetta* shook violently beneath Korvane's feet, the scream of twisting steel audible from somewhere far below decks.

'What the hell was that? Damage report, now!' bellowed Korvane, filled with a sudden dread. The sound had come from a part of his ship from which no such sound should ever come, even in the event of major battle damage. His gaze raced across the banks of data-screens clustered around the bridge, each choked with reams of rapidly scrolling figures.

Before he could even begin to decipher the data however, a second explosion sounded from the guts of his vessel, the bridge lights cutting out, leaving only the illumination that came from the static-filled screens.

'Where's that report?' he called, standing, and grabbing the nearest bridge officer, a junior rating, by the collar. 'You, go find out what's happening to my ship!'

Another explosion sounded, this time even deeper in the *Rosetta*'s innards. Korvane knew immediately that it was the drive section and his fears were confirmed a moment later as the ship began to list severely to port.

'Damage control parties!' Korvane ordered. 'Get the secondaries on line, now!'

'Yes, sir,' replied a hooded junior tech-adept, hauling open an access hatch in the deck plate, and clambering in to the cable-choked crawlspace.

Korvane experienced a moment of utter helplessness, the worst feeling a captain could ever have. Then, by the grace of the Emperor, the banks of screens flickered, went dead, and then awoke entirely, the machine spirit deep within the *Rosetta*'s cogitation banks reawakening them.

He strode to the main bank, leaning over the command lectern and gripping its edge hard as he felt the artificial gravity fluctuate. For an instant, he stumbled as the gravitic generators fought to maintain their normal output, their force doubling before returning to something resembling their normal level. He fought to concentrate on the endless figures scrolling across the main screen, suddenly gaining an inkling into what had happened.

Isolating the data committed by the *Rosetta*'s main bank augur array, Korvane reviewed the minute immediately preceding the explosion. Luneberg's vessels had closed in on the tau fleet, but their weapons had failed to fire upon their targets, that much was clear. More data scrolled across the screen, until, there! A signal had burst across local space and Luneberg's turrets had detonated.

So too had something deep within his own vessel.

'Sir!' A shout came from a rating in the bridge pit. 'Sir, damage control parties report fires on decks seven through nineteen, fore, spreading fast!'

'Damn it,' he cursed. 'Get me–'

Another explosion rocked the *Rosetta*, the deck plate buckling beneath Korvane's feet. The force threw him bodily against the main console bank, slamming the breath from his lungs and leaving him winded. He collapsed to the floor, rolling over and gasping to draw breath.

As he did so however, his lungs burst in agony as they drew in hot fumes, the stink of burning cables assaulting his senses. Coughing violently, he looked to the open access hatch in the middle of the bridge, from which a fountain of flames was erupting. He staggered to his feet, crossed the deck and hauled shut the metal blast hatch. His hands were burned as they closed on the superheated metal, but he gritted his teeth and slammed the hatch down, the flames spilling around its base for an instant, before they died.

'Damage control!' he bellowed, slamming his fist upon the nearest intercom plate, praying it still functioned. 'Damage control to the bridge!' He looked around the nightmarish scene. Thick, black smoke choked the space, sparks spitting from consoles and servitors both, while banks of static-filled data-screens provided the only, flickering, source of illumination.

For an instant, the smoke cleared and Korvane caught sight of the scene through the main viewing port. The *Rosetta* was listing drastically, and was drifting well out of station. She was moving, he saw with stark horror, right across the bows of the tau vessels. They were supposed to be on the same side, but he was filled with the sudden realisation that the alliance might well have been revoked in the light of his father's actions against the aliens. Would they respect the pact he had made with Droon?

His answer came an instant later, as the turrets of the nearest of the tau vessels rotated towards the stricken *Rosetta*. He saw with a rush of elation that, somehow, his vessel's shields remained raised, and were in fact holding strong at near full capacity. The tau vessel evidently saw this too, for it held fire, not wasting its shots.

Korvane watched in mute fascination as armoured blast doors opened along the tau vessel's flanks. Silhouetted against the pure, blue light that shone forth from within were rows upon rows of armoured figures.

As the distance between the two vessels closed to less than five hundred metres, the figures leapt into sudden movement, blue jets at their backs and ankles bursting into life and propelling them into space.

Korvane stood transfixed, barely noticing the damage control servitor stomping passed him, great jets of fire retardant gas spraying from the extinguisher units that replaced its arms. As the figures closed, he could see that they were some form of heavily armed and armoured suit, evidently built for extra-vehicular activity. What he could see were essentially torsos occupying the suits' central masses; small, head-like blocks perched atop them. The arms were great clamps, intended, he saw immediately, to attach themselves to any available structure, and hang on while the two great weapons mounted under each clamp burned through any but the most resistant hull. Upon the suits' backs were mounted complex manoeuvring jets, smaller clusters of which were also visible at the ankles and shoulders. He had never before seen their like, and two great waves were heading straight for his bridge.

Tracking their inevitable course snapped Korvane out of his shock. Praying that the communications arrays still functioned, he staggered back to the main command lectern, coughing as the powdery spray filling his bridge seared his already damaged lungs. He punched the console, awakening its machine spirit, and scanned the readouts for an open channel. He found one.

'Brielle!' he called, knowing that the ship-to-ship channel was open and that his stepsister's vessel was nearby. 'Listen, Brielle, I need you to–'

'Brielle?' he turned the dial, boosting the signal, and was greeted by an explosion of angry static. 'Brielle, if you can hear this transmission, this is *Rosetta*, Brielle. This is Korvane. I'm crippled, and I have multiple fast moving class nines inbound on my bridge. If you can hear me, Brielle, I need you to close to point defence range... Brielle?'

'Damn it!' he cursed, certain that the channel was open and that his stepsister should have been able to hear his transmission, and to reply to it. He looked once more to the viewer, seeing that the tau suits were half way across the gulf between the two vessels.

Just one chance, he thought, activating the intercom plate. 'Torpedo deck, this is your captain. Do you receive?' The intercom hissed and howled for a moment, before a voice replied, 'My lord? Yes sir, this is Second Under-Technician Kaerk, sir, the crew chief's dead sir, but I–'

'Chief Kaerk,' Korvane replied, promoting the man on the spot for his simple act of answering his master's voice. 'Listen to me carefully Kaerk. What is the status of the torpedo?'

'Sir?' the voice replied, the noise of a crash sounding before it returned. 'It's in tube one sir, as it always is. Should I–'

'Good!' replied Korvane, offering a brief but heartfelt prayer of thanks to the God-Emperor of Mankind. 'Do you have fire control?'

'Last thing the chief did sir, before he... was awaken the torpedo's spirit... said it looked like it might finally get its day!'

Thank the Emperor for the non-commissioned ranks, Korvane thought. 'Listen Kaerk, I want you to launch the torpedo, on a ten second fuse. That's all, do you understand?'

'Launch the torpedo sir? Launch "The" torpedo?'

'Yes! Now!'

'But it's the only one we've–'

'Launch it now or Emperor help me I'll–' the intercom sputtered, an explosion sounding in the distant torpedo deck and cutting the connection dead.

That's it then, thought Korvane. The torpedo had been his last chance, a last chance that the *Rosetta* had been hauling around the galaxy for over a decade; and now, he sighed, he would never fire it. He watched as the first of the tau suits closed on the wide viewing port, briefly debating with himself whether to lower the armoured blast shield. Little point, he decided, they'd be through it in seconds; it would only delay the inevitable.

Better to die with his ship, he decided, straightening his jacket and standing proud at the command lectern; as all good captains should.

The first of the tau suits closed on the armoured glass of the viewing port, its mighty clamps attaching themselves to protrusions on the vessel's outer hull. The under-slung weapons fired into life, blinding white light arcing from the short, rectangular barrel of each.

It began to cut, when Korvane felt the *Rosetta* lurch violently to starboard, causing him to stumble and grab hold of the lectern to maintain his balance. The movement was not that of the vessel suffering another explosion, but something else entirely, something he had not experienced since he had stood upon the deck of his father's vessel and watched in childlike wonder as the *Oceanid* unleashed upon a xenos vessel a fearsome torpedo attack!

The last torpedo in the Arcadius fleet ploughed through the dense formation of tau attackers, sending them scattering in every direction. Korvane barked the laughter of the insane, the laughter of those who know they have won, even as they welcome death. He locked his gaze with the single lens of the tau suit as it cut through the armoured glass, great gobbets of superheated, liquid material splashing across the metal deck of the bridge.

'Five,' he counted, watching the huge form of the torpedo as it dived into space.

'Four.' He saw manoeuvring jets flaring into life across the flank of the tau ship, less than half a kilometre distant.

'Three.' The suits turned, to race for their mother ship. He knew they would never make it.

'Two.' The pressure on the bridge dropped suddenly as the attacker breached the glass.

'One. Emperor bless you, Crew Chief Kaerk.'

The torpedo detonated, scouring the space between the *Rosetta* and the tau vessel, burning the surface of Korvane's vessel, instantly vaporising every last one of the tau battlesuits, raking the *Rosetta* with the cleansing fires of oblivion.

'Try again, damn it!' Lucian paced the length of his bridge, desperate for any response from his son's vessel. His earlier elation at having outwitted Luneberg turning to helplessness as he saw the *Rosetta* flounder, wracked by internal explosions.

'Helm!' Lucian called. 'Bring us alongside the *Rosetta*. Operations, all available hands prepare to receive survivors.'

The *Oceanid* ploughed on, the helmsman bringing her about to approach the *Rosetta* from astern. The manoeuvre would bring Lucian's ship into close proximity with the alien fleet, but he had no choice.

Meanwhile, he looked on as the alien vessels turned their attention from the first of the two Chasmatan cruisers to the *Borealis Defensor*. Luneberg's flagship was attempting to escape, but the aliens were evidently not about to let that happen. Four of the five tau vessels began a slow turn to starboard, their intention obviously to bring their prow-mounted weapons to bear against the *Borealis Defensor*'s rear section. The fifth alien vessel, Lucian saw, veered off to port, closing on the *Rosetta*.

'Best speed, Mister Raldi, the *Rosetta* needs us,' he said, willing, if it were required, to put his own vessel between the tau ship and his son's. 'Port weapons, prepare for firing.'

As the *Oceanid* closed on the *Rosetta*, Lucian watched as the four alien ships caught up with Luneberg's flagship. Prow turrets spitting blue flame, the invisible, hyper-velocity projectiles lanced across space and slammed through the vessel's shields. A second salvo tore a ragged line of punctures across her armoured drive section, breaching a secondary plasma conduit at a dozen points, superheated gases venting into space.

The tau vessels closed in for the kill, their turrets locked on their target's wound. Lucian held his breath, scarcely able to believe the destruction wrought this day.

However, the coup de grace was never delivered.

A searing, white light erupted to the fore of the *Rosetta*, Lucian throwing his arm across his face before the viewer even reacted by dimming automatically. Cautiously, he lowered his arm, and saw the remnants of a detonation of stunning magnitude, roiling energies spreading out in a searing bow wave.

The *Rosetta* was scoured by the explosion, the mighty vessel propelled away by the blast wave and spinning slowly clear. The tau vessel too was caught in the explosion, its entire starboard side erupting in secondary explosions as it was pushed by gargantuan energies across space. Lucian watched as the tau vessel spun clean through its four sister ships, each veering desperately to avoid it. At the last, the tau vessel collided with the *Borealis Defensor*, the two ships grinding inexorable together, twisting and melding together to form a terrible amalgamation of human and tau starship. Incredibly, neither vessel exploded outright, although plasma fires danced crazily across the surface of both, welding them together for all time, making a blackened tomb for thousands of men and aliens even as they perished within.

Lucian wasted no time mourning the xenos tau or the treacherous dogs of Luneberg's crew. He was more concerned for his son. The *Rosetta* was drifting, her drives clearly dead, and a hundred fires had erupted across the side of her hull that had borne the brunt of the explosion.

Worse, she was drifting across the bows of the remaining tau vessels. Lucian weighed the odds, immediately deciding upon his course of action.

'Helm, cross the *Rosetta*'s stern at ninety,' he ordered.

'Aye, sir,' Helmsman Raldi replied, a savage grin on his face, and Lucian saw that his helmsman had understood the order fully.

The *Oceanid* powered on, Lucian seeing that the remaining tau vessels were coming around for a salvo against the *Rosetta*'s aft section. Within minutes, his vessel was drawing across the *Rosetta*'s stern, crossing the T with the other ship's drive section.

'All stop!' Lucian bellowed. 'Starboard batteries, prepare to fire on my order.'

Lucian crossed his hands behind his back, counting off the range to the tau vessels. He knew they would open fire any second.

'Sir!' the helmsman shouted, collision-warning sirens screaming into deafening life across the *Oceanid*'s bridge. The ship pitched beneath Lucian's feet, throwing him to one side as he fought to keep his balance.

'Report!' he shouted.

'It's the *Fairlight*, sir,' Raldi replied through gritted teeth as he wrestled with the *Oceanid*'s helm. 'She's crossing our starboard bow.'

Lucian turned to see that the sight of the *Fairlight* coming alongside, entirely filled the starboard viewing port. He turned, looking to the holograph, to see that the alien fleet was veering off.

Thanks to Brielle's untimely and inexplicable manoeuvre, the aliens had escaped the wrath of the *Oceanid*'s broadside. Lucian fumed. His daughter might have thought she was aiding him, but she had cost him the potential opportunity to catch the entire alien fleet in one, devastating volley.

She would have some explaining to do, once he had seen that his son was safe.

'All stop,' Brielle ordered, the *Fairlight* coming to a stately halt two hundred metres to the *Oceanid*'s starboard. She stretched, catlike, in her command throne, and turned to the hooded figure standing beside her.

'One good turn deserves another, eh Naal?' she said, crossing her legs across the arm of the throne.

'Indeed, my lady,' the man replied. 'My masters will have much for which to repay you.'

CHAPTER FOURTEEN

'Shall we, then,' Lucian said, standing centre stage before Droon's throne, flanked by his son and his daughter 'discuss payment?'

'Payment?' replied Imperial Commander Zachary Droon, his courtiers and advisors fussing around him. 'I think you will find that the terms of the contractual arrangement between your son and me–'

'I think,' interrupted Lucian, a finger held out before him to silence the Imperial Commander, 'that you will find that I have decided to, alter, the terms of that arrangement.'

Droon's advisors erupted into outraged splutters of indignation, the reason not entirely lost upon Lucian. He chuckled inwardly, savouring the irony that, once again, a partner had altered terms on them.

'Now,' continued Lucian, 'this is how we are going to settle this.' He waited for any sign of dissension from Droon, continuing only when he saw the Imperial commander sit down upon his throne, resignation on his ascetic features.

'My son,' he placed a hand upon Korvane's shoulder, his son standing to his right, 'pledged the service of the Arcadius in the defeat of the traitorous forces of Mundus Chasmata. That pledge has been delivered upon, has it not?'

Droon nodded in reply, Lucian continuing before he could go any further. 'For that service alone I judge that you are in my, not inconsiderable, debt. However, there is the matter of the harm done to the person of my son,' he turned to Korvane, whose face and body bore the dreadful wounds done as, Lucian had since discovered, the family torpedo had detonated. Korvane's wounds would heal, of that Lucian was certain, but they would leave behind severe scarring, even disfigurement. 'Not to mention,' he continued, 'the large scale damage inflicted upon the *Rosetta* and the *Oceanid* during the course of the action.'

'That was hardly...' Droon spoke up, about to object to the fact that the damage to the *Rosetta* had been self-inflicted, and that done to the *Oceanid* had been caused in no small part by the weapons of the Mundus Chasmata Primary Orbital.

'Your fault?' Lucian growled. 'It was "hardly your fault" that you conspired with xenos to reject the just rule of the Adeptus Terra? It was "hardly your fault" that you did so entirely to settle an ancient grudge with a neighbour with whom you should have been cooperating in harmony?'

'What, then, are your terms?' Droon replied.

'Glad you asked,' Lucian grinned, handing a data-slate to a nearby page, who carried it across to Droon.

Droon read the slate, his eyes widening as he took in the enormity of the figures listed there. The Imperial Commander swallowed, hard, before handing the slate back to the page. 'And if I cannot settle on these terms?'

'Well, my dear commander, there are a number of reasons why I really think that you will. For one, my astropath has been monitoring the declarations of independence issued by every world in this region. You have been fooled, Droon: the tau were not fighting for your cause – they were fighting to stir the likes of you to rebellion. I can guarantee you that every other Imperial Commander on every other world in the Timbra Subsector and beyond has been approached, in one way or another, by these aliens' agents. Evidently, most have fallen to the temptations offered to them. In Luneberg's case it was exotic goods – his world was crawling with them – and weapons with which to equip his vessels. In your case it was mercenary service.'

'My astropath has picked up a new voice,' Lucian continued. 'The Imperium, Droon, has already heard of the situation out here.' He paused, allowing that to sink in, gratified that Droon's entire court had fallen to absolute silence. 'On my word, he can inform the very highest of authorities of the part you had to play in all this. You know what will happen then, Droon?'

When Droon did not reply, Lucian went on. 'If you are lucky, a

Guard army of occupation will arrive and you will be executed quickly. If you are unlucky, it might be the Astartes. They don't do occupation Droon, they go straight to the head and cut it off. It might even be the Inquisition. If it's them, you will not be executed quickly. They will execute very slowly, and very painfully.'

'Very well, Lucian Gerrit,' replied Imperial Commander Zachary Droon. 'I will have my factors draw the necessary bonds.'

Lucian suppressed a grin, clapping his son's shoulder, and catching the wry glance cast his way by his daughter. Following her manoeuvre: the manoeuvre that had allowed the tau fleet to escape, he had threatened to ship her off to take control of a grox-lard processing plant on Chogoris in which he owned a controlling interest. I still might, he thought.

The Arcadius had emerged triumphant, and the price he had exacted upon Droon for his not turning the Imperial Commander over to the first Imperial Navy warship he encountered would go a very long way to restoring their fortunes. Yes, Lucian thought, the Arcadius are back.

The *Rosetta*, restored to a semblance of running order, to the *Oceanid*'s port and the *Fairlight* to her starboard, Lucian stood upon the bridge of his vessel. He had been about to issue the order to make warp, when his astropath, Master Karisan, had rushed onto the bridge, breathless, and interrupted him.

'Speak, Karisan,' Lucian ordered distractedly, 'but make it fast and get back to your quarters. We make warp any moment.'

The astropath stood before Lucian, blocking the forward viewing port. The old man fidgeted and wrung his hands, a motion that instantly irritated Lucian.

'Report, man,' Lucian barked.

'Well, it's this...' Karisan cleared his throat before continuing. 'Not only has every world for twenty light years announced its secession from the Imperium of Man,' Karisan said, evidently catching his wind, and barely able to contain himself. 'Almost every such world has announced its joining of a new...' he paused.

'...empire.'

'Go on.' The astropath now had Lucian's complete, undivided attention.

'The forces of these aliens are even now flooding the entire region – everywhere to the galactic east of the Damocles Gulf. The secessionists are announcing, to all who will hear them, their joining of this alien empire: this tau empire.'

'But,' Karisan continued before Lucian could interrupt, 'but, I have been monitoring the distant voices of the Imperium.'

'What of them?' Lucian asked, sensing that life in the Timbra subsector was about to get very interesting indeed.

'A crusade!' The astropath's voice cracked as he yelped with something resembling religious ecstasy. Lucian had never before seen the old man so animated.

'A crusade is being preached even now my master. Cardinal Gurney preaches war against the tau. He denounces their lies and already, others have pledged aid or service to him.'

'Who?' Lucian's mind raced as he considered the possibilities unfolding before him. 'Who pledges aid to this Gurney against the tau?'

'Why,' replied Karisan, 'the fleet, of course, and Brimlock musters even now. Five regiments and more.'

'Five regiments of Guard have no hope of–'

'Not just them,' Karisan interrupted. Lucian let him continue. 'Inquisitor Grand of the Ordo Xenos! The Astartes! The Iron Hands! The Emperor's Scythes. Even,' and here the astropath leaned towards Lucian, 'the White Scars.'

Lucian leaned back in his command throne, feeling an exhilaration that he had not experienced for many years wash over him. Thoughts of the tales of old Abad and the others came to him, tales of his ancestors penetrating the outer dark at the head of vast, all-conquering fleets, Navy, Guard and Marines rallied to their Emperor-given banner.

Here, now, he, Lucian Gerrit of the Arcadius found himself uniquely placed to make such a thing a reality once more. This preacher, this Cardinal Gurney might prove troublesome, but Lucian could scarcely believe his luck that a contingent of the White Scars Chapter was present. The White Scars, those savage sons of Chogoris, who called the very same world home, as had Brielle's mother, and he was not without contacts there still.

'Master?' Helmsman Raldi turned towards Lucian, his hand still gripped upon the *Oceanid*'s tiller. 'Are we to make way?'

'What?' Lucian's attention was brought back to the here and the now. He looked to his helmsman, before addressing the whole bridge. 'Belay my previous order. We are not to return to the west.'

'Your orders then, my lord?' Raldi asked. Lucian saw the glint in his eye.

'East.' He glanced at a star map, taking in those systems that Karisan had indicated were now in the sway of the alien tau. He picked one.

'Kleist.'

As the bridge crew went about the business of enacting their new orders, Lucian smiled to himself. Perhaps the Arcadius would stay around for a while. It looked to him as if the Damocles Gulf was about to become a very interesting, and very profitable, place for a man such as he.

COLD TRADE

The Adeptus Astra Cartographica listed the world by the short form designator SK0402/78Φ, but the locals called it 'Quag.' It was an unpleasant little name for an unpleasant little world, but Brielle Gerrit, daughter of the infamous rogue trader Lucien Gerrit and next in line to inherit the Arcadius Warrant of Trade, had good reason to visit it. The corner of her mouth curling into a covetous grin, Brielle's hand was subconsciously drawn to the hidden pocket in her uniform jacket and the small object nestled within. Her costume was similar to that worn by the highest ranked officers of the Imperial Navy fleet of a sector very, very far away, and she most certainly did not bear the commission that granted her the right to wear it. But that just made the wearing of the deep blue frock coat with its shining gold epaulettes and fancy braiding all the more fun.

'Commencing final approach, mistress,' the pilot announced from the cockpit, snapping Brielle's attentions back to the here and now. She was seated in the astrodome of her Aquila-class shuttle, a small vessel configured as her personal transport and clad in the red and gold livery of the Arcadius clan of rogue traders. Really, she should have been strapped safely into her grav couch in the shuttle's passenger compartment, but she had always preferred to witness atmospheric interface first hand rather than relayed through a pict-slate. Her pilot, Ganna, was a trusted retainer of the clan and he had given up objecting to his mistress's habits years ago.

'How long?' Brielle said into her vox-pickup, the sound of Quag's atmosphere fusion-blasting the shuttle's outer skin making normal conversation impossible.

'We'll be through the upper cloud layer momentarily, mistress,' Ganna replied, the faintly mechanical edge to his voice betraying the latest of the machine augmentations he had recently been fitted with, at his own instigation. 'Stand by...'

Brielle gripped the handles beneath the armoured glass dome and raised herself upwards to look out. As she did so, the flames licking the shuttle's outer skin wisped away, and the scene opened up before her. The surface of the world below lurched upwards as Ganna brought the shuttle onto a new heading, the landscape resolving itself from the swirling mists.

'What a dump,' Brielle sneered, flicking her head back sharply as a stray plait fell across her face. 'Where's the settlement?'

'Just over the horizon, mistress,' Ganna replied. 'And if I might say so, I agree. It *is* a dump.'

'Hmm,' Brielle replied, settling in to watch the final approach, even if it was the final approach to an absolute festering boil of planet. As the shuttle gradually shed velocity and altitude, the landscape came into focus, not that Brielle paid it much attention. The surface of Quag was, as its name suggested, dominated by endless tracts of swamps, bogs, marshes and pretty much every variation on the theme of stinking, bubbling foulness. The planet's shallow seas were only distinguishable from its landmasses by the relative lack of trees, and even on the so-called land, these were twisted, stunted things that resembled skeletal limbs grasping for the wan skies. It wasn't pretty.

As the shuttle descended still lower, bucking sharply as it ploughed through the occasional pocket of atmospheric disturbance, Brielle caught sight of several small clusters of lights, out in the swamps and none closer to its neighbour than a hundred kilometres. The grin returned to Brielle's lips as she regarded the lonely, twinkling pinpricks. She knew exactly what they represented, though she would save that information for later.

At the exact moment that a burst of machine chatter spewed through the vox-net, Brielle located the shuttle's destination. Quagtown, some of the locals called it, while others preferred *the settlement*. Brielle's word for it wasn't fit to be expressed near those locals, though most would secretly agree with her general view of the badland town that even now was hoving into view. If the planet of Quag was a cesspit, then its only major settlement, below them, was the sump.

'Three minutes, mistress,' Ganna announced. 'Transmitting key now.'

As machine code blurted harshly in the background, Brielle watched Quagtown grow nearer. The first thing she saw was the towering rock column on which it was perched, a natural formation that looked anything but. The column was the only feature of its type on the entire world, resembling a flat-topped stalagmite rearing a kilometre into the air. At the summit was clustered the settlement itself, its oldest quarters built on the cap and the later ones clinging precariously to its sides. From this distance, the town looked like so many layers of festering metallic junk piled randomly on top of one another, and to be honest, it didn't look much different close up.

Both Brielle and Ganna remained silent as the machine chatter burbled away, and Brielle fancied she could discern the to and fro of electronic conversation in the atonal stream. After a minute or so, during which the shuttle continued its approach to the ramshackle town, the chatter ceased, to be replaced by a solid, grating tone.

'Did they go for it?' said Brielle, her gaze fixed on the command terminal before her. A small data-relay slate showed a line of text, but while Brielle was relatively conversant in such things, the code was unknown to her.

'I believe they did, mistress,' Ganna replied, his cranial feed allowing him to read the data faster than it could be deciphered and relayed through a command terminal. 'Stand by... confirmed. Sector three nine zero high,' he said, and Brielle saw him nod towards the rapidly closing settlement.

Following his directions and gesture, Brielle saw what her pilot was indicating, for the shuttle was now only a kilometre or so out from the top of the column and Ganna was bringing it around on a wide, lazy turn. A guttering fire had been lit at the summit of a thin, precarious-looking tower constructed from a jumble of metal stanchions from which protruded numerous aerials and revolving scanner dishes. As the distance closed still further, she could make out small figures clinging to the framework, many of which had scanning devices raised to their eyes. They were all clearly heavily armed.

As the shuttle banked, Brielle saw movement at the base of the tower, and just for a moment, the breath caught in her throat. What looked like a multi-launch missile system was tracking the shuttle as it approached, at least a dozen snub-nosed projectiles nestled in an oversized hopper just ready to shoot her down and really ruin her day.

But, Brielle realised, that was Ganna's point. If the missile launcher was going to fire it would have done so by now. Letting out the breath she had been holding, she scanned the bulk of the ugly settlement as the shuttle completed its turn and fired its manoeuvring jets for landing. Close in, the details of its construction were revealed, and it was a miracle that had nothing to do with the God-Emperor of Mankind that the place stayed together at all. Quagtown was constructed from a bizarre mix of junk, much of it evidently scavenged from small spacecraft and surface vehicles to judge by by the haphazard surface detail. These disparate elements were supported and conjoined by a twisted mass of wood harvested from the trees in the swamps far below, and the whole lot was lashed together by what must have been hundreds of thousands of metres of vine, again gathered from the lands all around.

And atop this confused, impossible mess of uncivil engineering was a vaguely circular landing platform roughly fifty metres in diameter. The pitted, blast-scorched surface was made from hundreds of deck plates welded crudely together and held up by a forest of wood and metal struts. It was crossed by dozens of snaking feed conduits and fuel lines, and numerous cargo crates were piled haphazardly at its edges. Guidance lumens set into the surface flashed a seemingly random pattern, no two of them the same colour, and Ganna fine-tuned the shuttle's approach, firing its landing jets as the vessel slowed to a halt above what Brielle assumed was its assigned berth.

From her vantage point in the astrodome Brielle was afforded a view of the entire landing platform, and she could see that three other vessels were already docked. One was a battered old Arvus lighter, and it was clear to Brielle's practised eye that it had once belonged to the defence fleet of a system spinward of Quag. Its new owner had made a very amateur attempt at painting over the livery of the vessel he had no doubt acquired via less than legitimate channels, and the spectacle brought a wry grin to Brielle's lips.

A second vessel was of a pattern Brielle had never actually seen in the flesh, though she had certainly seen it depicted in the Arcadius clan's archives held at the Zealandia Hab. In form it resembled some massively oversized insect, its domed, multi-faceted eyes forming its cockpit. Its wings were currently swept back into a stowed position, but Brielle knew they were fitted with an anti-grav array that granted the small ship such agility and grace it was no wonder its type was highly sought after by all manner of unusual or downright dangerous characters. Whether this was owned by an underworld lord, a powerful bounty hunter or even another rogue trader like herself Brielle could not say, though she silently resolved to be watchful.

The third vessel sat upon the uneven surface of the landing deck was a squat, armoured brick of a shuttle, and it was being tended by an indentured service crew, who were themselves being closely watched by a gang of heavily augmented and no doubt combat-glanded thugs. This was evidence of two primary facts. The first was that it had only recently arrived at Quagtown, its owner having paid for an immediate, quick turnaround service to ensure it was ready for an expeditious departure. The second fact that presented itself to Brielle was that the individual who she had come to this festering dump of a town to meet with had arrived ahead of her, exactly as she had anticipated he would.

'Set us down, Ganna,' Brielle ordered, a thrill of danger and expectation fluttering through her belly. 'Let's do what we came here to do...'

The instant Brielle and Ganna climbed out of the Aquila and took a breath of the air, she halted.

'Damn it,' she cursed as the stale air filled her lungs. 'Forgot my filtration plugs, this place stinks like an ork's...'

'Take my rebreather, mistress.' Ganna interrupted her unladylike outburst, unhooking his breathing mask from about his neck and passing it to Brielle.

But Brielle was already walking away from the shuttle, waving the offer away dismissively. 'Make sure the cargo's unloaded,' she called back as she stalked away across the deck.

Caught between his concern for his mistress and the need to fulfil her order, Ganna muttered beneath his breath as he turned hurriedly towards the open passenger compartment. At the head of the short ramp stood two burly figures, each as much metallic machine as biological flesh. The biomechanical, mind-scrubbed servitors carried between them a heavy, armoured chest, the expressions on their hybrid metal-flesh faces dead-eyed and blank.

'Imperative meta-nine,' Ganna barked at the servitors, the code phrase causing them to stir as they recognised and acknowledged the words of a duly authorised superior. 'Heeding signal zero zero actual,' he ordered, and stood aside as the mindless automatons marched down the short ramp in perfect lockstep and headed off after Brielle. With a final glance at the shuttle, Ganna punched a glowing rune plate mounted by the hatch, cycling the passenger bay to its sealed state, and followed after his mistress.

The metallic surface rang beneath the tread of Brielle's heavy, knee-high boots, and it took Ganna only seconds to catch up with her. The air was hot in the vicinity of the idling shuttles and scented by a nauseous mixture of fuel, filth and sin. Knowing that if anything untoward happened to Brielle, her father would hunt him down and feed him to the sump-rats in his cruiser's sub-decks, he determined to stay as close to her as it was possible to do, though he knew from experience that would really get on her nerves.

'Hey there!' Brielle called out to a cluster of ground crew struggling to affix a large feed-line to the intake on the armoured shuttle sharing the landing pad with her own Aquila. When the men seemed to ignore her, choosing instead to concentrate on their duty, she raised an eyebrow and planted her fists firmly on her hips.

Just as Ganna stepped up beside her, Brielle started forwards towards the ground crew, and at that very moment a pair of towering guards stepped in from nearby to bar her path. Obviously brothers, the pair were clearly in the employ of the local underworld, for they were heavily augmented as well as covered in the tattooed sigils that proclaimed the complex web of patronage commanding their loyalty. Brielle read it in a glance, and knew instantly that the pair belonged to one of the lowlife flesh brokers that dealt out of Quagtown.

Casting a seemingly casual glance over the bulk of the armoured shuttle the men were tending, Brielle craned her neck to look up into the face of the nearest thug. By the saints, they breed them homely around these parts, she thought to herself.

'Listen, boys,' she said sweetly, drawing a look of scepticism from both men. 'I need my lander overwatched while I'm doing business in town. What's the local scrip?'

Brielle knew full well what form of currency the locals would prefer, and how much of it they would demand, but she didn't want to play that card, not yet at least. After a moment of thinking hard on the matter, one thug replied, 'How much overwatch you need?'

'All of it,' Brielle replied on a whim, drawing a raised eyebrow from Ganna. In truth, it didn't matter what and how much she laid out for local security, not in the big picture, but she needed to make an impression in the right quarters.

'Half the crew're busy on *this* job,' the more talkative of the brothers replied, jerking the thumb of a mechanical hand towards the armoured shuttle.

'I'll pay double whatever they're on,' Brielle replied mischievously. 'In clan-bonded deaths-heads.'

The two thugs glanced at one another with eyes alight with greed, seeming to reach an unspoken agreement within seconds.

'Half now,' she interjected before either could reply, producing a single coin worth more than both men would normally earn in a month and holding it up where both could see. 'Half later, *if* you make me happy.'

'Done,' they said as one, clearly believing that Brielle had been.

'Then I'll leave it to you,' Brielle said, dropping the coin into the open hand of the nearest of the pair. She watched the two heavies pull their fellows off of the duty they were on and muster them to guard her own vessel. As the pair walked away, the two servitors close behind, the landing deck rang to the sound of the local hired muscle spreading the word that a sweet job was in the offing. Knowing it was unseemly to mock the hard of thinking, Brielle suppressed a sly grin and set off into Quagtown.

* * *

'Holy Terra,' Brielle muttered as the four turned into what passed as the town's main thoroughfare. 'It actually looks *more* of a dump than they say...'

The thoroughfare couldn't really be called a street, because it was more a valley between ramshackle buildings, and travel along it was not in a straight, flat line, but up and down across the numerous gantries, platforms, ledges and walkways that connected each building to the next. The buildings themselves were a tumbledown mess of sheet metals and unidentifiable machine components, with all manner of shipping containers providing the most desirable real estate. The numerous walkways were in many cases little more than parallel lengths of spar or rotted timber, with tread plate or mesh lashed crudely between with great lengths of dried vine.

But worst of all was the population. Every available space along the walkways and gantries was filled by the scum of Quagtown. Rag-clad beggars panhandled from the gutters while those afflicted by a variety of chemical addictions shivered and sweated in the shadows. Thieves and blaggers eyed Brielle and her party lasciviously, while meat-headed bullies and scarred mercs looked them over for hidden threats. The wealthy, a relative term in such frontier hellholes for the truly rich would pay to be anywhere else, promenaded along the gantries displaying what portable wealth their guards could be trusted to protect, while painted doxies fluttered their lashes from half-open doorways.

Brielle's eyes narrowed as she saw a number of mutants in amongst the press, individuals whose bodies were twisted and malformed and whose faces were more akin to those of beasts. Several of them sported skin and hair of garish hues; though it was possible the effect was artificial, as numerous subcultures across the Imperium pursued the most outlandish of fashions. Several had additional limbs, an effect which only the wealthiest could, or indeed would, pay for, for it required the services of the most skilled of flesh-crafters to carry out well. Clearly, these were true mutants, born into their genetic heresy.

On many of the million and more worlds of the Imperium, such debased individuals would be ruthlessly controlled or even culled. They might be allowed to repent their sin of impurity by toiling their short, bitter lives away in the lathes and foundries of some brutal labour-prison, but rarely were they allowed to show their malformed faces in such a public manner. Only on or beyond the frontier was it possible for such creatures to walk about openly, unchallenged by the authorities.

If the presence of the mutants was a rare sight on a human world, that of the creature stalking along the uppermost gantry was an outright spectacle. A spindly being, its body vaguely humanoid but its overlong, stilt-like arms employed as an additional pair of legs, was progressing with something akin to grace from one building to the next. Its skin was dusty grey with mottled, darker patches down its back, and instead of clothing it wore what could only be a combat rig, a form of webbing with numerous pouches and packs attached all over. Its head was long and aquiline, sporting three pairs of eyes along its sides, while its mouth was a tiny, leechlike opening at the end of its proboscis snout. Brielle was fascinated, for she had never before encountered its species nor read of it in all of her education.

A crude, grunting shout from another walkway made Brielle instantly aware of another type of alien, and one that she had encountered on numerous worlds. Indeed, the barbarous, green-skinned orks plagued the known galaxy, their anarchic empires forming great lesions of war and disturbance that meant that no Imperial sector was ever safe from their incessant invasions and migrations. A group of the hulking xenos was making its way along a walkway clinging precariously to the side of a building constructed from a huge, cylindrical fuel transport, shouldering people aside and growling at passers-by. Brielle's lip curled in disgust, for these beasts truly were the scum of the universe, and it was rare for them to be tolerated even in such recidivist sumps as Quagtown. The place got even lower in her estimation.

Brielle halted at a relatively open gallery, standing aside as a party of drunken lay-techs staggered by, and scanned the buildings and walkways before her. Reaching into a pocket, she drew out a small data-slate, aware of the numerous eyes amongst the passers-by that followed the motion while trying to look as if they weren't. With a flick of an activation rune, she awoke the slumbering machine, a rough schematic of the town appearing on its green-glowing surface.

As she studied the map, Brielle's brow furrowed. She'd paid a lot for it yet now, in the field, it seemed suddenly to bear scant resemblance to reality. The data had been purchased from an indentured sprint-skipper who supposedly knew the local wilderness zones better than anyone in the region, and the man had staked his reputation it was as accurate and up to date as it was possible to be. Brielle had made sure she had dirt on the skipper though, and knew exactly which interzone scum-ports he liked to haunt when off duty. If anything happened, he would be tracked down and shown the error of his ways in terminal fashion; she had made the arrangements before leaving.

But, despite the schematic's inconsistencies, Brielle was finally able to make some sense of it, and it soon became evident that part of the cause of the inaccuracies was the constant rebuilding of the ramshackle junk town. With nothing more sturdy than flotsam and jetsam to build their town from, the locals were forced to replace sections as they fell apart or came away from their precarious perch. A kind of pattern gradually formed, and Brielle was able to get her bearings. The building she was looking for was less than fifty metres distant, though it was not yet visible in the confused jumble of structures. To reach it she would have to wend her way up, down and across a crazy mess of walkways and galleries, passing through the mass of scrofulous locals. With a sense of cold dread, she saw that the path would almost certainly cause her to intersect with the group of orks, and with a weary resignation, she just knew they were going to be trouble...

Having climbed the winding stairs and walkways, the locals muttering with surly bitterness at the need to stand aside as the lumbering servitors marched through the crowd without any hint of concern for those forced to clear the way, Brielle's small party came face to face with the orks as both stepped on to a narrow gantry high above the thoroughfare.

Brielle halted as she stepped on to the walkway and looking downwards realised that she could see through the mesh under her feet to the crowded thoroughfare twenty metres or so below. Looking back up, she saw that the lead ork had also stopped, and was grunting some orky quip to its three mates, who laughed uproariously at the unheard comment.

'Something funny?' Brielle called out, knowing from experience that orks were a demonstrative species that respected action and attitude far more than words and thought. The biggest ork looked her over dismissively, and Brielle took the opportunity to appraise it in turn.

Like most of its species, the ork was massive, taller than an average human and at least three times the bulk. Its short legs were bowed and muscular, its torso hunchbacked and top-heavy. Its burly arms were almost long enough to touch the ground and its impressively ugly head sat so low between its shoulders it appeared to have no neck. It was carrying an array of weaponry, from pistols to cleavers, all stowed for now inside the bright red cummerbund wrapped about its middle. The barbarous creature's attire was a bizarre mixture of crudely stitched scraps and elements clearly intended to ape human modes of fashion. It wore a long, ragged frock coat, its hem frayed and dirty. On its head was perched a bicorn hat, and one of its beady, pig-like eyes was covered by a patch.

Brielle grinned ever so slightly as she saw the details of the row of medals and other adornments crudely attached to its chest. Each was a roughly stamped icon that served to identify the bearer, to one who knew how to read them.

'Move,' the creature growled, its voice a low, threatening rumble. Ganna cast a wary glance at his mistress, but Brielle remained exactly where she was, folding her arms across her chest and nodding smugly to herself.

'You speak well,' she said, and she meant it. The fact that the ork had used even a single word in the Gothic of the Imperium marked it out as a uniquely gifted individual. 'For one of Skarkill's boys, anyway.'

From the ork's reaction to her statement, Brielle saw that she had read its glyph-medals correctly. It was indeed a member of the same clan as the ork warlord she had named. The ork folded its arms in apparent imitation of Brielle's posture, the simple act serving to corroborate Brielle's suspicions. By aping human modes of dress and language, by copying her stance, and by its very presence in a human-dominated settlement, the ork revealed itself to be a member of the Blood Axe clan. That meant it was almost certainly an associate of the warlord Skarkill, a being that Brielle's family had encountered several times in this region of space.

'Who you?' it grunted, its single, leering red eye looking Brielle up and down. 'You Admiral wossname? Vonigut the turd?'

'No,' Brielle said dryly. 'I am not Lord Admiral Alasandre Vonicurt the *Third*.' The officer in question was a man of two centuries' service, Brielle knew, and well known for his exceptional girth and prodigious facial hair. Orks weren't the most observant of aliens, but still...

'I am Brielle Gerrit,' she said archly, suppressing her annoyance with an effort of will. 'Of the Rogue Trader Clan Arcadius.'

The ork seemed to think hard on that, for it evidently recognised the name despite its inability to tell one human from another. Brielle's fingers tapped against her arm and she flicked Ganna a glance that spoke volumes of her opinion of the greenskin's mental skills. She became aware that much of the noise and general hubbub of the thoroughfare had quietened down and that scores of upturned faces were watching the confrontation eagerly. What happened here might affect her entire visit to Quag, she realised. At length, the beast rumbled deep in its barrel chest, and it squinted its eye at Brielle.

'Hired Skarkill's mob?' the ork said. 'Big fight on church planet?'

'There we go,' said Brielle, relieved that the ork was indeed of the clan she thought it was, and an underling of the warlord Skarkill. 'The Arcadius had need of your clan's services on Briganta Regis. Skarkill's army took the city and hardly looted it at all. Everyone came away with a profit, and Skarkill said some nice words to my father. You remember those words?'

Now the entire thoroughfare went quiet as hundreds of the locals waited to see how things would play out. Brielle had no doubt that the greenskin mercenary would have terrorised many of these people, and that a fair few of them would be eager to see it put in its place. Others might have a vested interest in *her* being the one to come off the worse, though...

'He said,' the ork slurred, the effort to recall its lord's words clearly taxing its tiny mind. 'Ever you need something done, you just got to ask.'

'That he did,' said Brielle, moving towards the make or break point of the conversation. 'Now, I need something done, understood?'

'You want something killed?' the alien mercenary said, suddenly animated as it believed itself back on more familiar territory.

'No,' said Brielle, eliciting visible disappointment from the ork. Lowering her voice so that only those on the walkway could hear her, she said, 'I need you to step aside and let me pass.'

The crowds below had not heard Brielle's demand, perceiving only a protracted silence during which the woman in the frock coat with the elaborate eye makeup and outlandishly plaited hair seemed to face down an alien warrior several times her bulk, and which had refused to give way to a single one of *them* all the time it had been in Quagtown. A ripple of excitement passed through the crowd and someone started issuing odds. Soon, bets were being placed and money was furtively changing hands, and then, the confrontation reached its conclusion.

The massive, green-skinned brute nodded at the woman and grunted at its companions. Now utterly silent, the crowd was clearly expecting an explosive and highly entertaining outburst of violence.

But then, the ork stepped aside so that the walkway was clear for Brielle and her party to proceed across. The crowd exclaimed in shock and outrage, while several ruined bookkeepers made a sudden dash for the nearest side alley.

'Thank you,' Brielle said to the ork quietly and not without relief as she walked past, fighting hard to keep her voice steady so wildly was her heart pounding. 'Skarkill and my father will both be very pleased with your service, and I'm sure you'll be paid well.'

A moment later Brielle and Ganna were across, the two servitors stomping along after them, and the orks had continued on their way. 'Mistress,' Ganna hissed once he was sure that no one would overhear. 'If your father ever hears that I allowed you to do what you just did, he'd...'

'I know,' said Brielle, dismissing her pilot's complaint with a wave of a hand. 'He'd be furious at you. He'd be even more furious at me, though...'

Realising that his mistress was talking about more than he had knowledge of, Ganna slowed his pace and fixed Brielle with a dark stare. 'Might I ask why, mistress?'

'Because it wasn't him that hired the Blood Axes at Briganta Regis,' she said. 'It was the rebels. We were on the *other side*.'

Now Ganna halted entirely and rounded on Brielle as the colour drained from his face. 'What if he'd...'

'Remembered that little detail?' Brielle interjected. 'I was counting on him not being able to tell one human from another, as he proved when he mistook me for that pig Admiral Vonicurt. He had a choice between risking his warlord's wrath or losing face in front of a few humans. Luckily, he decided he cared more what his boss thought of him than us.'

Brielle's audacity was too blatant for Ganna to reply, so she fished the data-slate from her pocket and looked around for the building that was their destination. 'There it is,' she said, setting off again. 'Are you coming?'

'I think I'd better, mistress,' Ganna mumbled towards Brielle's retreating back. 'I think I'd better...'

'Hold it right there, miss,' demanded the stubjack guarding the door to the nondescript building. 'What's in the crate?'

Brielle looked the man up and down, determining in less than two seconds that he was wearing armour concealed beneath his scruffy overalls and padded jacket, and armed with at least one hidden pistol weapon. She could take him if she needed, she judged, but there were three others of his type loitering nearby, thinking they were acting casual but clearly in on the action.

'Nothing that should worry you,' she said, not feeling a tenth of the cockiness she put into her voice. 'Let me pass and we'll all have a far nicer day, is that clear?'

The stubjack cast what he obviously thought was a furtive glance at the nearby group, and Brielle knew for sure that they were guarding the place as well. 'I said, what's in the crate?' the man repeated as his fellows ambled over, his voice lower and more threatening than the first time.

'And I said, *nothing that should worry you*,' Brielle replied. 'Looks like we're stuck, doesn't it?'

'Not really,' the stubjack said as his three fellow, equally heavily armed and armoured guards appeared at Brielle and Ganna's back. The pair were surrounded by men much bigger than them, but still she refused to be cowed.

'Listen,' said Brielle, lowering her voice so that the guards were forced to lean in and concentrate to hear her clearly. It was a trick she'd learned from a particularly sadistic tutor growing up on Chogoris, and it forced the listener to concentrate on the speaker. 'I've already faced down a bunch of orks today, and they were far bigger than you. Let. Me. Pass,' she growled.

The man blinked as he held Brielle's gaze. Word had clearly spread quickly throughout the small town; hardly surprising, she thought, given the nature of its inhabitants. He glanced towards the crate held securely between the two servitors, evidently weighing up his desire to know what was inside it against his sense of self-preservation. Though he might try to hide behind the need to ensure that nothing dangerous was permitted inside the building he was employed to protect, Brielle knew that in reality, he was hoping it contained something he could take a cut of. Well, it most certainly didn't.

Swallowing hard, the man reached a decision. He nodded to his fellows and, with far more reluctance than the ork on the walkway, stepped aside to allow Brielle and her companions to pass. Grinning with theatrical sweetness, Brielle moved past him; allowing Ganna to push open the battered door, which appeared to be made from the rear hatch of a Chimera armoured carrier, for her to enter the darkness waiting inside.

Beyond the hatch, Brielle was plunged into shadow, which became pitch blackness the moment the guard slammed the portal shut after the servitors had passed through. Her heart pounding, she took a deep breath and straightened her back, before stepping forwards into the unknown with one hand held lightly out before her. She soon found the floor to be littered with small fragments of debris, though she couldn't tell, and didn't really want to know, exactly what she was treading on.

A moment later, she became aware of a muted, but rowdy noise from somewhere up ahead, and stepped forwards until her hand brushed against what felt like a metallic surface. The sound was definitely coming from the other side of what she guessed to be a second hatchway, and even as she listened she became aware of voices and wild strains of half-heard melody.

'Ready?' she said, as much to herself as to her loyal retainer.

Without waiting for an answer, she pushed on the hatchway, and saw for the first time the interior of the place where she had come to earn herself a small fortune.

The space was far larger than seemed possible from the outside, for what seemed like a random jumble of shipping containers and tumbledown shanties was in fact a cunningly wrought building, housing an establishment known, amongst certain circles at least, across the entire region. It had no official name, though those in the know often called it 'Quagtown Palace' and a variety of similar titles, all of them deliberately and sarcastically investing the place with an entirely undeserved grandiloquence.

The crowded interior was in essence a huge, shabby theatre, dominated by a stage at the far end that was framed by great swirls of crudely but ambitiously made baroque detailing. The stage blazed with light made hazy by the banks of acrid smoke drifting through the air, and as she stepped through Brielle found she could make out very little of whatever spectacle was being enacted on that stage, though it was clear that the crowd seated before it most certainly could. Row upon row of tattered, mismatched velvet and leather seating, much of it scavenged from a wide variety of vehicles, accommodated an audience of several hundred. Every one of them was shrieking, whooping and clapping at whatever was happening on the distant, smoke-obscured stage.

The sounds Brielle had dimly heard through the hatch were suddenly so loud they made her wince. An anarchic cacophony of raucous crowd noise and skirling, wild cadences produced by some unseen band competed with the hubbub of conversation, merriment and clinking drinking vessels.

Moving forwards to afford Ganna space to pass through the inner hatch, Brielle took in more of her surroundings. The walls were lined with shadowed nooks and counters that sold all manner of wares, most of them alcoholic and probably decidedly unhealthy to imbibe without a large dose of counter-tox taken beforehand.

Seated around the bar area, Brielle saw a variety of underworld scum. She recognised the types from a hundred frontier star ports and way stations: out of work crew, surly press gangers, harried looking lay-techs and in amongst them all, the dark-eyed, tight-lipped ship's masters and other higher-ranked crew. Serving staff shimmied through the smoky scene carrying trays of refreshments and soliciting the richer-looking patrons for whatever further services they might desire. The sight made Brielle's lip curl in disgust, but a part of her found the whole sordid spectacle somehow alluring, despite her upbringing in the tenets of the Imperial Creed.

'Is this the right place?' said Ganna as he appeared at Brielle's side, the two servitors still waiting in the passageway. 'It looks kind of...'

'Fun,' Brielle interrupted. 'And yes, it *is* the right place. Shall we find a table?'

'Drink, ma'am?' said the waitress, who appeared at the table several minutes after Brielle and Ganna had found themselves somewhere to sit. It was far from ideal, Brielle knew, but if things played out right she'd be moving on pretty soon anyway. The servitors were stood immediately behind her, eliciting numerous furtive glances from those nearby. The glances told Brielle who was who and what they were here for. Many *really* wanted to know what was in the crate, while plenty more were keen to look anywhere else, deliberate in their efforts to blend into the crowd and not to draw attention to themselves. They were the dangerous ones, Brielle thought with a small, wry smile.

'Hmm?' Brielle replied, leaning back against the scruffy, padded seat and propping her elbows on its back as she looked around at the crowd one last time before addressing the waitress's question. 'I don't suppose you stock Erisian Hors d'age?' she said, knowing full well they didn't.

The waitress looked blankly back at Brielle, and just for a moment she suspected the girl might have undergone some form of pre-frontal neurosurgery, though her forehead bore no obvious scars.

'Ganymedian Marc?' she pressed mischievously, her curiosity piqued by the waitress's continued silence. Maybe she was under some form of xenos dominance, Brielle thought, like those priests on Briganta Regis...

'Asuave?' she said finally, realising she wasn't going to get an entertaining reaction.

'Certainly, ma'am,' the waitress replied. 'Terran vintage is it? Void-sealed to give that complex flavour...?'

Brielle's eyes narrowed and Ganna coughed uncomfortably. 'Two shots of whatever you've got,' she said finally, slightly put out by the sudden feeling that it was *she* who had been made sport of. Before she could say anything more, the waitress had disappeared into the crowd, leaving Brielle and Ganna with a view of the large stage dominating the establishment.

'Mistress,' said Ganna. It was obvious he was about to chastise her as only a retainer as valued as he would ever dare. 'Do we really want to draw so much attention to ourselves?'

Brielle grinned widely as she settled in for the wait for the drinks. 'Yes, Ganna. That's exactly what we want. Now will you relax?'

With that, Brielle set her feet upon the low table, crossing her heavy boots as she tried to work out what was happening on the gilded stage. Entertainment varied so wildly across the Imperium it was often damn near impossible to decipher what was going on, each style depending on so many different cultural idioms they made little or no sense to outsiders. Even amongst those cultures that weren't rooted in a single location, the galaxy was such a huge place that what entertained one audience was utterly impenetrable to another. Nevertheless, Brielle had been raised in the uniquely free, wide-roaming culture of a rogue trader clan, and certainly considered herself open minded when it came to such things. What she saw unfolding on the stage before her however was quite some way from anything she had seen before.

The stage was obscured by banks of drifting smoke illuminated red, violet and purple by the array of lumen-bulbs mounted at its head, but as Brielle watched, the smoke drifted past, turning what was a hazy, half-seen blur into something shockingly solid. At the centre of the stage stood an impossibly tall, almost skeletally thin man wearing a bizarre costume that seemed to be made from a hundred different items of clothing thrown randomly together. On his head he wore a tall stovepipe hat and his eyes were made bug-like and bulging by a pair of heavy duty goggles inset with magnifying glass. He held in one hand an ancient brass vox-horn, while the other gesticulated towards the other dozen or so figures sharing the stage with him.

The stage show was clearly some form of exhibition, and the spectacle on display was a group of mutants whose bodies were so malformed by genetic deviation they would have been shot on sight on any civilised world, and most frontier or badland ones too. Brielle's first reaction was to reach for the laspistol holstered in her belt, but she caught herself before her hand could close around the grip. Clearly, if the mutants were dangerous they wouldn't be on show in such a way, she told herself, though in truth she was far from convinced that was the case.

The largest of the mutants was a hulking brute, and Brielle was only slightly relieved to see its ankles were clapped in irons, a long, heavy chain snaking off behind the striped curtain behind. It was at least as massive as an ogryn, one of the stable, largely tolerated mutant strains recognised by most of the Imperium as a sanctioned branch of the human family tree. But its size was the only thing the beast had in common with the ogryns. Its skin looked like pock-marked bark and its hands, which were clad in heavy metal straps, were long, serrated claws. Its face was barely visible off-centre in its chest, and consisted of a huge lower jaw, a massive brow and a pair of beady black eyes nestled in the folds between.

As if this hulking brute wasn't unusual enough, the rest of the mutants clustered on the stage were just as extreme, though thankfully none were anywhere near so large. One had multiple-jointed arms three times the normal length, while another had three heads, none of which had any visible mouth. One mutant was little more than a head mounted in a bizarre mechanical ambulatory contraption, while another had no head at all, its facial features set instead in the centre of a grossly distended belly.

With a flourish that brought forth another wave of applause from the audience, the scarecrow-like impresario introduced the next act. The lights dimmed to be replaced by a single, harsh sodium beam, and as the applause died away a stir of movement from overhead drew Brielle's attention.

To a flurry of wheezing, atonal music emanating from a pit out of sight in front of the stage, a garishly painted hoop descended from the rafters over the stage, and seated daintily upon it was a female figure that sent the crowd truly wild. Its legs were fused together into a shape resembling the body of a fish, but that was far from its strangest feature. Upon its shoulders sat two heads, each of which was dominated by hugely pouting, bright red lips. Neither face had any other features, yet the crowd clearly viewed the creature as the very pinnacle of female beauty. Even as Brielle watched, the figure stirred into motion, her hips writhing suggestively until the hoop in which she was perched began to swing back and forth, each pass taking her further out over the whooping crowd, who reached upwards with groping hands to get just a touch of the object of their devotion.

'Enjoying the show?' a voice said from behind Brielle, and she froze, determined not to betray the fact that she hadn't heard the speaker approach. She had been entranced by the figure swinging in the hoop, hypnotised by the truly bizarre spectacle, but her attention, if not her gaze, was now entirely fixed on the man who had spoken.

'Seen better,' she said casually as Ganna turned around to look at the speaker directly. Brielle herself waited a few seconds more, then turned her head languidly to face him, praying as she did so that the front would work.

The speaker was, as she had guessed it would be, the man she had come to Quag to meet. His name was Baron Gussy, though Brielle had been unable to discover if either or both were titles, affectations or nicknames. While at first glance he appeared a tall, slender man of indeterminate age, that effect was only short-lived. He wore the outfit of some ancient princeling, consisting of a jerkin made of brightly shimmering material, puffed sleeves, garish hose and an improbably large codpiece that brought a dirty smirk to Brielle's lips. But again, as outlandish as it was, it wasn't his attire that made his appearance unusual. It was his features.

Baron Gussy was a patchwork man, in every sense of the word. Every one of his features had been bought, or more often simply taken, from someone else, and recombined into the form standing over Brielle right now. His face was a jigsaw puzzle, each small section grafted to the next. Brielle had no idea how he thought the effect looked anything like natural, for no two parts were exactly matched. Perhaps that was the point, she realised. Perhaps he sought to deliberately project an air of macabre eccentricity, the better to put those he dealt with at a disadvantage.

Brielle's source had told her that the effect was not limited to the baron's face, however, and that every organ in his body had been sourced from someone else's; to create, so he told the loose-lipped doxies that kept him warm each night, the perfect example of mankind. Brielle couldn't see it herself.

His mismatched lips twisted into an unctuous grin, the baron bowed slightly at the waist and with a flourish indicated a shadowed alcove guarded by several more stubjacks of the type she had confronted outside. As she stood, she couldn't help but notice the covetous glance he cast towards the crate held between the two servitors.

'Shall we retire to somewhere more private, Madam Gerrit?' he said. Making her way past the baron, Brielle could not help but notice the furtive glances cast her way by many amongst the crowd. Many were appeared unhealthily curious, but the acid glares of a pair of richly dressed women nearby made her scowl with irritation, for clearly they thought her some morsel picked up for the baron's entertainment.

'Come on, Ganna,' she snapped as the waitress returned with their Asuave, a nasty little glimmer in her otherwise blank eyes.

Accompanied by a trio of obviously glanded house stubjacks, Baron Gussy led Brielle and her party through the crowded establishment, the masses parting without complaint as they advanced. Brielle fought the urge to pat the pocket hidden in the breast of her frock coat, and forced herself to be calm. She knew what she was doing, she told herself. She was walking right into the jaws of a trap, that was what she was doing, but that was the entire point of this little expedition...

At length, the lead stubjack reached an archway decorated with some mad artisan's idea of baroque finery, and turned to wait as the rest caught up. Brielle took the brief opportunity to study the scene, acutely aware that she might have need to exit it very quickly indeed if this all went wrong. The low arch led off to a private seating area, a low table set between plush, cushioned sofas. A low-hanging chandelier, its guttering flames blue from the gas that fed them, provided just enough light for clandestine business to be conducted comfortably in the shadowy nook.

'Please,' Baron Gussy demurred as he took position beside the arch, the stubjack looming behind him. 'Make yourself comfortable. But first, Madam Gerrit, you will understand if I take a few... precautions.'

Brielle's eyes narrowed in suspicion, but she remained silent until she had some idea what the baron was intimating. Eyes open, mouth shut; that was what her father had taught her, and he'd done all right for himself, she mused.

At a nod from the baron, the stubjack following on behind the group reached into the inside of his jacket, Brielle's breath catching in her throat as she and Ganna exchanged a silent look. She doubted Gussy intended harm, not quite yet at least, yet she was still relieved when the stubjack pulled nothing more dangerous than a portable scanning device from his pocket.

Brielle swallowed hard, but kept her expression as uncaring as she could as the stubjack ambled up to her, the scanner's main unit in one hand and its detectrix-wand in the other. She raised one eyebrow in mild surprise that the lump had the skills to operate the device. But then, she'd once seen a ptera-squirrel trained to serve drinks to the worthies of a minor Navigator House; only for the creature to enter the second stage of its life cycle, morph into a ravening beast of teeth and claws, and butcher half the family before the dessert course had even been fully served.

''scuse me, ma'am,' the man slurred as he approached, gesturing with the wand for Brielle to raise her arms. She felt a flush of irritation and the intense desire to knee the meathead in the groin, and the feeling only got more intense as he wafted the wand up and down, tracing the contours of her body as the control unit bleeped and burbled. Even when the machine chimed to indicate no hidden weapons had been detected, the stubjack continued to play the wand over Brielle's body, until a cough from his master caused him to step back, a sneer on his grox-ugly face.

'She's clear,' the leering goon announced, and ambled up to Ganna with less enthusiasm than he had Brielle. 'Up,' he ordered, but before the pilot could raise his arms, Brielle interjected.

'He's heavily augmented. He'll set that thing off even on its lowest threshold.'

The stubjack hesitated and looked to the baron for guidance.

'Then he can wait out here,' said Gussy, his tone sending a quiver of silent revulsion up Brielle's spine. 'He'll be well looked after; you have my word on that. Now, Madam Gerrit, shall we?'

Brielle met Ganna's eye, the pilot nodding slightly to assure her that he was fine with waiting outside, though he was obviously less than happy to allow her to enter the baron's lair on her own. Telling herself it would all work out to plan, Brielle waved the two servitors forwards towards the arch.

'That won't be necessary, madam,' Baron Gussy said, the faintest hint of triumph in his voice.

Brielle's heart thundered in her chest, but she managed to keep her voice level as she replied, 'Baron, the exchange?'

'Has nothing to do with that crate, Brielle. I've been in this business for a while, you know, and can spot a decoy easily enough. I assume the item is secreted about your person, in some shielded pocket perhaps?'

Brielle afforded the smug bastard a shallow tip of the head and flashed him an ego-quenching smile. 'Fair enough,' she said, and gestured for the servitors to set the crate down out of the way, before stepping beneath the low archway and into the private alcove.

Without waiting to be invited, Brielle seated herself amongst the plush cushions, leaning back in an effort to appear entirely at ease with the situation despite what she felt inside. The air was sweet with incense, and not the sacred type burned in the shrines of the Ecclesiarchy. Despite its veneer of luxury, the place was cheap and dirty, soiled with a heady mix of sin and ennui.

'Ah,' said the baron, his voice dripping with what he evidently thought was sophistication and charm. Brielle had been patronised by far better men than he and she only ever tolerated it when there was a profit to be made. Now, sadly, was one of those times. 'Make yourself comfortable, my dear, and we'll begin.'

With a curt gesture, the baron despatched one of the stubjacks to stand in the archway, before seating himself opposite the low table from Brielle. The flickering gaslight cast by the low chandelier seemed to exaggerate the patchwork effect of his skin and highlight the fact that each of his eyes was a different colour and size. In fact, the way he was sitting, it appeared almost as if his legs were a different length, the joints somehow wrong.

'I'm afraid we're all out of Erisian Hors d'age,' he said, a sly glint in his eye – the smaller, dark brown one. 'Though I was once offered an early first century M.37 amasec from the equatorial foothills of San Leor.'

Always the amasec, Brielle thought to herself. With a million worlds in the Imperium you'd think these people would try something different...

'I'm fine,' Brielle replied, not actually wanting to risk drinking whatever might be set before her.

'Quite sensible,' said the baron. 'Perhaps later, after we've done business, eh?'

Not on your life, Brielle thought sharply. 'That would be nice,' she said sweetly. 'Speaking of which...?'

'Indeed,' said the baron, reclining back into the cushioned seating as he spoke. It was clear from the predatory glint in his eye that he was about to play all of his hand at once, as Brielle had been counting on him doing. 'You have the item on your person. Please place it on the table where I can see it.'

Hesitating slightly for effect, Brielle smiled coyly. She reached up and slid her hand into the lining of her frock coat's left breast, watching him follow the movement with his mismatched eyes. With a deft motion, she unsealed the hidden, null-weave lined pocket and withdrew an object the size and shape of a simple, unadorned ring.

Reaching forwards slowly, she placed the ring in the centre of the table, before leaning back to watch the baron's reaction. By the gleam in his eye, the larger, blue one this time, she knew he was hooked.

'What is its pedigree?' he said, his gaze fixed with unwavering intensity on the small item.

'It was retrieved from one of the rediscovered fane worlds spinward of the Ring of Fire,' said Brielle, and as far as she knew it had been.

'By whom?' he demanded, his voice tinged with something akin to lust.

'By a flesh-wright clan out of the fourth quadrant,' she said, though that part of the tale was far from certain too.

'And you came into possession of it how?' he leered, his mask of sophistication and charm now almost entirely slipped. 'Tell me how you found this... *wonder*.'

'The flesh-wrights were contracted by a... competitor of the Arcadius,' she said, more certain of this part of the story, for she had been present throughout much of it. 'But they came off worse in a small war over trade rights with the Ultima Centauri annex. This,' she waved languidly towards the ring, 'was part of the settlement.'

'Have you... tested it?' the baron all but whispered.

You must be mad, Brielle thought. She knew full well what it was said to be capable of. The ring was said to be imbued with the power of some impossibly ancient and thankfully extinct xenos race that, when worn, reshaped the flesh of the bearer into new and extreme forms. It was said that it took a mind of great power to control the drastic process, but that the results were spectacular, or hideous, depending on the willpower of the wearer. Though Brielle herself was undecided on the veracity of the claims, she had little doubt that Baron Gussy was mad enough to believe them and to try to utilise the artefact's power, hence the exchange.

Speaking of which, Brielle thought. 'And you have the icon ready?' she asked, making every effort to sound casual and relaxed despite her fluttering belly. If he'd just produce the icon and let her get on her way, she knew an eldar corsair prince who was prepared to cede a paradise world for possession of it.

But she knew it wasn't going to be that simple.

Tearing his eyes from the small ring in the centre of the table, Baron Gussy leaned back in the sofa and as he did so, he reached up to his own collar, just as Brielle had minutes before. Undoing the first few buttons of his jerkin and the shirt beneath, he revealed far more than the patchwork skin of his chest. About his neck, secured by a simple leather thong, was a gleaming, bone-white pendant, a sacred icon a mad alien was prepared to pay an entire world to possess.

'How much is this worth to you?' said Gussy.

Here we go, thought Brielle. She knew he wouldn't be able to resist it, though a small part of her had dared hope he might be reasonable.

'How much are *you* worth?' he continued.

'Baron,' she said, interrupting him in the hope that he might allow himself to be diverted, and to avoid the otherwise inevitable unpleasantness. 'I'd far rather...'

'*I'd* far rather you listen, my dear,' he interjected. 'Rather than interrupt. It's so rude.'

Brielle nodded sullenly, allowing the fool his moment of vainglory.

'I've decided I want to expand my operations. I think a spot of extortion is in order.'

Brielle sighed and cast her eyes to the ceiling in what she hoped was a display of nonchalant dismissal. 'Go on then,' she breathed. 'Name it.'

The little display had the effect Brielle had hoped for, the baron's expression changing instantly from haughty pseudo-sophistication to flushed annoyance. Strange, she thought, how each section of the flesh on his patchwork face went a slightly different colour.

'You shall remain here,' he said coldly, all pretence of civility gone. 'Your father shall receive my demand when I've considered just what you might be worth.'

'You can't even *pronounce* how much I'm worth,' Brielle replied, her voice low and dangerous. This idiot was really starting to annoy her now.

'Oh, I wouldn't be so sure,' said Gussy. 'I'm told the trade routes on the far eastern fringe have been drying up for a few years now. They say there's a shadow out there, and that worlds are just falling silent, one system at a time.'

Brielle said nothing. Eyes open, mouth shut.

'Remind me,' said Gussy. 'Where does the Arcadius derive most of its wealth...?'

'You don't know half what you think you do, baron,' Brielle all but growled, though in truth it surprised her just how much knowledge of her family's business he had. It was true that something was stirring out beyond the eastern fringe and that it was affecting the trade routes the Clan Arcadius had relied upon for generations, but that was far from the whole picture.

'I know enough,' he snapped. 'Enough to know that your father might be keen to shed certain peripheral assets to have you returned safely to him.'

'Peripheral assets?' said Brielle. 'What are you...'

'I know the Arcadius owns half of Zealandia. How about that for an opening offer, hmm?'

Brielle was stunned. How this petty underworld crimelord thought he could get away with wresting ownership of a significant Terran conurbation was beyond her. Clearly, the man's ego outmatched his ability by some degree.

'Enough,' she said, waving a hand dismissively and leaning back once more. With a sudden motion, she swung her legs up and planted her booted feet on the low table, sending the priceless xenos ring pattering across the stained carpet. Gussy tried as hard as he could to look unconcerned, but his mismatched eyes tracked the ring as it rolled to a halt, then they switched back to Brielle. 'I'm offering you this one chance to play nice, Baron Gussy, then things get messy. Understood?'

The baron's lips twisted into a mocking sneer. Messy it is then.

Flicking her head back in a gesture that some might have taken for arrogance, Brielle caused one of her intricately plaited braids of dark hair to drop down across her face. She made to reach up and hook the errant strand away, but as finger and thumb closed about the braid, she squeezed, triggering the small, Jokaero-built device secreted within.

'This,' she said to the baron, 'is a ground to orbit transmitter.'

'Nonsense,' he replied, though he licked his lips with evident nervousness. 'There's no way you'd have got it through the scanner.'

'Perhaps I wouldn't have, if your goon had had his mind on his duty, and not my...'

'You're bluffing.'

'My light cruiser is, right now, holding geosynchronous orbit overhead. My spies have passed on the locations of a number of your holdings out in the swamps, and even as we speak, several macro-scale bombardment batteries are trained on each. If I'm not back soon, *with* the icon, those holdings are getting bombed right back to the Dark Age.

'Got it?'

'You're bluffing,' he repeated, before standing as if to intimidate her.

Her gaze fixed unblinkingly on his, Brielle brought the lock of hair to her mouth, squeezed, and said, 'Fairlight, target alpha, now.'

A bead of sweat appeared on one of the sections of flesh on Baron Gussy's forehead and he flexed his velvet-gloved hands as he stood over the reclining Brielle. The moment stretched on for what seemed an age, and then a ghost of a smirk appeared at the baron's lips as he evidently decided that Brielle was, as he had hoped, bluffing.

But she wasn't. His smile vanished as a sound like distant thunder rolled over Quagtown, a low, growling tremor passing up through the rock, transmitted through the metal and timber construction and causing the flickering chandelier to shake ever so slightly, yet ominously.

Gussy was the first to break the impasse, and he turned sharply to the house stubjack standing in the archway. 'Find out what that was, now!'

'That was your safe house twenty kilometres due south taking a direct hit from an orbital bombardment,' she said, not trying particularly hard not to smirk.

'What...?' he stammered. 'How did you...?'

'And that,' she said as a second, far stronger rumble brought a wave of panicked shouts from the crowd in the main part of the palace, 'was your *secret* clearing house on the ridgeline seventy east.'

'You spoiled little harpy!' the baron spat, his rage exploding as several of his guards pressed into the archway with concern and confusion writ large on their faces. Brielle simply smiled and remained outwardly nonchalant, though she knew the moment of truth was at hand.

'Give me the icon,' she said flatly, 'and your little pleasure lodge on the coast doesn't get flattened.'

His eyes wide with dumb horror, the baron reached up to the icon at this throat and grasped it in a fist. 'You're mad! I'm not giving you a...'

In the blink of an eye, Brielle was up off of the cushioned sofa, propelling herself through the air in a cat-like leap that brought her into contact with the stunned baron. The two went down in a confused tangle, and when they came up again, the guards pressing in with pistols raised, Brielle had Gussy by the neck. One hand was twisted about the thong on which the eldar icon hung, constricting his neck and cutting off his breathing. Even now, each segment of his patchwork face was going a different shade of purple. The other hand was reaching under the upturned table, retrieving something mislaid but a moment before.

'Back, meatheads!' Brielle shouted, putting as much authority as she could into the order. 'Ganna! Are you there, Ganna?' she shouted as the guards took a step back, clearly not knowing what the hell to do.

'Here, mistress!' the pilot's strained voice sounded from somewhere behind the wall of hired muscle. 'I'm a little...'

'Let him go or your boss gets it,' Brielle demanded, one hand twisting the thong still more and causing the baron to squeal in sudden panic while the other deposited a small object in a voluminous coat pocket.

'Do it!' he managed, his voice high-pitched and breathless. 'Do as she says!'

There was a moment of tense, uncertain silence, before the guards lowered their pistols and started backing out of the alcove, though they moved slowly and were obviously ready to react to any sudden movement.

Brielle jerked on the thong and shoved Gussy forwards, using his stumbling body as a shield should any of the goons open fire. It was a somewhat hollow gesture, she knew, and one that relied on them being more concerned that their boss lived than that she died, but it seemed to be having the desired effect. Within seconds, the goons had all backed out of the alcove, revealing Ganna and the servitors, the former's concern etched across his face, the latter as blank-eyed and vacant as ever.

'Time we were leaving,' said Brielle, moving backwards towards the entrance. Ganna voiced a word of command and he and the two servitors set off after her, the already spooked crowd scattering at the sight of so many drawn weapons.

Just then, one of the guards made the worst move of his career. Raising a knock-off Arbites-issue stubber, he shouted, 'Let him go or I'll shoot your damn head clean off your...'

The idiot never got to complete his sentence, a shockingly loud blast filling the air and turning his entire chest cavity into a smoking, ragged mess even as he looked down with incomprehension. A moment later, the guard crashed backwards to the deck, revealing

Ganna, his concealed, forearm mounted bolt pistol ready to fire at anyone else that fancied early retirement.

'*Now* it's time we were leaving...' said Brielle, dragging the squirming Baron Gussy by the neck as she reached the hatch.

The flight back to the landing pad took far longer than Brielle had planned, for the entire town was in uproar. It wasn't the panic at the Quagtown Palace that Brielle had unleashed that had got the population so stirred up, but the continuous stream of fire lancing down through the murky clouds to strike death and destruction at seemingly random points out in the swamplands surrounding the settlement. Though the target of every bombardment was in fact one of Baron Gussy's holdings, the rest of the criminal fraternity weren't to know that. Every petty crime lord in the town thought he was the target of the attacks, and that they were being mounted by some bitter rival suddenly possessed of an overwhelming weight of orbital firepower.

At length however Brielle, her prisoner, who was by now being carried between the two servitors, and Ganna reached the head of the ramshackle iron stairway leading up to the landing pad. The deck was a riot of activity as the ground crew fought to get craft ready for a hasty departure, but Brielle's shuttle was, fortunately, still present, and intact. The guards she had employed to watch over the shuttle, largely as a means of announcing her presence to the local crime scene, were milling nearby, more interested in the distant, blossoming explosions than doing their job.

Knowing her small party had but seconds before they were noticed, Brielle rounded on the baron and gripped the alien icon hung about his neck. 'Mine, I think,' she said, before tearing it free with a savage twist.

'The shuttle!' Brielle yelled to her pilot. 'Run!'

Ganna and Brielle powered forwards, but the servitors were left behind, the struggling Baron Gussy still held firmly between them in their vice-like, biomechanical grip. In seconds, the pair had reached the shuttle and the access ramp was lowering on screaming hydraulics. The baron started raving at the guards to apprehend Brielle and her pilot.

The ramp seemed to Brielle to be lowering far slower than it ever had. The roar of a handgun split the air and a hard round *spanged* off the hull right by Brielle's head, forcing her to duck down as Ganna tracked the firer with his concealed weapon.

A burst of stubber fire from off to the left told the pair that a stand-up fight wasn't a great proposition, and an instant later the hull where Brielle had been standing just a moment before was peppered with rounds, sending up a riot of angry sparks.

Fortunately, the ramp was now lowered enough for Brielle to throw herself inside, and within seconds Ganna was in too, scrambling for the cockpit even as Brielle threw the hatch into reverse and hard rounds continued to ricochet from the hull.

At the sound of the engines powering up to full output, Brielle collapsed onto the deck, her head spinning with a potent mix of adrenaline and relief. Those, and something more, she thought as she collapsed in a fit of dirty giggles.

It took Baron Gussy's minions almost an hour to prise the mind-locked servitors' grip off of his arms, and by the time they had, he was beyond furious. Stalking back to the Quagtown Palace, his guards barging the panicked locals out of his path, he raged at this turn of events. He had sought to take advantage of a rumour that the fortunes of the Arcadius were on the wane thanks to a decline in trade from the eastern fringe, but he was lucky to have come away with his life. Lucien Gerrit's daughter was a she-devil, he saw, but she had made one crucial mistake. She had left him alive, an enemy at her back. That thought fired him with a curious mix of dread and desire. How he longed to break the Arcadius, he thought, and how he'd like to...

Before he realised it, the baron was back at the palace, its main hall now empty of patrons and the floors strewn with the detritus of panic. Drinking vessels were scattered or smashed across the ground and tables and chairs were upturned. His mouth twisting into a nasty sneer, Gussy made for his alcove, determined at least to recover the ring Brielle had offered in exchange for the eldar icon.

It wasn't there. Of course it wasn't, he thought. That harpy must have snatched it up in the confusion of her escape, and left him with nothing at all to show for his attempted double cross.

He could really use a drink, but it looked like the serving staff had all fled, along with the stampeding patrons. Resolving to fetch his own, he looked about for a discarded bottle, but instead, his eyes settled on the stasis crate Brielle's two servitors had carried into the palace. They had set it down by the alcove, he realised as his eyes narrowed in suspicion, at her word...

'No...' he breathed as his eyes darted nervously about the dark, empty hall. Several of the stitched-together segments of skin on his forehead began to sweat, and one of his mismatched eyes started to twitch involuntarily. 'No, no, no,' he stammered as he closed on the box, his gaze fixating on the status panel on its side, a red tell-tale indicating that the stasis field had just deactivated. 'There's no way you...'

But she had. Three seconds after the blinking light turned solid, the overloaded core of the plasma charge that had been placed in stasis an instant before it went critical detonated. Baron Gussy saw his fate an instant before it overtook him, the second to last thing to enter his mind a curse on the Arcadius and all their daughters. The very last thing to enter his mind was the ravening nucleonic fires of the plasma charge as its core went into meltdown, the discreet blast wave expanding to neatly and utterly destroy the shabby interior of the Quagtown Palace whilst leaving its exterior with barely a scratch. To the denizens of Quagtown, the bass roar was yet more evidence of their impending doom, touching off a stampede as hundreds fled to be anywhere but in the centre of their tumbledown settlement.

For many months after, only the toughest of mutants would be able to survive the radiation within that ramshackle shell. By that time, Brielle Gerrit would be light years away, perhaps visiting the golden shores of a paradise world that had recently come into her possession...

STAR OF DAMOCLES

Lucian Gerrit, rogue trader and master of the heavy cruiser *Oceanid*, stood before the wide viewing port of his vessel's bridge, his arms crossed behind his back.

'Any minute now...' Lucian muttered, scanning the black vista. 'Any minute...'

Without warning, the low growl of labouring plasma drives rattled the deck plates and the bridge lights dimmed for just an instant, before flickering back to full power. Lucian grunted his satisfaction as a turquoise and jade orb swung into view across the viewing port, to settle in the dead centre as the *Oceanid*'s helmsman steadied the ship's course.

'Sy'l'Kell in range, sir. Closing as ordered,' the helmsman called out, working the great levers and wheels that controlled the *Oceanid*'s bearing, speed and altitude.

'Thank you, Mister Raldi,' replied Lucian, turning his back on the viewing port and striding across the bridge. 'Continue as planned,' he said, sitting down in the worn leather seat of his command throne.

With the press of a control stud on the arm of the throne, the area in front of Lucian was filled with a static laced, greenish projection. The holograph, a priceless example of nigh extinct technology, projected a three dimensional image into the air, a grainy, flickering representation of the space around the *Oceanid*. Lucian's vessel was at the centre of the image, and a shoal of other icons formed behind him, each representing another starship.

'Station three,' Lucian called, addressing the half-man, half-machine servitor hard-wired into the communications console. 'Open a channel to the *Nomad*.'

In response to his order, the bridge address systems burst into angry life with white noise, before the servitor slowly nodded to indicate that the communications link was established with the other vessel.

'*Nomad*,' said Lucian, 'this is *Oceanid*. Do you read?'

'Aye, Lucian,' came the reply over the address system. 'This is Sarik, and I hear you loud and clear. Are you sure you're ready?'

Lucian chuckled out loud, refusing to be baited. 'Yes, Sarik, I'm ready. Just don't bite off more than you can chew. Lucian out!'

As the communications servitor cut the link, Lucian grinned as he imagined the expression on Sarik's face. Sarik was a Space Marine, and Lucian did not doubt he would be outraged at having been spoken to in such a manner. But Sarik could take a joke, of that Lucian was sure.

'Sir?' Helmsman Raldi interrupted Lucian's chain of thought. 'The *Nomad* is accelerating to attack speed. Match her?'

Lucian glanced out of the viewing port as his helmsman spoke, catching sight of a distant point of light speeding ahead. The *Nomad* was a frigate, far smaller than Lucian's heavy cruiser, but being a Space Marine vessel it was far more deadly than the average ship of her displacement.

'Well enough, helm. Offset by one-fifty as planned.'

The speck of light that was the *Nomad* sped off towards the rapidly enlarging globe that filled a large portion of the viewing port. The planet was called Sy'l'Kell, but the vessels were not headed towards the world itself. Studying the holograph, Lucian saw that his vessel was still a good distance from its target. He scanned the other ships holding formation with his. The *Rosetta* sat at three kilometres astern, a rogue trader cruiser captained by his son, Korvane, and another two kilometres further on, the cruiser *Fairlight*, commanded by his daughter, Brielle. He was gratified to see that both were exactly in position, for he had cause to keep a close eye on Brielle's actions, following her increasingly unpredictable behaviour of late. Dozens of other vessels were spread out across an area of space spanning fifty kilometres port and astern. Battlecruisers, cruisers and escorts arrowed towards a single point in high orbit around Sy'l'Kell, while half a dozen smaller vessels, frigates of a class similar to the *Nomad*, formed up with Sarik's vessel, more Space Marine frigates, each carrying a deadly cargo of the Emperor's finest.

Lucian spared a thought for their target, but only a brief one.

'Comms,' he called, 'give me the *Rosetta*.'

The bridge address system burst into life once more, the white noise even greater than before, the channel laced with a harsh, almost sub-sonic growl.

'Korvane?' Lucian called, 'Korvane, do you read me?' The channel hissed and growled, before a voice cut in suddenly.

'...ferance from the outer belt, attempting to compensate. I repeat. This is *Rosetta*. I read you, father, but the planet's outer rings are playing havoc with our transceivers and primary relays. Over.'

'I read you, Korvane,' Lucian replied. 'I'm picking up the interference too, and I can only see it getting worse as we close on the target. We'll just need to let the Astartes carry out their mission and cover as best we can. *Oceanid* out.'

Lucian glanced out of the viewing port once more, noting that Sy'l'Kell almost filled the armoured portal. Its glittering, icy rings scored the blackness of space, causing Lucian to wonder what manner of substance or reaction might be generating the interference they seemed to transmit across a wide area of the void.

'*Fairlight*,' he said, the communications servitor at station three patching him through to his daughter's vessel at once. The channel opened, the interference bursting through the address systems before the *Oceanid*'s machine systems curtailed the signal.

'Duma's rancid left foot!' Lucian cursed. 'If you can't invoke the buffers I might as well work the vox myself.' The servitor nodded in mute response, incapable of taking offence at its master's scorn. Before Lucian could continue his invective however, another voice emerged from the howling comms channel.

'*Oceanid*? *Oceanid*, this is *Fairlight*. I repeat, do you read me, father?'

'Receiving, Brielle,' replied Lucian. 'Proceed as planned. No deviation. Do you understand?'

The comms channel howled its cold white noise for long moments, before the reply cut through, Brielle's tone as chilled as the interference plaguing the communications system. 'Understood. *Fairlight* out.'

Lucian sighed, but put aside his frustration at his daughter's continued obstinacy. He looked instead to the flickering holograph, the device, or more accurately, the sub-space sensor banks that fed it, evidently beginning to suffer from the same interference plaguing the communications systems. Amid the grainy, imprecise projection, he finally saw the target. Looking up, through the wide viewing port now entirely filled by the globe of Sy'l'Kell, Lucian could just make out a tiny, blue pinprick of light.

Lucian felt his pulse race as adrenaline flooded his system. These were the moments he lived for.

'Begin approach, my lord?' Helmsman Raldi enquired, Lucian noting the sardonic tone in the man's voice. Evidently, the master of the *Oceanid* was not the only man to enjoy the rush of ship-to-ship combat.

'Mister Raldi, you have the helm.'

Lucian leaned back into the command throne as he felt the pitch of the *Oceanid*'s mighty plasma drives deepen. The bridge illumination switched to a bloody red, and the apocalyptic wail of the general quarters' klaxon sounded throughout the vessel. The tone of the ancient drives grew lower as their volume increased, and every surface of the bridge shook visibly as virtually immeasurable power was bled from the plasma core and squeezed through the engines.

Lucian smiled as he watched the holograph, the relative positions of the other vessels swinging wildly as Raldi brought the *Oceanid* into a stately turn to starboard. Only the *Nomad* was ahead of Lucian's vessel, the small frigate all but lost against the lurid glow of the planet's oceans far below.

'Shields up,' Lucian ordered. 'Frontal arc, minimal bleed.'

Memories of his last space battle still only too fresh in his mind, Lucian determined not to take any risks against this foe. He looked at the holograph to check that the master of the *Nomad* had done likewise, when a curse from a sub-officer caused him to look up.

'What?' Lucian demanded of the man seated at the astrographics station.

'It's hard to tell with all the interference, my lord.'

Lucian rose to his feet and crossed the bridge to loom over the man's shoulder. 'Let me see.'

Lucian stared at the man's console, reams of data scrolling across its banks of flickering screens. His mind raced as he tried to piece together exactly what he was seeing. Interference, certainly, and there was something else, but what?

'Station nine!' Lucian called. 'Give me a near space reading, now.'

The servitor stationed at the adjacent console nodded, machine nonsense squealing from the speaker grill crudely grafted into the flesh of its neck. The main pict-slate at the centre of its console lit up with a representation of the gravimetrics readings of the area of space around the *Oceanid*.

Once more, Lucian's mind raced as he attempted to assimilate the information presented on the screen. No wonder he needed so many servitors, he mused, dismissing the thought as his eyes fixed on an anomaly.

There, in the lee of the target, into which his vessel's active sensors could not reach, there was a ripple in the fabric of the void, a signature he had seen before.

'Sarik!' He bellowed, the servitor at the comms station opening the channel immediately.

Through the wail of interference, Sarik's voice came back over the bridge address system.

'Gerrit? Go ahead, but make it quick. I'm somewhat busy.'

'Sarik, divert all power to your port shield, now.'

'Are you...?'

'Do it!'

The communications channel went abruptly silent. Lucian held his breath, not realising he was doing so, before the holograph showed that the *Nomad* was rapidly bleeding power from its main drives while its shield was being raised. He let out his breath. He'd apologise later, he mused, if he got the chance.

An instant later, and the viewing port was filled with a great, blinding flash of purest white light. Having closed his eyes by reflex, it took a moment for Lucian's vision to clear. Nevertheless, flickering nerve lights rendered him almost blind.

'Report!' He bellowed, not caring who answered.

'Ultra-high velocity projectile, my lord. We've seen them before,' Lucian's ordnance officer replied.

His vision clearing, Lucian looked to the holograph. The projectile had struck the *Nomad* amidships, half way down her port bow. Looking up, Lucian saw from where the projectile had been fired, as a long silhouette glided into view against the turquoise oceans of Sy'l'Kell.

'I knew it,' Lucian said. 'I absolutely knew the camel toed bastards would try it on.'

Exhilaration flooded through Lucian's body as he sat in his command throne once more, gripping the worn arms as generations of his forebears had done before him.

'Helm, twenty to port. Ordnance, prepare a broadside.'

As the helmsman laboured at his wheel and levers, Lucian watched as the opening moves of the coming battle played out before him. The target, towards which the stricken Space Marine frigate still sped, was now visible. A mighty space station, shaped like some giant mushroom, blue lights twinkling up and down its stalk, wallowed at the centre of the viewing port, its bulk black against the lurid seas of the planet around which it orbited. A vessel emerged from behind that station; the same vessel that had come so close to destroying, in a single shot, a frigate of the White Scars Chapter of the Adeptus Astartes. Lucian's grin became a feral snarl and his eyes narrowed as the tau vessel cleared the station it had been hiding behind.

'Enemy vessel powering up for another shot at the *Nomad*, my lord,' called the ordnance officer. 'She's going for the kill shot, sir.'

'That's what she thinks,' replied Lucian. 'Ordnance? Open fire!'

'But, sir,' the ordnance officer sputtered, 'I have no firing solution. We'll...'

'I said open fire damn you!' bellowed Lucian. 'Do it, or so help me...'

Lucian was glad to see that the officer had the presence of mind to order the broadside before his master could complete, or indeed enact, his threat. The *Oceanid* shuddered as the port weapons batteries unleashed a fearsome barrage towards the tau vessel. Lacking a solid firing solution for the war spirits of the super-heavy munitions to follow, the majority of the shells went wide, their fuses detonating them at random across the space between the two ships.

No matter. If Lucian had meant to destroy the tau ship he would have waited, but had he done that, the *Nomad* would now be smeared across a hundred square kilometres of local space. The tau vessel aborted its shot against the Space Marine frigate, its blunt nose coming around to face the greater threat presented by the *Oceanid*.

'My thanks, Gerrit. I am in your debt.' Sarik's voice came over the address system.

'You're welcome,' replied Lucian. 'Good hunting.'

Now, he thought, I've got a tau vessel to take out before it ruins everything. As the explosions cleared, the greasy black smoke left in their wake almost entirely obscured the other vessel. Lucian judged that the distance between the two ships would level at an impossibly close five hundred metres before they parted once more. Five hundred metres, he mused, remembering just how deadly another tau vessel had almost proved at such a close range in a previous engagement. There was too little time for an effective broadside, but he had other tricks up his sleeve that the tau had yet to see. Besides which, he thought, it doesn't pay to let the enemy get too used to one's tactics.

'Ordnance, I want a focused lance battery strike on the module aft of the central transverse,' he said, indicating one of the many blocky, modular units the tau vessel appeared to be carrying slung beneath its long spine.

'Aye, sir,' replied the ordnance officer, Lucian noting with satisfaction that the officer was plotting the lance strike against the exact point he had intended.

At seven hundred metres, Lucian could make out the details of the flanks of the tau vessel, though he could not fathom the meaning of the many symbols or icons applied to its surface.

'I have a solution, my lord,' the officer said. 'Fire pattern set.'

Lucian knew that even now, the sweating crews in the lance batteries atop the *Oceanid* would be toiling at the traversing mechanisms of their turrets, cursing crew chiefs threatening them with eternal damnation should they falter in their work.

At six hundred metres, the drifting smoke and debris of the

broadside cleared enough for Lucian to pick out the point against which he had ordered the lance strike. At five hundred and fifty metres, he saw it clearly, and so did the ordnance officer, who communicated a series of final adjustments to the turret crews. A horizontal line of clear blue light appeared at the centre of the module, gaining in height as it was revealed to be an armoured blast door opening upwards. A row of armoured figures was framed against the blue light, the like of which Lucian had seen before, from a distance, the last time he had fought the tau.

'You have fire control, Mister Batista.'

'Thank you, sir,' replied the ordnance officer, adjusting his uniform jacket, straightening his back and clearing his throat.

'Now would be good,' added Lucian.

'Yes, my lord.' The officer depressed the control stud that passed the fire order to the lance turrets. An instant later the lance batteries spat a searing beam of condensed atomic fire at the tau vessel, parting the smoky clouds, spearing the open bay, vaporising the armoured figures, and passing clean out of the other side of the module, accompanied by a rapidly expanding cone of fire and debris.

'Target well struck, sir,' the ordnance officer reported.

'Well enough, Mister Batista,' Lucian replied. 'Prepare for a second strike.' Lucian scanned the flanks of the enemy vessel as the range closed to five hundred metres, seeking further armoured bays from which the battle suits he had seen used before might deploy.

'Negative, my lord,' the officer replied, doubt obvious in his voice.

'Negative?' Lucian asked. 'Report.'

'Something's blocking the targeting mechanisms, overloading their machine spirits, my lord. I can't...'

'The interference?' asked Lucian, theorising that the incessant interference flooding from the rings of Sy'l'Kell was somehow confounding the *Oceanid*'s targeting arrays.

'No sir, there's something else.'

Damn these xenos to the Gideon Confluence, thought Lucian, at once irritated and impressed by the Tau's ingenuity. He crossed to the wide viewing port and looked out across the narrow span of smoky void between the two vessels. The ships were rapidly passing one another in opposite directions, the tau vessel veering to its port in a course that would take it away from the *Oceanid* and towards the station. Odd, thought Lucian. He had expected the enemy to close even further in order to make full use of the extra-vehicular armoured suits, as they had done against Korvane's vessel in the last battle.

Even as Lucian watched, the wound punched in the tau ship by his lance strike slid past, almost filling the entire viewing port. He judged the hole to be at least twenty metres in diameter, and as it passed across the dead centre of the port, he was afforded a view right through the enemy vessel, to open space beyond. The *Nomad* passed across that space, the tau ship turning towards her.

Lucian realised why the enemy ship was seeking to disengage from his own: it was seeking to hold him off while it swung around on the smaller frigate. He drew breath to order a change in course, when another sight greeted his eyes. A shoal of miniscule white objects, each propelled by a small, blue jet, was swarming across the gap between the two ships. So these were the cause of the fire control failure, Lucian realised. They were some kind of decoy, each, judging by their movements, possessed of some manner of machine intelligence, their density and erratic course confounding any effort to get a target lock on their mother ship.

'I can't get a solution at this range, my lord,' the ordnance officer reported. 'Whatever those things are, each one has an etheric signature far in excess of its size. All together like that, at such close range...'

'Saint Katherine's pasty arse,' Lucian cursed, causing the ordnance officer to blush and the helmsman to smirk. 'They're after the *Nomad*, and if they get her this whole operation will have been a waste of time. Mister Raldi, bring us in hard on the orbital, I want every ounce of power through the mains, but be ready on the retros.'

As the helmsman nodded his understanding, Lucian ordered a comms channel to the *Nomad* to be opened.

'Sarik, do you read?'

Lucian glared out of the viewing port as he awaited the frigate's reply. The tau vessel had passed from view, to reveal the tau orbital beyond, and in its shadow, the floundering Space Marine vessel. Fires raged across the *Nomad*'s port flank. Misty contrails snaking from her aft section betrayed a massive hull breach through which oxygen was bleeding uncontrollably.

An angry burst of static was followed by the distorted, barely audible voice of the Space Marine. 'Aye Lucian, I read. We're preparing for our run.'

'You won't make it at this rate, Sarik,' Lucian replied, knowing full well that he was pushing the Space Marine's bounds in speaking to him in such a manner, but continuing regardless. 'That vessel has you in its sights, and in your state you can't hold it off for long enough. Will you accept my aid?'

For a long moment, only hissing, popping static was audible over the communications channel. Lucian prayed that the Space Marine would put pride aside, just this once, and accept the aid of another. Then Sarik's voice came back.

'You and I shall have words, Lucian Gerrit, when this is over. In the meantime, speak your plan.'

Lucian felt relief flood his system, but saw that he did not have the luxury of time. 'We'll be with you shortly, Sarik. In the meantime, I suggest you continue on your course on momentum only, and shunt all available power to your aft shields. Understood?'

'Understood,' came the reply, this time without delay. '*Nomad* out.'

'Well enough,' said Lucian, as he sat in his command throne and turned his attention to the holograph. He took in the relative positions of the remainder of the fleet. He was gratified to see that his children's vessels had maintained formation with his own, keeping a distance as ordered, yet close enough to respond to any order he might issue. He was even more pleased when he saw that the other vessels, even further out, had yet to close in on the action. He smirked as he imagined the scenes on the decks of those ships, picturing the various captains raging in jealously as they watched Lucian save the Space Marines' bacon and take all the glory.

Steady, he thought to himself. The glory was not his yet, and he still had a Space Marine frigate to rescue, a tau cruiser to take care of, and a space station to capture. This would match the exploits of old Abad, if he could pull it off, Lucian mused. Abad had taken on a Reek voidswarm at the Battle of Ghallenburg, and single-handedly stemmed the tide of filthy xenos interface vessels as they made planetfall. Lucian would do likewise, he determined, and to hell with the others.

'Approaching orbital, my lord,' the helmsman reported, interrupting Lucian's rumination. He looked to the holograph and saw that the alien space station lay three and a half thousand metres off the starboard bow. The tau vessel was completing a stately turn that would bring it directly behind the *Nomad*. It had yet to open fire, but Lucian judged that it would not be long.

'Trim mains, Mister Raldi. Hard to starboard, full burn all port retro banks.'

Lucian stared at the holograph as the helmsman carried out his orders, feeling the enormous gravitational forces exerting themselves on his ship as it changed course sharply. The banks of mighty retro thrusters mounted along the length of the port side coughed into life as power was cut from the main drives, the *Oceanid* entering a manoeuvre that would see her slingshot right around the alien space station.

Then, the ordnance officer called aloud, 'Brace for enemy fire!' Klaxons echoed up and down the *Oceanid*'s companionways, warning the crew of incoming fire, but Lucian knew that his ship was unlikely to be the target, for the tau had a more choice prey in their sights.

Lucian closed his eyes against the bright discharge of the tau's ultra-high velocity projectile weapon, his vision turning red for an instant, despite the fact that his eyes were closed tight. An instant later the viewing port dimmed automatically, once again, its simple spirit too slow to respond to the flash.

'*Nomad* struck, my lord,' called out the ordnance officer. 'The enemy fired her port weapon, sir. *Nomad*'s shields took the worst of it, but I think her projectors took some feedback. Second shot any moment...'

The tau vessel fired a second time, and Lucian was thankful that the viewing port was still dimmed. Despite this, he saw the tau space station etched in stark silhouette, for the *Oceanid* was now on its far side with the tau ship on the other. He looked to the ordnance officer, who read off his report.

'*Nomad* struck again, sir. Port weapon again. Her shields are almost gone. I don't think she'll survive a third shot.'

'Hm,' replied Lucian. He'd seen the damage Space Marine warships could take, and was prepared to gamble that the *Nomad* would hold together. He had no choice, for his vessel would not complete its manoeuvre for several more, long, potentially painful minutes. Furthermore, he considered, why hadn't the tau ship fired its prow-mounted weapon?

As the *Oceanid* ploughed on, edging around the tau space station, Lucian's eyes were glued to the holograph. He saw that the tau vessel was trying to overtake the *Nomad*. The enemy ship was seeking to line herself up with the limping Space Marine frigate, which was careening towards the space station by way of momentum alone, every last portion of energy devoted to maintaining its rapidly failing rear shields.

Lucian saw hope in the tau's actions. If he could intercept their ship before they were lined up, he knew he would have them. If he could not, then all was lost, for the tau would have the perfect firing solution and the frigate would be doomed. Then the thought resurfaced: why hadn't they used their prow-mounted projectile?

'They're launching something,' reported the ordnance officer. 'More of the decoys.'

Why were the tau launching decoys? Lucian's mind filtered the possibilities, but he was interrupted before completing his chain of thought.

'In position, my lord,' reported the helmsman.

'Open fire, sir?' asked the ordnance officer.

'Hold, Mister Batista,' Lucian replied. 'There's something else going on.'

The *Oceanid* having completed its long arc around the tau space station, Lucian's vessel was heading straight towards the prow of the enemy ship. Crossing to the viewing port and squinting to make out the enemy ship as the distance closed, Lucian yelped in elation.

'I congratulate you, Mister Batista!'

'Sir?' The ordnance officer replied, confusion writ large upon his features.

Lucian laughed out loud for the sheer joy of it. 'Your untargeted broadside, Mister Batista. Evidently, something struck.'

As the *Oceanid* closed on the tau vessel, a great gash upon its blunt, armoured prow became clearly visible. The position, Lucian knew from prior experience against tau cruisers, of its forward weapon turret.

The question remained, Lucian mused, as to why the tau had launched the swarm of decoys, which was closing in on the *Nomad*'s drive section even as he watched. Then it came to him, and he bellowed for the communications channel to the Space Marine frigate to be opened one more.

'Sarik?' Only interference answered him, louder and more intense than ever. Lucian realised that the decoys, combined with the static coming from the rings of Sy'l'Kell, must be blocking the ship-to-ship channels entirely.

'Comms. Bleed all power from all available systems to near space vox.'

Lucian watched as the swarm of tau decoys arrowed towards the vulnerable aft section of the *Nomad*. They can't fire on me, he told himself, not with their prow turret out of action, but running with no shields in the middle of a space battle was considered bad practice, even by his standards.

A flashing tell-tale informed Lucian that the near-space vox was receiving all the power it ever would. This had better work.

'Sarik!' Lucian shouted, praying that his voice was being transmitted at full signal strength on all available frequencies. 'Sarik, power up your main drives right now!'

An instant later Lucian saw that his transmission had got through. The *Nomad*'s drives flared into life, crimson fire belching from them. The swarm of tau decoys was almost upon the *Nomad* when her drives spat into life, and they were incinerated in an instant, seared to ash and scattered into the void in a matter of seconds.

There, where the decoys had been clustered most densely, Lucian saw what he had guessed would be revealed: more of the tau armoured suits. Each was equipped with fusion weapons capable of ripping a crippled vessel to glowing pieces, and they had sought to approach the wounded frigate under the cover of the decoys. Now, the suits battled against the steadily increasing wash of the *Nomad*'s drives. Armoured plating, the likes of which Lucian had rarely seen, kept them going, even though the unprotected decoys had lasted mere seconds. The fire of the frigate's drives was so bright that Lucian was barely able to see. Nevertheless he watched the bulking forms as they blackened, their metal skins melting and running off in great billowing streams of vaporised armour. He watched as each suit took on the aspect of a comet rapidly shedding its mass.

At last, the armoured suits were blasted to their constituent atoms as the *Nomad*'s drives reached full output, the Space Marine frigate powering inexorably towards the space station, its ultimate target.

Lucian crossed his arms at the viewing port. 'Shields up, forward weapons target enemy ship's bridge. Fire!'

The scene that greeted Lucian as he stepped out of the airlock onto the tau orbital was one of unrestrained slaughter. He saw that the station had been, before the coming of the Space Marines, a well-ordered place, well lit and spacious. Now, it was a bloody mess, the formerly white, gracefully curved bulkheads bloody and scorched.

Having made their boarding action, Sarik's Space Marines had rampaged through the hasty and ultimately fruitless resistance mounted against them. The tau had put up a fight, retreating in the face of the Space Marines' righteous fury, falling back down the corridors of their station, firing their alien weapons from concealed ambush points for as long as they were able.

Lucian was shocked, not by the savagery of the fighting, but by the fact that the tau defenders had continued to fight in the face of such impossible odds. He was shocked that they had not surrendered, or attempted to flee in the lifeboats that the station must surely have been equipped with. The tau cruiser had surrendered once beaten, why hadn't they?

The corridor into which Lucian stepped bore grisly witness to the brief fight. Huge, smoking chunks were blown from the off-white walls of the curved companionway, and tau bodies were strewn across the deck. He stepped over the body of a tau warrior, sprawled face down before him, and then stopped to look upon the body of another. The second was propped against the corridor's wall, and though clearly dead, had not died instantly from its wounds. The loops of its guts had spilled over its legs, falling over the cradling arms that had attempted in vain to hold them in. A bolter shell fired at close range will have that effect, Lucian mused grimly, knowing full well that the explosive bolts fired by the Space Marines' weapons were lethal to any target of flesh and bone.

Lucian went down on one knee to look upon the dead warrior's face. The thought struck him that in his brief, ship-to-ship encounters with this new, previously unheard of race, he must have killed several thousand of their number, but until now he had not looked one in the eye. He had not known just who, or what he was dealing with. Now he looked upon the face of his foe, bloodied and broken as it was.

The face was narrow and noseless, with a small, lipless mouth, and was dominated by large, black, almond-shaped eyes. The skin was a blue-grey, and there was a slit in the centre of the forehead, an organ for which Lucian could see no obvious function. The alien was not tall, its stocky body certainly no taller than that of a man of average height. Its body was arranged in the same manner as a man's though, apart from its feet, which appeared cloven, though his son Korvane, who had met the aliens in the living flesh, had informed him they were not hooves, but more like wide-splayed toes.

Looking around him at the other bodies, Lucian marvelled that the aliens could have even thought to fight against the superhuman Space Marines of Sarik's small force. Blood was spattered across every surface, severed limbs scattered all around. The remains of a tau that had been cut in two by a single upward stroke of a chainsword lay nearby, split from groin to crown, the two halves of the body lying several metres apart. Lucian had never failed to be impressed by the Space Marines' skills, and was always reminded how fortunate he was that they were on the same side as him.

Lucian looked up from the bloody ruin as he heard footsteps approaching along the corridor. It was his son, Korvane, stepping gingerly across the headless corpse of a tau warrior. Lucian stood, a wide grin on his face, the scenes of death around him forgotten.

'Father,' Korvane said formally. Lucian noted that he appeared cold and aloof, but put it down to a reaction to the unpleasant surroundings.

'Korvane, what news?'

'The council, father. Gurney has called a session, right here, on the station, immediately.'

'Has he indeed?' replied Lucian, knowing that this news could only bode ill for him and his kin. 'He's riled that we got here ahead of him I'll wager. Ha! This should be fun. Come on, we can't keep the good Cardinal waiting now can we, son.'

CHAPTER TWO

Sarik gritted his teeth as the drop-pod disengaged from its cradle, his gene enhanced physiology coping with the punishing forces set into motion as the world of Sy'l'Kell leapt violently upwards to meet him. Course correcting retro jets fired seconds later, slamming the Space Marine's armoured shoulder into the padded, upright acceleration/deceleration couch into which he was strapped. The tiny vessel, with its cargo of ten of humanity's finest warriors was underway.

Sarik knew that the drop would be over as soon as it began. He had completed thirty-eight full combat drops before attaining the rank of Brethren, and he had completed, and commanded, many times more since. The pod shook violently, and a mechanical chime sounded in Sarik's ear. He glanced across at the tactical data-slate. The drop-pod was entering the upper atmosphere, its armour absorbing unimaginable energies as it began the main portion of its descent.

'Phase beta. The Khan and His Father protect us.' Sarik spoke the words of the Rite of Planetfall by rote, the other nine Space Marines echoing his words over the comm-net.

The White Scars were coming to Sy'l'Kell to bring death to the foes of the Emperor, and no alien that Sarik had ever fought could hope to stand against them.

'Your name, sir?' A very junior naval sub-officer demanded of Lucian, in the manner of a man revelling in unfamiliar authority. The officer stood at the end of the typically stark, white corridor, blocking a large round doorway stencilled with a square icon, the meaning of which was totally lost to Lucian.

Lucian halted as he approached, the officer barring his passage through the circular portal. 'What?'

'Your name, sir,' the officer faltered.

Lucian was in no mood to be challenged by officious flunkies. He drew himself up to his full height, savouring the opportunity to vent some spleen, when he was interrupted.

'This,' he heard Korvane snap from over his shoulder, 'is the Lord Arcadius Lucian Gerrit, Heritor of the Clan Arcadius, as well you know.'

The officer stammered, his mouth opening and closing in a manner quite unbefitting his rank. Would he really be so stupid as to bar the rogue trader's passage? Lucian prepared to unleash a tirade of invective, but saw that it would not be necessary. The man stood aside, evidently cowed by Lucian's stern manner, or by Korvane's recitation of his credentials.

Lucian grunted and put the fool out of his mind. He resumed his passage down the curved, stark white corridor of the tau orbital station, the armoured door rolling into the wall in near silence as he approached it.

Beyond the round portal, Lucian could make out the huge hall that the crusade council had commandeered for its latest session. The circular chamber, its ceiling entirely illuminated and glowing white, was home to a round conference table capable of seating two dozen and more delegates in the high-backed, shell-like seats mounted around it. The far wall was one sweeping window, affording an impressive view of the purple landmasses and turquoise seas of the world around which the station orbited.

As curious and attentive as Lucian was to such matters, however, the primary focus of his attention were the figures filing in to the chamber from a dozen other portals. The crusade council was made up of some of the most influential men on the Eastern Rim, each attended by a flock of scribes, servants and functionaries of indeterminate purpose.

Lucian stepped through the portal, unaccustomed to the stark white light illuminating the scene. The chamber, he was informed, had been the meeting place of the high council of the tau rulers of this place until mere hours before. A wide bloodstain smeared across the centre of the table attested to the fact that the station's previous owners had not relinquished it willingly. Lucian appreciated the theatrical conceit inherent in holding the council in such a place. He strongly suspected, in fact that whoever had decided upon doing so had ordered that the bloodstain remain in place, only to be washed away once its message had been well and truly imparted.

The drop-pod's assault ramps burst open on explosive bolts the instant the vessel struck the ground, its ten passengers disembarking with a clatter of armoured soles before its drives had even shut off. Sarik looked around, comparing the scene that greeted him with the tactical display overlaid on his vision by his helmet's systems.

'Squad!' he bellowed over the scream of more incoming drop pods. 'To me!'

Sarik scanned the landing zone as his cohorts took up position around him. Each Space Marine was a giant, his enhanced physique far taller and broader than any normal man. Each wore a suit of all-enclosing armour, capable of withstanding the harshest of environments and of protecting him from the fiercest of enemy fire. That armour was painted the white with red trim of the White Scars Chapter of Space Marines, the wild, proud sons of Jaghatai Khan, children of the feral *nomad*s of Chogoris, and one of the most celebrated and feared chapters in the Imperium.

The scene before Sarik and his squad was one he had witnessed many times before. He gave silent thanks to the war spirit of the drop-pod for delivering them safely through the world's atmosphere, to this place in which he would serve the Emperor, and if called upon to do so, die in his service.

The landing zone was atop a high plateau, a flat expanse between two spurs of the world's largest mountain range. The air was cold and clean, and low clouds scudded across the contrail streaked sky. The ground underfoot was rough and uneven, strewn with loose boulders, but of no hindrance to a Space Marine. It had been selected for one reason and one reason only: it was the site of the world's alien government, the single organ that, if excised, would spell the immediate death of the entire body. The Space Marines were the Imperium's terror troops. Their mission was to strike at the very heart of the Imperium's enemies, to rip that still-beating heart out, without mercy or delay, and in so doing to slay the enemy utterly, that none might rise in his place ever again.

'Objective Primus, five hundred, fifteen east, moonrise. On me!' Sarik used the battle-cant of his chapter, a series of clipped commands that his men understood without hesitation, but which any enemy able to intercept them would find entirely unintelligible. Sarik advanced, his men formed behind according to his orders. All eyes were fixed on their objective, a fortified building at the very edge of the plateau, melded into the nearest of the mountain peaks. Surface-to-orbit missiles streaked upwards from automated turrets atop the fort, while bright tracers spat incandescent death across the plateau. Sarik heard the ultra-high velocity rounds sing as they split the air nearby. He looked into the skies, to see more drop-pods descending upon columns of fire, retro thrusters screaming. Soon the squads of the Iron Hands and the other chapters would join his own, but for now, he thought with a feral grin, the White Scars were at the very spear tip of the assault on Sy'l'Kell.

'Sons of Khan!' he bellowed, unashamed of the joy and pride audible in his voice. 'Let us show our brothers how the White Scars fight!'

'I declare!' Lucian winced as the Cardinal's booming voice filled the chamber, 'Our mission here anointed by the Most Holy God Emperor of Mankind! The Damocles Gulf shall be crossed, the darkness pierced! So it has been decreed, and so it falls to us to enact!'

The Cardinal of Brimlock, Esau Gurney, had risen from his seat to pronounce the council in session. Lucian knew that he would proceed in such a manner for long minutes, declaring the benefaction of the Emperor upon the crusade's undertaking. He would make it abundantly clear, much to Lucian's chagrin, that it was through the cardinal's own authority that such benefactions were granted.

Lucian sighed inwardly and glanced around the table, the cardinal's words receding into the distance. He had heard the exact same speech on at least a dozen occasions now, Gurney's ranting tone growing more and more strident each time the council had sat.

The cardinal was placed directly across the huge, round table from Lucian, a flock of scribes and minor Ecclesiarchy officials clustered behind him. Those that were not engaged in recording their master's every word in spidery script across flowing parchment seemed intent upon producing a bank of cloying holy incense from wildly swinging burners. Such displays were not in Lucian's nature; he had been reared an Emperor fearing man, but placed little value in such ceremony. The Emperor, Lucian believed, helped those who helped themselves, ignoring those undeserving of his attentions.

To the cardinal's left sat a man for whom Lucian had far more respect. The hooded figure appeared capable of finding a shadowy space even below the direct lighting cast by the brightly illuminated ceiling above. This was Inquisitor Grand, an agent of the Ordo Xenos and no doubt the single most dangerous man in the entire crusade fleet. The inquisitor, for reasons Lucian had not yet determined, had chosen to ally himself with the cardinal. He preferred, it seemed to Lucian, to remain, literally, in the shadows. The man sat at council, casting his vote with the rest of the cardinal's faction, but rarely made any overt show of power. Such a man was to be watched closely, Lucian had determined, and watch him he most certainly would.

Looking to the inquisitor's left, Lucian exchanged a glance with General Wendall Gauge. A hard, battle-worn man from the death world of Catachan, Gauge had been appointed the commander-in-chief of the Imperial Guard regiments assigned to the crusade. Lucian considered him a sound choice, and had liked the taciturn old veteran the instant they had met, mere weeks after the pronouncement of the crusade. The General had until recently been serving as adjutant to the noted Lord Marshall Holt in his prosecution of the Wendigo Gulf rebellion, but had, he told Lucian, grown tired of the so-called "great man's" shadow. He had not expounded further, but upon hearing of the founding of the crusade, had exerted considerable influence to gain his rank. Lucian saw in Gauge a potential ally on the council, through whom he might gain power over the cardinal and his faction, though he knew he had a long way to go before he could bring such power to bear.

His mind brought back to the cardinal, Lucian focused once

more on the stream of oratory that Gurney was spewing across the table.

'To us falls the most holy task of eradicating these foul xenos beasts, of putting down the heresy of their existence. We who pledge allegiance...' The rant went on, Lucian deciding it was safe to ignore the man once more. He regarded the figure next to the general.

Admiral Jellaqua appeared to be in his early fifties, but must have been far older given his rank as commander of the Imperial Navy vessels assigned to the Damocles Gulf crusade. He was stout with a broad chest; a goatee beard and sly eyes his most striking features. Like the general, Lucian saw the admiral as a potential ally, one he would have to work hard to court, but a man whose aid would no doubt prove invaluable in the conflict to come, against the tau and the cardinal both. Jellaqua was a man who brooked no nonsense or affectation from any around him, whether subordinate or peer.

As the cardinal's address droned on, Lucian's glance passed to the empty seat to the admiral's left and his own right. It was the position in which Captain Rumann of the Iron Hands Space Marines would ordinarily have sat. Lucian had never before encountered the brethren of that chapter, though he knew them to be cold and methodical in their approach to war, and to bear an unusual amount of cybernetic enhancement. Rumann was absent, leading the Space Marine forces as they assaulted the tau centres of power on the world below, fighting and no doubt shedding their blood even as the council sat and the cardinal ranted. The crusade force was fortunate to be attended by detachments from a number of Space Marine chapters, and the captain of the Iron Hands had been elected by his peers to represent their interests on the crusade council, and was as such the most senior ranked Space Marine in the fleet. Rumann was a man the like of whom Lucian had seldom met. He was as aloof as any other Space Marine, but far colder and more distant than any Lucian had encountered. He really could not tell whether Rumann might prove a sturdy ally or a terrible enemy, or even whether the Space Marine had any awareness or concern of such matters. Lucian determined to pursue the matter further at the first opportunity.

To Lucian's left was an empty seat that belonged to the second Space Marine on the council, also absent, leading his forces in battle on the world below. Veteran Sergeant Sarik of the White Scars Chapter had been elected Rumann's second, and in Lucian's opinion provided the perfect counterpoint to the taciturn captain. In common with his kin, Sarik was hot-blooded and wild, yet surly and stubborn in the pursuit of victory. The White Scars hailed from the windswept steppes of the feral world of Chogoris. He preferred not to dwell on the savage beauty of that world, for it was the place that had given birth to his first wife, and the world upon which Brielle had been raised amongst the ruling classes of that race of noble savages. He cast the memory aside as quickly as it came to him, glancing instead to the next seat along.

Here sat the Magos Explorator Jaakho, a hooded figure whose face was almost entirely lost to a hissing cluster of pipes and cables, his eyes only barely visible as red-lit, cybernetic discs glowing from the depths of the explorator's hood. Jaakho was the fleet's most senior member of the Cult Mechanicus, the brotherhood of the Machine God, disciples and prophets of the innermost mysteries of technomancy and psience. It fell to the Magos to direct the crusade in its encounters with the technologies of the foe, to identify what might be exploited, and to combat that which must be resisted and destroyed. Lucian saw in Jaakho's position a potential ally, for the tech-priest's stance must surely be the opposite of the cardinals. Where Gurney preached that the tau and all their works must be ground to dust, reviled as unholy anathema, the Magos might look to exploit or to study new technologies discovered along the way. If such a possibility existed, Lucian determined that he would exploit it. Then he moved on, glancing to the next man at the table.

At Jaakho's left hand was Pator Sedicae, the most senior Navigator in the crusade, and the man ultimately responsible for the safety of the entire fleet. In common with many Navigators of his age and rank, Sedicae suffered from the genetic curse of his strain. The Navigators were a unique strand of humanity, gifted with the witchsight that allowed them to see the ebb and flow of the tides of the warp, through which they guided their vessels, navigating by the ever-constant light of the Astronomican on distant Terra. As each grew older, and more powerful, he was afflicted with terrible mutations, often causing him to retire from public view and devote himself entirely to his task from the lonely sanctuary of his navigation blister. Sedicae was quite unique in Lucian's experience, for his curse had not caused him to retire, though some would prefer that it had. Sedicae's skin was disturbingly translucent, his blood vessels, muscles, bone and pulsing organs plainly visible. The effect was ghastly, but it in no way impeded the Navigator in his duties, and so he went about his business, sitting on the crusade council and representing the interests of the other Navigators serving the fleet where a compatriot of a like age might be rendered unable to do so by the extent of his mutation. Lucian found the man hard to read, no doubt, he mused, due to the rigorous defences the Navigator, by necessity, surrounded himself with when traversing the daemon haunted depths of the warp.

To Sedicae's left sat a man for whom Lucian had felt a deep, abiding dislike the instant they had been introduced at the outset of the crusade. Praefect Maximus Skissor of the Adeptus Terra was a tall, hawkish man, whose haughty nature had infuriated Lucian from the off. Skissor was tasked with the political governance of the crusade, of overseeing the installation of new planetary governments, and of coordinating the crusade's efforts with the strategic concerns of the entire Ultima Segmentum. To Lucian, Skissor was a man promoted way above his abilities, due no doubt to some debt owed him by a compatriot, called in to buy him a seat on the council and to make his name along the way. Lucian had no problem with ambition, he welcomed it in the right sort of man, but here was ambition entirely divorced of potential, and Lucian had seen much death and destruction brought about by such a combination. He had already decided that when Skissor fell, for fall Lucian knew he would, he would not take any of the Arcadius with him,

Lastly, to Gurney's right sat Logistician-General Stempf of the Departmento Munitorum. If Lucian disliked Praefect Maximus Skissor, he positively loathed Stempf. The task of organising the crusade's logistics, of ensuring its supplies of ammunition, fuel, foodstuffs and a thousand other items would never run out, fell to the logistician-general. He was, Lucian believed, the worst possible crossbreed of autocrat and accountant, politician and statistician, warmonger and profiteer. Lucian's dislike of such men was bred into his line since the time of Maxim Gerrit, the ancient ancestor upon whose legacy the entire Arcadius dynasty was built. Well, Lucian thought, old Maxim would turn in his icy grave at the thought of an Arcadius having dealings with such a man, and as such, Lucian would have nothing to do with the logistician-general. He suspected that the man would throw his lot in with the cardinal anyway, and had long since written him off as a source of support.

'...should pledge his unconditional support in this matter,' Gurney was saying as Lucian turned his attention back to the cardinal's ranting. He became aware that an unusual silence had settled upon the council, and that each member was looking in Lucian's direction.

'You will, of course, support us in this matter?' said the cardinal, directly to Lucian.

His mind racing, Lucian cursed himself for a fool. He had let his mind wander whilst the cardinal ranted, and had missed some important point on which Gurney sought to entrap him. He heard a soft cough from behind him, and subtly turned his glance towards Korvane, who sat at one of the many seats arranged around the outer circumference of the chamber. With the slightest shake of his head, Lucian's son told him all he needed to know.

'I advise caution in this matter,' said Lucian, fully aware how glib his answer must sound, but determined not to allow the cardinal to win any victory over him, no matter how minor.

'Caution?' retorted the cardinal, sitting himself down and exchanging a silent glance with the inquisitor at his side. 'You would cast doubt upon the divine right of Mankind to rule this region? You would suggest that these xenos filth enjoy a higher place in the holy order of existence than we do?'

So that was his game. Lucian saw then the point the cardinal was trying to push through the council.

'My dear cardinal,' Lucian replied, warming to the confrontation now that he had the measure of his opponent. 'I have travelled from one end of the Emperor's Domains to the other. I have travelled far beyond of the realm of the Imperium. Though I have encountered many and various civilised xenos races, I have yet to discover one that is not of more value to us alive than dead.'

A murmur rippled around the table, some councillors evidently agreeing with Lucian's statement, others disagreeing and others still uttering noncommittal niceties. Within scant seconds, Lucian saw a new balance of power form, perhaps one that would ultimately shift the council in his favour. He saw that Jellaqua and Gauge agreed with his position; the tau should not be wiped out indiscriminately, but should be conquered for the benefit of the Imperium of Man.

Lucian's position on this matter was the product of his unique upbringing. As a rule, humanity was jealous of the galaxy's other races, for most were dire threats to the continued existence of the human race, and besides, felt that theirs was the right to rule the galaxy and not man's. Rogue traders, however, were unusual in that it was their duty to go out in to the dark places beyond human controlled space and to exploit what they encountered. In some cases this meant trading with alien races rather than destroying them outright. Rogue traders often held the view that not all xenos should be exterminated on first contact, a view at odds with the teachings of the Imperial Creed, the dogma the cardinal held as sacrosanct.

'What use to let them live?' asked the cardinal, now addressing the entire council. 'What use their continued existence? What might they teach us? What might they provide us?'

'I would suggest,' replied Lucian, also addressing the council as a whole, 'that the best way to find out might be to ask one.'

Another ripple of comment passed around the table, this time more urgent in its tone. Lucian saw that Inquisitor Grand was looking right at him, his hooded face making his expression entirely unreadable, only his frowning mouth visible in the shadows.

'You are suggesting,' the cardinal replied, once more addressing Lucian directly, 'that the pure form of Man should be sullied in body and soul by contact with a living, breathing alien?'

'If the crusade might benefit from doing so, and if the Emperor's cause might be furthered, then yes,' said Lucian, looking the cardinal straight in the eye. 'That is exactly what I am suggesting.'

''Ware the fore!' called Sarik, ducking behind an outcropping of rock, and resisting, barely, the urge to laugh out loud for the joy of battle coursing through his veins. A mighty explosion sounded a second later, the heat of the melta charge he had just planted evident even through his armour and from behind cover. He had led his squad across the cratered plateau, glorying in the fact that he had done so before the Iron Hands had even disembarked. Now, he would lead his brother Space Marines in an assault against the enemy bunker complex.

'With me!' shouted Sarik, rising from his position and striding into the smoke of the explosion. Through the enhanced vision granted him by the systems in his helmet, he saw that the armoured door had been reduced to glowing slag by the miniature nuclear charge he had placed against it, providing a way in to the tau command centre. Sarik's squad would be the first into the bunker, the glory of victory would belong to the White Scars.

Sarik passed through the ruined bunker entrance and slowed to allow his squad to catch up with him. He trained his bolter at the darkness before him, his suit's systems detecting no life forms within the shadows.

He opened his mouth to issue the order to advance, when he heard a high-pitched whine pass mere centimetres from his head. He turned, catching sight of a blue flash illuminating the shadows further down the corridor. It was the unmistakable signature of a weapons discharge, Sarik was sure of that, but despite that, he had no clue as to what type of weapon was being fired.

'Squad!' he called. 'Target ahead. Overwatch.'

Another whine passed dangerously close, but still the war spirit in Sarik's armour could not identify the position of the firer. He ducked back, but too late, as a mighty impact struck the armour of his right shoulder. He stifled a curse as the reactive actuators compensated for the impact. He was not hurt, but still he could not locate his foe.

'By the Great Khan,' he swore, releasing the catches that secured his helmet. The air of Sy'l'Kell greeted him as he lifted the helm, the smell of cordite and smoke filling his nostrils. He strained his eyes to pick out his attacker, and was rewarded with a brief glimpse of movement amidst the smoke.

He raised his bolter and fired two shots the length of the corridor. Sparks flew where the bolts struck, followed an instant later by two muffled explosions as they detonated within their target. But where Sarik had expected to hear the wet thump of a body hitting the ground, he distinctly heard the crash of a solid object falling, followed by a small explosion.

Seizing the initiative before any more foes could zero in on his position, Sarik rose and charged down the corridor, knowing that his brethren would follow his lead. The smoke parted as he reached the end of the low, dark corridor, and Sarik saw that he had come to a junction at its end. Burning scrap was scattered across the floor, the remains of a flat, dome-shaped machine with twin weapons mounted beneath. Sarik saw instantly why his suit's war spirit had been unable to detect an enemy.

'Squad, disengage target acquisition. Use your own senses, not those of your armour.' Several of the Space Marines removed their helmets as they took up position around their leader, while others spoke words of command that would render their armour's targeting systems dormant until revived. 'The enemy are using thinking machines to fight us, and they barely show up on autosenses.'

Such a thing was anathema to the White Scars, indeed, to all Space Marines. They were a warrior brotherhood, fighting and bleeding and dying together. To rely on a machine to do one's fighting was a blasphemy against their warrior honour, as well as against the religious dogma of their Chapter.

Sarik kicked the sputtering remains of the tau fighting machine, contempt writ large across his face. 'Brothers, we seek the tau leadership. I think they have need of a lesson in honour.'

'Which man here,' asked the cardinal, addressing the entire council, 'would consort with xenos?'

Lucian looked around the table, noting that none of the council members would answer a question so obviously weighted to implicate any who did so. If the cardinal can play that game, then so can I, thought Lucian.

'Which man here,' Lucian asked in reply, 'would throw away a chance to know more of his foe, that he might defeat him all the more decisively?'

At that, Lucian saw a number of heads nod in thoughtful agreement. Admiral Jellaqua and General Gauge were unashamed in their agreement, while other council members were more subtle and cautious, restricting their gestures to slight nods.

The cardinal saw this too, Lucian noticed, and evidently decided to change his tack.

'Gentlemen. I would point out that I could settle this matter entirely, and I would not need your permission or assent to do so.'

'Explain,' said the Magos Explorator Jaakho, the first time a council member other than the cardinal or Lucian had spoken up.

'By all means,' replied Gurney. 'I could simply order the world below us virus bombed. Believe me, I would do so.'

'How? replied the magos explorator, his voice mechanical and grating. 'How do you come to have such devices?'

Though the tech-priest's voice was nigh emotionless, Lucian caught the edge to it. Little could cause excitement in a senior adept of the Machine God, for they surrendered much of themselves in their integration with the mechanisms of their calling, merging and becoming one with the great cogitation banks with which they communed. A virus bomb, an example of high technology proscribed by ancient decree and available only to the very highest of authorities was just the type of thing to gain a reaction from such as he.

Lucian saw the answer coming, and looked to the cardinal's left, to Grand, as Gurney replied.

'There are those of the council who agree with my position,' stated the cardinal. Lucian saw that the inquisitor was looking right at him, the effect made quite disconcerting, because Grand's eyes were still obscured in shadow.

'My lords,' Lucian addressed the council, 'let us not be drawn into rash, unilateral action. Let us stand united in our efforts to prosecute the crusade, for is that not the task the High Lords have set us?'

He knew even as he spoke that he had made an enemy of the cardinal, and must work to draw the non-aligned members of the council to a new faction of his own creation.

'With me!' Sarik called, launching himself through the wreckage of the final armoured barrier between him and the inner command centre of the tau bunker. Even as the smoke cleared and his brothers crashed through behind him, he saw that he had reached the final phase of the mission.

Sarik and his brother Marines had fought through the winding corridors of the complex, facing and destroying more of the machine-warriors as they penetrated deeper. They burst into a massive chamber, its walls stark white and illuminated by the blue light of a thousand data screens. One such screen dominated the far wall, a massive projection plotting the course of the battle as it raged all around the plateau.

Silhouetted against that huge display, Sarik saw what he knew instantly was the alien he had come to kill, the head that when decapitated would spell the death of the entire body.

Attendants wearing oil-stained jump suits and bearing all manner of alien tools surrounded a mighty suit of armour far larger and more bulky than the armour worn by the White Scars. More accurately, Sarik saw, the figure did not wear the armour at all, but had climbed within it, to act not as a wearer but as a pilot.

Their task complete, the attendants stepped away from their leader. Relishing the thought of the upcoming duel, Sarik stepped forward, waving his brethren back as they went to follow. An unspoken understanding had, somehow, made itself apparent between the two leaders. Perhaps the tau did know of honour, Sarik thought, stowing his bolter and drawing his chainsword.

The tau commander drew himself to his full height, ignited his suit's jets and leapt to the floor before the Space Marine. Only ten metres separated the two warriors, affording Sarik a view of the weapons his adversary carried. He saw instantly that the tau was equipped for a ranged fight, apparently lacking any form of weapon that could be used in a melee.

'Man,' the tau said to Sarik's surprise, 'though we may be enemies, I am duty bound to offer to you our friendship. We need not fight, you and I. What say you?'

Though taken aback by his enemy's question, Sarik answered in the only way he could. 'Tau, we are foemen. If you wish to surrender, that choice is yours.'

The square device atop the tau's armour, which Sarik took to be some form of armoured sensor block, dipped, perhaps in sadness. 'You misunderstand me, human,' the tau replied. 'I do not offer you my surrender. I offer you my friendship and that of all the tau. You must join us, or we must fight.'

It took Sarik a moment to assimilate the alien's words, for no foe had ever asked him to surrender and to join him. Such a thing was utterly unthinkable, the very notion causing Sarik to bristle in anger.

'If you truly expect me to throw down my arms and join you, then you do not know honour after all,' said Sarik, thumbing the activation stud on the grip of his chainsword and causing it to growl into angry life.

'I do not ask you to throw down your arms, for I, like you, am a warrior and know well what that would mean. I offer you common cause. If you join the Tau Empire then you may fight for a cause truly worthy of your life. Join the Tau Empire, and we might fight together, not against one another!'

'You insult me with words, xenos,' spat Sarik by way of reply. 'Enough with words. Now, we fight!'

'I move,' Lucian addressed the council, 'that we vote on this issue.'

'And what motion would you table? asked Sedicae the Navigator, surprising Lucian and, it appeared, the rest of the council by choosing to speak up at this time.

'I ask that the council moves to delay any use of the cardinal's ultimate sanction,' Lucian replied, aware that the cardinal seethed with anger as he did so, 'until such time as the situation on the ground is fully resolved.'

'What right have you to naysay me, rogue trader?' growled the cardinal, his tone dangerous and his bearded face scowling.

'It is my right as a member of this council, should another member second me,' replied Lucian, knowing full well the gamble he was initiating.

The council knew the gamble too, so it seemed, for a tense silence settled on the chamber as each councillor considered his position. Lucian had taken a huge risk in calling for a vote, for should no other councillor second the call, then he would be humiliated, entirely isolated and devoid of power or influence. Furthermore, the councillor that seconded his call would be setting himself up against the cardinal as surely as Lucian had. A successful councillor might gain unimagined power, but a defeated one might be lucky to come out alive, so brutal could the power play become.

'I will second the Lord Arcadius's call.' Lucian let out a silent breath of relief, seeing that it was Admiral Jellaqua that had spoken up. 'If for no other reason than to settle this issue and move on to more pressing matters.'

Lucian nodded his thanks to the admiral, before addressing the council. 'I call then for a vote, on the issue of the enactment of the ultimate sanction against the taking of enemy prisoners. Gentlemen, please cast your votes.'

Lucian smiled to himself, pleased that he had worked the issue of taking prisoners into consideration, setting it up as the natural opposite of the cardinal's stance. And in his mind, it was, for if the cardinal convinced Grand to virus bomb Sy'l'Kell, then the taking of prisoners would be a moot point, and the crusade would be throwing away potentially vital intelligence.

The council's etiquette stated that the member nominated as chairman for the session should vote first, the voting passing around the table clockwise. The cardinal was the chairman. 'I vote against the motion,' he growled.

'As do I,' stated Inquisitor Grand, his voice dry and sinister, little more than a whisper emanating from the depths of his hood, but plainly audible nonetheless.

'I vote,' said General Wendall Gauge in his no-nonsense, gravel voice, 'for the motion. Arcadius has the truth of it.'

Lucian nodded his thanks to the general, and looked to the next man along.

'I hardly need to do so,' said Admiral Jellaqua, 'or I would not have seconded the call to vote, but I too vote in favour of Gerrit's motion. In war, one must marshal one's resources and know what weapon to use when. I believe it wise to capture and interrogate an enemy. It is not "consorting with xenos", it is common sense.'

Lucian savoured the outrage the cardinal fought so hard and unsuccessfully to contain, but knew better than to celebrate just yet.

The seat to the admiral's left, belonging to Captain Rumann of the Iron Hands Chapter, was unoccupied, the Space Marine being otherwise engaged with his role in the planetary assault in progress below. That meant that Lucian was the next in line to vote. He said simply, 'I vote in favour.'

To Lucian's left was the empty seat belonging to Sergeant Sarik of the White Scars. It was a shame the Space Marine was absent,

Lucian thought, for he suspected Sarik might have voted against the use of the virus bomb, even if he would have no great desire to interrogate prisoners.

The next councillor along was Jaakho, the Magos Explorator. Lucian counted two votes against his motion so far, and three for. He had no idea how the Magos might vote. A long silence preceded Jaakho's answer, punctuated by the slow wheeze of his augmetic systems and the rattle of the many pipes and cables draped from the facemask hidden beneath his red hood.

'I must,' the Magos stated at length, 'abstain from this vote.'

Lucian waited for some explanation from the tech-priest, but soon realised that none would be forthcoming. Jaakho's reasons for voting for or against any of the council's actions appeared to be couched in an entirely unreadable logic, one that Lucian believed was divorced from the reality in which he lived.

The next councillor to vote would be the Navigator, Pator Sedicae. As with Jaakho before, Lucian could not predict how the Navigator might vote, for he appeared to judge matters entirely by the unknowable concerns of his kin. The Navigators, as with the Techno Magi, moved in their own circles, and their ways were frequently alien and arcane to other men. The thought occurred to Lucian that Sedicae might feel the same about the circles in which rogue traders moved, so perhaps there was some possibility of finding common ground and of working towards an alliance.

The Navigator visibly gathered his thoughts, before casting his vote. 'On behalf of the Navis Nobilitie,' he said, referring to all of the Navigator Houses, of which he was the head of just one, 'I too must abstain.'

Lucian was not entirely surprised to hear the Navigator's vote, though he could not help but feel mildly disappointed. He looked at the two remaining councillors yet to cast their votes, cold doubt rising within him.

Praefect Maximus Skissor stood to deliver his vote, Lucian's view of the man plummeting even further. Skissor cleared his throat as he straightened his robes, before raising an ancient data-slate and lifting a tattered feather quill to its surface.

'I, Praefect Maximus to the Damocles Gulf Crusade, do hereby exercise the right and responsibility entrusted to me.' Skissor allowed a pregnant pause to drag on, apparently blind to the hostile glances that various councillors, not least among them Lucian, were casting his way.

'I choose to abstain.'

Lucian felt a cold sweat appear at his brow, but refused to let his discomfort show.

'I believe,' the Praefect continued, 'that to actively seek out tau prisoners to interrogate would be to create a line of communication between the aliens and ourselves. This I believe to be tantamount to recognising their empire and its right to exist. The purpose of this crusade is to challenge the tau, not to talk to them. Having said that, I believe it is my duty to consider how the tau might be of use to us, and I believe that to exterminate them would be to throw away what advantage we might gain by doing so.'

Lucian resisted the urge to rise to his feet and berate the councillor. Did he really believe his own nonsense? No, Lucian realised, that little speech was intended to bolster the Praefect's position, no matter how it sounded to the remainder of the council.

Looking across at the last councillor still to cast his vote, Lucian realised that he had, in all likelihood, lost this battle. The cardinal sat at the head of his faction, which included Inquisitor Grand, and, Lucian was sure, the logistician-general, even though Stempf had yet to cast his vote. Lucian could count on Jellaqua and Gauge, but with the abstentions and absences, it looked like that would not prove sufficient.

It was no surprise to Lucian then when the logistician-general cast his vote against the motion, putting the result at three for, three against and four abstentions; not enough to carry the vote.

Hot pain flared across Sarik's chest as high-velocity impacts cratered and buckled his power armour. The alien spoke no more, but would fight, that much was clear. Sarik offered a brief but heartfelt thanks to the Emperor that the ceramite armour was proof against the alien weaponry, for now at least.

Wasting no more time, Sarik launched himself at his foe, seeking to get within the tau's guard, from where the alien's weapons would be useless and his own lethal.

Before he could close on the tau, however, Sarik's enemy

launched himself into the air upon flaring blue jets, leaping clear of the screaming chainsword blade as it sliced through the space he had just vacated. Sarik cursed, and rose to his full height, reaching up and grabbing hold of one metallic foot of the battlesuit. The tau's upward motion was arrested as the Space Marine attempted to pull the suit back down to the floor. In response, the alien pilot increased the power to the jets, searing blue flames scorching Sarik's left arm and shoulder pad, the white paint peeling off and the metal skin below beginning to blister.

Sarik cursed as his flowing black hair set alight, forcing his right arm up against the jet wash, seeking to use the chainsword against his foe.

The tau, seeing his peril, twisted around in an attempt to use the downdraught created by the powerful jets to topple the Space Marine. But Sarik's power armour lent him superhuman strength, and he resisted the fierce blast even as his hair burned. He raised the chainsword and thrust it screaming into the battlesuit's primary thrusters, causing a spectacular chain reaction within the propulsion unit even as the blade melted and fused, its screeching gears jamming entirely.

Sarik threw himself clear as the battlesuit was engulfed in a series of small explosions, the pilot attempting to draw a bead on the Space Marine even as his suit disintegrated, blue bolts streaming from the rapidly spinning barrels of the suit's primary weapon system.

Drawing himself to his feet and shaking his face clear of his smouldering hair, Sarik could see that he had won. The battlesuit toppled backwards and fell with an almighty crash. The Space Marine watched in mute fascination as a series of tiny discharges popped the suit's front plates clear and a figure rose from the flaming wreckage and staggered clear, flames licking around its torso, to fall on its face at Sarik's feet.

Sarik grinned as the tau commander raised his blackened face and looked up at him.

'Surrender accepted,' Sarik said, 'you fought with honour.'

'It falls to me,' said the cardinal, addressing the council, 'to declare the result of the vote.'

Gurney's face was a mask of triumph, the cardinal evidently keen to consolidate the power he felt had come to him thanks to the result of the vote. Lucian looked away, unwilling to acknowledge that his gamble had failed. In so doing, he caught sight of his son, who indicated with a tap of his data-slate that Lucian should look to the console placed in the centre of the table.

A flashing light told Lucian that a priority transmission was incoming from the planet's surface.

'Wait!' Lucian called, standing and reaching across the table to activate the console.

'What is this, Gerrit?' demanded the cardinal. 'The vote is defeated. You are defeated.'

Lucian smiled as he pressed the control stud on the console. Three large pict-slates rose up, cables and purity seals snaking after them. The screens flickered to life, and a familiar face appeared for all the council to see.

'I repeat,' said Sarik, his face visible on the screen through banks of drifting smoke, 'this is Sarik to the crusade council, do you receive?'

'We receive you Sarik,' replied Lucian, the attention of every councillor glued to the screens. 'How do you fare?'

Sarik's face grinned, a feral glow evident in his eyes. 'We fare well, Gerrit. I have to report that the primary objective is secured. The enemy leadership is suppressed, and the world will soon be ours.'

A round of approval swept the council, but Lucian guessed there was more to come.

'I would also report,' continued Sarik, 'that I have captured the enemy commander. I recommend his immediate transferral to the fleet. I'm sure he will be of use to us.'

'I think,' said Lucian, turning his back towards the cardinal and addressing the council at large, 'that makes it four votes in favour, three against and four abstentions. The vote, by my calculation, is cast.'

CHAPTER THREE

The airlock door opened with an explosive hydraulic hiss. Brielle stepped through to the tau orbital, the first time she had left her vessel, the *Fairlight*, for many long months. She halted, taking in her surroundings, savouring the novelty after so long aboard ship.

The docking hub's inner ring was a wide area, its every surface from its deck to the high ceiling a brilliant white, unsullied except where long, crimson smears indicated that a fallen body had been dragged away. In all likelihood, an alien body, Brielle knew, for she had read the reports of the boarding action that had captured the orbital with such brutal efficiency.

Replaying in her head the account of the action, she set out along the lonely, deserted corridors. The White Scars, thanks to her father's intervention, had closed on the orbital in their wounded frigate *Nomad*, and had launched themselves in a boarding torpedo at the orbital's main docking station. The torpedo had breached the orbital's armoured skin, disgorging its contents of just a single Space Marine squad. That squad, led by veteran sergeant Sarik, had initially encountered few defenders, leading the crusade council to assume that the aliens had abandoned the station in the face of the Imperium's overwhelming attack.

As the White Scars had advanced further, they had encountered opposition, armoured and well-equipped tau warriors waiting in ambush at key defensive points. These would open fire before falling back to the next, prepared position, initially wounding three of Sarik's men, though none were put out of the fight permanently. Brielle could see the evidence of the accounts as she passed a junction between major companionways, the site, she saw clearly, of one of the tau defenders' early ambushes. The wall before her was pockmarked with a line of small craters. Each was surrounded by a dirty halo where a round fired from a Space Marine's bolter had entered the wall and exploded an instant later. The weapon was intended for use against lightly armoured enemies of flesh and blood, upon which the effect of the exploding bolt was quite lethal. A wide, red stain across the corridor's deck bore witness to just how potent the weapon was, testament to the price the tau had paid in discovering that fact.

Brielle walked right through the dried blood, a faint sense of revulsion welling up in her as the soles of her boots stuck ever so slightly as she passed. She forced herself to ignore the sensation, knowing she would see a lot more death, and from much closer quarters before this so-called crusade was done.

Passing a work crew of junior tech adepts engaged upon the installation of new, Imperium standard, phasic power transfer coils, Brielle considered just what her role in the crusade might turn out to be, and how she might prosper from it, so long as she could survive it. Her father, upon dealing with the renegade planetary governors of Mundus Chasmata and Arrikis Epsilon, had decided that the rogue traders should remain in the Timbra sub-sector. He had seen the opportunity to take part in the gathering Damocles Gulf Crusade, to revive some age-old family traditions and generally profit from the great undertaking as it got underway. All had gone well, Brielle mused, until the crusade had caught up with the rogue traders at the twin colonies of Garrus and Kliest, evacuated by small tau forces before the fleet proper could arrive and see them off by force.

The rogue traders had been introduced to the key members of the crusade council at those colonies. Its head, by way of influence rather than title, was the bombastic Cardinal Gurney, and ever lurking in the shadows nearby was his ally, Inquisitor Grand of the Ordo Xenos. The cardinal had held the crusade's reins, and had launched a series of courts of assize, putting to death hundreds of the liberated colonists whom he had accused of welcoming the recently departed aliens with open arms. The scenes of torture and execution had been etched into Brielle's memory, her hatred for the likes of the cardinal multiplying a thousandfold that day.

Then, she had heard of the assault on the world below. The tau presence on Sy'l'Kell was small, and like the defenders posted to slow the Space Marines' boarding action, were limited to warriors. The council had determined that the tau had evacuated all of their non-combatant personnel at the first sign of an attack. The cardinal's faction had declared this to be evidence of the aliens' inferiority to mankind, for whom every last man, woman and child was a combatant in the war against the xenos.

Brielle had watched the orbital assault as it had unfolded, for the Space Marines allowed a portion of their signals to be routed to the crusade's command network. She had listened as the blustering Sarik had led his squad in the attack on the tau command bunker, noting how the Space Marine sought to cover himself in the glory of victory, at the expense of his brothers of the other Chapters that had contributed squads to the crusade. She had been brought up around men like Sarik, and regarded them as little more than strutting wildedons, determined to prove their dominance over the lower ranked males of the herd.

When Sarik had reported over the command net that he had neutralised the tau bunker, Brielle had felt a stab of distain. When he had boasted that he had captured the alien leader, she had determined to meet this tau, or to look upon him as he was executed at the very least.

Approaching the last junction before the area of the station in which the tau prisoners were being held, Brielle felt a chill run down her spine. She came to an abrupt halt, hearing lowered, conspiratorial voices from around the corner as she did so. Even as she strained to make out the words, the voices stopped in mid sentence. Brielle held her breath for a moment, not really knowing why, her pulse thundering in her ears. Then she broke the spell, and stepped around the corner.

Standing as if interrupted in the midst of treason, Cardinal Gurney and Inquisitor Grand both looked up at her approach. She saw surprise writ across the face of the cardinal, but the inquisitor, from beneath his deep, shadowed hood, appeared to Brielle to have been expecting her. She floundered for words, but the inquisitor addressed her first.

'My lady,' Grand said, nodding as he did so, his voice, as ever, scarcely more than a grating whisper, but sounding as if he spoke from mere inches away nonetheless. 'What, may I ask, might concern you in a place such as this?' The inquisitor made an expansive gesture with both arms as he spoke. Brielle knew that he referred not to the station as a whole, but to this specific section of it, the section in which the tau prisoners were to be held, to be questioned and, she had little doubt, to be put to death.

'I have come...' Brielle said, her mind racing to justify her presence when she could not entirely explain her reasons for coming, even to herself. '...I have come to look upon the face of our foe, to watch as he dies.' She knew the words were lies even as she spoke them, but hoped it was the sort of statement that the cardinal and the inquisitor might appreciate.

'Indeed?' said the inquisitor. Brielle caught a glimpse of slitted eyes beneath the hood. 'You, unlike your father, would see these aliens die?'

'I would see them die, my lord,' Brielle replied, aware of the annoyance evident in her voice at the mention of her father.

'Good!' interrupted the cardinal, stepping forward to stand before Brielle, his arms reaching out to grasp her shoulders. 'Perhaps, my child, there is hope for you yet.'

Brielle resisted the urge to squirm at the cardinal's touch, standing defiant as she caught another glimpse of those eyes beneath the inquisitor's hood. She felt somehow... unclean in his presence. What is he? she wondered.

'I am an inquisitor of the Ordo Xenos,' Grand said, 'and as such it is my duty to persecute the xenos wherever it may be found. My lady, if you too would serve your Emperor in this manner, come and look upon the face of our enemy.'

Brielle stood frozen as the inquisitor turned, hauling open the armoured portal before which he and the cardinal had been standing when she had come upon them. Crimson light washed from the opening, its hue obviously at odds with the brilliant white and pale jade given out by the station's own illuminations. She knew that the light told of some human wickedness, though she had no idea what machinations of torture the inquisitor might have concocted.

Brielle watched from the shadows of the darkened interrogation chamber, intent upon the scene unfolding before her. She felt a thrill of tension, combined with the queasiness of apprehension at what she might be forced to witness. She had put aside her musings on just what had drawn her to this place; she would find out soon enough.

Brielle found herself in a low, wide chamber, its tau manufacture usurped by arrays of devices of human crafting. Tall banks had been placed against the walls, glass dials and rapidly blinking lights adorning their surfaces. Fat cables, some pulsing with obscene motions, writhed across the floors and connected the machines, paper seals, secured with holy wax, fluttering from each. Such machinery would soon become a common sight across the tau station, now that it was in the hands of the crusade forces, turning the orbital entirely to the function of serving the Imperium's mighty war machine.

A ring of tall, floor standing lighting rigs stood at the centre of the chamber, each casting its hellish red glow inwards. Brielle could just make out the shuffling figures of Mechanicus attendants within the ring, each making miniscule adjustments to the controls mounted on a further array of machinery. An empty surgical chair stood in the midst of the scene, mighty iron bands mounted where they might secure ankles, wrists and neck. Behind the chair a senior tech-adept tinkered with a device that resembled a crown of incredibly fine needles, each tipped with a tiny point of red glowing light.

Brielle saw clearly that the chair and its associated paraphernalia would be used to extract a confession from a tau prisoner. Sermons she had heard as a child returned to her, reminding her that the xenos must be shown no mercy, it must be sought out and ruthlessly crushed, lest its loathsome presence taint the very soil of the galaxy's worlds, worlds reserved for mankind by manifest destiny and the blood of the martyrs. Yet, her life as a rogue trader had taught her that such doctrines did not apply to all. Furthermore, at Mundus Chasmata she had caught a glimpse of something more, something offered not by conflict with alien races, but by contact. She had caught a glimpse, and desired to see more.

The heavy thud of an armoured portal swinging open caused Brielle to turn her attention to the centre of the chamber. Emerging from the shadows and into the red light stepped two bulkily armoured, helmeted figures. Each held a long staff, the wicked claw at the end of each shaft securely clamped around the neck of the tau prisoner.

Brielle pushed herself back against the wall, raising herself on her toes and craning her neck to gain a clear view through the jumble of machinery. Then she caught herself and shrank back into the ill-lit corner, not wishing to draw attention to herself, though she had the blessing of the cardinal and the inquisitor to view the proceedings.

Despite the clutter surrounding the scene, Brielle was afforded a clear view of the prisoner, the first tau she had seen in the flesh. He was tall, his limbs spindly and fragile in appearance, his neck forced sharply upwards by the mancatchers held by the guards. Brielle noted that the tau was indeed male, and naked, his blue-grey skin cast in a sickly hue by the red illumination. Despite the indignity of his treatment, Brielle noted that the prisoner bore himself with a degree of pride, not having been reduced to the snivelling creatures even many human convicts would be reduced to in such a position.

The guards shoved their prisoner forwards with a cruel jerk, manoeuvring him to a standing position before the chair, his back facing it. Then they yanked back on the mancatchers, forcing the alien down so that he was lying on the chair. The instant his limbs touched the device, the iron bands snapped shut with a vicious clang, securing him firmly against all hope of escape.

The mancatchers disengaged from the prisoner's neck with a metallic rasp, and the guards brought their weapons to their sides in parade ground fashion. The two armoured figures then turned and stomped off into the shadows, where Brielle assumed they took up guarding positions, though she could not make them out from where she stood.

Silence settled over the chamber. Brielle became aware of a stark, somehow acidic tension building in the air. Seconds dragged into minutes, the Mechanicus attendants shuffling around the prostrate alien, making unseen adjustments and mumbling prayers to appease the machine spirits. She watched as the prisoner's chest rose and fell, a fine sheen of sweat appearing beneath the heat of the lights.

Then, Inquisitor Grand emerged from the shadows, into the harsh red light. He wore his customary black hood and robes, but Brielle could see that he wore some manner of glove, long needles and fine, silvery wires protruding from his robes.

As the inquisitor approached the tau, Brielle saw that the prisoner too had caught sight of Grand. The tau's breathing increased as he strove to turn his head to look upon the inquisitor. Grand took up his position immediately behind the prisoner, and rested his hands on the device mounted over the tau's head.

'If the choice were mine,' whispered the inquisitor, his voice plainly audible despite its low tone, 'I would incinerate every last one of you. I would reduce you to ashes, and scour clean those worlds you have sullied with your filthy tread.'

The breath caught in Brielle's throat at the inquisitor's words, their sheer vehemence making her profoundly grateful that they were not directed at her.

'But, it has been decided that you may be of more use to mankind alive, for a time at least. Although I have the authority and the right to order you and all your kind destroyed,' said the inquisitor looking away from the prisoner and, it felt to Brielle, turning his head in her direction, 'I am willing to accede to the will of the whole, for a time at least.'

Brielle looked at the prisoner's face, to see what his reaction to the inquisitor's words might be. It occurred to her that the tau, in all likelihood could not understand Grand's words. She knew that some amongst the aliens had learned to communicate in passable Gothic, gleaned from the many systems throughout the entire region that they had infiltrated, but she had no inkling how widespread this had become. The tau's face betrayed no specific understanding of Grand's statement, beyond an evident appreciation of the inherent malice.

As if in answer to Brielle's musings, the inquisitor drew himself up to his full height. He lifted his hands and placed them on either side of the apparatus behind the tau's head, lowering the crown of needles and probes. The wires writhing at Grand's wrists snaked out of his voluminous sleeves, each linking up, and melding to a tiny port on the device.

Brielle realised that the inquisitor meant to undertake something other than a verbal interrogation.

The rise and fall of the prisoner's chest became faster and shallower, yet he closed his eyes as if in noble resignation of his fate. Brielle felt a prickling sensation crawl over her skin, realising that the feeling was more than one of simple unease at the scene unfolding before her. Her skin itched, and it took a supreme effort to resist the urge to scratch it with raking nails. She forced her attention onto the centre of the chamber, seeing that the inquisitor's hands were clamped around the prisoner's forehead, a halo of writhing, hair-thin wires joining human and tau in some cruel, blasphemous union.

Brielle watched as Inquisitor Grand used some form of witchery. He was tearing into the prisoner's psyche, using the wires to bridge the gulf between human and xenos. She felt revulsion well up within her; she felt unclean. She felt spiritually soiled by the psychic taint radiating from the scene before her. She felt literally revolted, as if she had not washed in a month, as if her skin, her organs were contagious, and to wear her own body was to wallow in corruption.

Brielle caught herself, shaking free of the sensation with a supreme effort of will. She leant against the wall behind her, realising that she was reacting to the inquisitor's use of his powers. She took a deep breath and gathered herself, before walking from the chamber in as controlled a manner as she could manage.

Ever-increasing waves of actinic corruption snapped at her heels as she walked through the chamber's armoured portal, the prisoner's alien screams echoing behind her before being abruptly cut off as the door rolled shut at her passing.

Having left the interrogation chamber, Brielle paced back and forth in the brightly lit, sparsely appointed atrium. She could not physically be in the room, sharing the space with the inquisitor as he went about his terrible business. Yet she feared the impression her leaving might create, and so she impatiently awaited the end of Grand's bloody interrogation. All the while, she was able to hear the prisoner's screaming, faint and muffled by the heavy armour of the chamber's entrance. Worse still, she could feel the psychic backwash of the inquisitor's probing, though thankfully the effect was but a shadow of what she had experienced within.

After an hour or more had passed, the portal rolled open with a heavy grinding, the deep red, infernal light washing through. Standing in the portal was the cardinal. He beckoned her to follow with a silent gesture.

Stepping across the chamber's threshold once more, Brielle was greeted with the overpowering stench of burned meat. As revolting as the odour was, more disturbing was the realisation that the taint was also spiritual, a stain upon the soul and upon the ether that would remain within the chamber even were it scoured with the cleansing flames of holy promethium.

'Be not shy, child,' the cardinal said as he turned to address Brielle, his voice low and threatening. 'We do the Emperor's work.'

'But you wanted them all dead,' she blurted, unable to comprehend why the cardinal and the inquisitor had interrogated the suspect when, by all accounts, they had opposed doing so in the recent council session.

'Oh, I do,' the cardinal replied, a twitching grin touching the corner of his mouth, 'I very much do, but the council has decided that we should know our foe, and so we shall.' With a slow flourish of his right arm, the cardinal stepped to one side to afford Brielle a view of the centre of the chamber.

She looked to the surgical chair, gave an involuntary gasp and spun around, her hand shooting up to cover her mouth. What she had seen upon, and scattered around, the chair filled her with utter horror.

'I understand,' the cardinal said from behind her. 'The xenos is a filthy creature, its form so different from the consecrated body of Man.'

She caught her breath as the cardinal spoke, feeling her heart beat return to something approaching a normal rate. She turned to face him, but pointedly avoided looking towards the chamber's centre.

'I thought...'

'Speak child, for you are among friends.'

'I thought,' she continued, 'you were going to question him.' She felt foolish even as she spoke, but went on nonetheless. 'Why did you...'

'Kill it?' the cardinal asked, his voice loud. 'The xenos has no right to live in the galaxy. The stars belong to Mankind. The council would have us question the prisoner, and so we did. Once questioned, it was disposed of, as is only fitting.'

Brielle felt cold dread at the cardinal's words, not that he should act in so callous a fashion, for such deeds were the price of humanity's survival in a galaxy of a million threats. No, she was filled with the notion that here was a man who would manipulate the entire crusade to achieve his own ends, and it mattered not a bit who suffered along the way. She saw in her mind's eye the course the crusade would take if the cardinal were to become the dominant figure on the council. The entire region, the Damocles Gulf and beyond would be reduced to ashes. None would survive to profit, whether from conquest or conflict.

'But,' the cardinal continued, 'the beast's death was not in vain.' Brielle looked up to see that Inquisitor Grand had come silently upon the pair, and was standing at the cardinal's shoulder.

'Indeed,' the inquisitor whispered, his eyes seeming to Brielle to flash crimson for just an instant, before being swallowed up beneath the shadows of his hood. 'I discovered much of interest before the prisoner expired.'

'What did he tell you?' Brielle asked, playing along with what she saw as the inquisitor's theatre.

Grand chuckled by way of explanation, a sound Brielle scarcely believed could have issued from a human throat.

'He told me nothing,' the inquisitor replied. 'I saw what I needed to see, but no words were exchanged between me and the prisoner.'

'So what did you see?' Brielle asked, annoyance spiced with fear rising within her.

'I saw a race entirely consumed with a false ideology. They believe they expand for the good of all, but I saw where they fear to look, and I saw it is fear that drives the tau ever outwards, and it is fear that will ultimately drive them to destruction as they are dashed against the ancient forces at large in the galaxy.'

Brielle felt confusion at the inquisitor's words. She had gleaned a little of the tau's philosophies, and did not recognise the drives that Grand described. So far as she understood, the tau sought to unite every race they came into contact with, through a desire for mutually constructive cooperation.

The inquisitor was studying her, Brielle realised, and she returned her attention to him, locking her thoughts away.

'I saw a race that believes the galaxy is a small place. A place they believe they can tame with childish ideologies and cold technologies. They hurl themselves across the void without an inkling of who or what awaits them. If they only knew...'

'They would run and hide,' said the cardinal. 'And so they should, for even now a force is being gathered to seek out and destroy a nearby colony that the inquisitor learned of from the prisoner's mind. Even as the battle rages below us, we shall send out our forces and destroy these aliens wherever they may be found. When every tau on this side of the Gulf is dead, we shall cross the void and raze to ashes every last world in their pathetic little empire.'

Brielle knew then that the crusade could not be allowed to continue if these two were to be its leaders. What had begun as an opportunity was rapidly descending into utter madness. Her mind reeled as she considered the scale of the disaster about to descend upon the Eastern Rim, upon man and tau both. She looked up and saw that the inquisitor's armoured guards were escorting in the next prisoner, and the Mechanicus attendants were shovelling the previous one into a large containment drum, to be jettisoned, no doubt, with the station's waste. As the cardinal and the inquisitor turned their backs on her, their attentions entirely shifted to their new task, she turned and walked on unsteady legs out of the chamber.

She maintained her composure almost the entire way back to her ship. It was not until she had boarded once more that she gave in to the urge to throw up violently across the deck. The confrontation had left her soiled. She was sure that it was not merely the exposure to Grand's witchery that left her feeling so compromised. It was the rank insanity that made her so ill, an epic lunacy that would spell the doom of the entire fleet and, perhaps, an entire race, if she did not act.

* * *

Later, Brielle lounged in her quarters aboard the *Fairlight*. She had welcomed the return to the familiar surroundings of her vessel. It might be cramped and ill lit compared to the tau station, but it was her home. The lighting was turned low, and a shadowed figure sat opposite her.

'I know enough of the Imperium,' the man said, 'to know that they will carry out their threat.'

Brielle sighed and took a sip of liqueur. Despite the fact that she had bathed, for hours, and scrubbed her skin raw, she still felt the horrific stain that had touched her in the interrogation chamber.

'I know that, Naal.'

'And you must act.'

'I know that too.'

Naal leant forward in his seat, his face, tattooed with an Imperial Aquila and lines of spidery text, came into the light. 'My masters aided you when you called upon them. They, in turn, require your aid.'

'I know,' Brielle replied.

CHAPTER FOUR

'The council is in session,' the orderly announced, the iron shod end of his ceremonial staff striking the floor. 'General Gauge has the chair.'

Lucian settled into the high-backed chair, still unused to the shape, for it was manufactured not for the comfort of the human council, but for the tau whose station they occupied. At least his eyes were adapting to the stark light, he mused, and he was getting used to the alien contours of the station's design. Thank the Emperor it was the general's turn to serve as chair of the crusade council, Lucian thought, for Wendall Gauge was a man that Lucian could respect.

'Please, gentlemen,' Gauge said as he sat, 'make yourselves comfortable. We have much to discuss.'

Lucian watched as the members of the council settled themselves in for what they all knew would be the final session before the crusade embarked upon its most ambitious phase. All members were present, including the huge figures of the two Space Marines who sat on the council, each barely fitting in the alien-made seats. Captain Rumann, the most senior Space Marine in the fleet, showed no apparent emotion at the victories he had commanded during the still-raging ground war on the world below. Sergeant Sarik however, sitting on Lucian's left, radiated steely martial pride at the actions he had personally led.

'I suggest we begin with reports to council. Who will speak first?' the general asked, casting his stern gaze around the table.

'I would address the council.' Admiral Jellaqua spoke up,

straightening his jacket and clearing his throat. 'My command stands at eight capital vessels and nine escort squadrons,' the admiral stated, his tone matter of fact, but professional pride glinting in his eyes. 'In addition, I have three deep space support echelons in place, each with the capacity to carry the fleet to the other side of the galaxy and back.'

Lucian allowed himself a small grin. He saw the truth through Jellaqua's boast. He knew that the admiral had put in place a formidable auxiliary fleet, a vast force of long-range tankers, freighters, service vessels and transports. It was an impressive achievement, and the admiral had Lucian's genuine admiration.

'All ships of the line are approaching readiness, and I estimate full capacity within three days. The *Regent Lakshimbal* has undergone a significant refit of her port drive section following the damage sustained during the Sy'l'Kell action. By bringing forward her major centennial service, we have significantly improved her combat potential. In addition, the *Duchess McIntyre* has a full complement following the mutinies she suffered at Garrus. The new crew is veteran and trustworthy, and unlike the last lot, they know how the Navy deals with mutinous bastards that try to take over one of the Emperor's warships.'

As the admiral sat, the council members nodded sagely at his last remark. The admiral referred, Lucian knew, to the fate of the several thousand mutineers who had been ejected, in long, flailing lines, from the *Duchess McIntyre*'s torpedo tubes once the commissars and naval provost parties had regained control of the vessel. Lucian had thought it an imaginative form of execution, and certainly one that would give pause to any more such plots lurking within the fleet's enlisted ranks.

'Thank you, admiral,' said General Gauge. 'Captain Rumann, might we hear of your victories?'

The Space Marine nodded in response to the general's invitation, and stood. Captain Rumann made for an imposing figure, towering over the table and the other councillors sitting around it. When he spoke, his baritone voice was cold and mechanical, his vocal cords having been replaced by a bionic vox unit.

'Council,' the Space Marine said, his cybernetic eyes scanning each member in turn, 'I have to report that the assault on the target world went according to plan. As you know, the assault on the orbital in which we reside was enacted by my forces, and spearheaded by three squads under Sergeant Sarik.' At the mention of his name, the White Scar grinned savagely. The Iron Hands captain continued. 'The station was cleansed within three point five hours, though no significant resistance was met. We believe that only a token defence force was left in place, while senior xenos were evacuated to the world below.'

Sarik snorted at the captain's assessment of the quality of the resistance, though Rumann showed no reaction.

'The planetary assault operation is still ongoing. Our forces, spearheaded by the Scythes of the Emperor have made contact with a number of xenos troop types that we have not encountered before. It appears this race makes extensive use of anti-grav technology, manifested in heavy armour and jump infantry. Casualties amongst the Guard are running at twelve percent, with a commensurate drop in combat effectiveness. Casualties amongst Astartes units are at less than five percent, with no drop in effectiveness.'

The Space Marine showed no emotion as he spoke of the first encounters with the tau armoured units, which had cost the crusade forces dear. The price had been paid in the blood and machines of the 17th Brimlock Dragoons, and Lucian had seen the pict captures of the Imperial Guard tank columns being ambushed by the fast moving tau vehicles. He knew that only the timely intervention of the crusade's army reserve units had averted the massacre of the entire regiment and a humiliating defeat at the hands of the aliens.

'Having secured the primary drop zone, Sergeant Sarik affected the capture of the tau high command facility. We believe the enemy's command and control capabilities are rendered entirely ineffectual. The 9th Brimlock Fusiliers are supporting a general advance on objectives 23 delta through 67 gamma. I expect all resistance to have collapsed within twelve hours.'

Polite applause rippled around the council chamber as the captain sat once more. Lucian leaned back in his seat, the reality that the crusade was really underway and achieving its ends beginning to sink in. He knew they had a very long way to go, for they had yet to even breach the Damocles Gulf, yet Lucian could not help but nurture a spark of hope, of ambition and of expectation at what might lie ahead. Yet, he knew too that this first battle would in all likelihood prove little more than an opening skirmish. The crusade had yet to utilise more than a portion of its strength, which included many more regiments of Imperial Guard and the towering, awesomely destructive war machines of the Adeptus Titanicus.

Lucian watched as the orderly who had announced the council session convened approached General Gauge and spoke to him in a muted voice. Lucian took the opportunity to turn to his son, who sat in a second tier of seats behind that positioned around the table.

Lucian leaned in towards Korvane. 'Our status?'

'Ninety nine percent, father,' Korvane replied. Lucian caught the intonation straight away and leaned in closer to speak.

'What is it, Korvane? I need to know if something's wrong.' As if to prove the truth of his comment, Lucian saw the orderly out of the corner of his eye as he moved from General Gauge and bent down to speak to Inquisitor Grand.

'Well,' Korvane said, 'I can vouch for the *Rosetta*, as you can the *Oceanid*, but I fear I cannot vouch for the *Fairlight*.'

Lucian looked his son straight in the eye. He noted as he did so that the rejuve treatments Korvane had undergone, following the terrible injuries he had received at the hands of the tau fleet at Arrikis Epsilon, had not been entirely successful. Lucian knew that his son would bear the marks of that battle for the remainder of his life.

'What of Brielle?' Lucian asked. 'Has she not made ready her vessel?' Even as he asked, he knew that even if Brielle had completed the preparations for her ship to cross the Damocles Gulf, she would not have volunteered such details to her stepbrother. She was becoming increasingly withdrawn, and had been for some time.

'I have spoken with her officers, father.' Korvane's expression became dark and brooding as he spoke of his stepsister. 'It appears that she delegated the task to her bridge crew and went aboard the orbital for some length of time. At that point, she had not returned.'

Lucian released a long sigh. This news did not surprise him, yet he could not help but be disappointed. He wished he could get up and leave, to track down his truculent daughter and shake some sense into her. But he could not, for even as he pondered the issue, he heard his name spoken as the general requested he apprise the council of his fleet's state of readiness.

Brielle would have to wait, he thought, standing to address the council.

'It's this way,' Brielle said, her voice hushed, but urgent. 'Three blocks in from the primary conduit.'

Brielle scanned the dark corridor ahead of her, satisfied that the way was clear, for now at least. She turned her head to the figure trailing her, the man who had got her mixed up in the affairs of the tau back on Mundus Chasmata.

'This had better be worth it, Naal. If anyone catches us I'm not sure even my father can protect me.'

'My lady,' Naal replied, 'please, rest assured my masters will reward you for your aid. The prisoners are senior members of their caste, and what they know of the Empire cannot be allowed to fall into the crusade's hands.'

Brielle paused, momentarily paralysed by the weight of her actions. She was faced, as she had been so many times before, with awful duplicity. She knew that the crusade had embarked upon an evil folly of epic proportion, its course set upon the destruction of a culture it had no knowledge of. She, however, did have some knowledge of the tau, and was rapidly coming to the conclusion that they offered far more even than life as a rogue trader held for her. Yet, she was born and raised a scion of a mighty dynasty, and loath to throw away millennia of prosperity, and the status that came with it.

'I understand that, and I agree that Grand and the cardinal must not be allowed to do to the other prisoners what they did to the first.' She felt her gorge rise as she pictured the tau prisoner after his interrogation, and recalled the inquisitor's scathing rant about the tau race. 'If the inquisitor could extract that much information from just one prisoner, I dread to think what he might find out from all of them.'

'Quite so, my lady,' replied Naal, 'and I offer you my personal thanks for your aid.'

Brielle did not reply, concentrating instead upon negotiating the warren of tunnels leading to the detention block. This section of the station was at present ill-lit, the tech-priests having shut down entire swathes of the station's systems while they installed generatoria of more appropriate, human-made, design. Brielle had noted how the station was already beginning to feel like a manmade, rather than alien-made, installation. Formerly bright-lit passages were now dark. Where the air had been filtered and clear, now holy incense circulated through the conduits, and where clean lines and unadorned surfaces met the eye, crudely draped cabling snaked along the walls, votive parchments fluttering in the camphor scented breeze.

She continued down the corridor, indicating with a glance that Naal should follow. The pair walked openly rather than sneaking in the shadows, yet neither wanted to be noticed. Brielle knew that questions would be asked were she to be observed and reported on. She also knew that Naal would be arrested instantly were he to be questioned by one of the Guard provosts or munitorum bully-boys who maintained order on the station. Naal had no official standing in the crusade, no provable rank or identity, and so would come under grave suspicion were he to be found in the vicinity of the detention block. Brielle knew that even her influence would do little do aid Naal should he be caught. She had already decided what she would do were that to happen, though she had yet to admit it fully to herself.

The pair came to a junction, and Brielle peered around one corner, while Naal craned his neck around the other. 'All clear, my lady,' Naal said, awaiting her lead. Funny, Brielle mused, that Naal, human envoy of the tau and therefore traitor to his race, should continue to address her in so formal a manner. They had shared the risks of battle at Arrikis Epsilon, and she had shared her bed with him many times since, yet still he maintained the role of servant or advisor, exactly the role he had performed under his previous human master, the traitor Imperial Commander of Mundus Chasmata.

'Which way, my lady?' Naal asked. Brielle knew that he was fully aware of the route to the detention block.

'This way,' she nodded to the left. 'We're on top of the conduit now, so get ready.'

Brielle saw Naal pat a concealed weapon under his left arm. Brielle drew her own, a laspistol of archaic design and priceless heritage, checked the charge, and returned it to its holster. She would rather settle this by stealth and subterfuge, but if she had to resort to violence she would do so. It was, after all, for the greater good, she mused, setting off along the corridor, the entrance to the detention block visible at its end.

'Thank you gentlemen,' General Gauge said, standing as the last of the councillors completed his address. 'Now, onto the real meat of the matter,' he said, activating a stud on his console, raising a triangle of three large pict screens from the centre of the table that flickered into life as they rose. 'Strategy.'

The general looked around the table, his scarred face turning to each councillor in turn. Lucian had heard the tales of how those scars had been attained, though he scarcely believed that a man could survive some of the encounters the old Catachan Guardsman was said to have won.

'Our plans to this point have assumed a jump off point here,' he said, pointing to a region of local space displayed on one of the screens. 'The fleet crosses the Gulf and musters here,' he continued, pointing to another grid, 'ready for further action. Comments?'

'That plan,' Lucian spoke up before the likes of the cardinal could interrupt, 'assumes we face no more than a handful of occupied and defended systems. I still say that if we go in all guns blazing and find ourselves up against well-defended systems we will have the worse of it.' Lucian saw the cardinal bristle at his words, but continued, 'We must offer them terms the instant we cross the gulf, and give them the impression we're just the spearhead. Then, they'll be ours.'

Cardinal Gurney surged to his feet. 'Nonsense! To show them mercy is to admit weakness, and thereby to blaspheme the Emperor! I will have no part in a scheme to pacify, where our mission is to decimate.'

'And pray remind me,' Lucian replied, feeling his blood rise, 'where in our charter does it state we are to exterminate the tau out of hand?'

'I care not for legal niceties, Gerrit,' the cardinal spat back. 'I can see no other course, and believe such an action would be entirely justified and ratified.' The cardinal looked pointedly towards Inquisitor Grand as he said the last, who nodded almost imperceptibly by way of affirmation.

Lucian had wondered at what point the cardinal would play his best card: his alliance with the inquisitor. He doubted that this was the last time Gurney would do so. Lucian had gone up against some powerful enemies before, from Imperial Commanders to retired High Lords of Terra, but had yet to cross swords with the Inquisition. He knew that to do so was madness, for the inquisitors had the licence to perform any act in the name of the Emperor, to command entire armies and to order the destruction of worlds. That Grand was apparently so subtle in exercising his power spoke to Lucian of a greater game, perhaps one in which the inquisitor was but the pawn of higher members of his order. Whatever the truth, Lucian resolved to tread carefully, to engage only the cardinal in open dispute.

'Gentlemen, please,' growled the general, 'we agreed at the outset that we would resolve the issue upon crossing the Gulf, for we have no idea what lies beyond it. The tau might only occupy a single system, in which case we can expect little trouble. They might occupy more, perhaps as many as five, but as yet we simply do not know what we face.'

'This is indeed the case.' Magos Jaakho stood as he spoke, the general sitting in response. 'This entire region is anathema to my order, for it bears no resemblance to the surveys submitted when last an explorator fleet passed through.' Lucian had read of that last survey, which took place almost six millennia past, but had yet to hear the magos speak of it.

'If it weren't for the stringent rites and procedures of my order, I would have concluded upon my arrival that those ancient charts were incorrect, for they bear no resemblance to what we see here before us.' The magos indicated one of the pict screens before the council with a sweep of his arm, a metallic finger emerging from a voluminous red sleeve to point out the swirling eddies of stellar matter that made up the entire region. Within that cauldron of stars lay the Tau Empire, and before it, the Damocles Gulf.

'According to the records in my possession, this region should bear no significant dissimilarity to any nearby cluster. Yet, it seethes with energies the natures of which I can only guess at. I would cross the Gulf, and discover what lays beyond, tau or no tau.'

'Well said,' said Lucian, seizing the half of the statement he agreed with. 'If we exterminate the tau we may never know what's behind the phenomenon. No doubt they have studied the matter in some depth.'

The magos nodded, giving Lucian some hope that he might have swung the explorator lord to his point of view, and in so doing, against the cardinal's.

'So then,' Lucian said, 'can we agree that upon crossing the Gulf, the fleet is to muster as previously agreed, whereupon the council will convene to decide the next course of action?'

The cardinal fixed Lucian with a venomous stare. 'What possible course of action could possibly face us, other than war?'

'I fully expect war,' Lucian replied, his voice low and dangerous. 'I am prepared for it, but I also wish to be prepared for what comes after it.'

Gurney smiled, his face taking on the leer of some daemonic gargoyle. 'What comes after, Gerrit? Nothing comes after. All that will remain of them, of the tau, will be bones and ashes.'

Lucian shook his head in silent disgust, looking around the table to judge which councillors might share his views. He saw that some might. General Gauge, Admiral Jellaqua, noble and honourable warriors both, appeared uneasy at the cardinal's words. Lucian judged the White Scars Space Marine to be a man of honour too, as intolerant of aliens as any of his brethren, but not a mass murderer in the sense advanced by the cardinal. He was less sure of others, and saw that he faced an uphill struggle to persuade any onto a course from which they might all prosper, and away from one in which the cardinal's hellfire and brimstone would lead to nothing but death.

Lucian's glance settled upon the figure of Inquisitor Grand, who was conferring with the council orderly, his manner both threatening and surreptitious at once. Taking a deep breath, Lucian went on.

'Council members, I am, as you know, the son of a great line of rogue traders. My family and a thousand others have penetrated the outer darkness for millennia, pushing back the frontiers of the Emperor's Domains, bringing lost worlds back to the fold of humanity, and exploiting all we encounter for the ultimate benefit of all mankind.' Lucian saw the cardinal smirk at this, but carried on nonetheless. 'We do so not by launching ourselves at any and all foes we encounter, but by measured conquest. Those we cannot conquer, we exploit, one way or another. I tell you, we must accept the possibility that the tau might prove too proficient a foe to crush so easily. If we are to have war, a reasoned war with a profitable outcome, then I pledge my support wholeheartedly. But if we are to slaughter these aliens for no reason other than their existence, at the cost to ourselves, I fear we might pay. Then I cannot, in all truth, promise my unqualified aid.'

Silence followed Lucian's address, and he sat once more, content that he had spoken his mind truthfully. Whether or not it would sway any of the council remained to be seen. Lucian turned to his son, and saw that Korvane was intently watching Inquisitor Grand, his expression glowering yet unreadable. Even as Lucian looked to the inquisitor, Grand stood, nodded briefly to the council, and left the chamber without a word. Perhaps Grand feared that Lucian had swayed the council, and had left before that power could be mobilised against him. Perhaps not, Lucian mused, for the affairs of inquisitors were best left well alone.

Brielle's heart raced as she approached the armoured portal, the entrance to the detention block. A heavy, circular door, tau iconography stencilled upon it in blocky white text, barred the way. The passage was dark and they were alone, and for that Brielle was thankful.

'Is it locked?' Brielle asked Naal as he appeared at her side.

In response to her question, Naal consulted a spartan console beside the door. He nodded. 'It is, my lady, from within.'

'What now then? Can you get it open?'

'Yes indeed,' Naal grinned, producing a small device of obvious tau manufacture from his jacket. She watched as he placed the device, which was no larger than his hand, against the door console. It adhered to the wall instantly. Lights began to blink across its slab-like surface, at first in apparently random fashion, before taking on a steady sequence. The screen upon the device's surface lit up, and Naal stepped back with evident pride.

Brielle looked to Naal, and then to the device. She stepped in closer, pushing her way in front of him to look upon the small pict screen. She saw what it showed, and turned her head to kiss Naal upon the cheek.

The viewer showed the scene on the other side of the portal, the device evidently having achieved communion with the station's native security net. Brielle knew that the tech-priests had yet to fathom the workings of the tau command and control network, and had been more concerned with superimposing their own machinery on the station than with shutting down the old. She was grateful, for it gave her an edge, and a chance of success.

Brielle watched a scene that she guessed was captured by a spy lens in the chamber beyond. The entire station was covered with the small, unobtrusive devices, and this room was no exception. It showed two munitorum guards, both female, both tall and broad, and both armed with shock mauls and protected by the heavy, interlocking plate of carapace armour. They were not the sort of women she would want to pass time with.

'This device communes with the entire station logister network?' Brielle asked, turning her head to look up at Naal, who looked over her shoulder.

'Yes, though the tau terms for what you describe differ significantly.'

'Fine,' Brielle said. 'We need to distract them, activate an alarm elsewhere to draw them away long enough for us to get in. Can you do that?'

'I can, my lady,' Naal replied, reaching around Brielle's shoulders to operate the device. Brielle watched as alien characters appeared on the viewer, Naal working his way through a series of menus and submenus, until he had located the function he sought.

'I have access to the master security net,' he said. 'From here I can trigger any alarm in the station. Which would you have me activate?'

Brielle smiled demurely, a sudden thrill coursing through her as she considered the mischief she could wreak with but a single command. She could trigger a core reactor leak alarm, and cause every soul on the station to abandon ship. She could trigger fire retardant in the council chambers; the possibilities really were endless.

But, she knew she had a task to fulfil, and could not risk discovery for so trivial a prank, though the thought of some of the pompous buffoons on the council soaked in foam did have a certain appeal.

'We need to activate something low level and nearby, something that'll get their attention, but no one else's.'

She watched as Naal scrolled through a long list of functions. Stopping, he asked 'Localised conduit overheat?'

'So long as it's just this compartment. We don't want the entire deck to evacuate. And make sure the threat is coming from our side of the door; we don't want them plundering right into us.'

Naal smiled, accessed another sub menu, and nodded. 'I can activate the alarm in such a fashion that only the guards will hear it. I'll make it appear as a precautionary, yet mandatory alert so they don't spread panic wherever they evacuate to. That should give us the time we need, my lady.'

'Do it.'

Naal activated the alert function, and switched the viewer back to the scene within the detention block. She watched as the guards' heads turned sharply, though she could not hear what they heard. The women looked to one another, and one shrugged, her lips moving in speech.

'Move, you witless bitches,' Brielle muttered, suddenly uneasy that the guards might decide it was more important to stay at their posts than to answer the alert.

Then, just as Brielle was considering increasing the alert level, she saw the guards shoulder their mauls and leave, exiting the detention block through a far exit. Brielle breathed a sigh of relief and turned around to face Naal.

'Come on then,' she smiled. 'Open the door and let's get on with it.'

'My pleasure,' Naal answered, activating the armoured portal, and detaching the control device.

Brielle moved to one side of the opening as the huge door swung inwards, peering through cautiously. The sound of the alarm came from within, its tone shrill and insistent. Naal pocketed the device and followed Brielle's lead, peering from the opposite side of the opening.

'All clear, my lady,' he said. 'Do you wish me to enter first?'

Annoyance flared within her at the suggestion that she might not be as capable as he was at dealing with whatever might await them through the portal. She drew her laspistol and stepped through the opening before he could do so himself.

The detention block was as dark as the passages through which they had approached it, though Brielle was struck by an air of oppression as soon as she entered. The clean lines and unadorned surfaces of the original tau structure were here, as elsewhere, subverted by the presence of man. She saw that the block was not originally intended as a prison, and doubted that the tau even had much use for such institutions. It had plainly served as some form of storage facility, the tech-priests having crudely welded great iron bars across the bays, each of which radiated out from the area in which Brielle found herself.

She looked down each bay, one at a time, catching movement in the darkness behind the bars on either side of the long spurs. She knew that one spur would contain the tau prisoners, but which?

'Look for a manifest, a log, anything that might tell us where they are.' She called to Naal, rifling through the parchments and scrolls piled on top of a bureau nearby. Papers scattered in all directions. 'And see if you can deactivate that alarm.'

Naal looked around the chamber, located a section of wall, and depressed a barely discernible panel. A small section of wall lifted up, to reveal a bank of bright-lit controls. Naal reached up and deactivated the alarm with a single motion.

'Thank you,' Brielle said. 'That was really getting on my...'

'I have them, my lady,' Naal said. 'Cell block Eta.'

'Good,' Brielle replied. 'Cover that up when you're done. Which one's Eta?'

'This way,' Naal said, indicating one of the dark passages radiating from the area in which they stood.

'Good. Follow me,' she replied, setting off for the cell block. She was soon engulfed in darkness, and she slowed lest she stumble. As her eyes became accustomed to the low light, she became aware of subtle movements within the shadows beyond the bars, and halted to look closer. She noticed too that the air in the block was even closer, the subtle taint of despair drifting upon a stale breeze. She squatted, determined to discover who, or what was imprisoned within.

A low moan emanated from the cell, sending a shiver up Brielle's spine. It was the moan of the damned, she thought, and had surely not been voiced by one of the tau prisoners. As her eyes adjusted to the dark still more, she began to discern lumpen forms within the cell, the source, she realised, of the movement and the terrible sound.

'Deserters,' Naal whispered from behind Brielle, causing her to start. 'Bound for trial, or what passes for trial in the Imperium.'

She turned and looked into his face, her eyes taking in the aquila tattooed across it. 'These men are criminals?'

'Who can say, my lady.'

'They refused to fight?'

'According to the records, yes.'

'Then they are criminals.'

'In the eyes of the Imperium, yes,' Naal replied, his voice low and dangerous. 'Perhaps they merely refused to fight against the Tau Empire. Perhaps they see what the crusade council, what the High Lords of Terra themselves, cannot.'

'Perhaps,' Brielle replied, 'but it matters not a bit. If they refuse to fight, they will die. That's how it is. That's how it's always been and how it always will be.'

'Not if more like them, like you and me, see an alternative.'

'There's a big difference,' Brielle said, looking back towards the forms within the cell, 'between aiding the tau, and actually turning on your own race.'

'No one has asked you to turn on your own, my lady. Though you yourself have asked...'

'Not yet, they haven't, Naal, but I'm not stupid. I know where this could lead. But know this. If I join, I do so on my terms, when I'm ready to. Do you understand?'

'I understand.' Naal stood as he spoke. 'All I can ask is that you do what you think right, for the Greater Good.'

Brielle stood without answering. She resumed her search of the black, peering into the darkness beyond the bars on either side as she passed along its length. As she approached the end of the passage, she knew that she had found what she had come for.

She halted, indicating with a gesture that Naal should do likewise. She saw a row of figures slumped across the deck, through the bars on her right, and by their form, they were obviously not human.

At that instant, a wave of nausea washed over her, and the air around her tasted suddenly tainted. She had experienced that horrible sensation once before, in the presence of...

A whisper, low and laden with menace, rasped from the cell to her left. 'My lady Arcadius.'

She turned, sweat appearing at her brow as the cell block felt suddenly humid and stifling.

'And our friend, Captain Delphi, though I doubt Brielle here knows him as such.'

Brielle knew that it was Inquisitor Grand. She felt, on some primal level, the corruption of his presence even before he had spoken. She felt paralysis clawing at her limbs, and knew that the inquisitor used his witchery against her. She tried to look at Naal, confusion at Grand's naming of him rising within her. She found she could barely turn her head, and through her peripheral vision saw that Naal was likewise afflicted. She looked back towards the inquisitor just as he emerged from the cell, a dark shadow against an even darker backdrop, only his mouth visible beneath the folds of his black hood.

'I'd hoped to find one of you here,' Grand said, his voice still low and rasping, 'but to find you both... surely the Emperor smiles upon me.'

Brielle heard Naal try to respond, but only a pained croak emerged.

'Hush, Delphi,' the inquisitor told Naal. 'There'll be plenty of time for confessions later. There's much for us to discuss, and much you'll wish to tell me, in time. You'll go to your grave, Delphi, but you'll be unburdened of your many sins against the God-Emperor of Man.'

Brielle heard Naal's response. Though unintelligible, its meaning was unmistakable.

'And you, my pretty.' Grand turned his attention back to Brielle. 'What shall we do with you? Is it even worth my while attempting to extract a confession from you? Or should I just practise my tender arts upon your soft flesh, beginning with your mind, perhaps, and working my way out. Maybe Delphi here would like to watch.'

Brielle spat an incoherent curse at the hooded inquisitor, hate welling within her. She screamed in silent, mental denial, directing all her rage and frustration at her capture.

'Now now, my dear, settle down,' the inquisitor said, turning his back on Brielle and advancing upon Naal. Feeling her rage boil out of control, she pushed with all her might against the mental bonds that restrained her. She focused on Grand's back, boring her hatred deep into his soul.

The inquisitor turned sharply, his attentions entirely focused on Brielle. She felt a strange sense of triumph; though she would likely die, she would do so with defiance and with honour. That much had been instilled in her by her upbringing amongst the savage nobility of the feral world of Chogoris.

'You are a strong one, aren't you?' Grand said, reaching out a hand towards Brielle's face. She felt his caress upon her cheek, reeling at the witch power coursing through it and into her body, the source of the paralysis against which she struggled.

'You can feel me, can't you?' Grand moved in closer, his hand snaking around to the nape of Brielle's neck, and grasping the flowing plaits of her hair. The sight of his hooded face filled her vision. She saw into the shadows beneath the hood, witchfire guttering in the depths of his shadowed eyes. 'Let me see you.'

As Grand closed in upon her, Brielle felt her soul begin to wither beneath his baleful gaze. Corruption radiated from him, focused and burning through his touch where it gripped the back of her neck. She screamed within against the pain of his touch, pushing against him with all the power her soul could muster, determined beyond reason to expel the paralysis entering her body, to push it back into his.

Alarm appeared in Grand's eyes, and Brielle was stunned to see him stagger backwards, backing into Naal as he did so. Unable to control his limbs, Naal fell to the deck with a painful crash, knocking him senseless against the bars.

'You think you can resist me do you, girl?' the inquisitor growled as he regained his balance. 'What little power you might have is insufficient. Now, you are mine.'

Focusing all her pain and rage, Brielle lashed out in one final effort to break the bonds paralysing her body. She felt her soul slipping from her, and her vision blurred into blinding white fire. She pushed one last time, feeling something yield beneath her effort. She realised with a start that it was her own flesh that yielded so, movement returning to her limbs. With a rush of sensation, her body was returned to her, and she collapsed to the ground before she could fully take control of her motor functions.

The sudden loss of control saved her life. A deafening report filled the cell block, followed an instant later by the unmistakable sound of an exploding bolt as it struck the bulkhead behind the space she had just vacated.

Brielle rolled, her vision clearing. She looked up and saw the black-robed form of the inquisitor advancing upon her, bolt pistol in hand, his eyes swirling with the ectoplasmic whirlpools beneath his hood.

As Grand lowered the pistol to draw a bead on her head, she lifted her arm and with a single flick of her thumb activated the tiny, one-shot flamer she wore in the guise of a ring. A cone of chemical fire erupted from the weapon, leaping the two metres between Brielle and the inquisitor, engulfing him instantly. The inquisitor's robes caught fire, and he gave voice to a scream that Brielle felt in her soul as much as heard, searing her mind and threatening to knock her out. She clambered to her feet and rushed to Naal's side as the inquisitor staggered against a wall and collapsed. She saw that Naal lived yet, but was still overcome by the paralysis inflicted by Grand's psychic attack. She hooked an arm beneath each of his shoulders, and pulled with all her might. Naal's body was a deadweight, but she succeeded in dragging him along the passageway and back to the entrance to the detention block.

'Come on,' she breathed, shaking Naal's shoulders in frustration. She knew that the guards might return any moment, and the conflagration still guttering at the end of Cell Block Eta might trigger a real alarm and bring damage control parties down upon them. 'Come on, Naal, fight!'

'My lady... I'm...' Naal's voice was weak, but Brielle felt overcome with relief as she saw movement return to his limbs.

'Don't speak,' she replied, standing while lending him a hand in doing likewise. 'We have to leave, right now.'

With a last glance over her shoulder before leaving, Brielle saw that the fire that had consumed the inquisitor was beginning to spread. She looked around and saw the console that controlled the locking mechanisms for the entire detention block. She slammed her fist down upon the master lock release, hearing the cell doors in each of the blocks swing upon.

Seeing the tau prisoners stir, she drew a breath and yelled. 'If you're coming, follow me!' Whether or not they could understand her, she saw that the prisoners were responding, creeping through the shadows to join her.

With that, she hitched an arm behind Naal's back, lending him what support she could as his strength returned, and left the detention block as fire and smoke engulfed it.

CHAPTER FIVE

Lucian winced as a titanic grinding echoed the length of the *Oceanid*'s drive service deck, the sound of the fleet tender *Harlot* being made safe alongside, her docking clamps grasping the *Oceanid*'s holding points with immense force. A glance to his side told him that Korvane had the same reaction, a poor indictment of the quality of the crews of the crusade's auxiliary vessels.

'Heave, you worthless scum!'

Lucian grinned as the petty officers below bellowed their orders to the press-ganged ratings crowding the service deck, each hauling on the mighty chains that secured the docking clamps.

'Well enough,' Lucian said, turning to the red-robed tech-priest at his side. 'Commence the operation.'

'Yes, my lord,' the adept replied, mechadendrites snaking from his back, the grasping claws of each arm operating a lever on the consoles mounted all around the gallery.

Lucian watched as the toiling crews below completed their work, and the petty officers corralled the cursing men from the service deck. The area below the gallery from which Lucian and Korvane observed was a vast, spheroid chamber, dominated in the centre by a mighty column from floor to ceiling that resembled nothing less than a vast stalactite grown so huge it had merged with the stalagmites below. Pipes and valves dominated the column's every surface, clouds of steam and other exhaust gases venting from spitting valves, rivulets of run-off pouring down its flanks to pool in great steaming, oily lakes across the deck.

'I've always hated this,' Lucian said, his son nodding in agreement with his words. Of all the practicalities of void faring, replenishing the warp drives had always been the task he loathed the most. It was quite unlike the taking on of the fuel required by the *Oceanid*'s myriad plasma generators, although thankfully, it was only rarely required. With the imminent crossing of the Damocles Gulf, all of the crusade's capital vessels had been replenished, with only the rogue trader vessels remaining to be tended.

The wailing of a siren filled the deck, accompanied a moment later by a low crash of the *Harlot*'s umbilical probe locking with the service deck's airlock. Warning lights flashed red as the airlock equalised, atmosphere venting from its release valves in angry plumes. Lucian watched intently, for he knew what to expect next. He heard Korvane mumble a low spacefarer's prayer, an imprecation against the perils of the warp, and all the dangers that awaited those who would cross it.

A low rumble filled the service deck, and the airlock's armoured door rose, a cloud of thick mist escaping, to creep across the deck. As the door receded into the bulkhead above, Lucian could just make out the silhouettes within.

A droning canticle emanated from the airlock, as a number of figures emerged from the mist. Soon, a column was snaking its way across the service deck, a funereal procession, the mourners carrying upon their shoulders great lead caskets glittering with etheric frost. Those figures were, even to Lucian who had seen some horrific sights in his time, disturbing in the extreme. Each wore long robes of woven, gunmetal grey metallic thread, and thick, lead gloves upon his hands. The robes were dotted with valves, to which long, pulsing cables were attached, each coiling behind the bearer to disappear into the airlock behind. The head of each bearer was bared, but his eyes, ears, nose and mouth were fitted with the same valves that covered his body. Forcing himself to look closer, Lucian could see that the bearers' hands, though protected by the thick mitts, gave off an oily smoke, as did the side of the face of each bearer that was closest to the casket he shouldered. Small, humanoid creatures walked at the side of each bearer, vat-grown cyber-constructs, mono-tasked to the whims of their masters.

The contents of each coffin-shaped casket was evidently hazardous in the extreme, for Lucian could see, even from the gallery on which he and Korvane stood, the flesh of each bearer slowly cooking, sloughing from his face to reveal muscle and bone beneath.

As the procession wound its course across the curved deck below, Lucian watched the tech-adepts of his own crew as they worked upon the many dials and levers mounted around the base of the great column at the centre of the chamber. Lucian knew that the tech-priests would have prepared long and hard for their task, for it was the most perilous operation a vessel could undertake, including, Lucian mused, actual combat. The consequences of a mishap were scarcely worth considering, and would cost Lucian and his crew far more than their ship and their lives.

The procession neared the column, and Lucian could see that the body of each bearer was beginning to disintegrate as time wore on, the pulsing of the hundreds of cables snaking behind growing more rapid as, Lucian presumed, some alchemical concoction that prolonged life was fed to them. He mumbled a prayer, as Korvane had minutes before, seeing the open distaste on his son's face.

The scene became even more ghastly as the first of the caskets neared the column. It's bearers visibly staggered beneath what must have been a terrible weight to bear. Singed matter trailed behind the bearers, great chunks of burnt flesh having detached from their limbs as they walked, only the ministrations of the horrific machinery keeping them animated as their bodies, quite literally, fell apart. The small attendants gathered the burnt remains into heavy chests carried between some of their number.

At the last, the bearers of the lead casket lifted their burden high upon arms almost bare of flesh. The casket was pushed forward into a gaping socket in the side of the column, the door of which swung wide as the *Oceanid*'s tech-priests pulled levers and voiced their prayers to the Machine God. With one, final heave, the bearers pushed their casket into the waiting maw, the frost encrusting it vaporising in a cloud of mist as it was slid home. With a crash, the door swung shut. The bearers collapsed, each lead robe almost entirely empty. With an obscene, sucking noise, the cables attached to the remains of each corpse tightened, before snaking back to the airlock, the small attendant gathering up the remains of each bearer, before turning back for the airlock.

'Emperor preserve us,' Lucian heard Korvane mutter, and turned to see that his son had developed a severe and quite spontaneous nosebleed. He touched his hand to his own nose, unsurprised to see blood upon his palm as he pulled it away.

'I've seen enough,' Lucian said, knowing that his duty as ship's master was done by ensuring that the first of the caskets was safely received. Many more would be delivered over the next hours, but he had little desire to watch the scene he had just witnessed repeated over and over again. 'Care for a drink?'

'Indeed, Father, I feel I need one,' Korvane replied, turning his back on the drive service deck.

Lucian and his son passed through the warren of the *Oceanid*'s companionways, trying to avoid the areas most crowded by work crews going about the business of preparing the vessel for the crossing of the Damocles Gulf.

'The last intake.' Korvane asked, 'Have they given you any trouble?'

Lucian chuckled as he watched a gang of ratings struggle to seal a defective plasma run, which, fortunately for them, had been bypassed lest they fail in their task and incinerate themselves in the process. 'Well, Craven's Landing provided some veteran crews, not surprising considering the trouble the port's had with the chartists.'

'And what of the Kleist intake?' Korvane asked.

'There weren't many left, after Gurney's courts,' Lucian replied, his mood darkening at his son's mention of the Cardinal of Brimlock. 'Just the dregs whose executions were commuted to service. What of the *Rosetta*?'

'The Arrikis Epsilon intake settled down well,' Korvane replied, referring to the massive draft of unskilled crew that the rogue traders had demanded from the Imperial Commander of that world, replacements for the hundreds of casualties Korvane's crew had suffered in battle weeks before. 'There're a handful that have made bridge crew, and one or two potential officers amongst them.'

'Hmm,' replied Lucian, distracted by the actions of the repair crew as they toiled with the plasma run. He saw that they were making a total hash of their work and their overseer was proving entirely inadequate in his role.

'You!' Lucian bellowed, the work crew and every other crewman in the area standing to immediate attention. He advanced upon the petty officer in charge of the crew, gratified to see that the man had the decency to go pale at his master's approach.

'What the hell are you trying to achieve here? You've got a dozen unskilled men screwing up a job that a pair of acolytes could complete to perfection in under an hour. Well?'

'Sir,' the man stammered, his uncertainty and fear evident in his voice. 'Sir, the adepts are all engaged on the drive service deck, sir. We were ordered to secure this plasma run as a matter of urgency though, and we...'

'For the Emperor's sake,' Lucian cursed, 'I'm afflicted by fools in all quarters.' Frustration rose within him as he considered that, even though the rogue traders' fortunes had improved in the wake of the encounters in the Timbra sub-sector, the flotilla was still being operated at something less than ideal levels. Though his crews were now larger, Lucian knew they still had a long way to go before attaining the experience and professionalism taken for granted in the dynasty until very recently.

'Wait until the adepts are available,' Lucian ordered the petty officer, 'but impress upon them the urgency of the task. If that run leaks in transit I'll hold you, not the adepts, personally responsible. Do I make myself perfectly clear?'

The man could only nod at Lucian's threat, knowing, as he must have done, the punishment that would await him were any malfunction to afflict the plasma relay. Lucian nodded, and the man took the hint and turned to gather his crew, who skulked off as fast as their dignity allowed.

Lucian watched the work crew retreat down the corridor, and then turned sharply on his heels to continue on his way. As he turned, he almost collided with another junior officer, a member of the bridge crew, though he could not remember the man's name.

'What the hell do you want?' Lucian bawled, the deck officer standing to rigid attention.

'Message from the bridge, my lord,' the officer replied, his voice steady in contrast to that of the work crew overseer. 'Visitor on board.'

'Who?' Lucian replied, knowing it must be someone important for the bridge to send a runner to inform him.

'General Wendall Gauge, my lord. He awaits you in the starboard bridge receiving room.'

Lucian turned to his son, who shrugged, clearly as surprised as he was. 'Well then,' Lucian said to Korvane, 'let's see what brings the general on board, shall we?'

'Lord Arcadius,' the general said as Lucian entered the receiving room, Korvane following close behind. 'Please accept my apologies for the circumstances of this visit.' Gauge cut an imposing figure, even in the ornately decorated chamber, though Lucian noted that he appeared uncomfortable in his general staff formal dress. Gauge was broad and muscled in common with all the men of Catachan, his face scarred and dour, a dangerous glint in his steely eyes.

'Not at all,' Lucian replied, instantly cautious. 'I had hoped we would have the opportunity to talk. I take it, however, that a specific matter brings you here, at this time?'

'Indeed,' Gauge said, turning his back on Lucian and Korvane, to look out of the brass-rimmed viewing port to the busy space beyond. After a moment of silence, the general spoke. 'It's bad news, Lucian, a bad business I'm afraid.'

Lucian caught his son's glance, before crossing to the general's side, looking out, as did his guest, upon the blackness of space and the myriad fleet service craft engaged on their apparently endless tasks.

'Tell me,' Lucian pressed, his mind racing to predict what council intrigue might have brought the general to his ship. He loathed the feeling of not being in complete control, of waiting upon another.

'Inquisitor Grand, Lucian. You have not heard?'

'Heard what?' Lucian demanded, his frustration growing. Had the inquisitor pulled rank on the council, he wondered? Had Gurney finally convinced him to use the influence he had, to date, held in check?

'He is wounded, badly,' the general said, looking Lucian in the eye as he spoke.

Lucian felt sudden guilty elation at the news, tempered an instant later by the realisation that such an event might well have serious implications for them all. He turned and lifted a crystal decanter from a polished wooden side table, and poured a hefty slug for himself and another for the general.

'How?'

Gauge took the proffered glass and downed the liquor in a single gulp. 'He was burned, eighty percent of his body. It was a deliberate attack, in the detention block, as he attended to his prisoners.'

'One of the tau? A break out attempt?'

'No, although they did escape.'

'All of them?' Lucian could scarcely countenance that the tau might have succeeded in escaping from an accomplished agent of the Orders of the Inquisition. 'They must have been helped. A traitor?'

'The inquisitor's staff believe so,' Gauge said, helping himself to a second drink, and pouring one for Lucian too.

'Lucian,' the general turned to fully face his host. 'What of Brielle?'

Lucian's breath caught in his throat, for he had not even thought of his daughter for several hours, so busy had he and his son been with the warp drive replenishment. 'What of her?' he asked. Though he respected, even liked, the general, Lucian's guard was fully up, for it was his family of which Gauge spoke.

'Grand's staff, Lucian. They have made certain... insinuations.'

'Korvane?' Lucian summoned his son. 'Find her.' Korvane nodded and left the room in silence, though Lucian noted a familiar glint in his son's eye. He thought that the old sibling rivalry was rearing its head again, though Korvane's expression grew darker each time his stepsister's name was mentioned.

'General,' Lucian said, turning back to his guest, 'please, be frank with me. I count you an honest man, and I believe we are both on the same side. I know nothing of the inquisitor, or it seems, my daughter. Tell me all.'

The general bowed slightly at Lucian's compliment, a gesture the old veteran rarely performed. 'Very well. As I said, the inquisitor has been assaulted, and lies in the medicae bay, even now, attended by his household apothecaries. His staff report that the prisoners are gone, and there is evidence of at least one intruder having infiltrated the detention block. Someone entered cell block Eta, attacked the inquisitor, freed the prisoners and escaped.'

'What has Brielle to do with this? I see no connection.'

'Neither do I, Lucian, but the inquisitor's staff wish to speak to her, and she is not answering hails to the *Fairlight*. I know not what evidence they might have to link her with the assault, but I do not believe they would ask unless they were very sure of themselves.'

'Of course they're sure of themselves,' Lucian spat, before lowering his voice, 'they're the Inquisition.'

'Lucian, I warn you...'

'To silence, general? On my own vessel? On this ship, Wendell, I am Emperor, Primarch, Warmaster and bloody executioner. I will not have some...'

'Lucian!' The general's voice was cutting, making Lucian look up and meet Gauge's eyes. 'Do not assume the inquisitor, or the cardinal for that matter, is anything less than dangerous in the extreme. We may all hold the same nominal rank, you, I, them and the rest of the council, but we both know what Grand truly represents.'

'Korvane!' Lucian bellowed, a moment before his son returned. 'Well?'

'Nothing, father.'

'Explain.'

'She is not aboard the *Fairlight,* her duty officer is quite sure.'

'And she is not aboard the station,' the general cut in. 'The inquisitor's staff are equally sure.'

'Whatever is going on, everything changes from here on in.' Lucian was thinking on his feet, his mind plotting a million potential ramifications of the news. What had his errant daughter done, why, and what might the inquisitor's response be?

'The council,' Lucian said, turning on the general once more, 'lines will be drawn over this. Can I at least assume that you and I shall stand on the same side of those lines?'

'I would not have come to you like this if it were not so, Lucian.'

'I thank you,' Lucian replied. 'What of Jellaqua?'

The general laughed out loud at the mention of his counterpart in the Imperial Navy. 'That old bastard? He curses Gurney for a motherless grox, and would oppose him and his allies on sheer principle alone.'

'Good, good,' said Lucian, smiling at the thought of the irascible old admiral voicing such an opinion over an oversized glass of after-dinner liquor. With an effort, he pushed the problem of Brielle to the back of his mind, and continued with his immediate concern.

'I think that Sarik and I see eye to eye,' Lucian went on. The White Scars Space Marine hailed from the world on which his daughter had been raised, and that might provide some common link that could grow to a more solid alliance. 'Rumann I'm not so sure of, he's a hard one to read.'

'As are all his Chapter,' the General replied, 'they have something of the machine about them, if you catch my meaning.'

'I do. The same goes for Jaakho, though he appears more disposed to our point of view in council recently.'

The general nodded by way of reply, before Lucian continued, 'And the Navis Nobilite, Sedicae?'

'Very hard to say,' Gauge replied, before Korvane interrupted.

'Father, might I speak?'

'Of course, Korvane,' Lucian said, mildly unsettled that his son should feel the need to ask permission to speak his mind. Of course Korvane should speak, Lucian thought, for he had been raised in the Court of Nankirk, studied at his mother's side the myriad intrigues of its nobles, and his guidance had true meaning.

'I believe the logistician general, Stempf, to be a lost cause. He has sought patronage since the outset, and found it in the cardinal. He has voted in favour of Gurney's motions on twelve major issues, abstained only once, and never voted against. I believe he is entirely beholden to Gurney, and will not be drawn away unless the cardinal is thoroughly defeated. Then, he will seek an immediate alliance with the stronger faction.'

'True enough, but let's not get ahead of ourselves,' Lucian nodded in agreement with his son's assessment. 'What of the Praefect Maximus?'

'Skissor has no loyalty and no great intellect. He is a man of high birth, but the youngest of many siblings and therefore the least likely to benefit from his connections and resources. He is from Kar Duniash, where the youngest born sons are sent to the planetary levy, for the commissions are less dear than those already purchased for the older sons. The fact that he is not serving in the defence force suggests to me that he somehow side-stepped that duty, probably by luck, but possibly through dishonest means.'

'So, he's out on a limb?'

'In a manner of speaking, yes, father. He certainly occupies a precarious position, despite his airs. I believe he would be amenable to supporting us, but only if we could prove, pre-emptively, that we are the stronger faction, and the one most likely to perpetuate his own, personal, status quo.'

'So,' said Lucian, thinking aloud. 'Me, you, the admiral and Sarik. That's four of us against Gurney, the inquisitor and Stempf. We can talk to Rumann and Jaakho, possibly Sedicae, but Skissor is unlikely. That puts us ahead, by my reckoning.'

'Yes, father,' Korvane hesitated.

'What? Out with it, Korvane.'

'It's Brielle, father,' Korvane continued. 'If she is implicated in this attack on Grand, there is no way the council could support you. The general and the admiral are generous in their support.' Gauge bowed his head to Korvane at the comment. 'But Grand need only invoke the power of his Inquisitorial Seal. The council might be disbanded. It would certainly be torn apart.'

'You are right, of course,' Lucian replied, inwardly cursing his daughter for any part she might have played in this mess. 'Whatever happens, he must not be pushed to do so. I'm sure only a higher authority than the inquisitor stays his hand, a superior with an agenda we are not yet aware of.'

'What will you do, father?'

'Well, my son, I've been in tighter corners, but not by much.' Lucian grinned. 'We find Brielle, and I face the council. This reminds me of the time I had to meet the prince of the Steel Eye Reavers, having earlier that evening stumbled upon his daughter and her maidservants engaged in an act that I'm quite sure no human had ever witnessed. I got through that, and I'll get through this.'

Later that evening, Lucian stood alone in an observation blister atop one of the *Oceanid*'s dorsal sensor pylons. The view from his vantage point was nothing short of stunning, even to such a seasoned spacefarer. The heavy cruiser stretched below, hundreds of metres fore and aft, from her armoured prow section to the clustered drives astern. The *Oceanid* was tethered to the tau station, the wounds of the first space battle still evident on the alien structure's flanks. The fleet tender, *Harlot*, was pulling away from Lucian's vessel, slow and gravid with her terrible cargo. Lucian recalled with distaste the replenishment of his warp drive, and was thankful such an operation need only be undertaken very rarely. It would take weeks for the stink of cooked flesh to be scrubbed from his ship's atmosphere, he thought, resenting the mechanicus and their practices, but knowing he had no choice in the matter.

Further out still, Lucian could see the various ships of the fleet: a dozen capital vessels, most of equivalent displacement to the *Oceanid*, some even heavier, some smaller. The *Blade of Woe*, Admiral Jellaqua's flagship lay at anchor three kilometres to the port. Her mighty armoured prow gleamed white in the light of the local star, for the irascible and eccentric Jellaqua had ordered a fresh coat of paint applied before the crossing of the Gulf, and press-ganged work crews had laboured triple shifts to carry out his order in time.

A number of escort squadrons were stationed around the fleet, each deployed to screen the larger, more valuable ships from surprise attack at what was perhaps the crusade's most vulnerable point. Each squadron consisted of three, sometimes four, vessels, whose role was to intercept any enemy attempting to close on one of the battle cruisers, and each captain knew that his ship and crew were entirely expendable so long as his task was done and his charge protected. Such was the tradition in the Imperial Navy, and it made Lucian glad he operated outside of its command.

Schools of smaller vessels, service craft and tenders of all classes, were clustered around each ship or moved to and fro between them. Last minute supplies were delivered, vital maintenance performed, and high-ranking officers ferried back and forth for last minute briefings and consultations.

In all, the sight was one to stir the heart of any ship's master, but for Lucian, it was overshadowed.

The crusade stood on the brink of crossing the Damocles Gulf, but Lucian could only ponder his daughter's fate. She had disappeared, and he had been forced to disown her to the council. The cardinal had ranted and raved, calling for the perpetrator of the attack to be hunted down and brought to justice, and Lucian had no choice but to agree with him. The cardinal had stopped short of naming Lucian's offspring as the attacker, but had noted her disappearance, and commented upon it in council. Whilst the inquisitor lay in the medicae centre, recovering from his wounds, Gurney would not press his case, and Lucian remained in good standing. But Lucian knew that things might soon shift dramatically.

In the meantime, the crusade would penetrate the dark region that was the Damocles Gulf. What lay within, or beyond, he had scarcely a clue, but a part of him, the scion of one of the greatest rogue trader dynasties ever to take the High Lords' charter, revelled in the adventure. Another part of him mourned, for he had, in all likelihood, lost his daughter, whatever had become of her.

Lucian crossed to the access hatch set in the deck. He had a ship to captain, fleet to usurp and an empire to conquer. Perhaps things weren't quite so bad, after all.

CHAPTER SIX

Lucian's gaze was fixed on the chronograph's hands as they counted down to the moment when the *Oceanid* would exit the warp. He could not say how long he had sat in his command throne and stared at the clock face; he had lost track of the passage of time, as it was so easy to do while traversing the depths of the Immaterium.

He blinked, shook his head and tore his eyes away from the slowly moving hands. It was just a trick of the warp, he told himself. He had only briefly glanced towards the chronometer despite what his mind was telling him.

'Mister Raldi.' Lucian addressed his helmsman. He got no answer.

'Mister Raldi, are you with us?' He caught a number of the bridge crew shaking themselves as if from a trance, looking around in mild confusion, before exchanging nervous glances. They feared the wrath of their master, expecting it to materialise at any moment.

'Mister Raldi!' Lucian called louder. The helmsman slowly turned to look at Lucian. Raldi's eyes were blank and unfocused, his head lolling slightly to one side. Lucian stood from his command throne and crossed the bridge. Facing his helmsman, he saw what his own face must have looked like only an instant earlier. But where he, and the other bridge crew, had shaken loose the fugue, Helmsman Raldi appeared entirely trapped. Saliva dripped down Raldi's chin. Lucian determined to take drastic action.

'Sorry old friend.' He threw a thunderous punch at Raldi's jaw, sending the man crashing face down to the deck in a heap. Lucian bent over the crumpled form, his hand on the helmsman's shoulder. Without warning, Raldi's body tensed, and he turned his head to look over his shoulder, almost eye to eye with Lucian. For an instant it was not Raldi behind those eyes, but as soon as the impression came, it fled once more. Lucian's officer shook his head and spat a great gobbet of blood upon the deck, coughing violently as he struggled to his feet.

'What?' Raldi gasped through his bloodied mouth, 'What happened, my lord?'

'Just the empyrean having its way,' Lucian replied, a cold shiver passing through him. 'Just the warp calling us home.' He shook his head again, knowing that he would not entirely rid himself of the feeling until they were safely out of the Sea of Souls, back in the material universe. The warp was home to all manner of evils, and few ever crossed it without feeling its effects. Whether nightmares, hallucinations or sudden mood changes, every spacefarer was afflicted in some manner.

Lucian looked to the chronometer once more, seeing that its hands had turned quite some way. The *Oceanid* was due to break warp in scant minutes. Satisfied that Raldi was back at his station, Lucian crossed to his command throne and sat back in the familiar, worn leather seat. He consulted the data-slates arrayed to either side, his expert eye taking in a thousand tiny details in an instant. His vessel performed as she should, despite her age and the rough treatment to which generations of the Arcadius had subjected her. All was as ready as it would ever be for the translation from the warp, to realspace. He lifted a polished brass cover mounted on the command throne's seat, an action only he could perform, for the cover was fitted with a genelock that responded only to his own touch. His finger hovered over the large stud beneath the cover plate, and after a moment he depressed it. The bridge lights flickered and died, to be replaced an instant later with the crimson light used when the vessel was at general quarters. With that simple action, Lucian had signalled to his Navigator, Adept Baru, who lay in his warp trance in his navigation blister high atop the *Oceanid*'s superstructure, that all was in readiness. Lucian hated the feeling of another having control over his vessel, but had no choice. Only a Navigator could take a vessel into the warp, pilot its capricious currents, and bring it home to safety at the other end. No mere human could hope to emulate such a feat, and to even try was to invite disaster and damnation as the ravenous beasts dwelling within the Sea of Souls tore the ship and its crew apart, body and soul. Lucian forced the notion from his mind. This voyage was affecting him more than any other had in quite some time, perhaps as much as his first run through the Wheel of Fire in fact, or his last journey to the borders of the Maelstrom.

A final glance at the chronometer told Lucian that exit was imminent. He took a deep breath and forced himself to relax. He'd done this a thousand times before, so why was he so...

Lucian's mind suddenly expanded, his perceptions stretched atom thin as the *Oceanid* reared up through the shallows between the warp and the material universe. He felt his vessel caught upon the crashing surf of impossible energies, surging through from the depths to burst into realspace. In less time than it takes to form a single thought, his mind's eye was presented with a swirling cascade of impossible images and impossible concepts: birth and death on a cosmic scale, and a million, billion futures rent from the fabric of time and space and re-knit into a new path. From one strand of fate were sown five, which were plaited back again into a single strand, the sum greater than the parts. A cosmic fate, orchestrated by ancient powers fleeing their inevitable...

Then the wound in the skein of reality snapped shut behind the *Oceanid* as she burst from the warp. Lucian's pulse thundered in his ears, and he forced his breathing back to a normal rhythm. He looked around the bridge, seeing that the crew had evidently been affected in a similar manner, except Raldi, it seemed, who stood at his station at the *Oceanid*'s mighty wheel, as he always did.

'Mister Raldi, how's my ship?' Lucian called, noting with approval that the bridge returned quickly and efficiently to a normal routine, despite the trauma of the warp exit.

'Number three's grumbling a bit, my lord, but nothing I can't contain.'

'Well enough, keep an eye on it. I don't want us to be the first to call in the support vessels, at least not this soon.'

'Also, my lord...'

'What else?'

'The sub-etheric veins are detecting a localised field of some sort.

There's some disturbance to station keeping, but again, nothing I can't compensate for.'

'Station nine,' Lucian said, addressing the servitor at the gravimetrics station, 'perform a primary scan as per Mister Raldi's parameters.'

'Astrographics,' Lucian continued.

'Yes sir,' the officer at station ten replied.

'Patch your readings through to the holo.'

The holo-plinth on the bridge deck before Lucian's command throne came to life, a green, spheroid representation of local space projected in three dimensions. The *Oceanid* sat at the dead centre of the projection, and the entire scene was shot through with gently waving tendrils of what appeared to be some gaseous liquid form.

Lucian looked to the bridge viewing ports on either side, but saw no such phenomenon. Evidently the weird, twisting forms were entirely invisible to the naked eye, though the *Oceanid*'s various augurs could detect them, and Raldi could feel their effects upon the helm.

Reams of data scrolled across the projection, and across the pict screens surrounding the command throne. The *Oceanid*'s logister banks sought to identify the source of the phenomenon, comparing the readings flooding across the screens to records held within the huge crystal memory-stacks. Lucian watched, seeing that the logisters would fail to identify the effect.

Turning a dial upon the command throne's arm, Lucian expanded the view of local space, the symbol representing the *Oceanid* at the centre shrinking as the view zoomed out. He saw, as he had hoped to, a number of augur returns, all within a quarter of a million kilometres, and all holding station. The returns resolved as the augurs locked upon them, Lucian seeing that they represented four capital vessels and an indefinable number of smaller ships, probably two or three escort squadrons. Lucian determined to congratulate his Navigator upon the accuracy of his warp jump, and ordered the ship-to-ship comms channels open.

Hours later, the *Oceanid* was within communications range of the fleet, and Lucian stood at the centre of his bridge, a cluster of pict screens arrayed around him. Each had been lowered from overhead upon thick cables, and upon each static-laced screen were the head and shoulders of a master of one of the other vessels of the fleet to have reached the first rendezvous point.

There were four of them: Master Florian of the Iron Hands Strike Cruiser *Fist of Light*, Natalia of the *Duchess McIntyre*, Captain Jephanim of the *Honour of Damlass*, and Commodore Ebrahim of the *Ajax*. According to their initial communications, each had arrived at the muster point within the last three days, an impressive feat of navigation, and one that belied the great skill of the Navigators selected to negotiate the unknown regions of the Damocles Gulf.

Master Florian was completing his report to the other four ships' masters.

'I can therefore conclude that intra-ship transfers are unwise, given the nature of the disturbance. I shall manoeuvre the *Fist of Light* to a position from which our superior augurs can cover the widest arc, though to be frank, I do not anticipate any contact with enemy forces.'

'Agreed,' Lucian replied. Although the four vessels and their tiny escort were undoubtedly exposed and vulnerable, the chances of any enemy locating and engaging them in deep space were microscopically small. Mind you, he thought, Lady Issobellis Gerrit had believed the same prior to the Battle of the Hydra, and look what that attitude had gained her.

'My readings confirm your own. There's something deeply anomalous about this region, as we all knew there would be. But still, there's something I can't quite...'

'You feel it too, Gerrit?' Natalia interrupted Lucian. Though her image upon the pict-slate was grainy and blurred, he could see in it an unsettling hesitancy nonetheless. It was in her voice, too, he thought, a lingering dread that all was not as it should be in the Damocles Gulf.

'I do, Natalia,' Lucian replied, 'and it's not just the local sub-etheric. It's the immaterium itself.'

'You are correct, Gerrit.' Lucian scanned the slates, seeing that it was Captain Ebrahim of the Ajax that had spoken. He had not met the man in person, though he had heard that Ebrahim was a well-regarded officer of the line. 'My Navigator was afflicted by some form of convulsion as we exited the warp. We very nearly didn't make it out. It was the closest I've ever come to...'

'Is he recovered?' Lucian asked.

'He assures me he needs only a day's rest, two at the most. I'm not sure what happened, but my crew are certainly unsettled by it. My provosts are on double shifts, keeping the mutinous bastards in line, but I am assured all will be well before the second jump.'

'Well,' replied Lucian, thinking as he spoke, 'with all of the disturbance in this region, I think it'll be some time before the entire fleet musters. Use that time well, Ebrahim.'

It was five days before the entire fleet mustered at the lonely rendezvous point. As each had arrived, the various ships' masters had arranged more ship-to-ship conferences. None would risk a shuttle journey to a host vessel, for the unusual disturbances afflicting the region continued. The risk of losing experienced captains so early in the crusade was unthinkable, and that of losing all of them at once for the sake of a face-to-face meeting was entirely unimaginable.

Lucian had participated in every such conference, taking on the role of chairman with a natural authority. He far preferred the company, even if it was not face-to-face, of his fellow ships' masters over that of the council. He considered these men and women to be his equals, while he considered many on the council to be his enemies. He listened to their reports with sympathy, for each told of some minor mishap during the first warp jump, and some of more serious incidents during the exit. None, however, suffered as serious an occurrence as their Navigator suffering convulsions during their warp exit. The thought of that still preyed on Lucian's mind, for he appreciated how close the Ajax had actually come to being lost in the warp. He knew that the fleet had additional Navigators amongst its complement, should any such event incapacitate one of their number, but in all likelihood, a vessel whose Navigator suffered such a fate would also be lost, with all hands.

The disappearance of his daughter was also troubling Lucian. In the aftermath of the attack on Inquisitor Grand, and the departure of the fleet, Lucian had very deliberately pushed the issue to the back of his mind. But he had spoken to Korvane of it before they had parted, and had been shocked by his son's attitude. Korvane, it appeared, had anticipated his stepsister's fall from grace, and had displayed an entirely dispassionate reaction to it. Lucian refused to write her off as a lost cause, however. In common with many of his standing, he felt that the mores of what passed as society in the galaxy held little sway over him and his clan. He had the curious notion that Brielle was in all likelihood pursuing her own fate, and he grudgingly admired her for doing so. She would be back, though he would certainly call her to account if her actions cost the Arcadius in any manner.

One of the final tasks Lucian and his son had been faced with before the fleet made warp on the first leg of the crossing of the Damocles Gulf had been the issue of Brielle's cruiser, the *Fairlight*. The pair had gone aboard and conferred with Brielle's officers. Lucian had determined that the ship be turned over to Brielle's chief of operations for the duration of her absence, making it clear to the *Fairlight*'s officer cadre, as well as to Korvane, that he considered that absence temporary. He had spoken with the ship's new, acting master, a long-serving officer by the name of Blaanid, whose line had served the Arcadius since the Fall of Kreel, his great grandfather being one of the petty nobles absorbed into the Arcadius officer cadre during that period. He had shared a bottle of *svort* with the man, and determined he liked him, even if he could not hold his drink. He had issued Blaanid precise instructions regarding the handling of the *Fairlight*, making it clear that he wanted the cruiser kept well out of harm's way unless given specific orders to the contrary. He was one child down on the dynasty already, and could ill afford to lose one third of that dynasty's space borne assets.

And so, on the fifth day after his arrival at the muster point, the last of the crusade's vessels arrived. It was one of the massive, bloated troop transports, each of which carried an entire regiment of Imperial Guard and sufficient supplies to keep it fighting for years if necessary. The transport's captain had immediately reported widespread lack of discipline amongst the troopers of the 12th Brimlock Light Infantry. General Gauge, travelling on Korvane's vessel with his staff corps, had insisted he shuttle over to put the unrest down in person, but had been persuaded against the idea by Lucian, who had convinced the old veteran of the danger presented by the anomalous sub-space disturbances when no other ship's master had succeeded in doing so.

The last captains' conference had been held, and the second rendezvous point confirmed. The fleet would travel another stretch of its journey, this jump somewhat longer than the first, the Navigators having familiarised themselves somewhat with the ebbs and flows of the warp in this region. The *Oceanid* was due to depart in less than an hour, and Lucian was pleased to note that all preparations were complete. He leant back in his command throne, the sudden inactivity not relaxing him, but quite the opposite. He felt an overwhelming tension, despite the years he had been about his business.

'My lord,' a voice from behind the command throne snapped Lucian from his reverie. 'Please forgive me my intrusion.' Lucian felt a mild irritation, for he had not noticed the arrival of anyone on his bridge. He turned to look over his shoulder, seeing that his visitor was the ship's astropath, Karaldi.

'There is no intrusion, adept. To what do I owe the pleasure?'

The astropath shuffled forward into Lucian's view. He was shocked at the man's appearance. Karaldi had, in Lucian's opinion, been burned out years ago, and he had considered petitioning the guild for a replacement when the opportunity presented itself. Somehow, that opportunity had never arrived, and against his better judgement he had come to like the old eccentric. Karaldi cared nothing for his personal appearance, which was at the very least dishevelled. His robes were dirty and tattered, his hair unkempt and his face unshaven. His eyes were empty sockets, in common with many of his calling, for the soul binding ritual that allowed him to exercise his powers safely had also blasted his senses to oblivion. The ritual, Lucian knew, blinded most astropaths, and some lost other senses too. He harboured the suspicion that Karaldi had lost his olfactory senses, either that, or he really did not care how bad he smelt.

'My lord,' the astropath said, bowing deeply to his master, 'I have communed with my peers, though only with great difficulty.'

'Explain,' Lucian replied, unsure of Karaldi's meaning, but suspecting he had some idea.

'There is something wrong here, my lord. I cannot explain it.'

'You are not the only one to believe that to be the case, adept. The Navigators describe the warp hereabouts in similar terms, and even I feel ill at ease. What of the astropaths?'

'We commune, but in doing so we hear not only the minds of our peers, but of others, or echoes of others. Forgive me, for I cannot easily describe the sensation to a...'

'Try. You cause no offence. I am master of this vessel and warden of countless souls. If I need to understand, please aid me in doing so.'

'Our minds, my lord, when we join in astropathic communion, we become entranced, distracted, as if called away from afar. It's as if our song, our astropathic choir, is subtly, but sweetly, corrupted. A note, a timbre, not of any astropath, joins our song, interweaving with our minds. It is so sweet that none will reject it, though we know we should sever the communion at the slightest outside interference.

Lucian's blood ran cold at the astropath's words. If Karaldi was telling him that some entity was working its way into the minds of the astropaths...

'Oh no, my lord! Never that!' Karaldi blurted, evidently having picked up on Lucian's surface thoughts. Lucian let it go, for now.

'I thank you,' Karaldi continued, his face a mask of tension. 'No, my lord, it is not some dark thing from the immaterium that whispers to the astropath. It is of this universe, of this place.' Karaldi gestured around him, suggesting that the phenomenon he described was specific to this region, to the Damocles Gulf.

'If that is so,' Lucian probed, 'can you ascribe a source?'

'In a manner of speaking, yes, my lord,' the astropath said, wringing his gnarled hands together, clearly uncomfortable, though determined to convey his concerns. 'It is all around us, in the ether, in the warp, in the weave of space itself. But it emanates from somewhere within the Gulf, of that we are certain.'

'So, the... effect... is likely to increase the deeper the fleet penetrates the gulf?'

'Most certainly, my lord.'

'And your ability to communicate with the other astropaths?'

'Oh, my lord,' Karaldi said, his face taking on a pained expression, his hollow eye sockets yawning gulfs beneath his creased brow. 'The note is so sweet, I fear our song might never sound the same without it.'

Lucian saw what his astropath was really trying to tell him. Though the ways of the psyker were foreign to him, they were not downright alien as they were to most men. 'You are telling me that to commune with your peers is to court disaster. Am I correct?'

'You are, master.' Lucian saw relief upon the astropath's distorted face.

'And have you shared these fears with the other astropaths?'

'Not openly, my lord, though I believe we all share an understanding of the nature of the disturbance. Some of my peers know that to commune is dangerous, but cannot help but do so. Others, I sense, long for the crossing to continue, so that they might close with the source. They crave it, my lord, yet know it might harm them.'

'I see,' Lucian said as he leant back in the command throne, thinking. 'I shall signal the fleet that astropathic communications should be kept to a minimum, unless absolutely vital. With luck, the effect will be limited to the Gulf. If not, we'll find ourselves with no long-range communications and at war with an alien empire. That would not do. Thank you Adept Karaldi, you have served well.'

The astropath bowed deeply, his expression suddenly one of gratitude as opposed to the tension he had displayed on his arrival. Lucian sighed deeply and considered what Karaldi had told him. Something called to the astropaths as they communicated, adding its psychic signal to their own, even as the Navigators reported disturbances within the warp, ships, crews were restive and sub-space was riven with abnormal and unidentifiable fields. Furthermore, the astropaths in some way craved the interference, perhaps being drawn by its call.

'Comms, open a channel to the flagship.' He would at least ensure that the other ships' masters were aware of the threat, even if it transpired there was very little they could do to avert any impending disaster.

CHAPTER SEVEN

'All stop!' Lucian called. 'Mains to idle. Station keeping please, Mister Raldi.'

The *Oceanid* gradually slowed to a standstill. Lucian stood from the command throne and crossed to the forward observation port. A bass growl passed through the vessel as the retro thrusters at the vessel's prow coughed to life, the deck plates vibrating with the titanic forces at play. Lucian caught the signs of discord within the familiar tones, and he knew that drive number three was grumbling again. Perhaps once this was all over, he mused, he would be able to put the *Oceanid* into space dock for the renovation that was so long overdue.

His mind curiously distracted, Lucian scanned the view from the armoured port. Out here, in deep space, there were few stars, the blackness of the void immaculate. Yet he knew that the stillness was deceiving, for the region seethed with anomalous forces. Ahead, Lucian could just discern the faintest smudge of lurid turquoise, the dense stellar cluster within which, if all went according to plan, the crusade would encounter the alien empire of the tau.

'Astrographics,' Lucian said, turning to the officer at station ten, 'give me local.'

The holograph projector powered up, its subsonic hum deepening beyond audible levels as the green, static laced representation of local space appeared above it. Lucian walked up to the three-dimensional projection slowly turning in the space before him, seeing the *Oceanid*'s icon at the dead centre. Once again, slowly undulating tendrils waved across the sphere, invisible to human eyes, but all too apparent to his vessel's augurs.

Lucian scanned the projection for the other vessels of the crusade fleet. He found none.

'Increase scan range. Boost gain,' he ordered. The projection shifted as the sensors quested further outwards, Lucian seeking what he expected to see at any moment.

'Nothing, my lord,' said the officer sitting at the astrographics station. 'We must be the first vessel to arrive on station.'

'Yes,' responded Lucian, thinking that he would have bet on that not having been the case. 'Increase scan range. Bleed secondary feeds into the main arrays.'

'Aye, sir,' the officer replied, his hands working the many dials and slides clustered upon his console. Lucian watched with growing impatience as three, non-critical functions were almost entirely stripped of power to boost the augurs as they scanned the local region. The three-dimensional holographic map now displayed a region several hundred thousand kilometres across, though great swathes of it were left blank as the *Oceanid*'s mighty augur banks were pushed further and further out.

The astrographics officer turned to address his master. 'I don't think we're going to...'

'There!' Lucian said. He walked around the globe of light, and pointed to a dimly glowing sensor return right at its edge. 'Full power on these coordinates.'

The officer worked his console once more, and three quarters of the holographic projection lapsed into an indistinct blur as power was bled from three arrays and shunted into the remaining one. The quadrant grew in relative size as the augurs scanned it, the return becoming more distinct all the while. Reams of text scrolled next to the icon representing the return, the *Oceanid*'s logister banks analysing its nature, comparing it to stored data.

'It's the Ajax, my lord,' The astrographics officer called, 'and there's something...'

'I see it,' Lucian replied. 'Boost output to maximum.'

Once more, the projection zeroed in on a single region, the return that was the Ajax shifting to the centre of the globe whilst the region beyond her became the object of the augur's attentions.

A second return resolved itself, but Lucian could see, had already guessed, that this was no starship.

'It looks like some kind of stellar body, my lord,' said the officer, his eyes fixed on the data wildly scrolling across his pict screens. 'And I'm picking up what must be false returns too, either that or there're a whole lot of dead vessels out there. It's as if there're a hundred other ships out there one moment, and none the next.'

Lucian's mind reeled. He dismissed the false returns, but the chances of encountering a stellar body, light years from any star, were so remote it was simply not worth calculating.

'Something's not right here,' Lucian said under his breath.

'Sir?' the astrographics officer said, unsure whether Lucian addressed him or muttered to himself. Lucian got a grip on himself.

'Helm, set course for the Ajax, but keep it steady and be ready for a change of orders.'

'Aye, sir,' the helmsman replied, working the *Oceanid*'s great wheel as he brought the vessel round on her new heading.

'Comms,' Lucian said, addressing the servitor at station three. 'Hail the Ajax. Bridge,' Lucian continued, addressing all of his officers as one, 'I want every one of you to keep a weather eye out. Comms, where's that channel?'

The bridge was filled with the sound of the open channel to the Ajax. Only static came back.

As the *Oceanid* had closed on the Ajax, Lucian had listened intently for any sign of a response to the continuing hailing signal. He had ordered the channel to be kept open, and endured the wailing and static lest he miss the smallest hint that the Ajax was alive. He had no reason to suspect anything more serious than a disabled transmitter, but somehow, he knew that would not be the case.

Lucian stood at the forward viewing port, leaning against the brass bulkhead. The Ajax would come into view any moment.

'Range?' Lucian asked, not taking his eyes from the view before him.

Silence.

He turned his head towards his helmsman.

'Range to target, Mister Raldi, now.'

The helmsman turned slowly to face Lucian, his eyes unfocused as if the man had drifted off into a waking dream.

'Helm!' Lucian bellowed, his patience growing thin. This region was playing havoc with his and everyone else's nerves, affecting each man differently.

'Sir,' Helmsman Raldi replied, his eyes clearing as his attention was forced back to the here and now. 'Please sir, I'm... I'm sorry. Range? Um... three kilometres, sir.'

'Are you sure?' Lucian replied, his irritation subsiding as fast as it had appeared. 'Check your readings, Raldi. I have no visual.'

Lucian watched for a moment as the helmsman adjusted myriad dials and knobs around the helm, turning his attention back to the view outside. This far from a star, visual ranges were extremely short, but a capital vessel was generally lit up like a...

'All stop!' Lucian bellowed.

Raldi heaved on the mighty lever beside the helm, bracing his legs for a better purchase on the steel deck. Lucian felt the *Oceanid*'s main drives die as their titanic output was routed through emergency vents in their flanks. The force of that alone squeezed the drives in towards each other, causing the vessel's vast metal skeleton to shriek in sudden anguish. An instant later and the banks of retro thrusters at the *Oceanid*'s prow coughed into life, their force forestalling the vessel's forward motion with a titanic juddering.

Fighting to remain upright, Lucian called, 'Bow arcs, full beam ahead.'

Looking once more to the view out front, Lucian was forced to shield his eyes when two great, white beams of light stabbed forward through the darkness. As his eyes adjusted, he watched as the two beams began a wide sweep from port to starboard, crossing each other in the middle before resuming their quest of the all-enveloping darkness.

As the *Oceanid* finally ground to a halt, Lucian saw the great beams settle upon the slab-like flanks of another vessel. As they tracked along its length, gothic lettering ten metres tall spelled out the ship's name: Ajax. Not a single running light gave any sign of life, and every last porthole and viewing port loomed as dark as the rotten eye sockets of the corpse of some long dead leviathan.

* * *

Lucian reclined in his command throne, a half empty glass of asuave in his hand. He brooded, his mood growing ever darker with each passing hour. The Ajax appeared, to the naked eye and to every augur trained upon her, to be dead in space. He seethed with frustration for he longed to assemble a boarding party, to cross the insignificantly miniscule distance between the two vessels and ascertain just what had transpired. But he could not do so, for the sub-space augurs warned that the ongoing disturbance in the fabric of the void made even the short hop to the Ajax too risky, unless no other course of action presented itself.

Another reason Lucian brooded so was the effect that the Damocles Gulf appeared to be exerting upon his crew. The bridge officers were steady enough, and the servitors obviously entirely unaffected, but of the other stations and ranks he was far less certain. The crew chiefs reported a growing number of infractions, each of which was met with increasingly harsh punishment. Drunken brawls and petty thefts amongst the conscripted ranks were to be expected, but of late the nature of the crimes had escalated, culminating in a number of serious assaults upon low ranked officers. Lucian had ordered the chiefs to impose the very harshest of penalties, for he knew that it was only a matter of time before some rabble rouser got a mob together and went on the rampage. That had not occurred on the *Oceanid* in over a decade, and on that occasion Lucian had been forced to lead a charge into the enginarium that the mutineers had captured. Lucian had taken the thuggish leader on in hand-to-hand combat, executing him out of hand, as was his right as master of the vessel.

But behind the ill discipline was quite understandable superstition. Lucian had no doubt that the Damocles Gulf was permeated with a tangible air of... something he could not quite put his finger on. It was a menace, but not in the sense of that experienced near the Eye of Terror. This was more a sensation of something... alien... permeating the very fabric of space, as if the region were not actually meant to exist at all.

The galaxy was home to many zones where the laws of conventional physics broke down, or offered scant explanation for the phenomena at play within them, regions such as the Eye of Terror and the Maelstrom, where the very stuff of the immaterium leaked into the material universe through great seeping wounds many hundreds of light years across. Others were similar in nature, yet nowhere near as threatening, such as the Storm of the Emperor's Wrath. Other features, such as the Wheel of Fire or Hangman's Void were entirely unexplainable, yet had become familiar, for want of a better word, hazards of spacefaring.

Lucian's mind returned to the question of the Ajax. She showed no outward sign of physical damage, and so he was faced with the awful possibility that some tragedy had overtaken her within the warp, or at the point of her exit. If that proved likely, he would be foolish to lead a boarding party onto her, for fear of whatever taint might linger aboard. Lucian doubted that he could muster a boarding party willing to perform the task in any case, and all his experience and every ounce of Arcadius collective wisdom told him that such a course was sheer folly.

Lucian took another sip of the thick liquor. He glowered at the slowly revolving holograph, his gaze moving from the pair of icons that represented the *Oceanid* and the Ajax, to the dark shadow beyond. It could only be a small, rogue planet, yet it appeared entirely impenetrable to the *Oceanid*'s augurs. The body barely even registered with the ship's scanners, but its presence seemed to cast a dour shadow, even though it was invisible to the naked eye, entirely swallowed by the interstellar darkness of the Damocles Gulf.

Lucian forced his train of thought back on to the here and now. The sensors appeared incapable of shedding any light on just what was going on, and there was no sign of any other vessel of the fleet arriving any time soon. He desperately needed to know what had befallen the Ajax, lest the same fate overtake his own vessel, or any other of the fleet. He had but one option.

'Summon Astropath Karaldi,' Lucian ordered the nearest bridge officer, 'and get me another drink.'

It was three hours before the *Oceanid*'s astropath appeared on the bridge in response to Lucian's summons. Having waited thirty minutes, Lucian had dispatched a junior officer to escort Adept Karaldi, but had been informed that the man was otherwise engaged. 'Astropathicus business,' the officer had reported.

Lucian had waited, but had seethed all the while. He was in no mood for Karaldi's eccentricities.

'My lord,' the astropath said, bowing deeply as he entered the bridge, 'please forgive my tardiness. I was performing certain rites, my lord. I could not...'

'Well enough, adept. You are here now.' Lucian walked to the forward observation port and looked out at the Ajax. The mighty spotlights still swept her cliff-like flanks, blindingly bright where they crossed.

'Yes, my lord.' The astropath appeared uncomfortable, though that in itself was not entirely unusual for the man. 'How might I serve you?'

'Come here, adept.'

Karaldi approached the viewing port, wringing his hands in obvious nervousness. He regarded Lucian, before following his gaze.

'The Ajax,' Lucian said.

'Yes, my lord,' Karaldi replied.

'We can't communicate with her.'

'No, my lord,' the astropath murmured, almost too quietly for Lucian to hear. But Lucian was close enough, so close that he could smell the liquor on Karaldi's breath.

'Yes,' Lucian said, his tone flat, yet entirely unequivocal.

'I cannot, my master.' Karaldi's eyes were wide as he pleaded. 'Please, do not ask me to...'

'To do your duty?' Lucian replied, his voice now icy cold. 'If I cannot call upon you to do this thing, what use are you to me? Why should I not petition the guild for a replacement, for one who can do his duty?'

Karaldi nodded, and looked out of the view port once more. Lucian caught the look of dread on the astropath's face as he squinted blindly at the Ajax. Karaldi lifted a golden aquila hanging from a chain around his scrawny neck, and cupped it in both hands. He bowed once more to his master.

'Might I have an hour to prepare?' Adept Karaldi asked.

'One hour,' Lucian replied, 'no more.'

Lucian had ordered the bridge crew to vacate their stations, all bar the servitor at the communications console, which monitored the still open, howling channel for any sign of life aboard the Ajax. Lucian stood in the centre of the darkened bridge, looking down upon the cross-legged astropath.

'My lord, you have witnessed an astropathic trance, but I must warn you that what I am about to undertake is something different from that. Remote prognostication is not...'

'I do not need to know the details, adept. Just tell me if I need do anything, and I shall do it.'

Karaldi sighed, his shoulders sagging. 'No, my lord, you need only watch. Though if you would...'

'What?'

'If you would pray for me, my lord. And if it is not me who speaks to you...'

'I know what to do, adept, have no doubt.' Lucian unconsciously patted the holster of his plasma pistol. Although he had but an inkling of what awaited the adept, he knew there were risks in what he had asked Karaldi to do.

The astropath did not answer, for he had already begun the rite. Lucian fought against the urge to prowl around the all-but empty bridge, forcing himself to stand still and look on whilst the astropath entered his trance. Lucian recalled the times he had witnessed Karaldi undertake an astropathic communion, and briefly wondered how different this might seem to those uneducated, though not entirely ignorant, in the ways of the psyker. His abiding perception in past instances had been of a sudden and dramatic drop in temperature. Would the remote prognostication be the same? he wondered.

In a moment, he had his answer.

The shadows of the darkened bridge suddenly closed in upon the astropath, flowing as liquid over the deck to engulf his body. Lost in a trance, Karaldi appeared not to notice, though Lucian could barely discern his features amidst the well of inky shadow that surrounded him. Then, the astropath's body began to sway gently from side to side, and Lucian saw that there was something odd in his movements. The swaying increased as Lucian looked on, Karaldi's motions becoming slow and languid, impossibly slow, in fact, as if viewed on a pict-slate with the playback set at one tenth the normal speed.

Lucian watched with increasing horror, his neck prickling. Karaldi's expression slowly transformed, until his face was a mask of terror. The astropath's mouth slowly opened as if he screamed the lonely wail of the eternally damned, though Lucian heard not a sound issue forth from his throat.

Lucian's horror mounted still further as he looked on. Karaldi's body tensed, every muscle pulled taut. Although the astropath's movements appeared impossibly slow, his face blurred as if in rapid movement. He screamed his silent scream as the shadows all around closed in still further.

Then Lucian caught, at the very edge of hearing, a sound that filled him with primal dread. The cold chill of the void filled his veins, the ashen stink of oblivion cloying at his nostrils. Yet still, he forced himself to look on, though he felt the claws of the warp tug and grasp at his very sanity.

The sound increased in volume as if its source grew nearer all the while. Lucian knew that it came from the astropath's still screaming mouth, as if it were the entrance to a tunnel along which something from a nightmare thundered ever closer. Karaldi's mouth filled Lucian's vision as the cacophonous wail grew louder and louder.

Then, the scream exploded from Karaldi's mouth and the shadows leapt back. The astropath's movements ceased their leaden blur, his body released as if he had been struggling against invisible bindings now suddenly released.

Lucian came forward as Karaldi collapsed to the deck, catching the man by the shoulders before he dashed his head against the steel plating. The astropath looked up at him with empty eye sockets, a crimson track running from each. What have I done? Lucian thought, cradling the man in his arms. He rejected the thought as quickly as it formed. I did what I had to, he told himself, for the sake of the fleet.

Lucian bellowed for a medicae servitor to attend the astropath. Blood pooled in Lucian's hands and spread in a wide pool across the deck.

'Can he speak?' Lucian asked, sitting beside Adept Karaldi's recumbent form. As he did so he looked around at the medicae bay. Odd memories of the place surfaced in his mind: memories of his grandfather lying mortally wounded in the very bed in which the astropath now lay; memories of countless others hurt in the course of their duties to the line of Arcadius.

The bay was stark white, a dozen medicae servitors permanently engaged in the simple task of scrubbing its every surface with caustic, sharp smelling antiseptic. Each bed along the bay's rectangular length was crowded with a halo of arcane equipment, the operation of many known only to the tiny staff that maintained them. That staff now clustered around the bed at which Lucian sat.

Adept Estaban, personal physician to Lucian, as he had been to an unspecified number of previous generations of Arcadius, stood at the head of the bed. Estaban was an enigma to Lucian, but he trusted him, quite literally, with his life. The chirurgeon had administered three courses of life-preserving rejuve, already having prolonged Lucian's life way past the span of a normal man's. The chirurgeon wore his white rubber smock, smeared with the blood of his patient, and a mask obscured his face. Various analytic probes and sensors were mounted around his head, through which he studied his patient intently. Estaban's staff clustered around him: three female medicae assistants, each adorned in a similar manner to their master, and each smeared in a quantity of blood. A medicae servitor stood beside each assistant, grossly pumping clear tubes and cables snaking from its body, directly into the patient's veins.

Estaban looked up at Lucian's arrival, his bloodshot left eye magnified grotesquely as it focused on him.

Realising that the chirurgeon had been so intent upon the astropath that he had not heard the question, Lucian repeated himself.

'Karaldi, can he speak?'

'Oh,' Estaban said, lifting the glass from his eye. 'The patient is conscious my master, though in some state of delirium, I fear.' The chirurgeon reached out a black rubber clad hand and touched the astropath's cranium. 'Quite what goes on in the mind of one such as he...'

Lucian took his gaze from Estaban, mildly repulsed, as he always was, by the surgeon's peculiar manner. He looked at Master Karaldi's face, stunned at how old the astropath suddenly appeared to be.

'Adept,' Lucian said softly, but insistently, gently squeezing Karaldi's wrist. There was no response.

He heard Estaban mutter to one of his assistants. The woman, her face obscured behind a white face mask, adjusted a series of dials mounted upon the chest of the medicae servitor standing next to her. She nodded smartly as the liquid pumping through the cable from the servitor to the patient changed colour, from a sickly yellow to an actinic green.

'Who...' the patient stammered. A second medicae assistant reached across Lucian and made some adjustment to the catheter inserted into Karaldi's bloody forearm.

'All better,' she said primly, smearing Karaldi's blood from her hand across the front of her white rubber apron.

'Karaldi,' Lucian said, determined to garner some response from his astropath. He prayed the man's sanity, or what was left of it, even before he had entered the trance, was not shot entirely. 'You must concentrate. I need to know what you saw. What's happened to the Ajax?'

'The Ajax?' Karaldi asked, some degree of lucidity returning as the intravenous fluid flowed from the servitor's body to his. 'My lord, nothing. Nothing has happened to the Ajax.'

Lucian looked to the chirurgeon, who shook his head slowly. One of the medical assistants leaned across and mopped Karaldi's sweating brow, her eyes regarding him with curious and mildly disturbing intent. 'Adept, please listen to me. Something has befallen the Ajax, and I need to know what, in case it–'

'No, my lord,' the Astropath cut in, 'it has not, not yet.'

The three medicae assistants shared knowing glances, and the chirurgeon shook his head yet again. They appeared to Lucian to have given up on the astropath, perhaps believing that Karaldi was in the grip of some fatal fever. Lucian, however, would not give up quite yet.

'What do you mean, adept? What do you mean "not yet"?'

Silence followed Lucian's question, broken only by the low humming of the medicae bay's equipment and the patient's laboured breathing. A cold suspicion crept into Lucian's mind.

'That's it, my lord,' Karaldi said, his blank eye sockets boring straight at Lucian as if the astropath met his very gaze. 'You have the truth of it. You know of what I speak.'

'No,' Lucian said, shaking his head in denial, refusing to accept what he was being told.

'Yes!' Karaldi spat back, the madness so often present in his tone coming entirely to the fore. 'Nothing has happened to the Ajax, yet!'

Lucian stood, his seat toppling into a bank of medicae equipment as he staggered back. His mind reeled as he looked upon the profusely sweating astropath, yet more blood seeping from his blank eye sockets to run down his cheeks in vile, crimson rivulets. Karaldi described what all spacers dreaded, a warping of time, in which the ghosts of events yet to pass haunted the present.

'Sedate him, for the Emperor's sake,' Lucian ordered. 'Put him out, and keep him out until I say otherwise.'

Adept Estaban fussed around the equipment as he issued terse orders to his staff. Karaldi convulsed as a new concoction of drugs was pumped into his body, a powerful mixture that knocked him out in seconds.

'Better now,' one of the medicae assistants crooned as she wiped the astropath's brow. 'All better now.'

CHAPTER EIGHT

'Master on deck!' the crew chief bellowed as Korvane stepped from the bulkhead portal, passing from the lifter shaft into the very guts of the *Rosetta*.

He paused, appraising the rabble before him. The wide thoroughfare was lined with crewmen, each of whom stood to attention, right arm raised in a perfunctory salute. He had travelled to an area of the ship that was scruffy and ill-kept, unlike the stately corridors he was used to. Korvane saw immediately that these were not the crisp uniformed officers of the upper decks, but the real crew of the rogue trader flotilla, the press-ganged scum, the indentured flotsam and jetsam of a thousand different ports. He hated them, and he was quite sure they hated him just as much.

Korvane cast a glance around the assembled men and women, crew members interrupted in the myriad tasks and toils they engaged upon each day, most of which Korvane had not the slightest knowledge of. Then, he noticed an unfamiliar element amongst the crewmen: tall, dusky skinned men and women, dressed in loose fitting, olive drab fatigues, dog tags clinking around their necks.

The chief had evidently followed his master's gaze, for he straightened up and puffed out his chest. The huge man, his bulky frame evidence of muscle run to fat with the encroachment of years, advanced upon the nearest group of strangers. Korvane's interest was piqued, leading him to follow silently behind the crew chief. He guessed what was coming.

Approaching a fatigue-clad figure leaning against a bulkhead, the crew chief raised himself to his full height. Eye to eye with the other man, the petty officer spoke so quietly that Korvane could barely hear him, though he followed close behind.

'When I says "master on deck"', the chief growled, 'I actually means, "bow down before he who on this ship is second only to the Emperor, praise be his name, you worthless Guard scum." Does I make myself clear?'

Silence descended. The Imperial Guard trooper, for it was obvious the strange figures were from one of Gauge's regiments being transported on the *Rosetta*, straightened, meeting the chief eye to eye.

Korvane felt the threat of imminent physical violence. He fingered his holster, reassuring himself that his las-pistol was close at hand. If the Guardsmen would not be cowed, he knew he would have to defend himself, and though he was well tutored in such matters, it was for the non-commissioned ranks, not for him, to impose discipline upon the crew. He knew that his father would have waded in and distributed summary justice the instant someone spoke out of line, but Korvane, to his own estimation at least, had been raised better than that. He knew his place, and considered it only correct that others should too.

The stand-off continued, the chief evidently allowing the trooper a moment or two to consider his predicament. The man's eyes darted from side to side, judging, Korvane guessed, the odds of his small group of warriors prevailing against the chief and the crowd of press-ganged scum that edged in upon the scene. A bead of sweat ran from the man's brow, yet the chief did not even blink. The trooper's eyes darted around once more, before meeting Korvane's. He held the trooper's gaze, before the man looked back to the chief.

'I didn't...' the trooper began to utter, before the chief unloaded a piston of a right-handed upper cut to his chin. The trooper was slammed back against the metal bulkhead, knocked unconscious by the impact. The man's form slid to the floor as a number of dislodged teeth clattered across the deck. The chief did not even look his victim, his gaze locked upon the trooper's compatriots.

'I will deal with this, my lord,' the chief said to Korvane, not turning around. 'A little bit of discipline needs dishing out.'

'Very well,' Korvane replied, looking upon the mess the chief's punch had made of the trooper's face, 'carry on.'

Korvane passed from this area into one far more crowded, yet thankfully far less unsavoury. The vast, central cargo areas of the *Rosetta* had been turned over to a number of Imperial Guard units, amounting, so General Gauge had informed him, to something in the region of five thousand combatants and a similar number of support personnel. A wide companionway ran the length of the vessel's spine, passing the vast bays in which the troopers were housed. The huge interlocking blast doors had been raised and the entire area was a hive of unfamiliar activity. Korvane saw one cargo bay given over entirely to rows of sleeping mats, so many that they stretched off into the distance along the entire length of the vast space. He had passed another bay in which the troopers practiced unarmed combat, several thousand warriors paired up, sparring with one another, all with blood-streaked faces and swollen lips. Assorted hangers-on, the regimental train as Gauge had called it, were to be found at every turn. Every regiment of the Imperial Guard relied on them as much as they did upon the Officio Munitorum. Lay armourers offered to service faulty weapons or patch up worn armour, cooks and peddlers plied their unsavoury wares, and sultry women offered other, vital services to the trooper keen to divest himself of what little funds he held.

Korvane was at once intrigued and repulsed by the spectacle of the Imperial Guard having taken over several decks of his vessel. Intrigued, for they had brought with them an almost entirely self-sustaining economy, complete with its unique cultural and societal mores. Repulsed, for he saw that outside of the disinterested and detached officer cadre, thugs and hoodlums ran this micro-society, with no regard for birth or rank. Korvane himself had been raised in the most rarefied of atmospheres, at the Court of Nankirk, where he had studied under the most refined of tutors. To him, these men and women inspired revulsion, and he would not be able to rest until they were off his ship.

Feeling his gorge rise, Korvane closed his fist over the small package he carried in his coat pocket. Pain shot the length of his arm, the lingering effects of the injuries he had sustained in battle against the tau at Arrikis Epsilon. He need only bear it a little longer, he told himself, striding on through the crowded decks as crewmen halted to stand to attention in his wake.

'My lord,' an officer called out as Korvane stepped on to the bridge. 'My lord, I must bring to your attention a number of troubling reports.'

Korvane regarded the man with weary indifference. He was about to reply when the officer continued.

'It's the Guard sir. We've been receiving some disturbing reports of ill-discipline and petty crime.' The man proffered him a data-slate, but Korvane pushed past.

'I don't have time,' he sighed, weary of the endless disruptions to his vessel's normally smooth running, weary, he realised, of the voyage across the Damocles Gulf.

'But sir,' the officer insisted, 'these really are rather urgent. They say it's the warp, sir, and they say it's getting worse. The armsmen fear things might get out of hand if something is not...'

'I said,' Korvane snapped as he rounded on the officer, 'I don't have time.' He felt an unfamiliar anger rise within him, one he knew his father would have had to fight hard against to suppress. His stepsister would not even have tried. Drawing on all the courtly etiquette with which he had been raised, Korvane steadied himself. The officer waited patiently, his face a mask of professional detachment.

'I shall review your reports presently,' Korvane replied. 'Dismissed.'

With a click of polished boot heels, the officer departed, leaving Korvane to pass across his bridge to the day room at its rear. As he crossed the deck, he could not help but be reminded of the terrible conflagration that had engulfed it during the battle against the tau at Arrikis Epsilon. Large sections of bulkhead had been replaced, often for the first time since the vessel's construction, the gleaming metal stark against the patina of a thousand years. Here and there, the metal had been melted by the intense heat of the battle, to blister and run like mercury across the deck. In places, these run-offs remained, set hard upon the bulkhead like solidified lava. The heat had inflicted a similar fate upon Korvane's body, though thankfully his father's chirurgeon had worked masterfully upon his scars, rendering all but the very worst invisible. He still felt his wounds though, deep inside, and he raged against the misfortune that had come so close to crippling him.

Passing in to his day room, Korvane sat heavily upon a padded and studded leather recliner, the peerless work, he dimly recalled, of the long extinct Dreyfuss artisan clan of New Valaxa. He slumped upon the recliner, vaguely aware that he should comport himself in a far more appropriate manner whilst sitting upon such a priceless artefact. Yet, he could not bring himself to care about the Dreyfuss, only about what was in the pocket of his jacket.

He withdraw his hand from his pocket, and opened it slowly. A small vial of clear liquid lay in his heavily scarred palm. The man in the enginarium had claimed that it was a potent analgesic, one that could reverse pain and transform it into something approaching pleasure.

Korvane sighed as he recalled the endless treatments he had subjected himself to in the aftermath of Arrikis Epsilon. Though each had lessened his outward scarring, they had in turn heaped upon him a concomitant pain deep within. At first he had taken standard pain killing drugs, then he had progressed to more potent metaopioids. Though he refused to fully acknowledge the fact, even to himself, he had developed a taste for the drugs, a taste far in excess of their medical efficacy.

As master of his vessel, not one of the medicae staff had dared refuse him access to the metaopioids. Yet, in time and with prolonged and ever-increasing use, the drugs' effects had reduced and the pain had slowly returned, this time far worse then ever before. He had been driven into the depths of his vessel, to the company of the lowest of the low amongst the press-ganged murderers and rapists, to seek out a source of pain killing drugs. He had found one, discovering to his great distaste that the vast majority of the engine crew were addicted to the stuff. They needed, he had been told, to stave off the crippling pain inflicted by their continuous exposure to the unstable fields that flooded the plasma containment decks. He cared very little for the fate of the scum who worked those decks, yet he ensured that his contact was moved to a safer station in the enginarium, lest he succumb to the effects of the fields.

The new substance, referred to by the crew who used it as

'd-sense,' had given back to Korvane some of the life he had enjoyed before. The pain went away each time he took the substance, and it did not even begin to return for days at a stretch. He hated it, yet, he knew, he needed the d-sense to function, for now at least.

He closed his fist around the vial, considering whether to take its contents now, or to wait a while longer until the pain increased to the point where he would have no choice but to do so. He looked up sharply as he caught a faint, unfamiliar sound at the very edge of his hearing. The Imperial Guard passengers were no doubt playing havoc with the orderly running of his ship. He opened his palm once more, hearing even as he did so the same faint tone. He felt distracted and annoyed, partly at the very fact of the intrusion, but equally because he simply could not place the sound. It was an eerie reverberation, an undulating tone that promised bewitchment if only he could pinpoint its source.

With a substantial effort of will, Korvane shook off the distraction and focused upon the vial. He would take it now, he resolved, if for no other reason than to throw off the weird fugue no doubt inflicted by the vessel's continued passage through the warp. With sudden conviction, he pulled the stopper from the glass vial and in a swift motion poured the liquid into his open mouth. The d-sense had no discernible taste, but the effect was almost instantaneous. Pain he had not even registered swept from him as if he were cleansed by the very purest of mountain springs. His spirit soared as he sank into the recliner's soft leather padding.

Even as he felt the last of the pain wash from him, he heard the weird sound once more. Perhaps, he thought, it had not been a product of the warp working upon his strained and overstretched mind. Perhaps, he felt with growing conviction, it was something he really should investigate.

Lifting his head from the comfort of the recliner's tall back, Korvane sought to identify the direction from which the sound emanated. He turned his head slowly, concentrating. As hard as he tried, he could not place a direction upon the sound. His pain quite forgotten, Korvane stood, straining all the while to keep the haunting tone at the very forefront of his attention.

Treading softly so as to avoid his footsteps drowning out the song, he crossed his ready room and, cautiously and deliberately, hauled open the heavy bulkhead door. All was as it should be upon the bridge, the *Rosetta*'s command crew busily engaged upon their myriad everyday tasks. The officer who had waylaid Korvane with the report turned, and upon seeing Korvane back on the bridge made to reach for his data-slate. Korvane flashed the man a look that left the officer in no doubt that his master was not to be disturbed, and crossed the bridge and went out of the main portal, on to the wide companionway beyond.

Once in the passage, Korvane halted once more, listening for the distant sound. He picked it up straight away, and could discern variations in its pitch and cadence; it was forming into a voice, giving song to the most heavenly sound imaginable.

He looked around, attempting to discern whether or not any crew nearby had noted the song. A number of junior officers and senior ratings passed by him, each saluting respectfully to their master. A couple appeared distracted, Korvane felt, but none appeared to be intently focused upon the sound. Perhaps, he mused, they too had put the phenomenon down to the tricks of the warp. Korvane knew, somehow, that the song was no trick. It was real, and he would find its source.

As Korvane had passed along the *Rosetta*'s companionways, the song had grown clearer and yet more entrancing. After a while, it became clear to him that others of his crew had heard it too, and it appeared that several hundred officers and ratings had found a reason to walk, slowly and deliberately, in the same direction. Korvane had resolutely ignored them. He determined that the song was none of their concern, though he did not go so far as to order them to return to their duties.

As Korvane had passed the central decks, those adjacent to the vast transportation bays, he had noted that the area was almost entirely empty of the thousands of Imperial Guardsmen who had crowded the place when last he had passed through. The cavernous holds were eerily devoid of life, though the warriors' equipment and personal effects were strewn all over the decks, as if cast away and forgotten in an instant.

Only now, as Korvane approached the *Rosetta*'s main flight deck did he come across a warrior of the Imperial Guard; and not just one warrior, but every last one of them. The entire regiment, it appeared, was filing onto the flight deck, clearly following the celestial song emanating from somewhere up ahead.

That song now filled Korvane's consciousness so completely that he scarcely cared about the sheer outlandishness of the events unfolding around him. The song was all that mattered to him, for it was so loud as to drown out all other background noise. Even the ever-present drone of the *Rosetta*'s plasma core was inaudible.

The wide passage leading to the flight deck was completely crowded with Guard troopers. All were moving towards the open portal that led to the vast space from which the *Rosetta*'s shuttles, pinnaces and lighters plied near-space when in orbit around a planet. Korvane joined the tide of bodies, passing along with them, his attention focused only on the song as it grew louder and clearer. As he passed through the portal onto the flight deck, the song grew clearer still, and he could easily discern a single voice amidst the beatific chorus, a voice that he was quite sure sang to him and to him alone.

The flight deck was several hundred metres wide, its hard pan surface pitted and scarred by the passage of many small vessels over the centuries. One entire wall was a mighty blast door, beyond which lay a small bubble of real space, and beyond that, held at bay by the *Rosetta*'s gellar field, the raging ocean of souls that was warp space. As the crowds spilled out onto the flight deck, each individual, whether officer, rating or Imperial Guardsmen, dispersed, each seeking the enchantment of the heavenly song.

Korvane slowed as he crossed the centre of the deck, noting distractedly the markings and guidance lights at his feet. He halted, his eyes upon the mighty armoured blast door as the song swept in all around him. It swirled in the very air, the ghostly voice whispering to him as if the singer pressed her lips to his ears and breathed her celestial promises straight into his soul. As Korvane watched, the mighty pistons above the blast door ground to life, a deep rumbling filling the deck as a line of impossibly bright, violet light appeared at its base.

Distant panic welled up at the edge of Korvane's psyche, to be soothed and born away in an instant, by flurries of ghostly voices. Korvane watched the blast door opening, but he knew the shielding that protected it even when the doors were opened to space would contain the atmosphere within the flight deck.

As the door rose, the violet light flooded the deck, casting long, diffuse shadows behind each individual. Korvane's heart leapt as his vision was engulfed, the others all around receding from his mind until he appeared to stand alone in the vast space, the light shining only on him. The song grew to a soaring crescendo, yet a single voice amidst the chorus sang for him and him alone. It was a voice of such sweetness and perfection that he felt he had known it all his life. Or perhaps he had simply sought it all his life, without knowing, unaware that such beauty could exist, yet still waiting for its promise to be fulfilled.

Korvane knew that he would now meet the creature whose voice had drawn him here.

A silhouette resolved itself from the blazing glory that flooded through the raised door to the *Rosetta*'s flight deck. Korvane stared into that light, knowing that here was the source of the song that he now heard not with his ears, but in his very soul. The shape became a figure, curvaceous and lithe, swimming through the air as if through water, darting lightly towards him in a series of rapid, stop-start movements. With each halt the figure made, its limbs waved as if caressed by a gentle ocean current, before moving onwards once more.

Korvane squinted, his breath catching in his throat. With a final, sudden movement, the figure glided, languid and sensuous, towards him, the song intensifying all the while. Her shape became clearer as she appeared from the light, the outline of her flawless body etched against the violet behind. He saw rounded hips and a supple back arched in motion. Gentle shoulders and delicate arms lifted as she settled directly before him, as if stepping from an ocean current onto a soft, sea floor.

Korvane knew that he was entirely bewitched. Yet he cared not, for damnation, if this was it, appeared to be a sweet eternity. Even as he watched, the figure resolved before him and he looked upon a kind of beauty never meant to be witnessed by mere mortals.

She stood before him, her beauty so complete it seared his soul. He looked upon a figure of such perfection that he could drink in the sight of but the smallest portion of her body and know complete satiation. She appeared human, yet Korvane somehow knew that such a term could never describe her; that she was so much more than such a word could encompass. He was humbled for a moment, almost shamed in her presence, an intense feeling of unworthiness causing him to cast his glance down to the floor lest his gaze somehow sully her. Then, as the celestial chorus softened, levelling out into a single, gently modulating note, he knew that he was meant to look upon her, that it was his destiny to do so, that he was always meant to do so.

Her hair was black, yet it shimmered with glittering iridescent hues, from pink, to purple, to blue, as scented oil swirls across the surface of dark water. It was cut across her forehead, framing her pale, oval face. Its dark coils tumbled gently down her shoulders and traced the contours of her body, to lie gently against her soft belly and round hips. Her skin was as pale as ivory, and every inch of it glittered as if dusted with the frost of the void.

His gaze finally settled upon her face. It was the face of perfect innocence, of sublime purity. He could scarcely believe he could look upon it and not somehow soil it with his own, inherent imperfection. Her face was turned down, but her eyes looked upwards into his. They sparkled with the violet light from which she had swum. With what he knew might be his last conscious action, Korvane dared to meet those eyes.

'I can take your pain away,' she told him, her perfect, rosebud lips barely parting as she spoke. The sound of her voice transcended mere human language, so that Korvane felt tears rising in the yawning silence that followed, mourning their passing as if a loved one had died.

'I can give you all you desire.'

Korvane sank to his knees, knowing that she spoke the truth. He raised his head, tears flowing freely down his face, to look up into her eyes. She regarded him with an expression of serenity, even love, and Korvane felt his soul wither before its light.

'How?' he made himself ask, the mere act of speaking a titanic effort.

The ghost of a smile touched the corner of her perfect mouth, before she lifted herself from the floor as if propelling her body into the non-existent ocean current. She propelled herself over him with a single motion, coming to rest at his back. He was afforded an unhindered view of the glorious light spilling through the launch bay, and he was almost blinded by its beauty. He felt lips pressed to his ear from behind.

'Come with me,' she whispered. 'Come with me and all will be perfect.'

Confusion welled within him. 'Come with you? But where?'

'Out there, my love.' The creature's lips settled upon the flesh of Korvane's neck, causing sublime electricity to course through his body. He fought hard to cling to his wits, but knew he was slipping away. Even as he gazed into the light, he felt the creature's mouth moving down his neck, planting impossibly gentle kisses as they did so.

Then, amidst the light and the sound, the scent of her skin and the touch of her lips, he perceived the faintest insinuation of discord. He turned his head just a fraction, so as to locate the source of the perception. Even as he did so, the creature's arms snaked around his waist, her fingers working the fastenings on his uniform jacket. Though almost entirely subsumed by the creature's touch, Korvane felt the disturbance again, and against all his desires, he fought to retain some measure of control. He looked once more to the light blazing through the launch bay doors, some distant part of his mind clinging to reality even as he slipped further and further away from it.

'Out there,' he muttered, barely able to concentrate as the creature's hands slipped inside his open jacket, 'but it's not safe out there.'

'Shhh,' the creature breathed.

'But it's not...'

Korvane felt pain flare across his chest as the creature dug razor sharp nails into his skin. He could not help but cry out.

'You like that, don't you my love.' She withdrew her hands from his jacket, and Korvane caught a glimpse of crimson upon them. He felt her pull back, and an instant later she was before him once more, having flipped as through water in one, graceful motion. She settled on the deck, her legs folded under her body, and leant forward upon her slender arms. She looked up into his eyes, her hair swimming around her and her eyes blazing with violet iridescence.

A drop of what he knew to be his own blood was smeared at the corner of her mouth.

'Come with me, my love, and I shall render unto you such secrets. I shall tell of creation and birth, of incubation and potential unbound. You shall walk at my side, amongst the gods of ancient times and of ages yet to be.' She reached out her hand, holding it palm upwards. 'Join me, Korvane Gerrit Arcadius, join us. Come with me.'

Korvane's mind swam at her words. Yet, a small voice deep within questioned what the creature had said. Did she really expect him to leave his ship, even while it traversed the warp? To do so was madness. Perhaps she had no understanding of such things, perhaps to such as her they were but petty, everyday inconveniences. Yet still, doubt welled up from the centre of his being.

'I cannot come with you,' he said. He choked on his words even as he spoke them, tears flooding down his cheeks. That small part of him that rebelled at what was occurring grew stronger, but still, doubt and grief threatened to drown him. 'Couldn't you stay here, with me?' He sobbed, knowing the futility of his words even as they left his mouth.

'Look upon me, Korvane,' she breathed. 'Look upon me and know that you will never again see such perfection should you refuse me. I know you, Korvane, I know you more than you know yourself. I know so much more. I know what she did to you, of the pain you fight everyday, and what you would do, what you have done, to visit justice upon her.' She pushed back with her arms so that she sat upright on her folded legs. She spread her arms wide, her hair swaying around her on the raging ocean current.

'I can help you,' she whispered. 'Before we depart, together, you and I, I can finish her for you.'

'But she's gone!' Korvane spluttered. 'For all I know she's dead!'

'She is not dead, Korvane. She is nearby. I could draw her here, if you like, and visit upon her such pains, or such pleasures, as I desire. What would you have me do with her, my love?'

Korvane's mind swam in turmoil. He had believed his bitch of a stepsister dead at the hands of Inquisitor Grand, or at least fled far beyond any capacity to return. But the creature claimed she was not dead, but nearby. Hatred flared within Korvane's soul, quite at odds with the sublime intoxication that had overwhelmed him since first he had heard the creature's song. The hatred drove out the bewitchment, the voice of reason begging at the back of his skull, screaming loud and clear.

'No!' Korvane bellowed.

The creature froze, her gaze fixed upon him. Though her face was purity and innocence personified and her body soft and curvaceous to the point of sublime luxury, her eyes were impossible wells of unknowable power. The all-encompassing violet light grew sickly, and Korvane caught ghostly motions at the edge of his vision.

With a supreme effort of will, he looked around. The flight deck was populated by half glimpsed apparitions, partly resolved figures growing more and more solid as the violet light dimmed. Even as he watched, the figures became solid. Each was a crewmen or a trooper, and before each stood a form. Before each, Korvane realised, stood the creature the individual most desired to see, to be called away by, to die for.

'Korvane!' a rough, male voice called from close at hand. He spun around, to see General Gauge and a group of his staff officers crossing the flight deck towards him. 'Korvane, down!'

Without thinking, Korvane threw himself to the deck. An instant later, an explosive roar sounded overhead. He rolled over as the sound passed by, to find himself looking straight up at the underside of one of the *Rosetta*'s shuttles. He lifted his head to see the launch bay, the last of the violet light disintegrating into tendrils of slithering energy. The shuttle, its course erratic and uncertain passed out of the bay, through the bubble of the atmospheric shielding, and out.

In a matter of seconds the shuttle had crossed the small space around the *Rosetta* within which the laws of the physical universe still prevailed, held in stasis by the all-enveloping gellar field. Korvane saw the blackness of space beyond, stained with swirling violet energies, and realised that the *Rosetta* was breaking warp, forcing its way back to the real, physical universe.

The shuttle was engulfed in raging energies as it breached the Gellar field. Corposant faces reared from the swirling clouds, claws and tentacles reaching out obscenely to grasp the vessel. Even as its engines flared, straining to escape the clutches of the warp, the vessel was ripped apart. A hideous keening went up, causing every individual on the flight deck to fall to the ground, hands over ears to shut out the wailing of the damned as they were dragged to the deepest infernal regions of the warp.

As Korvane's voice joined those of the damned, he felt consciousness slip away, his vision fading to blessed oblivion.

'What were they, general?' asked Korvane as he stared out of the conference chamber's viewing port. The lights were turned low, and he welcomed the encroaching shadows. 'How did they get on my ship?'

'I have no idea, Korvane,' General Gauge replied. 'I have consulted my confessor and his staff, yet none appear able to give me a straight answer.'

'What happened, then? To me, to the crew, to you?'

'That I cannot say either, Korvane. It appears that each man and woman experienced something unique to him or herself. Each was drawn to congregate on the flight deck, but then things got somewhat... confused.'

'How many gave in to their desires? To the... creatures?' Korvane asked, visions of the creature's glittering body coming unbidden to his mind.

'It seems that around five thousand congregated on the flight deck, mostly Guard, but not exclusively so.' The general appeared embarrassed, but Korvane nodded that he should continue. 'How many would have succumbed once there, I cannot imagine, though we know some attempted to escape via the shuttle.'

Korvane nodded, a shiver coursing through him as he recalled the soul screams of the deserters as the shuttle they had commandeered was swallowed up by the warp at the instant the *Rosetta* penetrated the thin skein between the warp and realspace. 'Where did they hope to flee to?' He asked, unsure he wanted to hear the answer.

'Where?' replied Gauge. 'Well, I'm told we're only half a dozen astronomical units from a stellar body of some kind. I can only imagine...'

'How?' Korvane interrupted, 'how did we come to exit the warp so near to such a body?'

'Korvane,' the general continued, 'you ordered the *Rosetta* out of the warp.'

Korvane was stunned. He had no recollection of issuing such an order. He vividly recalled the creature's promises, her silky skin, and the touch of her lips upon his neck.

'Korvane?' General Gauge leaned forward in his chair, his elbows resting on the polished wooden surface of the conference table. 'Korvane, when you issued that order, you saved the life and soul of every man and woman on this vessel. It was only the fact that the *Rosetta* was exiting the warp at the point where the Gellar field was breached that stopped... what happened to the shuttle happening to us all. You have my profound thanks, Korvane. You cannot know how much we owe you.'

Korvane turned back towards the viewing portal. The darkness was all-encompassing, matching the emptiness he felt might consume his soul now that the creature was gone. Somewhere out there, in the utter dark, was a stellar body, and beyond that, the rendezvous point at which the fleet would muster, half way across the Damocles Gulf. Further still, he mused, was an entire empire, but all of that paled into insignificance before one single fact. His stepsister was out there, and, if the creature's words were to be believed, she was not very far away.

It occurred to him that hatred had stolen him from the creature's embrace. His stepsister might have saved him, Korvane mused, but she would pay the very highest price for doing so.

CHAPTER NINE

'Welcome aboard our vessel,' the tall, robed alien envoy said, addressing Brielle. His face was wide and flat, and he lacked a visible nose, yet Brielle could see that his grey-blue skin was wrinkled and worn with age, just like a human's. 'I trust your voyage has been a comfortable one.'

Brielle, Naal at her back, stood in the centre of a wide, oval chamber, facing the envoy and his retinue. Long, scroll-like flags hung from the high ceiling, each adorned with the alien lettering of the tau. Having fled the system aboard a stolen tau shuttle, Brielle, Naal and the prisoners they had released had rendezvoused with a vessel of the so-called 'Water Caste,' the arm of the Tau Empire responsible, Naal had explained, for diplomacy and trade.

'I thank you for receiving me,' Brielle replied, as her mind raced with the lessons her father had insisted she undergo years before, lessons in etiquette and courtly manners. She had paid scant attention, reasoning that her native intelligence would see her through any such situations. Ordinarily, it had, but here she was dealing with a representative of an entire xenos race. She knew that the fate of that race and many human worlds besides might hang upon her words.

'It is an honour,' the tau replied, 'to have such an august individual as yourself aboard. I trust your voyage thus far was not overly taxing?'

Brielle forced her mind to a semblance of order, mentally filtering the alien diplomat's words for any sign of duplicity. She acknowledged that she lacked the skill in such matters that her father displayed, or even, she hated to admit, that her brother had learned during his upbringing amongst the highest Imperial courts. As a consequence of her uncertainty, she found herself studying the alien's flat visage, though she had great difficulty in reading his meaning beyond the words he spoke.

Naal coughed subtly, and she realised that the envoy was waiting for her answer. She felt annoyance at her performance, and her cheeks coloured. Hopefully, she thought, the tau would have little experience at reading human emotions, and she would be able to get through this.

'Please,' the envoy said before Brielle could speak. 'forgive me my ill manners. You have travelled a great distance to meet with us, and I have not allowed you to rest now that you are here.'

'Not at all,' Brielle replied, determined not to let any weakness show. 'We have undergone a long journey, but we are eager to meet with our new friends, the tau.'

The envoy dipped his head at Brielle's words, and spread his long, spindly arms wide in a gesture that caused the material of his formal robes to sweep backwards as if upon a sudden breeze. Brielle estimated that the fabric would be worth a small fortune on a number of coreward planets, for its decorative simplicity belied the obviously superior quality of its workmanship. Then, as the envoy raised his head once more, she realised that the role of trader was no longer hers, and might never be so again. She had to forge her own course now, wherever that might take her.

'In addition to welcoming you among us,' the envoy continued, 'I must express the gratitude of all the peoples of the Tau Empire for the return of those you released. I have heard only a small portion of the tale, but am given to understand that you have sacrificed a great deal in order to return to us those we believed lost.'

As one, the tau envoy and his retinue bent almost double, bowing in obviously heartfelt thanks. Silence filled the starkly lit chamber, and, all of a sudden, Brielle felt quite alone in the centre of the bright, white space. She felt too the sheer weight of the events unfolding around her, aware that her actions might ring down the ages in the annals of the Arcadius. If, she mused, her name was ever entered in them again.

After what felt to Brielle like long, drawn out minutes, the envoy and his retinue straightened. She took a deep breath, seeking to impose some order on her thoughts. Finally, she found what she hoped would be the correct words.

'I come to you in the hope that my actions might benefit both my people, and yours,' Brielle said, studying the envoy's implacable features intently. ' I am honoured,' she continued, 'to be received in such a fashion. I trust that we shall find common cause to the benefit of all.'

Once more, the envoy dipped his head in obvious approval of Brielle's words, the simple response filling her with relief. 'Indeed, Lady Brielle,' the envoy replied. 'I trust that through our actions, the Greater Good might prevail, to the benefit of us all.'

Lucian awoke with a start, gasping for breath as he sat bolt upright in his bed. Brielle... he had awakened from a nightmare in which his daughter had faced some terrible threat, alone in the dark, and there was nothing he could do to aid her.

Forcing his breathing to a normal pace, Lucian cast about in the dark for the carafe of water he kept at his bedside. After a moment of fumbling he located the crystal vessel and drank deep. The cold liquid helped his mind clear, the last vestige of the stark nightmare evaporating as he came fully awake.

The question of his daughter's fate had been gnawing at Lucian for weeks. As the voyage across the Damocles Gulf had dragged on, he had found himself dwelling upon it more and more. He had spoken of it with Korvane at the last fleet rendezvous point, but his son had appeared sullen and disinterested, as if in the grip of some deeper malaise. As the fleet had moved on, Lucian and his son had parted on bad terms, and that too preyed upon Lucian's mind.

Realising sleep would not return anytime soon, Lucian cast off his bed sheet, and stood and donned a plain, informal outfit. At such times as this, Lucian would often walk the long, winding companionways of his vessel, allowing his steps to lead him wherever they would as his mind pondered whatever problem was troubling him.

Not that this problem would withstand much pondering, Lucian mused, for the issue was plain enough. Brielle had assaulted an inquisitor, wounding him almost unto death, and she had fled, he knew not where. Even for a rogue trader, who would ordinarily exist far above the laws of the Imperium, such an action was unpardonable. Lucian counted himself extremely fortunate that Inquisitor Grand had not sought to wreak revenge upon the remaining Arcadius, though it had occurred to him that the inquisitor might yet decide to do so.

Where was she, Lucian pondered as he stepped out into the passageway? The ancient wood panelling on this deck appeared like the colour of blood under the red lighting of ship's night, and the brass fittings lining the bulkheads gleamed in the dark. Only the ever-present rumble of the *Oceanid*'s warp drive disturbed the silence, and few crew were to be seen at this hour. It was Lucian's favourite time, when the third watch were the only men on duty, the remainder fast asleep, or gambling and whoring in the lower decks.

He chose a direction at random and set off along the companionway. As he walked, he considered the problem at hand. Brielle, his daughter whom he loved dearly, had undertaken a course of action that he had no understanding of at all. It appeared that she had taken it upon herself to free the tau prisoners, but why would she do such a thing? Though he loved her, Lucian knew that Brielle could be selfish in the extreme, so he could not fathom what had caused her to attempt to free the tau prisoners. More to the point, what had she hoped to achieve in doing so?

As he passed through a wide bulkhead door into the *Oceanid*'s central thoroughfare, a thought occurred to Lucian. Had his daughter hoped to use the prisoners to gain some leverage within the crusade's command structure? Perhaps she hoped to help him, seeking some advantage that the Arcadius might bring to bear upon their rivals.

No, Lucian thought with a wry smile. He knew his daughter better than that. Though she would act for the benefit of the Arcadius, he did not believe she would have acted quite so selflessly as to put herself so squarely in harm's way, not unless she stood to gain enormous benefits from doing so.

And what of her fate now that she had fled the crusade? She was out there, somewhere, far beyond his capacity to aid her. She had fled in a tau shuttle, not even attempting to regain the *Fairlight*.

That in itself posed yet more questions. How had she piloted the alien vessel – had she coerced the aid of a tau pilot not captured in the initial assault upon the station? Did she intend to return at some point, and if she did, what could Lucian do to protect her against the wrath of Inquisitor Grand?

The thought of the inquisitor brought a silent shiver of revulsion. Lucian had met with the agents of the Inquisition before, indeed, he had worked closely with the Ordos of the Emperor's Holy Inquisition on several occasions, but Grand somehow stood out amongst its widely individual men and women. There was something deeply... unwholesome about Inquisitor Grand. For a start, he was clearly a political creature where many of his peers considered themselves far above such petty concerns. Grand, it seemed, was content to work within the crusade's power structures, lending the weight of his authority to its ends without bringing to bear the full power he was entitled to wield. Clearly, Lucian mused, the inquisitor and Cardinal Gurney shared some agenda, had some arrangement, or were perhaps both enamoured of some higher power. There were not many above a cardinal and an inquisitor, but the parent organisations of each man were notoriously complex, so anything might be possible.

Lucian wandered on, drawn along the central spine of his vessel. The companionways were still deserted, though he did catch sight of the occasional servitor engaged upon the endless tasks the constructs enacted upon his vessel. Many such tasks, routine maintenance of non-essential systems, were best performed at such a late hour, so as not to inconvenience the crew as they went about their duties during ship's day. Passing the central armoury, Lucian felt a faint tension in the air, and realised that the feeling had been with him for quite some time.

Lucian halted in the centre of the passageway. He told himself that it was the warp and the Damocles Gulf. He'd seen men driven mad by even the briefest voyage through the weirdling depths of the empyrean, and this journey had been particularly taxing. The entire region still pulsed and writhed with formless energy, entirely beyond the understanding of the fleet's most learned tech-priests. What effects, both physical and spiritual, those energies might be exerting upon the hundreds of thousands of crusaders none could tell. What Lucian did know, was that he, and others, were growing steadily more concerned as the crossing of the Damocles Gulf proceeded.

A distant sound drew Lucian's attention, breaking his chain of thought. From a junction up ahead, one passage from which led to the *Oceanid*'s cargo decks, he heard an odd chanting. The song was atonal, the voice cracked, but he recognised its owner straight away. He set off in the direction of the sound.

Turning starboard at the first junction, Lucian climbed down a short ladder, taking him onto the main cargo deck. There was a long corridor before him, which receded into the distance as it ran the length of the vessel. Large blast doors mounted in the bulkhead every twenty metres or so denoted the entrances to the smaller cargo holds. In front of him, the blast door leading to the primary hold was ajar, the wan crimson illumination of ship's night spilling forth. The chanting was clearly audible; it was coming from the primary hold.

His curiosity piqued, Lucian stepped through the open portal and out onto the vast cargo space. The bay was so large that its ceiling was lost to darkness, and even the outer hull doors were shrouded in distant shadow, several hundred metres away. The hold was nigh empty, the goods that the *Oceanid* transported kept in the many secondary holds, or held in deeper storage in the stasis chambers. Lucian fully intended the hold to be entirely filled on the return however, whether with trade goods or with booty.

As the chanting grew clearer, Lucian saw its source. A spindly, emaciated figure sat cross-legged in the very centre of the hold. It was, as Lucian had guessed, his astropath, Adept Karaldi.

Lucian approached cautiously, wary of the man's mental state following his encounter, and not entirely certain that Karaldi should even be out of the medicae bay. As he approached, he saw that the astropath still wore the blood-specked surgical gown that he had worn the last time they had met. Furthermore, catheters trailed from his twig-like arms, which were bruised and pinpricked with all the syringes that had impaled them.

Standing over the cross-legged astropath, Lucian cleared his throat. The man's chanting ceased, and after a long, drawn out moment, Karaldi craned his neck to look up at his master through empty eye sockets.

'My master,' the astropath said through dried and cracked lips.

'Adept. What is occurring? Why are you out of the medicae bay?'

The astropath's mouth worked soundlessly for a moment, before he replied. 'Please, my master, sit with me a while.'

Hesitating to do the bidding of a man obviously pushed way past the boundaries of sanity, Lucian squatted in front of the astropath.

'Speak, Karaldi. What ever transpires, I am your master, and you are my astropath. This vessel needs us both or all is lost.'

'Indeed,' Karaldi replied, a smirk creasing his purple lips. 'Right now, you need me more than you could know. That's what I was trying to tell them...'

'Tell who, adept. Please, speak clearly.' Lucian suppressed a growing impatience, knowing that the astropath could read his surface emotions only too well.

'The chirurgeon and his sisters of mercy,' Karaldi replied, his cracked voice straining with a fear that Lucian could not place. 'Something's coming, master. Something's already here, and I don't think I can do anything to keep it out.'

'What's here, adept? What's among us?' Lucian fought to keep his voice steady, feeling the strain of the voyage weighing down upon his shoulders as never before. 'What can I do, adept. How can I help you?'

At that the astropath merely smiled, though his expression was entirely devoid of mirth. 'It is not me you must help, my lord, not me.'

'What must I do then, who must I help?'

'You will know, my lord, when the moment is upon you. You will know what you must do.'

With that, the astropath lowered his head and resumed his chant. Lucian lingered a moment longer, before standing up straight and slowly looking around the vast cargo bay. The shadows appeared all the darker, as if formless horrors lurked within each, ready to snatch at any who passed too near. He shook his head, as if he might shake off the weird feeling that had stolen over him with the astropath's words. He could not of course, for only when the *Oceanid* had crossed the Damocles Gulf would he be free of the oppressive taint that enshrouded his very soul.

In the meantime, he had the astropath's warning to contend with. Some new threat evidently stalked the corridors of his vessel, or awaited it deeper within the Damocles Gulf.

CHAPTER TEN

'May I?' Brielle asked her tau host, indicating the bowl of purple fruit on the low table between them.

'Please do,' the envoy replied. 'The Tau Empire is both bountiful and generous.'

Brielle smiled demurely, though inside she considered the alien's words hollow and unsubtle. She took one of the round fruits and bit deep into it, considering her situation as she chewed. She cast her eyes around the chamber. It was the same, stark white she had come to associate with the tau. The lighting was diffuse and the furniture low and typically spartan. The only visible decoration was a round icon dominating one, otherwise plain, white wall; an icon she had seen repeated across the ship, and one she had come to regard as some form of national emblem.

This was her fourth meeting with the water caste envoy. He had introduced himself with a long and intricate name consisting of many interlinked parts, but she had come to call him by the first segment of that name, Por'el, and he had appeared quite content with that. After the initial, highly formal meetings, Por'el had appeared to take a more relaxed approach to his dealings with her. The envoy had appeared content merely to talk, to enquire informally on a whole range of subjects, but had not, as yet, made any solid proposal or proposition. Brielle knew that would not last; the tau wanted something from her, that much was obvious, and at some point she would have to decide exactly what it was that she wanted from them. Circumstance had driven her here, but, she knew, fate still had a lot more to reveal before her course would become clear.

'Por'el,' Brielle said as she finished her fruit, 'I am, as ever, grateful for your ongoing hospitality. May I enquire how I might serve you today?'

Por'el bowed his head, his black, oval eyes glinting in the stark white light of the small, but comfortably furnished chamber. Brielle had found him incredibly well informed regarding human social mores, though she suspected he had only the somewhat quaint, by high court standards, manners of the eastern rim sectors to go by. Nevertheless, Por'el seemed highly skilled at assimilating new social forms, and had adapted quickly to Brielle's more relaxed style. She knew that it was the sign of a highly accomplished diplomat, and she had resolved to be especially cautious in her dealings with him.

'Today, Lady Brielle, I had thought to tell you some more of our empire, that you might be more informed of our ways, and of our intentions.'

Brielle's guard was instantly up. She had guessed that the envoy was building towards something, and perhaps now, she might get some idea as to what. Perhaps, after weeks aboard the water caste vessel, there might finally be some form of deal on the table. She sat back in the recliner, catching herself before she placed her feet on the low table before her.

'I would be honoured to hear your words,' Brielle replied, determining to listen very carefully indeed to what the envoy had to say.

'I would tell you,' the envoy began, 'of our society. I and my masters wish you to see some of the perfection that comes from the Greater Good, that you might spread such knowledge amongst your own people, for the profit of all.'

Brielle nodded, her mind analysing Por'el's intentions even as he spoke. Did he expect her to return to the Imperium and proselytise the Greater Good?

'You see,' Por'el continued, 'the Imperium, as encountered by my people, appears to us fractured and disparate. It is spread across a wide area of space, so I am informed, yet each small group of worlds is almost entirely cut off from the greater community, or at least cut off from it for long stretches.'

The envoy looked to Brielle as if affording her the opportunity to correct him should he prove misinformed. She nodded that he should continue, for his words were true, even if he appeared more than a little ignorant of the Imperium's size.

'You enjoy mastery of many technologies still unknown to us. Yet, you have little understanding of the elementary forces at work in the universe. Instead of seeking such understanding, you indulge in needless ceremony and superstition, believing the cosmos populated by creatures that, in fact, exist only in your nightmares.'

Brielle raised an eyebrow at this, but allowed the envoy to continue without interruption.

'When you make contact with other races, you rarely open any form of dialogue with them. Instead, the human race sees enemies in every corner of the galaxy.'

Again, the envoy paused, giving Brielle the chance to correct him. She considered his words, judging them essentially true, even if they did not necessarily apply to rogue traders such as her.

'There exists among the ranks of humanity, however,' Por'el went on, 'those who do not share this view. Others such as I have established links with a number of planetary rulers, each of whom appeared quite content to have dealings with us, even though such a thing was proscribed by their own laws.'

'Those rulers,' Brielle interjected, 'have been replaced.'

'Of that I have no doubt,' Por'el replied, 'but the seed has been planted, for you are here, now, are you not?'

'I am,' Brielle said, 'though I am doubtful as to how that might serve your aims.'

The envoy smiled, though Brielle suspected the expression was for her benefit, for his wide, flat mouth appeared unfamiliar with the movement. 'Therein lies the path to the Greater Good we must all follow. Lady Brielle, it is quite beyond my station to decide how you might serve the aims of the Tau Empire. I am merely a servant, whose role it is to facilitate your journey. Therein lies the dialectic through which a resolution may be found.'

'Might I ask, Por'el, how you intend to do so?'

'Indeed, Lady Brielle. I propose to bring you before a council of my masters. I propose to take you to my homeworld, to show you everything the Tau Empire has built, that you might compare its glory to that of the Imperium, and make your own decision as to your true calling. Should you decide to act on behalf of the empire, then you will have all the support you require to do so.'

Brielle took a deep breath, seeking to steady her nerves lest she show any outward reaction to the envoy's words. What Por'el proposed could lead her to a position of enormous influence, perhaps one from which she could profit enormously. But it might also lead to her being labelled a grand heretic. The Damocles Gulf Crusade might throw its entire effort into bringing her to justice. But, she considered, perhaps there was a middle way. Perhaps, she could accomplish her original aim and stymie the insane ambitions of Cardinal Gurney and his tame inquisitor. Perhaps she could do so in such a way that she might return to her clan in a position of power, one from which her runt of a stepbrother could never assail her. Perhaps, she smiled as the idea formed, she could lead the Arcadius to glory, forcing her father to hand the dynasty to her, and her alone.

She realised that Por'el was watching her, his face returning to its normal, inscrutable expression. 'I thank you for the opportunity to serve,' Brielle said.

'That,' Por'el replied, 'is all any of us can ask for.'

Lucian was reaching for the decanter to pour a third glass of svort when the intercom by the cabin door buzzed. He considered ignoring the irritating sound, but decided to answer it. Too many unsettling events were occurring on his vessel for him to ignore even a routine communication.

He stood, and crossed to the intercom.

'What!' He spoke into the brass horn protruding from the ornate console. This had better be good, he thought, casting a glance back at the half empty decanter.

'My lord,' a female voice he did not recognise came from the horn, 'this is the medicae bay.' It was one of Estaban's assistants. 'The Chirurgeon, sir, he requests your presence, urgently.'

Lucian could hear an obvious element of panic in the woman's voice. 'What's the matter?' he asked. If the chirurgeon was unable to speak, then something very wrong was occurring.

'It's Master Karaldi,' she continued, her voice cracking even more. A voice raised in obvious anger interrupted her, before she continued. 'My lord, Master Karaldi has gone mad! He's ranting and raving that something is on the ship, that you are in great danger!'

'Well enough,' replied Lucian, the last effects of the two glasses of svort vanishing entirely. 'Inform Chirurgeon Estaban that I'll be with him shortly.'

'Thank you, my lord,' the woman replied, relief evident in her voice.

'And please,' Lucian added, 'ensure that no harm comes to Master Karaldi. Do you understand?'

'Yes, sir, but he does not respond to any of the sedatives we have administered, we fear he may...'

'Good!' Lucian cut in. 'We may need him, mad or not. Do not, under any circumstances, attempt to sedate him, that is a direct order.'

'Yes, my lord,' the woman replied, raising her voice over a background din of shouting. 'Please hurry!'

Lucian cut the channel and made to open the door. Something gave him pause, and he looked back into his cabin. He saw his holster lying over a high backed chair, and considered for a moment taking up his arms. No time, he thought, and besides, he would hardly have need of his plasma pistol or his power sword in the medicae bay, no matter how out of control the astropath had become.

Giving the matter no more thought, Lucian hauled open the heavy cabin door. Stepping through, he hurried down the corridor that led to his bridge, his mind rapidly filling with a thousand concerns as to what might await him when he reached Chirurgeon Estaban's medicae bay.

He was so distracted by such thoughts, that he was entirely unprepared for the scene that awaited him on his bridge. He came to an abrupt halt as the bridge door swung open, all thoughts of the astropath having fled his mind entirely.

The bridge resembled a slaughterhouse. Bodies and parts of bodies were cast across the deck, and blood dripped from every surface. The metallic taint of blood was in the air, as was the foul stink of stomach contents. It took Lucian a moment to take all this in, before he raised his head to meet the gaze of the one figure still living on the bridge.

It was his helmsman, Mister Raldi.

'My lord,' whispered the helmsman, his voice sounding distant, as if muffled by dense rolling fog. The man's body was drenched in blood, and he stood as if supported by a puppeteer's strings. His neck, it seemed to Lucian, was not supporting the man's head, for it lolled to one side, drool slowly pouring from his slack mouth.

'What in the Emperor's name...' Lucian started, before he saw Raldi's eyes. There was no point finishing the question.

'Daemon!' Lucian spat, knowing as he looked into his helmsman's eyes that the man he had known was far, far away. Whatever stood before him, clothed in the flesh of his officer, was not human, but some fiend from the depths of the warp.

'Please, my lord,' the whisper continued, sounding yet more distant, 'don't let it...'

The helmsman's body lurched forward, its movements grotesquely jerky as if the entity that controlled it had yet to master control of the unfamiliar form. Lucian was shocked into action, reaching instinctively for his holster.

'Damn it!' he spat, cursing himself for a fool for his decision to leave his weapons in his cabin. Knowing that he had no choice but to face the creature down, before it got loose on his vessel, he hauled on the bridge door and ran back down the corridor towards his cabin.

Once there, he retrieved his weapon's belt, and immediately unholstered the heavy, plasma pistol. Depressing the activation stud, he was profoundly grateful to hear the whine of the pistol's war spirit as it awoke. Pausing only to take a deep breath, Lucian returned to the passageway, steeling himself for the confrontation ahead. Checking one last time that his weapon was primed, he hauled open the bridge door and stepped into the opening, pistol raised.

The bridge was empty.

'Bastard!' Lucian cursed, seeing that the opposite door, the door leading to the *Oceanid*'s central thoroughfare, was ajar. Knowing that the entity was loose on his ship, Lucian saw no alternative but to hunt it down. He cursed the fate that had brought such a cruel turn of events upon him. Lucian knew that once a creature from the warp had control of a body within a vessel crossing the empyrean, that ship might be damned for all eternity. If he did not isolate the creature now, it would turn his ship into a charnel house.

Lucian crossed his bridge, cautiously, for entrails and unidentifiable organs were scattered across it, and all was drenched in steaming blood. Reaching the far door, he peered out warily, seeing that the companionway beyond was empty. Leaning back against the bulkhead, he slammed his fist into the intercom console, activating the ship wide address system.

'All hands,' Lucian said into the horn, feedback howling as his voice boomed from a thousand speaker grills. 'This is your captain. Adopt protocol extremis. I repeat, extremis.'

He leaned back against the bulkhead, scarcely believing that he had issued an order that none of his line had been forced to give in over three millennia. He knew that incursions by the things that dwelled in the warp could occur, it was his duty to know and to prepare for it, but he had never actually been faced with such an occurrence, and had prayed he never would be. He turned his face towards the console by the door, and punched the alert control. Instantly, the lighting of ship's day flickered and was gone, plunging the bridge into darkness, punctuated only by flickering pict-slate and flashing consoles. Seconds later, the red light of ship's night flickered on, indicating that the *Oceanid* was at general quarters.

Even as the bridge was bathed in light the colour of the blood that covered its every surface, a distant siren began to wail. The sound was taken up by another, this time closer. Within moments, Lucian could hear the apocalyptic wail start up all over his ship. At the last, the speaker grill over the bridge door came to life, almost deafening Lucian as it did so.

Focus, Lucian told himself; do what old Abad would have done. Not that Abad had ever faced down a fiend of the warp on his own ship, Lucian thought. Checking once more that his pistol was at full charge, he took a deep breath and stepped out into the corridor.

The flash of alert lights accompanied the wail of general quarters, and over it, Lucian heard the distant sounds of the crew rushing to their stations. But this was not ship-to-ship combat. This was something that every spacefarer dreaded far more than the clean death afforded when one's body was spat into the cold void or incinerated by plasma bolts as powerful as suns. This intruder should not exist, having infiltrated a weak soul and become real aboard his ship. The order he had issued, 'protocol extremis' was a desperate reaction to a situation few expected to survive. Those who could would close on his location. Those who could not, would lock themselves away in the darkest, deepest corner they could find and not come out until the alert was ended.

Lucian reached a junction, the flashing alert light directly over his head. He looked left, and saw nothing. He spun around, pistol raised, as if an enemy lurked in the shadows at his back. None was there, but as he lowered his pistol he saw a crumpled form sprawled across the companionway, one half of its head several metres from the other, and the body, further away still.

Stepping over the bloody mess, Lucian pushed on down the corridor until he reached another intercom console. 'To me!' he almost screamed. 'Command deck forward, passage delta one-one-one!'

Where were they? Lucian thought, feeling utterly alone despite the comforting weight of the heavy plasma pistol he held before him. A scream answered his question. They were in the service tunnel leading to the torpedo decks. He started running forwards along the corridor once more, his boots clanging on the metal deck plates all the way. Reaching another junction, he found the source of the scream.

A group of armsmen, the bully boys employed primarily to keep the press-ganged crewmen in line, stood in a wide utility area. Each carried a heavy gauge shotgun, but by Lucian's estimation, only a couple had found the time to don the crimson and gold armour they were issued. Before them, his back to Lucian as he entered the area, was the helmsman, or what used to be the helmsman, Lucian thought.

Lucian came to a halt as he took in the scene. He saw the creature spread its arms wide as in some mockery of benediction, its head lolling to one side. The uniform that Helmsman Raldi had worn was ragged and singed, as if contact with the skin the creature wore was toxic in itself.

A scream issued from the beast's mouth. Lucian bent double and dropped his pistol as he covered both his ears with his hands. Despite his best efforts, the terrible sound leaked in, forcing him to fight for consciousness lest it overcome him entirely. Raising his head, he forced himself to focus on the scene ahead, gritting his teeth against the infernal cacophony that filled the air.

The creature stood frozen before him, its arms raised above its head. In front of it, the armsmen had been caught in the full onslaught of its hellish assault. All had collapsed to the deck. One was coughing up his guts, almost literally, in a fountain of blood and bile. One bled from every orifice, his ears, eyes, nose, mouth and groin streaming red. Those armsmen marginally further back scrambled across the steel deck, made slick with the blood and vomit of their compatriots.

Drawing on reserves of strength he had no idea he possessed, Lucian raised himself to his knees as he reached out to grab his plasma pistol. He missed, sending the weapon clattering across the deck to land nearer the creature. The screaming died, and Lucian realised with stark horror that the creature was slowly turning to face him.

'My lord...' The creature's head lolled as it spoke. Its eyes rolled in their sockets, each facing in a different direction, before focusing on him. 'Please my lord, don't let this happen.'

The voice brought a choke of despair to Lucian's throat, for he knew it belonged to Helmsman Raldi. He guessed that the creature was yet to establish total control over Raldi's body, but knew that surely, it must soon do so.

'I promise,' Lucian said as his groping hands found the plasma pistol, his voice riven with anguish, 'I won't...'

Even as Lucian raised the pistol, the creature reacted. Its movements, though jerky as before, were impossibly fast.

The creature was in front of Lucian in the blink of an eye. He found himself on his knees before the wrecked form of his erstwhile helmsman, fighting to raise his pistol before the beast from the warp rent his body asunder.

'He's gone now,' said a new voice, little more than a whisper, but laden with all the pain and suffering of the abyss. 'Gone.'

'Get, off, my, ship,' Lucian spat, raising the pistol in both hands as its war spirit sang its high-pitched tone. He pulled the trigger, turning his head, squeezing shut his eyes and gritting his teeth. The weapon spat its payload of incandescent plasma straight into the creature's head, at point blank range.

The creature's head disintegrated as the plasma bolt passed through it to strike a conduit mounted overhead. As gas flooded the utility space, the body crashed to its knees, and tumbled to one side. An instant later an armsman was standing behind it, proffering his hand to Lucian.

'Sir? Are you...?'

The hair on the back of Lucian's neck stood on end as he saw the dead creature's arm shoot out, the distended claw taking hold of the armsman's wrist.

'Get back!' Lucian bellowed as he staggered to his feet, but he knew he was too late.

The armsman threw back his head and screamed, sickly light shining up from his throat as the daemon from the warp took over his body.

Despair threatening to overcome him, Lucian raised his pistol once again. But he never had the chance to pull the trigger, for the armsman, his body under the sway of the warp beast, flung out his arm and sent the pistol flying across the space.

It was gone a moment later, disappearing through the gases venting from the conduit overhead. Lucian looked up at the discharging pipeline as if only just becoming aware of it. He coughed, and looked around for his pistol. He could not see it. He risked losing the beast if he wasted time looking for the weapon. Throwing an arm over his face to shield his lungs from the gas, he plunged through the billowing clouds, after the beast that was slaughtering his crew.

All was darkness for an instant as Lucian passed through the cloud of gas, followed by nauseous disorientation as he emerged, to find himself in a narrow passageway that led from the utility area to the forward torpedo decks. He had no difficulty discerning the creature's path, for another two bodies lay up ahead; at least it looked as if the constituent body parts amounted to two people.

As the shock of the confrontation with the beast wore off, Lucian felt a primal rage well up within him. No Arcadius, to his knowledge at least, had ever lost a vessel to a warp beast, and he was damned if he would be the first to suffer such a fate. His anger grew as he considered that he had been forced to destroy the body of a man he thought of, if not as a friend then as a companion and a valued crew member. Even if he died in the event, which he thought entirely probable, Lucian determined that he would take this bastard of a creature with him. If he were to be dragged to hell by this beast, he raged, he'd make sure the beast went with him.

Passing the bodies, Lucian came to another junction, and was greeted immediately by the boom of a shotgun being discharged very nearby.

'Hold!' he called, rounding the corner cautiously.

He stepped towards a wide chamber, machinery clustered upon its every surface. A single armsman stood at the centre, and nearby a cringing group of ratings. The body last possessed by the creature lay before the armsman, its chest blown through by the force of a shotgun blast.

But Lucian dared not believe it had been defeated so easily.

The armsman with the shotgun turned towards him, his head tipping to one side as he did so. The mouth fell open and bloodstained drool pooled forth. Lucian met the armsman's eyes, experiencing a stab of despair as he saw that those eyes were filled not with the lucid gaze of the creature from the warp, but with sheer, unadulterated terror. Those eyes were the eyes of a man being dragged beneath the surface of the ocean by a voracious predator, knowing all the while that a quick, clean death would be denied him.

'Not again!' Lucian spat, casting around for something, anything he might use as a weapon. He did not care what; a pipe would do, if it would allow him to bludgeon the creature to death, to stave in its skull so that it could possess no more of his crew.

Before he could find a weapon, however, fate took a hand in events. One of the cowering ratings took the opportunity to flee, crossing the chamber and running behind the creature as he did so. The creature spun around to rake the man with its hands, its fingers split apart and the bones protruding to form wicked claws. It turned back towards Lucian, as if deciding which prey to pursue. Lucian judged that the beast was trapped, if only he could force it back to the next chamber. Summoning all his courage, he stepped forward, just as a group of armsmen arrived behind him. The beast stood motionless for an instant, before it evidently saw that it was outnumbered. The fleeing man dived for the access portal behind the beast, and the creature made its decision. It dived after him, through the small opening.

Lucian reacted in an instant. He knew that there was no exit from the chamber into which the creature had passed. As the creature overtook its prey, a terrible scream spilling forth to be cut off an instant later by the sound of rending flesh and bone, Lucian surged forward and hauled the portal shut. He spun the heavy wheel that engaged the locking mechanism, and sank to his knees with exhaustion.

As the chamber filled with armsmen and ratings responding to the emergency, Lucian raised his head, and laughed the laugh of one who has come far too close to the abyss. He saw his crewmen recoil in horror, and realised that he must appear a madman.

'Someone,' he said, forcing his voice to its normal tone, 'get me Karaldi.'

'It's in there, my lord?' asked Master Karaldi. Lucian was unsure whether the astropath asked a question or made a statement of fact. The man was impossible to read, the wild madness he had displayed on their last meeting now entirely gone. He nodded nonetheless.

'It's sealed, and there're no other exits,' Lucian replied, finding his eye drawn, as he spoke, to the small armoured porthole in the heavy bulkhead door. He could see nothing beyond, which made him even more uneasy.

'Apart from the tubes, my lord,' Karaldi said.

Aye, Lucian thought, the torpedo tubes. The creature was trapped on the loading deck for the forward torpedo tubes. There were no torpedoes in the area however, for the fortunes of the Arcadius clan had been so dire this last century as to preclude their replenishment. Lucian knew that the astropath referred to the possibility of voiding the chamber, in the hope of blasting the creature through the tubes and into the warp.

'No,' Lucian replied, 'that's not an option. The internal bulkheads aren't up to it.'

'Then what?' Karaldi asked, his blind gaze fixed on the small porthole.

'That's why I called you here,' Lucian replied, knowing he had no choice but to trust the mad old astropath. 'I have an idea, but I need your advice.'

'Please, my lord, go on. I am your servant.'

Lucian looked into the man's time-worn face, haloed as it was by his wispy grey hair. Lucian fancied he detected a change in the man, as if the astropath was prepared to face up to his duty in a way he had appeared reluctant to on prior occasions. Lucian had considered Karaldi burned out or washed up, of late, and had seriously intended to petition the Guild for a replacement. Something now gave him pause. Something in Karaldi might have changed, Lucian thought.

'Good,' Lucian began, 'I have a question for you, and I want you to be sure of your answer.'

'Of course, my lord.'

'I intend to destroy the body the creature inhabits, totally: to incinerate it to atoms.'

'Go on, my lord.'

'What then of the creature, with no new victim to claim?'

'Oh,' Karaldi replied, his hand reaching up to grip his chin, 'I see...'

'What then, without the body?' Lucian pressed.

The astropath hesitated, visibly considering his words before continuing. 'With no Rite of Warding, which would take many hours, I could not say, not for sure. It has certainly feasted upon enough souls to sustain it for some time, even in incorporeal form. But I know we do not have the luxury of time, so I say please do it, master. For the sake of us all, please do it.'

'You're sure?'

'Quite sure, my lord,' the astropath replied, his hands fumbling with the beads around his neck, an old and tarnished Imperial aquila hanging upon them.

Lucian turned and nodded to a tech-priest manning a console near the bulkhead door. The hooded figure bowed, and turned to the large array of levers, dials and meters before him. Lucian turned to the porthole once more, feeling the tension grow.

The tech-priest worked a series of levers, lowering each in succession and mumbling prayers to the Machine God all the while. The effect was immediate. The air in the chamber charged, the hairs on Lucian's body standing up, accompanied by a distinctly unpleasant sensation of something crawling over his body. The air pressure rose dramatically for a moment, before a bank of equalisation pumps mounted overhead started to life and quickly returned it to normal.

Then, Lucian heard a great commotion from the torpedo deck, and he approached the bulkhead door, cautious all the while. Peering gingerly through the porthole, he could make out only a small area of the bay, for the illumination was inactive, yet he caught an actinic flash to one side, followed an instant later by a great arcing bolt of energy that crossed the deck at the speed of light, grounding itself in the centre of the chamber in an explosive shower of sparks.

'Reactor bleed at optimum, my lord,' the tech-priest announced, monitoring his dials intently. 'Output shall remain constant until you order core flow resumed, but I advise against maintaining the output at the expense of primary systems.'

'Understood,' said Lucian, peering through the porthole for any sign of movement within. Another flash, and another arc, and a great whining went up from beyond the bulkhead door. The conduits that would have charged a plasma torpedo were discharging their raw power into the chamber. Lucian could tell that the system was straining to maintain the output that was even now scouring the bay with lashing arcs of raw power.

'There!' Karaldi shrieked, his voice almost drowned out by yet another burst of lightning from within the chamber.

As Lucian's eyes recovered from the massive blast, he caught sight of a figure standing in the centre of the torpedo bay. Its body was charred and smoking, the armsman's uniform incinerated entirely. Despite the apparent injuries done to its stolen body, the creature stood tall, though, as before, its head lolled to one side as if its neck muscles were weakened, and its mouth hung open, bloody drool pouring forth. The arms were held out wide, almost as if to welcome Lucian to him.

Lucian tore his gaze from the porthole, and turned to address Karaldi.

'The beast lends the flesh unholy vigour, my lord,' Karaldi said, evidently anticipating Lucian's question. Lucian suppressed his annoyance at having his surface thoughts read in such a manner.

'My apologies, my lord,' Karaldi said, his face deadly serious as he contemplated the creature.

'How long can it last?' Lucian asked. 'We cannot keep up the output indefinitely.'

'I feel,' the astropath said, his voice straining and cracked. 'I feel... it fights... it draws such power.'

Lucian turned to the tech-priest. 'Can you increase the core bleed?'

The tech-priest cast his mechanical eyes over his instruments, mumbling prayers beneath the hood of his crimson robes. Then he raised his head and addressed Lucian. 'I can, my lord, but to do so I must control the bleed manually.'

Lucian knew he was asking a great deal of his crew and of his vessel, yet he saw no alternative. If he did not get this creature of the warp off of his ship, he would have no ship, and no crew to man it. He knew that entrusting the core reactor flow to the tech-priest was incredibly risky, for the function was normally controlled by a hundred different, triple redundant cogitators. He scarcely believed a single, human mind could perform such a task, but he knew that the tech-priest would not have made the suggestion were it not true. The servants of the mechanicus might be taciturn and unimaginative, but such traits were, in times such as these, a benefit.

'Proceed,' Lucian ordered the tech-priest, gripping the frame of the bulkhead door as he turned his gaze back within.

The whine of the conduits venting their guts into the torpedo bay grew louder still, their pitch shifting upwards to a shrill howl. Lucian could faintly detect the touch of the tech-priest within the sound, a subtle modulation indicative of the workings of a human mind rather than that of a machine.

The creature still stood in the centre of the loading deck, but it was now bathed in stark, flickering white light. Around it danced a cage of arcing power, crawling up and down its body. That body blackened and blistered before Lucian's eyes, the skin slowly vaporising even as Lucian looked on, horrified, but knowing he must witness the creature's death.

'It fights,' Lucian heard Master Karaldi mumble at his side. 'It draws yet more power from the infernal planes.'

Lucian turned his head to regard the astropath, and was struck by the expression on the man's face. It was not the normal, crazed visage that Lucian had become used to. There was an unfamiliar calm upon Karaldi's face, he was almost placid.

Looking back to the chamber, Lucian could see that the creature was absorbing a staggering amount of energy. The body it wore should have been vaporised in an instant as soon as the reactor bleed was turned upon it, yet somehow, it was keeping the body together.

Then, Lucian saw that the creature's mouth was no longer hanging slack. It was smiling, and it was looking straight at him. Though he met its gaze for but a fraction of a second before violently turning his head away from the porthole, Lucian felt his soul seared by the raw stuff of the warp. He fought to remain standing, bracing himself with both arms against the frame of the bulkhead door.

'Increase bleed!' Lucian shouted, gasping as the air pressure increased and the equalisers overhead fought to remain on-line.

'My lord,' the tech-priest replied, an edge of uncertainty creeping into his normally even voice. 'Such a thing is...'

'Do it, damn you!' Lucian bellowed. 'Do it or so help me...'

'I obey, my lord,' replied the tech-priest. 'I can maintain point three variance for no more than forty seconds.'

'Understood,' replied Lucian, knowing this must surely be his best, and last hope. He dared to raise his eyes to the porthole once more, this time ready to avert his gaze should it meet that of the creature. He saw immediately that the core bleed output had increased even more, and that the creature's body was entirely black, a vile, greasy smoke rising from it in eddies. Yet still, it smiled, and held its arms out wide as if welcoming its fate.

'It mocks us,' Lucian scowled, hating the intruder with a depth of feeling he had not realised he could summon.

'Its power fails, master.' Lucian heard Karaldi at his back.

'How can you be sure?' he asked

Karaldi smiled, a trace of his former mania returning to his face. 'I can hear its thoughts, my lord.'

How could the astropath bear such a thing? Lucian thought. Just meeting its gaze had brought Lucian to his knees.

'I am soulbound, my master,' Karaldi whispered. 'It cannot hurt me. Not the bit that counts, at least.'

Lucian turned to look at the astropath, and saw that Karaldi held his hands across his chest, the thumbs interlocked and the palms spread wide. It was the sign of the aquila, and Lucian knew that it was meant as far more than a formal salute.

'The soulbinding, in which I received but a portion of the Emperor's infinite grace, warded me against the likes of this beast. Though it cost me my sight, I gained far more than I can tell you, my master.'

Lucian nodded slowly, and turned his gaze back to the torpedo bay. The creature's flesh was steaming from its body, blackened muscles visible as the skin peeled back and fell away in ashen fragments. A weird, guttering light flickered deep within the rapidly disintegrating body as its scorched bones became visible.

Even as Lucian watched in stark horror, the creature's body began to crumble. As power arced all around it, it stood as a rigid, petrified and charred statue, its arms still spread wide. A last great arc leapt across the chamber and grounded itself on the creature's form, and the remains of its body shattered into a thousand blackened fragments. All that was left was a retinal after image, seared across Lucian's eyes, as he looked on, not able to tear his gaze from the porthole.

'It is too powerful,' Lucian heard Karaldi mumble behind him as the whine of the core bleed died away. 'It is too near its home.'

'What?' Lucian began, blinking to clear his eyes of the retinal burn of the creature's death. 'But it's dead.'

'No, my lord, it is not.'

'Lucian blinked once more, realising with mounting terror that the ghostly image floating across his vision was not in fact the after-effect of the creature's violent death. What he saw was a glowing form standing exactly where the creature had stood, and it was there, in the torpedo bay, looking back at him.

'It's still...' Lucian never completed his sentence, for he felt himself shoved to one side, to slam into the frame of the bulkhead door.

'What...' he began, looking up as he caught himself, to see Master Karaldi struggling with the great locking wheel at the centre of the door. 'What the hell are you doing man?' he shouted, raising his voice as a shrill wail escaped through the door's seams as Karaldi pushed it open.

'Master,' the astropath called over one shoulder as the other leaned into the door, 'I have no choice. I cannot let it remain unbound.'

'It'll eat your soul, man!' Lucian shouted, pulling himself upright with one hand, and gripping Karaldi's arm with the other.

'No, my lord! You must let me do my duty!'

Karaldi turned his eyeless face on Lucian, and although the astropath's eyes were nothing more then empty sockets, Lucian felt that a fierce light had arisen within, where previously the astropath had radiated an aura of madness and despair. Karaldi shouldered the bulkhead door open, and Lucian relaxed his grip on the man's shoulder.

As the door fell fully open, an acrid stink assaulted Lucian's nostrils and scoured his throat. It was the scent of metal, ceramic and plastic ravaged by unholy powers. And mixed in with the chemical taint was something far worse. Lucian knew that it was the taint of the warp, made real through the destruction of the body in which the creature had infiltrated his vessel.

And that creature, shed of its mortal shell, stood in the centre of the torpedo bay. It was mighty, standing ten feet tall, its form an ever-shifting mass of dancing energy. It was, Lucian could only assume, made of the very stuff of the warp; souls coalesced in damnation, their eternal anguish giving form and energy to the being that stood before Lucian.

Even as Lucian watched from the portal, barely able to stand so cacophonous was the sound that roared from the creature's body, he saw Master Karaldi step before it. The astropath's steps were at first shaky and uncertain, yet with each, his stance became surer, and he stood more erect. Lucian looked back to the creature, and saw that it was looking around the chamber, as if acquainting itself with a new and entirely foreign environment. Yet, Lucian was astonished to note, it paid no heed to the man that walked straight towards it.

The creature turned its attention towards specific features in the torpedo chamber. It looked to the array of tubes, the massive hatch over each locked tight against the void. It's gaze swept upwards and across the ceiling, and then down and across the deck. Lucian realised then that it was not actually looking at the features in the chamber, but through them, sensing, he suspected, the souls of those in the decks above and below.

Then, the glowing, undulating apparition looked towards the portal in which Lucian stood. Lucian could not help but look back, his gaze drawn with shock and disgust to tiny, wailing faces swimming across the surface of the creature's insubstantial body. Each soul wailed its pain and anguish, adding its sundered voice to the thunderous cacophony flooding the chamber.

Raising its arms high to its sides, the creature started towards him. Yet, Master Karaldi stood in its path, his head held high.

'Karaldi!' Lucian bellowed. He was barely able to hear his own voice above the din, and had no clue if the astropath would hear him. 'Karaldi, beware!'

If Karaldi heard Lucian's warning, he made no reaction, other than perhaps a slight tilt of the head. The creature glided on, as if held aloft by the wailing souls of the infernal regions of the warp, its gaze entirely focused upon Lucian.

Then, Lucian saw Master Karaldi hold up his right hand, as if to bar the creature's way. Despair welled up within Lucian, for he knew that the astropath must surely be blasted to ashes at the creature's touch. Yet, the warp beast continued, apparently uncaring of the astropath's gesture, intent, it appeared on Lucian.

As it bore down upon Master Karaldi, Lucian turned his head. He would not look upon the astropath's death. He made to haul the armoured door closed, knowing all the while that there was no point in doing so. This thing would devour every soul upon his vessel, and there was nothing he could do to stop it.

Even as he made to slam the door, Lucian became aware of a change in the tone of the creature's wailing din. He looked back through the half closed portal, to see that the creature towered over the astropath. He watched as Karaldi's hand came into contact with the thing's ghostly body, and as it did so, the wailing cut off entirely.

The chamber was flooded with sudden, and complete silence.

Lucian dared not breathe. He strained his ears and became aware of a low mumbling. It was Master Karaldi, mouthing the words of the prayer every spacefarer knew, even if he knew no other.

'We pray for those lost in the warp,' the astropath said aloud, and a new sound rose from the silence. It was the sound of the creature, thrashing in a wild frenzy, its ghostly appendages distorting and stretching, its body arching as the souls trapped within fled from it, one by one. Each was a tiny, guttering spark that sped from the prison of the creature's form, across the bay to plunge into, and somehow through, the outer hull.

As the creature's form dissipated, its thrashing grew more violent, yet still Karaldi maintained his posture, arm held high as if to block the beast's progress and hold it in place. Though it screamed its unholy death scream, the astropath kept up his recitation of the prayer, his lips working as he mouthed the sanctified words. The creature shook, casting its ethereal limbs about it. Lucian saw that it was seeking, desperately, if it could possibly know despair, to escape the astropath's touch. At the last, it did, breaking free in an explosion of etheric lightning.

In the silence that followed the creature's departure, Lucian was blinded, so dazzling was the sight of its death. Yet he heard a sound any spacefarer knew, and dreaded above all others.

'Hull breach!' Lucian bellowed. His vision still slow to return, he stumbled through the portal in which he was standing, onto the metal deck of the torpedo bay. As his vision returned, he saw that one of the torpedo tubes had been ruptured, its loading hatch hanging from it, bent and twisted. He all but stumbled over the crumpled form of the astropath, and fell to his knees at Karaldi's side.

Bending over the man's body, Lucian took him by the shoulders and shook him violently. Even as he felt the air pressure drop, and heard sirens beyond the bulkhead door, he gasped in relief to see that the astropath lived yet.

'Up, damn you, Mister Karaldi,' Lucian cursed, heaving at the astropath's limp form. 'You don't go and,' he struggled for breath as the air rapidly fled the chamber, 'do something like that,' he gasped, 'and then... die on me.'

As Lucian felt consciousness slip away, he felt hands grab at his own shoulders, lifting him up as the cold of the void flooded the chamber. 'Karaldi,' he mumbled, barely able to form the words as the vacuum stole the last of the air from his lungs.

'He is with us, my lord.' Lucian heard the voice, barely registering the flat tones of the tech-priest. 'He is safe.'

'Good,' Lucian managed as he felt himself dragged through the portal and heard the door slam shut behind him. 'I think I'll keep him around.'

CHAPTER ELEVEN

Lucian stood at the wide viewing port, his arms folded before him. An area of space entirely new to him was arrayed beyond the inches-thick armoured glass. And not just new to him, for this was virgin space. To his knowledge, no human had travelled its depths and returned to tell the tale of what lay within.

'Range to fleet?' Lucian asked, stifling a wince as he spoke. His lungs had yet to fully recover from the vacuum effects suffered on the torpedo deck, but he had no time for extended treatment now.

'Three. Three. Two.' Intoned the servitor at the Navigation station. Regret stabbed at Lucian's heart, for Mister Raldi, the *Oceanid*'s long-serving helmsman should have answered him instead of the servitor at station one. Lucian could still scarcely believe what had occurred during the warp beast's attack. The effects were still being felt across the vessel. His bridge crew, for starters, would need rebuilding from the ground up, for all bar Mister Batista, the veteran ordnance chief, were slaughtered. The bridge still reeked of blood, despite the attentions of the maintenance servitors. Lucian knew that no amount of antiseptic decontamination would cover that smell. It would linger on his bridge, just as the sight of Raldi transformed into a slavering beast would linger in his memory.

With an effort, Lucian shoved such thoughts to the back of his mind. He had the here and the now to worry about. He turned his attention once more to the sight beyond the viewing port.

The region was dominated by vast gaseous nebulae, clouds of stellar matter dozens of light years across. The entire region was cast in the hazy blue light that emanated from deep within the formations. Even though they were many light years distant, Lucian could discern churning energies deep at the heart of each cloud. It was as if the very act of creation were being played out within the nebulae. Lucian felt something he had not experienced for many years, something akin to wonder.

Lucian also knew that he was not the only one to have reacted thus. He lifted the parchment he held in his hand, scanning its words for the third time since he had received it. Adept Baru, the *Oceanid*'s Navigator, had submitted his initial report of the voyage across the Damocles Gulf, and his first impressions of the region they had arrived in.

The first part of Baru's report, concerning the Gulf, made for unsettling reading. If Lucian's experience had been traumatic, his Navigator's had been truly horrific. For long weeks, the Master Navigator had guided the *Oceanid* through the raging torrents of the warp, assailed all the while by forces the like of which none of his kind had ever encountered. The more Lucian read the report, the more respect he had for the man. Baru said that the Gulf was quite unlike any other place in the galaxy. It was as if the Gulf was some barrier or boundary placed, entirely deliberately, to keep intruders from penetrating the region in which the Tau Empire lay. Beyond it, amongst the blue nebulae, lay something even more incredible.

The blue clouds of the region were, according to Baru, not entirely natural in their origins. Even to the naked eye they churned with stellar forces, yet to Baru's third eye, that organ the Navigators uncovered only when traversing the tides of the warp, they boiled with forces both physical and spiritual, both natural and positively unnatural. Such were the terms the Navigator used to describe the phenomenon to Lucian, and Lucian was well aware of the shortcomings of language when a Navigator attempts to explain such concepts to a normal man. It was akin to Lucian attempting to describe conventional space flight to a native of one of the Imperium's many feral worlds. In this case, it was Lucian who spoke only in grunts, and whose horizons defined the extent of his world.

It was the last portion of the report that gave Lucian pause. Baru's description of the region they had entered hinged on one word. It was, according to the veteran navigator, a 'young' region, as if time was turned back or the fabric of space cleansed of the passing of aeons. It was as if the region was a place out of time, still existing in the pristine state that would once have applied to the entire galaxy. It was charged with potential, as if the void just waited upon some wondrous event, as if it in fact existed purely to facilitate that event.

Lucian felt it too, as he raised his eyes from the parchment to look out upon those lambent nebulae once more. He knew, as only a rogue trader could, that the drifting clouds must be seething with life. He almost envied the tau their place in the galaxy... almost.

'Channel. Signus. Signus. Delta. Open.' The servitor's voice cut into Lucian's reverie. He tore his attentions from the viewing port.

'All stations stand by.'

The bridge became a hive of activity as the officers and servitors manning each console, from communications to astrographics, prepared for action. Lucian paced the length of the central walkway and sat in the warm leather seat of his command throne. An array of flat data-slates, clusters of fat cables trailing from each, closed in around him as he pulled on a lever. Each lit up with green static, before bursts of data began scrolling across the screens.

'Open long range channel.'

The comms channel shrieked into life, a wailing feedback bursting from the speaker grills before settling down into a gentle, modulated burbling. It was the quietest Lucian had heard the comms system, despite the odd background field. Makes a change, he thought to himself.

'This is Rogue Trader *Oceanid*, calling crusade fleet,' Lucian announced. 'Repeat, this is Lucian Gerrit of the *Oceanid*.'

'Receiving you,' said a female voice, the channel clear apart from the sweeping background tones. 'This is Natalia of the *Duchess McIntyre*. Glad you could make it, Lucian.'

Lucian grinned. He liked Natalia. 'How was your voyage?'

A moment of silence was followed by Natalia's reply. 'It was... eventful, Lucian. I suggest we hold a masters' conference.'

Understanding her tone, Lucian answered in the affirmative, and ordered the channel closed. Within three hours, the *Oceanid* had closed to medium range with Natalia's vessel, and Lucian had activated the three dimensional holographic display. A green, static laced globe was projected from the unit's base, filling the air before the command throne. The *Oceanid* sat at its centre and nearby a group of icons clustered together, representing the other vessels of the fleet that had, thus far arrived.

Aside from the *Duchess McIntyre*, the *Honour of Damlass*, the *Regent Lakshimbal* and Admiral Jellaqua's own flagship, the mighty Retribution class battleship the *Blade of Woe* were present. So too were three escort squadrons, which patrolled the fleet's outer perimeter lest any unexpected enemy appear. The *Rosetta* was not present, but Lucian had faith in his son's Navigator; he would arrive, soon. As Lucian had read off the label next to each icon, one name had halted him in his tracks.

One of the icons identified the *Ajax*. Less than thirteen thousand kilometres from the *Oceanid*'s current position lay at anchor a vessel that Lucian had last seen deserted, drifting in the cold interstellar space of the Damocles Gulf. She had been a ghost ship, yet here she was, safely across the Gulf, and station keeping with the rest of the fleet. Lucian felt cold dread grip his heart as he had looked upon the Ajax, all the superstition and fear bred into his spacer's soul threatening to overwhelm him.

As the *Oceanid* had approached the other vessels, Natalia had called her conference, each captain appearing in one of the pict-slates arrayed around Lucian's command throne. All had appeared to Lucian to be visibly relieved to be across the gulf, but it was Commodore Ebrahim of the Ajax who held his attention. Ebrahim had reported that his Navigator, who had suffered some form of seizure at the very outset, had recovered. Yet, Ebrahim had reported, the man had been afflicted by terrifying nightmares, and had been assaulted time after time in the waking trance in which he guided the vessel. The navigators of the other vessels had attempted, upon their arrival in this region, to convince Ebrahim's Navigator to relinquish his duties to a lower ranked individual. Yet he had refused, locking himself away in his Navigation blister and refusing to accept any visitors. The commodore had been visibly shaken, his face, even reproduced on the grainy, flickering screen appearing ashen. His eyes had been rimmed with dark circles, and Lucian had scarcely been able to bring himself to look into them, for it was akin to looking upon a ghost, or a man, who should, by all rights, be dead. Part of him knew that Ebrahim was already dead, despite what Lucian saw on the pict screen before him.

Then, as the masters had conversed, a message of the highest priority had been received. Its sending had immediately interrupted the masters' conference, a fact for which Lucian had, at first, been grateful. The message was from the remaining portion of the crusade fleet, which was, even as the conference broke up, closing. Lucian had scanned the sensor returns for any sign of the *Rosetta*, yet before he could locate his son's vessel, Cardinal Gurney had come on the channel. He had called an immediate council of war. His experiences crossing the gulf were such that he was convinced the entire region was populated by devils that must be wiped out in short order for the good of mankind. If the cardinal were not insane before, Lucian sighed, surely his experience crossing the Gulf had pushed him over the edge.

Lucian had stood from his command throne, and stalked off towards his cabin, without a word to his bridge crew. It was only as he made to close the bulkhead door behind him that word of the *Rosetta* came over the comms channel. It was Korvane, and he was safe.

'This is getting us nowhere,' Lucian spat. He turned in his council seat to regard his son. Korvane, however, appeared to have his mind on other things. His eyes were raised to the incense clouded vaults of the richly appointed conference chamber aboard the Admiral Jellaqua's *Blade of Woe*.

'Korvane!' Lucian hissed through clenched teeth. 'What's the matter with you, boy?'

Lucian remained twisted in his seat. He watched with mounting impatience as Korvane continued to ignore him, his head turned upwards, but his mind evidently light years away. Just as Lucian was about to turn his attentions back towards the council, Korvane's attention returned, his eyes coming into focus as they locked with Lucian's.

'Father?' Korvane asked.

What the hell was wrong with him? Their reunion had been stilted and awkward, and in the brief few minutes they had talked, Korvane had appeared distant and preoccupied. He clearly had no wish to attend his father at the council meeting, yet would not talk of whatever bothered him.

'Nothing. If you don't want to be here then lose yourself,' Lucian hissed, turning his back on his son. Seething, he turned his attention back to the council. Gurney appeared to be reaching the conclusion of his thirty-minute rant.

'...drown the tau in oceans of their own blood! We have the Emperor's will as our weapon. What have they?'

Though it was clearly a rhetorical question, Lucian took the opportunity to intercede. 'What have they indeed?' he rejoined. 'We have just words, extracted under torture, to go on. Do we commit on those words alone?'

As the cardinal turned on Lucian, Inquisitor Grand leaned forward: Inquisitor Grand, whom Lucian's daughter had assaulted, wounded almost fatally, who even now moved as one afflicted by terrible pain: Inquisitor Grand, who was the primary ally of Lucian's greatest opponent on the council. Despite mourning his daughter's unknown fate, Lucian cursed her actions, for she had made him an enemy powerful beyond reckoning. It just remained to be seen whether Grand would choose to exercise his full powers.

'Might I remind the council,' the inquisitor said, his voice the characteristic dry whisper, 'that the information extracted from the tau prisoners hardly took the form of a signed and witnessed confession.' Grand's words were laced with spite, his gaze sweeping the assembled councillors before settling on Lucian. 'The information we have was extracted directly from the prisoners' minds, and was thus quite free of deception.'

Lucian scowled, knowing full well the manner of the prisoners' interrogation. He knew that the inquisitor had used some vile form of torture on the tau captured at Sy'l'Kell. He had his suspicions that the inquisitor or one of his retinue had been utilising the psyker's arts to tear the information from the tau's brains, foregoing the need to study their language or risk them lying.

'And so,' Cardinal Gurney continued, casting a smug glance Lucian's way, 'we must devise our plan of conquest.'

'We know precious little of this region.' Admiral Jellaqua spoke up. 'We have entered an area of space of a quite singular nature, and have little idea where our foe lies within it.'

'Then he must come to us!' Gurney replied, leaning forward

across the table as he spoke. 'We must compel these xenos filth to commit their entire force against us.'

Lucian sighed in outright disgust. What had started out as an opportunity to lead a glorious conquest was rapidly turning into a chance to commit suicide following a megalomaniac on a vain-glorious xenocide. Prior to Brielle's attack on the inquisitor, he had been gathering council members to his cause, garnering support for his own approach to the crusade. But now...

'And how do you propose to draw them out?' Lucian asked. He made no attempt to disguise his contempt for Gurney's plan.

'We find the nearest population centre and descend upon it. We visit upon them the full extent of the Emperor's wrath. Leave no stone standing upon another.'

'You hope,' Lucian replied, 'to draw the tau into launching an all-out counter-attack.'

'I do, Lucian,' the Cardinal replied. 'Surely, you can see how this must work?'

'We do not yet comprehend,' Admiral Jellaqua interjected, 'the full extent of the tau's holdings. They may be limited to a single star system, though I doubt that, or they might occupy every system out there.'

The council fell silent for a moment, as each member appeared to mull over the admiral's words. Then, a voice spoke up. Lucian turned, though he knew from the voice's mechanical tones that it was Captain Rumann who spoke.

'Though I accept the view that the region is an unknown,' the captain said, nodding first to Jellaqua and then to Lucian, 'I do believe that a sudden strike with all available force is a doctrinally sound course of action. It is consistent with the mission of the Adeptus Astartes on this crusade, and may win a war before it has truly begun.'

'I agree.' It was Sarik of the White Scars, his eyes alight with feral glee as he spoke. 'My men and I have been cooped up for too long. We need the ground beneath our feet, a bolter in hand and an enemy to the fore.'

'Nonetheless,' replied Lucian, 'we must perform a proper reconnoitre first.'

'I agree!' said Admiral Jellaqua. 'I will not order my command into harm's way on the word of a captive. There is simply too much at stake.'

Gurney rounded on Jellaqua, leaning forward over the polished wooden table. 'Admiral, might I remind you that I am granted titular authority–'

'And might I remind you,' the stout admiral bellowed as he struggled to his feet, 'that I command the Imperial Navy. If any wish to continue without the support of my vessels, then they are welcome to do so!'

The admiral stood, red faced with rage, locked in confrontation with the cardinal. The council went silent, many around the table simply looking elsewhere for fear of setting either man off again. Lucian saw his chance.

'Gentlemen,' he said as he stood and walked around the table to stand between them. 'Clearly, this will get us nowhere. Such division plays into our enemy's hands, and we can scarcely afford to squander any edge we might have.'

'Quite so,' Jellaqua replied, nodding his thanks to Lucian.

The cardinal, however, was less magnanimous. 'To withdraw now would be treason,' he growled, his voice dangerously low where Lucian was more used to it being shrill. Jellaqua stiffened.

'No one is accusing anyone of treason,' Lucian interjected.

'Who among us,' the cardinal replied, 'is more fit to judge such a matter?' Gurney turned to his compatriot seated next to him. Inquisitor Grand nodded, his face barely visible beneath his dark hood.

'Indeed,' Grand rasped, 'treason is a word so easily applied, and yet one so difficult to take back.'

Lucian felt the inquisitor's gaze boring into him from beneath the hood, a queasy sensation rising in his stomach. A vision flashed across his mind's eye, a vivid image of his daughter, in pain and in desperate need. He knew stark dread for a moment, and knew then that he had made a terrible enemy in Inquisitor Grand. He recognised the touch of the psyker, and knew that Grand had placed the vision within his mind. The inquisitor, he had no doubt, was a psyker of some ability.

From where Lucian stood, interposed between the cardinal and the admiral, he noticed that Korvane was staring right at Inquisitor

Grand. Had his son shared the vision? Had the bastard inquisitor shown to all of the council that he might truly crush any power that remained within Lucian's grasp? He looked around the various faces, but saw nothing unusual. It was just him and his son, then.

'How shall we settle this matter?' Admiral Jellaqua asked, sitting once more with evident frustration.

'I'll do it,' said a voice from across the chamber. Lucian's heart sank. It was Korvane who had spoken up.

'What?' asked Jellaqua, seeking to locate the speaker.

Lucian saw his son rise and approach the council table.

'Korvane, please sit,' Lucian started.

'No,' interjected Inquisitor Grand, his relish all too evident. 'Let him speak.'

Korvane nodded his thanks to the inquisitor. Lucian felt a bitter stab of resentment. 'I propose,' Korvane continued, 'that I lead a scouting mission to locate a suitable target.'

'And why would you do such a thing?' Inquisitor Grand rasped.

'Because I believe such a course of action is in the best interests of the crusade,' Korvane replied.

'The *Rosetta* is no scouting vessel,' Lucian said, hating that circumstance had set him against his own son in such a manner, yet knowing he must intervene. 'She's not fast enough and she'll be detected within hours of breaking warp.'

'I know that, father,' Korvane replied, an unfamiliar edge in his voice. 'I'll lead a Navy deep space recon patrol. If there's a decent target within range, I'll find it.' He turned to the council at large. 'You have my word.'

'Can this be done?' Gurney asked no one in particular.

'Aye,' Jellaqua replied, 'it can be done, if it is agreed.' Here the admiral looked to Lucian. Lucian caught the hint of sympathy in the other man's eye, and appreciated it for the gesture it was no doubt intended to be. Though he seethed inside, Lucian knew that now was the time to show unity, to shore up what influence he still had within the council. To oppose his son's proposal would spell the end of any such influence, of that he was quite sure. Just what his son hoped to achieve by absenting himself from the crusade fleet at such a vital juncture, he had no clue.

'I propose,' Korvane went on, 'to proceed rimward thirty-eight by one-one-seven.' As he spoke, Korvane touched a polished brass control console mounted in the great wooden table. The vaulted ceiling space was filled with light all of a sudden, which gradually resolved itself into a representation of the surrounding space. The blue nebulae glowed serenely, casting their luminescence over the councillors as each craned his neck to look up. Lucian sighed inwardly, realising that his son's proposal had not been as spontaneous as it had at first appeared. No, Lucian mused bitterly, his son had planned this, and kept it from him.

The heading Korvane had prepared was scribed across the projection as the council watched, warp time differentials labelled at each waypoint. He's wasted no time, Lucian thought, seeing that the course led towards a system that Lucian would have chosen were he proposing the course of action, and not his son.

'This system,' Korvane announced, 'is, I believe, a viable target.'

'Not according to my data.' All eyes turned from the swirling blue eddies above, to Magos Explorator Jaakho, who had spoken. 'That cluster was subject to a delta seven survey when last my order passed through this region. I do not believe the tau would settle there, for it holds no worlds capable of supporting life.'

'And yet,' Lucian said, supporting his son's choice of target despite himself, 'the tau have developed into a highly proficient space-faring race, capable of crossing the Gulf and spreading Emperor only knows how far into the stars. With respect, lord explorator, that cluster occupies a strategically important position within the region. It provides an ideal staging post for expansion across the Gulf, or a bridgehead for any wishing to invade. Were we in the tau's position, we would occupy in force.'

Lucian's statement caused Gurney to simmer with barely contained outrage at the comparison of human and tau. Let him choke on his own bile, Lucian thought.

'Thank you, father,' Korvane said, nodding his head towards Lucian.

'You will need a strong recon element,' Lucian said. Though uncertain of his son's agenda, he was already calculating ways in which the situation could be turned to the Arcadius's advantage, 'Admiral?'

'Indeed,' replied Admiral Jellaqua, who had remained thoughtful as the discussion had taken this odd turn, 'I would not be averse to detaching a deep space reconnaissance wing to your son's command. I believe the 344th will suffice. I can order the necessary arrangements, if the council agrees.'

'You formally propose this course of action, admiral?' Explorator Jaakho asked.

'I do,' replied Admiral Jellaqua, tabling the motion that Korvane be allowed to lead a scouting mission to ascertain the crusade's first target.

'Who here will second this motion?' The explorator lord asked.

'I will,' replied Lucian. 'I will second the motion.'

Lucian and Korvane stood upon the vast crowded main flight deck of the *Blade of Woe*. A navy lighter waited nearby to shuttle Korvane to the scout wing patrolling the crusade's outer perimeter. The whine of the small vessel's idling engines was almost lost amidst the clamour of the bustling deck.

Lucian watched as his son's effects were loaded onto the waiting lighter, waiting for Korvane to offer him some form of explanation. He had been waiting since the council had broken up some hours before, and had yet to hear Korvane's account of his actions.

'So, you'll leave without telling me what's going on?' he finally asked, growing impatient with his son's silence.

'I believe it's for the best, father. I can do this.'

'Whether you can do this or not is beside the point,' Lucian growled, turning his back on his son and looking out across the busy flight deck. Small vessels arrived and departed by the minute, ferrying personnel and equipment between the capital vessels of the crusade fleet. 'That you chose to inform me of your plan of action in the manner you did was unforgivable.'

'I intended no disrespect, father. I sought merely to take the initiative in council.'

'That you did,' Lucian replied, turning towards his son once more, 'and you may have done our cause enormous benefit in the process.' Lucian grinned, unable to bear any malice towards his son, and certainly not when Korvane was about to depart into an unknown and hostile region of space.

Korvane however, remained impassive, his features dark and

sullen. 'You would not have heard me out were I to propose such a course to you, in private.'

Lucian was stunned. 'You think...'

'I know,' Korvane said. 'I saw the council turning against you, and I acted.'

Not entirely true, Lucian thought, for Korvane had evidently prepared a plot of the region prior to speaking up in council. He decided to leave it. 'What's done is done, Korvane. I do not wish us to part on ill terms.' He spread his arms wide, inviting his son to embrace him at his departing.

Korvane turned his head, his rejection of Lucian's gesture all too obvious and painful to behold.

'Go then,' Lucian said. 'Prove whatever it is you need to prove.'

Korvane turned towards the lighter's lowered access ramp and took a step up it.

'But Korvane,' Lucian said, his son halting, and turning his head towards him.

'Yes, father?'

'Try not to get yourself killed.'

'Yes, father,' Korvane said, and ducked into the lighter's small passenger bay.

CHAPTER TWELVE

The tau shuttle touched down with a barely perceptible jolt. Brielle looked across the small passenger bay at Naal, who nodded back at her. She touched the clasp holding the acceleration harness across her body, and it disengaged before retracting into its mounting on the wall behind her.

'Will there be much...' Brielle began.

'Ceremony?' Naal finished for her. 'No. Our host will wish to keep things low key, at least to begin with.'

'Until he's decided how much use I might be to him,' Brielle said. She really did not care that she sounded like a petulant child. She felt like one.

Naal smiled in a manner Brielle was coming to find somewhat patronising. 'To a point, yes, but don't forget, Brielle, that the tau do not mount grandiose ceremonies for the glorification of individuals. They may do so for the benefit of all, but this is not such an occasion.'

Brielle stood from the acceleration couch, stretching as she did so. The interface had taken less than an hour, and was far gentler than an atmospheric entry in many human vessels, but she felt cramped and tense nonetheless.

'So, I'm not important enough to make a fuss over?' she asked, a sly grin at her lips.

'Quite the...' Naal began, before he realised Brielle was toying with him.

'So, who is important enough?' she continued. 'Who's in charge around here?'

When Naal failed to answer her, Brielle turned and regarded him squarely. 'What?' she asked, instantly suspicious.

'The tau govern in a manner quite unlike the Imperium,' Naal answered. Brielle noted that he did not meet her eye as he spoke. Her suspicion was piqued.

'I know that, Naal,' she responded testily, 'the envoy briefed me. But I could tell that there was plenty he didn't tell me about.'

'It's true, Brielle, there is much more to learn,' Naal answered, ducking past her towards the boarding hatch. 'Please, be patient. The tau are in many ways a straightforward people, they shun affectation and pretence and are entirely selfless in the pursuit of the Greater Good.' Naal turned and looked Brielle straight in the eye. 'But there are some things they entrust only to friends. If you become their friend, you will be rewarded greatly.'

And if I don't? Brielle thought to herself as she held Naal's gaze for a long moment.

'As to your other question,' Naal continued, his tone light and conversational, 'no one is "in charge around here".'

She gave him her best incredulous look, and he continued.

'The tau practice a form of collective government. It's complex, but you'll come to see that it works.'

'Wait,' Brielle said, 'you mean to tell me there's no single tau in charge?'

'I do,' Naal replied. 'Various individuals may attain pre-eminence, enjoying great influence for a stretch, but they always accede to others when appropriate. Therefore, no one individual has total control, and he who may do so best exercises his influence while he may.'

'And this works? Brielle asked, genuinely incredulous.

'It does, and very well,' Naal said, smiling. 'You'll come to realise, Brielle, that the tau display a distinct lack of ego. It takes some getting used to, but once you do, it all makes sense.'

Taking this in, Brielle gave Naal one last look, just to ensure that he was not toying with her. His continued smile told her that he was not. It all seemed incredibly implausible, but then, the tau was an alien race, quite outside the human frame of reference. She approached the hatch, and stood at Naal's side as he reached out to activate the control at its side. With a barely audible hiss, the hatch began to open outward. The shuttle's small passenger compartment was flooded with the light that appeared around the lowering ramp.

Such moments always reminded her of a lesson she had been taught upon her first planetfall. Standing at her father's side in the equally cramped passenger bay of a human shuttle, he had told her that nothing could match the first breath of a new world. The memory was a precious one from her early adulthood, but it was sullied by the fact that the world in question had been Nankirk, where she had been introduced to her future stepbrother. Korvane had come into the Clan Arcadius that day, the result of a perspicacious joining of dynasties. Brielle, however, had lost her position as heritor of the clan, and, in her view, had lived in Korvane's shadow ever since.

Forcing such thoughts to the back of her mind, Brielle repeated the ritual she had first carried out on that day years before. She closed her eyes, and felt the gentle breeze on her face of the outside air as it rushed into the shuttle. Her eyes still closed, she took a deep breath. She savoured, as her father had taught her, the myriad subtle tastes and scents of this new world. The air was clean, with a faint undertone of some exotic spice. Something else was carried on the air too, the scent of artificial compounds, plastics, resins and the like. However, they were not the raw, harsh fumes belched out on many worlds of the Imperium, but something far more integrated into the society it served.

She breathed out and opened her eyes, to find the ramp entirely lowered before her. The bright light of the world's sun dazzled her for an instant, before the photochromatic lenses she wore in her eyes adjusted the light to tolerable levels. As her vision resolved, the view settled into a sight of breathtaking proportions.

The shuttle in which she had arrived was perched upon a small landing pad, which was itself an offshoot of a far larger, narrow, fin-shaped structure. A narrow walkway led from the landing pad to the larger building, although Brielle could see no obvious entrance in its surface. She looked around the landing pad for any form of welcoming party, but saw none. Despite what Naal had said about the tau not standing on ceremony, she felt mildly snubbed. Perhaps that was the point, she thought. It would hardly have been the first time a host had attempted to put an unwelcome guest at a disadvantage by affecting disinterest in their presence.

Looking beyond the landing pad, Brielle saw that they were a very great height above the ground. The structure from which the pad protruded appeared to be part of a far larger city, consisting of a great many such buildings. Each was linked to the next by walkways that soared high above the landscape, which appeared, from Brielle's vantage point, to consist of featureless, arid wastes as far as the hazy, distant horizon.

'No welcoming committee,' Brielle said, looking to Naal. 'You're the expert in these people,' she said. 'So what's next?'

'Please,' Naal said, gesturing forward, 'you are the guest, not I.'

She looked at him for a moment, not entirely convinced that all was well. No matter, she told herself; whatever happened, she would turn it to her own advantage soon enough. She had to, she mused; she could hardly go back and apologise to the council for killing one of their number.

Taking a deep breath, Brielle stepped down the ramp, steeling herself against whatever might await her on this world.

Having left the tau vessel on the landing pad, Brielle had allowed Naal to lead the way. He knew what he was doing, and had obviously been here before. She welcomed the opportunity to take it all in, to observe this new place, and to glean any advantage she could. She had followed Naal across a series of walkways, each of which passed through one of the soaring, off-white, fin-shaped structures, before continuing through the air to the next. At first, she had experienced vertigo, for the walkways had no hand holds, but she found that they were wide enough so that if she passed down their exact centre the effect was minimised. She had no idea who used these walkways, for the pair did not pass a single tau.

After a while, the walkways converged at a structure even taller than the rest. Brielle halted as it came into view, taking the opportunity to marvel in its construction. It must have been a thousand metres tall, and it rose in sweeping lines to a sail-like peak. Small clusters of what appeared to be sensor or communications gear were connected to its spine, and a great, gleaming spike pierced the sky at its very top, dancing blue lights chasing up and down its length.

Then, Brielle saw that small, floating machines were moving up and around the structure. She knew them straight away for the drones that the tau utilised at every level of their society, though these were far larger than the small utility drones she had witnessed onboard the tau vessel that had brought her to this world. The drones took the form of a flat, armoured disc, about a metre in diameter. Beneath the disc was a small sensor block, with its unblinking machine eye, and beside that, what was obviously a weapon of some sort. As she studied the drones, one detached itself from its orbit of the building, and approached her and Naal on a long, graceful arc through the air that brought it, hovering, before her.

The drone was so close she could almost have reached out and touched it, yet she sensed from its movements that such a gesture would not have been wise.

'What is it doing?' Brielle asked Naal.

'What you'd expect of any guard doing his duty,' Naal replied. 'It's determining whether or not we are a threat.'

'It's relaying back to someone in the tower?' Brielle asked, keeping an eye on the drone as she spoke.

'It is perfectly capable of making the decision on its own, Brielle.'

Brielle felt her hackles rise as she watched the drone begin a circuit of the pair. She knew that the tau utilised highly developed machine intelligences, but to see one close up was something else entirely. The teachings of the Imperial Creed warned against such things, and those admonitions had been drilled into her from a very early age. As she regarded the single lens mounted beneath the armoured disc, she felt that there was indeed some manner of intelligence at work within the machine, and the thought disturbed her to her core.

'When will it be done?' she asked Naal through gritted teeth.

'Please, Brielle,' Naal answered, 'such things are commonplace on tau worlds. You must get used to them.'

Now he was really starting to annoy her. She cast him a glare that told him the drone had better hurry up its examination or there would be consequences. But, before she could say any more, she heard the gentle sound of the door in the side of the structure before them opening.

A group of tau stepped through the opening.

Brielle quickly counted five of them. One, obviously the most senior, stood at the head of the group. He was tall and thin, and wore long, shimmering robes, but it was his face that made the greatest impression on Brielle. Although she had found it hard to read the expression of the envoy on whose vessel she had been brought here, she had at least found some similarities between tau and human facial expressions. This tau appeared maudlin to Brielle, as if he greatly regretted his role. To Brielle's understanding, the tau were born into their station, and all she had encountered to date had appeared quite content with their lot. Before she could ponder the matter further, the tau spoke.

'I welcome you, Mistress Brielle Gerrit of the Arcadius, to the Sept of Dal'yth. My name is Por'O Dal'yth Ulor Kanti. Please,' he continued, 'call me Aura. The translation is close enough for our purposes.'

Even his voice seemed sad to Brielle, almost wistfully mournful. Was this some affectation on his part to gain some advantage in their dealings? Not wishing to cause offence, she hastened to answer.

'Please accept my sincere thanks for the kindness you have shown me,' Brielle said.

'We have shown you no kindness beyond the spirit in which the Tau Empire approaches all the races it encounters. We do find ourselves, however, in a unique position.'

Brielle's guard was immediately up. She had been warned that the tau would not stand on ceremony, yet she sensed something more unfolding before her, something serious enough to disrupt the familiar course of any such meeting.

'Mistress Arcadius,' Aura said, 'you have arrived at Dal'yth not a moment too soon. Even now, the human fleet closes on this system.'

So soon? Brielle had assumed the tau vessel on which she had crossed the Damocles Gulf would have arrived a long way ahead of the crusade, affording her some time to turn the situation to her advantage and find some way of averting the disaster that would ensue if Gurney's plan was enacted. Now, she would have to think on her feet to turn things around.

'Might I ask,' Brielle said, 'how far out are they?'

Aura did not answer Brielle's question. Instead, one of the tau standing behind him took a step forward. Like his fellows, this individual was shorter and of more stocky build than the diplomat. The robes he wore were made of a far simpler, deep red, fabric, yet they did not disguise the tau's more muscular frame.

Aura made a shallow bow, before introducing him. 'Mistress Brielle, my colleague, Commander Puretide, will answer your question.'

'The human fleet is thought to lie only a few days travel gulfward of Dal'yth,' Commander Puretide said, his voice resonant and steady. 'The deep space piquets of the Air Caste have detected their communications, though the main body of the fleet appears to be mustering still, following its crossing of the Gulf.'

Brielle considered this information, regarding the commander as she pondered. She was struck by the air of calm wisdom he radiated. A breeze whipped up, causing the top knot on the commander's otherwise shaved head to stir. She felt a brief moment of vertigo, but forced her mind back to the issue at hand.

'Have they made any attempt at communication?' Brielle asked the commander.

'They have not,' replied the commander, transfixing her with his glare.

'And neither will they,' said a third tau, stepping forward as he did so. Brielle could tell that this individual was younger than Commander Puretide, and he stood taller and more erect. Something in the way the tau carried himself gave Brielle pause. This one was dangerous, she thought.

'Mistress,' Aura continued, 'please forgive me. These others are the commander's companions. I believe a better word, in your tongue, might be pupils or students, though neither word is entirely satisfactory.' Aura indicated with a graceful sweep of a long arm each of the tau as he spoke their names. 'Farsight, Shadowsun and Icewind.'

Each of the three nodded to Brielle as their name was spoken. Farsight was the tau who had spoken a moment before, and Shadowsun, a female tau stood next to him, her expression calm and unreadable. Next to her stood the tau introduced as Icewind, his expression one of calculated study of everything that transpired around him.

Brielle nodded in greeting to Puretide's pupils, before addressing the commander once more. 'The fleet will send out scouts to identify its first target. Tell me commander, which system lies closest?'

'Mistress Arcadius,' Commander Puretide replied, 'this very system lies closest.'

'Have you attempted to communicate with them?' she asked, a sense of dread mounting within her.

'We have not,' Aura interjected. 'We require that you do so on our behalf.'

Now Brielle's dread threatened to well up into panic. 'No!' She turned from Puretide, to Naal. 'I cannot, they will kill me before I...'

'You will have the might of the Tau Empire behind you,' Aura cut in. 'They will not dare harm you.'

'You don't know them,' Brielle said, her mind racing for an alternative even as she spoke.

'Nonetheless,' Aura said, 'you must do so, for the Greater Good. If you do not wish to join the tau, then you are free to return to your people.' The breeze whipped Brielle's plaited hair into her face, causing her to flick her head in irritation. 'But if you choose to do so, you do so alone. Join us, or return to them. The choice is yours.'

That's no choice at all, Brielle thought as Aura's words sank in. Return to the fleet as a traitor in the service of the tau, or do so as a cornered renegade with nowhere left to run.

'I need time to think,' Brielle said, desperately stalling for time.

'You have until sunset, Mistress Brielle,' Aura said, his mournful voice barely audible over the mounting breeze. 'Time is against us all, and I must have an answer before war comes to the Tau Empire.'

CHAPTER THIRTEEN

The cramped bridge of Korvane's scout vessel was dark and silent, every member of the bridge crew intent upon the operation of their sensor equipment. Korvane sat at the rear of the bridge space, the crew arrayed to his side and the pilot occupying the station below him. He stared out of the multi-faceted cockpit canopy, brooding at the system before him.

His hand trembled, and he gripped the seat's arm until his knuckles turned white. He forced his mind onto anything other than the pain and the substance that would mask it.

The crusade's charts listed this place as the Kendral sub-sector. It was a meaningless appellation as far as Korvane could tell, in all likelihood named for one of the explorators who had passed through six millennia before. Whoever Kendral was, he had not returned to settle the region named after him, and so no one would ever know what deed had earned him the right to have an entire region of space share his name. The system had no name, just a designation within the sub sector: KX122. Even now, Korvane's scout wing was edging into the system's outer reaches, each vessel on silent running lest they give away their presence to any tau in the locality.

'Report,' ordered Korvane.

A crewman, hunched over a glowing terminal, answered, 'Passive readings confirm the presence of at least a dozen stellar bodies, my lord. We are approaching the nearest as ordered.'

'Good,' Korvane replied. Looking through the canopy, he caught his first glimpse of the world in question. KX122/13 was expected to be a small, dense world consisting of little more than rock and ice. With only the passive sensors to rely on, the scouts would need to make a close pass in order to gather much more information, and this they would do as the world came into view.

Very little light fell upon KX122/13 this far from the system's single, cold white stare. Only the blue of the surrounding nebulae glinting from its icy surface caught Korvane's eye.

'Take us in low, pilot,' Korvane ordered. 'I doubt there's anyone about, but if there is, I don't want them to see us coming.'

'Confirmed,' replied the pilot. 'Activating ground following radar in point...'

'Denied!' snapped Korvane. 'I ordered passive sensors only and I meant it.' Korvane's rage was growing as the pilot turned to look up at him.

'Sir, without the...'

'I said,' Korvane said through gritted teeth, 'denied. You will follow my orders to the letter, or you will stand down. Do you understand?'

Correctly deducing that the question was entirely rhetorical, the pilot turned back to his task. Korvane stared at the back of the man's head for a moment, before looking out of the canopy. KX122/13 was coming into view, its blue, cratered surface dimly visible against the blackness of space. The pilot instigated a change of course that levelled the small vessel out. The horizon reared up from below, filling half of the view, the light of the distant star casting a ghostly halo above. Korvane leant back in the acceleration couch and scanned the read-outs around the bridge.

It felt both liberating and frustrating to be in command, not of a mighty cruiser with thousands of crew, but of a scout wing of four vessels, each with only a few dozen crew. It was the first time in his career that Korvane had undertaken such a mission, though he felt supremely confident in his ability to carry it through. He sighed as he admitted that in truth, he was glad to be away from the crusade fleet, from the myriad demands of running his vessel. He knew that he was also eager to escape his father's shadow, to ply his own course, for a while at least. He reflected ruefully how his stepsister had attempted to do something similar, and made such a mess of it. Well, he would prove that he was fully capable of making things work on his own, and to bring honour and profit to the Arcadius through his own actions.

In the meantime, he mused, if Brielle was out there, on the run, he would ensure that she never returned to the crusade fleet and to the Arcadius. Thinking of his stepsister brought a dark cloud down upon him. When he had learned of Brielle's assault upon Inquisitor Grand and her subsequent disappearance, he had been gladdened, though he had struggled to hide his reaction from his father. Recently, however, as the crusade had pushed on towards tau space, it had occurred to him that she must still be out there, somewhere. And so, he had seen the opportunity to place himself in a position of power, from where he could react should Brielle reappear. He had no idea exactly what he would do should he locate her, but, he brooded, he would worry about that if and when it happened.

'Sir?' The pilot said, breaking Korvane's reverie.

'Report,' he snapped back.

'Descending at your command.'

'Do it.'

Korvane felt an immediate change in the pitch of the scout vessel's drives as the pilot altered course, bringing the small ship's nose down towards the distant surface. Almost immediately, a series of small tremors passed through the vessel. Korvane looked to a pict-slate over the pilot's station, and saw from the readings scrolling across its blue screen that they had hit the outer edges of a very thin atmospheric envelope. A second series of shudders jolted the scout vessel, and Korvane checked that his harness was properly secured. The sound of the drives grew more intense, building to a deafening roar, as the angle of descent grew more acute. Looking from the pict-slate to the canopy, Korvane saw small trails of gas dancing across the armoured glass, the leading edge of the shuttle's blunt nose glowing faintly orange with the heat generated as it plunged through the atmosphere.

'Sir!' a crewman behind Korvane called out, raising his voice over the cacophony of atmospheric entry. 'Vox transponders are picking up a faint signal.'

Korvane's heart pounded as he read the data patched through to his console screen. He felt an exhilaration quite different to that he experienced at the bridge of the *Rosetta* in similar circumstances. Now, he sat not aboard a might cruiser able to take fearsome punishment from other vessels, but in a tiny scouting vessel that could take none, relying instead upon stealth and guile to survive. He struggled for a moment to make sense of the data, before realising that it represented not a weak signal, as the crewman had reported, but a very tightly focused one. And that, he surmised, could mean only one thing: a small tau presence, perhaps an outpost or research station, and the perfect target for his first action.

'Take us in, pilot,' Korvane ordered, thrilling to the prospect of an easy victory to report back to the fleet. 'Lock on to the signal source. Bring us in low and fast.'

The pilot hunched over his controls, driving the scout vessel lower. As Korvane watched, the view through the canopy became entirely obscured by superheated gases, and the ship bucked and jolted violently. Korvane saw that the pilot was flying entirely by the passive sensors, and by the uncanny instinct with which the pilots of the Navy pathfinder squadrons were rightly famed.

A moment later, the view through the armoured canopy cleared, and Korvane saw that the vessel was coming up on the end of an impossibly steep dive. He resisted the urge to order the pilot to arrest the descent, and an instant later the pilot hauled back on the control column with all his might. Korvane was forced back into the acceleration couch as the gravitational forces at work on the vessel mounted. Even as he felt he might pass out, the pilot brought the vessel out of the dive, and on to an even trajectory less than a hundred metres from the cratered surface. Korvane gasped for breath as gravity returned to normal, and released the harness strapping him into the couch. He leaned forward, over the pilot's shoulder, to gain a better view of the ground as it passed rapidly by below.

The surface of KX122/13 was cratered and scarred. Ice glistened dimly in the faint starlight, but Korvane could make out nothing obviously artificial or out of place. He checked the read-out above the pilot's station once more, and saw that they were closing in on the source of the signal.

'Sensors, I want a full, active scan the moment we reveal ourselves, understood?'

The crewman at the sensor station at Korvane's side turned and looked straight at him. 'Sir, standard doctrine is to...'

'I gave you an order!' Korvane spat, anger once more welling up. He felt his frustration growing steadily as the Navy crew felt it reasonable to question his orders. He would not have accepted such a lapse in discipline on the bridge of the *Rosetta*, and he was damned if he would do so here.

'But sir,' the crewman continued, evidently prepared to risk Korvane's ire, 'if they have any local defences they'll be able to lock onto us in seconds.'

'I am fully aware of that,' Korvane replied, barely able to keep his voice steady as his anger threatened to boil over, 'but an entire fleet is relying on us. We need only confirm the tau's presence, and then we can return to the fleet and report our findings. Do as I order, now, or your career is ended.'

'Understood, sir,' the crewman replied, turning from Korvane and working the controls at his station. Korvane watched for a moment, satisfying himself that the man was in fact preparing his instruments to perform a full, active scan the instant the scout vessel came into range of the signal source.

'Range?' Korvane asked. He felt a growing tension, but was damned if he'd let the Navy crewmen detect it.

'Three seventeen,' the pilot responded, not taking his eyes from the view outside.

'Descend to fifty metres,' Korvane ordered. He was determined that the scouts would have the advantage of surprise. If the tau did have any local air defence, then coming in so low might gain precious seconds in which the active sensors could scan the outpost. Any intelligence that Korvane could bring back would be invaluable in furthering the cause of the Arcadius against that of Cardinal Grand and his faction.

Korvane braced himself once more. The pilot pushed forward on his control column, the vessel descending so that the craters and ridges flashing by below lurched up into close proximity. Korvane could make out individual boulders on the surface, and could see that the deep blue colouration of the ground was caused by large dunes of drifting blue particles. A low, mountainous spine reared up on the horizon.

'Twenty seconds, sir,' the pilot intoned.

'Good,' Korvane replied. 'Sensors, prepare for...'

'Contact at three-three-six!' called out another crewman. Korvane spun to his right, looking over the shoulder of the man who had spoken.

'Identify,' Korvane replied.

'Four, belay that, five fast moving class fives, range... three kilometres and closing.'

Korvane forced down a mounting panic. 'Heading?'

The crewman turned to look Korvane right in the eye. 'They are inbound on our position, sir.'

Before Korvane could answer, the pilot spoke. 'Five...'

Korvane's mind raced to keep pace of events. He took a deep breath and forced himself to steady his nerves. He thought fast.

'Pilot, perform one pass and then break for orbit. Sensors, get as much as you can, while you can. Understood?'

Neither man answered him. As the countdown reached zero, Korvane felt the scout vessel lurch suddenly upwards, the low mountain range sweeping by beneath.

Then, Korvane saw the source of the signal. Beyond the ridge lay a wide depression, an ancient crater, the flanks of which were all but obscured by the drifting blue particulates. A tall, sail shaped structure soared into the sky at the centre of the crater. Korvane had only tau starship design to go on, but he knew instantly that this structure was of tau manufacture, the clean lines already familiar to him.

'Scanning,' called the sensor operator as the pilot brought the vessel down into the crater, skimming a mere twenty metres above the ground before bringing the ship upwards in a wide, banking roll.

'Comms,' Korvane said, addressing another crewman, 'I want a short burst transmission ready the instant we get clear.' Even as he spoke, Korvane tapped his report into his command terminal, sealed it with his personal cipher and shunted it on to the comms operator's station.

'Contacts closing at seven fifty kilometres per hour!' the sensor operator called out.

'Sir,' the pilot said, 'at this speed and heading I can't evade. We need to get clear, right now!'

Korvane forced down the urge to snap back at the man, knowing that the pilot was correct. He knew that they would not obtain a full scan if they pulled out now, but at least they would escape with their lives. 'Take us home, pilot,' Korvane ordered, hearing sighs of relief from the bridge crew behind him as he spoke.

'Hold on,' the pilot warned, before hauling back on the control column. The horizon dropped and the black of space hove into view through the canopy. Korvane felt his body forced back into the acceleration couch and struggled to fasten the harness.

'Contact closing,' the sensor operator announced, an edge of alarm in his voice. 'Speed increasing...'

'Incoming!' called out another crewman. Korvane looked around desperately for the cause of the warning, before the pilot heaved upon his controls and the vessel lurched violently to port. An instant later, what was obviously a high velocity missile streaked past upon a billowing contrail, before veering off and disappearing from view.

'It's coming round!' a voice called in outright panic. Korvane looked to his tracking screen, and saw that the missile was indeed beginning a wide arc that would bring it back on to the scout vessel's tail.

'Pilot,' Korvane called, 'bring us back around on heading seven six nine.'

'Towards the contacts, sir?'

'Towards the contacts. They clearly outmatch us for speed and reach. Call in the rest of the wing and close on enemy contacts.'

Korvane tightened the lock on his acceleration harness. If it's a fight they want, he thought, then it's a fight they'll get.

CHAPTER FOURTEEN

'Signal?' Lucian asked, not taking his eyes from the view through the forward viewing port.

'None as yet, my lord,' replied the newly appointed communications officer. 'All commands at alert status alpha crimson. We're on track for the assault when the *Blade* gives the word.'

'Thank you, Mister Katona,' Lucian replied, grateful that a flesh and blood human was manning the comms station. Lucian had petitioned Jellaqua for an intake of seconded officers following the disaster that had decimated his bridge crew during the crossing of the Damocles Gulf. The admiral had obliged, and not a moment too soon, in Lucian's opinion, for things were about to get very serious indeed.

Lucian continued his vigil at the armoured port. The scene was quite spectacular, even to one with the heritage of a rogue trader line behind him. The entire battle line of the Damocles Gulf crusade fleet was arranged against the lambent blue nebulae, ready and waiting to begin its attack on the tau system into which it had arrived. The *Blade of Woe*, Admiral Jellaqua's four thousand year old Retribution class battleship lay mere kilometres to the *Oceanid*'s prow. Several kilometres long, the vessel was slab sided and sharp-prowed, and bristled with weapons turrets and sensor arrays. She bore the scars of hundreds of battles. Lucian knew the battleship to be a fearsome opponent in a fight, her broadsides easily the match for any tau vessel he had yet to witness. Furthermore, Lucian had spoken with the admiral several hours earlier, and knew he would be taking a direct hand in his ship's operation when things got heated. Jellaqua might be a senior admiral of the Imperial Navy, but Lucian knew he would not be able to resist the urge to captain his flagship in person, leading from the front in a glorious example to the other captains of the line.

A kilometre off the *Blade of Woe*'s starboard bow lay the *Niobe*, an Overlord class battlecruiser captained by one Captain Joachim, whom Lucian had met once at council and had taken an instant dislike to. Joachim, it transpired, was the youngest son of the Cabiri dynasty, a rogue trader clan that Lucian's family had clashed with over trading rights three centuries earlier. Though Lucian bore the man no ill will, Joachim evidently felt that some form of feud existed between the two. Lucian had been in no mood to pander to Joachim's folly, and had given him no more thought since. He had decided, however, to keep a weather eye out, lest the son of Cabiri decide to renew his imaginary feud at some inopportune moment in the coming battle.

A pair of cruisers, the Gothic class *Lord Cedalion*, and the *Duchess McIntyre*, which was commanded by Captain Natalia, lay to the *Niobe*'s starboard side. Lucian had gained a solid respect for Natalia, viewing her as one of the most proficient and reliable captains of the fleet, and a definite ally in the incessant political manoeuvring that went on, even amongst the ships' masters.

The Lunar class cruiser the *Honour of Damlass*, and her consort, the Dauntless class cruiser *Regent Lakshimbal* rested at a distance, forming a pair of spiked, black silhouettes against the glowing blue backdrop of the region's nebulae. This pair would form a cruiser squadron tasked with guarding the fleet's port flank while the heavier vessels engaged the enemy head on.

Lucian's vessel sat at the rear of the formation, the *Rosetta* and the *Fairlight* in echelon to port behind her. Though he could not see her, Lucian knew that his stern was covered by the *Centaur*, a newly commissioned Lunar class cruiser yet to fire her first shot in anger.

The nine escort squadrons that the capital vessels would rely on to provide close protection against enemy vessels seeking to get in amongst their formation were scattered throughout this impressive armada. Each squadron consisted of three or four sword frigates or destroyers of various types, and each was led by a squadron leader proven in battle many times over.

Yet, even as Lucian looked out at the fleet, each of its vessels bristling with mighty weapons and laden with crew eager to fight for the cause of humanity, his mind drifted back, weeks before, to the encounter he had had with the derelict battlecruiser Ajax. Following Master Karaldi's prognostication trance, Lucian had been left in no doubt that the vessel was lost in the warp. Yet, when the fleet had mustered at its fourth waypoint during the crossing of the gulf, the Ajax had been there too, intact and fully operational. He had heard tales of such things, read cautionary accounts passed down generations of rogue traders from father to son, but never before had he been so close to witnessing such a phenomenon first hand. Lucian had withheld his account of his encounter with the Ajax, lest the morale of the fleet be adversely affected. He could not, and would not, tell anyone that he had seen the Ajax dead in space, before she had been seen alive and well and operating as part of the fleet, before disappearing once more at the final muster. The warp had inflicted some terrible fate upon the vessel, and he would keep his own counsel on the matter. He knew, however, that the event would stalk him in nightmares for many years to come.

For now, the position in the line normally covered by the Ajax would be covered by the *Oceanid* and the *Rosetta*, with the *Fairlight* in close attendance. Lucian was perfectly able to fulfil the role of a captain of the line, and he had briefed officers placed in temporary charge of the *Rosetta* and the *Fairlight*. Both were capable men, eager to prove their worth, and both had served the Arcadius for many long years. Though it pained him to entrust the two vessels to any other than his own blood, Lucian was glad that they were in good hands.

As he watched, Lucian saw the mighty plasma drives of the *Blade of Woe* flare to life. The armoured glass of the viewing port dimmed automatically, affording Lucian a view of the final jostling for position before the fleet moved to attack the tau world towards which they were ploughing.

'Any moment now, sir,' Katona said, anticipating Lucian's question. 'All commands have called in their final telemetries.'

'Well enough, Mister Katona,' Lucian replied, affording himself a wolfish grin at the prospect of the coming scrap. Turning from the port, he strode the length of the bridge, taking the time to look over the shoulder of each of the Navy bridge crew. All was well, each officer going about his duty as if born to it. They probably were, he mused, knowing that each man would hail from a naval line as old as the Arcadius.

'Let's get things moving, shall we?' Lucian asked no one in particular. 'Mister Ruuben,' Lucian addressed the seconded navy helmsman, 'you have control of my vessel. I care for her very deeply. Treat her well, understood?'

The helmsman, evidently a veteran of several calamitous battles by the terrible burn scars that marred his bald pate, turned at his station and bowed to Lucian. 'I'll take care of her like she's my own, my lord. You have my word.'

'I'll hold you to it, Mister Ruuben,' Lucian replied. He liked the man already, though he deeply mourned the loss of Raldi, and above all the manner of that loss.

Settling in to his command throne, Lucian savoured the feeling that few others could understand: to command a warship, to order her into battle, to hold in one's hand such awesome destruction as she could unleash, and to bear the responsibility of thousands of lives. It was his birthright and his burden, and he would not trade moments such as this for all Macharius's gold.

'Signal from fleet command,' Mister Katona called out.

'Patch it through,' Lucian ordered.

The bridge was suddenly filled with the open master command channel, the echoes of a thousand communications bleeding through the signal to produce a cacophonous riot of distorted and unintelligible noise. Then, the channel cleared, and a single voice rang out.

'Masters and officers of the Damocles Gulf crusade fleet.' Lucian smiled, recognising instantly Admiral Jellaqua's proud and authoritative voice. Gurney might exercise control over the council, but out here, in the cold of space and the heat of battle, it was Jellaqua and the ships' masters that wielded true power. 'We have come a long way, all of us together, but we now stand at the point of decision. Soon, we shall do battle with the tau. Where previously these xenos have infiltrated our systems and skirmished with our patrols, now we shall truly show them the might of the Imperial Navy. We know not what we might face here, but I know this: every one of you, I have no doubt, will give his all in the service of our cause. Whatever they throw at us, we shall counter them, with fire and shell, with blood and honour, with hatred and bile!'

Lucian saw the men and women of the seconded Navy bridge crew smile, as he had a moment earlier. Though they maintained an appropriate formality and discipline, he saw in the eyes of each a heartfelt respect and affection for the admiral, a genuine love of their master and commander. Such a thing was rare indeed in a Navy that relied as much on indentured or outright press-ganged labour as it did on the noble lines from which these officers were drawn. Many a ship's master was a figure of hatred and fear amongst his crew, and admirals even more so, for they wielded, and frequently exercised, the power to condemn thousands of souls to cold oblivion with but a word.

'The order is given, loyal servants of the throne,' Jellaqua's voice continued. 'I charge each of you with this sacred duty. Bring the tau to heel. Show them the fire in your souls. Do so with nobility. Be glorious in victory, and show honour to the defeated. Do this, and live forever at the right hand of the Emperor!'

'And one more thing,' Jellaqua continued, just as Lucian was sure he must be done, 'good hunting.'

The bridge crew erupted in cheers, even old Batista, Lucian's ordnance officer, joining in the impromptu show of emotion. Lucian caught Batista's eye, and the old man appeared suddenly guilty. Lucian smiled, and the man nodded. It was not Lucian's place to share in the moment, but he welcomed it nonetheless. He realised with a heavy heart that it had been too long since such a crew had served on his bridge. Over the past decade he had become too used to a station occupied only by mute servitors.

'Now then!' Lucian said, raising his voice to restore order to his bridge. The bridge fell silent. 'Jellaqua might be the master of this fleet, but I am master of this vessel.'

Lucian watched with a glint in his eye as the crew returned to their stations, each with a face stricken with guilt, apart from old Batista, who was clearly well aware of what his captain was up to.

'If we're to get through this, we all need to understand one thing. I'm in charge here, and you do as I order, the instant I order it.'

Lucian looked to Mister Batista. 'My Master of Ordnance here will tell you what happens to bridge crews on the *Oceanid* when they fail to do as I say. Mister Batista?'

'They get turned into servitors,' Batista grinned.

'Aye,' Lucian said, nodding his thanks to Batista, pleased that the man had discerned his intention so well. 'And what type of servitor do they get turned into, Mister Batista.'

The ordnance officer's face twisted in grossly exaggerated concentration. 'Waste ingestion servitors, my lord.'

Very good, thought Lucian, very good indeed. 'So, any of you wishing to avoid such a fate had better ensure that your station is one hundred percent battle ready.'

Lucian leaned back in his command throne, enjoying the scene on the bridge before him. The Navy crew were all veterans, and set to their task with efficiency bred of endless hours of training. Outside, he watched as the *Blade of Woe*'s plasma drives flared to full power, and the massed banks of manoeuvring thrusters that lined her cliff-like flanks brought her to her final heading. Within minutes, the other capital vessels of the line were orienting themselves to Jellaqua's flagship, whilst the escort squadrons of smaller vessels moved to their own positions around the armada.

'Helm,' Lucian said. The bridge went silent in anticipation. 'You have your course laid in?'

'Aye, sir,' Ensign Ruuben replied, 'awaiting orders.'

Lucian grinned, letting the moment stretch out. Then, 'All power to mains, Mister Ruuben, ahead full at best speed.'

The Navy helmsman worked the mighty brass levers, opening up the plasma core and bringing the main drives to full output. As the power mounted, the deck plates beneath Lucian's feet vibrated jarringly, then settled as the drives stabilised. With a shudder that passed down the length of the entire vessel, the *Oceanid* came around, taking her position in the fleet.

'Incoming signal,' Ensign Katona said. 'It's the *Nomad*, sir. Patch through?'

'Please do, Mister Katona,' Lucian replied.

'Gerrit?' asked the unmistakable voice of sergeant Sarik of the White Scars.

'Go ahead, Sarik,' replied Lucian. He recalled the last time the *Oceanid* and the *Nomad* had fought side by side, and wondered whether Sarik would warn him off or welcome his presence in the line. You could never tell with Space Marines, Lucian thought.

'Lucian,' Sarik continued, 'I owe you a debt of honour for your aid at Sy'l'kell.'

Lucian was surprised to hear a Space Marine make such an admission. He allowed Sarik to continue.

'Should you find yourself in a position whereby I might repay that debt, you have but to ask, whether in the coming battle or at any point in the future.'

Lucian felt deeply honoured by Sarik's words, knowing that they bore the weight and authority not only of Sarik and his small band of Space Marines, but of the entire Chapter of White Scars.

'Brother Sergeant Sarik,' Lucian replied, 'you have my word that I shall do so.'

'Good then.' Lucian detected a shift in Sarik's tone, as if the Space Marine's mood had lifted. 'With that out of the way, we have some fighting to do.'

Lucian chuckled. 'Aye, Sarik. I'm with you. Just try not to find too much trouble!'

The bridge crew went silent at Lucian's words, but he felt an understanding with Brother Sergeant Sarik. He knew he could say such things, where other men might fear terrible retribution.

'Lucian,' Sarik's voice came back, rough humour evident in it, 'what you and I consider trouble might differ considerably.'

Lucian laughed out loud as Sarik terminated the communication. He saw the *Nomad* heave into view through the forward port, before the smaller craft veered across the *Oceanid*'s path and powered on towards the fleet's very spear tip.

'Holo,' Lucian ordered, and the holographic came to life as the bridge lights dimmed. The revolving globe of green light mapped out the immediate area of space, each of the fleet's capital vessels clearly visible as glowing white icons, the names of each projected nearby. Lucian saw that the fleet had spread out in a broad and shallow arrowhead formation. The escorts and destroyers screened the larger cruisers, which in turn were to protect the *Blade of Woe*. The rogue trader flotilla, the *Oceanid* at its fore, was positioned to the rear of Admiral Jellaqua's battleship, from where Lucian's vessels could respond to the situation as the battle unfolded.

Studying the fleet's disposition and composition, Lucian was convinced it would take a major tau presence in the system to challenge it. His only concern, which he had expressed to Jellaqua at the crusade's outset, was the fleet's comparative lack of attack craft. It could not be helped, the admiral had responded, explaining how the only carriers within three sectors were laid up for major refits, or otherwise engaged in long-range patrols. Lucian reached up to a data-slate suspended from the ceiling above his command throne. He depressed a control stud, and the slate's pict screen came to life. The text of Korvane's hasty report was displayed upon it.

Although he had done so a hundred times, Lucian read over the report once more. The system into which the fleet was attacking was host to a small tau outpost. Korvane's scout wing had located this presence, before coming under attack by a small force of tau patrol vessels. Korvane was convinced that no major tau forces were in the system, and before moving on he had recommended that the fleet move in to consolidate and stage for the next phase of the campaign. The council had agreed, deciding that a hammer blow assault upon the small tau presence would serve as a suitable demonstration in the fleet's power, and intentions. If the tau mounted a defence of the system, or decided to counterattack, then they would be drawn into a war that they were ill-prepared to fight, one mounted entirely on the Imperium's terms.

Lucian sighed inwardly as he read over his son's words. Korvane was certain that the system was ill defended, yet Lucian knew better than to rely on such assumptions. As far as he was concerned, the fleet was moving into hostile territory, and should be prepared for any eventuality. Fortunately, Admiral Jellaqua was of the same mind, hence the fleet's disposition as it ploughed on towards its target.

That target was the small satellite designated KX122/13, a moon of a larger, though reportedly unoccupied body. Even as Lucian watched, the planet appeared at the very edge of the globe, projected into the centre of the bridge by the holograph. Very little of its nature could be discerned at this range, and no enemy activity could be detected. The task of flushing out and engaging enemy vessels would go to the Space Marines of the various chapters that accompanied the fleet, from the Iron Hands in their strike cruiser

Fist of Light, to the varied escort and destroyer equivalents of the Scythes of the Emperor, Ultramarines and White Scars Chapters.

'Signal from 27th Squadron,' called out Ensign Katona. 'They have a sensor return on KX122/13. Standby.'

If all was well, thought Lucian, it should be the tau outpost that Korvane had reported. He watched the holograph as the three Sword class frigates of 27th Squadron peeled off from their position ahead of the line.

'Confirmed,' continued Ensign Katona. 'The 27th reports corroborate the scout wing's report. Fleet has ordered 27th to locate and engage tau outpost. Remainder of fleet to continue on present heading.'

'Well enough,' replied Lucian. 'If we continue on our current heading we'll pass by the satellite and skirt KX122. I want every station ready for anything.'

Lucian felt the old, familiar tension that had preceded every space battle he had ever been engaged in. The bluster was passed, and total concentration was required lest the enemy gain an advantage that proved fatal. He watched the holograph as 27th Squadron bore down upon the small moon, before disappearing amongst the background noise of the satellite and its parent world. He traced the fleet's course forward, guessing that Jellaqua intended a slingshot of KX122, a manoeuvre that would flush out any enemy vessels lurking in the lee of either stellar body. Reaching for the control panel mounted in the arm of his throne, Lucian adjusted the holograph, panning forward, zooming in on the area between the satellite and its parent. The image blurred for a moment, before resolving once more, focused on the two planets and the static laced area of space between them. Something itched at the back of Lucian's mind. It was a feeling he had experienced before in similar circumstances, and one he had long ago learned not to ignore.

'Comms, signal the *Blade of Woe*,' Lucian said, his suspicions mounting as the fleet ploughed on.

'Sorry, sir,' Ensign Katona replied, 'receiving a signal from 103rd Squadron.'

It took only a second for Lucian to locate 103rd on the holograph. The two Sword class frigates were running seventy-five thousand kilometres ahead of the fleet's spear tip. With 27th dispatched to deal with the outpost, 103rd was the leading escort squadron.

'They have a return, in stationary orbit around KX122. The telemetry's coming through now.'

'Main screen,' ordered Lucian. He had a dreadful sense of premonition as the pict-slate mounted above the forward portal came to life in an angry wash of static.

The screen showed the sensor returns gathered by the leading frigate of 103rd Squadron. Less than a thousand kilometres to the frigate's fore was a large, solid return that was all too familiar to Lucian.

'Ensign Naveen,' Lucian said, addressing the Navy officer who had taken over station ten, 'consult the archives. Compare that return to the tau defence station the fleet encountered at Sy'l'kell.'

'Working,' Naveen replied, reams of text scrolling up the data screen before him. Lucian waited impatiently, his eyes on the main viewer all the while. Though undoubtedly more use in a fight, these men of flesh and blood communed far less efficiently with the *Oceanid*'s data stacks than did the servitors he had become accustomed to.

'Well?' he said, resisting the urge to cross to the station and stand at the man's back.

'Data probe reporting, sir,' Naveen said, turning in his seat to face Lucian. 'It's the same return, sir, only the power output is off the scale.'

'I knew it,' Lucian spat. 'Comms, get me Jellaqua, now.'

Lucian watched the holograph as Ensign Katona spoke, opening a channel to the *Blade of Woe*. Even as he watched, he saw the lead capital ships veer towards the return. Fools, he cursed inwardly. 'Comms, where's that channel?'

'The admiral is otherwise engaged, my lord,' replied Ensign Katona. 'He is in closed conference with Cardinal Gurney.'

That explains it, thought Lucian. Gurney must have overridden Jellaqua's authority, somehow, causing him to launch an immediate attack on the station.

'I want a masters' conference, now!'

Lucian stood and paced the length of the bridge as he waited for the other ships' masters to come on line. It felt like hours, but within a few minutes the pict screens clustered around the bridge's ceiling were filled with the faces of the other captains.

'This had better be good, Lucian.' It was Captain Natalia of the *Duchess McIntyre*, and she appeared distracted. 'We have attack orders coming through.' A chorus of terse agreement went up from each of the other captains.

'Listen to me for the Emperor's sake!' Lucian snapped. 'That station is a major threat. We need to approach it with caution or someone's going to get hurt, badly.'

'That's simply not true.' It was Captain Joachim of the *Lord Cedalion*. It would be, Lucian mused, but he suppressed any response, for now. 'The station we faced at Sy'l'kell was only lightly armed. We can take this one on without any danger. To suggest otherwise is to admit that the tau are superior to us, and that borders on treason.'

'It might appear the same to you,' Lucian responded, forcing himself not to rise to Joachim's insult, 'but I've faced the tau in ship-to-ship combat before, and I recognise the signature of their weapons. I'm telling you, that station is upgunned.'

Lucian looked to the screen bearing Joachim's image, only to see that the captain had cut the audio and was speaking to a subordinate. He looked to the other ships' masters, to see that several were obviously listening in on some other channel.

'Lucian,' Natalia began, 'I'm sorry. We have to...'

The pict-slates suddenly died, flickering to life again moments later. The distorted image resolved slowly, until Lucian saw what he had dreaded. It was Cardinal Gurney, and behind him stood Inquisitor Grand and Admiral Jellaqua. The trio stood on the command deck of the *Blade of Woe*, the flagship's massive bridge a hive of activity in the background.

'This is Cardinal Gurney and these are my orders.' Lucian stood stunned as the image was repeated across a dozen pict screens. 'The fleet will engage the xenos station immediately.'

Lucian could no longer restrain himself. 'By whose authority do you presume to make such an order?'

The cardinal's face took on a twisted leer. Lucian made a fist, imagining what he'd do to that face, were they in the same room. Gurney stepped aside to afford a full view of the inquisitor standing behind him. For the first time to date, Grand was wearing his inquisitorial rosette, a large red seal emblazoned with the 'I' of the Emperor's Inquisition. Grand said not a word; he had no need to.

So, thought Lucian, Grand had finally decided to exercise the full extent of his power as an inquisitor. Lucian had known he would do so at some point, when he felt the circumstances matched some agenda known only to him, and probably to Gurney. No doubt the old bastard had been waiting for this moment for weeks, and had timed it to do the maximum damage to his enemies' influence and credibility. Lucian looked to Admiral Jellaqua, seeing from his expression that he felt as Lucian did. Lucian knew that the admiral could not countermand the inquisitor's authority, and although Lucian's position as a rogue trader theoretically made him the inquisitor's peer, that relied entirely on the circumstances of any dispute. No, there was no possible way Lucian could fight this, not here, not now.

'All commands,' Gurney continued, 'will acknowledge receipt of this order.' The cardinal's face bore the expression of one entirely convinced that he had won. Lucian swore that the cardinal would pay for this. At some point in the future, perhaps when the inquisitor was no longer around to provide his support, Gurney would pay.

Lucian listened as each of the ships' masters and squadron commanders acknowledged the order. Most did so in clipped tones. When it was Lucian's turn to respond, he allowed a long, tense silence to precede his answer.

'Acknowledged,' he said, hating the cardinal all the more for the expression of victory that passed across his face as Lucian gave his response.

'New heading coming through, sir,' said Ensign Ruuben. 'We're to follow the fleet in to engage the station.'

'Do so,' Lucian ordered, his mood black. 'Ensign Sumiko?' The woman stationed at the shields station turned as her name was spoken. 'I want the shields ready at a moment's notice. If, or when that station opens up on us, I'm going to need one hundred percent output, no matter the drain, do you understand?'

'I understand, sir. I've operated this mark of projector before. I know how to get the best of her.'

Lucian smiled, though his mood did not lift. 'Well enough. Helm, take us in.'

The next hour felt like an impossible span of time to Lucian. He watched the holograph as the fleet closed on the tau station, looking for any sign of the attack he knew must surely come. If only the fleet had a strong enough complement of attack craft, he cursed. He was sure that one of the capital vessels would pay the price for Gurney's pride, when a fighter attack ahead of the main line might have crippled the station's weapons before they could cause the fleet any damage. As the spear tip of the fleet passed the five hundred kilometre mark, Lucian saw the energy spike he had anticipated. He looked to the holograph, and spat a colourful blasphemy when he saw which of the fleet's vessels was to the fore.

'Sarik!' He surged to his feet as Ensign Katona patched him through to the *Nomad*.

'I see it, Lucian,' said the Space Marine sergeant. 'I'm not as wet behind the ears as you seem to think, rogue trader, and I don't need warning twice. *Nomad* out.'

Coming to the viewing port, Lucian watched as the distant speck of light that he knew to be the *Nomad* altered its course sharply to starboard. A second later, a brief, blue light flashed for an instant and was gone, its source invisible at this range.

'The enemy has opened fire,' Batista called out.

'General quarters,' said Lucian, calm, despite what he knew was coming.

'Disposition orders coming in, sir,' called out Ensign Katona over the wail of the alert klaxon. 'The *Honour of Damlass* is being ordered to engage.'

'She'll be savaged,' Lucian snarled, knowing he had no time to intervene.

'Reading a second spike,' Batista called out.

Lucian braced himself against the bulkhead, though he knew that *Oceanid* was unlikely to be the target of the second shot.

A second wink of blue light appeared in the darkness up ahead. An instant later, a bright spark appeared as the ultra high velocity projectile struck its target.

'*Honour of Damlass* hit!' Batista said calmly. 'Damage reports coming in. Main shield array out of action.'

'Fleet are ordering the *Honour* to withdraw,' Katona said. Seeing a third flash of light flaring against the blackness, Lucian knew that it was too late. An instant later and a second explosion blossomed, describing the fate of the *Honour of Damlass* better than any damage report ever could. Even from this distance, Lucian saw the light of the *Honour*'s main drives gutter and die, leaving her crippled and doomed.

'We have to do something,' Lucian spat. He turned from the viewing port and strode across to his command throne.

'Signal Jellaqua, in person.'

'Aye sir,' Katona replied, understanding the order fully. 'Channel open.'

'Gerrit?' Admiral Jellaqua's voice filled the bridge, the channel flooded with distortion and crackles. 'Gerrit, I'm somewhat busy, make this quick.'

'Admiral,' Lucian said, 'I know you have your orders, but you have to break off the attack on the station. At least send in the escorts first, you know the cruisers are sitting targets.'

'I agree, Lucian, but I must... Standby...'

The channel fell abruptly silent. Lucian looked quickly around at the various readouts, hoping to discern the cause of the interruption. His blood ran cold as he looked to the holograph. There, at the very edge of the three dimensional projection, was a cluster of sensor returns, edging out from the lee of KX122.

'Jellaqua! You have to redeploy the fleet, right now. If those cruisers outflank us, we're all done for.'

'Agreed,' replied the admiral. 'I'm switching to fleetwide command broadcast.' The channel was filled with distorted comms chatter, followed by a burst of angry machine noise. Then the signal stabilised and the admiral's voice rang out, this time addressing the captains of each vessel in the line.

'All commands, this is *Blade of Woe*. We have multiple contacts closing from zero-zero seven two nine. All main line capital vessels will move to engage immediately. All escort squadrons to close on tau station and silence it. Form up on my lead and good hunting.'

'You heard the man,' said Lucian. 'Helm, bring us around on the *Blade* and match her speed. Echelon to port, two kilometres by fifty.'

'Aye, sir,' responded Ruuben, hauling on the *Oceanid*'s wheel. Lucian felt the gravity fluctuate as the vessel was subjected to the forces put into play by the change of heading. His head was forced back into the command throne for an instant, and he looked to station nine, one of the few manned by a servitor.

'Grav, I want those compensators on-line, or so help me I'll...'

He let the threat tail off. It was pointless threatening the servitor, for it had no independent will and felt no emotion. Besides, he was more intent on studying the holograph and its representation of the unfolding battle. The fleet was slowly moving to its new heading, though Lucian's practiced eye saw immediately that the arrow head formation was losing its former cohesion, the vessels becoming strung out in a long line, with the *Oceanid*, the *Rosetta* and the *Fairlight* at its centre. It felt to Lucian that the manoeuvre was taking far too long to complete, the tau vessels closing on them all the while.

They were closing on a single vessel that had drifted too far ahead of the formation. The Dauntless class cruiser the *Regent Lakshimbal* was isolated at what had previously been the extreme port flank, but was now the head of the line of vessels moving to intercept the tau. With no escort squadrons to picket the fleet's perimeter, the cruiser found the enemy bearing right down upon her.

As the range between the two fleets closed, the *Oceanid*'s sensors began to gather more data on the enemy vessels. There were eleven of them, and as the readings flooded across the pict screens above his command throne, Lucian sought out the configurations he had observed in his previous encounters.

He did not find them. At his previous battles against the tau, he had faced huge, lumbering starships with modular bays underslung beneath a central spine. He had come to discern that these bays might be swapped out for weapons, cargo or carrier duties, but that was not what he was seeing here. Instead of the comparatively vulnerable configuration encounter before, these vessels were smaller, yet evidently intended to carry out a far more aggressive role in ship-to-ship combat. Instead of a single weapons battery mounted to the fore, these bore multiple batteries. Lucian's professional eye saw immediately how the interlocking field of fire of each battery might combine with devastating effect. Even as he watched, he knew that the *Regent* was perilously close to entering those fields of fire.

'Full power to mains!' Lucian bellowed. 'Break formation if you have to, Mister Ruubens.'

'Aye, sir,' the helmsman called back as the roar of the *Oceanid*'s main drives was transmitted her entire length. We can make it, Lucian thought, if only the *Regent* can hold out against the first tau volley.

As Lucian's vessel swung gracefully to port, breaking formation with the main battle line, a mournful wail went up from somewhere deep in her bowels.

'What the hell was that?' Lucian spat. 'Report!'

'It's drive three, my lord,' responded Ruuben, even as he struggled with the great wheel in an effort to maintain the *Oceanid*'s heading. 'Something's wrong with...'

'Not now!' Lucian cursed. Drive three had been a concern for several years, but had never failed him when actually needed. He had delayed an overhaul, knowing that the Arcadius could ill-afford such an extravagant expense, and had intended to attend to the matter after the crusade had sufficiently lined his pockets.

Lucian's mind raced as he looked helplessly on at the *Regent Lakshimbal* as the tau vessel bore down upon her. 'Shut drive three down.'

'Sir?' replied Ensign Ruuben.

'I said shut it down, Emperor damn it! I want a full purge cycle, right now!'

'Aye sir,' replied Ruuben, before relaying Lucian's orders to the drive stations to the *Oceanid*'s aft.

Even as he watched, Lucian saw that the tau were in range of the *Regent*. He knew from bitter experience that the hyper velocity projectile weapons utilised by such vessels would outrange anything a Dauntless carried. Evidently, the captain of the *Regent* saw this too, for he brought his light cruiser around to face her armoured prow towards the enemy, and to present as small a target as possible against the inevitable salvo.

As the range closed, Lucian saw that the *Regent* had raised her shields. He knew the ship's master would be channelling every available reserve into the shields, for he would not be able to return fire until the tau vessels were within range of his forward lance batteries.

'The foremost tau vessel is powering up for a shot!' Batista called out, as Lucian had known he would.

Once more, the familiar wink of blue light appeared, marking the launching of one of the tau's projectile weapons. Though he knew he was not the target, Lucian gripped the arms of the command throne nonetheless. An instant later, and the attack struck the *Regent* square across the frontal shield arc, unleashing a blinding explosion as the shields converted the attack to energy and bled it off into space.

'She's holding!' Batista said. 'Shields maximal. Second shot incoming.'

This time, Lucian saw several of the tau vessel's weapons batteries open fire, and he realised that the first attack had been nothing more than a ranging shot. The *Regent* was struck a glancing blow across her armoured prow, and it was immediately evident that the shields had not absorbed the full force of the projectiles. A mighty wound was gauged along the starboard flank of the *Regent*'s prow, raging fires bursting forth and roiling black clouds billowing out into space.

'Ruuben?' Lucian called. 'What's the status of drive three?'

The helmsman took but an instant to consult a data-slate mounted above his station. 'Purge cycle at fifty percent, my lord.'

'Not good enough.' Lucian knew that the *Regent Lakshimbal* was dead if she continued to take the punishment being meted out by the tau. 'Push it to maximum, right now.'

Lucian saw Ruuben turn as if to voice an objection, but the helmsman evidently thought the better of it when he saw the look in Lucian's eye. Lucian knew the risks of forcing the plasma drive's purge cycle, but he was prepared to take that risk, however slim, if he might save the *Regent*.

Even as he watched, Lucian saw that the *Regent Lakshimbal* was doomed. Rising to his feet and crossing to the forward portal, he saw a second and third tau vessel close upon the stricken light cruiser. The range had closed, however, allowing the *Regent* the dignity of putting up a fight. The Dauntless class vessel's prow mounted lances spat incandescent death at the first tau starship, scoring a solid hit against its rear section. Lucian punched the air in bitter celebration, savouring the heroic act even as he knew the tau ship's shields had withstood the blow.

'Come on, Mister Ruuben,' Lucian growled.

'Ninety, sir.'

The second and third tau starships were moving to envelop the *Regent*, but in so doing, the tau showed the relative inexperience that Lucian had noted on previous occasions. The *Regent* wasted no time in punishing the xenos for their mistake, both her starboard and port weapons batteries unleashing a fearsome broadside at the approaching enemies. The tau, it appeared to Lucian, were caught entirely unawares, neither vessel managing so much as to offer its prow to the *Regent* so as to present as small a target as possible.

Lucian punched the bulkhead in savage jubilation as both broadsides struck home. He had never seen such a thing, and doubtless never would again, for surely the tau must learn from such an error. Both tau vessels were entirely enveloped in flame and smoke, and Lucian could tell right away that the *Regent*'s attacks had done significant damage, for flaming debris spread outward from the third vessel in an ever-expanding circle. Though not dead, Lucian was quite certain that the ship would be out of the fight, for a time at least.

Then, the third vessel emerged from the smoke and flame that had engulfed it. It edged slowly and gracefully through the debris of its wounds, appearing to Lucian to have taken on the aspect of some oceanic predator from prehistory, closing on the blood scent of its prey. The ship was scarred and pitted, greasy smoke and flame trailing from a dozen scars rent across its armoured flank. The formally pristine white hull was blackened and scorched, but Lucian could see that its weapons batteries were still all too operational. Lucian saw that the tau had just learned a valuable lesson in the nature of the galaxy, and one he doubted they would fail to act upon.

'Make it quick,' he whispered.

As it cleared the smoke and debris of the *Regent*'s broadside, the tau vessel opened fire once more. Blue flashes marked the discharge of its hyper velocity weapons, each propelling an indiscernibly small, but nigh impossibly dense projectile across space. Accelerated to an unbelievable speed, the projectile penetrated the *Regent*'s shields, unleashing a blinding storm of arc lightning.

Lucian winced, expecting a catastrophic explosion, but none came. Instead, the *Regent* unleashed a second broadside, the entire length of its mid-section obscured as the superheavy shells of its weapons batteries were flung across space.

The second broadside was just as unanticipated as the first had been, the tau caught unawares by a foe they thought dead. The tau vessel was wracked by mighty explosions, some blossoming across its shields and others penetrating them to strike its superstructure. The tau vessel veered drunkenly to port, and, through the debris and flame, Lucian made out that its drive section was aflame, ghostly plasma fire dancing across its rapidly melting armour.

Then, disaster.

CHAPTER FIFTEEN

The *Regent Lakshimbal* appeared to Lucian to shudder, faltering in her forward motion as she slewed about her central axis. He could see immediately that something had gone terribly amiss and that the shot that had struck her minutes before must have caused some unseen, yet fatal wound.

Lucian watched as the *Regent*'s mid-section buckled. He could scarcely believe his eyes as he saw the dying light cruiser fold around its spine, its thickly armoured outer hull cracking wide open. Debris burst from the great rent in an explosion of escaping gases. Though Lucian could not make out the details from this distance, he knew that hundreds of men were dying a cold, desperate death even as he looked on.

Lucian slammed his fist into the armoured portal. 'Status!'

'Almost there, sir,' replied Ruuben, calm despite the edge of threat that Lucian had put into the simple request.

Unable to watch as the *Regent Lakshimbal* spewed her guts into space, Lucian crossed to his command throne and threw himself down into it.

'Initiate purge cycle, Mister Ruuben, and hold her steady.'

The helmsman turned to meet Lucian's eye, and then nodded his understanding. Bracing himself against the mighty ship's wheel, Ruuben made a series of adjustments to the helm and then communicated Lucian's order to the enginarium.

Lucian too took the opportunity to brace himself, gripping the arms of his command throne against the shock he knew was about to overtake his vessel. He was too late to save the *Regent*, that much was obvious, but by the Emperor, he would make the tau starship pay for what it had done.

'Purge in ten...' called the helmsman.

'Now is fine, Mister Ruuben!' Lucian growled back.

Without answering, Helmsman Ruuben hauled back on a mighty, floor-mounted lever. For a moment, it appeared to Lucian that nothing would happen. Then, he felt a subsonic trembling rise up from the deck plate, growing in intensity until every surface on the bridge was vibrating violently. Lucian gripped the arms of the command throne still tighter as the lights gave out, the only illumination provided by rapidly flashing pict screens.

Then, these also died and the vibrating subsided in an instant. The *Oceanid* fell utterly, deathly silent. Lucian's fists dug into the fabric of his throne and he closed his eyes tight.

Drive three thundered into life, the nigh seismic force of its sudden reawakening transmitted like a quake throughout the entire length of the vessel. An instant later, the other three drives powered up, and then the bridge lights, and with them all of the ship's systems were restored.

All except the *Oceanid*'s cogitator.

'Let's see how good you really are, Mister Ruuben!' Lucian yelled. He was aware that an edge of mania had entered his voice, though he believed he was entitled to it. No sane man would attempt what he had just ordered.

Even from the fore-mounted bridge, Lucian could hear the roar of the *Oceanid*'s mighty plasma drives transmitted through the ship's structure. As they reached a crescendo, the vessel began to edge forward, riding the wave of the tremendous momentum generated by the ad hoc purging of drive three. Ruuben was struggling at the helm, putting all of his strength into holding the great ship's wheel on the course Lucian had ordered.

Still the myriad clusters of pict screens and data viewers around the bridge remained black. The *Oceanid* was for the moment running with no form of guidance or regulation from the massive cogitator banks secreted in her heart. Lucian knew that she could not survive for long without them, and neither could Mister Ruuben control the helm in anything other than a cursory fashion.

'Lieutenant Davriel,' Lucian said, addressing the Navy officer overseeing the cogitator banks at station five. The man appeared at least as much a machine as one of the servitors who had crewed Lucian's bridge until so recently, a cluster of data cables writhing around the back of his shaven head to interface directly with the *Oceanid*'s cogitation matrix.

Davriel's eyes had been closed shut as if he was in deep concentration, yet they snapped open the instant Lucian spoke his name.

'My lord,' the officer responded in a lilting whisper quite at odds with his appearance, 'I am communing with the custodians.'

Lucian knew that Davriel referred to the... creatures that maintained the *Oceanid*'s huge crystal datastacks. Each had once been a tech-priest of the Adeptus Mechanicus, who had, upon transcending the mental frailties of the organic body into which he was born, merged his consciousness with the Omnissiah, shedding his physical form to attain apotheosis with the Machine God. What was left behind once the tech-priest had merged his knowledge and experience with that of all his predecessors was a soulless husk. The Machine Cult used them to tend such cogitators as controlled the functions of the *Oceanid*. Davriel's station communicated with them.

'How long?' Lucian demanded.

'Primary functions?' Davriel asked, a damned stupid question in Lucian's opinion.

'Any bloody functions,' Lucian retorted. 'Helm control might be useful!'

'Aye, sir,' replied Davriel, apparently unflustered in the face of Lucian's wrath. Perhaps he wasn't so bad, Lucian thought.

Before Lucian could press the issue, the bridge was flooded with incandescent fury. Lucian snapped his head away from the forward portal, throwing an arm across his face in an effort to stave off the impossibly bright, pure white light. He clamped his eyes tight shut, and then dared to withdraw his arm, knowing that if the light remained he would see it through the membrane of his eyelids. Guessing it was safe to open his eyes, he saw that the portal had dimmed, an instant too late as ever, protecting the bridge crew from the worst of the inferno raging where once the dying *Regent Lakshimbal* had floundered.

Lucian was stunned. He had seen the *Regent*'s doom even

before the terrible damage inflicted by the tau's last attack had been revealed, but he had not anticipated the catastrophic fate that had engulfed her. He guessed that it was some form of reactor collapse, though he suspected none would ever know for sure, for scant evidence would be left to sift through.

Knowing the luxury of mourning must be deferred, Lucian attempted to get a hold of the events unfolding around him. He had no course data, and no holograph to consult, but he could see with his own eyes that the *Oceanid* was being propelled by the force of the drive purge straight towards the tau vessel that had murdered the *Regent*.

'Mister Ruuben,' Lucian said, addressing the helmsman as he wrestled with the ship's wheel, 'hold as steady as you can. I don't expect miracles, but I want to pass that tau bastard at point blank. I'm going to make them hurt.'

'Aye, my lord,' snarled back the helmsman. 'How about two thousand?'

Lucian smiled savagely, embracing the atavistic brutality of the battle. 'Give me two thousand metres, Mister Ruuben, and we'll have them stone dead.'

'Two thousand it is then, sir,' Ruuben replied, hauling upon the ship's wheel to bring the *Oceanid* about on her new heading. Without the cogitation banks to aid the manoeuvre, Ruuben was steering her unaided, in a virtuoso display of spacemanship.

'Mister Davrial,' Lucian said, turning to address the officer at station five, 'your turn to excel. Don't let me down.'

'Sub systems reawakening, sir. I'm prioritising helm, fire control and shields.'

'How long?'

'Minutes, my lord, I assure you.'

Lucian nodded, and leaned back in his throne. He took a deep breath as he looked around the bridge for any sign of the cogitation banks coming back on-line. Individual lights blinked where moments before consoles were dark, and quite suddenly every pict screen on the bridge burst into bright static. After another minute, the bridge was filled with the familiar sound of comms traffic as the many stations around the vessel re-established contact with one another. Many would have had no clue as to what was occurring.

Perhaps such ignorance was bliss, thought Lucian, considering what still had to happen for the coming manoeuvre to succeed.

Still lacking the bridge holograph, Lucian looked through the forward portal to make an estimation of the distance the *Oceanid* still had to close before she would pass the tau starship. Less than eleven kilometres, he judged, give or take a couple of metres.

'Helm function returning!' Mister Ruuben called out, relief evident in his voice.

'My commendations, Mister Davriel,' said Lucian, determined not express his own feelings of relief. Looking towards the tau ship as it manoeuvred around the wreckage of the *Regent*, he realised that he had a major decision to make, and he would have less than ten minutes in which to make it: shields or fire control?

If he raised shields before restoring fire control, the *Oceanid* would survive anything the tau vessel might throw at her as she passed, but with the cogitators off-line and unable to provide accurate fire control, that pass might be in vain. He could order a broadside without the aid of fire control, but even at two thousand metres, an impossibly close range at which to engage another vessel in ship-to-ship combat, he could not count on making his shots count. Unless...

'Mister Ruuben,' Lucian said, 'I need five hundred metres.' He leaned forward as the helmsman turned around and regarded him with ill-concealed incredulity. 'Can you give me five hundred metres?'

The bridge chatter fell silent, the tau vessel looming all the larger in the forward portal.

'Aye, sir,' Ruubens nodded, and then grinned like a madman, 'five hundred metres it is!'

'Emperor bless mad old spacers,' Lucian said. 'Mister Davriel, concentrate on the starboard shield projectors.'

Lucian did not wait for confirmation that his order would be enacted. He knew it would, for this new bridge crew was competent and professional, and evidently well drilled in following orders under pressure. Instead, he concentrated upon the tau vessel as the range closed.

The enemy starship was coming about. It had seen its danger then, Lucian thought. The tau must surely understand, by now, the danger an Imperial ship of the line posed at close range, where it could unleash the most fearsome of broadsides. He could see that the tau were moving to present their prow towards the *Oceanid*, thereby offering as small a target as possible to the coming attack. They were learning fast.

Lucian saw another threat as the distance closed. This new class of tau vessel with its multiple weapons batteries could present a threat from almost any angle. As the two vessel, neared one another, he could make out the details of his foe. Foremost amongst those details were the weapons turrets mounted across the forward dorsal section, turrets that were swivelling towards the *Oceanid* even as he watched, locking those devastatingly powerful hyper velocity weapons onto her.

'Mister Davriel?' Lucian snarled, not taking his eyes from the turrets.

'One minute, sir, and counting. Primary shield communion at fifty percent.'

'Work fast,' Lucian said. The turrets had the *Oceanid* in their sights. From previous experience, he knew they would fire at any moment.

'Energy spike!' yelled Mister Batista, the ordnance officer. 'Brace for impact!'

Lucian glanced across to the shields officer, but saw that Mister Davriel would not have the projectors on-line before the first shot was fired.

'Mister Ruuben, thirty to starboard!' Lucian shouted.

'Hard to starboard, aye sir!' yelled back the helmsman, bracing his feet on the deck and putting his entire weight into the ship's wheel.

The forward portal was enveloped in a blue flash, and Lucian gripped his throne all the tighter. The *Oceanid* veered hard to starboard, bringing her on a near collision course with the tau vessel. An instant later and the hyper velocity projectile struck the *Oceanid*. Lucian felt the attack strike his vessel as her armoured flanks were gouged savagely, a terrible rending sound echoing down the companionways, followed a moment later by the wailing of emergency sirens.

'Hull breach, sector seven-seven delta!' called out the Navy officer seconded to the operations station. 'Damage control parties dispatched.'

Lucian doubted whether the damage would be limited to the breach. He knew he would only get one chance at this.

'Mister Batista,' he said, addressing his ordnance chief, 'prepare a broadside. All starboard ports. Manual offset, twelve degrees.'

'Understood, my lord,' Batista replied. Of all his remaining crew, Lucian trusted his ordnance chief. Batista would ensure that the broadside struck home. If he did not, this fight would be over all too soon.

'Energy spike!' yelled Batista. 'Brace!'

'Shields up!' announced Davriel.

'Fire,' growled Lucian.

The *Oceanid* rocked violently as the broadside was fired. The superheavy shells crossed the short distance between the two vessels and slammed home with devastating effect. Fire erupted across the tau starship's flank, shearing off a vast portion of her drive section. The damage caused an instant destabilisation in the enemy's handling, and Lucian watched as his foe was thrown off course, beginning a drunken slew about its own axis.

Yet, despite the massive wounds inflicted upon her, it was obvious to Lucian that the tau vessel was determined to give a good account of itself. As he watched, the turrets mounted across its dorsal section swivelled as one, tracking the *Oceanid* with unerring stability, even as the tau starship came almost full about with the violence of its destabilised drives.

'Brace!' called Batista. Lucian held his breath.

Once more, the forward portal was flooded with the blue light of the tau weapons batteries discharging. At such short range, the impact came nigh instantaneously, yet to Lucian's enormous relief the newly raised shields held, the incredible energy of the projectiles being translated into raging energies that roiled out into space, but which caused no harm to the *Oceanid*.

Ruuben's previous manoeuvre, combined with the drastic change in the tau vessel's course following the damage inflicted upon its drive, left the *Oceanid* bearing right down on her. The tau vessel passed directly across the forward portal, its entire starboard drive section burning. As the flaming hull filled the entire portal, the tau vessel impossibly close, Lucian saw that the two ships were set to collide, and there was nothing he could do to avoid it.

'Full power, Mister Ruuben,' he ordered. 'All forward. Shunt her aside.'

It was the only way, though Emperor only knew what damage it would inflict upon his beloved vessel. The armoured sides of the tau vessel reared ahead, flames dancing across its pitted and scarred surface. Then, the prow of the *Oceanid* ground into the tau starship's side and a dreadful shudder was transmitted the length of Lucian's ship. A moment later and a terrible grinding roar filled the *Oceanid*, the bridge lights dying, and then coming back to life as the ship's reawakened cogitation banks re-routed the power conduits that fed them.

The fiery drive section of the tau ship ground across the upper hull of the *Oceanid*, the vessel so close that the flames licking its surface washed over the forward portal. An explosion to the fore shook the bridge crew, bright sparks exploding from consoles as their operators dived for safety.

'Keep going, Mister Ruuben!' bellowed Lucian over the deafening roar of grinding metal. He could not tell whether or not the helmsman had heard his order, but felt the *Oceanid*'s drives pour yet more power into the manoeuvre.

Raging flame and roiling black smoke entirely obscured the view through the portal. The bridge lights died once more and all was plunged into a stark darkness punctuated only by the guttering flames, and the small explosions of sparks that still spat from consoles. Yet another grinding quake shuddered through the vessel, and Lucian felt the *Oceanid* lurch upwards. Sweat poured from his brow and his heart pounded in his chest. If this didn't work, he thought, it would be a damn stupid way for the Arcadius dynasty to end.

The two vessels parted as the *Oceanid*'s drives swept across the tau starship's prow, propelling them apart and inflicting hideous damage in the process. The smoke and flame obscuring the view ahead parted.

What Lucian saw made him punch the arm of his command throne in celebration.

The Imperial Navy's battle line had followed Lucian in as he had drawn off the lead tau starship, which, even now, spun drunkenly away from the battle. Jellaqua's cruisers were trading devastating volleys against the tau ships, who appeared hard-pressed to keep them at bay. The entire area of space ahead was lit blue with the discharge of the tau's weapons, and fiery orange with the shells and torpedoes of the Imperial Navy's. Ships burned and men and aliens alike died as the vessels of each fleet sought to wreak nothing less than bloody slaughter upon one another.

'Comms on-line!' Katona announced. Lucian saw that the man's face was badly burned down his left side; evidently the man had refused to leave his station even while it burned, and he had restored the *Oceanid*'s communications system even while fighting the fire that had burned him. 'Incoming transmission on fleet wide band.'

'Thank you, Mister Katona,' Lucian said, nodding to the man, determining to reward each of the bridge's crew, assuming they all lived through this battle. 'Patch it through.'

'Imperial warships...' Lucian smiled as he recognised the voice of Admiral Jellaqua. 'The *Oceanid*'s unusual manoeuvre has taken the bastards by surprise! We have a new contact in amongst the escorts, and I am taking the *Blade of Woe* in to deal with it. Finish them off! In the name of the Emperor and the Imperium, give them hell!'

The bridge crew cheered, and this time Lucian joined them. As the last of the *Oceanid*'s cogitation banks came back on-line, the holograph spluttered to life at the centre of the bridge. Lucian leaned forward to study the unfolding battle, and smiled.

'Ordnance,' he said, 'I want every gun loaded and ready for firing. Shields, full power to frontal arc. Helm?

'Helm standing by, my lord.'

'We're going in.'

Brielle stood upon the observation deck of the tau vessel the *Dal'yth Il'Fannor O'kray*. The circular chamber was ringed with a single viewing window, and at its centre was projected a blue-tinged, three-dimensional representation of the battle unfolding around the nearby world. A dozen tau stood around the projection, conversing quietly and nodding as they watched events unfold.

Her heart raced as she saw an Imperial Navy vessel, a light cruiser, possibly a Dauntless by its displacement and configuration, die violently, its overloaded plasma reactor creating a new sun for an instant, which rapidly died to leave nothing but atoms to mark the ship's grave. The tau envoy she had met upon Dal'yth nodded to her at the ship's passing, quietly marking the victory. She nodded back, yet she raged inside.

The tau expected her to celebrate with them, but she could not.

As she watched, the defence station that had wrought such havoc in the early stages of the battle was overwhelmed by the Imperium's escort squadrons. Then, a senior tau of what they called the Air Caste, those responsible for the operation of the tau's fleet, issued an order. A mighty vessel, called a warsphere, belonging, she was told, to a subject race of the tau called the kroot, emerged from behind the planet and ploughed right into the escorts' formation. Though its weapons were close ranged, the warsphere took a fearsome toll amongst the far smaller escorts, before the Imperium's largest warship, undoubtedly the *Blade of Woe*, circled back and destroyed it with relative ease.

'They're winning,' she said, more to herself than to anyone around her. 'The Imperium is winning.'

'My lady,' replied Naal, standing at her shoulder, 'have no fear.'

Brielle turned her back on the projection and looked out into the blackness of space. Although the battle was too distant to see in any detail, pinprick sparks blossomed amongst the stars, each no doubt marking the passing of a thousand needlessly expended lives. What if one of those tiny lights was the death of the *Fairlight*? What if it were the *Oceanid* or the *Rosetta*? Then she would truly be alone, set adrift from all that had made her what she was.

She was a child of the Arcadius dynasty. She was born to explore and to conquer the dark regions that lay beyond the borders of the Imperium. She was not, she saw with sudden clarity, born to be some turncoat ambassador, and she would not act out such a role for the tau or for anyone else.

'My lady?' Naal asked, his voice low and urgent. 'The envoys, my lady. They wish that you should witness the fleet pull back before the next phase is implemented. And when you have, they will wish to have an answer to their proposal.'

Rage welled up inside her, but she beat it down savagely before turning to face the gathered tau. Let them gloat over their small victory, she thought. It can't possibly last. That would be her answer to their damned proposal.

Lucian sat alone in his stateroom, the lights down, a glass of strong liquor in his hand. They had won, he brooded, but at a terrible cost: four cruisers lost in a single battle. The names would be entered into the rolls of honour, but Lucian knew the *Regent Lakshimbal*, the *Centaur*, the *Niobe* and the *Lord Cedalion* would be missed grievously in the coming battles. The *Niobe* at least had been afforded the unusual luxury in space combat of its crew having time to escape, for the damage done to her had not been initially fatal. It was only three hours later, once the tau had finally disengaged, that the vessel's damaged plasma relays had lost containment and Captain Joachim had ordered his ship abandoned. Another hour later and the *Niobe*'s reactor had gone critical, engulfing her and those crew who had not escaped in roiling plasma. Lucian had not been surprised to learn that Captain Joachim had survived the death of his cruiser; he had not expected the man to be the last off of his vessel.

In addition to the four capital ships, the fleet had lost fourteen escorts, with another two almost certainly damaged beyond the fleet's capacity to repair them in space. The battle had been a victory, Jellaqua had announced, but it was obvious the Imperium could scarcely afford another such win.

Lucian could not guess how many lives had been lost, and this was only the first engagement in the crusade's mission. Downing the contents of his glass in one gulp, Lucian cursed the cardinal and his faction to the depths of the warp. If only the council had not been swayed by Gurney's rantings.

A chime sounded at the door to Lucian's chambers.

'Enter,' he growled.

The wheel at the door's centre spun, before it swung inward on creaking joints. A junior officer stepped through and saluted smartly.

'Report,' Lucian ordered.

'The pathfinder wing, sir...' Lucian slammed his glass down on the table beside his chair. 'We have them on the rangers.'

* * *

The holograph revolved slowly before Lucian. The augurs had picked up three returns, which even now were speeding towards the fleet at high speed. Both the *Oceanid* and the *Blade of Woe* had been hailing the three small scout vessels continuously for thirty minutes, but their long-range communications systems must have been down, for no signal was received back.

'Coming into range now, my lord,' announced Katona. 'Hailing on all short range channels.'

Lucian nodded, his heart pounding. If only three scout vessels of the elite pathfinders had returned from their mission, they must have run into serious trouble, for they were trained and equipped to escape enemy contact, not to seek it out. The thought that he might have lost a second child was too awful to consider, and so Lucian offered up a silent prayer that Korvane would be returned safely to him.

'Pict signal on screen now,' Katona said.

The main screen above the forward portal came to life. At first the signal was little more than static, but after a minute, the picture became more distinct. It was the small, cramped bridge of the lead scout vessel. The ship must have suffered terrible damage, for the small cockpit was wreathed in smoke, the figure sitting at the command station barely visible.

Then, the smoke parted as that figure waved his arm to clear it. Lucian knew blessed relief as he saw that it was Korvane.

'Son!' Lucian said. 'Thank the Emperor. What happened?'

'Father?' Korvane replied, his voice hoarse; the effects of the smoke, Lucian supposed. 'Father, it's you.'

'What is it, Korvane? Come aboard immediately.'

'No, father, wait.' Korvane reached across to his console and flipped a switch.

'We're on fleet wide,' Katona announced. Lucian knew that what Korvane was about to say would be heard upon the bridge of every vessel in the crusade fleet.

'I can see,' he said, before pausing to cough violently. 'I can see that a great victory has been won here this day, though not without a price, I judge.'

'Yes,' Lucian replied. 'The action cost us dear, but the tau are beaten back.'

'No,' Korvane answered, coughing once more, 'they are not beaten back. They have regrouped. The fourth body in this system is a major centre of population. We fought a small patrol and trailed the survivors home. We monitored their comms traffic. We couldn't translate anything, but we measured the signals and their sources.'

Lucian's blood ran cold. 'Go on.'

'As I said, the fourth body is a major world, as populous and as well defended as any sector capital. And it's not the only one. By the comms traffic we intercepted, this entire region is swarming with activity. Father, these tau are not some insignificant little race limited to one or two systems. There are millions of them, spread across the whole cluster. Whatever you faced here today is only the smallest part of their forces. And...' Korvane broke into another fit of violent coughing.

'And,' he continued, 'they are converging on the fourth body. It seems their entire fleet is converging on the fourth body of this star system.'

Lucian stood, looking up at the image of his son upon the main pict screen. The fleet wide channel broke out in chaos as those masters who had listened in demanded a million answers to a million questions, all at once. Lucian saw then that the crusade council had made a terrible error in underestimating the tau as it had. The council had decreed that the crusade would be sufficient to conquer the tau. Lucian had to admit that even he had believed the aliens would sue for peace rather than face the might of the crusade, somehow having convinced himself that no sane foe would risk the utter devastation the fleet could wreak upon any world it encountered.

Lucian saw then that the crusade might soon have to fight, not for conquest, but for its very existence. He doubted the dominant faction, led by Cardinal Gurney, would view the matter in quite the same way, however. Lucian knew that the crusade would continue blundering on into tau space until it ran out of momentum entirely and the tau unleashed the inevitable counter-attack.

Sitting once more, Lucian pondered further. Perhaps, he thought, the crusade might in the long run benefit from taking such a thrashing. Perhaps it might facilitate a seismic shift in the balance of power. Perhaps, he thought, warming to the idea, a sound defeat under the leadership of that bastard priest might cause the council to reject that leadership entirely.

Then, Lucian grinned savagely, he would step forward. He would fill the power vacuum left in the wake of Gurney's passing, and the rise of the Arcadius would be ensured.

AMBITION KNOWS NO BOUNDS

'Give me a reading, Joachim,' Brielle Gerrit shouted against the raging wind. 'I can't see a damn thing!'

'Augur says two-fifty, ma'am,' Brielle's companion and advisor called back, his voice barely cutting through the howling cacophony of the storm. 'We should have visual any–'

'There,' Brielle called, and halted, craning her neck to look upwards. Against the churning, dark, purple clouds there was revealed an even darker form. She attempted to gauge its height, but her senses were confounded and unable to decipher its alien geometry. The rearing, slab-sided structure could have been standing scant metres in front of Brielle, or it could lie many kilometres distant.

'Two-fifty.' Brielle repeated her advisor's estimate of the range to their destination. Even as she looked upon the structure's form, its cliff-like planes appeared to shift, as if new surfaces and angles were revealed by the slightest change in perspective. 'If you're sure. Is everyone ready?'

Brielle turned to inspect her small party, its members appearing from the all-enveloping shroud of the storm. She lifted the visor of her armoured survival suit, the cold air rushing in to sting her exposed cheeks. Squinting against the wind, she noted with satisfaction the deployment of the dozen armsmen that accompanied her from her vessel, the Fairlight, which waited in high orbit above this dead world to which she had come in search of riches for her rogue trader clan. Each was heavily armed, and appointed in rugged armour, their faces obscured by heavy rebreather units. Their leader, the taciturn Santos Quin, stepped forwards, shadowed by the far smaller form of Adept Seth, her senior astropath.

'All is ready, my lady,' Quin answered, his tattooed face just visible through his own suit's visor. 'But the storm rises,' he added, casting a glance upwards at the churning skies.

'Understood,' Brielle replied, nodding, before looking to the astropath. 'And you, adept, have you anything to report?'

The astropath stepped forwards, bowing his helmeted head to his mistress. Through his visor, the adept's face was visible as a gruesome mass of scar tissue; his eyes were hollow pits and his nose and mouth were barely discernible. The soul binding, the ritual by which the astropath had been exposed to, and sanctified by, the Emperor's Grace, had blasted his body such that the man was in constant pain. Yet, although the normal range of human senses was denied to him, Adept Seth was possessed of far greater perception than any ordinary man.

++This place is dead to me, mistress,++ the astropath replied. His voice was little more than a guttural rasp, so ravaged was his throat, yet Brielle heard the man's words clearly for he spoke with his mind, directly into her own. ++Dead, yet I hear echoes, reverberations of ancient thoughts, or the hint of a sleeper's dreams. I cannot tell which.++

Brielle caught the sneer that crossed the face of Santos Quin at the astropath's words, and knew that the man's feral world origins made him distrustful of Seth and his powers. Yet, she knew what the astropath referred to, for she imagined that she too had discerned the very faintest of echoes, distant thoughts carried on the unquiet winds. She knew not what alien mind might have given rise to such thoughts, but she believed, hoped, relied upon the fact that they were mere echoes of some ancient and long-dead power.

'Well enough,' Brielle said, lowering her visor. 'We continue, with caution.'

Brielle stood before the pitted, black wall of the vast alien structure. Although the surface was but an arm's length in front of her, she felt compelled to reach out and lay a palm upon it, just to be certain. Even through the tough glove of her survival suit, Brielle felt the cold radiating from the stone-like material, a cold that touched not only her skin, but her soul too.

'Mistress.' Brielle withdrew her hand at the sound of the astropath's voice. 'Please, try not to–'

'I know, Seth,' Brielle replied. 'I know.' She looked around, and addressed Quin. 'We need to find a way in. Have your men spread out.'

The warrior nodded silently, and moved away to speak to the armsmen. In a moment, they, as well as Brielle's advisor Joachim Hep, had departed, all bar Quin himself having moved out in search of a means of entering the vast structure. Brielle saw Quin test the mechanism on his boltgun, before lowering his sensor goggles to scan the depths of the storm. He would stand vigil over his mistress, no matter what.

Brielle resumed her study of the alien form. She craned her neck upwards, noting that either the storm clouds had lowered or the ever-shifting planes of the structure had elongated, for now the top appeared to be lost to the storm above. She pondered, not for the first time, the risk inherent in this expedition, but knew that vast riches were to be claimed on such worlds as this. As next in line to sovereignty of the mighty Clan Arcadius, it fell to Brielle to carve her name across the galaxy, to pierce the darkness in the name of the Emperor, to face whatever might lurk in the depths of the void and to overcome it, for the sake of humanity. And, she mused, smiling coyly behind her visor, to amass untold wealth and undreamed-of glory along the way.

It was Brielle's hope, and that of her clan, that this unnamed world, far out in the void between spiral arms, might yield such riches. The galaxy was strewn with the ruins of civilisations far older than the Imperium of Man, and planets such as this were home to dusty tombs sealed before mankind even looked to the skies above ancient Terra. Such tombs, when discovered, had been known to contain relics of long-dead alien races, artefacts of wonder for which the pampered nobility of the Imperium's ruling classes would pay a staggering price just to possess. The vast majority of these items were considered curiosities or art, having no discernible function. Others could be studied, their functions and exotic abilities unlocked. Brielle knew that dilettante collectors and self-proclaimed experts in the proscribed field of xenology would give their all for such items.

Yet, Brielle was struck with a cold sense of dread, an unutterable feeling that something was terribly amiss with this dead planet.

'Something stirs, my lady,' Adept Seth warned, as if giving voice to an unnamed fear gnawing at the periphery of Brielle's consciousness.

'What do you sense, Seth?' Brielle answered, casting around her for any sign of danger. Quin hefted his boltgun across his broad chest, and took a step closer to his mistress.

'I sense... a guttering flame... the flame is the soul, all but extinguished, yet it refuses to die...'

'I need a little more than that, Seth,' Brielle responded, biting back a less politic remark. 'Are we in danger?'

'Something knows we are–'

Before the astropath could complete his sentence, the vox-channel burst into life. Howling static assaulted Brielle's ears, before the voice of Joachim Hep cut in. '...a way in. Repeat, we have found a way in.'

'Stay where you are,' Brielle answered, not entirely sure whether or not Hep had heard her through the raging atmospheric interference. 'Quin, lead the way.'

'Recent damage, Joachim?' Brielle asked of her advisor. Though aged, the man stood almost as tall and broad as a Space Marine. She waited as he studied the vast rent in the cliff-like side of the alien structure, his eyes taking in every detail with practiced skill.

'I would say so, ma'am,' Joachim replied, without turning his gaze from the sight before him. 'Millennia of storm damage brought this about, but the damage itself has only recently occurred.'

Brielle's gaze moved from her advisor to the great fracture in the alien tomb. Though only a metre or so wide, the crack ran upwards what must have been many hundreds of metres, or would have been, if it weren't for the damnable geometry of the place. Brielle moved closer, aware of Quin keeping pace behind. She leaned in to examine the ragged edge of the crack, to glean some idea of the material and what might have damaged it.

++Time, my lady,' Adept Seth spoke into Brielle's mind. 'The only force which could damage such a place as this, is time itself.++

Brielle raised an eyebrow and cast a wry glance at her astropath, aware that he had read her surface thoughts. She turned back, leaning in yet closer to the damaged surface. She fancied she could see signs of repair, if only at a minuscule scale. Perhaps this place could heal itself, she mused. Perhaps that explained how it could have withstood the ravages of this storm-wracked world for so many long, lonely aeons.

'Let's go,' Brielle said, stepping into the fracture before Quin could take the lead.

Scant metres into the fracture, Brielle was plunged into utter darkness. She paused, allowing senses other than sight to come to the fore. She extended her awareness as far as she was able, attempting to gain some idea of her surroundings. She strained her hearing. The storm still raged outside, but now its howl was muffled and distant. She heard too the action of the rebreathers worn by her companions, and discerned the sure, heavy tread of Santos Quin as he sought to overtake her, to take the lead lest the party encounter danger and his mistress be threatened.

Savouring the darkness for but a moment longer, Brielle reached her hand to the mechanism at the side of her helmet, lowering a set of goggles over her visor. The headset buzzed as lenses whirred to focus on what Brielle's own eyes could not register. The goggles were capable of registering many different wavelengths, overlaying what they perceived over Brielle's own vision.

The blackness was replaced by a kaleidoscopic riot of colours, shot through with grainy static. Brielle adjusted a control at the side of her helmet, and the image resolved into something she could make sense of. Before Brielle, there stretched a circular tunnel into which she and her party had stepped. She looked behind, confirming that the tunnel stretched off in both directions, evidently running perpendicular to the outside wall through which, via the fracture, they had entered.

Satisfied that no immediate danger presented itself, Brielle used the control to cycle through a range of settings, the sight before her changing from one of vivid green hues to another of black with violet highlights, to yet another of purest white with shadows of turquoise. She paused on a vista of deep greens, seeing on the curved wall nearby an intricately carved icon. She stepped closer, aware that Quin did likewise. The icon was revealed to be a series of circles and lines, joined together into what must surely have been some long dead alien script.

'Joachim.' She turned to address her advisor, and he stepped forwards, past Santos Quin, who grunted as he stepped aside. 'Set your readers to sigma-twelve, and look at this.'

Joachim, his goggles already lowered, reached to his helmet and adjusted the controls. A moment later, his head scanned the walls of the corridor.

'I've never seen its like, ma'am,' Joachim Hep replied after a long pause. 'Though it puts me in mind of...'

'Of what?' Brielle replied, uncertain she wanted to hear her advisor's answer.

'Of the machine scripts of the servants of the Omnissiah, ma'am.'

'But this place is ancient,' Brielle answered, as much to assuage her own uncertainties as to answer her advisor. 'It predates the Mechanicus by countless millennia. There can be no connection.'

'Quite, ma'am,' Hep replied, nodding gravely to Brielle.

'Then let's continue,' Brielle ordered, 'this way.' She made to set off, but this time allowed Santos Quin to take the lead. The feral-worlder raised his boltgun as he advanced into the darkness, using his own set of goggles to pierce the gloom. The warrior used silent hand signals to direct his armsmen to the proper order of march, ensuring Brielle, Hep and Adept Seth were well protected in the centre of the line. Brielle allowed Quin to do so, grudgingly reminding herself that she would, after all, inherit the Warrant of Trade of her rogue trader house, and Quin was only doing the duty her father had bestowed upon the warrior.

Before making off along the tubular corridor, Brielle paused briefly, imagining she heard, at the very edge of perception, an out-of-place sound. She imagined she heard a metallic chitter. She listened intently, but heard no more. With a glance back beyond the rearmost armsmen, she set off.

'Not a sound,' Brielle whispered over the vox-net, edging forwards to peer over Quin's shoulder. She knew she need hardly have given the order, for the armsmen of the party followed the feral-worlder's lead, and he himself stood motionless and silent against the curved wall at the end of the corridor.

Brielle found herself gazing into a vast blackness. She was about to lower her goggles to scan the space in a different wavelength when she caught a glimpse of a dim, green glow amidst the darkness. Focussing, her eyes adapted, and after a few minutes she could make out a hint of the space before the party. What she saw made Brielle gasp.

The passageway in which her party waited opened out into some manner of chamber so vast that Brielle was struck by a nigh-crushing sense of insignificance as she tried in vain to comprehend its benighted dimensions. Brielle imagined herself an insect crawling across the worn flagstones of the mightiest of cathedrals, the vaults above lost in darkness. A cold shiver ran through her body as she realised the notion was not entirely her own imagining.

So vast was the space that its surface appeared to rise and fall with the curvature of the planet on which it stood. Brielle dismissed the notion; a structure so large would have been detectable from orbit, and the tomb had not measured so vast on their approach. Nonetheless, the geometry of the place played all manner of tricks upon Brielle's senses. Just as she had been unable to gauge the true size of the structure from outside, she now found herself unable to estimate its internal dimensions, and the sensation was deeply unsettling.

As Brielle's eyes adjusted further to the gloom, she saw that across the dark floor of the chamber there lay a gently undulating sea of what must surely have been dust. How long had this place stood, she pondered, that its floor should have accumulated such a layer of sediment? Looking closer, she saw low dunes, their crests gently aglow with the ever-present green illumination.

'Joachim,' Brielle addressed her advisor, who stood at her back. 'Do you see a source for the back light?'

Brielle waited while Hep scanned the vast space before them, then turned her head to look to his face as he answered. 'I do not, ma'am,' he replied. 'It may be the result of some background effect, an energy source not detectable by the augurs.'

'My lady,' Quin growled low. Brielle turned her gaze from her advisor to the warrior, instantly alert in response to his tone. 'Ahead, a hundred paces.'

Brielle squinted as she sought out the point Quin was indicating. After a moment, she found it.

'Tracks?' Brielle whispered.

'Aye, my lady,' Quin replied. 'Something small.'

'Vermin?' Brielle asked.

'Possibly,' Quin growled back. 'Though I see little for such a creature to hunt.'

Brielle nodded. 'When?' she asked.

The feral-worlder glanced back at his mistress. 'Hours, or decades, my lady. Such is the stillness of this place I can scarcely tell.'

Brielle made to answer, but Adept Seth spoke first. ++An aeon... and a day, mistress,++ he whispered, the sound of his voice whispered directly into her mind. ++An epoch past, yet still to occur.++

Growing uneasy with the astropath's manner, Brielle replied curtly, 'Speak plainly, Seth, please.'

The astropath turned his monstrous face towards Brielle. She knew that even though the man lacked conventional sight he was looking straight at her. 'My apologies, mistress,' he whispered. 'I know such things make little sense. But just as your eyes have difficulty perceiving the true dimensions of this place, so too do my own senses. This place is weighted, mistress, weighted with ages impossible for such as us to comprehend. Perhaps the gods themselves—'

'Enough!' growled Quin. Brielle's gaze lingered on the face of Adept Seth for a moment, before she turned back towards the warrior. 'Such words gain us nothing.'

Brielle took a deep breath, steeling herself to go on, before taking a step forwards into the vast chamber. She glanced back to her party, the dust of impossible ages rising around her boots. Looking back at them, she felt a moment of giddy recklessness, knowing her father would disapprove were he here to witness her actions. An instant later, the feeling passed, to be replaced with the crushing deadness of the tomb. 'Enough indeed,' she breathed, and set out across the ocean of dust.

Soon after setting forth across the chamber, the party had come upon the tracks that Quin had spotted from the passageway. The feral-worlder's hunting senses had told him that some form of insect perhaps a metre in length had made the tracks, and that the fine layer of dust overlaying them told him the trail was not recent. Despite this news, Brielle's feeling of unease had not been assuaged, but had instead increased the further into the dust sea the party had advanced.

At first, Quin had advised that the explorers should proceed with caution, treading softly lest great plumes of the thick dust carpeting the ground be thrown up with their passing. Brielle was soon forced to countermand this order however, for otherwise they would never have made any progress at all. And besides, she had mused, who might be watching? She had no answer to that question.

As she walked, Brielle attempted once more to gain some idea of the nature of her surroundings. She craned her neck to look upwards, and was immediately greeted with a wave of nausea as the distant planes high above shifted. She looked back to the ground, and a second wave of sickness came over her, causing her to stumble and come to a halt.

'Ma'am?' Joachim Hep was at Brielle's side in an instant, his firm hold grasping the shoulder of her armoured survival suit. A moment later, the rest of the party halted, the armsmen taking guard positions while their taciturn leader worked his way back down the line towards Brielle.

'I'm fine, Joachim,' Brielle answered. 'I'm fine. It's this place. It plays havoc with the senses.'

'That it does, ma'am,' replied Brielle's advisor, stepping back having satisfied himself that his mistress was able to continue. 'I cannot read it either.'

At this, Quin interjected. 'My lady, how much time do you perceive to have passed since we set out across this chamber?'

Brielle looked to the warrior, distracted, beguiled even, for a brief moment by the swirling patterns of his facial tattoos. 'How much time?' she repeated, turning her head to look back the way the party had travelled. 'I would say... Emperor's mercy...'

'How long, my lady?' Quin pressed.

Brielle looked back to the feral-worlder, her throat suddenly dry. 'Three, three and half...'

'Minutes?' Quin asked.

'Hours,' Brielle said, the sight of the passageway mouth, a hundred metres behind, still fresh in her mind.

'...aeons,' Adept Seth whispered.

'Behind us,' Brielle whispered into her vox-link, having subtly disengaged the external amplivox. She made an effort not to change her stance or the pattern of march as the party continued on its way across the dusty chamber.

'Yes, my lady,' Quin answered, having followed her lead and adjusted his own communications in the same manner.

'How long?' Brielle asked.

'For me?' Quin turned his head as he walked, raising an eyebrow sardonically.

'Fair point,' Brielle conceded. 'How long?' she repeated.

'No more than thirty minutes,' Quin said.

'Can you tell where?' Brielle asked. Brielle herself had been aware of movement to the party's rear for several minutes.

'In this half-light,' Quin answered, 'it's hard to be sure. But, I would say that we are being tracked by one observer, using the folds of the dust as cover, to our rear and left.'

It took a supreme effort of will for Brielle not to turn and look in the direction Quin had described. She could not help but imagine a crosshair aimed at the centre of the back of her head, making her skin suddenly itch beneath her armoured helmet. She felt an irresistible, inexplicable urge to pull the helmet free and shake out her plaited locks, which felt as if they were pasted to her scalp. She shook the notion off, adjusting her step, treading softly through the dust, focussing her every sense behind her for any sign of pursuit.

Brielle imagined she heard a distant voice, so quiet it was little more than a thought. She glanced towards the astropath, and noted that his head was cocked at an odd angle, as if he too were intently listening to something. She focussed upon that distant whisper, half-hearing the forming of alien words, yet not quite able to discern them fully.

++There are more, mistress++ the astropath's thought-message touched her mind, his withered, scarred mouth not moving at all.

++Where?++ She formed the reply in her mind, unsure whether the astropath would hear her. Evidently, he did hear, for the thought came back immediately, ++Everywhere, mistress. All around us. They slumber... yet they stir.++

With a conscious effort, Brielle closed her mind. She had felt the touch of madness in the astropath's thoughts, a cold dread verging on the insane. Her eyes met briefly with those of Quin, who nodded to the fore. Whilst Brielle's attentions had been otherwise engaged, the party had come upon the opposite side of the vast chamber. She looked back, seeing that they had somehow crossed the impossible distance in what felt to her like the course of barely five or six hours.

Brielle stood at the very brink of a wide chasm, cut with unreal precision into the black rock of the alien tomb's dusty floor. Far below, there emanated a lurid green glow, the same glow, she mused, as had suffused the chamber they had just crossed, yet here it was direct to the point of blinding intensity. Far above, the vaults were lost to blackness, and Brielle saw no other way forwards than to cross the vast chasm.

'Deploy the line,' she ordered.

Santos Quin motioned to one of the armsmen, who stepped forwards and unlimbered a heavy grapnel launcher. The man braced his feet wide, and aimed the launcher at a point on the ground across the chasm, some forty metres distant.

'Fire!' Quin ordered.

The launcher's report was deafening, the explosive crack filling the stillness of the tomb. Brielle experienced an instant of profound dread, as if their intrusion must surely be noted, as if the sound would bring attackers down upon them in an instant. She glanced all around, half-expecting the shadows on the black stone walls to resolve themselves into the dreadful forms of long-dead guardians. She shook off the notion, but guessed that the other members of her party shared it. Even Quin was casting cautious looks all about.

Brielle was brought back to the present by the impact of the grapnel as it struck the ground on the far side of the chasm. She watched as the module at the end of the line activated, power hooks springing forth to bite into the stone, before the energy was shut off an instant later, leaving the blades embedded in the ground. The armsman activated the mechanism on the launcher, and the line tightened. Using a similar system of power hooks mounted at the launcher's base, the armsman secured the device to the ground on the party's side of the chasm, and stepped back.

Brielle made for the line, before both Quin and Hep stepped forwards to block her path.

'With respect, ma'am,' Hep said, bowing as he did so lest he give undue offence. 'Please, Brielle,' he continued, his voice low. 'I cannot allow you to cross first. Your father would have me flayed by the bilge-rippers.'

Brielle suppressed a smile, despite her mild annoyance, for she was ever ill at ease with others taking risks on her behalf. Yet, she knew her advisor, one of her father's oldest friends, was correct. She smiled gracefully as she returned his bow and stepped aside.

'And I,' interjected Santos Quin, 'cannot allow you, Joachim, to cross first.' The warrior held up a hand to wave away any objection Hep might voice. 'I too have duties to observe.'

Brielle watched, amused, as Joachim Hep considered Quin's words, before he too stepped aside, allowing the feral-worlder to approach the secured grapnel launcher. With a gesture, the warrior deployed his armsmen so as to cover the far side as he prepared to cross. Unravelling a cord from his belt, Quin attached himself to the grapnel line, and lowered himself over the edge of the chasm.

Brielle watched as Quin progressed, slowly at first, but with increasing speed, across the wide chasm. She imagined for an instant that the green light blazing from below flickered for a moment, as if in recognition of the intrusion, but cast off the idea as imagination born of tension. A sound caught her attention, and she looked towards Adept Seth, noting that the astropath was mumbling under his breath, his ruined mouth working, the incoherent words muffled by the helmet of his survival suit.

'Seth,' Brielle called softly, mindful of disturbing the stygian silence of the tomb. The astropath appeared not to have noted his mistress's call. 'Seth!' she hissed, her teeth gritted.

'Mistress?' Seth replied, finally comprehending that he was being addressed.

'What is it, Seth?' Brielle asked, once more forcing down concern at the astropath's manner.

'I...' Adept Seth stammered. 'I think we should leave now, mistress.'

'Leave? What are you talking about, Seth? What's wrong?'

'It's the sleepers, mistress... it's their dreams... I can't...'

Brielle weighed the situation in her head. Her astropath appeared to be losing his grip on reality, but she needed him here, to communicate with her vessel in orbit, and for the edge his prodigious powers could provide in a dangerous situation. Yet, it appeared now that those same powers were proving his undoing, for it seemed to Brielle that the echoes of the dreams of the long-dead builders of this vast tomb were somehow afflicting him. If it came to it, she knew she could order one of the armsmen to incapacitate the astropath, to bind and drug him until the expedition was completed, but in so doing she would handicap their efforts significantly. She could not afford to lose the astropath, not yet, at least.

'My lady?' Brielle heard Quin address her over the vox channel. She turned, to see that the feral-worlder had made it safely across the chasm. 'My lady, I will have one of the armsmen attend to the adept, have no fear. Now please, it is safe for you to cross.'

'Thank you, Santos,' Brielle answered, noting that one of the armsmen had moved closer to the astropath, evidently responding to a surreptitious order from Quin. She approached the lip of the chasm, and stood at its very edge for a moment, gazing past her feet into the lambent depths far below. She experienced again a wave of disorientation, having little to do with any fear of heights and more to do with the subtly wrong geometry of the tomb. She could not quite place it. It appeared sometimes that no two planes intersected exactly how they should, as if perspective were somehow out of kilter. Taking a deep breath, she pushed such concerns to the back of her mind and withdrew a cord from her belt. She seated herself at the edge of the chasm, and clipped the cord to the grapnel line.

In a single motion, Brielle swung out beneath the line, suspending herself below it. She tested the cord attaching her belt to the line, and, satisfied that it was properly attached, began to winch herself across. Above her, Brielle could see little more than darkness, the vaults far overhead twinkling with what she took to be stray reflections from the actinic energies raging below her. Pulling herself along, one hand over the other, she concentrated not on the hundreds, perhaps thousands of metres below her, but on those minuscule points of green light twinkling in the darkness overhead. She judged herself halfway across the mighty gap before she noted that the lights above appeared to be growing in brightness.

'...dreams... the guttering flame... stirring...' Brielle heard Adept Seth over the vox-channel, and craned her neck to look towards Quin. Doing so, she saw that the feral-worlder's gaze was turned upwards, transfixed upon those same green lights that had held her own attention as she had crossed the gap.

She looked back upwards, to see that those same lights were now twice as bright, and were swooping down towards her!

'My lady!' Quin shouted. 'Beware!' The warrior raised his boltgun in both hands, bracing its butt against his shoulder. The weapon's staccato bark was deafening, and its discharge illuminated the darkness with blinding orange fire.

Hanging precariously halfway across the depthless chasm, Brielle felt suddenly painfully aware of how exposed her position was. She had no time to seek out the targets Quin was firing at, or to engage them herself. Instead, she gritted her teeth and hauled on the line, dragging her body into motion, hand over hand.

Even as she concentrated upon crossing the chasm, the air all around Brielle was filled with flashing light, the discharge of the armsmen's heavy-gauge shotguns as they blasted at the foe Brielle could not see.

'My lady!' Brielle heard, surprised by how close Quin's voice sounded. She looked around, to see that, somehow, she had traversed the chasm, and Quin was reaching out a hand to help her climb up over the lip. She looked to his outstretched glove, before something behind him caught her eye.

'Quin!'

The warrior followed his mistress's gaze, turning on the spot and bringing his boltgun up, one-handed.

The weapon barked, its report shockingly loud at such close quarters, even through Brielle's survival suit helmet. Something exploded, peppering Brielle and Quin with small metallic shards. With relief, Brielle saw that her suit was intact, its armour having protected her from the potentially lethal shrapnel.

'Are you hurt?' Brielle asked the warrior, aware that he had been closer to the detonation than she.

'Not badly, my lady,' Quin replied, before shouting a warning to one of the armsmen across the chasm.

Brielle looked across the gap, towards the remainder of the party. She was greeted by the sight of the armsmen arrayed in a semicircle, their backs to the edge of the chasm, with Joachim Hep and Adept Seth at the centre of their formation. While the fighters blasted into the darkness above, Hep was attempting to get Seth to cross the chasm.

From the darkness above the group flashed silvered, insect-like attackers, each little more than a metre in length. From what Brielle took to be the head of each creature, there shone a green light, clearly akin to that which blazed so brightly in the depths of the chasm she had just crossed. One of the metallic creatures swooped down upon an armsman, the green at its front increasing in brightness until the attacker was surrounded by a nimbus of pulsating energy. The armsman racked the slide on his shotgun and unleashed a blast at near point-blank range, but the creature swerved aside as it dived towards its target.

As the attacker fell upon the armsman, the green field surrounding it increased in intensity still further. At the last, his attacker closing, the armsman rotated his shotgun and drove its solid stock upwards, ramming it hard into his attacker's head. The green light exploded as the shotgun crunched into the attacker's fore section. The armsman was driven backwards, falling to land at the very edge of the chasm. His attacker plummeted, out of control, right above his supine form, and was lost in the pulsating depths far below.

'Everyone across, come on!' Brielle yelled, reaching for the bolt pistol holstered at her hip. Bracing the weapon in both hands, she drew a bead on the nearest of the insectoid attackers as it circled overhead.

'Hep!' she called. 'Get Seth over here, now!'

Not waiting for an acknowledgement, she squeezed the trigger. Brielle's pistol barked, and the shot struck home, burying itself in the outer shell of the creature's body. The impact caused the creature to swerve abruptly, but before it could correct its course, it exploded into a thousand metallic shards, the miniature explosive warhead of the bolt round having detonated itself with lethal effect after penetrating the target's armour.

As Hep forced the astropath onto the grapnel line and helped him cross, Brielle and Quin kept up their fusillade, the bolt rounds accounting for another three of the creatures. Then suddenly, the attackers broke off as one, as if in answer to some unheard order.

'Is anyone hurt?' Brielle asked Quin.

'Not seriously, my lady,' the warrior answered. 'I do not think these creatures were made for fighting.'

Brielle looked to Quin. 'Explain.'

'My lady, these creatures appeared to me to be testing our defences and our capabilities. I believe they were little more than sentinels.'

'Sentinels?' Brielle repeated. 'Sentinels guarding what?'

'This place, my lady,' Quin answered. 'They guard this tomb against intruders. Against desecration.'

'Against thieves,' Brielle finished, allowing herself a wry smile.

'They are close now, mistress... can't you hear them?' Brielle heard Seth mumble from her side as the party made its way through a maze of narrow passageways. Despite herself, she was beginning to lose her patience with the astropath, but knew there was little she could do about it now.

'What is it you hear?' Brielle replied. 'Please, Seth, speak plainly.'

'I hear these...' Brielle turned as she walked, and saw that Seth was trailing his outstretched hand along wall, his unfeeling, gloved fingers following the intricate engravings that covered its every surface.

'What do you mean?' Brielle asked, knowing that she was unlikely to receive a coherent answer, but preferring to keep the astropath from descending into total madness.

'It is all connected, mistress... all of it. They barely dream at all, mistress, not like we do...'

Brielle shook her head and turned her gaze back to the path ahead. The passages through which the group moved were narrow and dark, the only illumination provided by a green light emanating from the endless streams of alien script running along the walls. She tried not to look too closely at the script. To her, the interconnected circles and lines formed nodes and links, described hierarchies and progressions, told of alien domination and processes in which the human race had no part.

She shook her head once more, this time to clear it of the odd notions that crept into her consciousness whenever she looked too closely at the patterns on the walls.

'Seth,' she said. 'Do not lay hands upon the walls...'

'We must leave,' the astropath announced, halting in his tracks. 'We must turn back, mistress, now.'

Brielle stopped and turned on the astropath, ready to admonish him or order him sedated. And then, she caught an echo, a sound from the direction in which the party had come.

'It's the chasm, my lady,' Quin said as she looked to him for his assessment. 'The sentinel creatures.'

'It's them!' Seth shrieked, and turned as if to flee.

'Restrain him,' Brielle ordered. Quin motioned to a nearby armsman, who moved in behind the astropath and gripped both of his arms at the elbows.

'Why would the sentinels be active once more?' Brielle asked, not expecting any of her servants to answer. She shared a glance with Santos Quin as he raised his boltgun and made to continue along the passageway. She lingered a moment, listening intently to the last of the sounds from behind as they echoed and faded to silence. She imagined for a moment that the sentinels might be attacking once more, before rejecting the notion, and following after Quin.

Leaving the dark, sigil-lined passageway behind, Brielle stepped out into a vast, circular chamber. The space was dominated by hundreds of tiered galleries, each one stacked upon that below, the highest lost in darkness far above. Each tier was lined with alcoves, in each of which a dully gleaming, humanoid statue stood.

'Joachim?' Brielle asked, as her advisor stepped up beside her. 'What do you think?'

Hep's gaze took in the vastness of the chamber, scanning the galleries with an expert eye. 'I have never before seen the like, ma'am,' he replied. 'But I can think of half a dozen cartels that would pay a fortune for just one.'

'My thoughts exactly,' Brielle replied with a broad grin that was quite inappropriate on the lips of the daughter of a bearer of a Warrant of Trade. She crossed to the nearest of the statues. She stood before the metallic form, seeing that it had evidently been crafted to resemble some form of skeletal warrior, its face an impassive, skull-like death mask. Across its broad, ribbed chest, it held what was unmistakably a weapon.

'The Catacombs of Skard were attended by metal grave guards,' Brielle mused aloud, recalling gleefully an expedition into the subterranean vaults of that doomed world two years earlier. 'They bought the clan an entire world...'

'They did, ma'am,' Hep replied, standing beside his mistress. 'But they were cast of solid rhodium. These appear...'

'Mechanical?' Brielle interjected. Her eyes followed the many cables and pipes that led from sockets in the alcoves to points on the statue's body. Was one of those cables twitching? 'These are not mere grave-goods. Some manner of xenos technology is at work here...'

'They slumber...' Brielle heard Adept Seth sob from behind. The astropath had been restrained by two of the armsmen, but he continued to mumble an incoherent stream of nonsense. 'We must leave!' Seth bellowed, his voice echoing for long moments in the galleries high above.

'Sedate him, now!' Brielle ordered the armsmen restraining the astropath. She would save the apologies for later, when the party was back on the ship and its hold was full with xenos-tech.

Then, a voice filled the chamber.

'You would do well to heed his words.'

Instantly, Santos Quin was at his mistress's side, his boltgun raised as he scanned for the source of the voice. With a single gesture, he motioned for the armsmen to form a protective ring, with Brielle, Seth and Hep at its centre.

Raising the visor on her helmet, Brielle called into the darkness, 'Who addresses me?' As she spoke, she turned slowly around, seeking any sign of the individual who had spoken.

'I address you,' the answer came back. The voice was strangely lyrical in tone, not human, but not wholly alien either. Brielle followed the sound to its source, and saw a tall figure step from a dark portal on the other side of the chamber.

'We claim this place, by right of conquest,' Brielle called out, advancing towards the chamber's centre as she spoke, her servants aiming their weapons at the intruder. 'Be gone, or face the consequences.'

'Consequences?' the reply came back, the figure stepping forwards from the shadowed archway. A suspicion began to form in Brielle's mind. 'Pitiful idiots,' the speaker replied, scorn dripping from every word. 'You truly have no conception of your folly. Even as the galaxy crumbles to ash all around you, you flounder in your own filth, dragging yourselves and all of creation down with you.'

'Such arrogance I've only ever heard from the lips of the eldar,' Brielle replied, now certain of the intruder's species. She came to a halt near the centre of the chamber and placed her hands at her hips, surreptitiously loosening the catch on the holster of her bolt pistol and the scabbard of her chainblade.

The figure approached, and came to a halt opposite Brielle. Her intuition had been correct. Before Brielle stood a tall, lithe humanoid figure, dressed in a long cloak of shifting, chameleonic fabric. Across his back, the eldar carried a long rifle, confirmation, if Brielle needed it, of his caste.

'Pathfinder?' Brielle asked, seeking to wrong-foot the alien with her knowledge of his kind. As she spoke, she counted another three aliens waiting in the shadows not far behind.

'Indeed,' the eldar demurred, nodding his head a slight degree. 'If you have knowledge of my kin, then you know the folly of disregarding my warning. Leave this place. Do as your seer begs you. He has the truth of it, while you are blinded by avarice.'

Anger welling in her breast, Brielle raised a pointed finger as she advanced on the eldar. Her armoured boot thudded into an object on the dusty ground before her. 'I know that you speak in riddles. I know that you lie. I know that you can't be trusted,' she spat, jabbing her finger at the eldar. 'I know that you'd slaughter a million humans if your witches foretold it would save a single one of you from breaking a nail!'

'And what of it, child?' the eldar replied bitterly, ignoring the jibe but understanding Brielle's meaning all too well. 'My people have beheld the birth and the death of gods, while yours have barely crawled from the mud that begat you. What use reason, what use wisdom, when you seek nothing more than your own destruction, and care not if the galaxy burns along with you?'

'More lies,' Brielle retorted. She glanced down at the object at her feet. Half-submerged in the dust of aeons, there laid an ornate stave, a faint green glow shining at its bladed tip. 'More words to cover your own arrogant selfishness.'

'I say again,' the eldar said, his glance following Brielle's to the stave on the ground before her. 'Disturb nothing, and you may yet live. We all may yet–'

'You dare threaten me?' Brielle returned. 'You dare order me to do anything?' She reached down and lifted the stave. It was heavy, and cold. 'I'll disturb whatsoever I choose, xenos.'

'No!' the eldar shouted, his former arrogance wavering. The alien looked around, as if searching for something amongst the galleries, his slanted eyes wide with fear. He reached for the long rifle slung across his back.

Before Brielle could react, the air around her erupted as a dozen weapons discharged as one. The eldar staggered, his body hammered as round after round slammed into it. An instant later, the remaining aliens returned fire, their own weapons unleashing a hail of silent, yet deadly precision projectiles.

Bringing her right arm upwards in a sharp movement, Brielle unleashed the deadly payload of one of the miniaturised weapons she wore as ornate, yet lethal rings. A jet of chemical liquid arched forth, erupting into flame as it arrowed towards the nearest of the eldar's companions. The target saw his peril and rolled aside, the now-blazing liquid fire splashing down nearby. For an instant, Brielle cursed her misfortune, for the ring bore only a single charge. Then, a single gobbet of the fiery liquid splashed out, catching the eldar's flowing, chameleonic cloak. Before he even realised his peril, the eldar had been engulfed in the hungry fire.

With a cold outer ruthlessness that belied the disgust within, Brielle drew her bolt pistol, levelled it calmly at the living torch before her and put a bolt shell through the unfortunate's skull, ending his suffering for good.

Even as the dull crump of the bolt-round detonating inside the eldar's skull echoed away, a burst of alien fire scythed through the air around her. Brielle dived aside, the stave still in her hands.

She hit the dusty ground and rolled, coming up into a ready stance, to see that the firefight was already over. The aliens who had fired upon her lay dead, or grievously wounded, while the one she had killed with her concealed flamer guttered. Several of her servants were writhing on the ground, suppressing screams of pain from wounds that appeared no more than pin pricks, but had, she knew, probably wreaked havoc upon internal organs.

'The xenos!' Hep called out. 'He lives still, ma'am, beware!'

Brielle looked across to the centre of the chamber, seeing that the eldar lay in a rapidly expanding pool of his own blood. His head was raised upon his straining neck as he looked straight at her. Seeing that the dying alien presented little danger, Brielle stood, pulling herself up on the alien stave as she did so.

'Listen to me, human,' the eldar coughed, blood flecking his lips as he spoke. 'If you leave this place now, you may still avert a disaster you cannot possibly comprehend.'

Reaching the place where the alien lay, Brielle looked down upon his broken form. The hiss of venting gases sounded from one of the galleries high above. She knelt at the eldar's side, and leaned forwards to bear witness to his last words.

'There are forces in this universe you know nothing of,' the eldar whispered, his fading gaze sweeping the highest of the chamber's galleries. 'Minds that have slumbered for aeons turn their attentions upon us once more...'

A sharp, cackling laugh sounded from behind Brielle, and she was struck by the terrible realisation that Adept Seth's ravings might have contained something of the truth.

'What forces?' Brielle said. 'What minds?' She turned her head sharply as she thought she caught sight of movement in one of the alcoves nearby.

'My lady...' Quin said.

'Wait!' Brielle answered, aware that the eldar's life was fading before her very eyes, but knowing that she must bear witness to what he had to say to her. 'Tell me,' she demanded.

'Your race will discover, in time,' the eldar responded, coughing. He vomited blood across his chest. A loud hiss sounded from very nearby, causing Brielle to look to the nearest of the alcoves and the skeletal statue within. 'But you...' The alien smiled grimly through bloody lips, fixing his gaze upon Brielle as she turned back to him. 'You shall find out all too soon...'

Before the eldar could complete his sentence, the dusty ground on which he lay appeared to subside beneath him. Brielle looked on in frozen horror as the eldar sank into the dust. The alien's eyes widened in terror as realisation of his fate hit home. A moment later, an area of dust three metres across was sinking, and then, a wide, circular hole opened up. The eldar tumbled downwards, dust cascading after him, and was gone.

'My lady!' Quin shouted. Brielle stared down into the dark hole that had opened up directly before her, and then turned to face Quin. 'What?'

The feral-worlder's only answer was to look towards the nearest of the alcoves. Within it, a pair of green lights shone. Looking closer, Brielle saw that the eyes of the metallic statue had come alive. She looked upwards, turning as she did so to take in the row upon row of galleries lining the chamber all the way up into the darkness far above. Dimly glowing within every single one of the thousands of alcoves was a pair of lights.

Brielle brought up her bolt pistol, as a sub-sonic drone sounded from somewhere very far beneath the ground on which she stood. Before her, a lurid green glow appeared in the dark hole in the centre of the chamber. She took a step backwards as her servants appeared at her side, their weapons raised.

'Ma'am I strongly suggest we–' Hep started.

'I know,' Brielle interrupted. Anger filled her, along with cold dread. In an instant, her dreams of the riches this place might yield evaporated, to be replaced by the raw instinct to simply survive. She realised with a start that the stave she still held in one hand was now glowing fiercely at its bladed tip, its haft feeling suddenly cold even through the glove of her survival suit.

And then, a column of blinding green light appeared, lancing upwards from the hole before her. Motes of drifting dust glittered as if trapped by the shaft, and the low rumble rose in volume, the ground now visibly trembling.

'Fall back!' Brielle called.

A scream cut the air, almost deafening even over the steadily increasingly sound emanating from the trembling ground. Brielle turned, to see Adept Seth bent double, both hands clamped across his helmet as if the astropath tried in vain to cover his ears. At the sound of the roar of Quin's boltgun, she turned back towards the column of green light.

Within the shaft, a figure was rising. At first, all Brielle could make out was a humanoid form wreathed in a pulsating nimbus of light. As the figure rose upwards, she saw that it was floating, as if held aloft by the light itself. It was huge, easily three metres tall, its body a metal skeleton swathed in rags that appeared to writhe as if stirred by some unseen current.

'We leave,' Brielle ordered as the figure rose to a height of ten metres above the hole. 'Now!'

Before her servants could react, the figure's eyes came suddenly alive, aglow with the same green light that illuminated those of the statues, yet a hundred times brighter. Its death-mask head turned, as if it awakened, and regarded the sight before it.

That terrible gaze settled first upon the cowering form of Adept Seth. The astropath shrieked once more, and vomited inside his helmet, his face obscured by the dripping fluids. The skeletal figure's eyes blazed still brighter, and a wet crump sounded from within the astropath's helmet, the inside of the visor turning in an instant to the vivid red of fresh blood flecked with the grey of brain matter. Brielle watched in mute horror as Seth's body toppled lifelessly to the ground, a great cloud of dust billowing up from the ground around it.

Casting off the unadulterated shock, Brielle levelled her bolt pistol and drew a shaky bead on the figure's head. Breathing a silent prayer to the Emperor to guide her hand, she squeezed the trigger. Her shot struck the figure square across its metal brow, but the bolt exploded, leaving little more than a black smear to mark where it had landed. The creature appeared not even to register her attack.

A moment later, Quin bellowed a savage curse born of the barbaric world of his birth. The warrior raised his boltgun and in scant seconds emptied an entire magazine at his foe. Several dozen bolt-rounds, each sufficient to reduce a normal body to a bloody ruin, glanced harmlessly from the metal form above.

'Quin!' Brielle bellowed over the deafening roar of the armsmen's shotguns joining in the fusillade. 'It's no use! We're leaving!'

But the feral-worlder appeared not to hear his mistress's words, or was perhaps held in the grip of some barbaric death-frenzy. Brielle reached for his shoulder, but he shrugged her off as he reloaded his boltgun. 'Go!' Quin shouted.

Brielle made to repeat her order, but the savage fury in Quin's eyes told her that she would be wasting her breath.

'I made a pledge,' the warrior said, his eyes alight in his tattooed face. 'I promised your father... Please, my lady, allow me to keep my word.'

Looking around her, Brielle saw the metal statues in the ground-floor alcoves had come to life and were even now advancing towards the centre of the chamber. She saw too that Quin hoped to buy her time to escape, with his very life. For an instant she considered ordering him to leave, begging him to leave, but she knew that neither course would work. Unable to speak, she nodded silent thanks to the warrior, hefting her bolt pistol in one hand and the glowing stave in the other. A small part of her mind prayed the warrior's sacrifice was worth it, and his death would be a noble one.

'With me!' Brielle called out as she retreated towards the passageway. Joachim Hep appeared at her side, a laspistol raised before him, followed a moment later by a dozen armsmen. At the sound of Quin's boltgun opening up once more, she turned to run for the passageway.

A metallic warrior barred her path. Instinctively, she brought her bolt pistol to bear, opening fire from a distance of scant metres. At the same moment, her companions did likewise, and the foe was rocked backwards as its skeletal body was hammered by round after round of precision fire.

For a moment, Brielle feared that this enemy's metal form would prove as impervious to attack as that of the larger figure that floated above in the shaft of green light. She gave heartfelt thanks as she saw angry sparks erupt from within its chest, followed an instant later by a small explosion.

'Again!' She ordered, firing three more bolt-rounds into the enemy's chest. The armsmen pumped shell after shell at the foe, forcing it backwards still further.

And then, the metal skeleton blew apart, ripped asunder by an explosion deep within its armoured ribcage. Jagged metal shrapnel lanced outwards, one piece shattering the armoured visor of Brielle's helmet, and slashing a deep cut across her forehead.

Even as blood from her wound ran freely into Brielle's eyes, she rushed onwards, almost gaining the passageway before turning to take one last look at the scene.

Quin had stopped firing once more, evidently having emptied another two-dozen bolt rounds into the floating figure. Even as he ejected the spent, sickle-shaped magazine, the figure turned its gaze upon him, as if noticing his presence for the first time.

Quin slammed home a fresh magazine and looked up into the blazing eyes of his enemy. The figure reached out a metallic skeletal arm, ragged swathes of cloth flapping as if in some aetheric breeze around it. As Quin raised his boltgun once more, his tattooed face a mask of savagery, the figure's palm blazed with pulsating green light.

The feral-worlder convulsed, his boltgun slamming to the ground at his feet. Brielle screamed his name, but it was too late. Before her eyes, Quin's survival suit appeared to melt away. First the armoured plates dissolved, as if the metal were being peeled away, one layer of atoms at a time. Then the fabric too disappeared, to reveal the warrior's tattooed flesh beneath. For a moment, Quin stood naked before the metal daemon above him, and then the tattoos that covered his body faded, followed an instant later by his skin.

Quin's bloodcurdling death-scream split the dusty air of the tomb chamber as his skin dissolved and the raw musculature beneath was revealed. Layer by layer, the flesh was peeled away, atomised to nothing by the awful power of the green radiation. At the last, only Quin's skeleton stood, silhouetted against the blazing shaft of green light, and in an instant, that too was gone, the last of his marrow reduced to dust evaporating on the unnatural wind.

Before Brielle could react, the floating horror came fully to life, stepping from the column of green light before descending to the dusty ground with an earth-shaking impact. With a single motion, several thousand of its skeletal minions took a pace forwards, those on the ground level forming a circle around Brielle and her companions. Resigned now to the inevitable, but unwilling to go meekly, Brielle took a deep breath and raised her bolt pistol for one final act of defiance.

Before she knew it, the metal horror had strode across the chamber, and stood, towering over Brielle. Even as her finger tightened on the bolt pistol's trigger, it regarded her through blazing green eyes. It extended its hand. Brielle steeled herself for the same fate that had befallen Quin, her skin burning with dreadful anticipation of such a grisly end.

But instead of that metal hand erupting in green, pulsating light, it appeared to make a gesture. The breath stuck in her throat, and Brielle relaxed her finger, for but an instant. Her mind raced as she sought to decipher the figure's gesture.

Then it came to her. The metal daemon was demanding she surrender the stave she still held in her left hand.

'You want this?' She growled, girding her muscles and bracing her feet on the ground.

'Then have it!' With titanic effort, Brielle hurled the stave at her foe. The blade flared green as it crossed the space between them, almost blinding her. With unerring accuracy, the tip struck the skeletal figure in the centre of its ribcage, piercing armour that had proven impenetrable to dozens of boltgun rounds. A shaft of green light shot outwards, accompanied by a piercing machine howl, and the stave continued its course, burying itself up to the haft in the figure's chest.

The skeletal horror stood transfixed by its own weapon, blinding green light now splaying in all directions from its wound. It stood, unable to move, its hellish death-mask face staring at Brielle as it writhed as if in agony. For an instant, Brielle felt some unutterable hatred of truly cosmic scale turned upon her, and knew total, soul-rending insignificance before that impossibly ancient malice. And then, the moment passed, and she tore her eyes away from the dazzling sight before her.

Seeing that the skeletal warriors around the chamber appeared to have faltered in their advance, as if they shared something of the pain Brielle had inflicted upon their lord, she saw the chance to escape, and grasped it for all she was worth.

'Hep!' she shouted above the infernal metallic howl emanating from the transfixed metal giant. 'Gather the men. I've had just about enough of this place!'

* * *

Brielle stood upon the bridge of the Fairlight, Joachim Hep at her side. The wound at her brow was dressed, while Hep's right arm was set in a sling.

'A close call, ma'am,' Hep said flatly.

Raising an eyebrow at the understatement, Brielle turned to face her advisor. 'Aye, Joachim,' she replied. 'And costly. Santos will be missed. But,' she continued, 'it may not have been in vain.'

Hep rounded upon his mistress, unease writ large across his craggy features. 'Ma'am...' he started.

'Easy, Joachim.' Brielle smiled as she raised a hand to forestall her advisor's inevitable objection to what she was about to say. 'If what the pathfinder said is true, there must be more of these places, these tombs, out there,' she nodded towards the void through the viewing port. 'Just think, Joachim. Just think. We gained entrance to that tomb, and we had no idea what waited for us.'

'Ma'am...'

'That place makes Skard look like a downhive scav-mart,' she grinned. 'Just think what the Mechanicus would give to get their hands on that tech. They'd give anything to study just one of those machine warriors... what if we could broker contracts with each of the forges, one sample to each, exclusive rights...'

'Brielle!' Hep interjected. 'Your father would march me from the torpedo tubes if I allowed you to...'

'Next time,' Brielle pressed on, a mischievous light entering her eyes, 'we'll know what awaits us.' Feeling suddenly breathless at the thought of the riches she might bring to her house, she pressed on. 'Next time, Joachim, no conceited eldar will interfere with our efforts. Next time, we'll take it all...'

SAVAGE SCARS

'In the year of Our Emperor 742.M41, the most glorious forces of the Imperium launched a crusade of conquest into the Lithesh Sector, to regain control of those worlds so long estranged from the Rule of Terra by warp storm activity and the raids of the pernicious eldar. But woe, for it was discovered that far worse a fate had befallen those benighted worlds. A previously unknown xenos species called the tau had infiltrated and undermined the proper governance of a string of worlds along the edge of the celestial anomaly known as the Damocles Gulf. Foremost amongst those to have discovered this duplicity was the rogue trader Lucian Gerrit, patriarch of the Clan Arcadius.

The Imperium could not, would not, stand by as more worlds fell from the fold. The firebrand preacher Cardinal Esau Gurney of Brimlock preached a full crusade against the tau, holding that the Gulf must be breached, the tau home world located and the entire species exterminated.

The call to arms rang out across the sector and beyond, and was answered. The Space Marines of the Iron Hands, White Scars, Ultramarines and Scythes of the Emperor heeded that call, as did a dozen planetary governors who raised new regiments for the Imperial Guard to prosecute the Damocles Gulf Crusade. The rogue trader Lucian answered the call too, his Warrant of Trade earning him a place on the crusade's command council.

But so too did the figure of Inquisitor Grand, and

the council soon split into two factions – those centred around Grand and Gurney, who desired only the complete destruction of the xenos tau, and those allied to the rogue trader, who sought in various degrees honour, glory or profit, but not dishonourable slaughter.

The first battles were fought on the nearside of the Damocles Gulf, and saw the world of Sy'l'kell conquered with relative ease and a tau fleet bested at Hydass. But already the council was being torn asunder by internecine rivalries and Gerrit's daughter Brielle appeared to assault the inquisitor, for reasons unknown, and flee. She was assumed dead thereafter, much to her father's despair, though he still had his son Korvane to stand by him.

Having purged the world of Viss'el, the crusade pierced the Damocles Gulf, and fell upon the world of Pra'yen with the righteous fury of the faithful. But disaster almost befell the Emperor's warriors there, for it proved that the tau were a far greater threat than any had imagined. The tau were not some minor race residing on but a single world, but were possessed of an entire stellar realm.

As the crusade pressed in to capture the capital world of the Dal'yth system, Dal'yth Prime, more tau forces closed in. The fate of the Damocles Gulf Crusade would come to rest in the hands of three individuals – the White Scars Veteran Sergeant Sarik, the rogue trader Lucian Gerrit, and his daughter Brielle, who had fallen by her own hubris into the hands of the tau water caste envoy called Aura.

Mustering its forces, the crusade prepared for 'Operation Pluto' – the Dal'yth Prime landings. All would depend on those landings, and the actions of but three very different individuals.'

– Extract from preface of
The Truth of the Damocles Gulf Crusade
(unpublished, author unknown)

CHAPTER ONE

Deep within the dense stellar cluster that was the crucible and the cradle of the alien species known as the tau, the frigate *Nomad* was a dark shadow against the roiling blue nebulae permeating the entire region. The cluster seethed with anomalous energies not witnessed anywhere else in the galaxy, a phenomenon that the most learned of Navigator-seers and astro-cognoscenti had entirely failed to explicate. The stars here were young and the very fabric of space somehow charged with raw potential, and the same appeared to be true of the species that had evolved here. The tau had developed from primitive nomads to a heretically advanced, space-faring empire within a handful of millennia. The tau's very existence was now a threat to the Imperium's rule in the area, and the Damocles Gulf Crusade had been set in motion to restore order and adherence to the rule of the God-Emperor of Mankind.

But Veteran Sergeant Sarik cared little for inexplicable nebulae or esoteric stellar phenomena. He didn't even care a great deal about the tau or any other alien species, so long as they adhered to the one, defining principle by which he himself led his life. That principle was honour, and to Sarik, everything else was secondary.

Sarik was standing on the bridge of the *Nomad*, the lambent nebulae washing his weather-beaten, honour-scarred face and causing his folded eyes to glow with ice-blue luminescence. His polished white armour glinted in the light of alien suns. Sarik was the master of his vessel, a one-and-a-half-kilometre-long Nova-class frigate bearing the white and red livery of the White Scars Chapter of the Space Marines, but truth be told, he held little love for the role. He yearned to fight on solid ground, to engage his foe not in ship-to-ship combat at a thousand kilometres but in the brutal, face-to-face savagery of close-quarters melee.

Turning his back on the lancet-paned forward viewing portal, Sarik strode the length of the bridge, reading in every step the deep throb of the plasma drives as they propelled the *Nomad* through the void at full speed. The air was heavy with the smoky scent of the purifying unguents used to bless the vessel, its machine systems and the crew that tended her. The scent reminded Sarik of the cold, windswept plains of home, the world of Chogoris, for the Techmarines of the White Scars worked into the incense the resin of the rockrose gathered from the uplands of the north. Dozens of sounds filled the bridge, from the chattering of the cogitation banks and logic engines to the muted conversation of the bridge-serfs as they coordinated dozens of secondary operations, none of which were of immediate concern to the master of a vessel crewed by several thousand souls.

One of the bridge-serfs was a man called Loccum, a veteran with the rank of *conversi*, an appointment that honoured him with the right to address his Adeptus Astartes masters directly. Unlike many Adeptus Astartes, however, Sarik eschewed the aloofness so often displayed by the superhuman Space Marines, and while he might not converse with his crew or others as peers, he nonetheless valued their skills and their opinions.

Loccum glanced up as Sarik approached, and reported, 'Pathfinder squadron is approaching segment delta-nine, brother-sergeant.' The man was permanently connected to the frigate's machine-systems by a complex web of mind impulse link cables, and every fragment of visible skin was a matrix of Chogoran tribal tattoos. 'In-loading remote telemetry now.'

'Shunt it through, please, Loccum,' Sarik replied, frowning as he focussed on the icons tracking their way across the glowing blue screen of his command lectern. Machine chatter blurted out of the bridge phono-casters, a harsh sound that grated on Sarik's nerves whenever he heard it. He was reminded again how much he yearned for the howl of wind in his ears and the feel of a clean breeze on his face. The machine noise cut out as suddenly as it had appeared, a series of figures and icons resolving on the lectern's screen.

'Damn,' Sarik cursed, as he took in the full import of the lines of data scrolling across the lectern. A semi-circular form appeared at the edge of the screen, representing the enemy-held planet towards which the pathfinders were probing. In between the squadron and that planet three new returns blinked ominously. The Imperial Navy pathfinder squadron ranging ahead of the *Nomad* were the elite of the crusade's scout forces, the master of each vessel a man Sarik knew personally. He would not see them blunder into an alien trap, not while he could influence matters.

'Confirmed,' said Loccum. 'Three capital-scale defence platforms.'

'Initiate tight-beam communion,' ordered Sarik. 'We have to warn them.'

Loccum hesitated, causing Sarik to look up in response to his silence. 'Well?'

'Brother-sergeant,' the bridge-serf replied. 'Orders from fleet.'

'I am aware of fleet's orders, conversi,' Sarik said, using the serf's rank title to remind him of his status. 'If we must risk detection, so be it.'

Loccum bowed deeply in response to Sarik's order, and turned to a nearby vox terminal. The data script that was being fed back to the *Nomad* before being relayed to the bulk of the fleet continued to scroll across the lectern. The three icons that represented the alien defence platforms indicated that they were deployed in a relatively tight cluster, approximately 100,000 kilometres from the world they protected. Sarik's lip curled as he recalled the last time the fleet had faced one of those platforms. Then, it had been just one platform, but so heavily armed it had inflicted a fearsome toll on the Damocles Gulf Crusade fleet. Men had died by the thousand, screaming silently into the void as their vessels had burned around them, a death that Sarik considered an unsuitable one for such brave servants of the Imperium.

That station had finally been destroyed when Sarik himself had led a boarding action, consisting of a composite force of Space Marines drawn from the White Scars, Ultramarines and Scythes of the Emperor Chapters. The Space Marines had destroyed that platform's power plant, sending it burning like a meteor through the atmosphere of the world the alien tau knew as Pra'yen.

Sarik glanced up at the conversi, who noted his attention and replied, 'Seventy per cent, brother-sergeant.'

Grunting, Sarik resumed his study of the lectern's screen. He was looking for any sign of tau vessels, praying that the pathfinders would not be drawn into an ambush. The scout vessels were built for speed and stealth, and would stand little chance if they were engaged. The fleet had already faced a sizeable tau force as it had pushed into the system, and communications intercepts indicated that more were incoming.

A group of augur returns resolved out of the background noise, some distance ahead of the scouts.

'Tight-beam communion established,' announced the conversi. 'On main terminal now.'

'Nova-zero-leader,' said Sarik, using the pathfinder squadron leader's call sign. 'This is *Nomad*. I read multiple contacts inbound on your trajectory. Report status.'

'Received, *Nomad*,' replied the comms officer aboard the lead pathfinder, his voice clipped and metallic over the heavily shielded vox-link. 'Conducting passive augur reading of the platforms. Will relay to you when complete, over.'

The icons on the lectern blinked as the tau vessels rapidly closed on the pathfinder squadron. 'Enemy vessels have you in their sights, Nova leader,' Sarik growled. 'You don't have time for a full reading.'

There was a pause, before the pathfinder replied, 'We know that, *Nomad*, over.'

Sarik scowled and his grip on the edge of the lectern tightened as his frustration mounted. Inside, he honoured the pathfinders for their dedication to their duty, but he saw no reason for them to throw their lives away. 'They'll be on you before you can complete the reading, you know that.'

'We have our orders, *Nomad*. Fleet has to know of those platforms,' the comms officer insisted. 'Whatever it costs.'

Sarik forced himself to calm before responding. 'Nova leader, I honour your courage.' He did not say such a thing lightly, and many Adeptus Astartes would never have considered saying it at all. 'But if you do not take immediate evasive action, fleet will never hear your report. You'll be dead.'

'We can't simply–' the officer replied, but Sarik cut him off. 'Listen to me, Nova leader, and we'll get fleet their reading and share a victory horn together later. This is what I want you to do...'

* * *

As the Nomad had ploughed onwards towards the pathfinder squadron's position, Sarik had monitored the vox-channels. The elite crews of the scout vessels had accepted his plan, and were enacting it with supreme skill and courage. Even as the tau vessels closed, all but one of the scouts had veered off on a new heading, on Sarik's order, drawing the aliens away.

Only one pathfinder vessel now remained on station.

'Nova leader,' Sarik said, aware of how isolated the scout crew must be feeling. 'Status, please?'

'Preliminary readings compiling now, *Nomad*,' replied the comms officer of Nova leader. 'Initial cogitation suggests all three defence platforms are of a different configuration to those we have previously faced, over.'

Sarik's mind raced as he considered what devious new combination of offensive and defensive alien technology might await the fleet as it closed on the platforms. The tau had proved able to adapt rapidly, their forces displaying a wide range of unpredictable technologies. 'Different?' he said. 'How?'

'Unclear at this stage, *Nomad*–' the scout replied. Before he could complete his transmission, the channel burst with a sudden scream of feedback. Sarik knew from previous fights with the alien tau what such vox interference often foreshadowed. Yet another of their abominable weapons systems.

'Conversi Yosef,' Sarik addressed the tech-serf manning a station nearby. 'Source?'

'Enemy contact, brother-sergeant,' the crewman replied. 'Augur spirits sing of a homopolar energy surge analogous to mass driver weaponry previously encountered.'

Sarik had no idea what that meant, his gorge rising at the prospect of losing even a single fellow warrior of the Emperor to these aliens. Yosef's words spoke of the technological heresy of the tau, but they were as impenetrable and repellent as a sorcerer's hex to Sarik. 'Meaning?'

'The xenos are opening fire, sir.'

'At?'

'At the scouts, sir.'

A moment later, a bright blue pulse illuminated the scene beyond the bridge's armoured viewing port. Bitter experience had taught

Sarik just how lethal the aliens' weapons could be, and he braced himself against the sturdy lectern, even though he doubted the shot was aimed at the *Nomad*.

He was correct. Although the distance was far too great to see any detail of the attackers, the glowing readout on the lectern told him all he needed to know. The blurred return that was the group of enemy vessels was resolving into five separate icons as the scouts' augurs got a better fix on them. One of those icons, the vessel that had just fired, blinked as a line of cogitation data scrolled rapidly beside it. The machine script described just how alien the vessels were, their manoeuvring characteristics, displacement and weapons systems so different from the Imperium's warships and Sarik's anger rose at the thought of techno-heresy of the tau.

The vox-channel came to life as the comms officers of each of the scout vessels reported in. Sarik breathed a sigh of relief that none had sustained any major damage. Nova-zero-three had been the target of the attack, and had suffered a temporary failure in flight control as the shot had passed dangerously close. The scout vessel's tech-adept was even now tending to the outraged machine-spirits and nursing his systems back to life.

'They're going for it,' Sarik growled, as the icons representing the enemy ships changed course to power after the bulk of the pathfinder squadron. Nova leader still appeared mightily vulnerable, but at least the enemy were being drawn away. 'Helm,' said Sarik. 'Take us in.'

Helmsman Kuro, a bridge-serf who had served aboard the *Nomad* for three decades and whose voidsmanship was nigh legendary, hauled on his mighty brass control yokes, setting the vessel to come around to the new heading.

'Intercept at seven zero delta by five nine sigma,' Sarik snapped, before addressing Conversi Loccum. 'Do we have resolution yet?'

'In-loading now, brother-sergeant,' the serf replied, his face underlit by his readout and his eyes flicking impossibly fast as he rapidly scanned the reams of cogitation script passing across its glowing surface. 'Enemy vessels appear to be pickets, sir. Light displacement only.'

'Thank the primarch,' Sarik breathed. While the alien vessels might prove superior to the pathfinders, they would hardly be a match for the *Nomad*. That left the three defence platforms to face. Sarik determined to worry about those later. Right now, his attention was focussed on closing the trap without the loss of any Imperial lives.

Even as Sarik watched the icons swarming across the lectern screen, another bright blue pulse illuminated the bridge. Silence followed, during which Sarik fixed his gaze on the icons representing the pathfinder vessels. Far from machine phosphorescence, each was a crew of dozens of brave men and women.

Then one of those icons turned red. Involuntarily, Sarik held his breath.

'Pathfinder Nova-zero-two hit, brother-sergeant,' Conversi Yosef reported grimly.

'Damage?' Sarik replied, fearing the worst having seen all too closely the potential of the alien weapons.

'Port drive disabled,' the serf said. 'Reading grievous reactor failure.'

I'm sorry, Sarik said inwardly, no doubt in his mind as to what would happen next.

A second bright flash illuminated space, and a small sun flared into existence thousands of kilometres away, before collapsing in upon itself within the span of a second. The icon representing Nova-zero-two blinked once, then vanished. Sarik mouthed a silent Chogoran prayer to ease the passage of the dead into the halls of their ancestors, before resuming his duty.

'Helm, open her up,' Sarik ordered. Flicking a switch on his lectern to activate the internal vox-net, he said, 'Fire control?'

'Brother Qaja here,' the reply came back. 'Go ahead, brother-sergeant.'

'Qaja,' Sarik addressed the Space Marine who supervised the gun-serfs, a warrior Sarik had served alongside for decades and counted amongst his closest of brothers. 'I want your crews to concentrate fire on any enemy vessel that so much as *thinks* about breaking off from the decoy group to engage Nova-zero-zero. Understood?'

As Brother Qaja signalled his understanding, Sarik turned to Conversi Nord, the bridge-serf manning the shields station. 'Nord, we're about to draw a lot of fire, from the enemy scouts for certain, but possibly from the defence platforms too if they have the range. Be ready.' The conversi nodded his understanding, and Sarik turned his attention back to the screen on his lectern.

The tau pickets were closing on the bulk of the pathfinder squadron. The *Nomad*'s projected course would bring her into weapons range within minutes. The tau vessels opened fire on the scouts again. The scouts had scant point defence capability, but what few weapons they did have opened fire as one, stitching the void with streams of bright fire.

Screaming silently in, the tau pickets swept directly through the pathfinder's formation, reminding Sarik of a pack of silversharks attacking a shoal of moonwyrms. The brave pathfinders ploughed on, relying on their speed to push through the enemy. The tau vessels were fast, as Sarik knew they would be, but they were also supremely manoeuvrable, each vessel selecting a victim and latching onto it whatever evasive actions the pathfinder attempted. Just hold on, Sarik thought, counting down the seconds until his own weapons would be in range to intervene.

'Nova-zero-three's in trouble, brother-sergeant,' a crewman said. Sarik glanced upwards through the armoured portal, but besides the staccato flashes of distant weapons discharges, the opposing vessels were still far too distant to be seen with the naked eye. The readout on the lectern, however, told the full story.

The scout vessel with the call sign of Nova-zero-three was being closely pursued by a tau picket, the human pilot jinking sharply from side to side in an attempt to avoid the constant hail of high-velocity projectiles streaming through space towards him. The scout pilot was good, Sarik could tell, but so too was his pursuer. The scout's life must surely be measured in seconds.

'Intercept?' Sarik said, denial welling up inside him.

'Closing to long range now, brother-sergeant,' Conversi Kuro replied.

Sarik activated the vox-net link to Brother Qaja. 'Fire control,' Sarik said, 'Zero-three needs our help – I got him into this situation, and by the primarch I will get him out. Fire when ready.'

'Aye, brother-sergeant,' the other Space Marine replied. A line of targeting script scrolled across the readout beside the icon representing the enemy picket. 'Fire control cogitation plotted. Opening fire.'

A moment later, the *Nomad*'s weapons batteries spoke, the report shuddering through the frigate's hull as titanic energies were unleashed. Each shell was as large as a tank, and had been hauled into the breech of its cannon by gangs of sweating Chapter-serfs, who even now would be racing to load the next. A barrage of shells was propelled from the forward guns at supersonic velocity, tearing across the intervening gulf of space in a matter of seconds.

So close were the pursuer and the pursued that Brother Qaja had been forced to take aim at a point in space aft of the enemy picket, hoping to catch the alien in the shell's blast and avoid damaging the scout. More callous gunnery masters might not have taken such precautions, but Qaja knew his commander well and was in any case of a like mind. The first salvo of shells blossomed into raging orange fire, but Sarik saw instantly that the shot had fallen short.

'Nova-zero-three,' Sarik hailed the pathfinder. 'Cease evasion, full power to main drives and hold on.'

The scout did not reply, and Sarik had not expected him to, for all of his efforts would be focussed on simply staying alive. Nonetheless, Sarik's instruction was heeded. The scout vessel ceased its jinking and powered straight ahead, its forward velocity increasing now its path was true. Within seconds, the gap between the two vessels had increased.

A piercing shrill filled the small bridge.

'Enemy has cogitated terminal lock,' Conversi Yosef announced.

'Qaja,' said Sarik, his heart pounding with the ferocity of battle. 'Do it, do it now!'

The frigate shook as its forward weapons batteries roared a second time, unleashing another salvo of gargantuan ordnance into space. Even as the shrill warning tone continued, Sarik finally saw that the two vessels were entering visual range. The pathfinder streaked past to the *Nomad*'s starboard, and a second later the shells exploded violently to the fore.

A sheet of raging fire exploded across space, the infernal orange chasing away the serene blue of the nebulae. The glow lent Sarik the aspect of a fearsome beast from Chogoran legend, his polished white and red armour gleaming and his fierce eyes burning with reflected flames. His face twisted savagely in the furnace illumination and he pounded the lectern with a clenched fist with dark exuberance. The glass of the lectern readout cracked under the impact, but Sarik didn't notice.

The icon representing the tau picket was engulfed in a rapidly expanding circle that described the blast radius of the second salvo. The icon blinked out of existence. It had been caught in the blast, and even had it survived, it would not be in any state to continue the pursuit.

'*Nomad*,' the vox-channel burst to life, 'this is Nova-zero-three. Our thanks, we are indebted to you.'

'Never mind that,' Sarik growled, his hunter's instinct reasserting itself over his battle-lust as he scanned the readout. 'What's your status?'

'Alive,' the comms officer aboard Nova-zero-three replied wryly, causing Sarik to snort in amusement. 'But flight control is compromised and the machine-spirits are grievously angered.'

'Then get clear, zero-three,' Sarik ordered, 'before the Emperor gets bored of keeping you around.'

'Acknowledged,' Nova-three replied. 'Will form up on your trajectory.'

'Negative, zero-three,' Sarik replied. 'We'll catch you up. Out.'

'Sir?' inquired the helmsman, sensing a change in plans. 'Your orders?'

'Zero-nine by delta, offset three point five, helm,' Sarik ordered. A series of unfixed readings scrolled across the lectern readout, indicating the appearance of a potential new contact.

'Screen the defence platforms?' Conversi Kuro said over his shoulder as he hauled on the steering levers.

'Aye,' Sarik replied. 'Time?'

'Five minutes,' the helmsman replied.

'Nova leader?' Sarik said, opening a vox-channel to the squadron leader. 'What is your status?'

'Augur readings compiled, *Nomad*,' Nova leader replied. 'Communing with fleet now, but I think we have company.'

'I see it, Nova leader,' said Sarik, as a new augur return flashed on the lectern's screen. The *Nomad*'s cogitator banks set about analysing the return, comparing it to vessels the crusade had faced in its previous battles against the alien tau.

'Medium displacement, brother-sergeant,' Conversi Loccum

reported, his mind impulse link feeding him the raw information before it even appeared on the lectern screen. 'Cruiser analogue, similar to those faced previously.'

'Not something we want to face alone, then,' Sarik growled, the warlike side of his spirit battling with the veteran warrior-leader side. 'Nonetheless,' he continued, 'fleet needs those readings. Helm, bring us prow on with the enemy. Fire control?'

'Already there, brother-sergeant,' Qaja replied over the internal vox. 'Full yield lance?'

Sarik grinned savagely, his honour scars twisting into a swirling pattern as he gripped the lectern with both hands. 'Aye, Qaja. And make it count.'

Addressing the bridge-serf at the shields station, Sarik said, 'Nord, forward banks to maximum. This might hurt...'

The veteran sergeant had barely completed his remark when a blue pulse filled the forward vision port. Sarik braced himself, and a moment later, the tau's hyper-velocity projectile struck the hastily raised forward screen.

The entire view from the portal exploded with seething white energies as the enemy's attack was dissipated against the *Nomad*'s forward shield. Sarik squinted against the fierce illumination, but his pride refused to let him shield his sight entirely. The frigate shook violently as the projectors struggled to shunt sufficient power to counter the attack, warning klaxons sounding as the bridge lights flickered.

'Report!' Sarik shouted above the banshee wailing of the sirens.

'Shields holding,' Nord yelled back. 'But only just!'

Sarik's grip on the lectern redoubled as he imagined his hands strangling the life from the captain of the alien vessel. If only he could engage his foe face-to-face. Snarling, Sarik looked to the lectern screen, confirming that the pathfinders' squadron leader was finally coming about on a heading that would take the vessel back towards the fleet. His gaze followed the icon's projected course towards the far edge of the screen, where he saw...

'All stations!' Sarik bellowed. 'I want every last ounce of power on the shields.'

The frigate's main systems powered down one by one as the crew enacted Sarik's order, the siren dying away to silence as all available power was diverted to the shield generators. Soon, only the shrill whine of the labouring projectors was audible. Only the harsh light cast by the lectern screen lit the bridge, the surface laced with racing numerals. A new icon resolved in the mid-range band, to the *Nomad*'s aft.

'Energy spike!' Loccum reported, his voice seeming shockingly loud in the sudden near silence. 'Brace!'

Sarik didn't need to be told. Another cold blue pulse filled the portal, a white pinprick of light in the black void marking its source. An instant later, the hyper-velocity projectile slammed into the *Nomad*'s forward shield, and this time, the screen could not contain the terrific energy of its impact.

With a staggering release of blinding energies, the frigate's forward shield collapsed. The solid mass of the tau projectile was transformed into raw energy as it passed through the screen, and struck the *Nomad*'s blocky, armoured prow.

The gut-wrenching impact passed through the vessel in seconds, the deck beneath Sarik's armoured boots buckling with a tortured metallic scream. Secondary explosions ripped along the vessel's spine, scores of Chapter-serfs dying in an instant as ravaging flames scoured entire compartments or the cold vacuum of space plucked them away. The helm station erupted in a shower of molten brass, blasting Conversi Kuro backwards even as he was consumed in flames. The lectern screen died, plunging the entire bridge into near darkness, the only illumination that of guttering flames.

Bracing himself on the lectern, Sarik drew himself to his full height, looking around him as he did so to confirm his crew's predicament. His bridge, his personal domain over which he was undisputed master, was burning around him. Why had the conflagration-suppressors not engaged?

Sarik looked down at his dead command lectern, and realised that the impact of the tau weapon had ripped the soul from his vessel, its core logic engines and cogitation transmission conduits crippled, or at the very least silenced for a spell, at the worst possible moment.

The flames picked up as they rushed along the length of the bridge, consuming terminals as they progressed. Conversi Nord dashed across the deck towards the sprawled form of the helmsman,

Kuro, rolling his body over as he knelt down beside it. It was immediately obvious that the veteran bridge-serf was burned beyond aid, the flesh of his face sloughing away in smoking chunks.

Conversi Loccum's station was as yet untouched, but Sarik saw that it was directly in the path of the onrushing flames. Hard-wired into his mind impulse unit, there was nothing Loccum could do to avoid imminent and horrific death.

Having lost one valued servant, Sarik vowed in that instant not to allow the other to suffer a similar fate. He knew what he had to do.

'Bridge crew!' Sarik yelled over the raging flames and the shattering of glass terminal screens. Conversi Loccum had closed his eyes, his tattooed face almost serene in the face of death. 'Vacuum protocols, purging now!'

Sarik turned and hauled down on a large brass lever. The manually operated purge valve mounted in the vaulted ceiling irised open and the hatch to the rear of the bridge locked shut with a resounding clang. A new siren started up, its rapid rise and fall specifically keyed to the purge protocol. Those bridge-serfs not already at their station made quickly for their seats, following long-rehearsed purge drills. Sarik had no need to strap himself into a seat, his superhuman grip on the lectern sufficient to hold him against the coming storm of depressurisation.

Seconds later, that storm erupted.

With explosive force, the air in the bridge compartment was sucked through the valve almost directly above Sarik's lectern. He redoubled his grip, screwing his eyes tight shut and forcing the air out of his lungs to avoid internal injury. Loose objects were sucked upwards towards the valve, the grate across its surface stopping them jamming its mechanism. A bone-hewed Chogoran charm scythed through the air and cut a deep gash across Sarik's scalp, before shattering on the bulkhead overhead. Parchment strips affixed to terminals fluttered wildly in the rush of air, and then fell still. Suddenly, all was silent. Sarik opened his eyes to see that the flames, starved of oxygen, had extinguished.

Sarik pulled back on the lever, manually initiating the re-pressurisation cycle. The purge valve irised shut and the hiss of oxygen inlets filled Sarik's ears. He took a deep breath, unaccustomedly pleased to taste the stale shipboard air. The taste of burned metal would hang in the air for hours, he knew, and a fine mist was already forming as the newly pumped-in oxygen condensed in the chill space. Within thirty seconds the bridge was returned to one standard atmospheric measure, the emergency averted and Loccum and the other bridge-serfs saved.

'Sound off!' Sarik called out. As a Space Marine, his genetically enhanced biology was proof against the worst effects of the depressurisation, but Sarik was less certain how his bridge crew might have fared.

Coughs and splutters sounded from the darkness, before the first of the crew replied. 'Loccum!' the man called out. 'Vox-net awakening, but Kuro is down.' Sarik was filled with relief that Loccum had been saved from a horrible death, and immeasurably proud at how quickly the conversi resumed his duties.

'Nord,' the bridge-serf at the shield station called out. 'Residual only, projectors down.'

'Understood,' Sarik replied, looking down at the blank, cracked screen of the lectern. 'If you're out there...'

'Incoming vox communion, brother-sergeant,' said Conversi Loccum, his terminal awakening even as he spoke. A moment later the bridge was filled with churning static as the ship-to-ship vox-channel burst to life.

'*Nomad*,' a voice came over the static-laced vox-channel. 'Pathfinders are clear. Get your drives on-line and follow them out. We'll deal with this.'

Sarik grinned savagely as he recognised the voice of his friend and ally, the rogue trader Lucian Gerrit, master of the heavy cruiser *Oceanid*.

'You're sure you don't need help, Lucian?' Sarik replied. 'It wouldn't be the first time, after all!'

The rogue trader's only reply was a devastating broadside, which struck the closing tau vessel amidships and broke it in two. The enemy ship's drive section sheered away from its central spine, inertia and residual thrust carrying it forwards to pass the *Nomad* at perilously close range.

Two competing reactions welled up inside Sarik as he watched the spectacular destruction of the tau vessel. Part of him knew vindication, revenge for the deaths the tau had inflicted on his crew and the damage they had done to the *Nomad*. The other part, which Sarik rejected the instant he became aware of it, knew something akin to jealousy, for it had not been him, but another, who had dealt the killing blow. Sarik knew the emotion was ignoble, born of his fierce warrior heritage and nothing to do with the noble traditions of his Chapter or the Adeptus Astartes as a whole. He would confess his weakness to his ancestors later, he vowed.

As the flaming debris passed across the view from the bridge portal, Sarik saw the *Oceanid* move forwards, assuming a vector that would take it into battle with the three alien defence platforms.

'Lucian,' said Sarik, his momentary weakness replaced by concern for his friend. 'You can't take those platforms on alone...'

'Don't worry, Sarik,' the reply came back, and Sarik knew that the *Oceanid* was merely the tip of the spear. 'We'll save some fun for you.'

Sarik moved around his lectern and strode along the length of the bridge, coming to stand before the armoured glass of the forward port with his hands gripping the stanchions. As he watched, the entire fleet came into view, gargantuan battleships and cruisers gliding past in stately procession. In echelon behind the *Oceanid* came the other two vessels of the rogue trader's flotilla, the cruisers *Fairlight* and *Rosetta*. As the three ships began to open fire at extreme long range against the distant defence platforms, the majestic form of the *Blade of Woe*, the crusade's flagship, came into view. Even Sarik, who had seen the sight many times before and far preferred to prosecute his wars on land, could not help but be impressed by the battle cruiser's vast form. Its sharp prow was sculpted into the form of sweeping eagle's wings, and every square metre of its ancient armour was carved with litanies and the features of revered Imperial saints. Its portholes were delicate lancet windows, the armoured glass a riot of colours depicting scenes of glorious battle. One by one, the warships sailed past the *Nomad*, passing her by on every side and accompanied by their nimble escort squadrons and swarms of smaller vessels.

And then, the strike cruiser *Fist of Light* came into view. Though smaller than the *Blade of Woe*, the Space Marine vessel, which belonged to the Iron Hands contingent of the crusade forces, radiated menace as if the cold outer steel skin shielded a raging furnace at its heart. Where the Imperial Navy warships were stately, with sharp prows and covered in Gothic detailing, the Space Marine vessels were blunt-prowed and unadorned. Their flanks were not encrusted with devotional statues, but sheathed in the thickest ceramite armour known to man. The *Fist of Light* was the largest Space Marine warship in the crusade fleet, the remainder frigates and destroyers. Her armoured flanks were painted black, white and steel grey, the predominant colours of the Iron Hands heraldry, and they were pitted with countless thousands of small craters, each a battle scar earned over many centuries of service to the Imperium of Mankind.

The fleet crossed the point at which its longest-ranged weapons could open fire upon the alien defence stations. Initially, these weapons were those mounted in dorsal turrets, or torpedoes fired from cavernous tubes mounted in the armoured prows. The *Blade of Woe*'s weapons batteries spoke first, for they had the longest range, great salvoes of city-levelling ordnance blasting across the void to smash into the tau stations. Yet, the display was inconsequential compared to what would follow when the ships' masters ordered their warships to turn and present a broadside to the alien platforms. The Imperial Navy's battle doctrine dictated that its vessels' firepower was concentrated in mighty batteries on either flank. A single salvo could drive off, cripple or even destroy almost any enemy vessel, as the tau had already discovered to their detriment.

The *Nomad*'s systems began to reawaken, the lectern screen flickering to life, though it remained shot through with churning, grainy static. Though too far distant to be seen with the naked eye, even that of a Space Marine, the screen indicated the presence of a number of the crusade fleet's supporting vessels. Tenders stood by should a warship need repair or towing clear of the battle. Tankers and mass haulers carried vast quantities of fuel and other commodities. Transports carried the crusade's ground troops, each of them home to an entire regiment of Imperial Guard. Most of the ground troops belonged to one of the Brimlock regiments, raised from the planet on which the crusade against the expanding alien empire of the tau had first been preached. Right on the edge of the readout was an icon representing the huge conveyance *Toil of Digamma*, a vessel of the Adeptus Mechanicus that transported the Legio Thanataris Titan Legion, known as the 'Deathbringers'. The towering god-machines carried in its cavernous bays would be crucial in the forthcoming planetary assault.

As mighty as the crusade fleet was, Sarik was painfully aware that it lacked sufficient carrier capacity. Scant few interceptors were available to defend the larger warships against enemy fighter-bombers. These would be able to inflict a terrible blow were they to get amongst the lumbering transports that followed behind the main fleet.

Conversi Loccum spoke up. 'Signal from fleet, brother-sergeant. The platforms burn. It is done.'

Looking around him at his smoke-wreathed bridge, sparks still spitting from wrecked consoles, Sarik shook his head. 'It is far from done.'

'Addendum to signal,' the crewman said.

'Go on,' Sarik replied, a sense of foreboding rising inside him.

'All crusade council members are to gather aboard the *Blade of Woe*, brother-sergeant. Immediately.'

'Reason?' Sarik said.

'None given, brother-sergeant, but the signal has the highest priority level.'

'Better request *Blade* sends a cutter then,' Sarik sighed. 'We're going nowhere fast in this state.'

'Aye, sir,' the conversi replied, opening a channel to the *Blade of Woe* to arrange for a naval runabout to collect Veteran Sergeant Sarik, and ferry him to the hastily gathered council of the Damocles Gulf Crusade.

Sarik was the last to arrive at the majestic *Blade of Woe*, and he noted straight away that the atmosphere aboard the flagship was unusually strained. Ordinarily, following a victory such as that the crusade had just won, the mood would be celebratory, but right now it was tense. The feeling had only increased as Sarik had made his way from the main docking bay to the council chamber. Now that he stood at the ornate chamber doors, he had a feeling he was about to find out why.

The portal ground heavily aside, and the voice of the council's convenor announced, 'Veteran Sergeant Sarik, of the Adeptus

Astartes White Scars.' The convenor's iron shod staff of office slammed into the deck at his feet, indicating formally that Sarik was recognised and welcomed.

The sergeant stepped through the portal, into the council chamber.

Though a large space, the chamber was lit in such a way that little more than its huge, circular table was visible, illuminated by several dozen floating servo-skulls, the crown of each surmounted with a flickering candle, runnels of solidified wax covering their surfaces. The wan candlelight overlapped where the servo-skulls converged, illuminating the table below, while others picked out the councillors seated around it. Sarik saw immediately that four of the seats were unoccupied. One seat was his, and the remaining three had belonged to councillors lost in the crusade's previous engagements.

Apart from the table, the only other thing visible was a large pict-slate mounted on one wall. The slate's surface showed the image of the three enemy defence stations breaking up or burning to death under the fleet's withering bombardment. The scene had been slowed down and was being played in loop, as if the suffering of each was being repeated over and over again, so as to reiterate the Imperium's glory. In truth, the stations had proved not nearly so well armed and armoured as previous ones the crusade had encountered, a fact for which its leaders should be grateful.

As Sarik crossed to his seat, one of the councillors stood, a dozen candle-bearing servo-skulls converging on him from above. The position of chairman of the council rotated with each sitting, and for this convocation, Logistician-General Stempf of the Adeptus Terra fulfilled the role.

'The brother-sergeant has arrived,' Stempf announced, the tau defence stations reliving their death throes behind him. 'And so we can begin.'

As Sarik seated himself, he cast a glance to the man to his left. Lucian Gerrit, the rogue trader, met his eye and shrugged. Gerrit was in many ways the archetypal rogue trader, a privateer and something of a scoundrel, though Sarik found him far less vainglorious than most men of his class. Like Sarik, Lucian lived his life according to a strictly defined sense of honour, which, also like Sarik, was at times at odds with the machinations of the galaxy and of the fates. Lucian was a large man, his head shaved except for the extravagant topknot sprouting from his crown, a style not unlike that worn by Sarik and his Chogoran brothers. He wore a dress coat resembling that of the high-ranking officers of the Imperial Navy, but festooned with more gold braid than even the most decorated of admirals would dare display. Sarik had learned to see past the affectation, knowing it was part of the role that the rogue trader played and that, if anything, it was a ruse designed to hide the man's true self and confound the weak and the stupid.

Sarik looked back at Stempf, a man he had grown to strongly dislike over the previous months. The Logistician-General cultivated what he hoped was an ascetic air. Yet Sarik, gifted with the superhuman senses of the Adeptus Astartes, could not help but detect the cloying reek of illicit narcotics that permeated his adept's robes.

In common with the bulk of the crusade's Space Marine contingent, Sarik preferred to remain aloof from men like Stempf and from the incessant politicking that bedevilled its command council. The leaders had become increasingly factionalised, splitting into two opposed power blocs. No doubt the situation would get worse before it was resolved.

'Gentlemen,' Stempf continued, warming to his role as chairman of the crusade council. 'We have this hour received an astropathic communiqué of such import that I have convened this session of the council.' The other councillors exchanged glances. Stempf had not shared the details of the communication with any others, even with the leaders of the bloc to which he was aligned, the firebrand Cardinal Esau Gurney and the dark person of Inquisitor Grand.

The Logistician-General nodded to the council's convenor, who struck his staff of office against the decking again, the metallic thud resounding around the chamber. From the still open portal, a hunched, robed figure emerged, and made his way to stand beside Stempf.

'Master Karzello,' Stempf said as he stepped to one side, allowing the man to stand before the council.

Master Karzello was the crusade's senior astropath, the head of the choir whose psychic mind-voice allowed them to communicate across the interstellar voids with the distant Imperium of Man. Such distances made communications by conventional means impossible, but the most powerful of astropaths could receive and send messages across many hundreds of light-years of space. The seething aetheric energies and unknowable stellar phenomena that afflicted the region made even this means of communication unreliable at best, and next to impossible at worst. Nonetheless, Master Karzello was one of the most skilled astropaths in the entire segmentum, so his appearance before the council was greatly portentous.

A dozen candle-bearing servo-skulls swung away from the Logistician-General, to cluster around the master astropath, throwing his wizened features into flickering relief. The man was ancient, kept alive long past his natural span of years by repeated applications of the rejuvenat treatment available only to the most senior and valued of the Imperium's servants. The treatment was slowly poisoning the master astropath, even if it was keeping him alive. He was so thin that his skin looked like a paper-thin layer of crumbling parchment, barely covering his bones. He had no eyes, for as an astropath his sensory organs had been blasted away by the process that had created him. His body was only kept upright by an arrangement of clanking brass callipers and leather braces that bore his frame and animated his limbs. Furthermore, his robes, though crafted of the finest deep-green void-silk, were encrusted with filth, filling the council chamber with the acrid reek of bodily fluids.

When Master Karzello spoke his physical voice was no more than a whisper. His words were heard not by the ear but by the mind, for despite his bodily frailty, the astropath was gifted with one of the most powerful minds in the region.

'Honoured counsellors,' Karzello began, his psychic voice resounding with such vitality that it drowned out his real one. 'I bear a message. A message from the Inquisition.'

All eyes turned towards the black-robed and hooded Inquisitor Grand. Sarik's gorge rose as he considered what machinations the agent might have conspired in order to gain total power over the Damocles Gulf Crusade. At Pra'yen, Grand had used his rank to overrule the fleet's command structure, but in so doing had made himself more enemies than allies. Was this communiqué a means of cementing his power and taking total control of the crusade?

'Under what cipher?' the cold voice of Inquisitor Grand interjected. Sarik exchanged a second glance with the rogue trader by his side, for here was a mystery unfolding before them both.

The ancient astropath turned his skull-like face towards Grand, and replied, 'That of Lord Kryptman.'

All in the council chamber knew the name of Lord Inquisitor Kryptman, the scourge of xenos the length of the Eastern Fringe. The rogue trader at Sarik's side nodded subtly across the table, and Sarik followed the gesture, seeing that Grand and his arch-ally Gurney were engaged in hushed conversation.

'Please, Master Karzello,' Stempf pressed. 'Continue.'

The astropath's head turned back towards the table centre, the motion accompanied by the whining of dozens of tiny motors. 'Lord Inquisitor Kryptman states that his most trusted emissary shall soon be joining the crusade.'

Grand looked up sharply at this, though his face was unreadable beneath the black hood of his voluminous robes. It seemed to Sarik that the candle-bearing servo-skulls were giving the inquisitor a wide berth. He could hardly blame them.

'This emissary carries the seal, and her words are to be obeyed as those of Lord Kryptman himself. That is all.'

As Stempf stood and the master astropath shuffled out of the chamber, every counsellor began to speak as one. Taking advantage of the din, Sarik leaned towards his neighbour and asked, 'What do you make of this?'

'Ordinarily, I'd say the involvement of another inquisitor would seal Grand and Gurney's control of the crusade for good...'

'But?' Sarik pressed, frustrated with the need to involve himself in the crusade's politics, but knowing he might have to.

'But I'm not so sure. We both know Grand could just wave his Inquisitorial rosette at the council, dismiss us all and take personal control of the whole crusade.'

'Yet, he has not done so,' Sarik replied. The dealings of the Inquisition were even more obscure than the council's, and Sarik had even less desire to become embroiled in them.

'Indeed,' Lucian said thoughtfully, his expression shifting before he changed the subject. 'How go the preparations for the drop?'

'General Gauge has decided to take advantage of the aliens' delay in reinforcing their world,' replied Sarik, relieved to talk of something other than politics. 'We move within hours.' Sarik grinned. 'I for one look forward to the feel of solid ground beneath my feet, and a weapon held in my own hands once more.'

'The enemy fleet is moving in, my lady.'

Brielle Gerrit, daughter of the rogue trader Lucian, stood high up on a tiered gallery, looking down on the busy, brightly-lit tau command centre. The chamber could not have been more different than the equivalent on an Imperial vessel. The lighting was bright and the air clean, the stark white, curved structures pristine and devoid of the tracery and script applied to every surface of most Imperial vessels. Alien tau attended to their stations with calm efficiency, and not one of them was hard-wired into his terminal. Instead, the operators' hands worked effortlessly across banks of glowing readouts, utilising machine-intelligent interfaces considered heretical across the Imperium.

Like her father, Brielle wore the distinctive garb of her class, a flowing dress coat of the finest deep blue fabric lined with elaborate gold piping. Brielle wore her hair in a mass of flowing plaits, the natural black tipped with purple and violet streaks lending her an outlandish appearance entirely at odds with her surroundings. Her eyes were dark and brooding, and lined with painted swirls that further emphasised her exotic features.

Brielle's grip on the railing tightened and her knuckles turned white, but she made no response to the man who stood beside her. Naal, Brielle's companion, wore the dark grey, hooded robes of an Imperial scribe, but that was far from what he truly was. His face bore a tattoo of an Imperial aquila, bearing witness to a former life he had long ago abandoned in favour of service to the tau empire.

Brielle continued to stare fixedly at a vast holographic display below, her mind swimming with doubt as she desperately sought a way out of her predicament.

'My lady?' Naal repeated.

'Thank you, Naal,' Brielle said finally, not taking her eyes off the vast display that filled the centre of the command deck.

'The tau wish to remind us that we have a task to perform. The envoy will be with us shortly. He expects your full report on the crusade fleet's strength.'

I'll give him his report, Brielle seethed inwardly. I'll find a way out of this mess yet...

'Brielle,' Naal pressed, his tone low and conspiratorial. 'Brielle, you joined the tau willingly, and they offer you much in return. But there is a price, as well you knew.'

Brielle rounded on the man who was at once her co-conspirator, her lover and her jailor. 'They offer much,' she hissed. 'But how much of it is of any worth, tell me that?'

Naal glanced furtively about the command centre, before leaning in to speak. The whole space was brightly-lit and spacious, and there was nowhere for the pair to hide from suspicious eyes. 'The tau have made you their envoy to the entire Eastern Fringe, Brielle. Who amongst your line holds such power, aside from your father?'

Brielle resented the mention of her father, who she had no doubt believed her dead before the Damocles Gulf Crusade had even commenced its assault into tau space. 'I'm a rogue trader, Naal,' she said. 'Such power is hardly a novelty to me.'

'I understand that, my lady,' Naal said. 'But you joined the tau at least in part to recover what status you lost when your stepbrother was named your father's successor. Remaining in the clan was a dead end, or so you yourself believed when you agreed to join the tau and forge your own destiny.'

That much was true. Brielle had indeed seen something of value in the tau's collectivist philosophy, something which she could be a part of after her family had rejected her. But she had recently come to realise that she had acted foolishly, and in haste. In truth, she had allowed herself to be seduced by the aliens' words and ideals, seeing something in their notions of the 'Greater Good' that she could be a part of. Later, as the scales had slowly lifted from her eyes, she had seen that she had merely sought to escape the cruel twist of fate that placed her forever in the shadow of her stepbrother and robbed her of her rightful inheritance as bearer of the Warrant of Trade of the Arcadius Clan of rogue traders. Then she had sought to turn the situation to her advantage, her rogue trader's instincts asserting themselves once more. But it was now clear to Brielle that there was no profit to be made in working with or for the tau, no matter the plaudits they heaped upon her. She desired only to escape them, and already, a plan was forming in her mind...

'My lady?' Naal interrupted her brooding. 'Por'O Dal'yth Ulor Kanti approaches.'

Brielle looked up as the tau diplomat, who preferred to be addressed as 'Aura', approached. His long silver robes and fluted collar shimmered in the light of the command centre, dancing with the multihued reflections cast by the huge holograph below.

'Mistress Arcadius,' Aura said as he inclined his head towards Brielle. As with all tau, his face was flat and blue-grey in colour. Compared to a human's it was relatively plain, with black, almond-shaped eyes, a wide, flat mouth, no nose and an odd, slit-like organ in the centre of the forehead. 'The time is upon us. You will soon be attired as am I, in the robes of an emissary of the water caste, and you will go before the humans and demand their surrender. But first, as we have discussed, you must appraise us of their full military potential, that our brothers and sisters upon Dal'yth might put a stop to human aggression and force them to negotiate, as reasonable beings.'

Reasonable beings? Brielle suppressed a snort of derision as memories of Inquisitor Grand and Cardinal Gurney came unbidden to her mind. What they had done to the tau prisoner they had taken in the opening phase of the crusade was hardly the act of reasonable beings...

'Mistress Arcadius?' Aura repeated.

Gathering her thoughts, Brielle bowed to the tau envoy. 'Indeed, Aura,' she said. 'I will be happy to provide a full appreciation of the enemy's capabilities.' Aura turned, his silver robes shimmering as they swept behind him. Steeling herself for what she was about to do, Brielle followed in his wake.

CHAPTER TWO

Veteran Sergeant Sarik grunted as the drop-pod lurched violently and its retro thrusters flared to life. Not much larger than a tank, the drop-pod was essentially an armoured passenger compartment attached to a hugely powerful retro thruster, and although it would be recovered later, after the coming battle, it provided an essentially one-way journey directly into the heart of battle. Such operations had led to the Adeptus Astartes being labelled the 'angels of death,' warriors of vengeance who descended on their foes atop pillars of fire. The White Scars were masters of the lightning strike, drop-pod deployment just one of their many forms of attack.

The tactical cogitation readout in the centre of the pod's cramped passenger compartment told Sarik that it was seconds away from slamming into the surface of the world the alien tau called Dal'yth, the world the Damocles Gulf Crusade had come to conquer in the name of the Imperium.

'Steel your hearts, brothers,' Sarik called out to his four companions. The other five brethren of his ten-man squad were in another drop-pod, his squads deployed as five-man units for the initial drop. 'Your ancestors' eyes are upon you!'

The thrusters reached full power, and no more words were possible. Withstanding forces that would incapacitate any unaugmented human being, Sarik readied himself for the glorious moment when the drop-pod would touch down and release him into the crucible of battle. All that remained now was to mouth a final prayer to the primarch of the Chapter, honoured be his name...

And then the impact came. Even with its descent arrested by the drop-pod's potent thrusters, thc shock was stupendous. Every bone in Sarik's body was jolted, despite the huge bars that restrained him and kept him from being turned to pulp. The thrusters died and a klaxon wailed. With a pneumatic hiss the restraint bars lifted upwards. The bulkhead in front of each Space Marine dropped away to form an assault ramp, which slammed to the earth with a resounding crash. Harsh light filled the pod, followed a moment later by the unfamiliar air of the new planet.

'Out!' Sarik bellowed, surging forwards and grabbing his bolt-gun from the nearby quick release cradle. In an instant each Space Marine was bounding down his ramp and setting foot on the ground of the alien world of Dal'yth.

The ground was dry and sandy, coloured the dull ochre of a semi-arid land. The sky above was a serene shade of jade, and Sarik could see thin, column-like mesas rising into the skies all around the drop zone. The temperature was warm and the air appeared clean, though Sarik's armour systems would need a few more minutes to declare the atmosphere entirely free of toxic elements. Sarik's preparation told him that while other regions of the surface were host to cultivated farmland, this particular area had been left in its natural state, untouched by the aliens' hands or their heretical technologies, and not a single plant was visible.

Sarik rejoiced in the feel of solid ground beneath his feet and the knowledge that his enemies were nearby. Soon, the deaths of so many of the *Nomad*'s crew would be avenged.

'The ring of horns!' Sarik called out, using the unique battle-cant of the White Scars Chapter to order his warriors into a defensive perimeter around the drop-pod. The act of issuing orders to his fellow White Scars was a simple, long-missed pleasure; one denied Sarik at the bridge of his frigate. Hyper-velocity projectiles spat across the jade sky, fired from a distant defence turret towards more Space Marine drop-pods streaking through the air upon churning black contrails. The passage of the rounds through the sky was marked by silvery lines of disturbed air rather than the smoking black contrails of the Imperium's ordnance.

Sarik grinned savagely, knowing that even the aliens' heretically advanced anti-drop defences could not hit so small and fast-moving a target as a drop-pod, for the vehicles plummeted at impossibly fast speeds, slowing only at the last possible instant. Nonetheless, Sarik noted several shots coming perilously close to the drop-pods, evidence, if any were needed, of just how fearsomely effective the aliens' weapons truly were.

Sarik activated the tactical display within his helmet, reams of battlefield and command script suddenly appearing across his field of vision. Status runes indicated that the six White Scars drop-pods were all safely down, and the thirty warriors were all deployed as per their mission orders. A line of text scrolling across the lower portion of his vision told him that the other Space Marine contingents were also under way, each with the objective of destroying one of the sensor pylons that formed an extensive network across the entire surface of Dal'yth.

The White Scars were one of the smaller contingents amongst the two hundred or so Space Marines accompanying the crusade, the Iron Hands, Ultramarines and the Scythes of the Emperor far more numerous. The Ultramarines and the Scythes of the Emperor were each spearheading one of the other two main assault groups, with the smaller squads of the other Chapters each attacking a secondary objective. Despite this, or perhaps because of it, Sarik was determined that his Chapter would claim its share of the glory, and he would lead his brethren to victory. General Gauge's main force would only be able to land once a bloody wound had been torn in the heart of the aliens' defence network.

Satisfied that the assault groups were all on target, Sarik scanned the surrounding area for his own objective. A kilometre distant, in the midst of a cluster of tall rock columns, Sarik located the massive tau sensor pylon.

'White Scars!' Sarik shouted above the high-pitched whip-crack of tau projectiles splitting the air overhead. 'Move out.' With savage joy welling within him, he added, 'Let's complete our mission before the Ultramarines complete theirs!'

'White Scars deployed,' the chief of staff reported. 'Ultramarines groups in nine minutes, Scythes of the Emperor group in twelve minutes. All other sub-groups within twenty minutes.'

'Good,' replied General Gauge, turning from the huge pict screen that dominated the main wall of his command chamber aboard the

Blade of Woe. The entire space was crowded with command terminals, glowing readouts and blaring phono-casters describing every detail of the landing operations. Tacticae advisors and Imperial Guard staff officers manned dozens of stations, and vox-servitors and Munitorum logisters shuffled from one to the next, collating and dispensing raw data in ream after ream of parchment. Located in the heart of the *Blade of Woe*, the command chamber was Gauge's personal domain and it could have been a high command bunker at the front line of any of the Imperium's sector-spanning wars.

Gauge faced Lucian and the others of the crusade council who had assembled to witness the assault on Dal'yth Prime. 'Gentlemen,' the scarred, craggy-faced veteran soldier addressed his fellow councillors. 'Phase one of Operation Pluto is under way.'

The general nodded to the chief of staff, and then turned back towards the huge pict screen. The image resolved into a real time capture of the surface of Dal'yth Prime, transmitted by an orbital spy-drone controlled by one of Gauge's command staff. The dry atmosphere of the world below contained few clouds, so Lucian and the councillors were afforded a clear view of the main continent's eastern seaboard.

'As you can see,' General Gauge indicated the centre of the image, 'this region is ideal for our purposes. The land is relatively flat, and the sea to the east and the mountains to the north will mask our landing operations from those two directions.'

The staff officer worked the controls of his command terminal. The image on the pict screen blurred, and then came back into focus having magnified the central region.

'Sector zero shall be the site of the main landings,' Gauge said. Lucian caught a glint in the old veteran's eye, something that told him the general would be quite happy leading the planetfall operation from the very front. He smiled wryly as the general continued. 'The main landings can only commence once the tau's sensor network has been disabled,' Gauge gestured towards a number of blinking, red runes that represented the primary objectives being assaulted by the White Scars, Ultramarines and the Scythes of the Emperor, 'here, here and here.' Lucian saw that around a dozen secondary objectives were also marked, but the general was only interested in the primary ones, for now at least.

Each of the three primary runes represented a vital node in the planetwide sensor network. Taking out those nodes would blind the tau to the exact details of the main landings. The landings themselves could never be hidden, but at least the tau could be put at a major disadvantage if they could not clearly see what was happening at the landing zone. The defenders would be forced to commit their forces piecemeal, probing for the Imperium's armies.

'What of their air assets, general?' Lucian asked, his mind calculating every possible risk to the successful landing of the main crusade ground forces.

'That is the great unknown, Lucian,' Gauge answered, with unusual honesty for one of his station. 'All ground forces will be equipped with as many anti-air weapons as they can carry, and what sub-orbital fighter capacity we do have will be fully committed. But frankly, we really have no idea what the tau might throw against us.'

'Then why not wait, general,' said Cardinal Gurney, standing resplendent in the finery of his office. 'Or bombard the entire world into submission.'

'Cardinal,' Gauge bowed his head ever so slightly as he spoke. 'I am merely enacting the will of the council in this matter. I was given the task of conquering Dal'yth Prime, and that is what I intend to do.' Then he looked the cardinal straight in the eye. 'I have done this before.'

'General,' Lucian cut in, forestalling any further interruptions or objections from Gurney and his faction. 'When will the main landings begin?'

'That, friend Lucian, is in the hands of the Adeptus Astartes.'

The dry ground at Sarik's feet erupted into plumes of dust as the turret atop the sensor pylon brought its weapons to bear on him and opened fire. He continued running for another ten paces, before throwing himself to the right into the cover of a large boulder.

The other warriors of his squad, who had reformed into a single ten-man unit having disembarked from the two drop-pods, had caught up with him. Brother Qaja, the Space Marine who commanded the *Nomad*'s fire control station when the squad was serving as the frigate's command cadre, was the first to join him.

He seemed unencumbered by the huge plasma cannon he carried in both hands, and by the massive, humming power source on his back.

Sarik reached up and released the catches around his neck, then lifted his helmet clear and shook his long, black topknot loose. He took a deep breath, allowing his genetically enhanced senses to taste the air, testing it for contaminants and other indications of the nature of the immediate environment.

Qaja too had removed his helmet, and appeared to be laughing.

'Something amuses you, brother?' Sarik said, grinning with the joy of battle despite himself.

Brother Qaja shook his head, his long, plaited moustaches waving freely. 'My apologies, brother-sergeant,' Qaja said. 'I am merely grateful to be on solid ground once more, with my enemy before me and my battle-kin at my side.'

'Aye,' Sarik grinned. 'I feel it too, brother.' Sarik risked a glance around the boulder, hoping to get a fix on the turret that pinned him and his squad down. No sooner had he leaned around the outcrop than he was forced to pull his head back sharply. A torrent of rounds erupted against the rock, sending up plumes of vaporised stone and shards of razor-sharp shrapnel.

Nonetheless, Sarik had learned all he needed. The pylon was a mere fifty metres distant, its white tower rearing high above the arid landscape. Its form reminded Sarik of the funnel of a great sea-going vessel, and it was covered in domes and blisters that bristled with sensor veins. Sarik had seen a ring of smaller structures around the base of the pylon, and halfway up its flanks the turret from which the hail of blue energy bolts was being unleashed.

Furthermore, in the brief instant he had been exposed, Sarik had caught sight of at least one squad of enemy warriors about the base of the pylon, weapons trained on the boulder the Space Marines sheltered behind.

'Brother Qaja,' said Sarik. 'I want that turret silenced. Squad,' he called out, 'Cover him!'

With that, Brother Qaja hoisted the heavy bulk of his plasma cannon, his face split with a feral grin at the prospect of the coming destruction. Sarik nodded once, and the Space Marine stepped out from the cover of the rock and brought his heavy weapon to bear on the turret.

Even as Qaja raised his plasma cannon, Sarik and the remainder of the squad emerged from either side of the boulder, each taking aim at one of the enemy warriors. At the very same moment, they opened fire.

The boltguns spat explosive death towards the aliens, who should have been cut down in a bloody swathe. But instead of striking the tau warriors and exploding inside their bodies, the rounds detonated in mid air without striking a single one.

'Energy shield!' Sarik bellowed, frustrated once more by the perfidiousness of the aliens' technology. The tau warriors brought their own long-barrelled rifles to bear on Brother Qaja. Before the Space Marine could fire, a dozen blue energy bolts lanced towards him as the alien soldiers opened fire through what was clearly a one-way energy shield that allowed the tau to fire from behind its protection.

Brother Qaja was caught in the storm, the blue bolts slamming into his power armour and vaporising large chunks of ceramite and the flesh beneath.

Sarik bellowed a wordless curse at the sight of his closest battle-brother gunned down before him. The two warriors had shared such glories and such tragedies that a wound to one was a wound to the other. Rage and pain welled up inside Sarik and reason threatened to flee his mind entirely, so strong was the urge to avenge his fallen brother.

But Sarik's curse turned into a howl of joy as he saw that his battle-brother was far from dead. Dragging himself up onto one knee, his face a mask of grim determination, Qaja levelled his cannon at the turret.

As the turret's multi-barrelled weapons tracked him, Qaja opened fire. His target was high up on the side of the massive sensor pylon, and was not protected by the energy shield that had saved the alien warriors on the ground. The plasma cannon spat a roiling ball of raw energy, which lanced upwards and slammed into the turret. The side of the pylon erupted in an explosion of blinding violet light as the turret disintegrated, showering the tau below with liquid gobbets of the fabric of the pylon, turned molten by the plasma blast.

Sarik saw his opening. 'White Scars!' he bellowed, filled with battle-rage. 'On them!'

Limbering his boltgun and drawing his chainsword, Sarik surged out from cover, his battle-brothers close behind. As he passed Brother Qaja, he saw that the warrior was grievously wounded, but willing and able to fight on. The plasma cannon whined as it drew power for a second shot.

The world became a blurred rush of sights and sounds as Sarik powered across the open ground in front of the pylon. His armoured boots pounded the dry ground and his blood thundered in his ears. His heart sang with the sensations of battle and he roared a savage cry to lead his warriors onwards. As the range closed and the White Scars approached the nearest of the smaller structures circling the pylon, the enemy warriors opened fire again. The weight of fire had lessened, for a handful at least had been incapacitated or killed by the molten debris showered on them from above by the destruction of the turret. Small yet deadly bolts of blue energy split the air scant centimetres from Sarik's body or stitched the ground at his feet. Miraculously, Sarik crossed the open ground without being struck and slammed into the nearest structure, a projector for the invisible energy shield.

Sarik took cover behind the structure as a second bolt of plasma blasted through the air and struck the flank of the main pylon. Sarik could not see its effect, but he heard it a moment later. One of the tau was screaming in what could only have been pain, and another was coolly issuing orders in their alien tongue, the voice made oddly artificial by the helmet the leader wore. Trusting Qaja to do his duty, Sarik went about a hurried examination of the structure he had reached.

The projector was around three metres tall, and made of the same hard, white material as the main sensor pylon. Sarik pressed his hand against it, seeking to judge something of its properties. Even through the armour of his gloves, he felt the hum of machinery within, and judged that he had been correct in his guess as to its function.

Sarik's squad was closing on his position. He had but seconds.

'Keep going!' Sarik bellowed, activating the blade of his chainsword so that the diamond-hard, monomolecular-edged teeth came screaming to deadly life. Gripping the chainsword's hilt in both hands, he plunged it tip first into the side of the projector.

The structure had been built to survive small-arms fire, the white surface withstanding the strike until Sarik redoubled his efforts and the screaming blade began to pierce the armour. Another second and the chainsword was plunged halfway into the structure, and then Sarik felt its tip come into contact with the systems hidden inside.

A muffled explosion sounded from inside the projector, but Sarik gritted his teeth and forced the chainsword even deeper. His battle-brothers reached his side, and he pushed harder, bringing his full strength, augmented still further by the dense fibre bundles of his power armour, to bear.

A second explosion sounded from with the projector, and a crack appeared across its face. The air became suddenly charged, as it does the instant before a lightning bolt strikes the ground. Sensing danger, Sarik pulled his chainsword from the ragged wound it had inflicted, and pushed himself backwards.

The air pulsed with searing white light, and the projector exploded, showering the White Scars with fragments of shrapnel, their power armour deflecting the worst of it. The detonation of the first projector was followed a moment later by the next two along, and then by the next, until within seconds every projector around the main sensor pylon had exploded in sequence.

Sarik let out a joyous war cry as his battle-brothers charged across the ground that had previously been denied them by the invisible energy shield. Mad laughter came unbidden to his throat as he pulled himself upright, the sound of chainswords rending alien flesh and bone filling the air.

The main pict screen dominating General Gauge's command centre lit up with flashing runes as the tacticae logic engines plotted the progress of each of the Space Marine attack forces. 'All assaults now under way,' Gauge's chief of staff reported. 'First assault report their target was surrounded by some form of one-way energy shield; all commands advised.'

'Main viewer,' General Gauge said. As the assaults on the sensor nodes had developed, the command centre had become increasingly busy as Gauge's staff officers made final preparations for the main landings, which would follow as soon as the tau's sensor grid was disabled. As the image on the screen shifted, almost every head in the crowded centre turned towards it, the tension building as the stakes got higher with every passing minute.

Near silence descended, the only sound coming from the ever-chattering vox-net channels. The image on the screen now showed the scene of the White Scars' assault on their objective, and Lucian knew that his friend Sarik would be down there, at the very speartip of the Damocles Gulf Crusade.

As the spy-drone relaying the picts passed almost directly over the scene of the White Scars' assault, the shape of the main pylon came into view. A ring of burning structures was visible around it, and to the west a group of white-armoured figures moved relentlessly forwards towards their objective. A string of bloody corpses marked their defeat of the alien warriors that had defended the objective.

And then, Lucian saw movement at the top of the pylon, a number of circular shapes, each roughly a metre in diameter, detaching themselves from the structure to circle steadily about its flanks.

'General Gauge?' Lucian said.

Gauge had not yet seen what Lucian had, but Cardinal Gurney had. 'I am quite sure, rogue trader, that the mighty Astartes require no aid from us,' the cardinal sneered.

Though no professional soldier, Lucian was not a stranger to the battlefield, and as he watched it became clear to him that the White Scars had yet to detect whatever was deploying on the far side of the pylon.

'Wendall?' Lucian said, deliberately using General Gauge's first name. Gauge nodded smartly in response.

'Give me that,' Lucian said to the nearest staff officer as he grabbed the vox-set from the man's head. 'Patch me through,' Lucian said as he placed the set on his own head and adjusted the pickup. 'Now.'

'I really think–' Cardinal Gurney interjected, before General Gauge shifted sideways to block his view.

'Vox-communion established, my lord,' the staff officer reported.

'Sarik?' Lucian said, his eyes fixed on the screen as he spoke.

'Gerrit?' the response came back a moment later. 'Make it quick. I'm a little busy.'

'Understood,' Lucian replied, not wasting time with formalities. 'You have company. Two four, high, from your location.'

'Thank you, Lucian,' Sarik's voice came back. 'You just can't help it, can you...' The channel went dead as the Space Marine closed the link.

'You really should stop doing that,' came the amused-sounding voice of Admiral Jellaqua, who had crossed to stand beside General Gauge. The admiral was a large man bedecked in reams of naval finery and his jowly face was split by a friendly grin as he spoke. 'You'll only annoy him.'

'I know,' said Lucian. 'But someone has to...'

'The scythe-wing strikes at dawn!' Sarik yelled, his battle-cant warning providing the White Scars with more information than any formally composed order could have done in the scant seconds it took to issue. Two-dozen boltguns were raised towards the direction indicated, while the heavy weapons troopers braced themselves to open fire with heavy bolter and missile launcher.

Scanning the jade sky for contact, Sarik caught sight of movement near the pylon's summit. Within seconds, a fast-moving swarm of disc-shaped objects was swooping down, angling towards the White Scars.

'Gun drones!' Sarik called out, recognising the machines instantly, for he had faced them in the opening ground battle of the crusade. 'Aim for the undersides!'

As the drones descended towards the Space Marines, the twin-weapons mounted beneath their dish-shaped bodies opened fire. More of the blue energy bolts spat towards the White Scars, but before the tau machines could find their range, the Space Marines were following Sarik's order. Bolt-rounds filled the air, the force's heavy bolter adding the weight of its firepower a moment later. In seconds, the alien machines were blown apart as bolt shells penetrated the weaker armour of their undersides, detonated within, and scattered burning wreckage across a wide area.

The last of the debris pattered to the dry ground at his feet and Sarik activated his armour's strategium uplink. Runes blinked across his vision, and a stream of text told him what he needed to know. The battle-brothers of the Scythes of the Emperor were reporting their objective ready to take, the threat of another Space Marine force completing their objective first bringing a feral growl to Sarik's throat.

'Brother Kharisk, bring the melta charges,' Sarik called out. 'I want this place wrecked, now!'

Gauge's chief of staff looked up sharply from his command terminal, one hand to the vox-set at his ear. 'Enemy flyers!' he shouted over the noise of General Gauge's command centre. 'Inbound on all objectives!'

'Status?' General Gauge replied.

'Sergeant Sarik reports ready to place charges, estimate detonation within five minutes,' the officer replied. Lucian breathed a silent sigh of relief that his warning had got through in time, and the White Scars had been ready when the gun drones had attacked. By all accounts, the other pylons had been similarly defended, and the other Space Marine contingents had not fared so well. The Ultramarines had suffered one casualty, and the Scythes of the Emperor two, though none of the injuries was life threatening. To a Space Marine, few injuries were.

'Ultramarines ready to detonate charges,' the officer reported. 'Scythes still facing resistance from enemy infantry.'

'Gentlemen,' General Gauge addressed the gathered members of the crusade council as he turned from his chief of staff to face them. 'We arrive at the point of decision, the point at which all may be decided, the entire crusade. Given the previous... disagreements within the council, I would take this opportunity to show resolve, and to demonstrate that we are united in our purpose.'

'I propose the final order to begin the landings be put to a formal vote of the crusade council. Right here, right now.'

Lucian kept his expression outwardly calm, but inside his mind raced. The general had surprised even his closest allies on the council, as the expression on Admiral Jellaqua's jowly face confirmed. Perhaps he had done so as a precaution against the other faction, centred on Cardinal Gurney, catching wind. Inquisitor Grand was known to be a powerful psyker, and even if he did not resort to tearing the thoughts directly from the minds of his rivals, there were few secrets that could be kept from one who bore the Inquisitorial Rosette.

At the beginning of the crusade, before the mighty fleet had crossed the Damocles Gulf and plunged blindly into the region claimed by the tau empire, the council had consisted of twelve members. Three of that number, however, had been slain at the height of the crusade's last space battle, the ships on which they had chosen to travel lost, scattered to atoms in the void. Replacing those three councillors was a task the body had yet to undertake, but it would need to be done, and soon, if the council was not to become dominated by the likes of Cardinal Gurney. Two more members were absent, for they represented the Space Marine contingent of the crusade: Captain Rumann of the Iron Hands Chapter was aboard his vessel, the *Fist of Light,* directing his ground troops, while Veteran Sergeant Sarik of the White Scars was leading his own warriors from the front, as ever he did.

That left General Gauge, Admiral Jellaqua, and Lucian himself on one side of the council, and Cardinal Gurney, Inquisitor Grand and Logistician-General Stempf on the other. Ordinarily, Lucian would have been able to count on Sarik's agreement, not because the Space Marine had allied himself to a particular view, but because the two were simply of a similar mind most of the time. Captain Rumann was less predictable, keeping his own, inscrutable counsel in most matters.

'What motion do you propose, general?' said Inquisitor Grand, his voice low and threatening. 'And what is the alternative, should it be rejected?'

So that was Gauge's ploy. The tough old veteran, born on the Deathworld of Catachan and elevated through the ranks on the power of his will and the strength of his arm, was attempting to force the council's hand once and for all. In previous sessions, it had seriously been suggested that the crusade turn back, to return later with a fleet so vast it could reduce the entire tau empire to ruins. Thankfully, saner counsel had prevailed. While Lucian sought to profit from the enterprise, his allies sought honour, and neither outcome would be possible should the tau be completely obliterated.

'I propose the motion that we vote on authorising the landings or we withdraw the fleet,' Gauge said.

Silence settled upon the assembled council members, but each was painfully aware that the enemy's flyers were closing on the Space Marines on the surface below, every second bringing them closer to their targets.

'I second the motion,' Lucian stated. 'Let each cast his vote, while we can still make it count.'

'Very well,' rasped Inquisitor Grand, barely containing his displeasure. Why, if he was so displeased, did he not simply brandish his Inquisitorial rosette? The astropathic transmission relayed in the council chamber came back to Lucian's mind, before the inquisitor gave his answer. 'I vote in favour of the motion.'

Now things were really getting interesting, Lucian thought, his glance meeting that of Admiral Jellaqua for a fleeting moment.

'As do I,' said Cardinal Gurney, who stood beside the inquisitor.

'And I,' added the Logistician-General.

Within moments, Lucian, Gauge and Jellaqua had all indicated their agreement with the motion, and the vote was sealed. For the first time in the long months of the crusade, the entire council had, to all intents and purposes, presented a unanimous front. Even if the two Space Marines had disagreed with the motion, which was inconceivable, it would have been carried by a majority. But Lucian could not help but wonder what the vote had achieved, unless Gauge sought to demonstrate power over the rival faction.

Lucian's thoughts were interrupted as Gauge's chief of staff spoke up. 'Enemy flyers closing on White Scars objective. Contact in one minute.'

Sergeant Sarik hauled himself onto the platform at the top of the towering sensor pylon, directly below the structure's antennae mast. The platform was circular and ten metres across. It clung to the side of the pylon precariously, the dozens of spear-like antennae above swaying slightly as a stiff breeze rushed through them.

'Brother Kharisk,' said Sarik as a second White Scar climbed up onto the platform behind him, one more battle-brother following close behind. 'Get to work. High command reports we have enemy flyers inbound.'

Nodding, the Space Marine crossed the platform to stand directly beneath the antennae mast. Assessing the structure with an efficiency that Sarik had come to value highly throughout his tenure as the warrior's squad leader, Brother Kharisk unclipped three bulky, tubular melta charges from his belt, and set about placing them where they would do the most damage.

With Kharisk deploying the charges, Sarik turned to the next Space Marine to climb up onto the platform, Brother Qsal. The warrior carried a stubby missile launcher, which he handed to Sarik as he hauled himself up. Sarik took the weapon in one hand, and with the other aided his battle-brother onto the platform. Despite the additional strength afforded the brother by his power armour, Brother Qsal was carrying a double load of ammunition for his launcher, consisting of additional krak missiles to combat enemy aircraft.

'You know your duty,' Sarik said as he handed the missile launcher back to Brother Qsal. The warrior shouldered his weapon, and crossed to the platform's edge to begin his vigil.

With both of his warriors in place, Sarik took the opportunity to examine his surroundings. The surface of Dal'yth Prime spread out below Sarik, his vantage point several hundred metres up affording him a stunning view all the way to the distant horizon. The land was dry and sandy, and dotted with tall, flat-topped mesas of dark red rock. Over the curve of the western horizon, beyond the area that had been designated as the crusade's landing zone, were clustered a number of small cities. Assaulting those areas, General Gauge had claimed, would draw the tau to defend them, allowing the crusade to dictate the terms of battle. Sarik prayed the general was correct, for he had faced enough aliens to know that their reactions could rarely be predicted in such human terms. To the north, the dry land rose to form the foothills of a distant mountain range, which, it was hoped by the general, would protect the crusade forces from attack from that quarter as they carried out the landing operation. Again, Sarik determined not to put all of his trust into such a presumption, although the basic notion was sound.

Fifty or so kilometres from the pylon, the arid landscape gave way to the sea, which was a deep, blue-green band across the entire eastern horizon. The only vapour clouds in the jade sky were far out over that sea, and as a son of the wild steppes of Chogoris, part of Sarik's mind pondered what natural process kept them from sweeping in over the land and watering the parched earth. If it were true that the tau preferred their worlds dry, perhaps they used some form of planetwide atmospheric engineering, just as there were polluted industrial worlds in the Imperium where rain was made to fall at the end of each work shift to wash away pollutants.

Towards the south lay nothing but desert, dotted with the flat-topped, dark red mesas. The crusade's high command had discerned no threat from that quarter, ascertaining that the desert was empty and no enemy was likely to threaten the landings from that direction. The thought that the tau might prefer their worlds arid came back to Sarik's mind...

Brother Kharisk stood back, the melta charges all set at the base of the antennae mast.

'Brother Qsal,' said Sarik, his eyes fixed on the clear skies to the south. 'Do you detect anything out of the ordinary?'

'No contact, brother-sergeant,' Qsal replied, panning his weapon slowly across the skies.

'South, high,' Sarik said, a sense of foreboding welling inside of him. 'Maintain overwatch.'

Brother Qsal turned in the direction Sarik had indicated, and resumed his watch, though the skies looked empty. Perhaps the war spirit residing in the missile launcher's machine core would detect what the eye could not.

'Brother-sergeant?' Brother Kharisk said from behind him. 'Charges set.'

Command runes blinked across Sarik's vision, telling him that the other Space Marine contingents were also reporting that they were ready to begin the final phase of their assaults.

'Understood, prepare to...' Sarik answered, before he was suddenly struck by the notion that something was very wrong. He turned a full revolution, his eyes scanning the panorama intently. 'What was that...?'

'Brother-serg–' Qsal began, and then Sarik's world exploded around him.

A storm of blue energy bolts ripped into the platform, tearing great chunks from the white material. The air was filled with the ultrasonic whine of the bolts ripping through the air, and for a second, Sarik could hear nothing else. Sarik threw himself to the deck as a second blast of energy bolts ripped into the platform around him.

Something large screamed overhead and was gone before Sarik could identify it. He rose and looked about for the aircraft, but there was nothing to be seen, the jade skies as empty as they been but a moment ago.

The sharp scent of burned resins filling his nostrils, Sarik turned to his brothers, ready to order Qsal to locate the enemy flyer and engage it. He saw that the attack had chewed great wounds from the platform but left the sensor antennae masts completely intact and functional, a testament to the skill and the intent of who or whatever had fired on the Space Marines. Then Sarik saw that Brother Qsal was dead, torn into ragged chunks as dozens of the energy bolts had cut him apart. Brother Kharisk was simply gone, thrown from the high platform by the sheer weight of fire.

Sarik's next thought was for the mission. He would leave his mourning until later, as any good leader should. With Brother Kharisk gone, the melta charges could not be detonated remotely, for the warrior had carried their control device. Sarik would have to set the charges' timers manually, and get clear before they detonated. But such thoughts were instantly driven from his mind as a high-pitched whine caught his attention.

Following the sound, Sarik looked southwards, and caught sight of a rippling in the skies above the desert. Focussing on the sound, the source of which was travelling rapidly from south to east, Sarik saw it again, this time far closer, and knew what he must do.

Not taking his eyes from the subtle rippling in the air, Sarik went down on one knee, and without looking located and picked up the missile launcher Brother Qsal had carried. A moment later, the tube was at his shoulder, and he was squinting through the sights as the whine increased in pitch and volume, growing closer to the pylon as the seconds passed.

With a flick of his thumb, Sarik lifted the cover over the firing stud. Even as he did so, the air before him rippled, revealing for a brief moment the sleek, predatory form of a tau aircraft beginning a strafing run on his position.

Even as Sarik pressed down on the firing stud, the tau aircraft opened fire. The air was suddenly filled with a hundred blue energy bolts, stitching the platform at Sarik's feet or ripping through the air scant inches from his body. The moment his missile fired, Sarik threw himself to his right, diving into the cover of the base of the antennae mast as the platform disintegrated under the relentless tide of fire.

With a deafening whine, the enemy aircraft passed by overhead, its form fading again as it disengaged its weapons systems, shunting power back to whatever xenos-tech cloaking system had previously hidden it from the eye.

The tau flyer might be invisible to the eye, but it was not hidden from the senses of the machine-spirit guiding the krak missile that even now streaked through the air in the aircraft's wake.

The missile banked left, following hard on the heels of the invisible flyer. Then it banked suddenly right and dived straight down towards the ground, matching the invisible alien pilot's desperate efforts to evade death.

And then the missile exploded in mid-air, and whatever alien technology was hiding the flyer from view failed. Sarik voiced a feral war cry as the now visible aircraft shuddered and began to disintegrate. At the last, the main fuselage was torn apart as its drive section detonated, a thousand pieces of flaming wreckage plummeting to the ground several hundred metres below.

Sarik howled an ancient Chogoran victory chant, giving thanks to his ancestors that the human-forged weapon had bested the perfidious alien war machine. 'Command to Sarik,' the Space Marine's earpiece suddenly barked, interrupting his impromptu celebration. 'We read multiple additional flyers closing on your position, over.'

Glancing towards the melta charges at the base of the antennae mast, Sarik replied 'Understood, command. Detonation in three minutes.'

'Be advised,' Sarik added as he scanned the jade skies. 'Enemy aircraft are utilising some form of optical shielding. They're invisible to the naked eye.'

'Understood,' the voice replied. 'Disseminating to all commands.'

'The order is given,' announced General Gauge, the pict screen relaying the top-down scene of a vast mushroom cloud climbing into the air, marking Sergeant Sarik's destruction of his objective. Addressing his chief of staff, Gauge said, 'Commence landing phase.'

Scores of Imperial Guard staff officers and Departmento Tacticae advisors set about their preordained tasks, each relaying orders into vox-horns and putting into motion the planetary assault on Dal'yth Prime. This was the moment the crusade had been building towards for so long, from the earliest sessions of the crusade council when all of this was little more than a dream. Countless cogitation terminals lit up with rapidly scrolling lines of text, status reports flooding back and forth, describing the drama unfolding in orbit above the tau planet.

Lucian felt relief that his friend Sarik had completed his mission, though two of his warriors had fallen during the assault on the sensor pylon. Of the other Space Marine contingents undertaking their own missions against other pylons, a handful of injuries and two more deaths had been reported, all of which spoke volumes of their courage and dedication, and of the tau's readiness to defend their world. With the primary sensor pylons destroyed, however, the landings could commence, safe in the knowledge that the tau would be blinded to the true extent of the Imperium's invasion.

Lucian was reminded of the deeds of a number of his ancestors, those bold men and women who had earned the Arcadius Warrant of Trade and forged the clan's fortunes, carving its name into the annals of Imperial history for all time. The name of one of his forbearers rang especially loud, that of old Abad Gerrit, the hero of the Scallarn Pacification. As a child, Lucian had been enthralled by the huge holochrome rendition of old Abad, depicting the scene of the rogue trader leading an army of ten thousand followers against the orks that had enslaved the entire Scallarn Cluster.

At that moment, Lucian realised that above all else, he desired to be a part of such battles, to earn such glories for the Arcadius clan as had his predecessors. As much as he tried to dismiss the notion, his mind raced as he considered the possibilities. To join the crusade on the ground, to take part in its battles, would have both the immediate effect of elevating his position on the council, and of further securing the clan's long-term fortunes. Maybe someday someone would sculpt a holochrome of him, side by side with Sergeant Sarik as they conquered tau space...

As the landing operation began in earnest, Lucian marvelled at the sheer spectacle of the event. Dozens of screens showed fleet assets moving into position as lumbering troop transports prepared to disgorge hundreds upon hundreds of drop-vessels. These ranged in size from ships ferrying a single squad or platoon to the surface, to those carrying entire companies of armoured vehicles. The greatest and most impressive were those of the Adeptus Mechanicus, by which the mighty god-machines of the Titanicus would be deployed to the surface. For each man that would land on the surface, another hundred at least supported the action, each forming a vital link in the chain. In truth, the Damocles Gulf Crusade was a relatively minor undertaking in the grand scheme of the Imperium's wars, yet here and now, at the heart of the command centre, it had all the grandeur of any of the great battles of the last ten thousand years.

General Gauge stood at his command postern, surrounded by his cadre of staff officers, listening to a constant stream of reports and status updates. The central pict screen now showed the view over the landing zone as seen by a sub-orbital spy-drone a dozen kilometres overhead. Reams of data scrolled across a dozen smaller screens, each contributing to the general's picture of the grand invasion.

A winged death's head icon appeared in the centre of the main screen, indicating the successful landing of the first wave. That force was made up of a composite company of Space Marines drawn from several different Chapters. A second such company landed, via two-dozen drop-pods, five kilometres to the west of the first. It immediately deployed as a blocking force to intercept any tau ground forces that attempted to counter-attack along the road network that led to the western cities.

The operation unfolded over the following hours, General Gauge scarcely needing to issue any further orders, for the landings had been planned in meticulous detail. Regiment after regiment made the drop. While the elite Space Marines landed in small, five-man drop-pods, the Imperial Guard deployed in far larger drop-ships, each capable of ferrying an entire infantry company and its equipment, a troop of Leman Russ tanks, or an armoured infantry platoon mounted in Chimera carriers. The landings were not unopposed, however, for while the tau pulled back what ground units were near the landing zone, they committed large numbers of flyers to contest the landings, which General Gauge's force was hard-pressed to counter.

The tau air force launched sortie after sortie against the landing forces. The initial attacks were directed against the two composite companies of Space Marines, but that allowed the first wave of the larger transports to land largely without incident. The Space Marines withstood dozens of attacks by enemy flyers so fast that they stood little chance of engaging them. Nonetheless, the Space Marines did manage to shoot down a handful of aircraft using their missile launchers, each successful engagement being met with a hearty cheer from the staff of the command centre.

With the tau flyers concentrating on the Space Marines, the Imperial Guard were able to land several mobile air defence companies of Hydra flak tanks. Though one transport was engaged as it plummeted through the atmosphere and shot down with the loss of a dozen tanks and several hundred lives, the remainder were able to deploy successfully. Within three hours the landing zone was covered by an air defence umbrella that made it impossible for the tau to harass subsequent waves. With the immediate airspace secured, infantry companies from the Rakarshan Rifles and the Brimlock Dragoons pressed outwards to secure the ground in all directions. The bulk of their number headed west to establish dominance over the road network leading to the coastal cities.

At the last, satisfied that the landing zone was secure, General Gauge ordered the deployment of the crusade's heaviest units, the vast landers from which the mighty engines of the Legio Thanataris would walk. With the Deathbringers' fastest moving machines, their Warhound Titans, pressing forwards, the ground war could truly begin.

The view from the flat top of the rocky mesa was quite stunning, allowing Sergeant Sarik to take in the awe-inspiring scale of the landing operation. Several kilometres behind Sarik, the sensor pylon still burned, its once pristine white form reduced to a twisted, blackened mass as a column of choking smoke rose high in the atmosphere. The landings were well and truly under way, the white sun of Dal'yth setting in the rapidly darkening jade sky.

Having destroyed the sensor pylon and ordered the tending of his dead and injured battle-brothers, Sarik had linked his force up with the other Space Marine contingents to assist in the securing of the landing zone. The tau units in the area had swiftly disengaged, however, and mounted an impressively coordinated withdrawal before the Space Marines could engage them effectively. Sarik was forced to admit that the tau warriors were worthy opponents, and that they fought with honour. The aliens' fast-moving tactics reminded Sarik of those employed by the nomads of his home world of Chogoris, whose use of swift mounts allowed them to launch lightning raids before withdrawing in the face of enemy counter-attack. Already, Sarik had disseminated this point to the other Space Marine units of the crusade, and advised them how such tactics might be met, and countered.

The flat desert below the tall mesa was now swarming with troops and armoured vehicles. The first Imperial soldiers Sarik's White Scars had linked up with were the veteran light infantrymen of the Rakarshan Rifles. They moved quickly to press into the surrounding desert, and had begun aggressive patrolling in order to repel any enemy that sought to observe or interfere with the operation. The Rakarshans were followed by the crusade's more heavily armed and equipped units, whose tanks, mobile artillery and armoured carriers were even now filling the air with the roar of their engines, the grinding of tracks and the smoke of their exhausts. As more and more heavy landers touched down, the first streams of men and vehicles swelled to become rivers, until thousands of Imperial Guardsmen and hundreds of tanks were pressing outwards.

All the while, the tau flyers continued to contest the landings, and though few had penetrated the air defence umbrella the Hydra flak tanks had established, those that had been able to slew scores of men with each strafing run. Fortunately for the operation, only a handful of the flyers were equipped with the stealth field Sarik had faced on the pylon. The Departmento Tacticae advisors surmised that these were an elite wing of the tau air force. The Imperium would be ready for them next time.

Sarik's chain of thought was interrupted as he became aware of a deep, rumbling drone sounding from above. The heaviest lander yet was descending upon a column of fire and smoke. The vessel came ponderously in to land, and another three followed in its wake. The roar of the vessel's landing jets was deafening, even from several kilometres away. In basic form the lander resembled the drop-pod Sarik and the other White Scars had made planetfall in, yet its scale was truly vast. The vessel was three or four times taller than its width, its hull configured in a hexagonal form above the largest retro thruster Sarik had ever seen on a ship capable of atmospheric operation.

As the lander descended, an invisible anti-grav field was projected below it, an arcane and ill-understood system that would ensure the vessel's precious cargo was deployed with all possible care. The anti-grav field pressed down upon the earth as the vessel neared the ground, the invisible forces crushing everything beneath it flat, including a tracked cargo tender which failed to evacuate the landing zone in time. The grav field dampened the area so effectively that the clouds of dust that should have been thrown up by the retro-thrusters were crushed downwards to form a carpet of sand across the land.

As the first lander touched down, Sarik felt the desert beneath his feet tremble as millions of tons of steel and ceramite ground into the bedrock. It felt to Sarik as if he witnessed a primeval contest of the elements: that wrought in the forges of the Adeptus Mechanicus battling against the raw stuff of Dal'yth Prime's continental plates. The contest continued for long minutes, until eventually the tremors faded away, leaving Sarik with the impression that the world beneath his feet would remain scarred by the coming of the Titanicus forever. Soon, a dozen of the landers had touched down, each towering a hundred metres and more into air that shimmered with the residual heat of atmospheric entry.

The anti-grav fields deactivated, contingents of tech-priests and their servitors emerged from dozens of hatches and busied themselves around the heavy landers. Prayers and chants filled the air as the tech-priests supplicated themselves before the vessels, which in themselves were a manifestation of their Machine-God, the Omnissiah. The cloying scent of holy lubricant and incense oil drifted across the desert, mixing unpleasantly with the scent of burning resin blowing in from the ruined sensor pylon.

Finally, the sides of each lander lowered downwards like the petals of a titanic ceramite flower, accompanied by the grinding of metal gears and the thud of the huge ramps striking the earth. Vast clouds of dust were thrown up as the ramps hit the ground, and through them emerged a group of loping Warhound Titans of the Legio Thanataris. Each was a towering war machine bearing weapons of the scale normally only seen on starships. Though far from the heaviest of the Titans the Legio could field, these had the speed to range ahead of the crusade's ground forces, moving swiftly with a characteristic stooped gait, to engage anything the tau might be able to field. As they formed up into a predatory pack on the blackened earth of the landing zone, the Warhounds' heads, each sculpted to resemble a mighty wolf-like face, tracked back and forth across their new hunting ground. It almost appeared as if the Titans sniffed the air as they sought the spoor of their prey.

Sarik mouthed a prayer to the spirits of his ancestors, thanking them for the part he would enact in the coming battles as his heart yearned to begin the fight. Limbering his boltgun, Sarik turned to make his way from the mesa, filled with anticipation for the glory the coming battles would surely bring.

Deep in the bowels of the heavy cruiser *Oceanid*, Lucian and his son Korvane approached the mighty armoured portal of the vessel's armoury. This was no conventional store of arms and munitions, but the inner sanctum of the rogue trader dynasty, the holy of holies that kept safe some of the most prized of Lucian's possessions. Only the ancestral stasis tomb beneath the blasted surface of sacred Terra held more valued treasures, such as the Arcadius Warrant of Trade and the holy banner of the line's founding.

Lucian's mind was made up; he had decided to travel to the surface of Dal'yth Prime. He would lead a battle group of Imperial Guard units against the tau defenders, and in so doing bolster his position on the crusade council whilst continuing the glorious traditions of his line.

'Father,' said Korvane, the inheritor of the clan, as the pair halted before the armoured portal. Though a handsome man, Korvane's features lent him a shrewd aspect many found disquieting. Lucian's son wore the same style of clothes as his father, a dress coat styled after that of the Imperial Navy officer classes, though he had always eschewed the more overt forms of finery and naval affectation. While Brielle had been raised at Lucian's side, literally standing beside him on the bridge of the *Oceanid* as soon as she was able to walk, Korvane had been brought up in the refined surroundings of the Court of Nankirk, learning his trade in the cutthroat circles of the upper echelons of Imperial aristocracy. His experiences had taught him to conceal his passions and his thoughts, to shield them from potential rivals lest he reveal some exploitable weakness. Lucian knew that Korvane would disapprove of his plan.

'I really must–'

'I know, son,' Lucian interrupted, as hidden gears engaged and the portal ground slowly upwards. 'I know. But this is something I have to do.'

'Something you *want* to do,' said Korvane, as the pair stepped through the open portal and into the darkness beyond. As they passed over the threshold, hidden mechanisms detected their presence, confirmed their identity, and activated the lumens. The darkness fled as row upon row of arms and armour were illuminated.

'And what if I do?' Lucian countered, crossing to a row of armoured suits as he spoke. 'You were raised in the court, son, and I'm glad of it, for the skills you amassed there have served us well. Many of our battles of late have been fought with words, and others with lance battery and broadside. But sometimes, our battles must be fought in the traditional manner. Up close, and personal.'

'And General Gauge,' said Korvane. 'He agrees to this?'

'That he does, Korvane,' said Lucian. 'Gauge is a veteran of more battles even than Sergeant Sarik. He understands the value of one of our faction getting involved, of being *seen* to get involved, at the front line. I think he may be a little jealous, actually...'

'But what will it actually achieve?' Korvane replied. 'What good will this do our cause on the council?'

'Much,' said Lucian, selecting a suit of ancient power armour. Its scarred and pitted surface was polished to a sheen that reflected the overhead lights. 'Grand and his lap dog cardinal would have us exterminate the tau out of hand. They even state they have the means to do so, though I have yet to see evidence that any of the crusade's vessels is carrying anything like a virus bomb. If the landings go well, that position will become less tenable, and we can steer events to our own ends.'

'Which are?' Korvane pressed.

'You know as well as I, son,' said Lucian. 'Whatever happens, however the crusade is concluded, we must come out of it in the ascendant. The concessions we could win, the charters we could earn... Emperor, if we play this right, Korvane, we could end up as viceroys of this entire region!'

When Korvane did not respond, Lucian turned from his examination of the suit of power armour to face his son. 'What?' he said.

'Has it not occurred to you, father,' Korvane said darkly, 'that you might not return from this grand adventure?'

Lucian sighed, placing a hand upon his son's shoulder. It certainly had occurred to him.

'Son,' said Lucian. 'Before I depart for the surface, I have something for you. Just in case.'

Korvane turned his back on his father, but Lucian pressed on regardless. He raised his hand, palm upwards, to reveal a simple ring in its centre.

'You must take this,' said Lucian.

Korvane looked at the glinting ring held out before him. 'What is it?'

'It is the most valuable thing on this ship.'

When Korvane appeared not to understand, Lucian continued. 'It's a gene-keyed cipher bearer. The crystal contains the access codes for the Clan Arcadius stasis vaults.'

'On Terra?' Korvane said, the full import of Lucian's words slowly dawning on him. 'The warrant?'

'Indeed, son,' said Lucian. 'Should I fall upon Dal'yth Prime, it's yours, all of it. But not,' he raised his hand to Korvane, 'without this.'

For a long moment, Lucian thought his son would refuse the ring. After a pause, Korvane reached out and with obvious trepidation, gently took it.

'It was to be Brielle's,' said Lucian. 'But when I married your mother you become my son.' He nodded towards the ring in Korvane's hand. 'And that became your birthright.'

Korvane's expression darkened at the mention of his stepsister's name. Korvane's entering the clan had displaced Brielle, who was

Lucian's child from his first marriage, from her position as heir, and she had hated him ever since. Korvane still bore painful scars from a nigh catastrophic accident that had befallen his vessel, an accident which he, if not Lucian, believed to have been her last deed before she disappeared at the outset of the Damocles Gulf Crusade. As Lucian regarded his son's face, a new resolve appeared in his eyes, and he placed the ring upon a finger.

'While I'm gone, you will watch my seat on the council,' said Lucian. 'Do you understand?'

Korvane nodded, and Lucian continued. 'There are three empty seats that must be filled. They must be filled with men sympathetic to our cause, not to Grand and Gurney's. This is your battle, which you must fight here, while I fight below. Are we agreed?'

'We are agreed,' Korvane replied solemnly. 'I shall not let you down, father.'

'Good,' said Lucian, relieved that he had done what he must. 'Now, you can help me into this power armour.'

CHAPTER THREE

Sarik's command Rhino ground forwards as he led the Space Marine assault column across the inland plain west of the landing zone. Having boarded transports landed from orbit, the crusade's Space Marines had divided themselves into several groups, each approximately the size of a conventional company. Each group had then linked up with a pair of Warhounds. The spearheads would each advance along a separate axis, pushing hard and fast into enemy territory, and engaging and destroying any tau forces they encountered. In the unlikely event that the spearheads encountered resistance they could not simply smash aside, they would bypass it, leaving it for the heavier units behind them to deal with.

Throwing back the hatch of the Rhino armoured carrier, Sarik's ears were assaulted by the deafening tread of the nearby Warhound Titan. The huge bulk of the mighty war machine blocked out much of the dawn sky above. Sarik reminded himself that the Warhounds were but the lightest of Titans, and that their compatriots were at least twice as large again.

Shaking the tail of his long topknot out of his eyes, Sarik scanned the vista ahead. The land was still arid, but the column had left the majority of the towering rock mesas behind them. The column was following the tau road network, which led west directly towards their target, the city of Gel'bryn. The air was fresh, and Sarik's genetically enhanced senses could taste in it the underlying taint of pollutants unleashed into the atmosphere by the huge landing operation.

'Driver!' Sarik bellowed over the noise of the nearby Titan and the rush of wind. 'Loosen formation. That beast won't even notice if he treads on us.'

If the driver gave any response, Sarik did not hear it, but the Rhino soon veered off to the war machine's right. The going here was good due to the wide, smooth roads. Sarik's spearhead was advancing quickly as the roads allowed them to avoid the rougher terrain.

'Sergeant Sarik,' a voice said over the command channel. 'This is Princeps Auclid of the *Animus Ferrox*, do you receive?' Sarik glanced upwards at the Titan his transport had just passed, knowing it was the commander of that mighty iron beast that spoke.

'Go ahead, *Animus Ferrox*,' Sarik replied.

'Sergeant,' the princeps began. 'Augurs are reading a concentration of enemy armour a kilometre ahead. Be advised, we are adopting battle stance. I suggest you give us some room. Out.'

Fully aware of the dangers posed by remaining too close to a Titan engaged in battle, Sarik relayed the order to his squads. Titan weapons were capable of unleashing fearsome energies, which could prove lethal to nearby units. They tended to attract a lot of return fire too, which the Titans might be able to withstand, but that its friends almost certainly would not.

Sarik scanned the arid landscape, his warrior's eye ever alert for signs of trouble. The advance continued, the units of the spearhead adopting a loose formation in order to allow the huge Warhounds space to fight when the time came. The land rose as the spearhead came upon a range of low hills, and soon the Warhounds were cresting a shallow rise, each around a hundred metres ahead of the Rhino-borne Space Marine squads.

'Alert!' Princeps Auclid's voice came over the vox-net. 'Enemy missiles launched, source unknown.'

A dart-like missile streaked directly downwards from the sky and impacted on the invisible void shield projected around the Warhound.

The missile exploded ten metres above the Titan, erupting in a flash of white light, a roiling cloud of black smoke billowing outwards. The Warhound ploughed through the bank of smoke, its head, fashioned after the war machine's namesake, scanning left and right as it crested the rise.

Cursing the alien trickery, Sarik sent the dozen Rhinos of his force forwards with a curt order, whilst allowing the Scout Titans to continue at the front. The missile that had struck Princeps Auclid's war machine would have torn a Rhino wide open.

'Second missile inbound,' said Princeps Auclid. 'Still no source...'

The second missile struck the *Animus Ferrox* in the right flank, from a high angle, yet once again the void shield held firm and the iron beast strode on.

As Sarik's Rhinos reached the crest of the rise, the pair of Scout Titans were already stalking down the opposite slope. The land ahead was different to the terrain the spearhead had passed through. The arid desert gave way to a belt of scrubland, which ten kilometres ahead became arable land scattered with cultivated fields and stands of regular, planted trees. There was still no sign of the enemy that had fired the missiles.

'All squads,' Sarik voxed to his Space Marines. 'Increase visual scanning. Inform me the instant you see *any* sign of movement.'

The upper hull of each of Sarik's carriers featured a double-door hatch. These swung outwards as Space Marines emerged to scan the surrounding landscape for any sign of the enemy heavy weapons teams firing the missiles.

'Brother-sergeant,' a voice came over the net. It belonged to Sergeant Arcan of the Ultramarines Chapter, his Rhino following directly behind Sarik's own. The sergeant was riding high in the roof hatch and scanning the surroundings through a set of magnoculars. 'I have a contact. Twelve nine, high.'

Sarik followed the squad leader's warning, in time to see a salvo of rockets arcing straight up into the air from behind a stand of trees a kilometre distant. In the span of seconds, the missiles had streaked upwards through the sky, closed the distance, and slammed into the *Animus Ferrox*.

A blinding white light flashed, and the Scout Titan was engulfed in a billowing cloud of black smoke. At least some of the missiles had been stopped by the war machine's void shields, but in the process had overloaded the projector. The invisible shield had collapsed in upon itself.

The Warhound's torso swivelled left and right on its reverse-joined legs, its huge weapons eager to engage its tormentor. Sarik keyed his command terminal and sent Princeps Auclid the coordinates of the stand of trees the missiles had been launched from.

'My thanks, White Scar,' the princeps transmitted in reply. There was frustration in the man's voice, no different to how Sarik himself would have felt under sniper fire. The Warhound turned to bring both its weapons to bear at once on the coordinates indicated. The ammunition feeds of its Vulcan mega-bolter whirred as thousands of rounds were chambered ready to fire, and the coils of its plasma blastgun pulsated with the staggering energies it was ready to unleash.

Another salvo lanced upwards into the air, the launch point somewhere behind a stand of purple-leaved trees. This time, Princeps Auclid saw it too, and opened fire.

The Warhound's Vulcan mega-bolter was, in effect, a cluster of oversized heavy bolters, each one far larger than even a Space Marine could carry. The sound of the weapon firing was like a bolt of silk being ripped violently in two. Sarik gritted his teeth against the horrendous report, and fought the urge to cover his ears. Up ahead, the stand of trees the missiles had been fired from simply exploded into constituent particles. Trunks were ground to pulp, and the pulp to a fine mist, by the merciless fusillade.

Surely, nothing could live through that.

But something had. As the breeze carried the mist away, a curved and sleek form was revealed. It took Sarik a moment to register just what the form represented. It was a vehicle, but its construction was more akin to the gracefully wrought forms of eldar tanks than those of the Imperium, which were solid, brutal and supremely functional in their design. Then Sarik realised that the vehicle was not driven by a track unit like the majority of Imperial war machines, but by some manner of anti-grav generator. Once more, the similarity to the fiendish works of the eldar came to his mind. For such technology to be so widely employed was a sure sign of the depths of the technological heresy to which the tau had descended, and reason in itself, in the mind of the Imperium, to prosecute a campaign of extermination against their empire. Sarik's heart beat faster at the prospect of combat against such a foe, but the vehicle was already rising on its invisible anti-grav cushion. With a whine of turbo jets, it swung around and was gone.

As the mist of the pulped trees drifted across the road in front of the Warhound, Sarik caught sight of a thin, red beam of light scything through it, which disappeared the instant the mist was caught on the air and dispersed. He followed the beam to where it had originated, and saw another stand of purple-leaved vegetation.

'Princeps Auclid!' Sarik called into the vox-net. 'The fire is indirect, there are observers in the treeline, they're using some form of–'

Sarik's words were cut off as the Warhound opened fire on the nearest treeline. Sarik saw the red beam lance outwards a second time. The alien warrior holding the source of the beam did so with countless thousands of mass-reactive bolts thundering overhead in what must have been a deafening barrage. Despite his loathing of such alien technology, Sarik acknowledged the skill at arms such a feat represented.

And then another salvo of missiles came screaming in from a high angle. The faintest glint of red light reflected from the side of the Warhound's canine head. A second later half a dozen missiles slammed into that exact point. The Warhound's void shields had been stripped, and even though the ornate cockpit was heavily armoured, it exploded as the missiles struck. The mighty war machine staggered backwards, its machine systems suddenly bereft of control.

'Get clear!' Sarik bellowed, ducking back inside his carrier as the driver gunned its engines. '*Animus Ferrox* is wounded!' Folding down a periscopic sight, Sarik witnessed the last moments of the *Animus Ferrox* as his armoured carrier powered away from the Titan's awesomely destructive death throes.

The Titan shook, as if its war spirit fought to keep its crippled form upright even without the guidance of the princeps, who had been killed the instant the missiles had destroyed the head. Then one of its mighty clawed feet slipped and the towering machine listed precariously to one side. The last thing Sarik saw before his Rhino bore him away was the entire machine toppling to the ground, thick black smoke boiling from the ragged wound where its cockpit-head had been.

Then Sarik's Rhino was shaken violently as the Warhound hammered into the road and an instant later exploded. Secondary explosions ripped out, the Rhino's driver fighting all the while to maintain control of the bucking armoured transport. Orange flames licked at the edge of Sarik's scope, and the pristine white heraldry of his transport was turned to scorched black by the raging fires of the Warhound's destruction.

When the explosions finally ceased, Sarik ordered his driver to halt. The white of the road surface had been scorched black, great banks of smoke lit from within by airborne cinders gusting past. The *Animus Ferrox* was reduced to little more than its armoured carapace shell at the centre of a huge crater strewn with blazing wreckage. Sarik bit back his grief that such a mighty, proud war machine could be struck down by alien weaponry with such seeming ease. It was one injustice amidst a galaxy of wrong, but the tau would pay for it nonetheless, he vowed, in blood.

From out of the smoke reared the form of the Warhound's twin, the *Gladius Pious*. The second Titan paused a moment as it passed its slain companion, before stalking forwards to take its position at the head of the advance, its weapons tracking back and forth across the treelines either side of the road.

Sarik opened a channel to the *Gladius Pious*. 'Princeps, this is Sarik. I honour your fallen kin, and I suggest a change of plan.'

'Go ahead, Sarik,' the princeps replied, his bitterness and grief at the loss of his fellow obvious in his voice. 'But make it quick, I read multiple armour contacts.'

'Understood, Princeps...?'

'Atild, brother-sergeant,' the princeps replied.

'Listen to me, Princeps Atild,' Sarik continued. 'The tau are marking their targets with some sort of laser designator, which the missiles are following. They're being launched blind, and the launchers are redeploying as we press forwards.'

'I understand, Sarik. But what can we–'

'My force will press forwards,' Sarik said, aware that at any second another salvo of missiles could come streaking out of the skies. 'We'll clear the treelines of observers and flush out the launchers. If we force them to fire over open sights, you can engage them before they get a chance to do so. Agreed?'

'Sarik, you'll be exposing yourself to–'

'I know, princeps,' Sarik interrupted, growing frustrated with the exchange. Titan crews, even those of the comparatively light

Warhounds, were accustomed to dominating any battlefield. They were ill-disposed towards relying on infantry, even elite Space Marines, to clear the way for them. Nonetheless, Sarik knew that the princeps had just lost a valued fellow warrior of his order, and so he gave the man some leeway.

There was a pause before the princeps answered, during which Sarik scanned the sky impatiently, fighting back the urge to press the other man for a response.

'Agreed, Astartes,' the princeps finally replied. 'I am in your debt.'

'You can thank me later, princeps,' Sarik replied, finally able to enact his plan. In moments, he was leading the column of armoured carriers forwards to clear the treelines of tau spotters.

Even as the Space Marine spearheads were pressing westwards in their breakout from the landing zone, the crusade's Imperial Guard units were mustering to launch the second wave of the advance. While the Space Marines represented small but highly elite formations, the diamond-hard tip of the spear, the Imperial Guard would form the inexorable main bulk of the attack, an unstoppable mass that would roll over and flatten anything it encountered.

Lucian stood in front of the assembled ranks of the force that he himself would soon be leading into battle, his heart swelling with pride. No Arcadius had gone to war at the head of such a formation for several centuries, a fact that Lucian hoped would seal his place in the annals of the clan forever.

The Dal'yth Prime landings were still taking place, but the majority of the combat units had been ferried to the surface and local air superiority largely consolidated. The plain was filled with thousands of marching troops and hundreds of growling armoured vehicles, and overhead dozens of impossibly large heavy landers plied to and from the vessels in orbit. Lucian had made planetfall in his personal shuttle and made his way immediately to meet his new command.

The force was drawn from the veteran light infantry companies of the Rakarshan Rifles, an ad-hoc battlegroup of around a thousand men and women who were acknowledged as the finest infiltrators and mountain troops in the entire crusade. In addition to their reputation for highly professional soldiering, the Rakarshans were the subject of folklore amongst the peoples of the Eastern Fringe, their ferocity in combat making them greatly feared by their enemies. The tau had never heard of Rakarsha, but Lucian had promised his troops that together, they would give the aliens cause to dread their coming.

As the last troops took their places, the formation was called to attention by bellowing sergeant-majors. They were an impressive sight indeed. They wore uniforms designed to blend in with the predominant subtropical environment of their home world, and these had been retained, for the pale green and dusty brown patterning was well suited to the arable lands around the tau cities. While the camouflage was eminently practical, the Rakarshans carried plenty of reminders of the culture that had spawned them. Each carried a short, curved blade at his belt, which by tradition was not to be drawn from its jewel-encrusted scabbard except to taste blood. Some said that should a drawn blade not spill the blood of a foeman, it should do so from its bearer. In addition, the Rakarshans each wore an intricately knotted headdress made of rich, purple cloth wrapped about their heads. Mounted above the forehead was a single black feather taken from a mountain vulture, a creature held as nigh sacred by the superstitious peoples of Rakarsha.

A pair of officers stood at the centre of the formation. Major Subad would serve as Lucian's executive officer, enacting his orders and supervising the more mundane aspects of the battlegroup's operations. Sergeant-Major Havil would be the battlegroup's senior non-commissioned officer, in whose hands the discipline and moral well-being of the warriors would rest.

When the troops were finally all in place, formed up in perfect lines by platoons and companies, all fell quiet, apart from the ever-present background noise of the more distant tanks and the landers flying overhead. Lucian stood perfectly still, impatient for the ceremonial handover of command to begin so that he could be about the business of conquest.

The two officers walked smartly forwards. Major Subad was a tall, lean man who to Lucian's eye had something of the ascetic about him. One of his eyes had been replaced by an augmetic lens, which twinkled like a rare gem from his dark, sharp-nosed face. The major wore a headdress similar to those worn by his troops, not one, but three tall feathers mounted at its front. Though the major looked to Lucian more a man of intellect than of action, he bore an impressive, curved power sword at his belt. Lucian judged that by the man's bearing he was fully capable of using the blade to masterful effect.

At the officer's side came Sergeant-Major Havil, a giant of a man with a coarse beard and dark eyes that surely saw all that occurred in the ranks. He too wore the traditional headdress of his home world, surmounted by a single black feather. In his hand the sergeant-major carried a polearm as tall as he was. Its head was a huge, double-bladed power axe. Though the weapon was encrusted in gorgeous gems and was undoubtedly a regimental heirloom, Lucian suspected that it was also wielded in battle, and would reap a fearsome toll amongst the enemy.

Both officers halted in front of Lucian. Sergeant-Major Havil stamped his feet with parade-ground precision, and bellowed an order in the tongue of his home world so loud it made Lucian's ears ring. The rogue trader decided instantly that he liked the sergeant-major. The man reminded him of a cthellian cudbear.

In response to the order, every rifleman in the formation came smartly to attention, stamping down in flawless precision as they shouldered their lasguns. A gentle breeze stirred the feathers of their headdresses, but otherwise, the ranks stood perfectly motionless. It was a sight to stir the heart, making Lucian pleased that his political manoeuvrings had resulted in him taking command of such a splendid force of warriors.

Then, Major Subad bowed at the waist, straightened, and addressed Lucian. 'Battlegroup Arcadius is hereby commissioned, and its command is vested in Lucian Gerrit, bearer of the Warrant of Trade of the Clan Arcadius. Let it be recorded in the regimental rolls, and let the foes of the God-Emperor tremble!'

Lucian bowed in return, then took a step towards the major, holding out his right hand. The two clasped forearms, and the deed was done. Battlegroup Arcadius, Lucian smiled inwardly at the name, was his to command.

'My thanks, Major Subad,' Lucian replied, looking from the hawk-faced officer to the ranks of veteran warriors arrayed behind him. 'Is the battlegroup ready to receive orders?'

'That it is, my lord,' the major replied. 'All companies have been assigned orders of march and merely await your command to advance to glory.'

Lucian chuckled slightly at the officer's turn of phrase, filled as it was with beaming martial pride. The Rakarshans spoke an archaic dialect of Low Gothic and he would have trouble communicating directly with the ranks himself. The major, however, spoke High Gothic fluently, and would translate Lucian's commands as he passed them down the line. Nonetheless, Lucian thought it might be worth learning some of the Rakarshan dialect, as he might be fighting beside these fierce warriors for some time to come.

'Well enough, major,' Lucian said, grinning widely. 'The command is given. Let the advance to glory begin!'

Sarik vaulted the trunk of a large tree that had been felled by the Scout Titan's supporting fire, raising his boltgun one-handed and unleashing a rapid-fire burst at the tau warrior who sheltered in the foliage up ahead. Bolts stitched the alien's torso, his blocky, sand-coloured armour penetrated in half a dozen places. An instant later, the mass-reactive shells exploded within the warrior's body, and he fell to the ground a ragged mass of ruined flesh.

Sarik tracked his weapon back and forth across his surroundings, his squad moving up behind him.

'Clear.'

The chest armour of Sarik's victim was ripped wide open, as was the flesh beneath it. A pool of blood swelled outwards, seeping into the dusty ground. The alien's blood was not red, but a deep blue-purple. The xeno-genitors attached to the Departmento Tacticae postulated this was because their circulatory system relied not on iron, as in human biology, but on cobalt. The only thing that mattered to Sarik was that they bled, and that they died with honour.

Stooping, Sarik retrieved the weapon the dead warrior had carried. As with all the tau firearms Sarik had encountered, it was rectangular and hard-edged, lacking the ornamentation many weapons of human manufacture displayed. The grip was too small for his gauntleted hands. It was designed to accommodate the tau's hands, which featured an opposable thumb and three fingers.

Mounted atop the weapon was a device Sarik had not seen before, though he guessed straight away what it was. Lifting the weapon, he squinted into the device. As he suspected, it was a sighting mechanism. Tracking the weapon back and forth across the clearing, Sarik depressed a stud at its side and a needle-thin beam of red light lanced out from the front.

Sarik guessed that a second stud at the weapon's side would establish a machine communion with a remote, vehicle-mounted weapons system. The link would be maintained as the missiles homed in on the target indicated by the red beam.

Feeling suddenly tainted by his contact with the alien technology, Sarik threw the weapon to the bloodstained ground beside its former owner.

The alien that lay slaughtered at Sarik's feet was the third his squad had killed, and reports from the other elements of the spearhead indicated that a further dozen had been engaged. The Space Marines ranged ahead of the lone Warhound Scout Titan, clearing each stand of trees of the observers. The weight of missile fire had rapidly dropped off as the tau had discerned the Space Marines' tactics, allowing the advance to proceed again.

As the spearhead progressed, the stands of trees became increasingly regular as it pressed in to cultivated farmland. In the distance, small, white domed-shaped structures were nestled in amongst the vegetation, the first signs of the conurbations that the spy-drones had indicated lay all around the tau city.

Moving to the edge of the plantation, Sarik prepared to call his transport forwards towards the next area of cover an alien spotter might be concealed in. At the edge of his hearing, which was far superior to that of any normal man, Sarik detected a rising drone, like turbines slowly powering up. The sound was emanating from behind a low rise, and could represent only one thing.

'Squad,' Sarik called into the vox-net. 'Enemy armour located. I want the missile launcher forward, and all other brethren on overwatch.'

A battle-brother appeared behind Sarik and knelt down beside him. He shouldered the very same weapon that Sarik had used the previous day against the tau flyer that had slain its previous bearer. The sound increased in volume, and Sarik saw a curved prow edge its way out from behind the rise, followed by the low, almost piscine form of the rest of the tau vehicle. Last to be revealed was the splayed, wing-like structure of the multiple launcher mounted high upon its back, its paired vanes underslung with three missiles each.

The launcher was slowly rotating. An undetected observer must have managed to bring his laser designator to bear on the *Gladius Pious*. Sarik turned to the battle-brother at his side, about to issue the order to engage, when he saw a red reflection glinting from the Space Marine's helmet.

Sarik dived forwards, shunting his fellow Space Marine aside at the very moment a missile fired to life and streaked through the air towards the pair. Both hit the ground hard, rolling apart as the missile burst through the foliage. With a supersonic scream, the missile passed by a mere metre over Sarik's head and struck the bough of a tree on the other side of the clearing. The entire plantation erupted as the missile detonated, shards of wood transformed into potentially lethal shrapnel by the power of the explosion.

Rising, Sarik scanned the clearing, which had been reduced from an orderly plantation to a scene of devastation. None of his warriors was injured, but that would not last if the observer drew a bead on any of them a second time.

Opening a vox-channel to the *Gladius Pious*, Sarik said, 'Princeps Atild. The enemy have changed their tactics. They are targeting us, but the spotter remains concealed. I suggest you engage possible locations while we deal with the launcher, over.'

'Understood, Sarik,' the princeps replied. 'Activate transponders and stand by.'

Relaying the order to the squad leaders under his command, Sarik activated his transponder unit. The device would transmit the location of each Space Marine and Rhino in the spearhead to the Warhound's strategium, so that the Scout Titan's weapons would not be turned upon its allies. Ordinarily, the transponders might be left to continually transmit, but the Departmento Tacticae had warned that the tech-heresies of the tau were so dire they might be able to detect the transmissions. The Space Marines were not prepared to take that risk.

'All units, stand by,' Sarik said over the command net, the blood rising within him.

Then the skies erupted as the Warhound turned its Vulcan mega-bolter on the nearby treelines, sweeping the weapon left and right as thousands of explosive bolts hammered into any and every possible location a tau spotter might be concealed in.

'Squad forward!' Sarik bellowed, praying his voice would be carried over the vox-net, for it was not audible over the deafening torrent of fire. 'Take it down!'

Sarik burst from the cover of the plantation and emerged into the open. A second later the warriors of his squad were at his side, and the black-armoured Scythes of the Emperor were not far away. Before them, the tau grav-tank had engaged the huge thrusters mounted on its flanks and was rising up as its retractable landing treads folded into its underbelly. The thrusters swivelled downwards to give it additional lift, and as the power built they emitted a high-pitched whine so loud it was soon competing with the thunderous report of the Warhound's mega-bolters.

Stowing his boltgun, Sarik drew his chainsword and brandished it high so that his warriors would follow his example. Then he brought the snarling blade downwards, pointing it directly at the tau grav-tank. A missile lanced from the treeline the Space Marines had just left and slammed into the side of the slowly rising grav-tank.

The missile struck a thruster unit on the grav-tank's side, and although the vehicle's thick armour deflected the worst of the blast, the engine was crippled. The vehicle slewed around, its remaining thruster screaming as it fought to maintain lift.

The grav-tank's nose dipped towards the ground, and Sarik sprang forwards, putting all his strength and that granted him by his power armour into sprinting across the open ground before the vehicle could recover and escape. As Sarik closed with his target, the pilot finally regained control and the vehicle began to rise again.

Finally, Sarik was on his foe, his battle-brothers a mere step behind. As the grav-tank rose, the air beneath it rippling with the anti-grav field that kept it aloft, Sarik leaped upwards, and caught hold of one of the secondary control vanes at the grav-tank's prow.

Pulling himself up onto the curved surface, Sarik looked for a handhold. Finding none on the alien machine, he located a crew hatch high on its spine and threw himself towards it even as the grav-tank gained altitude. The barking report of half a dozen bolt-guns sounded from below as Sarik's warriors opened fire on the anti-grav generators keeping it aloft.

His grip on the curved surface threatening to desert him, Sarik finally got a hold on the small hatch, and dug his armoured fingers in around its collar. Hauling with all his might, Sarik bellowed a wordless war cry, which turned into a joyous outburst of savage victory as the hatch peeled back under his efforts.

The grav-tank dipped violently, whether from the effects of his battle-brothers' fire or the pilot panicking Sarik could not discern. A red battle fury descended upon him. He plunged his arm inside the hatch right up to his shoulder plate, and pulled furiously on the first thing he grabbed hold of.

As Sarik retracted his arm, the grav-tank dipped crazily forwards. He dragged the pilot through the hatch and held him in the air victoriously. Then he brought the tau's body downwards upon the spine of the vehicle. He broke his victim's back across the hard armour, before flinging the ragged form to the ground below. It was only then that Sarik's berserker rage lifted, as the grav-tank slewed wildly out of control towards the structure it had been hidden behind.

In the final seconds before the tau vehicle slammed into the dome-shaped building, Sarik threw himself from its back, propelled clear by a last, powerful thrust of his legs against its hull. Even as he fell backwards towards the ground Sarik saw the grav-tank strike the building, gouging a great wound through the structure. Sarik struck the ground, the breath hammered from his lungs by the force of the impact. Then the vehicle upended itself, its nose ploughing through the building, before the entire structure collapsed upon it with a mighty release of dust, smoke and falling masonry.

'One down,' Sarik snarled, rising once more to his feet. An entire empire to go...

The landscape ahead of Lucian was dominated by low rises and dense vegetation, making it a perfect hunting ground for the veteran light infantry of the Rakarshan Rifles. To the south, a vast column of black smoke rose many kilometres into the sky, marking the death of one of the Legio Thanataris Scout Titans. Lucian had monitored the advance of Sarik's spearhead over the command-net, and warned his own companies to be vigilant for the missile grav-tanks and the observers directing their fire. Perhaps because the Rakarshan Rifles used no vehicles, they had not attracted the attentions of these supremely deadly armour killers.

Now, Dal'yth's sun was high overhead, and the battlegroup's advance was proceeding well. The Rakarshans had been transported forwards on Officio Munitorum conveyances, each large enough to carry a whole platoon and its equipment, before pressing forwards on foot. The warriors were well suited to the terrain, and were able to make intelligent use of the folds in the land and the regular stands of cultivated trees, whilst maintaining a rapid and steady advance.

Enemy resistance had been relatively light at first, with the lead platoons pressing through what ambushes they had encountered. The Rakarshans had proved themselves fearsome attackers and many had blooded their ceremonial blades already. The ambushes were growing in frequency, however, as the tau adjusted to the Rakarshans' tactics and redeployed their highly mobile forces to counter them.

'Communiqué from command,' Major Subad said, his hand raised to the vox-set at his ear. 'Spy-drones report a substantial concentration of enemy infantry amassing in the conurbation ahead.'

Lucian raised a gauntleted hand to shield his eyes from the white sun, and squinted in the direction indicated. The land rose and fell in a series of low hills, the eastern slopes of each covered in row upon row of the now familiar, purple-leaved fruit trees. Nestling in a shallow valley around five kilometres ahead, Lucian saw a cluster of white, domed structures, and in amongst them, evidence of enemy infantry moving to and fro.

'Looks like they intend to make a stand,' Lucian said, as much to himself as to his second-in-command. 'If they want a fight...'

'Standing orders require us to bypass them, my lord,' Major Subad interjected, 'and leave the main body to engage them while we press on.'

Lucian looked the officer in the eye, gauging the tone of his statement. 'How far behind is the main body?'

'Command states the advance has become stalled on several fronts, my lord,' said Major Subad.

'So there's a very real chance that if we bypass the enemy position, they will escape before the main body can engage?'

Major Subad's bionic eye glinted in the sun. 'A very real chance indeed, my lord,' he said.

'Then clearly, it is our duty to engage the enemy. Pass the word, major.'

Lucian remained at his vantage point, maintaining his watch on the tau while his forces prepared for the assault. During a brief conference with the company commanders it was decided that the battlegroup's heavy weapons, mainly missile launchers and heavy bolters, would deploy to the enemy's front and pin them down. Meanwhile, one third of the battlegroup would advance north-west, hooking around the enemy's flank to assault them from what should be a lightly defended front. Finally, the remainder of the battlegroup's companies would work their way around to the enemy's rear, block his escape route and guard against enemy reinforcement.

When the three elements were finally ready to begin their advance, Major Subad approached. 'My lord,' the major said. 'Will you be joining us?'

Lucian looked to his second-in-command and raised an eyebrow. 'It would be an honour, major,' said Lucian. 'Where would you have me?'

Subad's face lit up, and he bowed to his commander, before answering. 'The flanking group would very much benefit from your presence, my lord. I myself shall lead the blocking group, while Sergeant-Major Havil directs the heavy weapons. I shall vox you when all units are ready.'

'Well enough,' Lucian answered, keen to press on. Taking his leave of his officers, Lucian strode towards the companies he would be leading into battle, an adjutant vox-operator close behind him. The companies were mustered amongst a large cultivated fruit tree plantation, each platoon having moved forwards to its ready position in near total silence. Lucian felt suddenly very aware that while his troops were lightly equipped and camouflaged, he himself was wearing hulking power armour adorned in the deep red and gold trim of his clan's livery. No matter, he told himself. A good commander should be seen and heard, leading from the front, as much an inspiration to his own troops as an object of fear to the enemy.

The Rakarshans were eager to advance. Each was grim-faced and dark-eyed, every movement fluid and ready for battle. Lucian had seen hardened Imperial Navy armsmen look more nervous before boarding a harmless cargo scow, and he almost felt pity for the tau warriors. Almost.

'All units in position, my lord,' Major Subad's voice came across the vox-net. 'Advance at your command.'

'Stand by, major,' Lucian replied, locating the riflemen of the foremost platoon. He crossed to the unit's position, and nodded to its lieutenant before replying to Subad. 'You may begin, major.'

There was a brief pause, before the sound of a missile launcher being fired from Sergeant-Major Havil's fire support element filled the air. The missile streaked from its launcher upon a billowing black contrail, its firer hidden amongst the fruit trees of another plantation south of Lucian's position, and detonated upon striking one of the dome-shaped buildings. The resulting explosion was the signal to the entire battlegroup that battle was joined.

The air was suddenly filled with the deafening roar of dozens of heavy weapons opening fire at once, thousands of rounds of explosive ammunition hammering into the settlement.

Taking his cue, Lucian drew his power sword from its scabbard and turned to the platoon commander beside him. Though the man was much younger, his eyes were filled with the desire to advance. Lucian nodded, and the man yelled an order in the Rakarshan tongue.

An instant later, the riflemen were charging from cover and so too was Lucian. The sunlight was harsh after the shade of the fruit plantation, and it took Lucian a moment to get his bearings. Ahead of him was a cluster of low, white buildings, towards which the Rakarshans were advancing. The riflemen moved quickly, darting from one piece of cover to the next, each platoon covering another with weapons sweeping the buildings ahead. Despite the disciplined manner of the advance, Lucian knew that the final seconds would be a wild, ferocious charge as ceremonial blades were drawn.

Then came the whip-crack of a hyper-velocity projectile splitting the air nearby. The tau had seen their advance, and were firing on the flanking group.

The leading riflemen opened fire on the cluster of buildings, from where it appeared the shot had been fired. Lucian pressed forwards, making use of what cover he could, knowing that to fall to an alien sniper at this stage would be an ignominious way to start, and end, his military adventures. Lasgun rounds sang through the air, hammering into the white buildings and stitching dirty black scorch marks across their flanks. A second hyper-velocity shot scythed past, and Lucian imagined he saw a thin line etched through the air in its passing. A grunt sounded from somewhere behind, followed by the thud of a body hitting the ground. First blood to the tau, Lucian thought grimly, knowing that his flanking group could not afford to become stalled so soon in its advance.

'You men!' Lucian shouted to a platoon opposite from his position behind the trunk of a tall fruit tree. 'With me!'

The riflemen looked back at Lucian, their faces blank. He might as well be offering to make them a cup of recaf. Raising his power sword high, Lucian decided to lead by example.

Lucian stepped out into the open and swept his power sword towards the tau position. The Rakarshans got the idea immediately, and those nearest to him limbered their weapons and drew their ceremonial blades, springing forwards to join him.

A shot whined past Lucian, way too close for comfort, and sent a shower of grit into the air scant metres behind him.

'Forward Rakarshan!' Lucian bellowed, to be answered a moment later by the ululating war cry of the riflemen.

The charge towards the cluster of buildings was a mad dash, Lucian only absently aware that a relentless rain of blue energy bolts was being unleashed from somewhere up ahead. He heard several screams of pain from the accompanying riflemen, but he knew that to falter now would be fatal.

Closing on the nearest building, Lucian was confronted by a tau warrior emerging from cover to bring a long-barrelled weapon to bear. The warrior wore a blank-faced helmet, its single lens locking on to him as the alien swung his weapon upwards to draw a bead.

As he closed the final metres, Lucian brought his power sword up and back, and then finally his charge hit home.

Lucian's blow struck the alien warrior's weapon, scything it in two in a shower of blue sparks. The tau uttered an unintelligible curse and stepped backwards, even as a second warrior emerged behind him. Lucian let his momentum power him forwards, and shouldered his full weight into his enemy's chest, pinning him with a bone-crunching impact to the wall of the building.

The alien slumped to the ground, his body pulverised. Lucian drew his plasma pistol with his free left hand and swung it upwards towards the second tau.

Before the pistol was fully raised, the other fired his weapon, a shorter, carbine type firearm well suited to the close quarters battle. The carbine's discharge was almost blinding at such a short range, the energy bolt slamming into Lucian's shoulder armour. The impact blew Lucian backwards, his body striking the ground with a gut-wrenching thud. An instant later, he was looking directly up into the barrel of his enemy's weapon.

'*Gue'slo*!' the tau said, the words sounding metallic as they came from his helmet speaker.

'I've had guns pointed at me by far more scary people than you, tau,' Lucian sneered.

On hearing Lucian speak the name of his race, the alien cocked his head slightly. '*S'nae'ta...*'

'*S'nae'ta* indeed...' Lucian replied, playing for time as the Rakarshans pressed forwards.

The word must have been an insult, for the tau shouldered his weapon, his finger closing on the trigger.

Then the tau's head snapped back violently as a las-bolt slammed into it from the side. The alien warrior dropped heavily to the ground at Lucian's side, the blue-grey of its face visible through the smoking crack in the helmet. A hand appeared in front of Lucian's face.

'Rha ji?' the Rakarshan trooper said.

'Great,' Lucian grunted as he took the rifleman's hand and got to his feet. 'Does no one speak the Emperor's holy tongue around here?'

Before the Rakarshan could answer, the air was filled by a storm of las-bolts as the rifleman's platoon charged forwards and passed the building. As they closed on the tau positions, the riflemen drew their ceremonial blades and unleashed an ululating war cry that stirred cold dread in Lucian's heart. He could scarcely imagine what it would do to the tau.

The tau defending the cluster of buildings fired a last, desperate fusillade and half a dozen Rakarshans went down. The high-velocity weapons tore straight through their bodies, but unlike many weapons used by the Imperium, they did not kill outright. Instead, they left the victim to bleed out on the ground, out of the fight but a drain on resources as medics would have to deal with them and stop their cries demoralising their unwounded fellows.

Then the Rakarshans were upon their foe, and their blades were drinking deep of the purple blood of the tau.

'Leave some for fleet intelligence!' Lucian yelled as he rejoined the riflemen. 'Leave some... Emperor's balls, will you just...'

With the Rakarshans unable to understand Lucian's words, he had no choice but to wade in amongst them, locating a rifleman whose blade was raised to deliver the killing blow to a tau warrior at his feet. Lucian stepped in and grasped the man's wrist, staying his blow.

'No!' Lucian said firmly. 'Intelligence. We need to get at least...'

'Band'im?' the Rakarshan said, the savage light of battle fading from his eyes.

Lucian relinquished his grip on the other's wrist, and the rifleman lowered his blade. 'Aye lad, band'im. Band'im right now.'

The Rakarshan nodded his understanding, and then drew his ceremonial blade across his palm, drawing blood, before sheathing the weapon in the jewelled scabbard at his belt. A crowd of riflemen was gathering about the scene as Lucian turned on the tau.

The warrior's helmet had been torn off in the melee, and he had a blackened wound at his shoulder where a las-bolt had struck home. There was no blood; the heat of the blast had cauterised the wound, but would have flash-boiled the surrounding tissue making the entire arm useless and collapsing the adjacent lung. If they even had lungs. 'Looks like the war's over for you, tau,' Lucian said. Then, remembering the mess Inquisitor Grand had made of the first tau the crusade had taken prisoner, he added 'Better get you to Gauge's staff...'

An explosion sounded from somewhere amongst the settlement,

followed by a last burst of heavy bolter fire before the sounds of battle finally ended. The sound of whining turbines came from the far side of the cluster of buildings, rising in pitch before fading as the vehicles fled.

'Vokset, sir,' the vox-operator said as he handed Lucian his headset.

'That I understood,' Lucian said. Like most Low Gothic dialects Lucian had encountered, the Rakarshan tongue contained elements common across the Imperium. It was just a matter of deciphering the underlying terms. 'Gerrit here. Go ahead.'

'The enemy are retreating, my lord,' said Major Subad over the vox-net. 'They put up an honourable fight, but they are now fleeing west by anti-grav carrier.'

'Understood, major,' Lucian replied. 'Congratulate the men on a battle well fought and meet me here. Have Havil deploy a screen to the west in case they counter-attack. Out.'

As the rifle platoon's lieutenant arrived and set about ordering his men to secure the area, Lucian took stock of the tau settlement the Rakarshans had captured. The dozen or so buildings were constructed of the off-white, resin-like compound he had encountered in previous battles, and were low and domed. They were so unlike anything humanity built or dwelt within, all clean lines devoid of ornamentation. Despite their functional appearance, there was something elegant about the design of the buildings, for there was obviously some alien aesthetic at work.

Lucian located the door of the nearest building, comparing its design to that of the defence station that had been captured at the outset of the war and used for a brief time as its base of operations for the planetary assault on the tau-held world of Sy'l'kell. A shallow recess to one side of the door concealed a simple command rune, which Lucian pressed, causing the door to hiss as pneumatic systems engaged and opened the portal.

Lucian stepped inside, his eyes adjusting to the relative gloom. He kept his plasma pistol drawn, just in case any defenders lurked inside. As his eyes adjusted, Lucian saw that the room he had passed into was some sort of workshop, with dozens of tools arrayed in orderly rows across the walls. A moment's study told Lucian that the tools were little more than agricultural implements, but they appeared not to be designed for use by the tau, whose four-fingered hands would surely be unsuitable to wield them. The tools looked more like they were designed for use by some sort of...

A shadow swung across the periphery of Lucian's vision, and his plasma pistol was up and pointing right at it in an instant. Floating two metres off the ground directly in front of Lucian was a small, dome-shaped machine, a single lens blinking red as if it were studying him. Beneath the curved dome hung a cluster of multi-jointed limbs, each terminating in an empty socket that Lucian guessed was designed to use the tools arrayed across the walls.

Lucian kept the plasma pistol levelled at the drone as it bobbed in the air in front of him. 'So you're the hired help,' he said, marvelling that the tau should use such a wondrous machine for the simple task of tending crops and fixing broken fences. The red-lit lens blinked, and the machine emitted an electronic chatter, less harsh, but not unlike the sounds Lucian was accustomed to hearing around the cogitation terminals aboard his starship.

'Intelligence,' he said, lowering his plasma pistol a fraction. 'Of a sort at least. You'd be popular with the tech-priests. They'd take you to bits, not be able to put you back together again, then declare you a heretic...' he added wryly.

As if in reaction to Lucian's comment, the drone backed into the shadows with a sharp movement.

'You understood that, didn't you,' Lucian said, part of him feeling faintly ridiculous, another estimating how much the machine might fetch amongst those who collected such items of 'cold trade' curiosity. 'Of course,' Lucian muttered. 'Your masters have been in contact with isolated colonies for decades.'

'My lord!' Major Subad said as he burst into the room. 'I have it covered, back away slowly...'

Lucian could not help but smile as the Rakarshan commander entered the room in full combat stance, a gold-chased laspistol fixed on the bobbing drone. 'It's just a glorified shovel, Subad,' Lucian said, but the major's expression told him the man was on the verge of blowing the harmless drone to pieces. The drone seemed to see this too, and backed even further into the corner of the room.

'My lord,' Subad said, not taking his eyes from the drone. 'This is heresy. Crusade intelligence warned us of them. You must have read the briefing slates.'

'Those were gun drones, major,' Lucian said. 'This is no war machine.'

The major looked far from convinced. 'But it thinks, my lord, look at it!'

'Aye,' Lucian said. 'That's curious, isn't it?'

Major Subad's eyes widened and he turned his glance to Lucian. '*Curious*, my lord?'

'Well enough,' Lucian sighed. He could hardly expect the man to share a rogue trader's attitude to the unknown. 'Why don't you post a guard at the door and we'll keep it safe in here?'

The major nodded fervently at Lucian's suggestion, and began backing away towards the door. When Lucian had stepped out into the light, Subad sprang out, his laspistol still trained on the shadows inside.

Lucian pressed the command rune and the door hissed shut, locking the infernal thinking-machine inside the building.

'Major,' Lucian said as the officer finally lowered his weapon. 'You and your men are going to have to learn the difference between a gun drone and the sort of machine in there. If the tau use such machines as warriors, they probably use even more as menials.'

'They employ techno-heresy as servants?' Subad said, his expression incredulous.

'I would guess so, major. We know they espouse some extremist collectivism they call the Greater Good, so perhaps...'

'My lord!' Subad hissed. 'Please, we have our orders. That obscene doctrine is not to be mentioned. It is *unclean*.'

'Yes,' Lucian sighed. 'I've heard that Cardinal Gurney fears the troops might desert in droves if they got wind of the notion that all were equals...'

'Indeed, my lord,' Subad said, apparently not noticing what Lucian had hoped was a witheringly caustic tone. 'The Commissariat are alert for signs of taint.'

'Pfft!' Lucian said. 'Myopic fools who can't see past the muzzles of their own bolt pistols. Please, if one of those jumped-up demagogues so much as looks at one of our boys, you'll let me know, won't you?'

Now Major Subad's face was a mask of horror.

'Come on, major,' Lucian said, deciding it would be better to steer the conversation away from such dangerous topics as techno-heresy and xenosyndicalism. He slapped a hand on the officer's back as the two walked away from the building towards the main body of the troops. 'Update me, if you would be so kind.'

Subad nodded, visibly composing himself. 'Yes, my lord, forgive me...'

'Nothing to forgive,' Lucian interrupted. 'I've just seen much more of the galaxy than you. I should have taken that into account.'

Subad straightened up and tugged down the front of his battle dress. 'The assault went as planned, my lord, with one exception, for which I offer my most humble and sincere apologies.'

'Go on, major,' Lucian said raising an eyebrow.

'A number of the enemy escaped using carriers we had not previously detected. If you want patrols platoon flogged I can–'

'Flogged?' Now it was Lucian's turn to be horrified. 'Why would I want them flogged?'

'You want them put to death, my lord?'

'No!' Lucian said, exasperated. 'Neither. Not now, not ever. Is that clear?'

Major Subad managed to look both relieved and confused at the same time, but nodded his understanding before continuing. 'The battlegroup inflicted at least one hundred and twenty kills.'

'Captives?' Lucian asked.

'Captives, my lord?'

'Yes, major. Captives. Band'im.'

'Oh. Band'im, yes. Just the one.'

'The one I took.'

'Yes, my lord.'

'Have the Band'im passed back to Gauge's staff cadre at sector zero,' Lucian said. 'Not to Grand's goons. Understood?'

Major Subad nodded his understanding, though he looked distinctly uneasy at the mention of the inquisitor's name. Lucian pressed on. 'Casualties?'

'Twelve dead, my lord. Twenty or so light wounds, twelve are being mustered for medicae evacuation to sector zero.'

At least the wounded wouldn't be flogged for getting in the way of enemy bullets, Lucian thought, though he kept the idea to himself in case it gave the officer ideas. 'What of the general advance? Any reports?'

'Yes, my lord,' Subad said, producing a data-slate from a pouch at his belt. His face grew dark as he scanned the first few lines of text.

'Initial advances pushed back what few enemy units opposed them,' Subad said, paraphrasing the information presented on the slate's screen. 'But the main advance has been opposed by multiple hit and run attacks and ambushes. It has broken up into separate thrusts, and each is facing increasingly heavy resistance.'

Lucian scanned the settlement, which was crawling with riflemen dashing to and fro doing whatever it is soldiers do straight after a firefight. 'Then we'd better push on then, hadn't we, Major Subad? Remind me,' Lucian added absently. 'What's the tau name for the city we're taking, major?'

Subad consulted his data-slate. 'Gel'bryn, my lord?'

'Gel'bryn,' Lucian said. 'Something tells me the road to Gel'bryn isn't going to be an easy one, major.'

The *Gladius Pious* stalked ponderously away, its huge armoured feet uncaring of the destruction wrought in their passing amongst the plantations and farm buildings. Princeps Atild had informed Sarik that the Warhound had been ordered to reinforce another of the spearheads. The Iron Hands had encountered heavy resistance in sub-sector delta twelve, while the spearhead Sarik led had made far better progress once it had broken through sector beta nine.

Sarik's Rhino ploughed onwards along the road towards the distant city of Gel'bryn, the column heading westwards as it penetrated ever deeper into alien territory.

According to Sarik's command terminal, the city was still some fifty kilometres away. His force was the furthest forwards, a fact that stirred fierce warrior pride in Sarik's heart, even though the White Scars made up only one part of the spearhead he commanded. The column, consisting of three squads from Sarik's own Chapter, two from the Ultramarines and three from the Scythes of the Emperor, plus supporting Predator tanks and Whirlwind missile tanks, had sustained multiple casualties and three deaths as it had pushed onwards. The fallen had been evacuated by Thunderhawk gunship, and the composite Space Marine company was travelling through a sector almost entirely given over to agriculture.

'All squads,' Sarik said into the vox-net. 'Remain vigilant for ambushers. Maintain overwatch on all arcs.' The terrain was closing in again, the crops and plantations offering ample hiding places for the spotters that had directed the tau grav-tanks to fire so effectively on the Warhound.

'Lead,' Sarik transmitted to the Ultramarines Rhino travelling ahead of his own. 'Watch your forward sinister. There's cover there the enemy might use.'

The Rhino's Ultramarines tank commander swung his pintle-mount storm bolter in the direction Sarik had indicated, covering the dense stand of fruit trees as the vehicle rumbled by.

The Ultramarines carrier cleared the trees and the column wound its way past a cluster of what appeared to be abandoned agricultural machines. Sarik studied the machines as his Rhino ground past, studying their pristine white, gracefully rounded forms and considering for a moment whether he should order them destroyed in case the enemy should use them as weapons.

Even as Sarik decided the machines were no threat, the air was split by a hissing roar. Sarik recognised the sound of a fusion reaction boiling the air up ahead, and shouted from his open hatch: 'Ambush! Pattern Nova!'

A sharp explosion split the air and the lead Rhino shuddered to a halt, its left track splaying outwards as its armoured flank was flash-melted to white hot slag. The Rhino veered right as flames belched from its left-side traction unit, shedding the track entirely.

Sarik hauled himself from the top hatch of his Rhino and vaulted over its side, bolt pistol drawn in one hand and chainsword in the other before his armoured boots had even touched the ground. The rear hatch slammed down and his squad emerged, each brother taking position to cover a different arc with his boltgun.

Last out was Brother Qaja, his plasma cannon tracking back and forth as he came to kneel beside Sarik. The battle-brother had been patched up following the injuries he had sustained at the sensor pylon, but Sarik had been told by his force's Apothecary that the warrior would need heavy cybernetic augment-treatments when Operation Pluto was concluded.

'Target, brother-sergeant?' Qaja said as he swept the land ahead with his heavy weapon. 'Do you see them?'

'I see nothing, brother. Get the squads dispersed,' he said, before running forwards towards the lead Rhino, which was now almost entirely engulfed in flames as the melted armour on its flank began to solidify. None of the Ultramarines riding inside had yet disembarked.

As Sarik reached the rear end of the carrier, a secondary explosion burst from its foredeck. It was the pintle-mount's ready ammo cooking off, telling Sarik that the damage was far greater than was visible from the outside.

'Sergeant Arcan!' Sarik bellowed over the roar of the flames. 'Sergeant, do you hear me?' When no answer came, he sheathed his bolt pistol and chainsword and moved right up to the rear hatch.

'Can anyone hear me?' he bellowed. Again, no answer. There was only one thing for it. Flexing his armoured gauntlets, Sarik fed power to their fibre-bundle actuators to bolster his own, already formidable strength. He reached an arm out to either side of the hatch, locking the armoured shells covering his fingers to provide an anchor. After a final deep breath, Sarik hauled on the rear door with every ounce of his strength. The carrier's armour was designed to be proof against the many and deadly threats it would face whilst fighting across the numerous battlefields of the 41st Millennium, and was not so easily beaten. Sarik took a second deep breath and bled more power from the fusion core at his back to his armour's actuators. Warning tones sounded as the armour's war spirit protested its mistreatment, then the hatch buckled at either side and Sarik hauled one more time.

With a roar, Sarik tore the rear hatch from its mounting and flung the metal down. A dense cloud of greasy black smoke billowed out to engulf him and Sarik's genetically enhanced senses filtered and analysed the taste and scents assaulting him. The strongest was burning flesh.

'Apothecary!' Sarik bellowed before diving inside the stricken carrier. In a moment the smoke had begun to clear and Sarik's eyes, well capable of operating in darkness, beheld a tragic sight.

The blast that had struck the Rhino's flank had burned a concentrated jet of nucleonic fire into the passenger compartment. Sergeant Arcan had been standing in the open rooftop cupola, and his entire lower body had been seared to atoms, its upper half still slumped in the hatch. The three battle-brothers nearest the wound in the side of their vehicle must have been boiled alive inside their armour, which had been melted into a hideously deformed parody of its former shape.

A movement caught Sarik's eye as an Ultramarine stirred. A second fusion blast sounded from somewhere outside, and Sarik heard running footsteps approaching from behind; the Apothecary, he hoped.

'Help is on the way, brother,' Sarik told the Space Marine, whose once deep blue armour had been reduced to scorched black by the titanic energies unleashed inside the vehicle. 'Hold on, and have faith.' Another secondary explosion sounded from the forward area of the troop bay as more ammunition detonated, showering the sergeant with micro-shrapnel. He reached forwards and grabbed the nearest Ultramarine by the shoulder plates, hauling the stunned warrior from the open rear hatch as the Apothecary joined him.

The Space Marine medic added his strength to the effort, and the wounded Ultramarine was dragged clear by their combined efforts. In another minute, the two warriors had pulled another three clear, and more Space Marines had arrived to aid the rescue effort.

'Do what you can, brother,' Sarik told the Apothecary before rushing back to join Brother Qaja.

'Status,' Sarik said.

'Squads are deployed as per Pattern Nova,' Qaja said.

'Enemy?'

'None located, brother-sergeant,' Qaja said, not taking his eyes from the terrain as he spoke.

'None?' Sarik growled. 'These xenos and their trickery...'

A third fusion blast roared through the air, burning a searing orange wound across the flank of one of the Whirlwind missile tanks further down the column. The blast was hard to track, twisting and distorting the air as it was boiled by nucleonic forces. Nevertheless, Sarik got an idea of the origin point.

The only problem was, he could see nothing there. A ripe Chogoran curse escaped his lips as he scowled at the thought of yet more alien technology at work against his Space Marines.

'All squads,' Sarik growled into the vox-net. 'Suppressive fire, delta nine, two hundred metres, wide.'

Every battle-brother deployed on the column's left flank opened fire at the kill zone. The air was filled with hundreds of mass-reactive bolts, the crops in the target area ripped to shreds as the ground was pounded by exploding rounds.

'Cease fire!' Sarik called out, watching intently for signs of movement in the kill zone. 'Just wait...'

Then the sound of some kind of rotary gatling weapon powering up came from further down the column and an instant later a storm of blue energy bolts sprayed towards the Space Marines. Most struck the sides of the sturdy Rhino transports without inflicting any damage, but a battle-brother of the Scythes of the Emperor was thrown violently backwards as a bolt struck his shoulder plate. The warrior was unharmed, but he was forced to discard the wrecked shoulder guard and jettison the arm section as he stood to regain his position in the firing line.

'Tau infantry,' Sarik said. 'But they're using the same stealth devices we've seen in their elite flyers.'

'Orders, brother-sergeant?' Qaja said.

Sarik scowled as he scanned the surrounding terrain. It was dominated by low rises and depressions, a patchwork of crop fields and fruit plantations receding into the distance. The rise and fall of the land reminded him of the Baatarn Lowlands, an area his nomadic tribe had passed through when he was a child. His uncle, the tribe's seersman, had told him a tale of the mist-spirits said to haunt the place...

'Smoke...' Sarik muttered.

'Brother-sergeant?'

'Did you ever hear the tale of how the Tuvahks defeated the Kagayaga at Baatarn?' Sarik said, a sly grin forming on his face.

'Of course, brother-sergeant,' Qaja replied. 'Codicier Qan'karro related it at the last Feast of Skies. I don't see what–'

'All squad leaders,' Sarik said into the vox-net. 'Have one of your men gather smoke grenades from the Rhino launchers and stand by.'

Another burst of blue bolts sprayed through towards the Space Marines, this time from further down the column still.

'They're circling us like blood-sharks on a wounded mooncalf,' Qaja said through gritted teeth.

Within thirty seconds the squad leaders had all reported back over the vox-net that they were armed with smoke grenades taken from the multi-barrelled launchers at the front of each carrier. 'How did the King of the Tuvahks escape the Kagayaga, brother?' Sarik said, a feral light gleaming in his eyes.

'He...' Qaja said, before realisation dawned. 'He smoked them out, brother-sergeant.'

'All squads, deploy smoke grenades. Wide dispersion, fifty metres. Now!'

As one, the battle-brothers of each squad armed with the smoke grenades hurled them forwards. Upon striking the ground, each grenade detonated, creating an instant cloud of white smoke that billowed out from the impact point. Within seconds, a wide area fifty metres in front of the column's left flank was enshrouded in drifting banks of smoke.

'What now, brother-sergeant?' Qaja said.

'Wait and see, brother,' Sarik said. 'All squads, maintain overwatch. Look for movement in the smoke.'

Quiet settled the length of column as the Space Marines on its left flank focussed their attentions on the drifting smoke. Clipped exchanges went back and forth between the squad leaders as they coordinated their arcs, ensuring that every quadrant was covered.

'Contact!' a battle-brother from a Scythes of the Emperor Devastator squad on the extreme end of the line reported. 'Zeta nine, transient.'

'Hold your fire,' Sarik ordered. 'What did you see?'

'Movement, brother-sergeant,' the Space Marine said. 'A parting of the smoke, but nothing solid.'

'Your vigilance does you honour, brother,' Sarik replied. 'Stand by. Qaja, you have the squad.'

Sarik moved swiftly along the column, exchanging brief words with the squad leaders as he passed them. As he reached the Scythes of the Emperor Devastator squad, its sergeant indicated the battle-brother he had spoken to.

'Show me.'

The warrior lowered his heavy bolter, resting its gaping barrel across his knee, and pointed into the drifting smoke bank with his free hand. 'There, brother-sergeant. The smoke parted for a moment, as if something were about to emerge.'

'But nothing did.'

'Contact!' another of the Scythes of the Emperor hissed, bringing his missile launcher to bear on a point to the squad's extreme left. Sarik saw it too.

'They're working their way around us,' Sarik said. 'All squads. Ten round fusillade, fifty metres, delta quad, on my mark.'

As the squad leaders signalled their acknowledgements and ordered their firing lines ready to enact Sarik's direction, the sergeant looked to the next squad along, a Scythes of the Emperor tactical squad. Clapping a hand on the shoulder of the Devastators' sergeant, he said 'Remain on station.' Then turning to the sergeant of the tactical squad, he said, 'Sergeant, I need five men.'

The squad leader selected five of his warriors and with a curt gesture sent them over to Sarik. 'Brothers, remove your helmets. Our foes are hidden to our sight, but not to our other senses. With me!'

As the five Scythes stowed their helmets at their belts, Sarik turned and was off, running towards the roiling bank of smoke. He crossed the fifty metres and plunged into the mists, halting the instant his vision was swallowed up by featureless white. A moment later, he heard the Scythes move in behind him and likewise halt. Even at a range of two metres, the warriors were barely visible. It was only their black armour that made them stand out at all, while Sarik's white armour would make him all but invisible even at that close range.

Sarik took a deep draught of the air, slightly overemphasising the action so that the other Space Marines would hear it and follow his example. To Sarik's enhanced senses, the air tasted overwhelmingly of garlic, though in reality that was the phosphorus employed in the smoke grenades. Sarik sensed his multi-lung implant engage as it protected his kidneys from the toxic effects of the chemical smoke. Taking another deep breath, he mentally filtered out the strong odour of garlic, and detected something else, something sharp, like bleach.

'Ozone?' one of the Scythes of the Emperor whispered at Sarik's side.

'Indeed,' Sarik whispered back. 'Some sort of energy field. Follow me.'

Sarik rose and commenced a stooped run, breathing steadily as he followed the sharp scent. As he moved, the smell grew in intensity, until his suspicions were confirmed. The tau were nearby, and the energy fields they were using to shield their movements were giving off the sharp smell of ozone as they reacted with the atmosphere.

Sarik halted, and was joined a moment later by the five Scythes of the Emperor.

'Follow my lead,' he hissed as low as possible. 'And stay close and quiet.'

Then he was up again, the Scythes close behind. The smell of ozone grew almost overpowering and Sarik could sense he was almost upon his prey. Then the mist parted as if something just larger than a man was walking through it, and Sarik dived forwards headlong.

Sarik's dive was arrested in mid air as he slammed into something invisible. The unseen form must have been substantially armoured, for the impact almost took the breath from Sarik's lungs. He went down, the invisible opponent beneath him, and felt the figure thrashing wildly as it fought to escape.

The dark shadows of the Scythes of the Emperor passed by, and Sarik knew they too were engaging more unseen enemies. None made a sound.

Sarik made a fist and punched down hard towards the smoke-shrouded ground. His fist stopped half a metre from the ground, striking a hard surface. A muffled grunt sounded, confirming that the tau warrior was clad in some form of hard, but not invulnerable armour. Guessing where its head was, he made a grab, and found its neck, clamping his fist around it.

Sarik used his free hand to draw his combat knife. The enemy struggled all the more, and something blunt slammed into Sarik's left shoulder plate. It could only have been a weapon, for a moment later Sarik heard the universal sound of ammunition being chambered. Knowing he had but seconds to prevent the enemy from firing its weapon and at best giving his presence away and at worst blowing his head clean from his shoulders, Sarik plunged the monomolecular-edged blade towards where he judged the enemy's chest must be.

The blade struck solid armour, but Sarik brought it downwards until it found yielding flesh. With a brutal upwards thrust, Sarik plunged the knife deep inside the enemy's innards, feeling the tau shudder and thrash as he did so.

Then hot, purple blood spilled out of the invisible wound, staining Sarik's forearm. He withdrew the blade, and a shower of blue sparks, accompanied by the overpowering stink of ozone, erupted in front of him. He stood, and before his very eyes, his enemy faded into existence.

The warrior was wearing an armoured suit of matt black. The armour covered most, but not all of its body, and Sarik saw that his knife had found the soft joint between thigh and groin armour plate. The warrior's right arm carried a blunt, tube-shaped heavy weapon, and at its back was a device that Sarik judged to be the generator that powered its stealth field.

A series of muffled grunts and impacts told Sarik that the Scythes had encountered, and violently neutralised, more of the enemy stealth troopers. He listened until all had gone quiet again, and a moment later the five Space Marines reappeared.

'There are more of them, brother-sergeant. At least twenty, to the north.'

'Did they hear you?'

'Yes. They are inbound.'

'Good,' Sarik said, assuming a prone position on the ground. The smoke was beginning to clear. 'You might want to take cover, brothers.'

The Scythes of the Emperor took position beside the White Scar, and the six warriors concentrated on the smoky depths where the enemy lay. 'Come on then...' Sarik whispered.

Then he saw it. The smoke parted as at least a dozen figures ghosted towards the Space Marines.

Sarik opened the vox-channel. 'Mark!'

The air erupted and the ground was churned as bolt-rounds hammered in from the Space Marine gun line. Heavy bolters added their throaty roar to the sharp staccato of the boltguns and the smoke banks sizzled as balls of plasma lanced through. Though un-aimed, the fusillade could not help but strike the foe. Sparks flew as rounds struck invisible bodies over and over again. Then the tau attempted desperately to return fire and a stream of blue energy bolts spat out from the invisible heavy weapons. But the tables were turned; the tau could not see their targets, and they were cut down before Sarik's eyes. As each fell, their shattered forms resolved, broken armour and body parts scattered across the ground.

The return fire died away, and within seconds ceased as the surviving tau retreated in the face of the Space Marines' overwhelming fusillade.

'Brother-sergeant,' a voice cut in over the vox-net. 'Estimated fifty contacts, closing in behind us'

Lucian and his two subcommanders looked west through their magnoculars into the setting sun. The skies had turned a deep turquoise the like of which Lucian had never seen before, with a faint glimmer of stars appearing overhead. Below the white sun, the distant towers of Gel'bryn glinted in the fading light, tempting the rogue trader with the riches and opportunities to be found there.

The city was small by human standards. In the Imperium it was often convenient to pack the multitudes in as tightly as possible, as near to their workplaces as could be achieved, in order to control the means of production with brutal but vital efficiency. The ultimate expression of this harsh reality was the hive cities of such worlds as Armageddon, Ichar IV and Gehenna Prime, each of which could equal the industrial output of any other planet in the Imperium short of a forge world of the Adeptus Mechanicus. Instead of packing their population into a relatively small number of massive cities, the tau evidently preferred to establish thousands of smaller settlements across an entire planet, and Gel'bryn was the largest of those on Dal'yth Prime. Lucian suspected that each city was relatively self-sufficient too, if the surrounding farmland was anything to go by. The use of advanced technology, forbidden or simply lost in the Imperium, for such simple tasks as farming was beyond anything he had seen in his decades of contact with all manner of xenos species. It suggested a highly ordered society in which individuals were free of the drudgery that was the reality of everyday life in the human Imperium.

But despite their seeming reliance on technology and their aberrant social order, the tau had proved a highly capable foe. While their skills in close combat were no equal to the sheer ferocity of the Rakarshans or the Space Marines, their advanced weaponry made up for that deficiency. The Departmento Tacticae was slowly piecing together a picture of the tau's capabilities, which it was disseminating to the ground force commanders as quickly as the reports could be compiled. The Imperium had learned more about the aliens' battlefield doctrines in the last forty-eight hours than it had in the entire crusade, for in previous ground battles Imperial forces had encountered little more than line infantry. Now reports were flooding in from all fronts of anti-grav armoured vehicles, target designator-equipped artillery spotters and a myriad of equally unanticipated, yet highly deadly foes.

'Be advised,' the voice of the Departmento Tacticae advisor crackled over the vox-net. 'Spearhead Sarik reports contact with enemy heavy infantry equipped with some form of stealth field. Ex-loading tacticae script now.'

Lucian lowered his magnoculars and took the data-slate handed to him by Major Subad. He scanned the reams of information being transmitted from General Gauge's command centre on the *Blade of Woe*, ignoring large portions of it and zeroing in on what was most relevant.

Item; main advance stalling, Imperial Guard units engaged by multiple ambushes resulting in fractured progress. Regimental Provosts to increase activities pending Commissarial intervention.

Item; advance to be consolidated into three main fronts. Battlegroup Arcadius to advance along present axis to probe city outer limits. Space Marine composites to amalgamate as soon as possible to reduce main enemy concentration. Titans to amalgamate ready to face enemy destroyers.

Item; second wave Imperial Guard units to proceed in attached order of march. Armoured and cavalry units to be made ready for push against enemy units consolidating along River 992. Armoured infantry to move up in support of armour. Mechanised units to muster as per attached orders.

'Havil, better get the boys fed and watered,' Lucian told the sergeant-major as he lowered the data-slate. 'Subad, draft a warning order. We're going in. I want us moving by nightfall.'

The outskirts of Gel'bryn lay ahead, the details lost to the static-laced, monochrome green of Lucian's prey-sense goggles. Battlegroup Arcadius was advancing towards a small conurbation on the eastern shore of the watercourse designated 'River 992', beyond which lay the city and the bulk of the tau defenders. Patrols platoon was a kilometre forward, the very finest of the Rakarshans' scouts leading the rifle companies forwards under cover of darkness.

Though he had wanted to go in with the foremost platoons, Lucian had been told in no uncertain terms that he was nowhere near the equal of the Rakarshans when it came to stealth and field craft. His insistence on wearing his ancestors' suit of power armour tipped the argument. Lucian was currently positioned halfway down the line, where he was less likely to give away the Rakarshans' approach.

Lucian knew that the advance into the outskirts would not go undetected for long, for it had been established that the tau had their own low-light technology. Though he kept the heretical thought to himself, it seemed likely to Lucian that the tau's technology was superior to the Imperial forces' in this, and many other fields. Though the Rakarshans' own night-vision devices were offset by the tau's, they had other advantages and skills to draw on. The Rakarshans moved with such utter silence that one could be marching right next to Lucian and he would not have heard. Their use of cover and concealment was beyond any human unit Lucian had ever witnessed. In fact, they were almost supernaturally good.

With a slight start, Lucian realised that he was alone, no Rakarshans visible in the darkness around him. He continued his advance nonetheless, knowing that there were probably over a dozen of the stealthy riflemen within ten metres of him. The terrain dipped as it ran down towards the distant river, beyond which the Tacticae advisers reported a concentration of the enemy units gathering.

'Sir!' an urgent whisper hissed out of the darkness. Less than three metres in front of Lucian was a Rakarshan section leader, barely visible in the shadows behind a low shrub. Spread out behind him was a whole rifle section, which Lucian had not even known was nearby.

Lucian halted, lowering himself into a kneeling position beside the corporal. 'Report.'

The section leader clearly spoke a small amount of standard Low Gothic, for Lucian could just about understand him when he said 'Enemy, right flanking.'

Lucian adjusted the gain on his goggles and studied the terrain to the right of the group. The land continued to dip as it ran towards River 992, which sparkled in the middle distance. Three hundred metres to the east was an orderly plantation of the ubiquitous purple fruit trees, but to Lucian, they harboured nothing but dark shadows.

'You're sure?'

'Yes, sir. Ghosting in the thick.'

'Well enough,' Lucian said. 'If you're sure.' Lucian looked around for the signalman who had been his shadow for the last day or so. He was not surprised when the man appeared from the darkness nearby.

'Advise Subad we've detected movement in the woods to the east. Tell him I've ordered a sweep, but the advance should continue.'

The signalman passed the message on, shielding the pickup of his vox-set with his hand as he spoke in hushed tones.

'Right lad,' Lucian whispered to the corporal. 'Let's go see what we have.'

The man's eyes narrowed in disapproval and he nodded to indicate Lucian's power armour. 'You go first then,' Lucian conceded.

The section leader saluted silently and in a moment was gone, along with his men. Lucian engaged his prey-sense goggles again, and could just about make out the Rakarshans' thermal signatures as they dashed across the open ground towards the plantation. Lucian cycled through his goggles' range bands, looking for any sign of an enemy in the treeline. He found none, but that did not mean there was no enemy there. If the enemy the Rakarshans had detected were the stealth-fielded heavy infantry the White Scars had encountered, then it was incredible the Rakarshans had detected them at all. According to the tacticae reports disseminated to the various commands, the stealthers were not just shielded from the eye, but from other targeting devices too. Perhaps even from the war spirit that animated Lucian's prey-sense goggles.

Lucian was overcome by the notion that someone was watching him. He told himself it was nonsense and moved out in the Rakarshans' wake, but could not entirely shake the feeling. Wanting to be ready for combat, he drew his plasma pistol, and was just about to activate its power cycle when the signalman put a restraining hand on his forearm. He was right of course; the high-pitched whine of the containment coils drawing power from the plasma flask would ring out like a bugle signalling a cavalry charge. Lucian nodded his thanks to the signalman and re-holstered the pistol, drawing his power sword instead, but not activating it for now. The sword could be powered up in a second, so he could leave doing so until really needed, whereas the pistol could take long seconds to be readied to fire.

Lucian continued as quietly as he could, leaving a generous distance between himself and the leading Rakarshans. He was painfully aware of every little sound his suit made, marvelling that he had never noticed any of them before. The fusion core of his backpack gave off a low hum, while the actuators at the suit's joints hissed and strained with his every movement. Ordinarily, the sounds were practically inaudible, but in the dark night, with a concealed enemy potentially training a crosshair on Lucian's forehead, they were appallingly loud.

'Sir!' the signalman hissed, dropping to a crouch. Lucian followed the man's example, and scanned the treeline through his goggles. Still nothing.

'What?' he whispered, his voice barely more than a breath.

'The riflemen, my lord,' the man said. 'They have detected movement beneath the trees. It must be an ambush.'

Lucian located the riflemen, who were spread out in a line about a hundred metres ahead, each taking cover behind the low lying shrubs that studded the area. Lucian felt suddenly that whatever would happen next was down to him to decide. He was used to such situations in the void, where his actions in a space battle might doom himself and thousands of crewmen, but this was something else. What would Sarik or Gauge do, he thought?

Both would fight through the ambush, he knew. And they would do so from the front.

Turning back to the signalman, Lucian was about to give the order to press on when a thunderous burst of gunfire erupted from the treeline. Five Rakarshans went down, dead or wounded, Lucian could not tell which. 'Damn this,' he spat, and drew his plasma pistol from its holster.

'Charge!' Lucian bellowed, uncaring of the high-pitched whine of his plasma pistol powering up. He stood, the signalman following his example, and strode forwards. A second burst of gunfire sounded, pale blue bolts whipping through the air all too close.

'That's it!' Lucian yelled as he picked up his pace towards the treeline. 'Come out and play!'

Lucian strode past the Rakarshan section leader, the man's face staring up at him with a stunned expression. 'Now's your chance, lad,' Lucian hissed. 'Get moving!'

Understanding dawned on the Rakarshan's face and Lucian grinned like a fool. In an instant, the man was leading his riflemen away, starting a wide loop that would bring them towards the hidden enemy's left flank.

Now Lucian was picking up speed as he neared the dark treeline, and a third volley of gunfire split the air. The projectiles were the same condensed energy packets fired by other tau weapons, but the discharge of the weapon firing sounded distinctly different, somehow cruder and certainly noisier.

The signalman was directly behind him, and thankfully, so too were several other sections. Lucian brandished his power sword and thumbed it to full power, arcs of white lightning leaping up and down its length. The nearby Rakarshans followed his example, limbering their lasguns and drawing their ceremonial blades.

Now the treeline was only twenty metres ahead, and Lucian heard a ripple of lasgun fire from fifty metres to the left. The Rakarshans had engaged. An ululating hoot sounded from within the trees, and was repeated along its whole length. The sound was utterly alien and savagely barbaric, and not like any other Lucian had heard so far on Dal'yth Prime.

Then the trees rustled, and a dark shape leaped to the ground in front of Lucian, followed within seconds by a dozen more. The figures glowed bright green in Lucian's prey-sense goggles, and were tall, muscular and whip-fast in their movements. In the last few moments, Lucian tore his goggles free, knowing they would hinder his three-dimensional awareness in the brutal melee to follow.

The creature in front of Lucian let forth a high-pitched, almost avian-sounding cry, and charged in. It lifted its rifle, which was fitted with wickedly sharp spikes at barrel and butt. Lucian brought his power sword high to parry the blow, and the rifle erupted in sparks as it was cut in two.

The creature kept on going, brandishing the two halves of its ruined weapon like hatchets. If anything, it was now more dangerous. With a twist, Lucian turned his forward momentum into a sideways lunge and brought his power sword down in a wide arc aimed at the creature's middle. It anticipated the move and sprung backwards with an angry hoot.

The war cries of the Rakarshans and the whistling calls of the aliens erupted all about, and a swirling melee engulfed the entire treeline.

Lucian's foe leaped through the air, directly for him, and he raised his power sword again. In a split second, he saw that he could not hope to deflect both of the alien's weapons, so he parried one, reducing it to a useless stump, and turned his shoulder to the other causing it to glance harmlessly from a shoulder plate.

The creature hissed its anger in Lucian's face, its sharp, beak-like mouth open wide as if it meant to bite into Lucian's flesh. The alien came on, barrelling into Lucian and forcing him backwards as its weapon scraped down his chest armour. Lucian saw an opening and brought his power sword up to plunge it into the thing's chest, but again, his foe twisted aside and sprang clear.

For a second, Lucian and the alien circled one another, the shadowy forms of bitterly interlocked combatants swirling around them in the dark and grunts of pain and anger filling the air. Its beady eyes were fixed on his and sharp quills at the back of its head rattled as they stood on end like the hackles of some enraged predator.

Lucian feinted to the left, and the creature dodged his blade with preternatural speed. But that was what he had hoped it would do. With his left hand, Lucian brought the plasma pistol up, levelled it directly at the alien's head and pulled the trigger.

The darkness erupted into violet brightness as the plasma bolt spat from the blunt pistol's barrel and consumed the alien in a roiling ball of searing energy. Lucian's vision swam with nerve-light and he was momentarily blinded. As he blinked furiously to clear his vision, Lucian heard the wet thud of meat striking the ground and knew his foe was dead.

A Rakarshan yelled something from nearby. Though Lucian did not understand the words, he guessed their meaning and ducked blindly. The sharp hiss of air parted by a razor-sharp blade sounded a hand's span above his head, and Lucian knew the rifleman had just saved his life. He straightened again and as his vision finally cleared he saw another three of the alien warriors closing on him.

'Daem'ani!' a Rakarshan yelled, an unfamiliar note of fear in his voice. The shout was taken up by a dozen other riflemen, and in a moment Lucian was surrounded by Rakarshans.

The aliens threw themselves forwards at the exact same moment the Rakarshans charged. The two lines crashed together in a thunderous explosion of steel and blood. A rifleman beside Lucian was struck hard in the face by the spiked stock of an alien's rifle, the blade lodging itself in the man's head. Before the creature could pull the blade free Lucian lashed out with his power sword and severed both of its arms in a single sweep. The creature hooted in pain as it collapsed writhing to the ground, blood spurting from its wounds.

Even before the wounded alien had been trampled flat beneath the Rakarshans' boots, another had stepped into its place. A rifleman leaped forwards, repeating the earlier cry of 'Daem'ani!' at the top of his lungs, his ceremonial blade lashing outwards to gut the creature. The alien saw the blow coming and parried it with its rifle, using it as a duel-bladed stave and slamming its end into the soldier's stomach. The Rakarshan doubled over under the impact and the alien brought the other end of the rifle down across his back, crushing him to the ground beneath the brutal strike.

A high-pitched whine from Lucian's plasma pistol told him it had recharged and was ready to fire another blast. He raised the pistol and this time brought his right forearm across his face as he squeezed the trigger so he was not temporarily blinded by its discharge.

Lucian had no time to aim his shot, but had no need to. The enemy were coming on in such numbers that he could scarcely miss. The plasma bolt burned a hole right through the torso of the first enemy in its way and incinerated the one behind it. The enemy faltered in their assault, and in that moment Lucian saw that scores more of them were pouring from the treeline.

'We're outnumbered!' Lucian bellowed. *By at least three to one, and rising.*

The section leader was nearby, and Lucian grabbed him by the shoulder. The man's eyes were glowing with madness, as if he were consumed by overwhelming and unreasoning fear of what the Rakarshans had named 'daem'ani', and a berserker's rage to destroy the foe. The man appeared not to notice Lucian, so he shook him violently until his eyes came into focus. 'Order your men back, now!'

More hoots and whistles sounded from the woods, and Lucian knew the small force had no chance if it did not fall back straight away.

'Fall back!' Lucian yelled. 'Move and cover, you know the drill!'

But the Rakarshans did not understand. 'Damn you,' Lucian growled, looking about for his signalman, who he knew to speak near flawless Gothic. The man was on the ground, bleeding profusely from a wound across his chest, a dead alien warrior sprawled out next to him.

'How do I tell them to fall back?' Lucian said as he crouched next to the signalman. 'What's the word of command?'

'Fall back, my lord?' the signalman said through gritted teeth. 'There is no word for fall back in our tongue...'

Lucian bit back a curse and sheathed his power sword. Hooking his free arm around the signalman's waist, he raised his plasma pistol at the onrushing aliens and let off another blast. The shot struck an alien square in its roaring, beaked head, decapitating it and setting its still-standing body alight.

The aliens nearest to the conflagration leaped back from the fire, hissing and whistling in obvious fear. Lucian took a step back, dragging the wounded signalman with him. 'Tell them to follow me,' he growled. 'You must have a word for that!'

'Mu'sta,' the signalman grunted as Lucian dragged him back. 'Tell them that...'

'Mu'sta!' Lucian yelled. 'Mu'sta, ya bastards, mu'sta!'

Within seconds, the surviving Rakarshans were gathering about Lucian, two of their number taking the wounded signalman from him and propping the man up between their shoulders. Lucian fired another plasma bolt at the aliens, who were even now recovering from the shock of seeing one of their number decapitated and immolated at the same time.

The Rakarshans followed Lucian's example, firing into the aliens even as more emerged from the treeline. Lucian backed away, though he kept firing as he went, and soon the Rakarshans had the idea. The corporal appeared to have recovered his wits too, for he set about ordering the sections to deploy or cover one another alternately. Soon the Rakarshans were halfway back up the rise and out of immediate danger.

Lucian lowered his prey-sense goggles over his eyes again, in order to judge the numbers of aliens the Rakarshans had fought. Zooming in on the scene, he saw something that filled him with utter revulsion. Three of the aliens were crouched over the body of a fallen rifleman. One was scooping up a great, looping handful of the man's guts and sucking on the end. Another was biting down hard on a forearm, while the third was doing something behind the corpse's head that Lucian was glad not to be able to see clearly.

'You sick, sick bastards...' he muttered, unaware that the section leader had come up beside him.

'Sir?' the man said.

Lucian turned from the horrific scene and lifted his goggles. 'Nothing son, nothing. Come on, we need to get the battlegroup organised, and I need to talk to someone from Tacticae intelligence...'

Brielle stood in the centre of the domed viewing blister high on the spine of the tau vessel *Dal'yth Il'Fannor O'kray*. It was like standing on the outer hull of the ship itself, for the blister was made not of solid material, but an invisible force field. Brielle felt a combination of trepidation and thrill as she looked out past the gleaming white hull to space beyond. A swarm of spacecraft traversed to and fro across the void, every possible class and configuration represented, from pinnace to mass transport.

Brielle turned slowly on the spot, taking in the full panorama of the scene until she came to face Naal.

'What?' Brielle said, her dark eyes glinting with mischief.

'You lied to them, Brielle,' Naal said, and gestured to the vista beyond the invisible field. 'And this is the result.'

Brielle turned from him again, her mood growing dark. Of course she had lied, it was the only way she could see to avert disaster and dissuade the tau from using her as an emissary to demand the crusade's surrender. The vessels crossing the void beyond the energy dome were preparing to evacuate huge numbers of tau civilians from Dal'yth Prime, while a warfleet was mustering further out to retake the planet with overwhelming force. If the tau knew what Brielle did, they would chase the humans all the way back to Terra. The crusade had been launched in haste with no idea of the tau's capabilities, was riven with internecine rivalries and massively overextended following the months-long crossing of the Damocles Gulf into tau space.

'The *result* is that the tau have pulled back from Dal'yth,' Brielle said. 'I've saved thousands of lives.'

'For now,' Naal said. 'But that wasn't why you told them the Imperium has twenty more battleships inbound. You wanted to create chaos and confusion. Why, Brielle?'

The observation blister was plunged in shadow as a huge refugee transport passed the *Dal'yth Il'Fannor O'kray*, a shoal of tenders and launches buzzing around. It was just the first of several hundred such transports the tau had rushed to the Dal'yth system with the intention of evacuating as many civilians as possible. Brielle's warning of how humanity treated aliens was no lie, and the tau had taken it to heart.

'Because this has got to end, Naal,' Brielle sighed. She felt a great weight lifted as she finally said what she had been feeling for weeks.

'Then you have to go before the crusade council as Aura requests, and settle this.'

'That isn't what I meant.'

'Then what, Brielle? What do you-?'

'I want out!' she said, stalking away from Naal towards the invisible shield that held the void at bay and kept her alive. 'I exaggerated the crusade's strengths so the tau would pull back. We both know that the crusade council is split. Gurney and Grand, if he's still alive, want total war, my father wants profit and the others want honour. If my father can turn the council around before the tau can muster a big enough force to repel the crusade, this can all be settled. And I can go home.'

Naal's face showed his utter shock at Brielle's revelation. The Imperial eagle tattoo on his forehead, a relic of past military service, seemed to fold its wings as he frowned at Brielle, then cast his glance to the floor.

'Why did you not tell me earlier?'

'You may share my bed, Naal,' Brielle said as she rounded on the man. 'But we both know where your loyalties lie.'

'What are you saying?'

'You're for the tau. You always have been. I don't know what led you to them, and I know you can't go back. But I can.'

'Brielle,' Naal sighed. 'I was just a Guard captain before I joined the tau, before I heeded the Greater Good. I was just a captain and yet I'm marked for death across an entire segmentum. You're the daughter of nobility, Brielle. There's nowhere you can hide. You have no choice.'

'My father can protect me from the likes of Grand.'

'Your father thinks you're dead.'

'Then he'll be happy to see me again then, won't he?'

'Please, Brielle,' Naal said with an edge of sadness to his voice. 'Look around you. There are no inquisitors here. There is no judgement and no repression.'

'So long as you do *exactly* what they say, Naal, come on...'

'That's the point of the Greater Good, Brielle,' Naal pressed. 'They don't have to tell you. You just do it, for the good of all.'

'And if you don't?'

'You do.'

'And if *I* don't?'

'You will, Brielle. In time...'

'You can't really think this is right, Naal, not deep down.' Brielle reached up and tenderly caressed the eagle tattoo on his temple. 'Does this mean nothing to you?'

Naal took Brielle's wrist in his hand. 'Of course it does. I love the Emperor. I just hate the Imperium. The aquila represents the former, not the latter.'

'What made you this way, Naal?' Brielle whispered, her eyes narrowing as she tried to find something, anything, inside his.

'You wouldn't understand, Brielle.'

'Then why not come back with me. Put it right. Together.'

'Brielle, if I did that, he'd–'

Naal's words were cut off as the circular iris-hatch set into the deck hissed and a column of white light shone upwards as the opening widened. Brielle and Naal stepped apart like guilty lovers, both turning to face the tau envoy, Aura, as he rose upwards on a platform through the hatch.

Aura looked around, casting his sad gaze out into space for a moment before turning it upon the two humans and affording them a shallow bow. 'Lady Brielle,' the envoy addressed her in his usual formal, yet strangely maudlin tone. 'As you can see, the transport fleet gathers to deliver our people from destruction.' Did he count Brielle in that 'our people'? 'And the fleet musters even as we speak.'

Brielle inclined her head, acknowledging Aura's statement without saying anything herself.

'When the fleet arrives, there will be much bloodshed, on both sides. Even now, with our enemy attacking us in such great force, we would avert disaster and bring peace.'

Brielle and Naal shared a furtive glance before the envoy continued.

'You will go before the enemy's leaders and demand their surrender...'

'Their *surrender...*?'

'Yes, Lady Brielle,' Aura continued. 'You must inform the humans that if they do not submit and take their place in the tau empire according to the dictates of the Greater Good, they will be destroyed. Utterly.'

'You will be briefed and prepared for your duty, Lady Brielle.

You will go before their leaders adorned as I, as an envoy of the tau empire. This will be your finest hour, Lady Brielle, and it will be remembered across the entire empire.'

'Of course,' Brielle said, though her mind was in turmoil. She had been so sure the tau would have seen sense when she had so grossly overstated the crusade's strength, yet they wanted not just a ceasefire or even a surrender, but to coerce the crusade's forces to join them...

'Of course,' Brielle repeated. 'For the Greater Good...'

CHAPTER FOUR

Sergeant Sarik's force was pushing forwards now, driving the tau stealth-troopers back towards a low rise as the light of dawn filled the skies. The Space Marines had taken casualties when the tau had attacked the rear of the column, including both Whirlwind missile tanks being taken out of action as stealthed tau infantry used their equivalent of the Imperium's tank-busting melta weapons from close range. Sarik's warriors had rallied, and over the course of a three-hour firefight learned how to detect the presence of the infiltrating tau.

As Sarik advanced at the head of his tactical squad, he saw another such sign. The air would ripple just before the tau opened fire, as if their weapons were bleeding power from whatever generator powered the stealth field. Sometimes, if an observer was looking in their exact direction, a change of light would cause the enemy to become visible for a fraction of a second, and if they were not moving and the light remained unchanged, they might solidify and become plain to see.

Most importantly, the Space Marines were learning how to predict the enemy's movements and where to look for them. The details had already been voxed to the other Space Marine commands, and the stealthers were being driven back all along the front.

'Contact front!' Sarik called out as he opened fire at the half-visible foe. 'Strike them down!' A line of small explosions stitched the ghostly figure and its stealth generator failed with an eruption of blue sparks. The enemy resolved into a black-armoured warrior, its helmet blank-faced and with blocky, segmented armour plates across its chest, shoulders and thighs. Mounted on one arm was a tubular heavy weapon, which it was raising to point directly at Sarik.

The sergeant shouted a warning to his squad and weaved sideways as he advanced. The tau fired and a hail of blue energy bolts scythed the air where the Space Marines had been advancing a fraction of a second earlier. The alien stepped backwards as it fired, tracking its weapon left and right. The ground at Sarik's feet was churning with dozens of impacts as he powered on, and several shots glanced from his shoulder plates and greaves, biting neat-edged scars across the ceramite.

A grunt of pain sounded from behind Sarik as a Space Marine of the Scythes of the Emperor went down, an energy bolt having clipped his cheek and torn off half his face. The warrior went into a roll as he fell, and having barely lost momentum was up again. His enhanced physiology caused his blood to clot the instant it met air, his features a mass of scabby tissue with the inside of his jaw visible through the ruined cheek.

Sarik's warriors returned fire as they ran, the combined boltguns of his own squad and the nearby Scythes of the Emperor hammering into the alien stealther. The enemy lowered his heavy weapon and assumed a wide-legged stance. A second later he leaped straight backwards, having activated a short-distance jump generator on his back. This was the first the Space Marines knew of the capability, and although it took them by surprise, the alien did not get far.

At the height of the alien's powered leap, a missile streaked in over the Space Marines heads, fired from one of the Devastator squads at the column's rear. The missile slammed into the alien with unerring accuracy, its war spirit predicting its target's trajectory and altering its course at the last possible second. Both missile and alien exploded three metres up, showering chunks of ruined armour and flesh across a wide area.

As Sarik approached the crest of the rise he saw another ripple in the air, followed by a burst of blue flame. Three more tau stealthers resolved in the air, their jump burners drawing power from their stealth generators. Sarik opened fire and his squad followed his example, filling the air with fin-stabilised, deuterium-cored bolter rounds. But the aliens were fleeing the Space Marines and with their jump packs engaged were soon bounding down the opposite side of the rise and away from the Space Marines.

'All squads,' Sarik said into the vox-net. 'Let the cowards flee. Consolidate on me.'

The squads of Sarik's spearhead were soon in position near him, the sergeants ensuring each was correctly deployed. There were obvious gaps in the line, where squads had taken casualties. Most of the wounded were able to fight on thanks to their genetically enhanced physiques, but the worst, in particular the Ultramarines caught in the stealthers' ambush, had been evacuated for treatment.

'Rhinos,' Sarik voxed the vehicle commanders further back. 'Maintain position and overwatch. All squads, form up on me for probing advance forward.' Sarik had to remind himself not to use the White Scars' battle-cant, which used context- and culture-specific references that could not be deciphered should a transmission be intercepted. But with warriors from more than just his own Chapter under his command, Sarik was forced to use more standard battle-code.

'Brothers,' Sarik addressed the squads. 'We advance around this rise. Devastators,' he indicated the Ultramarine and Scythes of the Emperor heavy weapons squads, 'overwatch just below the crest. White Scars tactical squads,' he nodded to his own squad and the other two of his Chapter, 'right flank. Remaining squads to the left.'

'Brothers,' he went on, conscious that the enemy stealthers were unlikely to have withdrawn far. 'This could be a trap.' Consulting his data-slate, which displayed a grainy, low-resolution aerial reconnaissance image marked up with numerals and symbols, he went on, 'Limit of exploitation is Hill 3003, to the west. Move out in one minute.'

As the Space Marines checked ammunition levels and swapped out depleted magazines for fresh ones, Sarik consulted his data-slate for an update from crusade command. Almost a hundred reports had been disseminated since the last time he had checked, most of which he felt justified in ignoring as they related to matters outside of his immediate concern. He skimmed reports on the enemy's aerospace strength, noting that the crusade had managed to land a small number of its precious fighter-bomber wings. Understandably, these were being kept in strategic reserve to be used only when desperately needed. The Imperial Navy deployment officers and the Departmento Tacticae intelligence advisors considered launching them into anything but totally empty airspace practically suicidal.

Noting the fighter-bombers' call sign, Sarik read on through the list of reports. Space Marine spearheads to amalgamate – Captain Rumann of the Iron Hands had ratified that order and the other Space Marine units were moving towards the rendezvous point even now, meaning Sarik's would be the last unit there. The Titans were amalgamating too, preparing for a push further down the line. The tau were massing beyond River 992, and the Rakarshans had encountered resistance on its east bank.

At the mention of the Rakarshans, Sarik opened the report, knowing that the unit was led by his friend Lucian Gerrit. The report was vague, having been penned in a hurry, but warned that the tau were not the only xenos on Dal'yth Prime. Lucian's battlegroup had encountered a group of tall, agile and highly aggressive alien savages. Tacticae had cross-linked them to troops encountered on Sy'l'kell at the outset of the crusade, and concluded they were the same group. Sarik's gorge rose as he read the grisly account of the aliens consuming the bodies of the fallen. He promised there and then he would not allow such a fate to befall even one of the battle-brothers under his command.

Then a minute had passed and the squads were ready to move out. Sarik stowed the data-slate and unlimbered his boltgun. He took his place at the head of his squad, which would be the second to move through the low defile around the base of the rise.

Checking that the two Devastator squads were in position to cover the Space Marines' advance, Sarik ordered his warriors forwards.

As Sarik rounded the base of the rise, the land ahead opened up into a dense patchwork of fields and plantations. Hill 3003 rose from amongst the crops and trees, and beyond it, glistening silver in the morning light, was River 992.

Beyond the distant river, made hazy and indistinct by the small amount of vapour still lingering in the morning air, was the city of

Gel'bryn. The city's towers shone bright in the full light of the sun, and each was revealed to be gracefully curved in form, almost as if it had been grown rather than constructed. The tallest of the towers must have been five hundred or more metres in height, and a myriad of walkways connected each to its neighbour. Small points of light glinted all around the city, and Sarik guessed that each was an anti-grav flyer of some sort, or perhaps one of those fiendish, thinking-machine drones.

Sarik tracked back from the city, locating the enemy troop build-up the Departmento Tacticae had reported on the western side of River 992. There it was, a dirty haze marking an area where the tau's grav-tanks were gathering, throwing dust up from the dry ground. From this distance, Sarik could make out very little of the gathering, other than suggestions of multiple armoured vehicles and the scurrying of infantry at the perimeters. No matter; he would soon be facing that force, regardless of its strength.

'Sergeant,' Brother Qaja said, nodding towards the extreme left end of the city. Sarik followed the gesture, tracking along the horizon and locating what must have been a star port, the skies above it clustered with hundreds of aircraft. Some were coming in to land, while others were departing, but all were travelling to or from orbit.

'Reinforcements?' Qaja said.

Sarik studied the scene for several moments as he advanced, noting as best he could from such a great distance the sizes and types of vessels. 'I don't think so,' he said. 'It looks to me like the tau are evacuating their city, brother.'

'Why would they do such a thing?' Qaja said. 'Why would not every citizen muster to defend his home?'

Sarik's eyes narrowed as he considered the situation. Qaja was correct, but only in so far as that was what most enemies would do. Rebels would man their barricades with men, women and children, while most aliens made no such distinction between the members of their population. Almost every foe Sarik had ever fought regarded the defence of hearth and home as sacrosanct, holy ground for which they would fight and die regardless of the chances of winning. Yet, here was a tau army clearly gathering to defend the city, while others were being evacuated rather than mustered to join the defence.

'They are truly alien,' Sarik said. 'We cannot know how they will fight or what drives them to do so. If they are evacuating non-combatants, then perhaps they believe they have already lost and their warriors intend to make a stand for the sake of honour.'

'You think they believe in honour, brother-sergeant?' Qaja said.

Sarik nodded as he walked. 'I will grant them that, brother,' he said. 'Until or unless they prove me wrong.'

Brother Qaja made no reply, though he appeared less then convinced at the notion of affording aliens anything akin to honour. The battle-brother merely hefted his plasma cannon, and fell back into the line of march.

The lead squad, another group of White Scars, had reached a cluster of boulders as the land ran down towards the distant river, and halted. With a gesture, Sarik ordered the entire force to halt, and with another to take up overwatch of the surrounding terrain. Crouching, he opened the vox-net and spoke to the squad's sergeant.

'Brother-Sergeant Cheren, report.'

'It's one of the tau stealthers, brother-sergeant. It appears that he died of wounds sustained before the rise and was left behind.' Sarik and Qaja shared a glance at the idea of leaving the fallen behind, a concept that was anathema to the Space Marines, and especially to the White Scars Chapter, whose people practised highly ritualised funerary rites and afforded the dead great respect.

'Hold position, brother-sergeant,' Sarik said, before leading his squad forwards from the column. He was painfully aware that the body might have been left there as a trap, to distract the Space Marines while a tau force deployed nearby. There was no honour in it, but he had seen such tactics used before, especially amongst the mortal followers of the Ruinous Powers.

His boltgun tracking left and right as he advanced, Sarik crossed the open ground, Brother Qaja at his back all the while, and soon stood over the alien body. He thought it was the stealther he had hit minutes before, but had no way of telling for sure.

'They were either fleeing, or it's a trap,' Sergeant Cheren said. 'Either way, there is no honour in it.'

'Aye, brother-sergeant,' Sarik replied. 'Or perhaps both. These tau have proven tactically flexible. Even if the body was not left here to draw our attention they may take advantage of the distraction. Get your squad moving, we have a...'

Sergeant Cheren's body erupted before Sarik's very eyes. It happened so suddenly Sarik saw it almost in slow motion. An entry wound appeared in the centre of Cheren's chest armour, the ceramite actually rippling and distorting around the impact point. Then the sergeant's power pack shattered outwards as the projectile exited his body. So drastic were the forces exerted on the sergeant's body that it was liquefied inside his armour, reduced to a red gruel which sprayed outwards from the exit point like a burst in a high-pressure conduit. The Space Marine behind Cheren was standing directly in the path of that fountain of gore and his pristine white armour was turned deep red as he was covered head to foot in the sergeant's pulped remains.

'*Kuk...*' the blood-splattered Space Marine cursed, reverting instinctively to his native Chogoran tongue.

'Down!' Sarik bellowed, and the two squads of Space Marines nearby dived for cover amidst the boulders.

The air was ripped apart as two more hyper-velocity projectiles passed overhead in quick succession.

'Devastators!' Sarik said into the vox-net. 'What do you see? Report!'

'Stand by, brother-sergeant,' came back the voice of the Sergeant Lahmas, the sergeant of the Scythes of the Emperor Devastator squad. 'Tracking contact on Hill 3003.'

A deafening crack split the air and a hyper-velocity projectile slammed into the opposite face of the boulder Sarik was sheltering behind. It must have weighed ten tons, yet it visibly trembled and a jagged fracture appeared on the rock face right before Sarik's eyes.

'It's the same ordnance they use on their warships,' Sarik growled. *Come on Lahmas...*

'Sergeant,' Lahmas's voice cut in to Sarik's chain of thought. 'I have eyes on nine enemy heavy infantry. Each has twin shoulder-mounted weapons of unknown type. Range too great to engage.'

Another projectile struck the boulder that Brother Qaja was sheltering behind, razor-sharp spall spraying from the opposite face and catching the battle-brother across one cheek. Qaja gritted his teeth, one eye remaining closed and bloody as he hefted his plasma cannon and shouted something at Sarik.

The sergeant realised only then that the tremendous pressure wave of the impact had partially deafened him, but his hearing came back in a rush.

'...I said,' Brother Qaja repeated, 'Breakout?'

'Hold your fire, brother,' Sarik said, and risked a look around the edge of the boulder. Though he dared only expose his head for a couple of seconds, in that moment he located the crest of Hill 3003. Atop the hill's summit was a line of enemy warriors, clearly wearing some sort of heavy personal armour. The ground battle of Sy'l'kell came to Sarik's mind, at the height of which he had fought a tau commander wearing a battle suit of similar design. Yet these were even larger, and bore weaponry akin to that of a battle tank.

Sarik reached to his belt and un-stowed his battle helm, placing it on his head and re-opening the vox-link to Sergeant Lahmas. 'Seen. Lahmas, I want you to patch your sensorium exlink directly to my system. Keep eyes on, I'm calling this one in.'

The Scythes of the Emperor sergeant signalled his understanding, and a few seconds later Sarik's vision froze, then dissolved into static. A moment later a rune blinked into being, and then the view was replaced by the scene from the other sergeant's point of view.

'Machine communion established, brother-sergeant,' Lahmas said. Are you receiving?'

'Aye, brother,' Sarik replied. 'Stand by and hold still.'

Sarik had to focus his thoughts and concentrate hard to control the other's sensorium system, but after a moment he made the view magnify as much as it was able without the aid of magnoculars. The scene zoomed in on the summit of Hill 3003, where the enemy heavy infantry were clearly visible. Each was half as tall again as a Space Marine, their blocky armour reminding Sarik of one of the mighty Space Marine Dreadnoughts, though it was not quite so bulky. Like the Dreadnought, however, the battle suit was more piloted than worn, for the large torso must have housed the operator, who viewed the battlefield through the armoured sensor block mounted atop the body.

A flash of blue from further down the line of battle suits caught Sarik's attention, and Lahmas tracked across to it, guessing correctly that Sarik would wish to see more clearly. Before the movement was complete another boulder nearby was split in two, the Space Marine behind it only just managing to dive clear, and coming up near Sarik. Then the sound of the discharge rolled across the landscape, giving Sarik some idea of the speed the projectile must have been travelling to exceed its own report. He re-called the sensorium archive, re-playing the last few seconds at ten times slower speed, his eye on the timestamp as the projectile came in. He estimated that the enemy projectiles must have been travelling at between eight and ten times the speed of sound.

No wonder Sergeant Cheren's body had been liquefied inside his armour.

Sarik opened the crusade command channel. 'Sarik, beta-nine, zero-delta,' he said, the call sign and context routing his transmission straight through to the fighter command duty officer.

There was a brief pause, overlaid by machine-chatter as vox-exlink systems authenticated the identity of sender and receiver.

'Fighter command, go ahead, sergeant,' the duty officer replied. The channel was distorted, for the signal was being routed back to the more powerful vox-unit on board one of the nearby Rhinos, and then through hundreds of kilometres of atmosphere and orbital space to the *Blade of Woe*.

'I need a fighter-bomber fire mission, urgent, my authority.'

'Sergeant,' Sarik knew by the man's voice he was about to attempt to haggle. 'We have only...'

'Listen to me,' Sarik interjected. 'I know assets are scarce, but you can't keep them hidden away like your daughters at the victory feast, I need...'

'Repeat last, sergeant...' the duty officer said.

'Never mind,' Sarik said. 'I need a fire mission, right now, and if you can't process it I'll have to speak to General Gauge directly. Do you understand?'

There was a brief pause before the duty officer replied 'Understood, sergeant. Call it in.'

'Better,' Sarik growled. Before he could continue, the enemy battle suits opened fire again, blue pulses rippling up and down their firing line. Viewing the scene from another's point of view was faintly disconcerting, but Sarik focussed on the task at hand.

The channel clicked several times as the transmission was shunted through multiple relay and encryption conduits. The background whine of powerful jets cut in, telling Sarik he was through to a fighter pilot. 'This is Silver Eagle leader, holding pattern east of your position. Go ahead, sergeant.'

'Good to hear you, Silver Eagle leader,' Sarik said. 'I have multiple hard targets atop Hill 3003. Heavy battle suits. I want a rapid-fire pass, full effect, from one-sixty, over.'

'Understood, sergeant,' the squadron leader replied, the background sound changing pitch as his fighter dropped five thousand metres in mere seconds. 'Splash two-zero,' the pilot said, his voice strained by the g-force inflicted on his body by the rapid dive. 'Keep your heads down, and good luck.'

Splash two zero. Twenty seconds to attack.

Sarik disengaged the sensorium link to Sergeant Lahmas, his vision locking for a moment before being replaced by a wall of static. After a few more seconds his armour's war spirit awakened and his vision was returned to his own perspective.

Craning his neck upwards, Sarik searched the eastern skies for the Thunderbolt ground attack squadron. Within seconds a distant roar filled the skies, but the fighters were travelling too low and too fast for Sarik to make them out.

The sound grew in volume, until it was almost upon the Space Marines. Four dark shapes appeared to the east, diving in low and following the undulating terrain, lines of bright shock diamonds trailing behind their engines. The tau heavy infantry turned towards the oncoming fighters, some raising their twin hyper-velocity projectile weapons towards the oncoming threat. But none fired; there would have been no point with the fighters travelling in excess of fifteen hundred kilometres per hour.

In the final seconds, the tau battle suits took a ponderous step backwards, evidently lacking the short-burn jump jets that made the smaller stealthers so agile.

The roar of the fighters' turbofans became a deafening scream, and then the Thunderbolts opened fire. The first shots were from their nose-mounted lascannons, lancing out towards the tau in an incandescent blast.

One battle suit was struck square in the torso, vanishing in a pulsating explosion and leaving just shrapnel scattered across the ground. Another las-bolt struck its target a glancing blow to one of its arm-like appendages, its end terminating in a boxy weapons mount that must have been some sort of short-ranged, anti-personnel multiple missile launcher. The missiles in the weapon's tubes detonated spectacularly, causing the battle suit to stumble sideways as the one next to it was peppered with shrapnel. The last two beams split the air between two of the battle suits, setting the scrub behind them alight.

But the lascannon blasts were just the beginning. As the Thunderbolts screamed onwards they came within the range of their nose-mounted autocannons. The relentless hammering of multiple rounds split the air and the tau were caught in a storm of metal as thick as driving rain. Though many rounds churned into the ground around the battle suits' mechanical feet, so heavy was the torrent of fire that dozens struck their targets. Smoke and dust was thrown upwards, small white flashes of incandescence shining through, each sent up by an autocannon round striking its target and turning for a brief instant into a small, superheated ball of plasma. Sarik's helmet autosenses activated, momentarily darkening his field of vision so that his eyes were not damaged by the searing white lights that flickered up and down the entire crest of Hill 3003.

Before Sarik's vision had entirely cleared, he felt the sharp impact of a metallic object rebounding from his shoulder plate to patter to the dry ground at his feet. It was a brass shell casing, ejected from the first of the Thunderbolts as it screamed overhead, and it was followed by hundreds more raining down on Sarik and the other Space Marines. In a split second, all four Thunderbolts had passed overhead and were already gaining altitude as they banked east in the jade skies.

Sarik readied himself to issue the order to press on and assault the hill, for nothing could have survived that hail of autocannon fire. Sarik studied the distant crest as the smoke and dust was caught on a gust of wind and drifted clear, revealing the destruction the Imperial Navy fighter squadron had unleashed on the tau.

As the scene cleared, it became evident that somehow, at least three of the tau had survived. Sarik had seen even the fell war machines of the followers of Chaos reduced to smoking wreckage by such attacks and could scarcely believe that the tau battle suits, even as heavy as they were, could be so well armoured as to survive. Though each of the surviving battle suits was visibly damaged, the ochre yellow of their armour blackened and dented by numerous impact scars, two of them were regaining their feet and levelling their heavy, shoulder-mounted hyper-velocity weapons on the Space Marines.

'Silver Eagle leader to Sarik,' the squadron leader's voice came over the net. 'Report status, over?'

'Silver Eagle leader,' Sarik called back. 'Multiple effective survivors, over.'

There was a pause, then a crackle on the line before the squadron leader replied, 'Understood, sergeant. Remain in position. Returning to previous heading for full-effect bomb drop.'

The four Thunderbolts continued their wide bank towards the east, dropping low as they came about for a second pass.

A whip-crack report split the air not three metres from Sarik's position as the first of the tau opened fire again. Sarik guessed that whatever fire control systems they used must have been disrupted by the Thunderbolts' attack, for it was the first shot to have missed the boulders behind which the Space Marines waited. And a good thing too, for the huge boulder near Sarik was fractured in several places and would not provide cover for much longer.

Two more shots cracked the air, sounding like a steel cable at full tension suddenly cut. Sarik opened the vox-channel to address his force. 'All squads. The navy are going to flatten that hilltop. The second the bombs are down I want all units moving, tactical dispersion delta delta nine. I want that hill taken. Out.'

'Silver Eagle leader to Sarik,' the squadron commander's voice came over the vox-net again. 'Beginning attack run. Be advised, this is going to make a mess of everything within half a kilometre of that hill. Good lu...'

'Repeat last, Silver Eagle leader?' Sarik said.

'Stand by, sergeant...'

The squadron came in low across the eastern plains, then split into two pairs, one piling on the G's as it sped south, the other executing a tight turn that brought it on an approach vector back towards Hill 3003.

'...not falling for it...' the squadron leader's voice cut into the command channel. 'Half loop, execute!'

The group heading back towards the target rose suddenly into the air, the pilots executing one half of a loop. As one completed its manoeuvre and streaked back east, the other was engulfed by fire as its starboard wing was torn apart by a storm of gunfire.

'Silver Eagle leader is down,' a new voice filled the command channel. 'Eagle four, complete the run, I'll try to draw them off...'

As the squadron leader's Thunderbolt exploded across the sky shedding multiple smoking contrails behind it, his wingman dived towards the ground, the air rippling two kilometres behind. The other two Thunderbolts executed a rolling turn and came back on the attack vector, arrowing towards Hill 3003 at supersonic speed.

'All squads!' Sarik yelled into the vox-net. 'Brace for air strike, then follow me!'

The sound of the approaching jets increased to a deafening roar, doppler-shifting as they screamed overhead so low the backwash sent up plumes of dust from the ground.

'Payload deployed!' one of the pilots called, and Sarik went down on one knee beside the boulder as four 1,000 kilogram bombs dropped from the rapidly receding Thunderbolts, directly towards the crest of Hill 3003.

The hilltop erupted in such a devastating explosion that the entire rise was consumed in a plume of black smoke that blossomed rapidly into the air. An instant later the sound and pressure wave struck Sarik, showering his armour with grit and small stones pushed before it by the blast. Had he not been wearing his helmet the breath would have been torn from his lungs. Just a few hundred metres closer to the hill and his lungs might have been torn from his chest.

Then debris began to rain from the sky, large chunks of rock thrown up in all directions by the massive explosion. Sarik forced himself to his feet, still fighting the blast wave which continued to rage as the air pressure sought to right itself. He opened the vox-channel again, and bellowed, 'With me! If there's anything left on that hill I want it dead!'

Sarik burst out from the cover of the boulder, his squad close at his heels. The ground churned in front of him as debris rained down from the skies. The hilltop was now capped by a plume of black smoke rising ever higher into the air and blossoming outwards as it rose. Sarik pounded the ground, determined that any tau still alive on or near the hill would soon be struck down by his blade. Sarik's heart pounded and his blood rushed in his ears. He tore his helmet off and cast it to the ground without thinking, and unleashed a fearsome Chogoran war cry in the tongue of his people.

As he closed on the foot of the hill, the black cloud rearing high overhead, the ground became jagged and uneven with huge chunks of rock torn up by the explosion. Soon Sarik was climbing up the base of the hill, clambering over the uneven ground and shoving boulders aside as he powered upwards.

The cloud began to clear and the hill in front of Sarik became visible. Pausing in his climb, Sarik craned his neck to look upwards, to locate the foe he would soon be rending limb from limb.

Then it struck him. There were no enemies. They had been disintegrated. The entire crest of the hill had been disintegrated.

'They're gone, brother-sergeant,' Brother Qaja said as he came up beside Sarik, his voice ragged as he regained his breath. Qaja had kept pace with his sergeant as he had closed on the hill, despite the fact that he was bearing a weapon that weighed nearly as much as he did.

'No,' Sarik growled. 'There'll be more nearby. We take the hill.'

Qaja held Sarik's gaze for a moment, before nodding. 'By your command, brother-sergeant,' he said, bowing slightly as he spoke. As Sarik turned back to gaze up the rubble strewn slope, he heard Qaja bellowing commands as he strode off to muster the squads closing on the hill.

Leaving Qaja to organise the battle-brothers, Sarik unlimbered his boltgun and set off up the broken slope. His blood was still up, but he was thinking clearer now, and he scanned the skies for any sign of the surviving Thunderbolts or the stealthed tau fighter that had engaged and destroyed Silver Eagle leader. There was none; the jade skies were clear of all but the plume of smoke towering overhead.

It did not take Sarik long to reach the top of Hill 3003, for so much of its crest had been destroyed that it had lost half its height. As Sarik dragged himself up over the last chunk of debris, he found himself looking down, straight into a huge, smoking crater more resembling a semi-dormant volcano than a hill.

As Qaja led the Space Marines up behind him, Sarik started out around the crater rim, the view beyond it towards the river still obscured by thick smoke and drifting clouds of dust. Sarik pressed on, eager to gain the opposite side of the crater and the commanding view it would afford of the river and the city of Gel'bryn beyond. It took him another five minutes to work his way around the rim, and by the time he had reached the other side Qaja had directed the tactical squads to split into two groups and press around the rim.

Finally, Sarik stood on the opposite edge of the smoking crater, looking down at the opposite slope. Though it was as broken and jagged as the slope he had climbed, it was also wreathed in smoke and dust, and the view of the terrain leading down to the river was all but obscured.

'Your orders, brother-sergeant?' Brother Qaja said as he appeared at Sarik's side. 'Devastators are working their way around the base, they'll be in position to cover an advance towards the river within five. And, brother-sergeant?' he added.

'Yes, Brother Qaja?' Sarik said.

'You may have need of this,' Qaja said as he proffered Sarik the helmet he had discarded as he had charged across the open ground in the wake of the air strike. There was a note of reproach in the other's voice, and not without justification. Sarik nodded his thanks, knowing that he had committed a failing that a neophyte would have been punished severely for. Brother Qaja was an old friend, and only fate had placed Sarik as his senior; it could so easily have been the other way around. Qaja's unvoiced reproach was punishment enough for Sarik, but he would mount a vigil of prayer after the battle was over, and ask the primarch, honoured be his name, for guidance.

'Thank you, brother,' Sarik said as he took the helmet and clipped it to his belt. 'I'm not sure I would have...' Sarik stopped, turning his head sharply towards the smoke-wreathed downward slope. Qaja followed his glance, instantly alert.

'You hear it?' Sarik whispered low.

Brother Qaja nodded slowly, his eyes scanning the drifting smoke below. 'Sounds like...'

A dark shape appeared in the smoke. Qaja hefted his plasma

cannon and engaged its charge cycle. The rapidly rising whine of the plasma coils energising was shockingly loud.

'Get the squads forward, quickly!' Sarik said, now uncaring whether his voice was heard or not. He limbered his boltgun and drew his chainsword, thumbing it to life so that the monomolecular-edged teeth growled with sudden violence.

The shape in the smoke solidified as Brother Qaja beckoned the tactical squads forwards, and two more appeared at its side. It was tall, at least half as tall again as a Space Marine, and broad across the blocky, armoured shoulders. The first parts of the shape to become fully visible were the tips of the two long, rectangular hyper-velocity cannons mounted on its shoulders.

As the battle suit trod ponderously out of the drifting smoke, the cannons levelled out to point directly towards the crater rim where the White Scars, Scythes of the Emperor and Ultramarines tactical squads were taking position.

'No time,' Sarik growled. 'Cut them down!'

Brandishing his chainsword high, Sarik leaped from the crater rim onto the rubble-strewn slope below. The cannons tracked him, but he was moving too fast for the battle suit's targeting systems to get a solid lock.

As Sarik powered down the slope, small boulders cascading all around him, the sound of armoured boots striking the ground behind filled the air. Another three battle suits emerged from the smoke, and a detached part of Sarik's mind understood that the force that had held the crest of Hill 3003 must have been just a vanguard of a far larger group.

As Sarik closed to within thirty metres of the first of the battle suits, the air was turned livid violet as Brother Qaja unleashed a blast from his plasma cannon. The roiling ball of pure energy spat downwards, its backwash burning a channel clear through the smoke before it engulfed its target.

The solid matter of the battle suit was consumed in an instant, its very stuff feeding the plasma ball. The energies expanded briefly, the heat so intense that the armour from the nearest battle suit was reduced to wax-like liquid. The entire roiling mass exploded outwards, burning the dusty ground and turning loose rocks into a liquid lava rain.

The heat and blast wave of the explosion struck Sarik as he closed on his target, and it felt for an instant as if he was running into the open hatch of a starship's plasma furnace. Then the energies disappeared and Sarik was upon his foe.

The battle suit Sarik had fought on Sy'l'kell came to mind again. That opponent had been similar in form, but equipped with lighter weaponry and short-burn jump jets similar to those used by the lighter stealthers. The enemy Sarik now faced was heavy and ponderous, made slow by the weight of additional armour and its heavy weaponry.

Knowing that the battle suit could not make use of its weapons at such short range, Sarik circled around it, chainsword raised in a two-handed guard position, looking for a weak spot in the tau's formidable armour.

The battle suit began to back away, its heavy tread crushing boulders to dust. Space Marines appeared all around Sarik, each following his example as they closed in on an opponent.

'Not so deadly now, are you...' Sarik growled as he pressed forwards. Locating what he judged to be a weak joint between leg and torso, Sarik feinted left, then swept his chainsword in low as the battle suit sought to avoid him.

The teeth of Sarik's blade howled as they struck the impossibly hard metal, grinding across the ball joint. The tau raised an arm terminating in a large multiple missile pod in an attempt to fend off another strike, and as it did so took a heavy step backwards. The damaged ball joint locked and the battle suit staggered as it fought for balance. Sarik pressed his advantage.

Sarik's blade lashed out and tore a ragged scar across the battle suit's torso, but the armour there was too heavy and solid to penetrate. Sarik bared his teeth in a feral snarl and brought the blade in a horizontal sweep that smashed the lens in the centre of the sensor block mounted atop the torso. Evidently blinded, the pilot of the battle suit tried to back away again, and toppled backwards as the ball joint failed entirely.

As the battle suit slammed into the ground, Sarik leaped forwards, his feet pinning his opponent's arms. He reversed his grip on his chainsword and raised it high.

The battlefield resounded with war cries and angry shouts, and the screaming of chainswords and the reports of bolt pistols fired at point-blank range. The Space Marines were laying into the battle suits, which were desperately outmatched and seeking to break away. But their enemies' armour was holding firm and the fight was far from won.

Sarik plunged his chainsword directly down into the centre of the battle suit's torso. The teeth ground against the hard armour, shrieking like some spirit from Chogoran legend. The blade slipped, gouging a wound across the face of the armour, and lodged in a recess between the plates. Redoubling his efforts, Sarik took advantage of the purchase he had found and put his whole weight into forcing the howling blade downwards. Smoke poured from the wound, the chainblade's teeth began to glow red, but the blade finally began to sink into the battle suit's torso.

Then the blade was through the outer armour, and it suddenly sank halfway up its length. Sarik growled and hacked the blade downwards, tearing off an entire panel of armour. He withdrew the blackened, smoking blade and cast it aside.

Consumed by battle rage, Sarik took a two-handed grip on the red hot edge of the wound he had torn, and forced it wide with his armoured gauntlets. A part of him was astonished at the armour's resilience, for rarely had he seen such strength on anything less than an armoured vehicle. Then the armoured plate gave and Sarik stumbled backwards as it came free in his hands.

Breathing heavily, Sarik looked down on the ruined battle suit. With the entire front torso armour torn away the pilot was visible within. The tau was compressed into an impossibly small, padded cockpit in an almost foetal position facing forwards. He wore a jump suit that resembled a glossy second skin, and numerous sensory pickups snaked from points on his body to terminals inside the suit. The pilot's face, spattered with his own purple blood, stared back at Sarik with unmistakable hatred.

'You fought with honour, foeman,' Sarik said, stepping forwards again to deliver the killing blow.

'*Ko'vash*,' the pilot coughed as he raised his fist out of the hole in the suit's torso. The pilot was holding some form of control device, and its thumb was raised above a flashing red stud. '*Tau'va. Y'he...*'

Even as Sarik brought his chainsword down, the dying pilot

depressed his thumb on the control stud. Sarik's blade ground through the pilot's body as if it were not even there, a geyser of purple blood gushing upwards to stain Sarik's arms up to his shoulder plates.

'Brother-sergeant!' Qaja's voice penetrated Sarik's battle fury. 'The enemy are breaking off!'

But Sarik did not reply, for his gaze was fixed firmly on the blinking red control stud held in the pilot's death grip. The blinks were getting faster, and a sharp, electronic tone was sounding from within the gore-spattered cockpit.

Sarik's berserker rage lifted entirely and realisation dawned. 'Fall back!' he bellowed. 'Everyone back up the slope, now!'

Sarik's tone brooked no argument, and even if any of the Space Marines had sought to pursue the remaining battle suits as they backed into the smoke bank, their conditioning was such that it was all but impossible for them to ignore an order from a superior. Sarik turned, retrieving his chainsword, and pounded back up the slope, ensuring that his battle-brothers were all heading for cover.

As he climbed the last few metres Sarik overtook Brother Qaja, who despite his nigh legendary strength and the load-bearing mechanisms of his armour was impeded by the bulk of his massive plasma cannon. As he came alongside his battle-brother, Sarik hefted the weapon's snub barrel to share its weight and the two White Scars climbed the last few metres together and threw themselves over the crater rim.

For a moment, Sarik and Qaja were face to face. Sarik's battle-brother opened his mouth to ask the inevitable question, before it was answered for him.

The sky beyond the crater rim was consumed by a blinding white light and a staggering blast wave slammed into the crater rim behind which the Space Marines sheltered. The rim edge disintegrated, showering Sarik and Qaja with hot stone. The air burned and Sarik's multi-lung clamped its secondary trachea tightly shut so that he did not breathe in the searing atmosphere. Without his helmet's auto-senses to protect his eyes, Sarik was forced to screw them shut lest he be blinded. Even with his eyes tightly closed Sarik's vision boiled red as the light burned through.

Then all fell silent, and Sarik opened his eyes. Brother Qaja was on all fours, spitting blood from his mouth from a wound caused by flying debris. Further away, other battle-brothers were struggling to their feet, stunned by the sheer devastation of the explosion. The sergeants were restoring order, ordering battle-brothers to the crater rim and to cover all approaches an enemy might take.

As Sarik rose and looked down at the slope, he knew it was most unlikely that any more enemies would come that way. The entire slope had been scoured clean of everything but scorched black bedrock. Whatever device-of-last-resort the battle suit pilot had activated, it had afforded his companions the time they needed to break away from the Space Marines. With the smoke of the air strike blown clear by the explosion, the remaining battle suits were visible, half a kilometre away as they retreated back towards the river and the tau army that was even now mustering on the opposite shore. As he watched, the heavy battle suits reached another rise, where more of their kind had assumed a firing line with a commanding view of the surrounding landscape.

As Sarik surveyed his battle-scarred force, it occurred to him that the Damocles Gulf Crusade might have far more vicious a struggle ahead of it than even its most bullish of leaders had anticipated.

'Qaja!' Sarik called. 'Gather the squads. We're far from done here yet...'

Twenty kilometres to the north-west of Hill 3003, Lucian Gerrit was scanning his data-slate and considering his next move. As the crusade ground onwards towards Gel'bryn, the force mustering on the other side of River 992 launched a series of daring hit and run attacks. So accomplished were the tau mechanised forces at this style of warfare that the more ponderous units of the Imperial Guard were barely able to react. As the battles progressed, cadres of tau anti-grav tanks swept in towards the crusade's flank, disgorging up to a hundred warriors who unleashed a devastating volley of short-ranged fire before being carried away again by their transports. General Gauge fed more and more forces towards the river in an effort to overwhelm the tau defenders. Even as he did so ever-greater numbers of tau converged on Gel'bryn from the west, reinforcements sent from the other cities to stall the invasion.

The main advance split into three spearheads. The engines of the Deathbringers Legion gathered together into a formidable battle group that sought to push its way into the city's outer limits by brute strength alone. The Titans' initial assaults saw them destroy dozens of enemy armoured vehicles and hundreds of infantry. The fast-moving and agile Warhound Scout Titans made rapid gains in the first few hours of their advance. It was only several hours later, when the Warhounds had pressed so far forwards they had outrun the anti-air cover provided by the Hydra flak-tank companies of the Imperial Guard, that they were engaged by heavy tau flyers. To the great surprise of the advisors of the Departmento Tacticae, these flyers proved to be the very same machines the tau utilised as gunships in space, revealing the hitherto unknown capability of operating in both deep space and planetary atmosphere.

The Space Marines had largely amalgamated into a single force, though Lucian noted with concern that his friend Sarik had encountered heavily armed and armoured battle suit infantry at Hill 3003 and his force was still engaged in that area. The remainder of the Space Marines, consisting of the Iron Hands, Scythes of the Emperor and Ultramarines, along with individual squads from a handful of other Chapters, had formed a single, large contingent under the direct control of Captain Rumann of the Iron Hands. That force had pressed towards the river, but had encountered large numbers of the jump-capable battle suit infantry. The Departmento Tacticae reported that the tau term for these particular battle suits, which the crusade had encountered a single example of, was '*hereks'vre*', which in their tongue meant the 'mantle of the hero.' Already, the Tacticae had bastardised that term to codify the battle suits as 'XV' class rigs, with various sub-classes already identified.

Even Lucian was surprised that the Space Marines were having such a hard time of it, for the XV-class battle suits appeared their equal in almost every respect. They were heavily armed, each carrying anything up to three weapons systems, some of which were capable of scything down a Space Marine in a single shot. Their battle suits provided at least as much protection as the Space Marines' power armour, and appeared to incorporate a number of additional systems such as advanced sensor and communication arrays. The XV-class battle suits were highly manoeuvrable too, for every one of them was equipped with a short-burn jump pack that made them as agile as an Assault Marine.

The numerous skirmishes the Space Marines had fought against the various types of battle suit infantry all pointed to a single weakness, details of which the Tacticae had disseminated to all commands. The tau were proving lacking in the field of all-in, hand-to-hand fighting. Many theories as to why this might be had been posited, from a biological deficiency that meant the tau could not focus on close-up and fast-moving objects as quickly as a human, to a fundamental moral weakness born of their alien philosophies. Lucian had his own ideas, which he knew would not find many sympathetic ears amongst the Tacticae and might even bring about the wrath of Inquisitor Grand were he to voice them too openly. Lucian was beginning to suspect that the tau regarded close combat as a brutal and dishonourable slaughter. They excelled in manoeuvre warfare, using speed and agility to dictate the terms of battle. When it was necessary to commit to a close-quarters assault, Lucian guessed the tau utilised the savage aliens his force had encountered the previous night. He wondered if they were the only alien allies the tau used, recalling how ready they appeared to be to subvert the human worlds on the other side of the Damocles Gulf.

Lucian's own battle group had performed well, pressing towards the outlying suburbs of the city on the eastern side of River 992. The Rakarshans had met and defeated more groups of the savage aliens, and for a while the two groups had fought on more or less equal terms. Both were adept at taking full advantage of cover, and a running battle had developed amongst the outlying settlements. The aliens had launched repeated ambushes, leaping from the tops of low buildings to engage the Rakarshans in brutal close combat. Having witnessed the aliens' despicable trait of devouring the corpses of the fallen, the Rakarshans' morale had initially suffered, for the superstitious riflemen believed their foe to be the mythical daemons of their world's dark legends. But Lucian had led them throughout the night, spearheading assault after assault and demonstrating that whatever else the aliens were, they were made of flesh and blood and could therefore bleed and die. The Rakarshans had learned that lesson well, and by morning the outlying suburbs were in their hands.

In the wake of Battlegroup Arcadius's assault came a huge force of Imperial Guard armoured and infantry units. As these gathered, the tau increased their hit and run attacks, and a front line had stabilised across the northern shore of the river where it looped around the flank of the city. The Imperial Guard had been forced to dig in, and it was only the aggressive and determined patrolling of the Space Marines into the no-man's-land between the two foes that kept the alien forces largely at bay.

Reaching the last of the latest batch of Tacticae updates, Lucian suppressed a curse. Concerned that the ground forces had reached an apparent impasse, Cardinal Gurney was shuttling down to the surface to imbue the warriors with his own particular brand of motivation. The cardinal's lander was due at the front within the hour. Leaving the battle group in Major Subad's command, Lucian left his warriors to head off whatever damage Gurney was no doubt intent upon inflicting on his own agenda, and that of his faction.

Lucian took his place in the line of regimental commanders as the cardinal's lander swooped in on screaming landing jets and settled on the dry ground, throwing up a plume of dust as its landing struts flexed and touched down. Behind the commanders were gathered several thousand Imperial Guardsmen and hundreds of tanks, all lined up in parade ground formation to receive this most august of visitors. The vessel was one of the ubiquitous 'Aquila' landers, the name taken from the highly stylised swept wing configuration that gave it the appearance of an eagle. Lucian could not help but give a snort of derision, for the vessel was far from standard in appearance. It was painted gold, as if it had been chased in priceless leaf, and every flat surface was covered in line after line of spidery devotional script. The coffers of the Ecclesiarchy were deep indeed.

Ground crews rushed forwards to service the lander, and Lucian and his companions waited for the vessel's passenger pod to lower and its hatch to open. Lucian's eyes narrowed as the minutes dragged on, and he caught the furtive glances of those on either side. The minutes passed slowly, and Lucian's annoyance rose. What by the warp was Gurney playing at; did he really think the assembled warriors had nothing better to do than wait on his convenience?

Then the air was filled by the sound of chanting blaring out of a vox-horn mounted under the shuttle's blunt nose. The sound was amplified so loud that the horn was distorting, resulting in little more than a discordant racket and certainly not the heavenly chorus Gurney no doubt imagined it to be.

Then the passenger pod at the shuttle's rear engaged, accompanied by the sound of whining servos. The pod thudded to the ground, and a moment later the hatch lowered.

First to step out of the hatch was a robed and stooped attendant, an ornate censer held before him. A bluish cloud of sweet-smelling incense billowed from the orb, and the bearer voiced a loud imprecation, the gist of which was that the cardinal would not have to breathe the same air as the alien tau.

As the censer bearer marched forwards, the cloying cloud blossoming in his wake, three more attendants made their way down the hatch. Each was carrying a large book, the pages held open so that all about might gaze upon the wisdom of the saints and martyrs that had composed them.

Finally, Cardinal Esau Gurney appeared at the hatch and made his way down the walkway. The cardinal was regaled in the outrageous finery of his office, his robes the colour of ancient parchment lined with impossibly intricate, hand-stitched tracery. At his belt and around his neck Gurney wore dozens of holy relics, ranging from the smallest finger bones of saints to shining gold rings and other revered icons. He wore a cloak of deepest crimson silk, which trailed five metres and more behind him as he descended the ramp, and upon his head he wore a mitre bearing the sunburst skull of the Ecclesiarchy.

Gurney paused before stepping forth onto the dusty ground, and spat upon the earth. It was a clear message to all who saw it that the cardinal considered the entire planet cursed by the presence of the xenos tau. Then, he stepped from the walkway and made his way with his procession towards the gathered warriors.

Gurney halted in front of the gathered warriors, and stood there arrayed in his Ecclesiarchal finery, his dark gaze taking in the assembled ranks. Here was a side of the cardinal's personality that Lucian had not yet witnessed. He knew that Gurney was a firebrand, and it was by his sermons that much of the military forces of the crusade had been gathered in the first place. Many months previously, Gurney had preached first on the world of Brimlock and then across an entire sector, bullying, inspiring and cajoling the Imperium's leaders to contribute forces to the endeavour that became the Damocles Gulf Crusade. Many of those gathered here today would have heard those fiery sermons, and no doubt hold the cardinal in high esteem, regardless of what Lucian thought of the man.

'Warriors of the Imperium!' Gurney shouted, his voice so loud that even those warriors in the rear ranks would have no trouble hearing him. 'I salute you! Much blood has been spilled these last days, and many fell crimes committed by the foul xenos, but you are sons and daughters of the Emperor, and no vile xenos can possibly stand before you!'

The assembled Imperial Guardsmen were visibly moved by Gurney's opening words. Previously weary eyes came alight with faith, and stooped shoulders straightened as pride returned to warriors who had known little more than frustration at the tau's constant hit and run attacks and devastating ambushes.

'Today, you are blooded and weary, for the xenos foe is possessed of many forbidden technologies,' the cardinal continued. 'It uses tricks and treachery, and is devoid of honour and faith!'

The cardinal's eyes burned with the light of righteous zeal as he pressed on. 'But you are men of blood and faith! You bear the sanctified weapons of the Emperor, and all you need to conquer our foes is courage and cold steel, duty and honour!'

'Duty and honour!' the assembled Guardsmen repeated. 'Duty and honour!'

'Death or glory!' The cardinal bellowed.

'Death or glory!' the warriors repeated. 'Death or glory!'

Lucian stalked away from the impromptu rally, his mood darkening. He was forced to concede that Cardinal Gurney's sermon, which continued behind him, was certainly having a positive effect on the crusade's morale. He had discovered that Gurney would be touring the entire front, with the exception of the Space Marine positions, and repeating his words until every Imperial Guardsman in the crusade had heard them.

Lucian had no doubt that Gurney's presence on the surface would serve to rally the army and get the warriors inspired again. But Lucian's concerns were of a far more strategic nature. What happened afterwards, when Gurney returned to the crusade council with a string of victorious battles under his belt? That was what Lucian had sought to do, and it appeared to him now that Gurney was seeking to go one up on him, not by leading a force to victory, but by inspiring the entire army to slaughter the tau wholesale.

If that were allowed to happen, then Gurney and his ally Inquisitor Grand might take control of the crusade council, and nothing anyone could do would stop them doing things their way. The tau would be wiped from the galaxy, their empire cast down in flames. As a rogue trader, Lucian considered that a crime of unimaginable proportions, for it deprived the Imperium of so many potential resources. If the tau could be forced to a weak negotiating position, the Imperium could benefit from the natural resources their region harboured. At the very least, Lucian's clan could make a fortune in trade, but only if there were any tau left to force to the negotiating table and to actually deal with.

As he approached the lines of Battlegroup Arcadius, Lucian located his signalman and gestured him over.

'Patch me through to Korvane Gerrit Arcadius,' he ordered. '*Blade of Woe*.'

The signalman saluted smartly and set to work on his vox-set. After a minute, he had established the uplink and handed the headset to Lucian.

'Father?' his son's voice came through the static-laced channel. 'Father, are you well?'

'Well enough, son,' Lucian said. 'But Gurney's making a power play. What's the situation with the council?'

There was a pause as Korvane gathered his thoughts, during which Lucian could hear renewed cheering from the assembled Imperial Guard companies. Then Korvane's response came through. 'It's been quite anarchic here, father, but I've made inroads towards filling the vacant council seats.'

'Go on,' Lucian said impatiently. Even in the midst of a major planetary invasion, he could not entirely relinquish his role of patriarch of a rogue trader dynasty.

'Tacticae-Primaris Kilindini,' Korvane said. 'How well do you know him?'

'Not well,' Lucian said as he recalled the man his son was referring to. 'He's the head of one of the Departmento Tacticae divisions?'

'That's our man,' Korvane replied, warming to his subject. 'He's the overseer of codes and ciphers, but I've looked into his service record and I think he might be agreeable to our faction's agenda.'

'How so?' Lucian replied. 'Isn't he more concerned with breaking alien comms?'

'Yes, father,' Korvane said. 'But I've uncovered details of his serving alongside an Adeptus Terra diplomatic mission. The mission was to an eldar craftworld.'

'Interesting,' Lucian said, his mind racing ahead of him, aware that such contact was rare, but not unheard of. 'I take it this particular mission was especially out of the ordinary?'

'That it was, father.' Lucian could hear the smile on his son's lip's as he spoke. 'In that it did not end in mass bloodshed or planetary devastation.'

'Then you think Primaris Kilindini would be willing to back our intent. He'd be willing to enter talks?'

'He is willing, father,' Korvane replied. 'I've spoken to him already.'

'You've already...' Lucian bit back a stern reproach. He had after all left his son to deal with things. 'You've got his agreement? He'll join us?'

'He will, father. And both Gauge and Jellaqua will back him too. You'll have to speak to Sarik and Rumann though.'

'Agreed,' Lucian replied. 'And son?

'Well done.'

CHAPTER FIVE

Brielle gripped the railing as she looked down from the high gallery at the operations centre below. The whole chamber was shaped like the inside of a huge sphere, with row upon row of galleries working downwards towards the projector of a massive holograph in the very centre. Hundreds of tau officers manned stations all around the galleries, with each of the four castes of the tau race represented. Fire caste warriors coordinated ground operations, while air caste representatives controlled impossibly complex fleet manoeuvres like it was second nature. Earth caste leaders coordinated the logistics chain, while the water caste facilitated communications and the smooth operation of the entire endeavour. The tau war fleet was on the move again, a massive force heading in-system towards Dal'yth Prime.

'There's no way they'll do anything but accept your terms when they see the size of this fleet,' Naal said. Brielle's response was to grip the white rail all the tighter, lest she make some remark she would later come to regret.

'The evacuation is ninety-eight per cent complete,' Naal continued, oblivious to Brielle's feelings on the matter. 'Ground forces are massing at Gel'bryn. The crusade has stalled before it's even got going.'

'Will you just...' Brielle started, but Naal interrupted her.

'Main viewer, Brielle,' Naal gestured towards the operations centre below.

As Brielle followed Naal's gesture, the holograph came to life. A huge, semi-transparent globe grew from a single blue point of light in the dead centre of the spherical chamber. It expanded to become a representation of local space the size of the entire chamber, so that even from the high gallery it filled Brielle's field of vision. A tau icon showed the location of Dal'yth Prime, and a cluster of smaller symbols indicated the position of the crusade's main ships of the line. A string of smaller icons showed the Imperium's supply vessels as they plied to and fro from the edge of the system, and, presumably, towards the Damocles Gulf.

Then the globe expanded still further, its outer surface almost within arm's reach, and Brielle was struck by how flawlessly the projection device operated compared to its equivalents in humanity's service. Her father's flagship, the *Oceanid*, had such a device on its bridge, but much smaller and far less reliable. The secret of the manufacture of hololiths, as the Imperium called them, was a closely guarded secret known only to a handful of Adeptus Mechanicus forge worlds, and Lucian's had been gifted to an ancestor of the Arcadius as reward for services rendered during the liberation of such a world from an ork invasion.

The globe stabilised, the individual icons representing the Imperium's warships amalgamating into a single, distant rune. At the edge of the blue globe there appeared a series of tau symbols that Brielle recognised as indicating alien naval battle groups. Naal was right. The fleet that Brielle was travelling on massively outnumbered the Imperium's force. Even if the crusade could summon reinforcements from across the Damocles Gulf, there was no way any would arrive in time to save it.

But, according to Aura's plan, the crusade would not need saving. It would need reasoning with, negotiating with. The tau still believed, despite all the evidence to the contrary, that the Imperium could be convinced to join the tau empire and sign up to the Greater Good.

The tau were nothing if not optimistic, Brielle thought, a state of mind rarely seen in the Imperium.

'Mistress Brielle,' the voice of the tau water caste envoy Aura sounded from behind her. She forced herself to appear unconcerned, despite the fact that she had not heard him coming. She was normally very good at detecting people creeping up on her...

'Aura,' Brielle replied, bowing as the envoy came to stand beside her at the railing. 'I trust all is well?'

Aura nodded back, his features set in the now familiar sadness they always showed. If it were not for the fact that the alien's voice sounded equally as melancholic Brielle might have concluded that he had some sort of condition, or had perhaps been dropped on his head when he had been hatched.

'All is very well, Mistress Brielle,' Aura replied. 'We are closing to within tactical communications range and a link with the troops on Dal'yth Prime is now possible. Such a link has been established, and is about to be displayed in the unit below.'

Brielle was instantly suspicious. Was Aura planning on showing her the tau gloriously defeating human troops? If so, why?

Aura's black, almond-shaped eyes held hers for a moment, and then he turned to the scene below. The representation of local space faded away, a mass of tau symbols scrolling through the air, before the projection flickered and was replaced by a monochromatic image that could only have been captured from a lens mounted on a warrior's armour.

'What am I seeing?' Brielle said, as much to herself as to the tau envoy.

'This is a real-time uplink from one of our glorious warriors, who even now is deploying against the invaders. His name is Cali'cha, which you might translate as "quick purpose", though the term has no exact analogue in your tongue. He is the leader of a crisis team, and he is closing on a group of the warriors you call Space Marines.'

'He'll be slaughtered,' Brielle muttered, causing Naal to cast a warning glance her way.

'Have no fear, Mistress Brielle,' Aura replied having overheard, but misconstrued her remark. 'Cali'cha is a warrior of great experience and skill. He has served the Greater Good with peerless dedication and knows well the ways of human warriors.'

'Has he ever fought Space Marines?' Brielle said.

'His battle suit is well equipped to counter their armour, Mistress Brielle, of that you may be certain.'

'Space Marines are more than armour...' Brielle started, but Aura had turned his attentions to the holo projection.

It was night, and the tau were moving out from the outskirts of Gel'bryn city, moving in graceful, bounding leaps powered by the thrusters mounted on the suits' backs. Cali'cha set down at the western shore of a river, and his two companions appeared in his field of view. Each wore one of these 'crisis' battle suits, boxy missile launchers mounted at their backs and stubby energy weapons on their arms. The team exchanged what Brielle took to be ritualised, pre-battle words, each touching the tips of their weapons to a representation of a ceremonial blade painted onto their armoured torsos. In the background, the night sky flickered with distant explosions and tracer fire rose with seeming laziness high into the air.

'The Imperium have moved their anti-air assets forwards, Mistress Brielle,' Aura said, having seen her following the tracers as they arced high overhead. She merely nodded, and Aura turned back to the projection.

Their ritual complete, the three warriors moved out, gathering speed as they approached the river. At the very shore, they leaped high into the air, soaring through the night sky with a grace Brielle had only seen amongst the alien eldar. As they reached the height of their bound, the land ahead was revealed. Distant artillery boomed and flashed, and insect-like gunships swept in low over the shadowed terrain. A huge flash lit the entire horizon, and for a second, Brielle saw the towering silhouette of what could only have been a war Titan of the Adeptus Titanicus.

'They have commenced a bombardment of the city's outer limits, Mistress Brielle,' Aura said. That was not good, Brielle thought, knowing that her father would have objected to such a course of action had he the power to affect it. Clearly, the more hawkish elements of the crusade council were gaining the ascendancy.

The crisis team set down on the opposite edge of the river, splashing down in the shallows before making its way past a cluster of dome-shaped buildings at its edge. Evidence of war was all around, from the scorched surfaces of the nearby structures to the wounded tau warriors being evacuated by teams of earth caste medics. It struck Brielle how well the tau treated their combat wounded, each individual casualty being tended by an entire team of medical staff as they were rushed away on anti-grav stretchers towards waiting medical vehicles. In the Imperium, especially in the Imperial

Guard, the wounded were often treated at best as an inconvenience and at worst as malingerers. They would be treated, most certainly, but not through compassion or sympathy, but more to get them back in the fight as soon as possible so that their duty to the Emperor might be done.

The crisis team passed quickly through what must have been a forward assembly area, and came to rest in the lee of a dense fruit tree formation. A group of gangly aliens rushed by, squawking and whistling as they disappeared into the trees and were gone. The view panned left and then right, and Brielle saw that the team had joined a larger force, consisting of at least five more groups of battle suit warriors.

'Flawless,' Aura said to himself. 'Mission commences in four...'

Now every tau in the chamber focussed their attentions on the huge projection, an expectant silence settling across the scene. The crisis teams turned towards the east, the sound of a heavy weapon pounding away nearby filling the chamber. Then they were leaping forwards and the fruit trees were rushing past below, the shadowy forms of the rangy aliens weaving through the plantation.

Tracer rounds scythed upwards towards the battle suits as they powered through the air, at first appearing to move as if in slow motion, but speeding up as they closed. Brielle knew that only one in four or five of the heavy bolter rounds would be filled with the chemicals that made them burn bright red, and that the air must have been filled with a storm of shots far greater than the eye could see.

As the crisis team came in to land, the source of the firing came into view. In the ruins of an outlying agricultural building the heavy bolter sprayed death in a wide arc. The stream of tracers followed the tau as they bounded forwards, several rounds clipping the battle suits. The command centre resounded to the harsh metallic thuds and clangs, but the tau pressed on, unharmed.

The next sound was that of Cali'cha issuing last-second orders to his teammates. Brielle could not understand his words, although their meaning was universal.

The view from the battle suit as it closed towards the enemy position jolted and swung crazily as the tau evaded incoming fire. Then the crisis team was in range, and a targeting reticule appeared in the centre of the projection, hovering just above and behind the spluttering muzzle flare of the heavy bolter.

A missile streaked out from behind the crisis team leader's field of vision, and rose rapidly into the air. Within a second it was streaking downwards, its predicted trajectory etched in the glowing line through the air of the command centre. Then it struck, and the gun position disappeared in a blinding flash. Seconds later the heavy bolter's ammunition started to cook off, filling the ruins of the building with whip-crack flashes.

The crisis team pressed onwards, swooping in amongst the ruins as the last of the heavy bolter's rounds crackled and fizzed across the ground. The view point tipped downwards as Cali'cha looked down at the dead gunner, evidently keen to afford the command staff a view.

The breath caught in Brielle's throat as the gunner's ruined body resolved in the air in front of her. He wore power armour, painted white with red detailing in what could only have been the livery of the White Scars Chapter. His face was almost entirely gone, just blood-smeared bone and hair visible as dead eyes stared upwards at the Space Marine's executioner.

'You see, Mistress Brielle?' Aura said sadly. 'The Space Marines are far from undefeatable...'

The envoy's words were cut off as the air was filled with the unmistakable sound of massed boltguns being fired from nearby. Rounds clattered loudly from Cali'cha's battle suit and sparks danced across the field of vision. The view point swung across to the left towards a second ruin, where a line of white-armoured figures was advancing on the tau, weapons blazing.

The battle suit pilot issued a calm order, and the team leaped backwards, the energy weapons mounted on their rigs' arms spitting incandescent beams of blinding blue fire towards the enemy. One went down, and several others appeared to have been wounded, but still the line came on, the night air filled with rapid-fire death.

Then the command centre was filled with a savage war cry, several dozen of the tau manning the control stations visibly flinching before the terrifying sound. Cali'cha panned further left, in time to see a chainsword-wielding, white-armoured figure emerging from the darkness. The warrior's screaming blade lashed outwards and severed the arm from the battle suit of one of Cali'cha's team mates, before leaping forwards to drive the weapon straight into the square sensor block atop the armoured torso.

The channel howled with the sound of the chainsword's teeth grinding through the battle suit's systems, and an instant later the death scream of the pilot joined it. Then the channel went abruptly silent. Brielle could not tell whether the pickups had been destroyed or the tau below had severed the connection in order to spare the viewers from the terrible sound.

'Savages...' Aura said, glancing sideways towards Brielle. 'So callous, and brutal.'

Brielle made no reply, her eyes fixed on the projection. The crisis team had been caught in an anarchic melee, and were desperately seeking to back away from their enemy. The field of view swung back to the right, showing the first line of white-armoured Space Marines charging in to join the fray. A second member of Cali'cha's crisis team was pulled down as he attempted to engage his suit's thrusters, one Space Marine gripping a mechanical leg while another used a bolt pistol to hammer shot after shot into the jet's innards.

The battle suit's propulsion system erupted in seething energies as a bolt-round bored through to its generator. The Space Marine pulling the suit downwards towards the ground was thrown clear by the explosion, though his armour was visibly damaged by the energies, his left shoulder plate torn off as he came upright again. The second Space Marine backed away, but continued to pump rounds into the writhing battle suit until finally its torso split wide open under the relentless barrage and the pilot inside was pulped to a bloody mess.

'*Mon'at*...' Aura said sadly, as Cali'cha finally broke clear and the scene of devastation receded below him.

'He is alone,' Naal said. 'His team is reduced to one. It is a sad fate indeed for a servant of the Greater Good.'

Brielle nodded, though in truth she had no sympathy for the surviving warrior. His commanders had drastically underestimated the Space Marines if they thought them so easily defeated. She had even tried to warn them...

'Reinforcements,' Aura said, and the projection was filled by the scene of a dozen more battle suits swooping in to join Cali'cha. The air filled with the Space Marines' war cries and the deafening report of boltguns, and battle was joined again.

Sergeant Sarik loosed a feral grunt as he yanked his screaming chainsword from the torso of the ruined battle suit, bracing an armoured boot against its groin as he pulled the weapon clear. The blade was coated in purple fluid and its teeth almost clogged with small chunks of the pilot's flesh. Raising the chainsword to a guard position, Sarik looked around for another foe.

A sharp explosion sounded from nearby as Sarik's battle-brothers finished off the second of the battle suit team, and a third was lifting high overhead on hissing blue jets.

'Regroup!' Sarik bellowed. 'On me!'

Within moments, Sarik's warriors had gathered at his side and Sergeant Tsuka's squad was inbound, loosing a hail of fire at the retreating battle suit as they came. The scene was one of utter devastation, the Imperial Guard's bombardment of the settlement on the nearside of River 992 having ruined every structure and cast flaming debris over a wide area.

'We'll need more squads moved up fast, brother-sergeant,' Tsuka said when he reached Sarik's side. 'It appears the enemy are attempting to probe the Guard lines.'

It was only by repeated Space Marine combat patrols throughout the area bordering the northern loop of River 992 that the tau had been held at bay. General Gauge knew that the Imperial Guard's possession of the area beyond the river was by no means secured, and it would take only a determined enemy thrust to disrupt the entire area of operations. Captain Rumann had approved the patrols, which had been in action throughout the night. Significant progress had been made, the patrols keeping the enemy away from the Guard as they moved their heavier units forward.

'Sergeant Rheq,' Sarik said into the vox-net as he opened a channel to the Scythes of the Emperor contingent leader. 'Sarik. What is your status?'

Sergeant Rheq's reply was half drowned out by the sound of gunfire in the background, the Space Marines' bolt-rounds competing with the tau's energy rifles. Then the hissing streak of a missile cut across the channel, a muffled explosion sounded, and the tau weapons fell silent. 'Grid three-alpha-nine secure, Sarik,' the Scythes of the Emperor squad leader replied. 'Enemy probe neutralised.'

'Good,' Sarik replied. 'Sergeant Rheq, can you spare two or perhaps three squads?' Although technically Sergeant Rheq's superior under the terms of the Space Marines' contribution to the Damocles Gulf Crusade, Sarik knew diplomacy would get him a lot further than rank in multi-Chapter operations.

'I can spare two tactical and two Devastator combat squads,' Sergeant Rheq replied. 'That's including three heavy bolters and two tubes. Is that sufficient, brother-sergeant?'

Sarik's eyes scanned the dark skies above the river, where he caught sight of another group of battle suits zeroing in on his position. 'I am sure it will be, Rheq,' Sarik said. 'My thanks.'

Closing the channel to the Scythes of the Emperor leader, Sarik opened a transmission to all Space Marine squad leaders in the area. 'All commands,' he said. 'Enemy heavy infantry multiple inbound on grid seven-theta-nine.'

A ream of acknowledgements came instantly back from the Ultramarines and Iron Hands squad leaders operating in adjacent grids, each promising immediate reinforcement of Sarik's section of the front.

There was time for one last batch of brief orders to Sarik's squads before the enemy battle suits touched down in the lee of a ruined building one hundred metres to the south-east. Bitterly won experience had taught Sarik that the tau battle suits preferred to keep their distance, bounding into weapons range, unleashing a torrent of fire and then retreating to cover before a counter-attack could be staged. But they could be beaten, as Sarik had discovered. The tau were highly accomplished technically, but they displayed an almost paralysing fear of close assault that could be used to blunt their advances and counter their technological trickeries.

Leaving a Devastator squad to cover the dead ground, Sarik led his warriors into a wooded area that ran down to the river, passing the ruin the battle suits had touched down behind.

'The third moon at the false dawn,' Sarik said. Both of the squads accompanying him were of the White Scars Chapter, meaning he could use the battle-cant to impart information far more efficiently, and secretly, than he could with the larger, composite force.

Following Sarik's battle-cant order, the White Scars spread out into two long columns. Such a formation afforded rapid movement through the dark, dense terrain within the plantation, and allowed for superior arcs of fire. Though the White Scars were born of the nomad tribes of the plains of Chogoris, they were superior warriors even in the dense, wooded plantation. Their white-armoured forms took on the aspect of ghosts moving implacably through the dark woods, backlit by the occasional explosion or streak of tracer fire from beyond.

The sounds of artillery and gunfire receded as the White Scars pressed into the plantation, though the vegetation caused the sounds to echo unpredictably. Something caused Sarik to slow down, some inkling that something was not quite right. He halted, and gestured for the silent order to be passed down the line. Within seconds, the two squads had stopped moving, each Space Marine stood motionless against the night.

Then Sarik realised what it was that was niggling at his subconscious mind. To his enhanced senses, the complex but entirely natural aromas of the fruit trees tasted somehow... tainted, as if some other substance had been mixed in with them. Or, he realised, as if the juices of the fruit were being used to mask something else...

Sarik made a hand-gesture warning to alert the battle-brothers of a potential ambush. He took another deep breath, and this time he was sure. The fruit scents were being deliberately employed to mask something entirely different, something oily and alien.

Sarik raised his bolter and scanned the ground up ahead. The plantation was well tended, so there was very little in the way of ground cover in which an ambusher could conceal himself. Sarik tracked first left, then right, seeing no sign of an enemy using what little cover the tall tree trunks would offer. Then a gentle gust of wind sighed through the plantation, carrying with it a cocktail of smoke, cordite, blood and...

Sarik froze, forcing every muscle in his body to remain still. Though he kept his eyes locked on the path ahead, he knew that his enemy was directly above, suspended in the canopy.

Sarik breathed again, and this time there was no mistaking the oily scent of alien skin. It could only have been the alien savages his friend Lucian had reported. His gorge rising, he recalled the promise he had made himself when he had first read of these aliens' repulsive practices. Not a single one of his warriors would suffer such a fate.

Not wishing to give the alien ambusher any clue that he was aware of its presence, Sarik continued tracking his raised weapon across the ground up ahead, but his eyes were not scanning the ground, but the tree canopies. It was only when an air-bursting explosion half a kilometre distant cast the entire scene in a brief, flickering glow, that he caught sight of a mass of bodies suspended high up in the trees to the right.

Guessing the alien in the canopy directly above him was a sentry for the larger ambush group up ahead, Sarik made his decision. In a single, fluid motion he bent his arm at the elbow and fired a burst directly into the air. The bolts struck flesh, and exploded an instant later, showering Sarik with a fine rain of oily gore.

Proceeded by the snapping of branches and the rustling of leaves, a ragged mass of limbs and quills slammed to the ground in front of Sarik. He had no time to waste with an examination, but a brief glance confirmed that this alien was not a tau. It must be one of the carnivores Lucian had faced the previous night.

'The night-howler!' Sarik bellowed in battle-cant. 'Swooping from the peak!'

He had never used that particular phrase before, but the beauty of using battle-cant was that his warriors could infer his meaning with reference to the culture of Chogoris. Night-howlers were creatures of legend. According to the old tales, they had once lurked in the equatorial mountains, waiting for passing travellers whose bodies they would drag away to consume in their caves.

Sarik was up and firing as his warriors pounded forwards to his side. His shots slammed into the canopy up ahead, and without needing to be told his warriors followed his example, adding the weight of their fire to his own. The throaty *thump thump thump* of a heavy bolter opened up from the right flank, and an entire tree was torn to shreds, along with the three aliens that had waited in its canopy.

A piercing shriek filled the air, sounding to Sarik like some wailing banshee from nomad myth. Shadowy figures dropped from the trees all around, landing silently and bounding forwards on whiplash-muscled legs.

And then the Space Marines and the aliens were upon one another. Curses and oaths clashed with screeches and hisses, and both groups loosed a final volley of fire before clashing in the brutal mass of hand-to-hand combat. The aliens fired their musket-like rifles from the hip as they closed, livid bolts of blue energy slamming into white power armour. A battle-brother of Sarik's squad was struck square in the chest, a chunk of his chest armour torn away to reveal the flesh beneath. Another was struck a glancing blow to the helmet, the entire left side of his faceplate shorn away.

But the Space Marines' weapons were far more deadly, for the aliens wore no more armour than the occasional shoulder pad. Sarik fired his bolt pistol at the closest alien as it screamed in towards him. The bolt buried itself in the rope-like tendons of the creature's hip, lodging in amongst the flexing musculature. Then the mass-reactive round detonated, and the savage's entire leg was shorn off to cartwheel through the air trailing a comet-like plume of blood. The alien crashed to the ground at Sarik's feet, but still it came on, screeching hatefully as it used its barbed rifle to pull itself upwards.

Sarik put a bolt-round into the alien's head, and it went down for good.

Then the entire plantation seemed to erupt in savage fury as the two groups merged into one another. A spiked rifle barrel swung in towards Sarik's head and he ducked, the spike catching on a vent of his back-mounted power pack. That was all the opening he needed, and he pistol-whipped his attacker, staving in its bird-like skull with the butt of his bolt pistol.

Another creature leaped in from the right, its spiked rifle held two-handed like a stave. The alien came in high, feet first, and before Sarik could reach his chainsword it had slammed into him, one foot on each of his shoulder plates. The savage was surprisingly heavy, and its muscles so powerful that Sarik was pushed backwards under the weight and power of the impact. Instead of resisting the weight, Sarik rolled backwards with the alien's momentum, his back striking the ground as his opponent was suddenly forced to struggle for balance. Then Sarik brought his legs up sharply, his knees striking the alien in the back and powering it overhead to strike a nearby tree. Sarik was up in an instant. The alien was stunned, struggling to regain its feet. Sarik made a fist and unleashed such a pile-driving punch that the alien's head was pulped into the tree trunk.

A brief lull in the melee allowed Sarik to draw his chainsword and thumb it to screeching life. The fight was finely balanced. The aliens were no match for the Space Marines on a one-to-one basis, but they outnumbered Sarik's force three or four to one. Sarik looked around for a means of tipping the odds in the White Scars' favour. Then he saw it.

Twenty metres away, beyond the swirling combat, stood an alien that Sarik knew instantly must have been their leader. It was tall, and robed in a long cloak of exotic animal hide. Its olive green skin was daubed with swirling patterns of deep red war paint, applied, Sarik guessed, from the blood of the fallen Rakarshans. The alien was screeching loudly and gesticulating wildly as it issued its shrill orders to its warriors.

'You!' Sarik bellowed, pointing his chainsword directly towards the alien leader and gunning its motor so that its teeth wailed a high-pitched threat. The alien heard him and turned, its beady, bird-like eyes narrowing as they focussed on him. It seemed for an instant that the swirling mass of the raging close combat parted between Sarik and his foe, affording a clear path between the two.

The alien ceased its racket, and turned fully to face Sarik, the dreadlock-like quills sprouting from the back of its skull bristling with evident challenge.

'You hear me,' Sarik called mockingly. 'Face me!' Knowing the alien would not understand his words, Sarik put as much symbolism into his tone and body language as possible, so that even a brain-damaged gretchin would get the message and understand he was being issued a one-to-one challenge.

To Sarik's surprise, the alien nodded. It might have been coincidence, but Sarik was struck by the impression that the savage somehow understood his tongue, though he could not see how. It screeched again, and every one of its warriors nearby leaped backwards, disengaging from the Space Marines. Several of Sarik's warriors pressed instinctively after their foes, but Sarik stilled them with a curt order, and silence descended on the plantation as both groups of warriors eyed one another grimly.

Sarik stepped forwards, and the alien leader strode to the centre of the clearing to meet him. Another air-bursting shell exploded high overhead, and for the first time Sarik was afforded a clear view of his enemy. The alien was tall, taller even than a Space Marine, who were counted giants compared to the bulk of humanity. Its muscles were like steel cables, and it appeared not to have an ounce of fat on its lean body. The leader wore its ragged animal-skin cloak as if it were a stately robe of office. Apart from that it wore no other garments, but numerous leather belts and bandoliers hung with pouches and fetishes were wrapped about its torso.

As it came to a halt, the alien threw one side of its robe back over its left shoulder, revealing a sword scabbard at its belt. Sarik's eyes narrowed as he saw that the blade was obviously a power sword, its guard worked into the form of the aquila, the Imperial eagle and icon of humanity's faith in the Emperor. It appeared then to Sarik that the alien was actually boasting of its possession of the weapon, as if the Space Marine was expected to respond in fear or admiration.

'I've seen a power sword before, bird brain,' Sarik growled.

The alien's beak opened and it issued a sibilant hiss. Its warriors repeated the sound until it echoed around the entire plantation.

Sarik decided to play along. 'I come in the name of the primarch,' he called.

'Honoured be his name!' his gathered warriors responded, drowning out the aliens' hissing.

Energised by his brothers' proud war cry, Sarik raised his chainsword high and rushed in towards the alien. He expected his opponent to reach for the power sword and attempt to parry the attack, but to his surprise the alien made a casual gesture with its clawed hand, and Sarik's blade rebounded as if from an invisible barrier.

'Psyker...' Sarik spat, raising his chainsword to a guard position. That changed things.

'So the power sword's just for decoration,' he said, seeking to distract his foe and buy time to engineer an opening. The alien hissed in response, its worm-like tongue writhing in its beaked mouth.

'The Librarians will hear of this,' Sarik said, as much to himself as to the alien. 'Even should I die.'

As he spoke, Sarik worked his way around his opponent, then circled back the other way, all the while seeking to gain the alien's measure. He feinted to the left and the alien gestured again, invoking its invisible psychic shield. He feinted right and it did so again. A third feint further to the left told Sarik all he needed to know.

Sarik gunned the chainsword to maximum power and raised the weapon high for an obvious downward strike. The alien raised its hand and as the blade descended its screeching teeth were deflected once again. But the ruse had worked. Even as the chainsword came down, Sarik was drawing his bolt pistol with his left hand. The alien never saw the pistol coming, and Sarik had correctly surmised that the shield was a highly localised effect only able to protect the alien leader from one quarter at a time. The bolt pistol spoke, and a mass-reactive round penetrated the alien's chin, lodging deep inside its skull.

Amazingly, having a large-calibre micro-rocket slam into its head barely registered with the alien. It stepped backwards beyond Sarik's reach, and screeched its anger at the Space Marine, its eyes wide.

Then the bolt-round detonated, and the alien's headless body toppled heavily to the ground.

'Take them!' Sarik bellowed, and twenty boltguns levelled on the aliens. Within seconds, the ground was littered with shattered and burned alien corpses, trampled beneath the armoured boots of the rapidly redeploying White Scars.

Brielle seethed inside, drawing on every ounce of her noble-taught discipline to remain outwardly calm. She was standing in a ceremonial robing chamber belonging to the water caste, and it was lined with rail after rail of garments of office. Having been disrobed by water caste attendants, Brielle was being fitted for the finery of an envoy such as Aura.

Aura had not joined the spectacle, leaving it to a group of more junior members of his caste. The first time she had sworn at one, Brielle had learned that none of them spoke her tongue.

Everything was happening too fast. The tau had fallen for Brielle's gross exaggeration of the crusade's strengths, and that had without a doubt bought her time and saved lives on the ground. But the tau empire was small and concentrated, and its fleets were able to respond to local threats far quicker than would be the case in the Imperium, where populations were separated from their neighbours by huge gulfs of space. The tau fleet, of which the *Dal'yth Il'Fannor O'kray* was now a part, was inbound for Dal'yth Prime in massively overpowering strength.

'Ow!' Brielle spat with unconcealed irritation as one of the attendants manhandled her ankle. He was trying to get her shoe off, but he was unfamiliar with the human ankle arrangement, for the tau's lower legs were reverse jointed. She flicked her foot and the shoe came off, the attendant scurrying off after it.

That was another thing that annoyed her. Though the tau were treating her with politeness, they had no idea of personal space. She had submitted to the ritual disrobing, though only grudgingly, and the attendants had treated her more like a mannequin than a living being. It occurred to her that the tau's collective philosophies were probably the cause, the needs of the individual being secondary to the needs of the many. At first she had been reticent to stand bare before the attendants, but they had proven entirely disinterested in her body. She told herself that was a good thing, but it just served to annoy her even more...

Another attendant approached, carrying in his arms a folded shimmering, silver robe. It was made of the same material as the robe worn by Aura, though Brielle noted its embroidery was not quite so intricate. The attendant came to stand in front of her, and with a gesture he ordered her to hold her hands out to either side. Another attendant joined the first, and together they draped the silver robe over her shoulders so that it covered her body from neck to feet. The material felt cool, and although it covered her entirely, Brielle was nonetheless pleased with the way it draped across her form and accentuated her curves. Her thoughts were not rooted in vanity, however. Even as a second layer was being lifted over her head and fastened around her waist, she was calculating which of the Imperium's merchant families might be interested in acquiring such fabrics, and how much they might be prepared to pay.

More of the attendants closed in, the idiot who had had such trouble with her shoes lifting one of her feet gingerly. She looked down and saw the monstrosity that he was about to place on her foot. 'You've got a lot to learn,' she told the uncomprehending alien. 'No way am I wearing those... hideous things. I'll go barefoot, thank you.'

The water caste attendant looked up at her as she spoke, and seemed to get the message, backing off and taking the ugly, tau-made shoes with him. Others closed in from behind, and a fine array of interwoven braids was applied around her waist and neck, cinching the silver fabric and completing the costume.

Brielle regarded herself in the wide mirror. Her robes glinted in the white overhead light and her dark, plaited hair tumbled down her shoulders and across her back. The costume resembled nothing she had ever seen a human noble wearing, and she felt a deep unease at the sheer alienness of her reflection. Then a soft hiss sounded from behind as a door slid open, and she saw in the mirror the envoy Aura step into the chamber.

'Mistress Brielle,' Aura said as he came to stand beside her. 'Your transformation is almost complete. Soon, you shall not only wear the trappings of a senior water caste envoy, but you shall wield the power of one too.'

Almost complete? Brielle turned towards the envoy, her mind racing but her expression congenial.

'This,' Aura reached towards Brielle's neck and pulled aside the robe's collar. 'I bring you a gift; a far more appropriate adornment for one of your station.'

Brielle looked down and saw that Aura was holding the aquila pendant she still wore on a slender chain about her neck. In his other hand, he held the tau equivalent, a bisected circle, with a smaller circle within the first.

Her gorge rose as Aura's alien hand closed around the eagle, the symbol of humanity's faith. Despite all she had done in turning aside from her family and the crusade, she had nonetheless never abandoned her faith. And now, that was exactly what the tau expected her to do.

It was too much.

Brielle stood stock still, staring at her own reflection as Aura removed the eagle and passed it to a water caste attendant. Then he took the chain of the pendant, and placed it over her head, the symbol of the tau empire settling on her chest.

'Now, you are one of us,' said Aura. 'The fleet closes on Dal'yth Prime, and your duty awaits.

'The Greater Good, awaits.'

'I'm going alone, Naal,' said Brielle. 'This is complicated enough already.'

Naal turned his back on her, stalking to the opposite side of Brielle's quarters to stand at the wide viewing port. Dal'yth Prime glinted in the distance, and the blue plasma trails of a hundred tau vessels formed a blazing corona around the planet.

'You won't be coming back,' said Naal.

Brielle forced down a blunt reply. He was right, but she had to make him think she was sacrificing herself for the Greater Good, and not thinking of her own future.

'I may be,' she said softly. 'If I am able, I will.'

'They won't let you, Brielle,' said Naal. 'Grand will have you in his excoriation cells the instant you step foot on the *Blade of Woe.*'

Brielle sighed, knowing that the possibility was all too likely. 'Not if my father is willing to protect me. He wields the Warrant of Trade. That still means something.'

'And Grand wields the Inquisitorial rosette,' Naal replied. 'As well you know.'

'We are beyond the borders of the Imperium,' said Brielle. 'The rosette grants no formal power here, just influence.'

Naal turned his back on the viewing port as he replied. 'How much influence?' he said bitterly. 'You're counting on your father carrying the will of the council. That's a pretty big assumption to make, given the charges Grand will level on you, and on anyone who supports you.'

Brielle closed on Naal and took his hands in hers as she replied. 'I have faith, Naal. I have to do this.'

'For the Greater Good?' he said, his eyes locked on hers.

Brielle held his gaze, but hesitated to answer.

'Or for your own, Brielle?'

She let go of his hands and walked back to the centre of the living area. 'Perhaps both,' she said finally. That was as much as she would give him, though she knew inside that he deserved more. Since the two had met on the Imperial world of Mundus Chasmata, they had gone from co-conspirators to lovers and eventually to friends. But Brielle knew enough of herself to see how this would all end. Naal had sought, through genuine conviction, to show her something different from the Imperium. He served the Greater Good even though it made him a traitor to the entire human race. He sincerely believed that humanity could change, could embrace the Greater Good and stand side by side with the tau and others, rather than simply exterminating any race it could not enslave.

She knew he was wrong. She was leaving, but not on the shuttle the tau were even now preparing for her diplomatic mission.

'I'm to leave soon,' Brielle said. She turned, a coy smile at her lips. 'That gives us just enough time...'

She was in his arms before she had finished speaking, his kiss stealing the words from her mouth. The tau would have to wait a little longer.

Lucian stood in the midst of his battle group's command post, Major Subad nearby poring over a large map while the voice of Sergeant-Major Havil bellowed in the background. A gaggle of Departmento Tacticae specialists had joined the Rakarshans and were busy attempting to disseminate the reams of intelligence the crusade had gathered, and learn what they could of the aliens from those who had fought them. The Rakarshans had done a lot of that recently.

Putting some distance between himself and the anarchic command post, Lucian brought the vox-set to his mouth. 'Go ahead, Korvane.'

'Father,' Lucian's son replied. 'Would you prefer the good news, or the bad?'

Lucian scowled, knowing that his son rarely joked about such things. 'Give me the good news, son. Sugar the pill.'

'I have two more candidates for the council, father. It looks like they'll be accepted at the next sitting.'

'Who?'

'The first is Pator Ottavi. He found me in fact. He's been pronounced Pator Sedicae's successor by his House, making him the senior Navigator in the crusade.' Sedicae had been killed when the *Regent Lakshimbal* had been destroyed by tau warships, and it made sense that his successor would desire a seat on the crusade command council. Well enough, thought Lucian, so long as he showed a little more interest in the running of the crusade than his predecessor, who was almost entirely concerned with predicting the currents of the warp.

'He'll support us?' Lucian said, lowering his voice and moving further away from the command post.

'I believe so, father,' Korvane replied. 'He seems to agree that this region should be exploited, not put to the torch.'

'Well done, son,' said Lucian. 'And what of the other?'

'The Explorator, Magos Gunn,' Korvane said. 'I sounded him out and eventually discovered that he's a member of a Mechanicus faction that seeks to study the type of technology the tau use. He doesn't care if they all die, but he wants something left behind to study, and that puts him on our side as far as I can make out.'

'I know the man,' said Lucian. 'Something of an outcast amongst the wider Mechanicus, but not so much for an Explorator. Make it happen, then.'

'Did you want to hear the bad news, father?' said Korvane.

'Not really, son,' said Lucian. 'Give me it anyway.'

There was a pause, during which Lucian guessed that his son was checking the channel was secure and the conversation was not being listened in on. 'Something's happening,' Korvane said.

Lucian glanced back at the command post, and the Tacticae advisors busying themselves at their temporary cogitation-stations. 'Go on.'

'I think the fleet is preparing to face another force, father,' Korvane said. 'I think it's a big one.'

'The tau?' Lucian said, though he knew it could be no other. 'They're reinforcing?'

'More than that, father,' Korvane replied. 'I think the Tacticae are in the process of re-assessing the tau's capabilities.'

'Re-assessing?' Lucian said. 'As in, voiding themselves because they're coming to realise the tau aren't dirt-grubbing primitives that can be rolled over with a single crusade?'

'Well, I wouldn't put it quite like that, father,' Korvane replied. Lucian wouldn't expect his son to, for he had been raised in the Court of Nankirk, one of the most refined in the quadrant. 'But essentially, yes.'

'Have they informed the general?' Lucian asked.

'No, father,' Korvane replied. 'I don't think they've told anyone yet. Perhaps at the next council sitting...'

'Leave this with me, Korvane,' Lucian said, his mind racing as a hundred possibilities sprang into being. 'See about calling a council session as soon as possible, even if we have to conduct it remotely. Understood?'

As Korvane signed off, Lucian walked back to the command post, his eyes on the Tacticae advisors all the while. There was certainly something... furtive about them. It was as if they were desperately trying to piece together a puzzle they really didn't want to complete.

It all made a kind of sense, Lucian thought as he stepped back into the post. The crusade had already met far greater resistance than any had thought possible, first in space, and then here on the surface of Dal'yth Prime. The landings had started off well, but the advance had all but ground to a halt along the northern bank of River 992. Tau reinforcements were by all reports flooding east from the world's other cities, and now it appeared that a new fleet was inbound for Dal'yth Prime.

Things were just about to get interesting...

CHAPTER SIX

'Lucian,' said Sarik as the White Scar strode into Battlegroup Arcadius's bustling command post. The staff were preparing for a session of the Damocles Gulf Crusade command council, with each councillor attending from a remote station. Large pict screens were being erected in the centre of the tented command post, each connected by snaking cables to a central field-cogitation array.

The rogue trader turned from the tacticae-station he was leaned over, and grinned when he saw his friend. With a last word to the Rakarshan trooper manning the station, Lucian crossed to the Space Marine, and the two clasped hands.

'How goes the war?' asked Sarik.

Lucian's expression darkened before he replied. 'We've been ordered to dig in,' said Lucian. 'The whole operation's grinding to a halt.'

'Aye,' said Sarik. 'It's the same along the whole front. The tau have evacuated non-combatants and their reinforcements are flooding in. We've been fending off probing attacks all night.'

Lucian nodded, and leaned in conspiratorially. 'Have you spoken to any of Gauge's staff?'

Sarik noticed that the command post was manned by a large number of Departmento Tacticae staff, and guessed that the rogue trader was not entirely happy about the fact. 'Indirectly. Talk plainly, friend.'

'Well enough,' Lucian replied quietly. 'I think something's up. I think the Tacticae are reassessing the strategic situation.'

'To what end?'

'I think they're coming to realise that the crusade is overextended,' Lucian said. 'My son reports that the fleet is struggling to protect the supply trains, and if things get any worse dirt-side will be hard pressed to support orbital and ground operations together.'

'It's only a matter of time before Gauge receives this information, then,' Sarik said. 'And when he does?'

'Hard to say,' Lucian said. 'If I read Gauge right, I think he'll press for a breakout, but something will have to be done quickly. My son believes there is a substantial tau war fleet inbound, so time is at a premium.'

'Is this to be the crux of the council session?'

Lucian grinned. 'Possibly, but there is other business too. My son has been busy, finding prospective replacements for the vacant council seats. I aim to propose three new members, all of whom are sympathetic to our faction's agenda.'

Something inside Sarik stirred, for he disliked being dragged into the crusade's politics. Far better to leave such things to Chapter Masters and their peers, he believed, and leave sergeants such as himself to lead the troops. Still, he had accepted the responsibility of a seat on the command council, and could scarcely expect to avoid such things, no matter how tedious he found them.

Before Sarik could answer, one of the Tacticae staff called out, reporting that the pict screens were all in place and the council session ready to convene. Sarik and Lucian strode to the centre of the command post, the screens arrayed in a circle around them. 'Ready?' Lucian asked.

'Ready,' Sarik replied. The advisor gestured to a technician, and the screens burst to life as one.

A respectful quiet descended on the command post, and the static on the screens resolved into a dozen images of the face of the council's convenor. The man's expression looked distinctly stern, and he was obviously unhappy with the nature of the session, which was being conducted with each of the councillors widely separated rather than together in the council chamber aboard the *Blade of Woe*.

After a brief moment of silence, the convenor spoke. 'This extraordinary session of the Damocles Gulf Crusade command council is hereby convened. In attendance are Inquisitor Grand of the Most Holy Ordos of the Emperor's Inquisition, General Wendall Gauge of the Imperial Guard, Admiral Jellaqua of the Imperial Navy, Captain Rumann of the Adeptus Astartes Iron Hands, Lucian Gerrit of the Clan Arcadius, Veteran Sergeant Sarik of the Adeptus Astartes White Scars, Logistician-General Stempf of the Adeptus Terra and Cardinal Esau Gurney of the Adeptus Ministorum. Cardinal Gurney has the chair.'

With that, the convenor slammed his staff of office against the deck, and his face disappeared from the pict screens, to be replaced by the councillors. Four of the screens remained blank.

Cardinal Gurney now addressed the council, the scene behind him indicating that he was near the front line, his attendants gathered around him. 'It is my honour to chair this session of the council at this most auspicious of junctures. The first order of business is to answer the petition of Korvane Gerrit Arcadius regarding the election of three new councillors to our august body. I call Korvane Arcadius to address the council in this matter.'

Now one of the previously blank screens showed Korvane's face. Lucian's son was stood on the bridge of his vessel, the *Rosetta*.

Something occurred to Sarik, and he leaned in to speak to Lucian. 'Was that too easy? Would we not expect the cardinal to place obstacles in the path of this petition?'

Lucian appeared to be thinking the same thing. 'Aye, Sarik,' he replied in a low voice. 'Something isn't right here...'

'Honoured members of the command council,' Korvane said. 'It is my intention to propose Tacticae-Primaris Kilindini of the Departmento Tacticae, Explorator Magos Gunn of the Adeptus Mechanicus and Pator Ottavi of the Navis Nobilite be called to serve the council. I would like to–'

'The council thanks you, Korvane Gerrit,' Cardinal Gurney interrupted Korvane's petition. 'Given the urgency of the situation I call upon those in attendance to cast their votes.'

Now Sarik knew that something was definitely awry. Gurney had sidestepped procedure and gone straight for a vote, as if he was not even concerned that those proposed for council seats might be sympathetic to his rivals' agenda. Within a minute, each of the councillors had cast their votes and the three were elected, their faces appearing on the three remaining screens.

'Welcome, then,' Gurney continued. 'With that settled, I call upon General Gauge to appraise the council of the strategic situation.' Sarik could not help but read a note of smugness in Gurney's voice, as if he looked forward to his rival being forced to recount bad tidings.

'Thank you, cardinal,' Gauge scowled, his flint-hard eyes narrowing as he spoke. 'I have this hour received a full report from the Departmento Tacticae, presenting a reappraisal of our enemy's strengths and capabilities. Needless to say, I have not had the time to fully assimilate the report, but I can summarise what I have read simply enough.'

Sarik glanced around the screens, gauging the reaction of each of the councillors. Admiral Jellaqua looked as dour as Gauge, while Captain Rumann was as unreadable as ever. Gurney still looked smug, while Inquisitor Grand looked downright triumphant. 'He knows already,' Sarik whispered to Lucian, nodding towards the screen showing the inquisitor's face. Lucian nodded slightly in reply.

'It now appears that the tau are a substantially more established race than previous intelligence maintained,' Gauge continued. 'Their domain is larger by a factor of ten than initially estimated, and their technology far more dangerous.'

'And what do you propose, general, to overcome this situation?' Cardinal Gurney interjected. 'Given the evident perniciousness of our foe, how shall we defeat it?'

It was obvious that Gurney was attempting to bait the general, to force him to admit that conventional military tactics would not prevail. Sarik doubted the veteran warrior would rise to so crude a tactic, and was pleased to be proven correct.

'My staff have been busy preparing a new plan, cardinal,' Gauge replied, his voice dry and dangerous. 'I propose Operation Hydra.'

'I don't think–' Cardinal Gurney began, before he was interrupted by Lucian.

'I would hear the general's plan,' Lucian said.

'So too would I,' said Sarik.

Admiral Jellaqua and Captain Rumann added their ascent, and Gauge continued. 'I propose a rapid breakout across River 992, crossing using the bridge at the settlement designated Erinia Beta. By massing the Titans and the armoured units of the Brimlock

Dragoons, we can take the city's star port and push the enemy back against the southern coast.'

'And what then?' Inquisitor Grand spoke for the first time. 'When the star port is in your hands and the tau beaten back, what would be your next course of action?'

General Gauge's cold eyes swept the screens in front of him, evidently measuring carefully his next words.

'Having taken the star port, we will have reached a tipping point,' Gauge said. 'The tau will not be able to bring in any more reinforcements, and the city will be ours for the taking. In fact, we can use it to bring in our own, without the need to bring units through the desert from the landing zone.

'But there is this,' Gauge continued, his voice suddenly low. 'The reinforcements we were promised at the outset of the crusade have not materialised. Without these, we may have to consider–'

'There are to be no reinforcements, general,' Inquisitor Grand interrupted.

Silence descended on the council and in the command post, all eyes now focussed on the inquisitor.

'Explain,' Gauge said, his eyes glinting with murderous incredulity. 'What do you mean, inquisitor?'

'This crusade is over,' Grand said, pulling back his hood as he spoke. His features were twisted and scarred, the result of Lucian's daughter attacking him with a flame weapon before she had fled the crusade and disappeared. In amongst the scars, Grand's face was decorated by a swirling mass of tattoos, describing esoteric runes and symbols. His eyes had no lids, a deliberate message that his gaze would see all and never falter. At his neck was the red-wax seal of the Inquisitorial rosette, the irrefutable font of an inquisitor's power and authority.

The message was quite clear.

'The tau are to be exterminated, one world at a time. I have heard all I will of pride and honour. They are xenos, and they deserve no mercy. Exterminatus shall commence in precisely twenty-four hours, by which time any ground units not evacuated will be left to their fate.'

A stunned silence followed, before Admiral Jellaqua spluttered, 'The council must vote–'

'There is no council!' Grand boomed, the first time he had raised his voice above a sibilant whisper in all the council sessions Sarik had attended. 'I hereby invoke the authority invested in me by this rosette. My orders are to be obeyed as if they came from the High Lords themselves.'

The Inquisition had such power throughout the Imperium that in theory, its servants could do as they pleased, enacting every possible sanction from summary execution all the way up to planetary devastation, for the survival of humanity. In practice, however, the extent of an inquisitor's power relied on his standing within the Inquisition, and the broader strategic and political situation. To Sarik's mind, Inquisitor Grand was on anything but firm ground, dealing as he was with highly placed officials and far from the Imperium's borders.

Sarik reached a decision, and was on the verge of speaking when Lucian gripped his forearm, and subtly shook his head. Anger welled up inside the White Scar, a feeling that honour and duty were being set aside for the aggrandisement of the inquisitor and his pet firebrand cardinal. The thought of the inquisitor unleashing a virus bomb and enacting Exterminatus filled him with seething fury, for where was the honour in reducing every last scrap of biological matter on Dal'yth Prime to a rancid gruel?

He took a deep breath, and Lucian redoubled his grip on his forearm. 'Sarik!' Lucian hissed. 'We'll deal with this, but not now, not like this...'

Sarik forced himself to calm, and nodded back at Lucian. The rogue trader was correct; Sarik knew that. Then his attention was turned back to the screen that showed Gurney's smirking face as the cardinal addressed the council.

'So there it is,' Gurney crowed. 'I suppose it falls to me as chair to close this convocation. Each of you shall be receiving his orders in due course, and these will be obeyed without question, on the authority of the Inquisition. That is all.'

'That is all?' Sarik fumed as he and Lucian stalked away from the command post. 'How dare he speak like–'

'Friend,' Lucian said, coming to a halt and placing a hand on the Space Marine's shoulder armour. 'You are a warrior of great renown, and I have nothing but admiration for your battlefield skills…'

'But?' Sarik interjected. It was obvious there would be a 'but'.

'But,' Lucian smiled as he went on. 'The council is not your native battleground. I don't mean that–'

'I know, Lucian,' said Sarik, smiling himself. 'You are going to say that around the council table, my skills are no more deadly than those of a neophyte.'

'Well, I wasn't going to go quite that far,' Lucian said. 'But essentially, yes. There is far more going on here than we just witnessed.'

'What else is happening?' asked Sarik, frustrated once more by petty politicking. 'What did I miss?'

Lucian looked back towards the command post, where several dozen staff officers and Tacticae advisers were already starting to break down the tacticae-stations and pict screens.

'I think we need to speak with Gauge and Jellaqua, Sarik. I fear there's a lot more fighting ahead of us yet.'

Quietly, so that she did not wake the slumbering Naal, Brielle pulled the glittering water caste robes around her body and made for the door of her living quarters. She made no attempt to arrange the formal attire in the intricate manner it had originally been arrayed in; she had no intention of taking part in Aura's plan, and would not be playing the role he had ordained for her.

Pausing at the hatch, Brielle looked back into the chamber. Naal stirred, but did not awaken. She was leaving, not just Naal, who she had shared her life with these last few months, but the tau and the Greater Good. On the dresser beside the bed was the pendant Aura had given her, the symbol of the tau empire. She was leaving that too.

Brielle took a deep breath, knowing that she once again stood upon the precipice. She had been here before; the last time when she had made the decision to leave Clan Arcadius and follow Naal into the service of the tau empire. Now all of that seemed like a dream from which she was slowly waking. The tau, she now knew, were no different from the clan or the Imperium. They expected her to play her part in their great games, to subsume herself within the greater ideal. How was that any different from her former life?

The only difference she could discern was that the tau offered her no way to forge her own destiny, while her life as a rogue trader at least allowed her some control of her fate.

Her hand hovered above the hatch control rune, and for a brief moment she considered rejoining Naal and accepting her fate. But the notion passed as quickly as it had come, and her mind was made up. She blew the sleeping Naal a last kiss, and opened the hatch.

The door slid open silently, and in an instant she had slipped through into the brightly-lit passageway outside. As the hatch closed behind her, she took a second to straighten her robes and brush down her dishevelled, plaited locks. She doubted the tau would notice the state of her hair, but they had taken great care in the arrangement of her ceremonial robes, and she did not want a stray glance to raise suspicion. Barefoot, for there was no way she was wearing the hideous shoes the tau had given her, she strode forth along the passageway, her mind racing as she formulated a plan.

She knew that she had to return to the crusade and throw herself upon her father's mercy. That much was clear, for Inquisitor Grand would try to execute her the instant he discovered she was still alive. During their last encounter Brielle had assaulted him, burning him almost fatally with a burst of the micro-flamer secreted in one of the ornate rings she wore. She still wore that xenos-crafted ring, but it contained only enough fuel for one more burst. Hopefully, she would not have to use it.

She continued along the passageway, passing several earth caste technicians going about their business with typical efficiency. None appeared to pay her any notice. She was headed along the vessel's central spine, making towards the shuttle bay she knew to be located amidships in one of the huge modular sections slung beneath the ship's backbone. Several possibilities came to mind as she padded along the hard white floor.

The first possibility she had already discounted. She could have played along with the whole charade, playing her role as envoy to the crusade. Instead of delivering the tau's message that the Imperium should surrender itself to the Greater Good, she could simply have told the truth. But that would not work, because Inquisitor

Grand was sure to be amongst those she addressed, and there was no way the mind-thief psyker would let her live after what she had done to him.

The next possibility was to steal a shuttle and make for the crusade fleet. Again, that was extremely dangerous, for not only would she have to penetrate the shuttle bay and force a pilot to ferry her to the fleet, she might simply be blasted by the first picket vessel she encountered. Still, stealing a shuttle could work, if she could find a way of getting to the fleet or to her father without appearing in the crosshairs of a trigger-happy naval gun crew.

That left the third option, which Brielle was rapidly deciding was the only way to come through this alive. She would head to the shuttle bay and commandeer an interface craft. She would make for the surface, and from there try somehow to rejoin the crusade's ground forces. Perhaps agents of her father were down there, or even her father himself. Even if they were not, she could find a way of infiltrating the staff and from there make her way back to the fleet.

Her mind resolved, Brielle arrived at a junction. There were more tau here, technicians and soldiers busying themselves with preparations for making orbit. The *Dal'yth Il'Fannor O'kray* was approaching Dal'yth Prime from the opposite side to the Imperial war fleet, in the hope that the tau would gain the element of surprise when they revealed themselves and demanded the crusade receive their envoy. As large as a warship was, it was still a speck of dust compared to the bulk of a planet, and there was a lot of orbital space. Brielle calculated the odds, and came to the conclusion that even if the tau were discovered on their final approach it would still take several hours for the crusade fleet to deploy into a battle stance.

Then Brielle turned another corner, and the sight she saw her made her halt. The passageway opened up into a long processional chamber, banners hanging from the tall walls. The entire ceiling was transparent, affording a breathtaking view of space. It was not only the black of the void that was visible, but the upper hemisphere of the planet Dal'yth Prime.

The tau war fleet had arrived in orbit around the embattled world. Brielle knew that she had mere hours to escape, if even that.

The sound of a thousand boots stamping the deck resounded through the hall, and Brielle lowered her gaze from the sight above. The chamber was filled with tau warriors arrayed in such precise ranks that the sternest of Imperial Guard commissars would have been proud. They wore the distinctive, hard-edged armour plates protecting shoulders, torsos and thighs, as well as the blank-faced, ovoid helmets. The armour was painted a mid tan colour, which Brielle knew from her talks with Aura to be the most appropriate scheme for the dry worlds that the tau favoured.

The warriors stood perfectly still for several minutes, and Brielle was considering pressing on along the hall, through their midst towards the exit at the other end. Then a swirling blue light appeared in the air over the warriors, cast by projector units set flush into the walls of the hall. The light resolved into a face, and with a start, Brielle realised it was the face of the water caste envoy, Aura.

Brielle took a step backwards, her back pressing against the wall of the long chamber. Every tau in the hall was looking towards the face of the envoy, which towered high above. Aura appeared to be looking down at the assembled warriors, making Brielle curse the fact that tau buildings and vessels were so starkly lit there were no shadows she could retreat into.

Then the envoy started to address the warriors. Brielle was far from fluent in the tau language, but she had been taught its basics and picked up more as she had interacted with the race, especially those of the water caste. Aura appeared to be briefing the warriors, informing them of the plan to use Brielle as an envoy to the human fleet and to demand its surrender. The whole scene struck Brielle as odd, for Aura was a diplomat, not a military leader. She could think of no case where an Imperial diplomat would even think of explaining an operation to the rank and file. Certainly a military leader might give the troops a rousing speech to get their blood up, but briefing them on the behind-the-scenes intricacies appeared to Brielle almost a complete waste of time. It only served to remind her how alien the tau were from the human mindset, and how out of place she really was.

After something like ten minutes, Aura concluded his address, and the massive projection of his face appeared to sweep the ranks, something akin to pride in his glassy, oval eyes. Then he said a phrase Brielle knew well from her time amongst the tau. '*Tau'va*': '*for the Greater Good.*' The thousand assembled fire warriors repeated the phrase in unison, a thousand clenched fists striking a thousand rigid chest plates. To Brielle's great relief, the image of the envoy faded, and the warriors filed out of the hallway.

After another five minutes, the warriors had left the hall, leaving only ship's crew passing along its length. Brielle cast another glance upwards through the transparent ceiling, where Dal'yth Prime's northern pole was still visible. So too were several dozen other tau warships, the blue flare of their plasma drives telling her they were assuming a station-keeping formation in high orbit. A swarm of small motes of blue light clustered around each vessel and plied the space between them, each the drive of a small picket, tender or dispatch boat.

Clearly, the tau were readying for what they saw as their victory over the Imperium. Brielle suppressed a snort of derision as she recalled her conversations with Aura about the extent of human held space. No matter how she had tried to convince him that the Emperor's domains spanned two thirds of the known galaxy and had stood for ten thousand years, he had refused to take her seriously. He had talked often about how the peoples of the Imperium would be welcomed into the tau empire, how they would willingly throw off the oppressive regimes of despotic planetary governors when the truth of the Greater Good was revealed to them. Eventually, Brielle had stopped trying to convince him otherwise.

But out here, beyond the borders of the Imperium, the crusade was isolated and exposed. The tau war fleet could certainly destroy it, though not without great losses. All the more reason to get back to her father, Brielle knew, and turn a potential disaster into an opportunity for gain.

Brielle smiled slyly as she hurried along.

The processional hallway several minutes behind her, Brielle was padding along another starkly-lit passageway when she was forced to duck into a recessed portal. Up ahead, she had seen a group of junior water caste envoys, and they were heading in her direction.

The seconds dragged on as Brielle waited for the envoys to pass.

She could not be sure whether Aura had been amongst the group, for even though she was well used to his features, tau faces still appeared to her far more homogenous than those of humans. Several technicians strode past, followed by a fire warrior in light armour carrying a long rifle across his shoulder. Just when she thought the envoys had turned off, she heard their voices getting nearer, and she simultaneously shrank back into the recess whilst straining her ears to catch their conversation.

She thought she caught something about armed escorts, and then her own name was mentioned. A moment later the envoys passed by the recess, and she held her breath. Then they were gone, their voices receding down the corridor, and she could breathe once again. Aura had not been amongst the group, but they had been talking about her...

Gripped by a sudden sense of urgency, Brielle straightened up and stepped from the recess as if she had every right to be there. She continued along the passageway towards the shuttle bays, knowing that time was rapidly running out.

Eventually, Brielle came upon the *Dal'yth Il'Fannor O'kray*'s cavernous shuttle bay. Sensing danger ahead, she had ducked into a technical bay as soon as she had entered. Whatever intuition had made her do so, she was grateful indeed, for Aura, a number of his water caste juniors and a group of at least two-dozen fire warriors were waiting on the hardpan in front of the shuttle she was expected to be taking to the crusade fleet.

The shuttle bay was huge, at least a hundred metres tall and three hundred long. In common with the interiors of so many tau buildings and vessels it was brightly-lit and constructed of the ubiquitous hard resin material. Unlike most other areas, the bay showed some small signs of wear and tear, though even these were as nothing compared to the uniform state of decay and disrepair an Imperial facility of the same type would display. Small burn marks scuffed the hardpan, the only evidence of the coming and going of countless shuttles and other small vessels, at least a dozen of which were sat upon its surface. The far wall was open, the cold void beyond held at bay by an energy shield which glittered with dancing blue motes of light as a small lighter passed through and settled on hissing jets to an area indicated by tau ground crew waving illuminated batons.

Through the open bay Brielle could see the surface of Dal'yth Prime. At least two-thirds of the visible surface was land, and most of that dry and arid. Nonetheless, there were patches of green dotted regularly across the land, which Brielle guessed were belts of arable land surrounding each of the planet's cities. The seas were especially eye-catching, for they were a deeply serene turquoise, sparkling with the light reflected from the Dal'yth system's star.

From behind a row of fuel drums, Brielle strained her ears to catch what Aura was saying to the group. Such a thing would have been impossible in a shuttle bay on an Imperial vessel, which would have resounded with screaming jets, shouting deck crew, the thuds and scrapes of cargo being dragged about, the tread of lifters and a thousand other raucous sounds. The bay in front of her was eerily quiet compared to that, with little more than a background hum audible.

Aura was speaking in the tau tongue, but Brielle was by now well used to his manner of speech and could pick out a fair amount of what he was saying. He was telling the assembled tau to be ready to depart soon, for he was to return to the vessel's command centre from where he would be transmitting a communiqué to the human fleet. Aura's message was to inform the crusade that their lost daughter was returned, that she served the Greater Good with all her heart, and that she was to go before them in the spirit of peace. Brielle's heart sank, for she knew that such a message would damn her. Even her father would find it next to impossible to protect her from Grand, and then only if he did not reject her and abandon her to her fate.

Brielle's options were rapidly narrowing. It was too late to return to the tau, and if that message got out to the crusade she would be doomed. Her earlier notion of commandeering a lander to take her to the surface was looking increasingly impracticable, for it appeared that the tau warriors assembled in front of the shuttle were to be her honour guard.

Events were moving fast, but Brielle's mind even faster.

Hunkering down in her hiding place, Brielle considered her priorities. First, escape the tau vessel, then later, worry about getting a message to her father. She had to get moving before Aura could deliver his message, to somehow contact her father before the envoy ruined everything. She just had to get to the surface...

Then it struck her. She did not need a lander to get to the surface. Her heart raced as she leaned out from behind the drums and scanned the shuttle bay's outer bulkheads. Surely, there must be a...

There it was! A row of small hatches in the vessel's outer skin, each edged with yellow. It was what she had been looking for. All she had to do to get to the surface was to reach a saviour pod, an emergency life raft designed to ferry crew from a crippled vessel and if possible, to land them safely on the nearest world.

The shuttle bay's pods were out of the question, for she would have to skirt the brightly-lit space in full view of her honour guard. But she knew there must be others nearby, and so she hoisted her silver robes and padded off, back to the bay entrance and the corridor beyond.

Once back in the passageway Brielle assumed an erect stance and forced herself to walk at a normal pace. It became all but impossible for her to maintain her composure as she saw in the middle distance another row of yellow-edged hatches. She just had to pass a wide, open portal into a technical bay, and she would be away.

Her head held high, Brielle walked past the entrance, hearing as she passed the chatter and hum of the tau's advanced, the Imperium would say heretical, communications systems... the systems that Aura would soon be using to transmit his damning message to the Damocles Gulf Crusade command council.

Brielle halted as she passed the entrance to the communications bay. Aura would be on his way to the command centre at the vessel's fore, but the transmission systems were here, right in front of her. She turned her gaze from the row of escape hatches not twenty metres away, and looked into the communications centre, a sly grin curling her lips...

CHAPTER SEVEN

Lucian's command post was all but abandoned, the fleet staff having dismantled the majority of the tacticae-stations. It was dark outside, the cool night air gusting in through the open portal as Lucian and Sarik entered. A trusted cadre of Rakarshan staff officers manned those tacticae-stations that had not yet been removed, and these stood up and left as Lucian dismissed them with a curt gesture. Most of the remaining screens were blank, but two were not: those showing the faces of General Wendall Gauge and Captain Rumann.

'Are you with me or are you not?' the general growled, his face looking to Sarik even more craggy than normal. He swore he had seen Chogoran qhak-herders in their eightieth year with fewer lines.

'You ask much, general,' Captain Rumann said, his voice metallic but harbouring within it something of the raw furnace heat at the heart of the forge. The Iron Hand's voice was hard to read, but his features were even harder, for both eyes and much of his face were made of metal, the weak flesh replaced with infallible steel.

'I know, captain,' Gauge said. 'But I repeat. Operation Hydra must go ahead regardless of the inquisitor's proclamation. We can take that star port and scatter the tau before us, and within the twenty-four hour limit he has imposed. If we do that, he'll have no choice. We'll have got the crusade moving again, and he'll have to call off his Exterminatus.'

'And if we take the star port,' Lucian added, 'we still have the option of using it to transport our own troops. In whichever direction.'

Sarik's eyes narrowed as he considered Lucian's words. The general and the rogue trader were right; capturing the star port would put the crusade's ground forces in a powerful position, and force Gel'bryn's defenders up against the southern coastline. Sarik did not want to countenance using the star port to evacuate, for there was little honour in doing so, but the plan opened up more possibilities than simply going along with Grand's order.

'I agree,' Sarik said, his mind made up. 'There is no honour to be found in evacuating now, and even less in enacting Exterminatus.'

General Gauge nodded his thanks, and Sarik and Lucian looked towards the pict screen showing Captain Rumann.

The Iron Hands Space Marines were in many ways the polar opposite of Sarik's Chapter, and they measured such things as honour and duty according to a different standard. Sarik's people were the savage, proud children of the wild steppes of Chogoris and much of their home world's wildness flowed in their veins. The Iron Hands, however, were often held to be aloof and distant, a seemingly contradictory mix of emotionless, cold steel and the implacable, burning heat that forged it. Sarik knew such a view point was overly simplistic, but as with most stereotypes did contain a kernel of truth. Even though he had served alongside Rumann for several months now, Sarik still had great difficulty reading the captain's intentions.

'Exterminatus is without doubt the most efficient means of defeating our foe,' Rumann said. 'But much has been committed to the ground offensive. Veteran Sergeant Sarik is correct; there is no honour in evacuating as per the inquisitor's proclamation.'

'Then we are all in agreement,' General Gauge said. 'Operation Hydra is to go ahead, regardless of the inquisitor's orders.'

Sarik nodded gravely. As Space Marines, he and Captain Rumann were at least partly insulated from the wrath of the Inquisition. Lucian's standing and his rogue trader's Warrant of Trade afforded him, in theory at least, some protection. The general, however, was taking a great personal risk.

'You are a man of great honour, general,' Sarik said, nodding his head slightly towards the pict screen displaying the general's face. 'You alone of our number have much to lose. I shall not allow that to happen.'

'Nor I,' growled Captain Rumann.

Perhaps for the first time in the long months since the Damocles Gulf Crusade had been launched, General Wendall Gauge looked genuinely speechless, perhaps even moved. Sarik grinned, keen to avoid embarrassing the old veteran any more, and pressed on. 'Friends, I move that this session of the command council be wrapped up.' Lucian laughed out loud at that, and Gauge's normally cold eyes twinkled with amusement.

'Let our next meeting be convened at the Gel'bryn star port,' Sarik concluded. 'No more than twenty-four hours from now.'

Several hundred kilometres overhead, in orbit around Dal'yth Prime, death incarnate was slowly awakened from a timeless slumber. Deep in the bowels of the Blade of Woe, *in a section of the mighty warship given over to the use of Inquisitor Grand and his staff, ancient and all-but forbidden devices were being activated. Inside a huge and lightless vacuum-sealed chamber sat a sleek, black form, enveloped within a stasis field and blessed by the wards of a thousand exorcists. A secret word of command had been uttered, and a cipher-sealed communication heeded. The stasis lock was opened, and that which had been held within stirred once more.*

The stygian darkness was pierced by a wailing klaxon, an apocalyptic forewarning of the end of a world. Flashing red lights penetrated the dark, their illumination sliding across the black form like oil mixed with blood.

Within that sleek form, a billion viral slayers were freed from aching stasis. Suspended in a blasphemous medium of hybrid cell nuclei, the slayers set about the one and only task they were capable of doing. They replicated, and with each reproduction tore in two their hapless cell-hosts. In a living being, such catastrophic cell damage would lead to death within minutes, sometimes seconds, as the host's cells were literally torn apart and their body reduced to a writhing sludge.

The process set in motion, death was inevitable. Either the viral slayers must be unleashed upon a world, to infect the nuclei of every living thing, or they would expend the artificial gruel they were suspended in, and potentially break free of their prison. At that point, the slayers would have to be slain, jettisoned into space or scoured by nucleonic fire lest a single one remain.

A deep, grinding moan echoed through the chamber, and the sleek black form was in motion. The deck beneath it sank on well-oiled gears and jets of superheated steam spurted from release valves. With a final mournful dirge of sirens, the deadly payload was swallowed whole, inserted into the transport conduit that would carry it to the launch bay.

The countdown to Exterminatus had begun.

As the sun rose, Operation Hydra got under way. Sergeant Sarik was at the speartip of a mighty war host, and the sight of it filled his savage heart with pride as he rode south in his Rhino.

Ahead lay the settlement codified Erinia Beta, and its strategically vital bridge. Behind Sarik was the crusade's entire contingent of Space Marines, the livery of their Rhinos proudly proclaiming the colours of the White Scars, Ultramarines, Scythes of the Emperor, Iron Hands and several other Chapters. The Rhinos were accompanied by Predator battle tanks, Whirlwind missile tanks, land speeder grav-attack vehicles and mighty Dreadnoughts. The skies above the column were filled with the whining of jump packs as Assault Marines advanced in great, bounding leaps towards the enemy.

As impressive a sight as the Space Marines were, they were merely the smallest fraction of what followed in their wake. Nineteen entire front-line Imperial Guard regiments surged forwards as one. First came the armoured regiments, each consisting of dozens of battle tanks, their huge cannons levelled at the distant settlement with unequivocal threat. Behind the armoured spearhead ground forwards the Chimera-mounted regiments of the Brimlock Dragoons, scores of armoured personnel carriers throwing up a storm of dust into the air overhead.

The host's right flank was made up of the lighter regiments, including the Rakarshan Rifles and the Brimlock Fusiliers. These would move forward on light trucks, then fight on foot, following in the wake of the armoured thrust and consolidating its victories whilst guarding the flanks and rear against enemy infiltration.

But it was towards the army's left flank that Sarik looked as he rode high in his transport's cupola. There was to be seen the most impressive sight of all. Even through the haze thrown up in the host's passing, the distant figures of the crusade's Titan contingent were visible. Gauge had massed the gigantic war machines into a single force, which even now strode forwards towards its position at the head of the advance. The first Titans to move forwards were six Warhounds, their characteristic stooped gait and back-jointed legs giving them the appearance of loping dogs of war. Behind the Warhounds strode the even larger, upright Reaver-class Battle Titans. Each of these was half as high again as a Scout Titan, with huge banners streaming from their turbo-laser destructors proclaiming the symbols of the Legio Thanataris. High atop the carapace shell of each Reaver was an Apocalypse missile launcher, each carrying as much destructive potential as an entire Imperial Guard artillery company.

Yet even the mighty Reavers were small in comparison to the single Warlord-class engine that followed in its companions' wake. As the Warlord strode forwards, it broke through a drifting bank of dust, parting it as a huge ocean-going vessel emerging from a seaborne fog. Even at a distance of several kilometres, the ground shook as the Warlord advanced. Its head was wrought in the image of a long-dead Imperial saint, its gold-chased features ablaze in the white morning light. The Warlord's right arm was a gatling blaster, each one of its multiple barrels many times larger than a tank's main weapon and capable of rapid-firing a storm of shells. Its left arm was a volcano cannon, one of the most powerful weapons in the Imperium's ground arsenal, and capable of obliterating even another Titan in a single shot. A pair of turbo-laser destructors was mounted on its shell-like armoured carapace above each shoulder, in all probability making the Battle Titan the single most lethal combatant on the entire planet, if not the whole region.

As the Titans strode in from the flank, the Chimera-mounted Brimlock Dragoon regiments took position behind them. Gauge intended to use this mighty armoured force to smash through the main body of the tau forces and press into the city itself without even stopping. Aside from the tau destroyers, the Departmento Tacticae had not identified anything in the enemy's arsenal heavy enough to confront a Titan. On the evidence gathered so far, the tau did not utilise Titan equivalents, as so many other races did.

That scrap of good news had been disseminated throughout the army, and was very welcome indeed.

As the tread of the Titan force shook the entire landscape, a deep roar passed high overhead. Squinting against the harsh morning light, Sarik saw the massed formation of the crusade's fighter and bomber force streaking south. Gauge and Jellaqua had committed the crusade's entire sub-orbital air force to a single, vital mission. The force was tasked with intercepting the tau's destroyers and bombing their airfields, protecting the Titans from their super-heavy weapons. Both leaders knew that they were asking the veteran aircrews to embark on a nigh suicidal endeavour, and the crews themselves knew it too. Nevertheless, the men and women of the Imperial Navy tactical fighter wings were amongst the most dedicated servants of the Emperor in the crusade, and every one had vowed to undertake the task given to them so that not a single Titan would be lost. Most of the aircrews had already received the last rites from Gurney's army of Ecclesiarchy priests.

As the massed fighter and bomber wave plied south on miles-long white contrails, the Imperial Guard's artillery opened up. Several hundred Basilisk self-propelled artillery platforms lobbed their shells high into the air from the army's rear, the first strikes blossoming amongst the pristine white structures of the tau city. The outer suburbs on either side of River 992 had already been relentlessly bombarded, and these were targeted for yet more devastation so that the enemy infantry defending them would be driven to ground. Missiles streaked overhead from Manticore launchers alongside the Basilisks. These fell amongst the defended ruins and sent up vast mushroom clouds as they exploded. What little cover the tau might have found amongst the ruins was blasted to atoms, reducing the settlement to a scarred wasteland.

'Five hundred metres to phase line alpha,' Sarik's driver reported.

The sergeant turned his attentions from the vast spectacle of the crusade army going to war, back to his own small part in the mighty endeavour. Sarik's objective was to take the bridge over River 992 at the Erinia Beta settlement. Though the mission sounded simple enough, the success of the entire operation would hang on that single bridge being taken intact, and without delay. Without that happening, nineteen regiments of Imperial Guard would be forced to bridge the river individually, an operation that could not possibly be completed in the face of enemy opposition and within the brief window before Inquisitor Grand carried out his threat of enacting Exterminatus upon Dal'yth Prime.

Sarik's grip tightened on the cupola's pintle-mounted storm bolter as he tracked the weapon left and right to test its action. The terrain grew denser as the Space Marine column neared the river, and Sarik trained his weapon on every potential hiding place he passed in case enemy spotters were concealed within.

Where were they? Sarik raised his magnoculars to his eyes and tracked across the ruins up ahead as best he could with the Rhino bucking and shaking as it ground forwards. Smoking ruins filled the viewfinder, and fresh craters were visible across the road leading towards the bridge. Still, no enemy troops were to be seen.

Had they fallen back in the face of the crusade's advance? The tau had displayed such an ability at the tactical level, when individual squads would pull back and re-deploy with well drilled precision and often-deadly effect. But for the tau to enact the same doctrine at the operational level was not something the crusade had anticipated.

'Two fifty, sergeant,' the driver reported.

Sarik's Rhino was now passing through the outer limits of the wrecked settlement, the scorched, dome-shaped structures clustered near the river.

'Slow down to combat speed,' Sarik ordered, before he opened the command channel. 'I want all Predators and support units forward, now.'

Sarik's driver steered the Rhino to the left of the road, its tracks grinding over a low wall and crushing it to a powdery residue. Three Predator battle tanks prowled past, one belonging to the White Scars and two to the Ultramarines. Their turret-mounted autocannons and sponson-mounted heavy bolters tracked back and forth, while the tanks' commanders rode high in their cupolas in order to spot any enemy that might lurk in the ruins armed with short-ranged but devastating tank-busting weapons.

As soon as the three Predators had ground past, three Rhinos followed close behind, two of the Scythes of the Emperor Chapter and one of the Black Templars. Each of these would shadow one of the battle tanks, ready to deploy the squads it carried to counter-attack any enemy infantry that approached through the cover of the ruins.

As the column pressed forwards, the bridge over River 992 came into view. It was an impressive structure, a hundred metres across and twenty wide. It was by far the largest bridge across the river, and far larger and sturdier than anything the Imperial Guard's combat engineer units could have erected even had there been time to do so. The bridge was pristine white, unmarked by the devastation that been unleashed on the buildings of Erinia Beta. Even a single stray artillery round or rocket could have rendered the bridge unusable, but the bridge was perfectly intact.

But that in itself raised further questions. The reason the Space Marines were ranging ahead of the main crusade army was to ensure that the tau did not have time to destroy the bridge should they fall back. Clearly, the tau had gone, but why then had they not undermined the bridge?

The lead Predator, a venerable Ultramarines vehicle with the title *Son of Chrysus*, edged towards the ramp of the bridge, its autocannon tracking left and right threateningly. Sarik's vox-bead clicked, and the tank's commander came onto the channel.

'Phase line reached, veteran sergeant,' the commander reported. 'Your orders?'

From his position further back in the column, Sarik had only a limited view of the bridge. He needed to know more before he committed his force.

'Choristeaus,' Sarik addressed the commander of the *Son of Chrysus*. 'Can you see any evidence of demolitions being set?'

There was a pause as the vehicle commander scanned the base of the bridge and the supports that were visible from his vehicle. 'Negative, sergeant,' the commander reported. 'No evidence at all. Request permission to proceed.'

Sarik had no time to consider the implications of the commander's request, for the crusade army was following hot on the heels of the Space Marine column. To delay the crossing of the bridge and the securing of the far shore would impose an intolerable bottleneck on the army, and the momentum of the entire advance would be lost. The consequences should that occur were too dire to ponder.

'Proceed, sergeant,' Sarik answered. 'But with caution. All other units, follow on when *Son of Chrysus* is halfway across.'

Dozens of acknowledgements came back over the vox-net as the Ultramarines tank powered up the bridge's ramp. The next two Predators edged forwards, their weapons tracking protectively back and forth, covering any scrap of cover that a tau spotter could be using to train a laser designator on the *Son of Chrysus*.

His Rhino halted by the side of the road, Sarik raised his magnoculars again, and trained them on the far side of the river. More ruined domes lined the shore, palls of smoke drifting lazily upwards. Dotted all around the ruins were stands of fruit trees, reduced to little more than splintered skeletons by the relentless bombardments. Sarik increased the magnification, his view almost entirely obscured by banks of smoke and darting cinders. He tracked left, towards the great loop in River 992 that led south around Gel'bryn. Seeing nothing but wreckage, he tracked the magnoculars right, his view temporarily obscured by the blurred mass of the *Son of Chrysus* as the Predator ground inexorably forwards. The shore five hundred metres to the right of the opposite end of the bridge was even more obscured, a pure white bank of smoke sizzling with inner turmoil making it impossible to see anything more.

Something about the white cloud made Sarik pause. He reduced the magnification so that the entire right side of the bridge was visible. With the view widened, Sarik could see what had raised his suspicions. The area of white was an anomaly, for the smoke rising from the rest of the ruins was grey or black. Where the banks were lit by orange fires deep in their innards, the white area seemed to shiver and pulse, as if charged by some unknown energetic reaction.

Then the wind changed, and the sharp taint of bleach filled Sarik's nostrils. Ozone.

'Choristeaus!' Sarik called into the vox-net. 'Ambush right, six-fifty, the white patch of smoke!'

Sarik did not need the magnoculars to see what happened next. The Predator's turret tracked right as sergeant Choristeaus located the area Sarik had indicated. 'My thanks, sergeant,' the tank commander replied. 'Standby.'

Then the white smoke was parted by the passage of an invisible, hyper-velocity projectile. It left no trail or wake, and struck the Predator's glacis plate at an oblique angle. The entire front left section of the tank was vaporised, tearing a ragged wound in the prow, peeling back layer upon layer of armour and exposing the Predator's mangled innards. The driver was killed instantly, his body directly in the path of the projectile. No trace of it was ever found.

'Power loss,' the tank's commander reported, his voice calm and steady even as death closed in on him. The white smoke that had parted when the projectile had been fired now drifted clear, revealing that it had been generated by some hybrid gas/distortion charge device mounted on a grav-tank. The tank prowled forwards threateningly, lining up a second shot with its massive, turret mounted gun.

'Choristeaus!' Sarik bellowed over the vox-net, though loud enough that the tank commander probably heard him with his own ears. 'Bail out, brother, now!'

'Negative,' the sergeant replied calmly. 'Engaging capacitor surge.'

With its power systems crippled, the Predator was unable to traverse its turret to fire on the enemy vehicle. But the tank was not dead yet, as Choristeaus knew. By activating the capacitor surge device, every ounce of power remaining in the Predator's machine systems would be flooded to the turret actuators. Enough power would be provided to turn the turret and line up a single shot, even as every fuse in the entire vehicle blew out. It was a last resort, and Choristeaus grasped it.

A dozen angry sparks went up from various points on the wounded Predator's hull as the capacitors were squeezed dry and the vehicle's fuses blown. Then the turret tracked right, and the autocannon lowered. The *Son of Chrysus* opened fire even as the tau grav-tank found its mark. The Predator's first shot struck the enemy's left thruster pod, the cannon shell slamming right through the slatted armour protecting the intake and exploding within.

Sarik fought the unseemly urge to punch the air in celebration. Before the second autocannon round could cycle into its chamber, the tau grav-tank fired. The alien gunner's aim must have been spoiled when his vehicle's thrusters had been struck, for the shot clipped the rear of the Predator, tearing through the armour protecting its rear section. The hyper-velocity slug was transformed into plasma as it impacted against the solid mass of the Predator's armour, which in turn burned its way through one of the tank's ammunition hoppers. A hundred shells detonated as one, and blow-out panels intended to protect the crew against such catastrophic damage were automatically jettisoned from the rear, a great gout of fire and burning debris erupting forth.

Less than a second passed between the projectile striking the Predator and the second autocannon shell cycling into its chamber. Even as the ammunition hoppers detonated, sergeant Choristeaus fired the last shell, which boomed from the cannon mouth and struck the tau grav-tank a metre to the left of the first shot. The joint between the grav-tank's thruster unit and its main hull was shattered, and the entire pod split off to slam to the ground.

The enemy tank slid sideways through the smoke, its pilot struggling in vain to control his vehicle now it was bereft of the thruster. He failed spectacularly, the solid bulk crashing into a nearby dome, slewing sideways and then flipping over entirely. At the last, the upturned tank ploughed into the ground, kicking up a spray of dirt as flames spouted from its wounds.

But that was not the last of the engagement. The rear of the Predator blew outwards as more of its ammunition detonated, its failsafe systems unable to contain the extent of the damage the hyper-velocity weapon had inflicted. Sergeant Choristeaus braced his arms against the rim of his cupola and pulled himself upwards, even as gouts of flames erupted around his waist. Then the rear of the Predator blew apart, the over-pressure escaping via the open wound at the tank's prow and the open hatch through which the tank commander was attempting to escape. The blast propelled the sergeant from the hatch and he was hurled through the air. He slammed to the ground hard ten metres behind his now furiously burning tank, and miraculously, rose to his feet.

Sarik had seen enough. He opened the vox-channel and bellowed, 'All commands, I want that bridge taken, now!'

Tank engines gunned to life and the Space Marine column ground forwards towards the bridge, dozens of weapons trained on the far bank lest any more ambushers show themselves. The two Predators that had followed the *Son of Chrysus* forwards powered up the bridge's ramp and sped towards the wreckage of their fellow. Then the three Rhinos that Sarik had ordered to support the Predators powered forwards, the first one slowing and dropping its rear ramp so that Sergeant Choristeaus could board.

As the first of the Predators approached the wreckage in the centre of the bridge, Sarik's Rhino started moving. The sergeant stood tall in his cupola, his magnoculars trained on the banks of drifting smoke on the far shore. He zoomed in on the scene of the destroyed tau grav-tank, the view jumping wildly as his Rhino pressed on. Flames were guttering from the tank's flank where its thruster unit had been blown away, and they were spreading, greasy black smoke spouting from several vents across the vehicle's hull.

Then the grav-tank's commander clambered out from the vehicle's rear hatch. He was obviously wounded, his entire left side blackened and his chest armour shattered. As the commander staggered from the wreck, several figures appeared behind the tank. Within moments, a squad of fire warriors was surrounding the wreck while two of their number dragged the wounded commander to safety.

At a shouted order from the aliens' leader, another warrior clambered under the grav-tank's upturned prow, risking the flames to reach the driver's hatch.

'I have a clear shot. Engaging...' the voice of a Predator vehicle commander came over the vox-net. It was Sergeant Larisneaus, the commander of the Predator called *Wrath of Iax*. The Ultramarines battle tank was aiming its autocannon directly at the fire warriors, its commander keen to avenge the destruction of the *Son of Chrysus*.

'Negative, Larisneaus!' Sarik snapped. 'They recover their fallen. Let them do so.'

'Sarik,' the tank commander replied. 'They killed my kin. It is my–'

'Negative!' Sarik shouted. 'They honour their fallen, as we do our own. You will obey my order, Sergeant Larisneaus.'

The other tank's autocannon lingered on the scene of the fire warrior dragging the unconscious or dead tau pilot from the burning grav-tank. The Predator pressed forwards at combat speed, its turret tracking to the right as its commander kept the object of his wrath in his sights.

The *Wrath of Iax* slowed as it passed the smoking wreck of the *Son of Chrysus*, forced to manoeuvre through the gap between the bridge's edge and the ruined Predator. Sarik's Rhino mounted the bridge and he was afforded a clear view across the shimmering waters of River 992 to the devastation beyond. He trained his magnoculars on the wrecked enemy tank, seeing that the pilot and commander had been dragged clear. The alien squad leader was shouting orders, gesturing for his fire warriors to re-deploy.

Then the scene in the viewfinder exploded in purple blood and orange flashes. With the wounded tau clear, Sergeant Larisneaus had opened fire. The Predator's turret-mounted autocannon and its two sponson-mounted heavy bolters opened fire as one, unleashing a terrible storm of explosive metal that caught the tau in the open. Rounds tore through alien bodies, ripping them apart in a welter of blood as limbs were sent cartwheeling through the air. The flank of the grav-tank erupted in sparks as stray rounds hammered into its armour, gouging huge ragged chunks out of the alien material. Within seconds, the fire warriors were reduced to smoking meat scattered around the upturned grav-tank, their blood splattered across its side.

'Honour is settled,' Sergeant Larisneaus said flatly over the vox-net. Sarik could scarcely argue.

'Contact front!' another voice yelled over the vox-net. It was Sergeant Jhkal, of the White Scars Predator *Stormson*. An instant later the sound of the tank's autocannon and heavy bolters opening fire rang out.

On the far side of Bridge 992, the tau were counter-attacking.

Battlegroup Arcadius, Lucian Gerrit and his officers at its head, charged through the ruined settlement on the nearside bank of River 992. Explosions erupted all around and deadly bolts of searing blue energy whipped through the air. The Rakarshans were at the army's extreme right flank, guarding against the possibility of the enemy launching rapid strikes against the host's otherwise exposed edges. Five minutes earlier, such a strike had been launched.

Lucian threw himself against a mass of burned-out machinery as a volley of energy bolts scythed through the air not a metre from him. The air sizzled as the bolts zipped past and he felt his skin tingle at their passing. Looking back along his path, Lucian saw that a platoon of Rakarshans were following close behind, Sergeant-Major Havil at their head.

'Havil!' Lucian called out, but the warrior ignored him, running past his position with his power axe raised two-handed and his beard trailing behind him. More shots whined past and Lucian momentarily lost sight of Havil.

'Well enough,' Lucian growled. 'We'll do it the Rakarshan way.'

Lucian propelled himself to his feet, his plasma pistol instantly raised as more of the riflemen ran forwards. He tracked the pistol left, then movement from the right caught his eye and he brought his weapon to bear on it. A tau warrior had risen from a previously concealed position, a short, stubby carbine braced against his shoulder and pointed straight at the charging sergeant-major.

Lucian fired, and the roiling blast of raw plasma took the tau's right arm off at the shoulder, the backwash of lethal energies spraying across his blank faceplate. The alien screamed horrifically as he fought with his one remaining hand to tear the rapidly melting helmet away before the liquid energies melted through.

For an instant, Lucian felt a stab of guilt for inflicting such a grisly death upon another sentient being. He was just about to fire again, to end the alien's obvious suffering, when Sergeant-Major Havil did it for him. Voicing a shrill, ululating war cry that drowned out the alien's pain-wracked wailing, Havil stormed in and brought his power axe in a wide, horizontal sweep that scythed the tau's head clean from his shoulders. The decapitated head flew in one direction, while its helmet spun away in the other.

Lowering his plasma pistol, Lucian glanced around, scanning the ruined buildings for more targets. Furtive movement further ahead suggested the tau he had just shot was not alone, but no solid targets showed themselves. The sergeant-major's maddened voice sounded a second time, and Lucian saw an arc of purple blood spurting outwards from behind a shattered dome. He started forwards, the platoon of Rakarshans at his side. As they closed on the cover where Lucian had seen movement, the riflemen drew their blades and uttered their own chilling war cries.

Lucian and the riflemen pounded forwards after the sergeant-major, rounding the corner to see Havil standing over the bodies of three more tau. These wore lighter armour that the main line infantry, suggesting they were scouts or spotters of some sort. And where there were spotters, Lucian knew, there was inevitably something to be spotted for.

Lucian turned to find the platoon commander, seeing the officer running towards him in the midst of his men. He opened his mouth to order the man to get his men to cover, when he saw a red light paint the ground at his feet.

'Get-!'

It was as if lightning struck the ground not ten metres from Lucian. An instant before, the air became charged and his skin stung, then everything went white. He was propelled backwards to crunch painfully into the side of a building, though his power armour absorbed the worst of the impact.

Temporarily blinded, Lucian had little idea what had struck the Rakarshans. The air had crackled as a deafening wail had screamed in from somewhere to the south, and it sounded as if the air itself had been ripped in two.

Even after the explosion, the air was filled with crackles and buzzes, not unlike the sounds that dominated a warship's generatorium.

Then, just as Lucian's vision began to clear, the screaming began.

'What the...' Lucian started. The surface of the road along which the Rakarshan platoon commander had been running was a blackened crater, seething with arcs of bright energy. Inside the crater was scattered the charred remains of the officer and at least five of his riflemen, every single bone of their bodies pulled apart, their flesh burned away by whatever had struck them.

The screams were coming from those riflemen not caught in the blast's full effect, but who had been close enough to suffer from its blast wave. Men writhed upon the ground, arcs of what looked like electricity sweeping up and down their bodies and burning their flesh wherever they passed.

'Medics!' Lucian bellowed into his vox-link. 'All commands, I need immediate-'

Lucian stopped, the channel howling with interference that popped and crackled in time to the energies spitting from the crater. He looked around, and located his signalman, who had only recently returned from treatment for the wounds he suffered at the hands of the alien savages what seemed like many weeks ago.

The vox-officer was furiously working his vox-set, desperation written clearly on his face.

'It won't work,' Lucian said as he grabbed the man's shoulder. 'Go get help. Find Subad and tell him to get some anti-tank up this way too. Now!'

The signalman nodded, hoisted his vox-set onto his back and dashed back through the settlement towards the battle group's rear. As he ran he passed another platoon pushing forwards, grabbed the command section's medic, and pointed towards the crater. The medic followed the gesture, nodded grimly, and in an instant was at the side of the nearest wounded rifleman.

Lucian's skin tingled, and this time he took the warning. He dived across a low, ruined wall and rolled into cover just as a seething ball of energy crackled overhead. He did not see where the shot impacted, but he heard the detonation, and guessed that it had been aimed at the second platoon pressing forwards through the settlement.

'Damn it...' Lucian spat. 'Havil!'

When he heard no response, he raised his head above the ruined wall and looked about for the sergeant-major. It was no wonder the man had not heard his call, for he was up and running already, a handful of Rakarshans at his heels. Then Lucian saw what the sergeant-major was charging towards. It was a tau grav-tank, its turret surmounted by the previously unknown weapon that had unleashed the devastating energy ball. The tank was moving down the far end of the street, several dozen tau infantry flanking it as they passed quickly through the ruins on either side.

'Mad bastard...' Lucian growled, stepping out from the ruins. 'Rakarshan!' he bellowed, drawing his power sword and raising it high so that every rifleman nearby would see him and have no doubt as to his meaning. 'Rakarshans, forward!'

'Rakarshan!' dozens of voices repeated, accompanied by the metallic ringing of ceremonial blades being drawn from jewel-encrusted scabbards. Seconds later, scores of Rakarshans were charging headlong down the street, and Lucian was caught up in the ferocious charge, carried forwards by its inevitable momentum.

The Rakarshans discarded all notion of tactics and subtlety as they closed on the tau. Though expert stealthers and mountain troopers, when it came to the charge the Rakarshans fell back on the atavistic nature of their ancestors. The tau unleashed a desperate fusillade as the Rakarshans closed, felling at least a dozen in the last seconds. The rifleman to Lucian's left was felled by a gut shot, doubling over as he grasped his stomach to keep his innards from spilling out of the smoking wound. The rifleman to Lucian's right was shot in the knee, his entire lower leg blown away as he collapsed to the ground. Lucian bellowed along with the Rakarshans as he closed on the tau warrior only twenty metres ahead.

The alien raised his carbine and brought it to bear on Lucian's head. For one awful second which felt to Lucian like an eternity, he felt the alien's crosshair settle right between his eyes. Then an alien voice called out an order, and the alien lowered his weapon to the ground. He pumped the action of an underslung launcher, and a projectile spat from a secondary barrel. It slammed into the ground between the aliens and the charging humans, and Lucian's vision was filled with flickering motes of energy.

He kept going, as did the Rakarshans. Everything around him swam as the air distorted and perspective slewed out of kilter. Colours bled into one another and the spectrum abruptly reversed. Then he was through the bizarre effect, which was evidently intended to disorientate an assaulting foe, and upon his enemy.

The tau in front of him raised his carbine instinctively as Lucian swept his power sword downwards. The energised blade scythed the weapon clean in two, and then did the same to the alien's torso, spilling its internal organs across the ground at Lucian's feet before the two halves fell apart. Lucian continued forwards, and the next tau warrior died as its head was split in half by a high strike.

On either side of Lucian, the Rakarshans were butchering the tau infantry. What little resistance the aliens had been able to mount was rapidly turning into a rout as the enemy sought desperately to break off. The melee swept into the ruined buildings on either side of the road, and for a moment, Lucian found himself alone in the open, his power sword smoking in his hand as he took a great gulp of air and looked around for another enemy to slay.

A high-pitched whine assaulted Lucian's senses, and he looked up. Thirty metres ahead, the grav-tank was advancing, its huge main weapon lowering towards him.

'Sir!' the voice of Lucian's signalman rang out. 'Down!'

Lucian dived to the right and an instant later a hissing roar thundered down the street. He came up in a roll as the missile streaked overhead, and flung himself into the cover of the nearest ruin.

Less than a second later, the missile struck the grav-tank with a deep, resounding wallop. Then something detonated within, and the entire tank blew itself apart. The blast wave vaporised the road surface, throwing up an instant curtain of dust within which flames danced. The grav-tank's turret was thrown directly upwards into the air, the barrel of its weapon shearing off and spinning away into the distance. Then the turret crashed down into the ruins of the building Lucian was sheltering in, showering him with shrapnel and embers.

Lucian's power armour took the worst of the shrapnel, though its livery would have to be lovingly reapplied much later, and triple-blessed by a confessor. Though the skin of his face felt singed and bruised, Lucian was alive.

The jade sky above darkened as a figure was silhouetted against it. 'Sir?'

Laughter came unbidden to Lucian's throat as he focussed on the signalman standing over him. He let it out, giving voice to a deep, booming laugh that must have sounded to the officer like that of a madman.

'Sir?' the signalman repeated, bright cinders dancing around him.

'Glad to see you, lad,' Lucian said when the laughter had passed. 'Now help me up.'

The signalman took hold of Lucian's power-armoured forearm with both hands, and put all his weight into hauling Lucian up. As he stood, dust and ash fell away from Lucian's armour, the dark red and gold trim of his clan's colours almost entirely obscured by debris and burns.

The street outside the ruin was wreathed in smoke and a driving rain of glowing embers thrown up by the burning wreckage of the tau grav-tank. Riflemen were rushing past, firing into the ruins as they drove off the remnants of the tau counter-attack. Major Subad was striding towards him, another signalman hurrying behind him. Lucian was relieved when he heard the booming voice of Sergeant-Major Havil further ahead, pushing the riflemen onwards against the remaining tau.

'My lord,' said Major Subad as Lucian stepped outside into the street. 'What happened to you?'

'Never mind me, major,' Lucian said as he looked back down the street towards the scene of the grav-tank's first attack. Company medics were already getting to work on the wounded. 'Call in a medicae lander,' Lucian said. 'I want those men evacuated.'

'Yes, of course, my lord,' Subad replied, gesturing to his signalman to enact Lucian's order. 'But...'

'What?' Lucian said. It was obvious that the major had bad news.

Subad hesitated. 'What?' Lucian repeated, on the verge of losing his temper.

'I have just received word straight from General Gauge's a.d.c,' Subad said. It was going to be very bad news.

'What did he say?' Lucian pressed. 'Out with it, man.'

'He wished that you be informed that Cardinal Gurney has just left the front line, and is returning to the *Blade of Woe*.'

'He's what...?' Lucian started. But he was interrupted by the sight of a shining gold shuttle streaking overhead. A moment later a deafening sonic boom rolled across the ruins, and the shuttle was gone.

'Bastard...' Lucian growled. 'Subad? Pass me that vox-set.'

Word of the Space Marines' assault upon River 992 was disseminated quickly through every level of the crusade's ground army, the command echelons of the nineteen front-line combat regiments passing it down to their line companies, who informed the platoons. The Titans, now in position at the army's head, strode forwards, ready to support the Brimlock Dragoons as their massed armoured transports raced towards the bridge. As the army advanced, enemy counter-attacks gathered momentum, and soon it was not only Battlegroup Arcadius that was fighting to keep them at bay, but every light infantry unit at the army's flanks.

But the Space Marines were forcing their way across the bridge, and the order was given. Cardinal Gurney himself had been at the head of the force, bellowing his battle-sermons and filling the hearts of tens of thousands of Imperial Guardsmen with resolve and courage. When the first of the tau counter-attacks struck at the army's flanks, Gurney redoubled his efforts, ordering that his words were relayed through the command-net and amplified through the vox-horns on each signalman's set so that every warrior would hear them and take heart.

Gurney's sermons drove the beleaguered flank units to superhuman efforts, his furious imprecations ringing in the ears of the combatants, lending strength to the arm of the Guardsman, succour to the wounded and dying, and even planting fear in the hearts of those tau warriors close enough to hear them. Enemy units mounted in fast-moving grav-effect carriers looped wide around the Imperial army, the passengers disembarking to unleash fusillades of withering fire at the flank companies. At one stage the fastest of enemy cadres threatened the army's mobile artillery concentrations at the rear, which were moving forward in great, bounding advances while keeping up a storm of supporting fire for the front-line regiments. The Brimlock Light Infantry moved swiftly to counter the sudden threat, redeploying seven companies and holding the enemy at bay long enough for the heavy weapons companies to set up their field pieces and drive the enemy off completely. The fight was bitter and intense, but Gurney's words rang out across the battlefield as the sun reached its zenith in the jade sky, pushing the warriors of the Emperor to ever-greater feats in the service of their lord and god.

Then something happened. It would never be known who sent the original transmission, but as quickly as word of the Space Marines' assault across the bridge had reached the lowest levels of command, so this new piece of information spread equally as fast. Cardinal Gurney, so the message stated, had quit the field of battle to return to orbit. Yet, how could this be? The cardinal's voice boomed out of every vox-horn on the battlefield. Surely, Gurney was at the very leading edge of the army, only waiting for the Space Marines to take the bridge before he would lead the faithful across, into Gel'bryn and on to victory.

Then where was he? Concerned that this rumour would undermine morale, commanders and commissars alike hounded their vox-officers to seek clarification. But every channel was filled with Gurney's sermons, and no other transmissions could penetrate.

The rumour spread far and wide, sowing confusion in its wake. Where Guardsmen had fought with righteous fury, now doubt gnawed at the edges of their courage. Where previously las-rounds had flown with vengeful and unerring accuracy, now they wavered. Where men had stood firm in the face of overwhelming odds, now they cast wary glances backwards. Where the order to fix bayonets and charge into the very teeth of the enemy had been obeyed without question, now men hesitated.

And still, none could locate the cardinal.

Runners were sent from regimental commands, intelligence cell liaison officers seeking out their opposite numbers in the other units. Where is Gurney? Is he with the armour? The infantry? The artillery?

He was nowhere to be found, for he had indeed quit the field of battle. His transmissions were recorded phono-loops, broadcast by a vox-servitor left at the landing zone while Gurney sped away in his gold-liveried personal shuttle towards the waiting *Blade of Woe*. This fact took longer to discover and disseminate than the previous rumour, but despite the best efforts of the Commissariat, it could not be contained for long. As the runners returned to the regimental commands and informed their superiors of what they had heard, others overheard and repeated the tale.

Gurney was gone, so the initial rumours stated. Gurney was dead, so others said, but that could not be so for his voice still rang out from the vox-horns, dominating every channel. Gurney had fallen hours before, others said, and his sermons were being looped over and over so that none would ever know. Gurney was dead, still others claimed, and was preaching to the faithful from beyond the grave!

Regardless of the exact rumour men heard, the effects were universal. The advance lost momentum even as the Titans closed on the nearside shores of River 992 and prepared to wade across. First the armoured and mechanised units slowed, the gap between them and the Titans increasing all the while. Then the infantry faltered as first confusion, then panic swept through the ranks. Men refused to advance, and the commissars were forced to execute dozens.

As the advance stalled, the tau redoubled their attacks on the army's flanks, and men previously galvanised by the cardinal's presence were suddenly terrified by his absence. Those platoons at the battle's leading edge began to fall back, and soon entire companies were retreating in the face of an enemy they had previously had no fear of whatsoever.

It was midday, and Operation Hydra hung in the balance.

Sarik yanked his screaming chainsword from the torso of a tau warrior, the screeching teeth back-spraying a torrent of purple blood as he used his armoured boot to force the body down. The far end of the bridge was less than thirty metres away, but the tau were making his force bleed for every metre the Space Marines took. Already, over a dozen battle-brothers lay slain on the once-pristine, now bloody and scorched surface.

'Missile launcher!' Sarik bellowed as yet another battle suit dropped out of the air, coming to a smooth landing thirty metres in front of him. Sarik was learning to recognise the tau's weapons, and their capabilities. This one's arms were twinned fusion blasters, each capable of melting a fully armoured Space Marine to bubbling slag.

'Ware the fore!' a battle-brother yelled, and Sarik pushed himself sideways, right to the edge of the bridge. He turned his head, and for an instant looked directly down into the glistening waters of River 992. Then the missile screamed overhead, and Sarik gritted his teeth against the imminent explosion.

But none came. He rolled over, raising his boltgun as he looked back towards the end of the bridge. The battle suit had leaped high, the missile streaking beneath it and off into the roiling smoke beyond the bridge. It was coming down to land right in front of Sarik, its deadly blasters locking onto him.

Sarik squeezed the trigger of his boltgun, unleashing almost an entire magazine of mass-reactive explosive bolts directly into the enemy's torso. The first shots sent it reeling off-balance and it stumbled backwards on its claw-like mechanical feet. As more shots impacted against its armour, detonating with furious staccato flashes, it swivelled around again, bracing itself against the fusillade as it raised its blasters.

Then a crater appeared in the centre of its torso armour, and Sarik concentrated his last few rounds on that exact spot. Round after round buried themselves in the wound, and detonated as one. The battle suit quivered as its systems sought to respond to the nerve signals coming from the dying pilot's mind; then it shook violently as a jet of purple blood and gristle spurted out of the wound.

The battle suit collapsed in a still-quivering heap in front of Sarik, and in an instant he had leaped upon it and was brandishing his chainsword high. Utter savagery filled Sarik's heart, his conscious mind struggling to maintain control over his battle-rage. That part of him that was a supremely trained, genetically enhanced, psycho-conditioned warrior-champion of the Emperor of Mankind was fighting a constant battle against the other part, perhaps the greater part, that was a wild, untamed, undisciplined son of the windswept steppes of the feral world of Chogoris. No amount of conditioning or training could entirely rid a son of the steppes of that warrior spirit; indeed, it was the very heart of all that the White Scars were.

At times such as these, it was the savage that won the battles.

Sarik swept his chainsword down, pointing it directly towards another squad of enemy warriors rushing forwards in a desperate, last-ditch attempt to hold the far side of the bridge. He snarled an incoherent oath, and leaped forwards as his warriors joined him. As Sarik and his battle-brothers closed the last thirty metres of the bridge, the tau opened up with a fusillade of energy bolts so dense it felt as if he were charging through raging sheet lightning. A brother went down, his head split in two; Sarik could not see who it was. He bounded over the body even before it came to rest, gunning his chainsword to full power as he closed the last few metres.

Then he was in amongst the tau. His chainsword hacked left and right, and aliens died with its every stroke. Purple blood sprayed in all directions and stringy gristle threatened to jam the blade's action. He roared with savage battle lust as enemies fell at his feet to be crushed to paste beneath them. The white-armoured forms of his battle-brothers pressed in, and behind them came warriors bearing the deep blue of the Ultramarines and the black and yellow of the Scythes of the Emperor. Bolt pistol fire rang out from all about and combat blades flashed in the midday sun. The white of the bridge's surface was stained purple with tau blood and the air was filled with the mingled sounds of the Space Marines' battle cries and the aliens' terrified screams.

Quite suddenly, there were no enemies within Sarik's reach. Those not slain in the charge were fleeing headlong towards the ruins of Erinia Beta. Sarik bellowed in frustration and denial, and sprang forwards after them, cutting the closest down from behind with a horizontal sweep of his chainsword that hacked the alien's legs from out beneath it.

Not breaking stride, he powered onwards, the remaining tau fleeing before his wrath. The first aliens to reach the ruins turned to raise their weapons to cover their companions' retreat, but upon seeing Sarik's fury abandoned the notion and fled deeper into the wreckage and out of his sight.

As the last of the tau disappeared into the smoking ruins, Sarik came to a halt. His breath came in great ragged gulps. He spat, surprised to see blood in the spittle, and wiped his bloody face with the back of his gauntlet as a hand settled on his shoulder plate.

'It is done, brother-sergeant!' shouted Qaja.

Sarik stared his battle-brother in the eye, but it took him a moment to recognise his old friend. Then reason dawned on him and the red mist lifted. Qaja's face was stern, his eyes dark and unreadable. After another few seconds, Qaja nodded back across the river, and Sarik followed his gesture.

The Warlord-class Battle Titan was striding through the ruins of eastern Erinia Beta, every tread of its huge mechanical feet crushing an entire building. The settlement, already reduced to ruins by the crusade's bombardment, was now flattened to rubble as the engine strode forwards towards the edge of River 992.

The ground trembled with the Titan's every step, the waters of the river quivering as crazy patterns sprang into being across its surface. Its sculpted head gleamed blindingly bright in the harsh noon sun as its gaze swept across the scene on the far side of the bridge. It looked to Sarik as if that beatific face was casting its benediction on the battle fought to capture the bridge, granting its approval of the alien blood spilled in the Emperor's name.

The Warlord came to a halt at the river's eastern shore, its Reaver-class consorts stepping to its side, three on its left and three on its right. The seven Titans halted, forming a towering line along the river as solid and massive as a fortress's curtain wall. An odd stillness settled upon the scene as the Titans stopped moving, the only sound that of pulsing plasma generators and sizzling void shields.

Then the sirens spoke. The Warlord's voice was deep and resounding, its war horn filling the air with a slowly rising and falling dirge that sounded to Sarik like the dying cries of a gargantuan beast. But this was no mournful lamentation; it was a warning, and a dire one at that.

Friend or foe; be warned. I am the God-Machine, and I am your doom.

'All commands,' Sarik was forced to shout over the terrible drone. 'Heed their warning and get your heads down!'

Then the six Reaver-class Titans added their own voices to the Warlord's, and now it sounded like the end times were truly come to Dal'yth Prime. Space Marines boarded their Rhinos, which made for the one place nearby they knew the Titans would leave untouched – the bridge. As the apocalyptic chorus wailed on, the Space Marines formed up in a long column along the bridge, the vehicles packed closely for mutual cover. The assault squads, who did not have their own transports, swept down amongst the armoured vehicles, each Assault Marine taking what cover he could find.

Then the sirens powered down, the pitch and volume falling to the subsonic. A brief moment of utter silence stretched out, and then the line of Titans opened fire.

The first weapon to fire was the Warlord's gatling blaster. Rounds the size of men were cycled into the weapon's chamber, and fired with explosive force before the next barrel rotated around to fire the next shot. If a man-portable assault cannon sounded like a bolt of silk being torn in two, then the Titan's equivalent sounded like the air, the sky, the very fabric of reality being torn apart.

Round after round hammered from the rotary weapon in impossibly fast succession as the Titan swept its fire from right to left across the far bank. Each round was as powerful as a heavy tank shell, blowing out the already damaged structures across the river one by one as the line of fire swept along their length in seconds. Sarik had only previously seen such devastation from a low-level bombing run conducted by an entire wing of fighter-bombers, each successive explosion coming microseconds after the last as the detonations walked across the line. It was an impressive sight, even through his Rhino's vision block, and his transport shook violently with successive blast waves.

As each shell pummelled into its target, a blinding white blast preceded a rapidly expanding cloud of dust and rubble. Seconds later, shrapnel and debris began to fall on the Space Marine vehicles, some pieces razor-sharp fragments that zipped through the air and pinged on armoured plates, others large chunks that clanged heavily upon upper hulls.

Within seconds, the entire line of buildings on the Gel'bryn side of the river were reduced to dust. The Titans' sirens started up again.

The Warlord stepped forwards first, one foot setting down into the waters of River 992. As its armoured shin sank, the waters churned, huge waves crashing around. The tidal effect caused the waters to surge up and over the riverbanks, flooding either side of the settlement and dousing many of the fires with a billowing of white steam. The waters rose up the bridge's pilings, but the bridge was just high enough over the river to avoid being swamped.

The engine's leg sank down to its knee, and then it set its other foot down and set out across the river. A moment later, the six Reavers waded in too, the waters coming right up to their waists and completely swallowing the heraldic pendants slung between their legs. The Warhounds appeared on the shore at the formation's flanks, their torsos swivelling left and right as they maintained overwatch for their far larger companions. The river was too deep for the Scout Titans to wade across safely, for the waters would swamp their arm-weapons. They would have to cross via the bridge, once the Space Marines were clear.

Though the warning klaxons still howled their doom-laden song, Sarik judged that it was time to get moving. As the Titans passed the midway point of the churning river, he opened the vox-net to order his units forward. 'All commands, Predators forward. Column, advance.'

As his driver gunned the Rhino forwards, Sarik hauled open the hatch above his head and took position at the cupola's storm bolter. In the open, the Titans' klaxons were all but deafening, drowning out the roar of the Space Marines' armoured vehicles. The Titans passed the middle of the river, huge bubbles and gouts of steam churning from the waters all around. Then the air was filled with multiple howling shrieks as the Apocalypse launchers atop each Reaver's carapace shell unleashed a salvo into the settlement. So dense was the smoke enveloping the shore Sarik could not see their targets, but the Titans were gifted with arcane sensorium systems capable of detecting a target in the most adverse of conditions. With each salvo, distant buildings erupted in seething explosions and defenders died by the score.

Sarik's Rhino rolled forwards, picking up speed as it cleared the end of the bridge, a dozen others, as well as Predators, Whirlwinds, Dreadnoughts and land speeders, following close behind. Sarik ordered the grav-attack speeders to range forwards, to scour the ruins for any sign of surviving tau, while the vehicle column formed up into an advance pattern before plunging into the ruins.

'All squad leaders,' Sarik said into the vox-net. 'We need to get clear so the main body can cross the bridge. Spread out as soon as you are across.'

There was a brief pause, then Sergeant Lahmas of the Scythes of the Emperor came on the channel. 'Brother-sergeant,' Lahmas said. 'I'm at the rear. I have no visual contact with following forces, over.'

'What?' Sarik said as he turned in his cupola towards the column's rear. Through banks of drifting smoke and dust he could just about make out Lahmas's carrier at the far end of the bridge, but virtually nothing beyond it for the smoke was too thick.

'Confirmed, brother-sergeant,' the pilot of one of the circling land speeders reported. Sarik glanced up and located the speeder. 'I have visual contact on the approach. There are no Imperial forces visible at all, over.'

'Where the hell are they...?' Sarik growled. If the army did not cross River 992 at Erinia Beta and take Gel'bryn before Grand's ultimatum expired, they would all be dead.

Several kilometres east of Sarik's position, Lucian pushed his way through a crowded regimental muster. Grumbling Chimeras filled the air with acrid exhaust fumes and the shouts of hundreds of Imperial Guardsmen assaulted his ears. Hospitaller staff in a hastily erected medicae station did their best to succour scores of wounded troopers, and winding processions of Ministorum preachers threaded their way through the masses, dispensing the Emperor's blessings to all and sundry. Haphazardly parked armoured vehicles and knots of exhausted troopers spread out across a wide expanse of land, and evidently, they were going nowhere in a hurry.

By the time Lucian had located Colonel Armak, the commander of the Brimlock 2nd Armoured and brevet-general of the ground force, Gurney's transmissions had abruptly cut out. The cardinal's vox-servitor had been discovered and deactivated, and the Imperial Guard's command channels were finally clear of the incessant phono-looped sermons.

'Why aren't you moving?' Lucian bellowed as he crashed the colonel's orders group. Armak and his subordinates were clustered around the flank of the colonel's command tank, a huge map suspended from its side. A dozen heads turned towards him as he approached.

'I said–'

'Lord Gerrit,' the colonel interrupted, removing his peaked cap with one hand and sweeping back his stark white, sweat-plastered hair with the other. 'It's a miracle we're here at all and the entire army isn't hightailing it for Sector Zero. You were saying?'

Lucian forced his way into the throng of commanders and aides, coming to stand in front of the colonel. 'Good answer, colonel,' he grinned. 'But we need to get this force moving again, or we're all f–'

'Thank you for your astute observation, Lord Gerrit,' Colonel Armak said, a wry smile touching his lips. The distant roar of a Titan's gatling cannon thundered across the land from the south, and Armak continued. 'This is a mess, Gerrit, but I'd appreciate your input.'

'Well enough,' Lucian replied, coming to stand by the tactical map hanging from the command tank's side. He consulted his chrono, then looked to the map to locate the phase line the army should have reached. 'We're well behind...' he said.

'And the Space Marines and Titans are pushing forwards,' the colonel replied. 'Word's just come in that they've taken the bridge and are pushing towards the city.'

'Then we have some catching up to do,' Lucian said. The commanders exchanged surreptitious glances. 'Well?' Lucian continued. 'What's the problem?'

Colonel Armak sighed as he replaced his battered cap. He looked around at his subordinates, before answering 'Morale is the problem, Lord Gerrit.'

'Gurney,' Lucian said flatly, noting that many of the assembled officers were now looking at their feet, the ground, or anywhere other than their commander. 'His departure.'

'Yes,' Armak replied. 'His sermons bolstered the advance, got it going, kept it going when the enemy counter-attacked...'

'But now he's gone,' Lucian finished for the colonel. 'And without him, the men have lost their spirit.'

Colonel Armak held Lucian's gaze for a moment, then nodded. Lucian understood then the colonel's problem. The Brimlock commander and all of his staff knew that Gurney's departure had caused the advance to falter and stall, yet they could not bring themselves to say as much. These men were from the same world as Gurney himself, had in all likelihood grown up with his planet-wide sermons. It had been his words of fire and brimstone that had instigated the Damocles Gulf Crusade. He had been the Brimlock regiments' totem, and they had been his favoured sons and his praetorians. When their home world's planetary forces had been raised to the Imperial Guard, they had been proud to pledge themselves to his service, and follow him into the xenos-pyres across the Damocles Gulf.

Now, he had left them.

Cardinal Gurney's departure had left behind it a vacuum. A grin split Lucian's face, for politics, as with nature, deplored a vacuum.

'Then we need to resurrect that spirit, Colonel Armak,' Lucian said.

The officer remained blank-faced, his eyes darting around the group to meet the gazes of several of his subordinates. 'How?' he said finally.

'Someone needs to speak to the men,' Lucian said. 'Whatever it was the cardinal gave them, they need to get it back.'

The colonel's eyes narrowed. 'Who?' he said.

Lucian recognised the officer's disquiet, and trod gently. 'You?' Lucian said. 'A commissar? That's what they're trained for...'

'Or you,' Armak said flatly. 'Is it command you seek here? You're known as an ambitious man, Lord Gerrit.'

Lucian forced himself not to appear too triumphant as he answered, 'That's been said, I'll grant you that. But I know my limits. I have no desire to take over your command, Colonel Armak. And none to preach against the cardinal.'

'Then what do you propose, Lord Gerrit?'

The scream of a mighty salvo of missiles being fired by the Titans rolled across the land and receded into the distance. Lucian turned towards the battle, marked as it was by a column of black smoke where Erinia Beta burned. He fancied for a moment he saw the dark shapes of Battle Titans moving amongst the dark stain.

'That we follow the example already set us,' he answered, gesturing with a nod towards the battle. 'You command, and I'll lead.'

Colonel Armak nodded, at first a slight gesture as if he were considering Lucian's words. Then the motion became more resolute, and he held his hand out towards Lucian.

The rogue trader took the proffered hand, and the two men shook on it. 'Let's get things moving then,' Lucian said, casting a glance heavenwards as he imagined Inquisitor Grand's gnarled hand hovering impatiently over the command rune that would doom them all.

Brielle held her breath as another tau technician walked past the recess that had become her hiding place. She had infiltrated the communications bay with the intention of disabling its systems so that Aura could not contact the human fleet, but getting in had been the easy part. Carrying out her plan, which in truth she had not entirely thought through, was proving far harder. She glanced back along the service passage, the bay entrance through which she had come now impossibly distant. At ten metre intervals, the passageway's walls were inset with a recess like the one she was hiding in now providing access to machine systems, and it had taken her far too long to penetrate as far as she had. But now she was committed, for she was nearer to the communications control system than she was to her escape route.

Not for the first time in the last few months, Brielle questioned her seemingly unerring ability to get herself into the most ridiculous of situations...

The technician was gone and the passageway was clear again. Brielle peered cautiously along its length. No more crew were in sight, so she carefully eased herself out of the recess, keeping her back to the wall and her eyes on the far end of the communications bay. She darted forwards silently on bare feet, and ducked into the last recess.

Peering from her hiding place, Brielle confirmed that the communications bay was empty. As she had proceeded along the service corridor she had noted the comings and goings of the tau. It appeared that regular checks were made on the bay's systems, but it was not permanently attended. Such a location on an Imperial vessel would be staffed by dozens of crewmen, and its systems maintained by even more man-machine servitors, many hard-wired directly into the machinery. The tau utilised what they considered to be highly advanced technologies, reducing the reliance on living and breathing, and fallible, crew. The Imperium warned against the folly of relying too heavily on machine intelligence, many considering it a blasphemy capable of bringing about the doom of the entire human race. Indeed, Brielle had read texts that claimed that such a thing had come about in humanity's pre-history, texts that ordinary men and women had no access to whatsoever. She shook the apocalyptic visions that text had described from her mind, offering thanks to the God-Emperor of Mankind that the path ahead was clear.

Taking a deep breath to steady herself, Brielle checked the charge on the compact flamer hidden in the workings of her ring. It read the same as it had the last dozen times she had checked – one shot left. She had not used the weapon in months, not since the deed that had forced her to flee from the crusade into the all-too-ready arms of the tau. She had been cornered by Inquisitor Grand, who had been intent upon probing her mind for signs of the traitorous thoughts he, quite correctly, suspected that she harboured. She had unleashed a blast from the disguised flamer, immolating the inquisitor almost unto death, and fled in the aftermath.

Judging that the way ahead was clear, Brielle slipped from her hiding place and entered the communications bay. It was a circular area, a good twenty metres in diameter, the ceiling a solid white light source. The circular walls were lined with large screens, across which endless streams of tau text scrolled. The characters meant very little to her, though she had learned a little of the aliens' script. Five narrow access ways led from points around the wall, and Brielle could see that each led into the bowels of the communication bay's systems. Picking one at random, she made towards it, then came suddenly to a halt.

The slightest of movements had caught her eye, and she slipped sideways, ducking into the next access point along. As she sank into the shadows, she watched as a small, disc-shaped drone, floating two metres from the deck, emerged. The tau, Brielle had learned, made extensive use of such machine-intelligent devices, some for basic security tasks, but many more for maintenance and other menial jobs. The heaviest examples carried weapons underslung beneath an armoured disc. Fortunately, this one must have been a maintenance drone, for while it was equipped with a jointed appendage beneath the disc, it carried no obvious weapons.

The drone floated on its anti-grav field into the centre of the bay and stopped. Its single, red-lit eye blinked slowly as it revolved on the spot, its machine gaze lingering on each of the access points.

Brielle looked behind her, desperately seeking any implement she could use as a weapon should the need arise. She cursed the tau's efficiency, for there were no loose objects to hand. As the drone completed its scan of the bay, its lens-eye turned on her, and the blinking turned into a slow pulse.

She made a fist, ready to activate her concealed flamer, though she was loath to use its last charge. But how else could she defeat the drone if no other weapon was to hand?

Two million, three hundred thousand kilometres was impossibly far from a safe distance from a planetary body for a vessel to break warp and translate back to real space. Not even the most legendary of Navis Nobilite master Navigators would attempt such an operation, for in all likelihood their vessel would be smeared across interplanetary space, and every soul on board smeared across the depths of the empyrean.

Nonetheless, at a point in space two million, three hundred thousand kilometres coreward of Dal'yth Prime, a wound was ripped in the flesh of reality. Were it not for the vacuum of space, the gibbering of ravening, hungry monsters and the wailing of every damned soul ever to have lived and died might have echoed from that wound, and driven any mortal that heard it utterly insane.

Writhing aetheric tentacles quested forth from the wound, some impossible leviathan sensing the lush feeding grounds on the other side of the gate. Then, as by a surgeon pulling tight on the sutures around an incision, the wound was drawn shut, the tentacles, if they were ever really there, slurping back inside.

The blackness of the void reasserted itself once more. But the starry backdrop of space was somehow darker than before, a patch of stars missing. Stars do not simply go missing, of course, but they can be obscured.

A black patch of space started moving, slowly at first, but rapidly gaining speed. Whatever systems propelled the sleek black form, they cast no signature on any spectrum the human race could read, though several older races might have detected them. It angled towards the distant globe that was Dal'yth Prime, and speared silently through space towards its destination, two million, three hundred thousand kilometres away.

CHAPTER EIGHT

After taking the bridge over River 992, the Space Marine column pushed rapidly through the ruins of the settlement designated Erinia Beta and was soon fighting its way into Gel'bryn proper. Prior to their entry into the city, the Space Marines had fought amongst the low agri-domes and service habs of the small settlements surrounding Gel'bryn. Now, the true character of tau construction revealed itself as the smoke clouds of burning Erinia Beta parted.

The city was built on a grand scale, yet it was wholly different from the sprawling hives of the Imperium. Gel'bryn had obviously been planned with meticulous precision, its wide thoroughfares and graceful, almost organic structures arrayed according to some grand, unifying scheme. Where humanity's cities continued to grow for centuries, even millennia, buildings often constructed in layer upon layer of rockcrete sediment, the tau built their cities according to need, and built another when that need was exceeded. It was a process of continuous dynamic expansion, but one that could only lead to confrontation with other races as space and resources dwindled.

As the Space Marines pressed on, it became evident that their assault had achieved some measure of surprise. Either the tau had not expected the Space Marines to defeat what forces had defended Erinia Beta, or they had fatally misunderstood the crusade's capabilities and intentions. Much later, Tacticae savants would postulate that it was the presence of the mighty war machines of the Legio Thanataris that caused the initial disintegration of the tau defence, the sight of the huge god-machines striding along the wide streets striking awe and terror into the defenders' alien hearts. The Titans, however, did not move as fast or penetrate as far as the Space Marines, for speed was of the essence. Besides this, the central areas of the city were ill-suited to Titan combat, and the Legio was relegated to a support role, for the time being.

And all the while, Sarik was keeping an eye on the column's rear, hoping he would see evidence of the Imperial Guard's armoured units following on in the Space Marines' wake. So far, there had been none.

The column passed through the wide-open spaces between rearing structures that resembled gargantuan fungus made of the ubiquitous white resin. The buildings were interconnected by walkways hundreds of metres in the air, along which the Space Marines could make out defenders moving hastily to pre-designated strongpoints.

The Space Marines smashed aside all opposition, the column becoming the very tip of the spear blade that plunged into the heart of the tau city. The manner of the defence made it clear that the tau had not expected any enemy to ever penetrate so deep. The lead Predators gunned down lone squads of the enemy's fire warriors. Many were attempting to re-deploy when they were forced to make a desperate last stand, their bodies crushed to pulp beneath the tracks of the Space Marines' armoured vehicles.

Individual tau snipers took position on the high walkways, their pinpoint fire striking a number of the Assault Marines from the sky. One Space Marine, the sergeant of the single tactical squad contributed by the Subjugators Chapter, was shot clean through his helmet's eyepiece while riding in his Rhino's hatch by a sniper at least two kilometres distant. Even as they had raged against the loss of such a valuable warrior, Sarik and his battle-brothers had saluted the enemy's obvious skill at arms.

As the column penetrated the city, pressing ever onwards towards the star port, the enemy's defence became more organised. Where before there was little coordination between defending units, soon the defence took on an altogether different character. Isolated groups of defenders were quickly and efficiently brought into a coherent command and control structure. Some defenders fell back towards more defensible positions, while others provided them with deadly accurate fire support.

But still the Space Marines had the upper hand, for they were able to bypass enemy strongpoints and render them entirely ineffectual. The column was within ten kilometres of its objective when General Gauge's chief of staff came on the vox-net to issue Sarik a warning.

'Be advised, sergeant,' the officer said, the channel interlaced by pops and crackles. 'Fleet augurs have detected a pattern of destroyers moving to and from the star port. Tacticae believes the enemy is ferrying rapid deployment units to defend the objective.'

'My thanks,' Sarik replied. 'What type of units?'

'Unknown at this time, sergeant. But tactical analysis would suggest battle suits.'

'Understood,' Sarik said. 'Interceptors?'

'All but expended neutralising enemy airfields,' the officer replied, sadness evident in his voice. 'The tau air force is now so hard pressed they are forced to use their remaining destroyers to ferry reinforcements to the star port.'

'Well, at least that keeps them off the Titans,' Sarik said. He looked to the column's rear, before asking, 'What word of the Guard?'

There was a pause while the officer consulted his tactical readout, then he came back on the channel. 'Brimlock 2nd Armoured is now across River 992,' the officer said. 'As are the Rakarshan Light Infantry.'

Sarik's brow furrowed at that – how had a tank and a light-role infantry unit crossed at the same time? 'Explain last?' he said.

'The Rakarshans are riding the tanks, sergeant.'

'Lucian?' Sarik said, smiling.

'Indeed, sergeant,' the officer replied. 'By all accounts, Lucian had a few choice words for the rank and file, and he got them moving again. The Dragoon regiments are close behind the 2nd Armoured, and the rest not far behind them.'

Sarik performed a quick calculation, then saw movement amongst the buildings up ahead. 'So we can expect to link up by what, plus eight hours?'

'Give or take thirty minutes, yes, sergeant,' the officer replied. 'Your intention?'

'Enemy inbound,' he said. 'We'll attempt a breakout, and I want it coordinated with the Guard. We'll hold the enemy off until the

2nd and the Rakarshans reach us, then we break out for the star port, regardless.'

'Understood, sergeant,' the officer said. 'Good luck. Out.'

Sarik closed the channel and turned his attentions back to the road up ahead. Two huge structures towered overhead, interconnected by a dozen precarious walkways up and down their length. He tracked along the walkways, left and right, to the points where they joined the towers. There, lurking in the shadows of portals at the end of each walkway, were the now familiar shape of tau battle suits.

'All commands,' he said into the vox. 'Enemy heavy infantry concentration, twelve high. Assume static defensive posture and hold them here.'

Acknowledgements flooded back as the armoured vehicles ground to a halt on the roadway, forming up into a ring with Predators covering every angle and Whirlwinds in the centre. The last voice on the channel was that of Brother Qaja, who was in the troop bay of Sarik's own transport. 'We're holding, brother-sergeant?'

'Aye, brother,' Sarik said as he lowered himself through the hatch, grabbed his bolter and located the heavy weapons specialist in the cramped bay. 'The Guard are delayed, but inbound, and we have a large tau concentration closing from the front. We link up here, and then break out together.' Sarik braced himself against a bulkhead as the Rhino came to a halt, the entire vehicle swinging forwards on its suspension before settling. Qaja nodded his understanding, then bellowed, 'Hatch open! As the hunter in the dawn mist!'

Sarik smiled at Qaja's use of the White Scars battle-cant, for he had barely heard it amongst the mixed Space Marine force. The battle-brother was a highly capable second in command, and the members of Sarik's squad were out and deployed around their transport in double quick time.

Sarik was the last to exit the Rhino, his armoured boots clanging on the ramp as he strode down and stepped on to the white road surface.

The buildings of the tau city reared all around and stretched upwards to dizzying heights far above. The squads were deploying exactly according to his orders. Sarik strode to the centre of the circle as the spearhead's missile tanks raised their boxy launchers ready to engage the enemy. It was relatively unusual, though not unheard of, for such a mixed force to operate together. Sarik had served alongside other Chapters before, most recently the Harbingers Chapter at the Battle of Sour Ridge. But in that action, the white of Sarik's battle-brothers had remained distinct from the deep purple of the Harbingers livery, and their chain of command uninterrupted. Yet here, the White Scars livery co-mingled with the blue of the Ultramarines, the black of the Iron Hands and the Black Templars, the black and yellow of the Scythes of the Emperor, the jade green of the Subjugators, and a handful of other colours. Sarik realised that he found the sight quite inspiring.

Silhouettes appeared on the walkways above and to the fore. Sarik judged he had less than a minute before combat was joined.

'Battle-brothers!' he bellowed.

The warriors, who had taken up defensive positions on and around the laagered vehicles, kept their weapons trained to their front, but turned their heads to heed his words.

'We stand this day, together, united!' Two-dozen bulky silhouettes dropped from the nearest walkway, bright white jets flaring as they descended.

'Our primarchs watch our every deed!' The air was split by a searing blue fusillade of energy bolts as the silhouettes found their range and opened fire on the nearest of the Space Marines. Shots whined in to slam against the armoured glacis plates of Rhinos and Predators. The battle-brothers simply waited, listening for Sarik's order.

'For the primarchs!' Sarik bellowed, raising his boltgun one-handed and tracking the nearest of the dropping battle suits as it neared the ground, its jets flaring to slow its final descent.

'Honoured be their names!' Brother Qaja bellowed.

'Honoured be their names!' three hundred voices repeated as Sarik opened fire. A moment later, the entire force followed suit as more battle suits appeared at the walkways all around and began their descent. A Dreadnought bearing the blue and white of the Novamarines Chapter, mere metres from Sarik, engaged its rotary assault cannon, the multiple barrels spinning faster and faster as it prepared to fire. The cannon raised as the venerated pilot of the ancient suit expertly selected his first target. The weapon locked onto a rapidly-dropping battle suit, and opened fire.

The burst of fire lasted only three seconds, but in that brief period, several hundred rounds were cycled through the six barrels from the huge hopper at its rear. The sound of those rounds leaving the barrel was a continuous, deafening scream. The battle suit was caught in the torso at a range of eighty metres and a height of thirty, and it simply disintegrated before the Space Marines' eyes. One moment the armoured opponent had been descending of jets of white flame, its weapons spitting seething blue balls of energy, and the next it was a rapidly expanding ball of flame and vapour. Tiny chunks of debris rained down on the Space Marines, not one of them larger than a man's thumb so thoroughly was the target destroyed.

From every walkway, scores of battle suits now dropped down on the Space Marines' position. The jade sky was filled with the yellow-tan forms, each spitting round after round of livid blue energy down upon Sarik's warriors. The tau were dropping down all around the laager, unleashing devastating bursts of fire and then taking to the air once more with bursts of their jets. The tactic was designed so that the Space Marines could not concentrate fire on one target before the battle suit was gone, leaping through the air to repeat the process elsewhere. There was no point moving squads around, for to do so would be to fall for the enemy's ploy. Sarik ordered the sergeants to direct the fire of their squads as best they could, concentrating their fire on the targets in their fire arcs with ruthless efficiency.

Meanwhile, Sarik concentrated on the larger picture, reading the ebb and flow of battle and predicting every probing attack the tau made. When a large horde of the olive-green-skinned alien carnivores appeared in one quarter, he ordered the Whirlwinds to open fire. Two-dozen missiles streaked from the launchers atop the tanks on boiling black contrails, sweeping high into the air before plummeting down on the aliens. The resulting explosion engulfed the entire horde, slaying a hundred or more as missile after missile detonated in their midst. When the smoke cleared, the surface of the road the enemy had advanced along was a mass of black craters, several hundred aliens blown to charred meat scattered across the whole area.

When the arcane sensors of the Novamarines Dreadnought detected the presence of tau stealthers working their way around to what they assumed was a weak point, Sarik ordered the column's land speeder squadron forwards from the holding pattern the flyers had been engaged in overhead. The five two-man craft descended on the invisible enemy like predatory razorwings swooping on a defenceless prey, unleashing a solid wall of fire from their assault cannons and heavy bolters. As the smoke cleared and the land speeders climbed back on screaming jets, the now visible remains of at least twenty enemy stealth suits could be seen, scattered across a wide area. The flank of the structure the stealthers had been sneaking around was splattered by great arcs of purple blood.

But the Space Marines were surrounded until the Imperial Guard caught up with them, and casualties were inevitable. The hated tau battle suits carried a fearsome range of weaponry, from rapid-firing burst weapons similar to the Dreadnought's assault cannon, to short-ranged but devastating fusion blasters designed to cut through vehicle armour as if it were not even there. Some carried flame projectors, but these were short-ranged and of limited use against the Space Marines' ceramite power armour, while others used longer-ranged missile systems to fire warheads fully capable of slaying a Space Marine or cracking open a tank with every shot.

The Dreadnought attracted a heavy weight of enemy fire, leading Sarik to the conclusion that the tau had never seen its like and were concentrating upon it out of fear and awe. The mighty war machine shrugged off missile after missile and its intricately engraved sarcophagus was reduced to a mass of smoking scars by round after round of energy weapon fire. Every time a missile exploded against its armour, the iron beast would stride through the smoke to return fire, earning cheers of adoration from Space Marines of every Chapter, not just its own.

Then the Dreadnought shuddered, swaying back and forth for a moment. With a crash like a granite column toppling, it struck the ground, sending up a plume of pulverised resin roadway. The Dreadnought was down, but Sarik mouthed a prayer of thanks that it appeared still intact.

'Overhead!' Brother Qaja yelled, and Sarik looked up to see a line of the heavy battle suits arrayed on the highest walkway. They were the same type the Space Marines had encountered at Hill 3003, their three-metre-long, shoulder-mounted main weapons angled almost straight down towards the Space Marines.

This time, Sarik knew there were no Imperial Navy Thunderbolts on station, and no 1,000 kilogram bombs to be dropped on the heavy battle suits.

'Land speeders,' Sarik ordered. 'Work your way around the heavy suits, but do not get too close.'

As the pilots acknowledged Sarik's order, he opened the channel to the commanders of the Whirlwinds positioned in the centre of the laager. 'How many Hunter missiles do you have?'

There was a pause as the commanders shared load-out manifests, then the answer came back, 'Twenty-eight Hunter missiles, brother-sergeant. But if you mean to use them against–'

'Duly noted,' Sarik interjected. Each of the Whirlwind missile tanks carried a load of anti-air missiles called Hunters, in addition to their regular, anti-personnel ordnance. The Hunters were effective against air targets, but whether or not they would be any use against the heavy battle suits was unknown. There was only one way to find out, and no alternative.

Another of the hyper-velocity projectiles hammered down from above, striking an Iron Hands Predator battle tank square in the commander's hatch. The tank was buttoned up, its commander ensconced within, but the shot penetrated easily. The projectile turned to superheated plasma as it impacted on the armoured hatch, and the jet went straight through the commander, the tank's innards and out through its belly armour. The entire tank seemed to be pushed down as if by an invisible fist, as far as its suspension would allow. Then it sprang back up as its systems reversed the impact, but not before something deep inside detonated. There was a sharp explosion and a fountain of crackling flames erupted from the top hatch. Another three seconds later, the entire tank exploded, shunting sideways the Rhinos on either side, killing three Space Marines outright, and slamming a dozen more to the hard ground as the blast wave overtook them.

A chunk of blazing armour scythed through the air, forcing Sarik to throw himself aside as it passed less than a metre overhead. The projectile was as dangerous as any weapon. It carried on, striking a Black Templars Space Marine from behind and severing both of his legs at the knees. The warrior collapsed to the ground, but even as Sarik watched, retrieved his bolter and continued firing into the mass of enemy battle suits his squad was defending against.

'Whirlwinds!' Sarik bellowed as he pulled himself to his feet. Those heavy suits needed to be shut down, right now. 'Target the suits with Hunters, full spread, now!'

The twin launcher boxes atop each Whirlwind whined as they traversed, elevating almost to their maximum angle. The augur dishes between the boxes tracked their targets, pinpointing coordinates and calculating trajectories. The war spirits in each missile tank communed silently as the firing solutions were communicated and the shots plotted. Then the missiles fired, one after another, until all twenty-eight were streaking upwards on hissing contrails.

The missiles banked and climbed, the machine-spirit in each warhead homing in on its designated target. The heavy battle suits saw their peril as the missiles rose in a wide spread, climbing towards, and then past, the walkway. Sarik saw the battle suits tracking the missiles as they reached their maximum ceiling, some of the tau taking a step backwards on the narrow, rail-less walkway.

Then the missiles dived directly downwards, and slammed into the line of heavy battle suits. As each impacted against its target it unleashed a blinding white burst of light and the suits disappeared in a devastating line of explosions that sent fragments of burned armour shooting off in all directions. The staccato *crump* of the explosions came a second after impact, and rolled out across the artificial valleys of the alien city.

'Land speeders,' Sarik said into the vox-net. 'Close and engage any survivors, now!'

As the grav-attack flyers banked high and dived down upon the smoking walkway, Sarik turned his attentions back to the tau attacking the laager, just in time to see a trio of battle suits closing from the east. A Devastator squad of the Scythes of the Emperor unleashed a fusillade of heavy bolter fire at the fast-moving suits, but the enemy came on regardless, seeking to close the range.

Then Sarik saw why the enemy were prepared to brave the storm of mass-reactive bolt-rounds. All three of them were carrying twinned weapons that Sarik had learned were the tau's equivalent of meltaguns, fusion effect blasters capable of reducing an armoured vehicle to slag in a single shot.

If the battle suits got close enough, they could open a breach in the laager. Sarik would not let that happen.

'Squad!' Sarik called to his battle-brothers. 'With me!'

Sarik limbered his boltgun and drew his chainsword, gunning it to screaming life as he charged towards the Devastators and the Razorback armoured fighting vehicle they were using as a makeshift fortification. The twin lascannon turret on the back of the vehicle spat a double lance of searing white light towards the enemy, striking the lead battle suits full in the torso. But amazingly, the blast, which was amongst the most powerful armour-piercing weapons in the column's arsenal, did not penetrate. At the last possible moment, a bubble of blue energy sprang into being, and the lascannon blasts were absorbed.

As Sarik reached the Devastator squad, he bellowed 'Weapons down! Chainswords and pistols!'

The Devastators obeyed without question, disengaging quick-release weapons couplings and discarding their bulky heavy bolters. Each Devastator carried a bolt pistol as a personal side-arm, for just such a necessity. As the Scythes raised their pistols, Sarik charged past, vaulting over the glacis of the Razorback and pounding towards the battle suits with a feral snarl on his lips.

The nearest of the battle suits raised its twinned fusion blasters towards Sarik as he charged in towards it. The pilot hesitated, the suit actually taking a step backwards. The tau might be inexperienced in the realities of a galaxy at war, but they were fast learners, that much was clear. They were quickly learning to keep the Space Marines at arm's length, though doing so was easier said than done.

The berserk fury descended on Sarik again as he closed the last few metres. The fusion blasters powered up, nucleonic energies pulsating through their vents as they prepared to fire. The blasters zeroed in on Sarik, and he dived forwards as they fired. As he struck the ground, the twinned blasts turned the air above him into a roaring inferno. The heat caused the skin on the back of his head to blister and cook, and the hair of his topknot to melt and sizzle. So immense were the tightly contained energies that he could feel their effects even through his power armour, the war spirit within flooding his system with combat drugs to negate any pain that might otherwise have slowed him down.

As the blast dissipated, Sarik came up with his chainsword in both hands. He was right in front of the battle suit, too close for it to bring its fusion blasters to bear. He bellowed and brought his screaming blade directly upwards, seeking to damage the vulnerable ball joint between leg and pelvis. But as the chainsword swept in, the energy shield activated again, sheathing the battle suit in pulsating blue energies for but a moment, and repulsing Sarik's blade.

Sarik was pushed back by the forces unleashed by the energy shield. He ducked to the left as the battle suit brought its fusion blaster to bear, and as he did so he saw the first of the Devastators closing on another of the suits. Sarik shouted a warning as the other suit raised its twin blasters, but his words were drowned out by the furnace roar of the weapons discharging at close range.

The two blasts converged on the nearest Space Marine, turning his entire body into a seething lava-orange mass. In an instant, his armour was reduced to slag, great gobbets of liquefied ceramite blowing backwards and splattering across the battle-brothers following close behind. In less than a second, the Devastator was gone, nothing but a long smear of rapidly cooling, bubbling liquid marking his passing.

Bolt pistol shots rang out at close range, successive blasts driving the battle suits back one step at a time. Through his rage, Sarik saw that his opponent's jets were powering up, ready to leap into the air and re-deploy nearby, so that he could fire from outside of Sarik's reach. Sarik needed to disable the battle suit so that he would have the time to drive his chainsword through its armour, but the energy shield was making it impossible to find a weak point.

Frustration and anger raging inside him, Sarik made a crude upwards thrust. The energy shield sprang into being again, rebounding the attack, but this time, Sarik saw that the energy was being projected from a small, disc-shaped device mounted at his opponent's shoulder.

Throwing caution to the wind, Sarik sprang forwards, grabbing hold of the battle suit's sensor unit head with one hand while he gunned his chainsword with the other. Bracing himself, he set his armoured boots on the battle suit's thigh panels, and hauled himself forwards to grapple his foe, or otherwise embrace it in a furious death grip. There was no way the pilot could have anticipated such a reckless move, and the energy shield generator activated half a second too late.

Sarik was inside the shield.

Hauling himself onto the battle suit's upper torso, Sarik fought for balance as his weight caused the pilot to all but lose control. The jets fired, but encumbered by the combined weight of the Space Marine and his power armour, the tau could only rise three metres. Sarik roared in utterly incoherent savagery, and forced the sensor block backwards as if it were the head of a living enemy and he was baring its throat to sever its jugular. He brought the chainsword down, its teeth grinding into the armoured joint between head and torso, sending a fountain of sparks arcing upwards into his face as if from an angle grinder. The battle suit crashed back to the ground, the pilot barely able to keep it upright under Sarik's weight. It bent almost double, whether through a deliberate attempt to throw Sarik off or simply as a desperate random reaction the Space Marine could not tell.

The chainsword shrieked, then its monomolecular teeth were through the neck joint's armour and Sarik sheathed his weapon. Using both hands, he tore the head from the torso, and threw it savagely to the ground.

Blinded, the pilot attempted to raise the suit's fusion blaster arms towards his tormentor. Sarik dodged back, his one hand grasping the wound in the torso for purchase while the other alighted on the shield generator. He grabbed the disc-shaped device and yanked it back with all his might at the exact moment that the pilot tried desperately to fire his blaster at the Space Marine, at perilously close range.

The heat blast turned the air to nuclear fire, half a metre from Sarik's face. He turned away, putting his left shoulder plate between his head and the impossible heat. The livery of the entire left side of his armour blistered and was scoured away in a second, leaving only the bare, dull metallic surface beneath, charred and blackened by the fusion blast.

The fire died, but the weapon was cycling up for another burst. Pulling himself up on top of the bucking battle suit, Sarik rolled over the upper surface of the torso and reached downwards to grab the weapon's barrels, one in each hand.

The weapon's systems had shed much of the heat, but it was still impossibly hot. Even through his armoured gauntlets, Sarik felt the flesh of his hands cooking. His power armour pumping ever more palliative elixirs into his system, Sarik strained, hauling the weapons around as the feed chambers peaked at full capacity.

The pilot could not possibly have known Sarik's intentions, and in truth, neither did he, for he was acting on pure instinct, his body flooded with adrenaline and potent combat drugs. The fusion blasters discharged, the furnace-beams enveloping a second battle suit, towards which Sarik had tracked the weapons' barrels.

The other battle suit's energy shield cast a shimmering blue bubble. Sarik bellowed as he held the weapons on target, forcing the fusion beams to burn through the shield. Overwhelmed by the titanic energies, the shield pulsated, before collapsing in upon its projector.

The battle suit's armour withheld the raging sun storm for all of three seconds before the panels peeled back, one laminate at a time, each layer disintegrating into billowing black gas. The instant the armour was gone, the rest of the suit was turned to liquid fire which scattered on the hot winds stirred up in the wake of the devastation.

Finding that his gauntlets were fused to the barrels of the weapons, Sarik hauled with all his strength to tear them free. The battle suit bucked and kicked beneath him, but could not dislodge his bulk. Then one hand tore free, pain flaring until his armour systems administered yet another dose of elixir. Though he could barely feel his free hand, he made a fist and powered it down into the open wound atop the battle suit's torso. It crunched through a layer of internal systems, before striking something soft. The battle suit went immediately limp and as it crashed to the ground, Sarik finally tore his other hand free and rolled clear.

As Sarik braced himself to bound upright and engage the last of the three battle suits, he heard a voice bellow, 'Sarik! Keep down!' Bolt-rounds tore overhead, followed by a missile streaking in from a position further behind. He was barely able to hold his berserker fury in check, the urge to spring to his feet and charge the last enemy almost overcoming the danger of the gun and missile fire.

He rolled sideways, and saw the last battle suit enveloped in a roiling mass of flames and smoke as the missile struck its energy shield and detonated. The shield defeated the missile, but the battle suit's pilot was retreating and was outside of the effective range of its fusion blasters. As the smoke cleared, the suit's back-mounted jets flared to life and it sprang up and backwards in a great bounding leap.

Sarik was overcome with the desire to tear the battle suit's pilot from the infernal machine, and surged to his feet with a snarl on his lips.

'Sarik!' he heard from behind.

He started forwards, his chainsword raised, before his name was called again, this time from closer behind. 'Sarik!'

Something in the voice caused him to pause. It was Brother Qaja, his old friend, who he had known since both had served as scouts in the 10th Company. For a brief moment, he was back on Luther McIntyre with his fellow neophytes. Qaja was wounded and Kholka cornered by the mica dragon...

...Sarik drew his bolt pistol and threw himself forwards, determined to save his fallen brother from the beast's rage. Qaja called his name and tackled him to the ground, pushing him away from the creature's snapping maw. The beast distracted, Kholka darted clear, helping Sarik as he dragged the wounded Qaja from the cave. Only Qaja's shouted intervention had saved him from a fool's death...

Reality crashed back in on Sarik, and he realised he was standing in the open twenty metres beyond the laager. Brother Qaja had hold of his blackened, fused shoulder plate and was dragging him around to face him. Shots whinnied all around and savage explosions rent the air.

Sarik turned and looked his fellow White Scar in the face. For a moment, it was not *Brother* Qaja that stood there before him, his face a latticework of honour scars. It was *Scout* Qaja, his face untouched and unlined.

'Never do that again!' Scout Qaja had said as the three neophytes had cleared the mica dragon's cave.

'You said you would never do that again!' Brother Qaja said angrily. 'There is honour, and then there is foolhardiness... I thought you understood the difference!'

Sarik's rage lifted as his battle-brother's words sank in, and he allowed himself to be pushed towards the laager. The Devastators were falling back in pairs with disciplined precision, one covering the other with his bolt pistol as they fought their way back to the vehicles. A lull seemed to have settled on the scene of the battle, the tau pulling back to regroup after their failed attempt to breach the Space Marines' defences. In less than a minute, Sarik and Qaja were back within the circle of armoured vehicles.

'This time, brother,' Sarik said as he caught his breath. 'This time, I mean it.'

Qaja's face was grim as his dark eyes bored into Sarik's. Then he nodded, and said, 'This time, I believe you. You are master here, you must rein in your battle-lust, but you know that already, I am sure.'

'Aye, brother,' Sarik said, looking around the laager and noting the casualties suffered in the first wave of assaults. 'Too many rely upon me for me to indulge in such things.'

'Not unless you truly have no alternative,' Qaja said. 'I shall say no more on the matter.'

But Sarik was not content with that. 'No, brother,' he said. 'If you need to do so, you must. I shall seek the counsel of the Chaplains later, but in the meantime, you must be my confessor.'

'And if you do not heed my words?' Qaja said, a wry grin creasing his scarred face.

'Then you can strike me down,' Sarik smiled, 'just like you did on Luther McIntyre.'

'I promise it, brother,' Qaja replied. 'I–'

The air shuddered as the Whirlwinds opened fire again, three-dozen missiles streaking overhead to detonate amongst another wave of the savage alien carnivores surging towards the laager. Sarik clapped his battle-brother's shoulder, then bellowed orders as he strode to the nearest squad, ready to man the defences. Qaja hoisted his plasma cannon and checked its power cycle, then followed after his friend and commander.

* * *

'Repeat last, Korvane!' Lucian shouted into the vox-horn, one hand clamping the phones around his head. 'You're breaking up!'

Lucian was hitching a ride in a Chimera belonging to the 2nd Armoured's regimental intelligence cell, and the transport bucked and jolted as it hurtled at top speed along the road to the Gel'bryn star port. The passenger bay was cramped, filled with staff officers working field-cogitation stations and yelling into vox-sets. Lucian could barely hear himself think, let alone what Korvane was saying.

'I said,' Korvane's voice cut through the burbling static, 'I'm going to try to rally the council against the inquisitor. I've got to do something. I can't just stand by and watch him go through with this!'

'I understand, Korvane,' Lucian said. 'But there's nothing the council can do. It's been dissolved, as well you know–'

'Only because he says it has, father,' Korvane interjected. 'And only because the councillors accept his authority.'

'He's an inquisitor, Korvane,' Lucian hissed, trying not to be overheard by the other passengers of the command Chimera. It was practically impossible, but it seemed the staff officers had their own concerns and none were at all bothered with his. 'He can do what he wants.'

'Father,' Korvane said, his tone almost chiding. 'You know as well as I that his authority beyond the Imperium relies on others acknowledging it. His rosette holds no more inherent authority than your warrant, or the council's charter. The council only accepts its dissolution because its members are scared of him.'

'And with good reason, son,' Lucian said. 'You're right; we're all peers out here, but what happens when we get back to Imperial space? If we make an enemy of him, a real enemy, we make an enemy of the entire Inquisition.

'And besides,' Lucian continued, 'he has a damned virus bomb.'

There was a pause, punctuated by popping static and low, churning feedback. Then Korvane answered, 'Father, I'm going to try to stop him. I don't know–'

'You cannot!' Lucian growled. 'Son, you're the sole inheritor of the warrant. There is no second in line!' Not since Brielle had disappeared, presumed dead. There was a third in line, but he was a pampered imbecile, and aside from a few distant cousins Lucian had no desire to see the Clan Arcadius go to anyone but his son on his own death.

'Leave this to me, father,' Korvane replied, his tone resolved. 'I have to do something, and I will. You are needed at the front; I am needed here.'

'Well enough, Korvane,' Lucian said, his words belying what he felt inside. He looked across the command Chimera's transport bay, towards the glowing map displayed on a nearby tacticae-station. The 2nd Armoured was coming up on ten kilometres from the star port, and would soon be linking up with Sarik's Space Marine force. Five other regiments were close behind, and the Deathbringers moving in support. If the combined force could push through the tau and take the star port, Inquisitor Grand might call off his insane plan to virus bomb Dal'yth Prime. If not, Lucian might be able to return to orbit and stop his son getting himself killed.

'Good luck, son,' Lucian signed off. 'Damn fool offspring...'

Brielle held perfectly still as the drone approached, its slowly pulsing, red-lit lens-eye closing on her as she waited in the shadows of the recess off the communications bay. She pressed backwards into the shadows, feeling her way behind her with her left hand while with the other she prepared to unleash the last, precious load of her digital flamer. As she ghosted back, the drone came on – surely, it had not discovered her presence, for it would have raised an alarm had it done so. Perhaps it had just glimpsed movement and was following some pre-programmed imperative to investigate. Or perhaps it had raised a silent alarm, and a squad of armed warriors was rushing to detain her even now.

A small, levered arm unfolded from beneath the drone's disc-shaped body, an unidentified tool clicking at its end. It was less than three meters away, level with the end of the shadowed recess, and still it had not seen her. From her hiding place, Brielle studied the drone, deciding that it must be some low-level maintenance machine, with a correspondingly low level of intelligence or will.

The tool levered out in front of the drone, and touched a piece of wall-mounted machinery. Brielle's eyes followed the movement, and she saw that the drone was more interested in the communications sub-systems lining the recess than in her. In fact, she saw with a small smile, it was straightening up a piece of looped cabling she had disturbed as she had pressed backwards.

A thought struck her. Keeping her eye on the drone's pulsing eye-lens, she stepped backwards still further, the recess becoming all the more narrow and cramped as she penetrated deeper into the communication bay's innards. Her hand behind her tracing the wall, she located another cable run, and took it in her grip. Then she looked around slowly, careful not to make too sudden a movement in case she drew the drone's attention, and found another. She knew enough of the tau script to understand the meaning of the characters stencilled across a junction box the second set of cabling led to: danger.

Last chance, she thought as she flexed the finger on which she wore the concealed flamer. Use the last charge, or take a risk on the cabling. She had never shied away from risk, and would not be starting now.

The hand that gripped the first loop of cabling tightened, and Brielle committed herself. She pulled hard, and yanked the cable from its terminal, darting backwards beyond the second cable's junction box as she did so. A sharp, bright discharge filled the dark recess, and Brielle was blinded for a brief moment. She felt her way along the walls, and crouched down. As her vision returned, she saw that the drone had closed on the damaged cable, its tool-arm re-seating the ripped-free cable even as she watched.

Knowing it was now or never, Brielle reached up and gripped the second cable. This time, she closed her eyes as a bright arc of power leaped from the end. Raising the spitting cable high, she stabbed upwards, and plunged its end into the drone's exposed underbelly.

With a high-pitched, electronic screech that sounded disturbingly organic, the drone's systems erupted in sizzling lightning. Small arcs of power seethed around its body, up and down its levered tool-arm and along the cable it was holding. The drone hovered there, shaking violently as smoke begun to belch from vents around the upper facing of its disc.

It hovered there for another ten seconds, Brielle watching from the very end of the recess. Then it shuddered one last time and exploded, white-hot, razor-sharp fragments of its body scything in all directions. When the smoke cleared, a dozen small fires had sprung into being amongst the systems hidden in the recess, but Brielle was unscathed.

Brielle suppressed a wicked laugh as she realised that the drone's destruction might be the perfect way of crippling the communications bay. Then she heard a hissing sound, and glanced upwards. Some manner of fire suppression system, mounted in the recess's ceiling. It hadn't yet kicked in, but it would, within seconds. She guessed that whatever gas would spring forth would starve the fire of oxygen, hence there would be an in-built, if slim, delay to allow crew the chance to get clear.

Brielle's eyes tracked the pipework emerging from the suppression vent, across the ceiling, down the bulkhead, along, to a junction box three metres away. She crossed to it quickly, intently aware that she might only have seconds before the lethal gases erupted from directly overhead. The box was stencilled with a line of unfamiliar characters... she ripped the front off, and stared into a mess of cables and blinking control studs, three blue, one red.

'Never press the red one...' she said, her fingers hovering over the blue control studs.

The fires were taking hold, and the hissing overhead was increasing as the fire suppression system prepared to pump oxygen-starving gases into the communications bay. She pressed the red one.

The hissing immediately died. She turned, and saw that the fires were now engulfing the recess, and spreading towards her. A small explosion *crumped* from somewhere nearby, followed an instant later by the sound of glass shattering across the floor of the main bay. The damage was spreading faster than even Brielle could have expected.

Time to be somewhere else.

The Space Marine armoured column was once more advancing through the thoroughfares of Gel'bryn City, smashing the tau defence aside as it speared towards its ultimate objective, the star port. As the spearhead advanced deeper into the city, the structures became ever more imposing until the Space Marines and their vehicles were dwarfed by the towering buildings. The tau had disengaged soon after Sarik's slaying of the battle suits, though the sergeant suspected the two events were not connected. More likely, the tau had detected the Brimlock 2nd Armoured moving to link up with the Space Marines and quite sensibly determined they were outnumbered and outmatched.

The instant the tau assaults lessened, Sarik ordered the laagered Space Marine vehicles to assume an attacking formation once more. Within minutes, several hundred Space Marines of a dozen different Chapters were aboard their transports again, which moved out in a long column punctuated by Predator battle tanks, Whirlwind missile tanks and stomping Dreadnoughts. Space Marine assault squads moved forwards in great bounding leaps, guarding the column's flanks against enemy counter-attack. The Assault Marines engaged dozens of the laser-designator-armed spotters, slaughtering the aliens before they could bring indirect missile fire onto the armoured vehicles. The assault squads were by now well-practised in locating the spotters' hiding places, and what mere days ago had been a lethal threat was now expertly countered.

Land speeder squadrons soared overhead on screaming jets, providing Sarik with a continuous reconnaissance of the tau defences further ahead. Several times, the land speeders were intercepted by heavy gun drones. Two speeders were lost in the first engagement, one belonging to the White Scars and one to the Iron Hands, though two of their crew survived, to be rescued by an Ultramarines assault squad and join the ground forces. Later engagements saw the land speeders avoid dogfighting with the heavy gun drones, and call in ground-to-air Hunter missile fire from the Whirlwinds stationed along the length of the column.

The advance was a stop-start affair, for the tau forces were highly mobile and well able to mount localised defences at key points in the city. Sarik soon realised that the tau were either falling back to the star port, or they had guessed that it was the Imperium's objective. As the column pressed on, it encountered hastily mounted defence positions from which the tau would attempt to ambush the Space Marines before falling back in their on-station anti-grav carriers. Sarik's orders were clear – such defences were to be bypassed, and engaged where necessary by the trailing forces of the Imperial Guard. In most cases, the positions were abandoned long before the Imperial Guard reached them, the tau re-deploying to the next ambush point ahead.

As the sky darkened with the approach of evening, the combined advance of the Space Marines, Imperial Guard and Adeptus Titanicus developed into a series of running battles against a seemingly piecemeal defence. While the Space Marines spearheaded a focussed assault, the Imperial Guard spread out onto multiple axes as they pressed on, the better to take advantage of their numbers. Entire regiments of tanks rolled aside any opposition they encountered, though only the heavy battle suits even dared make a concerted stand against such forces. Dragoon regiments moved forward rapidly, armoured fist squads using their Chimera transports as mobile bunkers and fire support bases as they dismounted and cleared enemy-held positions with bayonets fixed. While the Rakarshans rode forwards on the backs of the 2nd Armoured's tanks, other light infantry units followed on foot, using their skills in fieldcraft to move rapidly through the urban terrain.

The Titans of Legio Thanataris split into smaller formations, each moving out to support the advance on its far flanks. The Titans unleashed holy hell on every tau defence point they encountered, flattening structures hundreds of metres tall and striding through the high walkways, causing hundreds of defenders to plummet to their deaths in the streets far below.

With their remaining destroyers committed to ferrying troops to the star port, the tau were unable to oppose the Titans, though they made repeated and numerous attempts to do so. Tau stealth suits launched desperate and often suicidal attacks against the Titans, leaping from high structures in an effort to board the mighty war machines.

Using fusion blasters, the stealthers attempted to cut through the Titans' ceramite armoured shells and disable the systems within. One group swarmed over a Reaver Battle Titan in an attempt to overwhelm its armour and inflict death by a thousand cuts. At first, the Reaver's princeps was dismissive of the threat, determined to ignore the attackers as beneath his notice and deserving of no more than contempt. Only when his Titans' Apocalypse launcher was disabled did he take the threat seriously. His answer to the boarding attempt was to smash his Titan through a nearby building that was taller than his war machine. The entire structure burst apart as the Reaver strode through it, the collapsing debris scouring the stealthers from its body and leaving the Titan coated in a layer of bone-white dust that lent it the aspect of a gargantuan apparition.

Soon after, the Warlord Battle Titan was assaulted by at least sixty tau stealth suits deployed from the bowels of an armoured transport that soared high overhead. The battle suits descended on their target like drop troops onto a bastion, and immediately turned their fusion blasters on the turbo-laser destructors. The Warlord's princeps was not so fast to dismiss the threat, yet his war machine was too tall to repeat the Reaver's act of smashing through a building. Instead, the princeps ordered three nearby Warhound Scout Titans to turn their Vulcan mega-bolters on him.

The Warhounds' princeps were loath to fire on their commander's sacred engine, but were ordered to do so on threat of disciplinary action. The three Warhounds opened fire, and the Warlord's entire upper body was stitched with thousands upon thousands of rapid-firing, mass-reactive explosive shells. Though the Warlord suffered multiple minor systems damage, the enemy attackers were utterly wiped out. Their purple blood was smeared across the Titan's upper hull in garish patterns that would stain its livery for years to come despite the best efforts of legions of artificers.

The battles did not go entirely in the Imperium's favour. Inevitably, some units became separated as the advance penetrated deeper into the city and became encircled and destroyed entirely by rapidly counter-attacking enemy units. One of the 4th Brimlock Dragoons heavy weapons companies was engaged by a wing of extremely agile tau skimmers, their Chimeras outflanked and torn to shreds as the squads attempted to deploy their heavy weapons against a foe they could not get a fix on. The 4th Storm Trooper company turned back from its advance to attempt a link-up with the dragoons, but was outflanked and pinned down by the skimmers. A Warhound Titan was in turn ordered to aid the stormtroopers, but by the time the skimmers were driven off by the war machine's sustained Vulcan mega-bolter fire, the dragoons were all but wiped out.

As nightfall approached, it became evident to the Departmento

Tacticae advisors, on the ground as well as in orbit, that something was awry with the tau's command and control systems. While many individual tau units mounted a competent and disciplined retreat in the face of their enemy, a feat considered amongst the hardest of manoeuvres to accomplish, coordination between the tau units became notably degraded. It was Sarik who noted this phenomenon first, as he witnessed two tau battle suit groups falling back as one. In previous engagements the two groups would have coordinated their retreat, one covering the other as it redeployed so that a constant fire-and-movement was kept up. Before Sarik's very eyes, both groups fled, neither offering the other any fire support. As a consequence, both battle suit groups were cut down as the Space Marines forced their advantage, punishing the tau for their tactical error.

And that error was being repeated all over the front. Sarik communicated his observation to Colonel Armak of the Brimlock 2nd Armoured while the Tacticae ensured it was disseminated to all other commands. Fleet intelligence turned its efforts to uncovering the roots of the degradation, and the elite Codes and Ciphers division under Tacticae-Primaris Kilindini reported that command and control signals between the tau ground forces and off-world contacts had become garbled and weak. It was soon discerned that the tau defending Gel'bryn had been coordinated by a higher command echelon in space nearby. It appeared that the tau's much vaunted and feared technology was turning against them, though none amongst the Tacticae could offer a plausible explanation as to the cause.

As darkness engulfed the city, the battlefield was illuminated by strobing explosions, the glowing contrails of missiles streaking high overhead and a thousand lasguns and boltguns gunning down the tau wherever they were encountered. The only sound audible was that of the engines of the Space Marines' armoured transports and the tanks and carriers of the Imperial Guard. The air was filled with the stink of exhaust fumes, ozone and fyceline. The sky was etched with tracer fire and the flaring jets of hundreds of battle suits and anti-grav transports as they fell back in a long stream towards the star port.

Three hours after nightfall, the advance elements of Sarik's column were within five kilometres of the star port, and the tau's defences appeared to have collapsed entirely. The column paused while Sarik sent his land speeder squadrons forwards to undertake a reconnaissance of the objective. Minutes later, the land speeders reported that the traffic around the star port was now entirely in one direction: outwards. At some point during the closing hours of the day the tau had ceased ferrying reinforcements into the city and were now ferrying those same troops out as fast as the destroyers could carry them. The land speeder crews relayed images of masses of alien troops and machines flooding towards the star port's multiple landing pads. The activity was disciplined, but the intent was clear: the tau were retreating.

The Tacticae advisors passed word to the Commissariat, who approved the dissemination of a simple communication to the troops. Word that the tau were in full flight was welcomed with cheers and celebration, but the morale officers were sure to impress upon the men that there was much fighting yet to be done.

Higher up the chain of command, a debate was set in motion. Some commanders pressed for the advance to continue without delay and the tau to be slaughtered even as they fled. Others counselled that there was scant honour to be earned in slaying a retreating enemy, even the xenos tau who, it was largely accepted, had fought thus far with honour and tenacity.

A brief operational pause set in as high command considered the next phase of Operation Hydra. And all the while, unknown to most of those on the surface of Dal'yth Prime, the countdown to Exterminatus ticked inexorably down to zero...

General Gauge stood calmly in the midst of the controlled chaos that had engulfed his command centre aboard the *Blade of Woe*, his arms folded across his chest. He was the calm at the centre of the storm, his razor-sharp mind the cold focus of the entire invasion of Dal'yth Prime. His expert eye took in the reams of information scrolling across a dozen pict screens. First-hand accounts and tactical updates streamed in from the surface, Tacticae officers rushing to and fro as they collated the data and entered it into cogitation banks. Maps and charts were updated on a minute-by-minute basis, the information becoming obsolete within moments of being entered. Staff officers yelled into vox-horns as they sought clarification from their opposite numbers on the ground, desperately trying to piece together a coherent picture of exactly what was happening as the crusade army advanced.

Gauge glanced to his chron. It was almost an hour since his last vox conversation with Colonel Armak, and it would soon be time for another. He was just about to order his aide-de-camp to patch him through to the colonel when the officer appeared at his side and handed him a data-slate coded for his personal attention.

His eyes narrowing, Gauge entered his personal cipher and scanned the message header. It was from Tacticae-Primaris Kilindini and penned by the man's own hand.

My lord general. My division has traced the enemy's command and control net to a node in high orbit on the far side of Dal'yth Prime. My staff conclude that enemy ground forces are being coordinated via a tight-beam conduit from a high command element off world. Back-trace cogitation reveals that this node has been controlling enemy ground forces for at least twelve hours, but the signal has been steadily degrading. At zero-nine-nine, the signal cut out entirely. My conclusion: enemy operational command and control capacity has been severed and is at this time defunct. Recommend this intelligence be acted upon as best you see fit.

Gauge allowed himself a ghost of a smile as he closed the message and handed the data-slate back to his aide. He checked his chron again, his mind performing a hundred calculations and filtering a thousand possibilities all at once. Inquisitor Grand's deadline would expire before the sun rose over Gel'bryn, and the ground forces were within five kilometres of their objective. They could take it, he knew. If they pushed on, driving the tau ahead of them, they could take it. The enemy would be forced to abandon the star port, and trapped en masse against the sea to the south of Gel'bryn.

'Get me Sarik, Armak and Gerrit,' Gauge said to his aide. 'I want the advance moving again and that star port taken.'

'All commands,' Sarik said into the vox-net as he rode in the cupola of his Rhino. 'Objective in sight. Repeat, star port in sight, five kilometres. Form up on me and advance like your primarchs are watching! Out.'

Sarik's driver gunned the Rhino's engine and the transport gained speed. Sarik's blood was up, but he had finally mastered the raging berserker fury that had consumed him earlier. In fact, he now felt as if that fury had been lurking within him for years, and he had only just acknowledged its toxic presence. He felt as if he had passed through some form of trial, one that he had come perilously close to failing. He had walked the precarious line between control and unfettered rage, and he had seen, with his battle-brother's assistance, how close he had come to stepping over an invisible threshold. The previously hidden delineation was now entirely clear to him, and he knew himself, his limits and his capabilities, as he had never done before. He would harness this newfound realisation, nurture the wisdom he had uncovered, and turn it to the execution of his duty and the pursuance of honour above all things.

Sarik swept his pintle-mounted storm bolter left to right, tracking the buildings on either side of the road that led as straight as an arrow towards the star port. The buildings were growing closer together, and every portal and window harboured deep shadows within which an enemy might be lurking. The Assault Marines bounded alongside the column, ensuring that no tau spotters waited to call in the lethal, indirect-firing missiles that had accounted for so many armoured vehicles, and even a mighty Titan, since the opening of Operation Pluto. No spotters had been encountered for several hours, yet the Assault Marines still carried out their task, for even a single spotter left undiscovered could wreak havoc amongst Sarik's force.

Sarik reviewed his force's disposition as the Rhinos, Razorback, Predators and Whirlwinds advanced. Though many squads of the crusade's Space Marine contingent were engaged in detached duties elsewhere, the bulk of the battle-brothers were under his command. His heart swelled with fierce, martial pride as he watched the column on its final advance towards the objective. The white and red livery of his own Chapter was but a small proportion of the colours displayed by the vehicles of the dozen Chapters, and it was the greatest honour of his service to act as their force commander. Though many had fallen in the advance, untold acts of individual heroism had earned every Chapter represented untold honour. The histories of a dozen Chapters would record the name of Operation Hydra and the Battle of Gel'bryn as a prized battle honour, and the chronicles of the White Scars would recall his own squads' actions for all time.

The lights of the star port were now coming into view. Sarik recalled the surveillance images captured by the fleet's orbital spy-drones, mentally comparing them to what little he could see in the darkness up ahead. He knew that the star port was a sprawling complex of raised landing platforms, each served by a grav-dampener that both cushioned an incoming craft's final approach and aided the launching of outgoing ones. The crusade's Adeptus Mechanicus greatly coveted those generators, for while their construction was known to them, they were eager to learn how the tau had come about knowledge of a technology considered arcane by their order. The star port was lit by intense arc lights that cast their stark illumination upwards into the night sky, creating six square kilometres of bright day in the midst of Dal'yth Prime's night. Control towers speared the sky, warning lights chasing up and down their flanks, and the entire complex was ringed by what the Departmento Tacticae advisors warned were probably automated gun turrets.

Sarik's vox-bead came to life. 'Ancient Mhadax to Sergeant Sarik,' the machine-modulated voice of a Scythes of the Emperor Dreadnought said. Sarik spun the cupola around one-eighty degrees, and saw the hulking walker containing the mortal remains of the celebrated Captain Mhadax striding along two hundred metres behind. To the White Scars, internment in the sarcophagus at the heart of the mighty war machine was anathema, for the Chapter far preferred to let its mortally wounded heroes die, their spirits to return to the wide open steppes of Chogoris, than to keep them alive indefinitely in such a manner. It was always a trial to contain such notions when confronted with Dreadnoughts from other Chapters.

'Sarik,' he replied. 'Speak, honoured one.'

'My prey-sense augurs are detecting movement amongst the structures up ahead, sergeant. Be warned.'

'My thanks, Captain Mhadax,' Sarik said, deliberately using the ancient's rank, though the vast majority of those interred in the iron body of a Dreadnought relinquished their right to command. Sarik was technically Mhadax's commander, but it would be hubris of the worst kind not to accept his words.

'All commands,' Sarik said in the vox. 'Prepare for contact, minus twenty to plus twenty.'

Sarik's driver allowed the Rhino to fall back slightly as two Predators growled forwards, one bearing the black and yellow livery of the Scythes of the Emperor, the other the jade green of the Subjugators. Both trained their heavy weapons on the structures on either side of the road as they pressed on, their commanders riding high in their cupolas so as to spot any sign of movement in the shadows.

'Sarik!' Ancient Mhadax's machine voice cut in urgently. 'Zero-seven high, twenty metres. Beware!'

Sarik spun the cupola round to the position the Dreadnought had indicated, tracking the storm bolter up the side of a tall structure. The barest hint of movement caught his eye and he swung the weapon upwards sharply...

With a blink of muzzle flare, something fired from a shadowed recess high on the side of the rearing structure. An instant later, an energy bolt zipped past Sarik's head, so close it made his scalp sting. The round impacted on the Rhino's rooftop hatch.

'Contact!' Sarik bellowed, but he had no need to issue any more orders, for his force was already reacting. Bolt-rounds were stitching through the air, tracing death across the shadows of the building's flank. Another enemy shot whined past, only missing him because the Rhino had bucked sharply at the last possible instant. This time Sarik caught the exact location of the firer, and zeroed his storm bolter on the shadows.

More energy bolts rained down on the Space Marine vehicles, and Sarik knew that multiple firers were engaging the Space Marines. Settling the storm bolter on the patch of shadow where he knew his assailant to be hiding, he squeezed the trigger and loosed a rapid-fire volley.

The rounds exploded as they plunged into the target's position, the backwash of their detonations casting hellish, strobing illumination on the sniper's nest. A body was flung backwards against the wall behind, then flopped forwards over the edge to plummet the twenty metres to the ground below. Sarik saw instantly that the body was not that of a tau, but of one of the savage alien carnivores he had encountered in the plantations what seemed like a week before.

As the alien's gangly body crunched to the hard surface below, Sarik brought his storm bolter around, seeking other enemies lurking in similar hiding places. The Predators were already passing the building, and slowing slightly. Their sponson-mounted heavy bolters coughed to life as the commander of the Subjugators tank came on the vox-net. 'Brother-sergeant, multiple xenos carnivores ahead. Engaging.'

'Carnivores' was the term by which these savage aliens were becoming known amongst the crusade's army, and it described them well. From his position, Sarik could not yet see the targets of the Predators' fire, but he could well picture the vile creatures as they threw themselves onto the tanks' guns. While he had come to afford the tau with a certain amount of respect and ascribe them something akin to honour, these other aliens were something else entirely. They were possessed of a fearsome degree of fieldcraft, Sarik granted that, but their habit of consuming the flesh of the fallen cast them beyond redemption.

'Kill them, sergeant,' Sarik growled to the Subjugators tank commander. 'Show them no mercy.'

As the Predators' fire redoubled in fury, Sarik opened the channel to address the entire column. 'All commands, heavy contact ahead. All squads dismount to repel enemy infantry, but do not allow yourselves to get bogged down. Out.'

As Sarik's Rhino closed on the two Predators, he got some idea of how many carnivores must be inbound. The tanks' turret autocannons were belching round after round of explosive shells, tracking back and forth as they gunned down the alien horde's front ranks. The heavy bolters mounted on the flanks of each tank were keeping up a constant, thunderous fire, a continuous stream of spent shell casings ejecting from side ports to clatter across the hard white road surface.

Still, Sarik's view of the horde was obscured by the tanks and the fyceline haze thrown up by the heavy weight of weapons fire. 'Brother Kjanghis,' Sarik addressed his driver over the transport's internal vox. 'Halt here.'

'Yes, brother-serg–' the driver began, before a sound like a piledriver hammering into the side of the Rhino cut him off. The Rhino lurched violently under the impact, throwing Sarik forwards in the cupola. A sharp metallic clatter sounded from the right-side track nacelle, and Sarik knew instantly the transport had been struck hard on its tread unit and thrown a track.

As Sarik righted himself, the driver brought the Rhino to a halt, the right-side track unfurling behind and the foremost road wheels grinding into the road surface with an ear-rending squeal.

Sarik dropped down inside the vehicle. 'Brother Jek,' Sarik nodded to one of his warriors waiting in the troop bay. 'Aid Brother Kjanghis with the track. The rest of you, with me.'

The warrior nearest to the Rhino's rear punched a bulkhead-mounted command rune and the rear hatch thumped downwards to form an assault ramp. The squad was out in seconds, Brother Qaja's plasma cannon sweeping left and right as the Space Marines secured the immediate area.

The air roared as a solid round sheathed in blue energy thundered from the smoke up ahead and passed directly through the Space Marines' formation without striking one of them. Sarik traced the shot's trajectory back towards its source, offering a silent prayer as he did so that the huge round had not struck any of his battle-brothers. The round had been of a type the Space Marines had not yet encountered, some kind of solid projectile encased in the seething blue energies fired by many of the tau's weapons.

As the following Rhinos ground to a halt behind Sarik's squad, Space Marines pounding down assault ramps to take position around their vehicles, Sarik waved his warriors forward. He kept his gaze fixed on the arc the projectile had come in from as he ran forwards into the smoke, his battle-brothers close behind.

The squad plunged into drifting banks of stinking smoke, made all-enclosing in the dark night. The thunderous report of the Predators carried weirdly through the dense smog of battle, and the ringing of brass casings pattering across the ground was almost louder than the sound of the weapons firing. Then Sarik heard another sound – a gruff snuffling. A low, birdlike chirrup followed, and the first sound ceased. The bird sound was undoubtedly that of a carnivore, but Sarik could not place the other.

He raised his hand to indicate a cautious advance to contact, allowing Brother Qaja to come level with him. The squad moved forwards with weapons raised to shoulders, spread out with each battle-brother covering a separate arc.

Then a gust of wind ghosted across the scene, and the haze thinned for just a moment. Sarik and Qaja both saw the beast at once as it reared on stumpy hind legs, its apelike forearms raised high overhead.

For an instant, both battle-brothers took the creature for a *rok-chull*, a demonic beast of their home world's most ancient legends. Its body was grossly muscled, its face low between massively humped shoulders. That face was grotesquely akin to that of the alien carnivores, as if the two were but strains of the same xenos genealogy. Its face was dominated by a huge, beak-like mouth, the lower jaw protruding so its jagged edge formed an underbite. Its beady eyes were aglow with dumb malice and it opened its mouth wide as it reared on its hind legs.

As Sarik and Qaja brought their weapons up as one, they saw that the beast had a rider. A single carnivore was clinging onto the creature's back, manning an overlarge, crudely manufactured projectile weapon lashed to the mount's shoulders by strips of cured hide. It was that weapon that had fired the solid round at the Space Marines.

Sarik had no need to issue Qaja the order to fire on the beast with his plasma cannon while he targeted the rider with his boltgun. Qaja's weapon completed its power cycle an instant after Sarik's boltgun spat a full auto burst that thudded a line of rounds into the rider's torso. The alien was torn apart in a welter of gore as the mass-reactive rounds detonated, its arms still flailing as its limp, broken body toppled backwards from its saddle.

A high-pitched whine announced that the war spirit within Qaja's plasma cannon was ready and eager to slay its foes. The weapon's containment coils blazed a livid violet, and then the blunt nose erupted as a concentrated ball of super-heated plasma cascaded forth. The beast was so close it had no chance to avoid the shrieking ball of energy. It was engulfed in seething arcs of raw plasma, its beak gaping wide as it threw its arms out as if in denial of its imminent death, roiling energies spilling across its muscular form.

Then it exploded. The beast was torn apart as the raging power of the heart of a sun transformed the solid matter of its body into another state entirely. Sarik and Qaja were blasted by a wave-front of black ash, all that remained after the hideous transformation. The air was filled with the flash-stink of body fluids turned to super-heated steam and the blast wave scoured away the smoke of battle.

Sarik and Qaja looked to one another in the wake of the explosion. Each saw that the other was a blackened mess, his face streaked with bloody soot. Both warriors' proud white and red livery was almost entirely obscured, and Sarik's armour was blistered and deformed down one side.

'You look like a ghak-sifter, Brother Qaja,' Sarik grinned, his white teeth bright in the midst of his blackened face. 'You're a disgrace.'

'And you look like a midden-herder, Brother-Sergeant Sarik,' Qaja replied. 'If I may be so bold.'

Sarik's brow creased as he considered Qaja's words. 'A midden-herder?'

'Aye, brother-sergeant.'

'Hmm,' Sarik said, as he turned towards the horde of at least a thousand screeching carnivores thundering towards the Space Marines.

'Glad we've got that settled.'

Lucian saw staccato lightning a kilometre up ahead, and lowered his prey-sense goggles to get a better idea what was happening at the head of the advance. He was riding in the turret of the Chimera, the vehicle lurching and jolting so hard he could barely keep the image through the goggles steady.

Activating the goggles, Lucian's world became a grainy, green wash, but he could now see something of the Space Marine column where before all that had been visible was smoke, shadow and muzzle flare. Advanced elements of the 2nd Armoured were pushing through the middle distance, and beyond them, the Space Marines' Rhinos were formed up and stationary, their rear hatches down. The battle-brothers were spreading out and forwards while the column's support vehicles ground to a halt behind the Rhinos.

Guessing that the Space Marines had dismounted to deal with some threat they could not either bypass or smash straight through, Lucian shouted down to the vehicle's commander. 'Slow down! The Space Marines are engaging on foot, we need to give them space.'

The commander nodded, and relayed the information to the company officers of the Brimlock 2nd Armoured. The Brimlock tanks up ahead slewed off the road to either side and ground to a halt, and a moment later, the Chimera that Lucian rode in did the same. Behind, the entire regiment was strung out in a line of tanks, transports and support vehicles three kilometres in length. And that was just the first regiment of nineteen, all of which were pushing hard for the star port at the heart of Gel'bryn.

Tracking his goggles from the view up ahead to the nearest tau buildings, Lucian saw a cluster of luminous blobs moving across the flank of a tall, sail-shaped structure. With a twist of a dial at his temple, he increased the magnification. The side of the building was swarming with long-limbed and nimble figures, scuttling across the surface like insects.

Lucian activated his vox-link at the same moment as he swung the pintle-mounted heavy stubber around. 'Contact right, high.'

The turrets of two dozen nearby tanks and armoured transports swung around to the right in response to Lucian's warning. He squeezed the stubber's trigger plate with his thumbs, thumping off a three second burst that would tell the gunners exactly where the enemy were. Tracers streaked towards the enemy, and Lucian was surprised to see several of the carnivores blown to bloody chunks as his un-aimed fire thundered in. Realising they had been detected, the remainder of the carnivores redoubled their speed as they crossed the surface, jumping down to the ground as soon as they reached a safe height to do so.

Then C Squadron opened fire. Twelve Leman Russ battle tanks fired as one, the flaming discharge from their battle cannons turning night into day. The shells slammed into the side of the building the carnivores had been scaling, blowing out the entire façade in a mass of blossoming explosions. Clouds of pulverised resin swelled upwards, illuminated by raging inner fires, and then the whole face collapsed, burying the aliens beneath tons of debris.

'Contact left!' a tank commander from B Squadron called.

'Contact right!' D's squadron sergeant-major called.

'Movement rear!' B Echelon's commander reported.

* * *

'All units,' the voice of Colonel Armak cut into the channel, his code overriding the transmissions of his subordinates. The colonel's tone was measured and calm, exactly what his men needed at that moment. 'We're surrounded on all quarters by large numbers of xenos carnivores. We can't push forwards until the Space Marines get going again, and I'm sure as hell not going to be the first commander in this regiment's history to order a retreat. All units, prepare to address! Don't stop firing 'til they're right on you, then up and at 'em!

'Good luck.'

'Battlegroup Arcadius,' Lucian said into his command-net once the colonel had finished his address. 'Dismount. Keep well clear of the tanks while they fire, then address as the enemy close. Out.'

Closing the channel, Lucian tracked the heavy weapon back and forth, seeing movement in the darkness. He magnified the view through his goggles, penetrating the thick banks of smoke drifting across the scene. What at first appeared a blurred, undulating mass resolved into the front rank of a thousand-strong horde of alien carnivores. The gangly xenos were bounding forwards in great leaps, their dreadlock-like head spines erect like the hackles of an attack canine. They bore their long, primitive rifles, firing from the hip as they advanced, though not with any accuracy. Their beaks were open wide as they hissed and screeched, their vile war cries filling the air.

'Enemy at three hundred metres!' Lucian called down to the Chimera's crew. 'Prepare to–'

'Father, this is Korvane,' the voice of Lucian's son came over the vox. 'Father, do you receive?'

Settling the heavy stubber's aiming reticule over the front rank of the advancing aliens, Lucian replied, 'Korvane? This isn't a good time. Can it wait?'

'No, father, it cannot!' Korvane replied. There was no mistaking the urgency in his voice. Lucian's son had been raised in the rarefied atmosphere of the high court, and was not given to inappropriate shows of emotion. If he was spooked, there was a damn good reason.

'Go ahead,' Lucian said, as the aliens surged forwards, his fists tightening on the stubber's twin-grips.

'Father,' Korvane continued. 'You have to get off the surface, right now...'

'What?' Lucian said as the vehicles on either side opened fire, their deafening reports drowning out Korvane's voice and flooding the channel with interference. 'Repeat last!'

'I repeat,' said Korvane. 'You must evacuate, now. All of you... everyone!'

'Why?' shouted Lucian over the sound of heavy gunfire. 'Calm down and tell me what's happened.'

There was a pause as Korvane got a grip, then carried on. 'Father, Grand has brought forward the deadline. The Exterminatus is–'

'What?' Lucian cursed. 'And he was going to tell us when...?'

Another pause, before Korvane replied, 'He wasn't, father.'

'Understood, son,' Lucian replied as the alien horde closed and he opened fire with the heavy stubber. The thump of the weapon firing and the bloody ruin it inflicted on the aliens' lanky bodies drowned out the rage rising within him...

A gnarled, scarred hand caressed a sleek, black form, its owner cooing words of power that penetrated the armoured housing and reverberated through the cell-hosts. Death heard those words, and heeded their meaning. A trillion murder-cells quivered with hungry life, as if each and every one tasted the scent of their prey, far below.

The vessel of death, the Exterminatus torpedo, waited, held securely in a cantilevered launch cradle. The hand receded, and the words of power fell silent. Wait... death was told. Wait, and soon you shall feed...

CHAPTER NINE

Brielle pulled the hatch closed behind her, the hiss of the saviour pod's life support systems engaging filling the small space. The sound of alarms and the shouts of emergency response crews receded behind the armoured panel, and everything was suddenly very quiet.

The interior of the pod was sparsely appointed and illuminated with a blue light that Brielle assumed was the equivalent to the low, red glow the Imperium's vessels utilised in similar circumstances. The bulkheads were covered in crash padding, and the deck consisted of an arrangement of ten grav-couches radiating from a central command terminal.

Now what? Brielle stepped over the couches and peered out through a porthole. The glowing orb of Dal'yth Prime filled the circular viewer, the arid surface clearly visible. It was day below, but Brielle knew that the battle at Gel'bryn was currently being fought at night. That meant she was half a world away from where she wanted to be.

She studied the world's surface for a moment, half entranced by the intricate patterns of mountain ranges, coastlines and the sparkling reflections of Dal'yth's star cast from the pristine turquoise oceans. The other half of her mind was committing the world's topography to memory, tracking trajectories and calculating the flight path she would have to take to reach the Imperium's forces at Gel'bryn.

There were so many other risks and variables there was simply no point worrying about them all. What if the pod would only take one path, directly to the surface below? What if it was programmed to make for tau territory? Even if she could control the descent, what if it landed her in the midst of a battle instead of near friendly forces?

She cast all such things from her mind and lowered herself into the nearest grav-couch.

As she settled into the couch, the padding expanded to grip her body, holding her firmly in position. Only her bare feet were left loose, for they were too different from the tau's reverse-jointed lower legs to be accommodated. As she leaned back, giving in to the unfamiliar loss of freedom of movement, a command terminal lit up on the bulkhead above her. Its screen displayed a single, flashing word in the angular tau script.

She struggled to decipher the text, recalling the lessons Aura had conducted weeks ago as she had been transported across the Damocles Gulf. Tree? No, that made no sense. Nostril? Come on, concentrate... Propel, perhaps... Launch!

But she did not want to launch, not yet at least. She wanted to enter a flight plan, to ensure the saviour pod took her where she wanted to go. If it took her to the surface by the most direct route, she would be dumped in the middle of the desert, to be picked up by the tau, or starve to death in the arid wastes. She hated arid wastes. They played havoc on the pores.

There must be some way to...

A voice outside the hatch, raised in question.

Brielle's breath caught in her throat. She was trapped in the grav-couch, barely even able to move her head. She looked down the length of her body to the access hatch, and heard the voice again. What she had taken for a question was in fact a statement. Something like... 'Safe to come out.'

Whoever was out there, he thought that Brielle was a tau crewman who had fled to the saviour pod at the sound of the alarms, assuming the fire raging through the communications bay would engulf the entire deck, perhaps the entire ship, and necessitate escape.

The voice came again, this time more insistent. She was being *ordered* out of the pod.

She looked back to the blinking text on the screen above as a thud sounded against the hatch. Whoever was out there was now pounding on the outside, evidently losing patience. She knew it was only a matter of time before a crewman with the sense or authority to override the lock arrived and dragged her out.

She had no choice. She would have to worry about plotting a course to the crusade's ground forces once she was in transit.

'Launch,' she said out loud, as it occurred to her that there was no lever or command rune to activate to set the pod in motion. The terminal over her head beeped loudly, and the text changed.

Confirm launch order.

So it was voice activated, she realised. Another thud came from the hatch as she struggled to recall the pronunciation of the tau word for 'confirm.' Then she realised that she had said 'launch' in Gothic, and the pod's systems had understood her. Clearly, the tau had extensive knowledge of the Imperium, and had disseminated that knowledge throughout their empire.

'Confirm,' she said.

The blue illumination inside the pod dipped, then came back, assuming a pulsating rhythm. A siren started up as the pod's systems cycled into life, the air pressure change causing her ears to pop.

There was a grinding sound as an unseen launch cradle disengaged, accompanied by suddenly frantic knocking at the hatch. A low, subsonic machine hum started up, rising through the audible range to a high-pitched whine that made the hairs on the back of Brielle's neck stand on end.

With a jolt, the saviour pod propelled itself from the launch tube. The grav-couch enveloped Brielle's body even tighter, pressing in around her so that only the extremities of her legs, torso and arms were visible. Then a dampening field powered up around her, entirely cancelling out any sense of acceleration. The view through the porthole changed as the globe of Dal'yth Prime swung away, to be replaced by the white, cliff-like flank of the *Dal'yth Il'Fannor O'kray*. The now-empty tube that the pod had launched from was revealed as one in a line of dozens, and yet more were visible on every deck of the vessel.

A plume of silent flame, flaring as if in slow motion from a black wound on the warship's side, drew Brielle's attention. She smiled wickedly, proud of her work in wrecking the communications bay. She guessed that the flame was the result of the entire bay being voided, so as to starve the fire of oxygen since she had disarmed the suppression systems.

The pod's manoeuvring jets flared, the hissing sound especially loud in such a small vessel. The tau warship spun around as the pod changed attitude, and Brielle caught sight of a point defence weapons blister nearby. The blister sported a twin-barrelled weapon, which swivelled around to fix on the pod. Brielle's heart almost stopped beating as she fixed on the gun turret, willing it not to fire. Now would be a damn stupid time to die, she thought... Please, don't fire.

It didn't, the weapon lingering on the pod for a moment before tracking back in the opposite direction.

The manoeuvring jets flared again and the pod swung around so that its base, which consisted of one, huge retro jet, was pointing directly towards the planet below.

The terminal above Brielle's head bleeped and the display changed from the tau text, to a graph plotting the craft's insertion, descent and landing. The three stages were shown in simple graphics, each labelled with the time it would take to complete. The chart showed a direct descent, lasting twenty-two minutes from now to landing. The craft would be in position to begin the descent in less than six minutes.

'No you don't...' Brielle said under her breath, another manoeuvring jet firing.

Repeat instruction, the text blinked, superimposed over the trajectory chart.

'What?' Brielle muttered.

Repeat instruction, the text flashed again.

'Erm...' Brielle said, feeling at once foolish and guilty. She had grown accustomed to the tau's use of thinking machines, but actually talking to one dredged up the teachings of the Imperial Creed in no uncertain terms. 'Alter, er... landing point?'

Input new landing point, the screen flashed. A moment later the text was replaced by a flat representation of the surface of Gel'bryn, overlaid with a fine grid. Brielle understood the system straight away, and recognised it as intended for use under the considerable pressures of an emergency evacuation from a stricken spacecraft. She searched her memory for a rough idea of the location of Gel'bryn, and scanned the area where she estimated it would be found. That stretch of the main continent's eastern seaboard contained a dozen cities. She recalled the conversations with Aura, and the scenes she had witnessed in the command centre. It must be the eastern-most of the twelve cities, the one nearest the ocean.

There it was. 'Nine, nine, seven, zero two, er...' she read off Gel'bryn's coordinates from the grid, 'by, er, two, nine, two, five, zero.'

The graphic changed, the flat grid replaced by an image of the globe. A line traced the course from the pod's current position to its interface point, then almost straight downwards towards the surface.

Confirm course change, the text blinked.

'Confirm,' Brielle said, swallowing hard at the finality of the statement. The manoeuvring jets flared again as the saviour pod came around to its new heading. Brielle forced her breathing to a calm rate, and tried to relax her body, but she could not rid herself of the mental image of the vessel being transformed into a streaking meteor as it plunged towards the surface of Dal'yth Prime.

The voyage to the interface point took less than an hour, and Brielle watched through the porthole as the saviour pod crossed directly over the terminator line where day turned into night. Throughout that time she was gripped by a feeling of helplessness; that her life was in the hands of a machine that appeared to be able to think and hold, albeit rudimentary, conversation. She was entranced by the patterns of light glinting from the serene seas far below, and the faint, wispy cloud formations gracefully whirling over them.

Several times throughout the journey to the interface point, the pod's vox system had blurted into life, only to cut out after delivering several seconds of distorted garbage. She had no doubt that the *Dal'yth Il'Fannor O'kray*'s main communications banks would be out of action for quite some time, and guessed that these transmissions were coming from vessels further away, or from less powerful, secondary transceivers on the warship. She could just imagine the confusion and concern the tau must have experienced as the saviour pod cleared the ship. Perhaps they imagined it to contain an over-reacting crewman convinced the ship was crippled. After her failure to make any attempt to reply to the hails, they had probably concluded that the pod had malfunctioned and been fired in error, and would just let it slip away. After all, they had far more pressing concerns.

The pod had been over Dal'yth Prime's dark side for twenty minutes when its manoeuvring jets fired for the last time. The view through the porthole shifted, the world gliding out of view to be replaced with the star-speckled blackness of the void. The pod's interior lighting dimmed, then started to pulsate as it had when it had first launched from the *Dal'yth Il'Fannor O'kray*. Brielle looked straight up at the pict screen, and guessed that the descent to the surface was due to begin.

Again, that feeling of utter helplessness came over her. She had made planetfall countless times, but always, she had been in command. Although she had only rudimentary piloting skills and was no drop-ace, she had always been in charge. The pilot of whichever vessel she had rode had invariably been her servant, and that, she realised, was the root of her unease. She hated not having someone she trusted to rely upon, or if it came to it, boss around.

As the saviour pod began its descent, Brielle realised that she did have someone to rely on. She closed her eyes, not wishing to watch the blinking icon on the screen above her as it rode the trajectory line in a hell-dive to the surface of Dal'yth Prime. Someone very far away. Forty? Fifty thousand light years? Certainly, half a galaxy at least...

'Imperator,' she began, sacred words she had not spoken in years coming unbidden to her lips as a shudder ran through the pod. 'From the cold of the void, we beseech your protection. From the fire of re-entry, we implore you to shield us, from the...'

The saviour pod began its dive, surrendering to the inexorable pull of gravity. For the first few minutes, not a lot seemed to happen, but Brielle could feel the slow build-up of gaseous friction on the outside of the pod. Then she realised she was sweating, and not from the tension of her situation. The temperature inside the pod was rising, even with the life support systems cycling at full power. A foolish notion appeared in her head: what if the tau's biology was more resistant to the trauma of re-entry than a human's, and the pod's tolerances designed with that in mind? Nonsense, she told herself. Those of the air caste might be more comfortable in zero-g, while tau of the earth caste were better suited to hard work, but the pod would have to accommodate them all.

A fluttering tremble passing through the hull cast the thought from Brielle's mind. She looked towards the porthole, and saw ghostly flame dancing across the black void beyond. In any other circumstance the effect would be quite entrancing, she thought, but being strapped into a lump of alien tech plummeting at Emperor-knew-what speed through the sky above a warzone took the edge off it.

Another tremble, and the whole pod started to vibrate. The craft was entering Dal'yth Prime's upper atmosphere. While still incredibly thin, the air was still dense enough to cause friction on the pod's outer hull, though the energy shield projected below was absorbing the majority of it. The Imperium's military drop-pods and emergency saviour pods were only rarely fitted with such a feature, the utilitarian planners regarding it as a luxury in most cases. By all accounts, planetfall in one of those junk buckets was almost as dangerous as taking your chances on a burning assault ship.

Despite the energy shield protecting the pod from the worst of the turbulence, the whole interior was shaking. The effect increased to a violently quaking crescendo as the pod neared terminal velocity and the heat in the interior rose still further. Brielle squeezed her eyes tightly shut, wishing only that she could free her arms to clamp her hands over her ears to deaden the screaming rush of burning air consuming the pod.

Then, the pod's retro thruster kicked in. The grav-couch cushioned the worst of the violent arrest in downward momentum, but every cell in Brielle's body felt as if it were being squeezed, flattened and compressed, all at once. Brielle felt at that moment that the pod really was a small compartment bolted onto a huge jet thruster, which belched and roared just below her supine form. She could feel the incredible energies being unleashed in that terminal burn, and abandoned herself to them.

Quite suddenly, the roaring inferno that had raged outside was replaced by a shrill whistling. Brielle opened her eyes and looked towards the porthole. The view outside was of the dark-jade, night-time skies of Dal'yth Prime.

In the last few minutes of the descent, the manoeuvring jets kicked in one final time, and the pod altered attitude. The stars swung upwards and the distant horizon hove into view. An anti-grav generator powered up, guiding the pod towards its final crashdown.

According to Imperial Navy doctrine, as well as sound military principle, a fleet undertaking offensive operations should maintain an extensive counter-penetration defence screen. A network of picket vessels, of every displacement from interceptor to frigate, should provide three hundred and sixty degree, three-dimensional surveillance before, during and after any engagement. The fleet of the Damocles Gulf Crusade was not particularly large by naval standards, especially given its losses at Pra'yen, and its carrier capacity was woefully short, but nonetheless, no enemy vessel should have been able to get within five thousand kilometres of its flagship, the *Blade of Woe*.

Thus, it was something of a surprise when Admiral Jellaqua's vessel was hailed by an unknown vessel from less than a thousand kilometres away, and well within its picket screen.

'*Blade of Woe*,' the unknown sender said, his voice relayed through the vox-horns on Jellaqua's bridge. 'This is theta-zero. Requesting immediate dock, over.'

'Who the *hell* is it?' Jellaqua scowled at none of his bridge officers in particular. 'Who the hell *dares*...?'

'Augur scan collating now, admiral,' a crewman called out. Jellaqua crossed to the station, his eyes scanning the reams of scan data scrolling across the flickering pict screen.

'Run it again,' Jellaqua said. 'That makes no sense. Run it again.'

'Erm, admiral,' the officer stammered. 'I have, sir. This is the third run. Whatever that vessel is, it matches nothing in the registry.'

Jellaqua turned from the augur station and crossed to the comms station, half a dozen aides trailing in his wake. 'Well?'

Jellaqua's Master of Signals was as much machine as he was man, a dozen snaking cables running from grafted terminals in his cranium to the cogitation array in front of him. The Master of Signals nodded, as if listening to something very far away, before replying. 'A sub-carrier wave, admiral.'

'What seal?' Jellaqua said, guessing the answer before it came.

'Magenta, my lord.'

'Confirm docking and alert all commands,' Jellaqua said, two-dozen staff officers rushing off to enact his orders as others started yelling into vox-horns. 'Prepare to receive Inquisition boarders.'

The light infantry companies of Battlegroup Arcadius were advancing on foot through the streets of Gel'bryn, and Lucian could see the lights of the star port visible mere kilometres ahead. The tau were disengaging across the entire city, the last of their units falling back on the star port to be evacuated by huge, wallowing transports. The tau were still mounting a defence, but it was poorly coordinated and piecemeal, and the crusade armies were pushing them back on every front. By all accounts, the enemy's command and control network had completely collapsed, and the tau leaders on the ground had proven ill-prepared to adapt. Lucian had no idea what had caused the collapse, and Gauge had claimed that it was none of the crusade's doing. Whatever had caused it, Lucian and the other commanders gave silent thanks for this one nugget of good fortune.

It seemed to Lucian now that the tau were suddenly the lesser of two enemies, and that it might be Inquisitor Grand that defeated the entire undertaking.

The last hour had seen the tempo of Operation Hydra attain a new urgency, which Lucian impressed upon his subordinates as the other regimental commanders did on their own. Unlike the vast multitudes of the rank and file, the commanders knew the reason for the sudden haste. An operation that had previously been allowed an extremely tight twenty-four-hour window to achieve its objective now found even that deadline brought forward. The problem was, not even General Gauge knew exactly when that deadline would expire.

Lucian seethed inwardly as he moved along the street. The elite patrols platoon of the Rakarshan Rifles were ranging ahead of him, while two rifle platoons was close behind. What the hell was Grand playing at? The inquisitor's initial threat to enact Exterminatus within twenty-four hours had been extreme enough, but the remnants of the crusader council had thought themselves able to call Grand's bluff and make the devastation of the entire world unnecessary. Lucian was coming to suspect that Inquisitor Grand had intended to bring the Exterminatus forward all along, and Lucian and his allies had played right into his hands in pushing towards the star port, well beyond their capability to return to Sector Zero and evacuate.

'Warp take him...' Lucian cursed, for the tenth time in as many minutes. The madman was prepared to slaughter thousands upon thousands of Imperial Guard and several hundred Space Marines just to prove a point...

'Excuse me, sir?' Lucian's signalman said from close behind as a barrage fired by a troop of Manticore missile tanks streaked through the night sky overhead.

'Nothing, son,' Lucian growled, bitterness rising inside as he recalled his actual son, and the risks he had taken to discover and communicate the fact that Grand had brought forward the Exterminatus order. The Manticore barrage walloped into a tau position a kilometre distant, setting off a staccato burst of secondary explosions that lit the edge of the star port with a hellish orange glow.

Lucian was torn, his duty to the crusade conflicting violently with his duty to his dynasty. He could leave within the hour, he knew, by calling a lander from the *Oceanid* to return him to the fleet. He could confront Grand and ensure his son's safety, though he suspected doing so might cost him his life. But to abandon his duty now, as his battle group closed on the objective it had fought and bled so hard to capture, would be the act of a self-serving coward.

No, Lucian knew that the only course of action open to him was to lead Battlegroup Arcadius forward in glory, and take that cursed star port as soon as possible. Korvane would have to do what he could, as would General Gauge and his staff, though that was precious little. As dire as his own predicament seemed, Lucian did not envy Gauge. The general was faced with an apparently insane inquisitor, an individual who wielded authority to all intents and purposes equal to that of the High Lords of Terra themselves, as well as the pressing need to win a major victory and evacuate tens of thousands of troops.

'Sir?' the signalman said again.

'Nothing,' Lucian repeated, distracted by his train of thought and not really paying attention to his surroundings.

'Sir!' the man said, the urgency of his tone snapping Lucian back to the here and now. The signalman was pointing up ahead, and Lucian slowed as he followed the gesture. Patrols platoon had disappeared, and the street was empty.

No, it was far from empty. The elite scouts and trackers of patrols platoon had simply melted into the shadows on either side of the wide street, and that could only mean trouble.

'Tell the column to stand by,' Lucian said, and the signalman passed the order along.

Cautiously, Lucian advanced along the street, lowering his prey-sense goggles to pierce the smoke and darkness beyond patrols platoon. Whatever the scouts had spotted, he could not yet see it, but his goggles would detect what even the elite trackers could not see.

Lowering the brass headset over his eyes, Lucian tuned the viewfinder. The smoke appeared to lift like a morning mist dispelled by the rising sun, revealing a group of boxy vehicles at the far end of the street. After a moment, Lucian realised that the vehicles were Space Marine Whirlwind missile tanks, and that his battlegroup had almost caught up with Sarik's spearhead. Lucian knew that the Rakarshans would have to slow their advance so that the two groups did not become mixed up, frustrating given the haste to reach the star port, but that could not have been why patrols platoon had gone firm.

'Signals,' Lucian hissed, waving the adjutant to his side while keeping his gaze fixed upon the vehicles up ahead. He heard the signalman speaking low into his vox-horn, and the hushed, distorted chatter of return traffic. Then he saw...

'Carnivores, sir,' the signalman reported, passing on the report from the Rakarshan captain leading patrols platoon. 'They're just about to–'

'I see them,' Lucian hissed, not taking his eye off the dark shadow moving towards the rearmost of the Space Marine vehicles.

Then the boxy twin-launchers atop that vehicle angled upwards on whining servos, and a flaring jet of flame belched from the rear vents. A missile spat outwards from one of the launchers, and the scene at the end of the street was fully illuminated in the sudden flare.

Something big was moving towards the Whirlwind, something so large the carnivores around it seemed little more than scuttling vermin. It was some type of beast, its long body supported on massive hind legs. Its front legs were little more than vestigial claws, while its head was dominated by a jagged-edged beak and quills sprouting from the crown. As the light cast by the missile guttered away, Lucian saw that the beast carried some form of oversized howdah or saddle, and that two or three more carnivores were mounted on its back, manning some kind of primitive, crossbow-like heavy weapon.

'Get some tubes forward,' Lucian ordered, then activated his own vox-link, cycling through the channels until he found the one reserved for the Space Marine commanders. Ordinarily, the channel would be locked out to anyone other than the Adeptus Astartes, but Lucian had friends in high places. The channel burst to life, curt orders cutting back and forth as squad sergeants called targets and coordinated fire and movement between their units. He waited for an opportunity to cut in, but the beast was closing on the Whirlwind too fast to stand on ceremony.

'Rearmost Astartes Whirlwind,' Lucian said. 'This is an urgent transmission, over.'

The voices went silent, the tinny sound of gunfire bleeding in. 'Last sender, identify yourself,' a gruff voice said.

'Stand down, Sergeant Rheq,' the familiar voice of Sergeant Sarik came over the channel. 'Make it quick, Lucian.'

'Carnivores closing on your rearmost launcher. And they have something big,' he said. 'I'm moving up anti-tank, so I suggest you get your vehicles clear.'

'Understood, Lucian,' Sarik replied. 'My thanks. Out.'

As Lucian closed the link, three two-man missile launcher teams came level with him, one man in each carrying the shoulder-fired tube while the other bore a case of three reloads. Sergeant-Major Havil followed in their wake, his long-hafted power axe slung over his shoulder. Havil immediately set about bullying the missile launcher teams into setting up their tubes in double time, and soon they were ready to fire.

Meanwhile, the Whirlwinds' engines were gunning to life, thick smoke belching from their side-mounted exhausts. Lucian saw the carnivores react, halting as they crept forwards, their primitive, spiked rifles raised. The beast was reined in, its vile face glowering at the source of the sound.

Yet, while Lucian could see the scene clearly thanks to the arcane systems of his prey-sense goggles, the smoke was obscuring it entirely from the missile launcher teams.

The carnivores were gesturing towards the nearest Whirlwind as it juddered forwards. The heavy weapon on the back of the huge beast was turning around to engage the missile tank from almost point-blank range. Even such a primitive weapon could cause damage at close enough range, especially against the tank's rear armour.

Realising the beast-mounted weapon was about to open fire, Lucian made up his mind. He rushed towards the nearest of Sergeant-Major Havil's missile-launcher teams, and grabbed the tube from the grip of the stunned Rakarshan. The man was about to voice a protest, when Havil thumped the non-lethal end of his power axe into the back of his head. The Rakarshan hefted the weapon from his shoulder and passed it to Lucian.

Raising the tube to his shoulder, Lucian realised that he would not be able to sight using the weapon's onboard system, for it could not penetrate the smoke. Steadying the tube with his right hand, he used his left to pull a cord from his goggles, which he jacked into a port on the side of the launcher's sighting unit. Lucian prayed that the war spirits within the two devices would achieve communion, and not reject one another as often happened. A moment later the vision through his goggles was overlaid with the launcher's targeting reticule, the two devices operating as one.

His thumb closing on the firing stud, Lucian took a moment to still himself, breathing out as the reticule settled on the beast. He played the aim across its body, rejecting the sure kill, but possible miss of a headshot for a sure hit, but less likely kill, body shot.

'Clear!' Lucian called, issuing one last warning to anyone behind him that he was about to fire.

'Clear!' he heard Sergeant-Major Havil confirm.

He pressed the firing stud, and the missile streaked from the tube. The backblast blew hot, sharp-smelling gases into his face, before the main charge ignited ten metres out and propelled the missile along the length of the street and into the smoke.

The missile struck the huge beast square in the howdah, exploding the heavy weapon which had been preparing to fire on the Whirlwind. The two carnivores manning the weapon were enveloped in a white flash, leaving only their legs, fused to the wreckage on the beast's back.

'Missed,' Lucian spat. 'Reload!' he said to the Rakarshan beside him.

'No need, my lord,' Sergeant-Major Havil said, a broad grin splitting his black-bearded face.

Lucian lifted his goggles to see that the missile's explosion had blown away the smoke at the end of the street, exposing the carnivores to the Rakarshan's view. Though Lucian's missile had not struck the huge beast square as he had hoped, in winging it and killing its riders he had caused it to go berserk. The beast was enraged, lashing out with its beaked head and stomping the ground hard with its huge, taloned feet.

The beast spun around as the carnivores scattered. Several were too slow. One was bitten in half at the waist by the beast's snapping, razor-edged beak while another was pounded flat by a crushing foot. Some of the carnivores dashed into side streets, but the majority backed off along the main thoroughfare, towards Lucian's force.

Seeing his opportunity, Lucian stood, and bellowed, 'Rakarshans, address!'

Then he realised the Rakarshans probably had no idea what 'address' meant. He turned to the sergeant-major, who was still grinning. The whip-crack ripple of coordinated section fire sounded from patrols platoon's position, and the street lit up with white, strobing light.

Dozens of carnivores were cut down as the veteran riflemen of patrols platoon rose up from their concealment, unleashing rapid-fire death on the foe. The enemy were caught in the open and in the crossfire of the two halves of the platoon, one on either side of the street. Gangly bodies danced and spun as las-rounds lanced into them, and within seconds the ground was littered with smoking, twitching, alien bodies. The Rakarshans had a debt of honour to settle, and the carnivores had much more to pay.

The enraged beast roared, its savage face whipping left and right so fast its head-quills rattled loudly. The Rakarshans held their fire, knowing that to shoot the beast would probably draw a charge. Then it roared again, and stomped off down a side street, the pounding of its heavy tread receding into the distance.

'Get patrols platoon forward, sergeant-major,' Lucian ordered, passing the missile launcher back to its original owner. 'Secure the area, but let the Adeptus Astartes press forwards.'

'Understood, my lord,' Havil replied, before striding off down the street to pass Lucian's orders to the captain in charge of patrols platoon.

Lucian looked up into the night sky as Rakarshans dashed past. The eastern horizon was touched by the merest hint of green, the first visible sign of the coming dawn. Hardly believing that the night had almost passed, Lucian checked his chron, and cursed. Time was running out.

A fiery light streaked overhead, another missile barrage, Lucian assumed. He glanced up, but saw that the light was travelling north-east to south-west, so could not have been a missile fired from the Imperial Guard's lines.

The light passed almost directly overhead, casting a flickering luminescence over the scene, and Lucian saw that it was not a missile, but a small craft making a controlled crashdown following planetfall. The air beneath the craft seethed with burning atmosphere, the heat absorbed and simultaneously shed by an energy shield projected below it.

No Imperial lander that Lucian knew to be in orbit employed such a device.

The object disappeared from view as it sped past one of the city's hundred-metre-tall structures. The sky flashed white behind the tower, and the sound of the craft's violent crashdown rolled down the street. Whatever it was, the battle group would be passing it soon.

Seeing that the path ahead was secured and the rearmost

vehicles of the Space Marine column had ground ahead and were out of sight, Lucian looked around for his executive officer.

'Major Subad!' he called.

A moment later, Subad was running towards him from further down the street. 'My lord?' he said as he came to a halt and saluted.

'Get the companies moving, major,' Lucian said. 'The objective is in sight.'

CHAPTER TEN

Sarik pulled his shrieking, gore-streaked chainsword from the broken torso of the barbarous alien carnivore, and brought it up into a guard position as he sought another opponent. The only enemy left were the dead and the dying, the Space Marines pushing forwards with boltguns raised as they secured the area.

A muffled *thump-crack* rang out as a battle-brother put a bolt pistol shell through a wounded alien's head.

'Clear!' Brother Qaja shouted, and a dozen similar acknowledgments flooded over the command net.

'Transports forward,' Sarik ordered, the roar of several dozen engines revving to life sounding from behind as his order was enacted. The Space Marines had reached a junction, and the outer limits of the Gel'bryn star port lay around the next turn in the road. The ground was strewn with the spilled blood and severed limbs of the alien carnivores, which crunched and split under Sarik's armoured tread as he walked forwards towards the corner.

The aliens had fought like nightmarish creatures from Chogoran legend, though why, Sarik could not tell. The tau themselves had almost entirely evacuated the city, and none had been reported for an hour at least. It seemed that the tau had deployed the carnivores as a rearguard, but one that they must have regarded as expendable given the imminent fall of Gel'bryn and its star port. Perhaps the carnivores were bound to the tau by some unknown blood oath. Perhaps they had simply been paid so handsomely they considered the nigh suicidal defence worth attempting. All that really mattered was that they were xenos, and their mindset quite literally alien.

Sarik cast such thoughts from his mind as he approached the turn. He skirted the wall of one of the massive tau buildings, and as he came to the corner, edged around to get his first look at the star port complex.

A huge, flat expanse of ground formed the bulk of the star port, with numerous circular pads raised on fluted stilts providing the launch terminals. Control and sensor towers soared high overhead, and arc lights shone down from others, bathing the whole scene in a cold, white light. The nearest of the landing pads, a mere three hundred metres from Sarik, was the scene of bustling activity as tau ground crew rushed to and fro in preparation for a fat, vaguely ovoid lander with four huge thruster units swivelled downwards and spitting a backwash of flame. As the lander neared the pad, its engines cut out, and Sarik thought for a moment its systems had failed. But no, the vessel had been caught in the anti-grav sheath projected by the pad's systems, and was being carried safely downwards towards its docking station.

As the lander came in, Sarik saw a stream of tau warriors emerge from a structure near the landing pad's base, and make their way across the dry ground, towards the elevators inside the structure's supports. These must be the very last of the tau, Sarik thought; the last shuttle out of Gel'bryn.

A squadron of sleek tau flyers rose from a landing pad further away, and moved in towards the lander, assuming an overwatch formation, hovering as their multiple-barrelled heavy weapons scanned the star port's edges. That changed things, Sarik thought. While he might have been prepared to let the lander go unharmed, the presence of the heavily armed escorts made it a matter of military necessity to engage it. The star port had to be captured without delay, and the enemy flyers were an obstacle to be overcome.

'Your orders, brother-sergeant?' Qaja said as he appeared at Sarik's side.

Sarik thought a moment, a plan forming in his mind. His gaze tracked downwards from the rearing landing pad, and across the flat expanse of the complex. The entire area was ringed with a line of low bunkers, and behind them a ring of shield projectors, exactly the same as the one his force had broken through at the very beginning of Operation Pluto.

'No delay,' Sarik told Brother Qaja. 'Grand's deadline may already have passed, so this finishes, now.'

'Agreed, brother-sergeant,' said Qaja. Sarik had no need of his agreement, but he valued Qaja's opinion nonetheless.

'Those bunkers appear to be configured for anti-personnel work.' Qaja nodded his confirmation as he studied the bunkers' low gunports, seeing the multiple-barrelled cannons pointing out threateningly. 'We advance on foot behind the Predators and Rhinos, then use krak and melta on the shield projectors beyond,' Sarik continued. 'After that, we take the landing pad. The enemy surrender, or they die.'

'More likely they die,' said Qaja. 'None of them have surrendered yet.'

'We haven't yet given them the chance, brother,' said Sarik.

'Understood,' said Qaja, understanding well that Sarik was referring as much to his own previous losses of control as to the breakneck speed of the advance. 'I'll pass the order along. Ten minutes?'

Sarik smiled grimly as he took one last look at the line of bunkers. 'Ten minutes.'

The instant the Predators and Rhinos moved out, the bunkers opened fire. Twinned cannons spat an incandescent rain of energy bolts from the dozen or so bunkers that had the range and arc to target the Space Marines, hammering the frontal armour plates of the vehicles. Even as dawn edged the horizon a deep jade, the air was lit by livid blue pulses that chased the shadows from the streets.

Sarik had deployed his lascannon-equipped Predator battle tanks and Razorback armoured transports to the head of the formation. Six tanks from four different Chapters ground forwards across the open ground leading to the bunker line, Rhinos fanning out on either side. Energy rounds spat across the two hundred metres between the bunkers and the tanks in constant streams, every round as bright as a tracer, washing back and forth across the tanks. Where the energy rounds struck, they produced a dull wallop and gouged out a lump of armour the size of a clenched fist, but none could penetrate the tanks' forward plates.

The tanks moved at a stately pace, cautious not to advance too rapidly for Sarik's squads were following on foot. While Sarik judged the tanks to be all but impervious to the bunkers' fire, he was less certain about the power armour his warriors wore. What the energy bolts lacked in armour penetration capability, they more than made up for in raw ballistic force, meaning they could wreck a Space Marine's armour systems and cripple the warrior even without cracking open his protective suit.

Striding along behind the lead Predator, Sarik rued the fact that the crusade's Terminators were being held in strategic reserve. All of the heavy-armoured veterans belonged to the Iron Hands Chapter, and Captain Rumann had made it quite clear they were being held back for boarding actions should the fleet find itself engaged in orbit. Sarik conceded that he would have done the same thing, though a squad or two of Terminators teleporting into the bunker line would have made the current advance unnecessary.

'Fifty metres!' Brother Qaja called out over the roar of the tanks.

'Proceed,' Sarik said into the command-net.

Every armoured vehicle that was armed with a lascannon opened fire on its prearranged target. Searing white lances of focussed energy speared the air, slamming into the bunkers and blowing three to atoms within seconds. The weight of fire immediately lessened, but the remaining bunkers swung their fire across to the tanks that had fired, hundreds of energy rounds scything into them with relentless ferocity.

The tanks ground on, their frontal armour plates soon transformed into cratered slabs of smoking ceramite by the constant fusillade. One Predator, the *Executioner* of the Scythes of the Emperor Chapter, sustained three successive shots to the armour plate immediately fore of the driver's station, and a fourth shattered the whole glacis. The round passed through the wrecked armour and struck the driver a glancing blow to his left shoulder, rendering the arm limp and useless. Despite his wound, the stoic driver continued with his duty, keeping the *Executioner* steady while its commander directed round after round of lascannon fire, taking revenge on the enemy in lethal fashion.

As the vehicles closed on the bunker line, a clear breach was opened where three ruined structures smoked and spat fire into the dawn air.

'Squads forward!' Sarik bellowed. He had no need to use the vox-link for the Space Marines were pressed in behind the armoured vehicles, ready to move forwards and smash aside any resistance that still stood.

Squads deployed in pairs, one group using their boltguns to cover the other as it rushed forwards to storm the bunkers with bolt pistols and grenades. Sarik drew his chainsword with one hand, and took up a melta bomb in the other. While Qaja and the rest of his squad covered him, Sarik joined an Ultramarines assault squad deploying on foot rather than by jump pack, and joined the charge.

As he stepped out from behind the cover of a Rhino, Sarik located the nearest operational bunker and gestured for the assault squad to follow him towards it. The bunker was low and dome-shaped, with the twinned energy burst weapons sweeping left and right from the fire port. The Space Marines came in at the extreme edge of the bunker's firing arc, but still the gunner saw them, sweeping his fire in a wide fan that pulverised the ground and sent up fountains of dust. The charge took only seconds, though Sarik was intensely aware of every single energy bolt as it buzzed through the air towards him and his warriors. Seething blue points of strobing light passed by, etching a trail of vapour where they passed. One bolt struck an Assault Marine square in the chest, gouging a deep wound, its edges flickering blue as the warrior went down. Sarik knew instantly the Ultramarine would fight again.

Seconds before Sarik reached the bunker a final burst of defensive fire spat directly towards him, and he dived to one side. The Assault Marine behind him was not so fast to react. A dozen energy bolts slammed into the Ultramarine's helmet, the first handful destroying the armour, the remainder vaporising the head. The warrior's body continued to run for several seconds, his nervous system locked on the last imperative it had received. Or perhaps the body was driven even beyond the point of death to serve. Perhaps it was just the armour's actuators failing to register that the wearer was slain.

The dead Ultramarine only stopped moving when he slammed into the side of the tau bunker, the headless body finally realising it was slain and toppling to the ground in a heap. Sarik was the next warrior to reach the bunker, followed within seconds by the eight remaining Ultramarines. The twinned cannons continued to spit their blizzard of energy bolts, homing in on more distant targets now that Sarik and the Assault Marines were too close to engage. The stream of fire split the air in a thunderous barrage almost within arm's reach, charging the air and creating small crackles of energy that played across the Space Marines' armour plates.

Sarik edged around the curved form of the bunker, gesturing for the three closest Assault Marines to follow him. The warriors carried bolt pistols in one hand and frag grenades in the other, ready to storm the enemy fortification the instant Sarik's melta bomb had cracked it open.

Aware that enemy infantry might be guarding against an attempt to penetrate the bunker, Sarik moved fast. As he cleared the bunker's rear he looked for an entry hatch, but to his surprise, found none.

'Thinking machines,' Sarik growled, realising that the turrets were automated, controlled by the same heretical machine intelligences that animated the tau's gun drones and other such hated devices. He activated the melta bomb, set it to a three second delay and clamped it to the base of the bunker wall, praying that the charge would be sufficient to penetrate the armour.

The charge set, Sarik retreated back around the wall. He turned to the Assault Marines, and nodded to the frag grenade the nearest was carrying. 'Krak grenades,' he ordered, and a second later the melta bomb detonated.

A ripple of nucleonic fire spread outwards from the bomb, eating the bunker's outer shell and reducing the material to streams of superheated lava. The reaction lasted only seconds and was accompanied by a nigh deafening roar and an instant pressure change as the air was consumed and more rushed in towards the vacuum. When the reaction ceased, the entire rear of the bunker was a blackened mass, a great bite taken out of it to reveal machine systems within.

Sarik had been correct; there were no tau gunners within, merely an automated, machine-controlled gun system. 'Go!' he ordered, and three Assault Marines stepped past him and lobbed their armour-piercing krak grenades inside. The charges detonated with the ear splitting report that gave them their name, and the sound of the twin cannons instantly stopped. Thick black smoke belched from the wound, and the line was silenced.

Now the breach in the bunker line was sufficiently wide for the entire Space Marine force to break through. The Predators ground forwards and assumed overwatch positions, their turret weapons tracking back and forth ready to engage any enemy that counter-attacked from the star port. Rhinos and Razorbacks followed, while the first eight dismounted tactical squads formed two assault groups that pressed left and right along the bunker line to suppress and destroy any bunkers that had the arc and range to harass the force's flanks. Within minutes the sound of melta bombs and krak grenades being brought to bear on more bunkers filled the air, and the bunkers fell silent.

'Brother Targus,' Sarik addressed a Techmarine of the Red Hunters Chapter. The warrior was studying the line of energy shield projectors that lay beyond the bunkers, his articulated servo-arms stretched out from his backpack, the sensors at their ends blinking. 'Mines?'

The Techmarine's sensors tracked back and forth for a moment, before the warrior answered, 'None detected, brother-sergeant. But the xenos may have some method of hiding them from the gaze of the Omnissiah.'

'Understood, Brother Targus,' Sarik replied. 'Please continue your vigil.'

'Predators forward,' Sarik then ordered. 'Breaching duty to positions.'

Five of the battle tanks not standing overwatch moved forwards through the breach, their dozer blades lowered. Behind each, a tactical squad took position, the battle-brothers equipped with extra supplies of krak grenades.

Sarik moved up to join a squad from the Aurora Chapter, the green-armoured warriors in position and ready to advance. 'Be advised,' he said into the vox-link. 'If this is a minefield, it does not register. Advance.'

The Predators gunned their engines and lurched forwards, and immediately a torrent of burst cannon fire rippled through the air overhead. The flyers overseeing the extraction of the last tau warriors had opened fire, but were remaining protectively close to their charge.

'Your status, brother?' said Sarik.

Brother Qaja's voice came back straight away, 'Enemy infantry have reached the landing pad, brother-sergeant. Crossing towards the lander now.'

'Let's get moving then!' Sarik bellowed, and the Predators began their advance. The tanks moved slowly but surely across the flat expanse of ground between the bunker line and the shield projectors, their dozers lowered and scraping across the packed earth in order to trigger mines that might be waiting just below the surface. Sarik studied the ground at his feet as he strode behind the Predator, looking for tell-tale signs of booby traps amongst the tilled soil.

More rounds screamed in, thudding into the ground behind the Space Marines. The enemy flyers were increasing the volume of their fire, sensing that the tau warriors would soon be overtaken. But the angle was poor and the shots whined harmlessly by over the Space Marines' heads.

It was only when the breaching group was exactly half way across the open ground that the first mine detonated. The ground a mere three metres behind Sarik erupted in a geyser of dust and a mine spat directly upwards. It exploded at a height of two metres, a blinding pulse of booming energy radiating outwards.

One of the Aurora Chapter Tactical Marines was almost directly beneath the explosion. He was slain in an instant, his armour transformed into a deadly wind of razor-sharp shrapnel that tore into a battle-brother nearby. The fragments buried themselves in the warrior's armour, penetrating it in a dozen places and passing straight through in several locations. Another Tactical Marine further out from the blast wave was blown clear, his helmet and half of his face torn from his head by the raging energy pulse.

Sarik had time to turn his shoulder into the blast and brace himself against the wave-front. He felt the hot, actinic energies wash over him, his already ruined shoulder plate absorbing the worst of the damage. As he straightened up again, a second detonation sounded from further along the line, right in the midst of Sergeant Rheq's Scythes of the Emperor tactical squad.

Realising that the mines must have been command operated, Sarik opened the vox-net to address all commands. 'All overwatch units. Locate enemy spotters. Someone must be calling in the detonations.'

The weight of incoming fire redoubled as the tau flyers sought to pin Sarik's force down in the open. Ordinarily, an assault group exposed in such manner would be forced to take cover or retreat in the face of such overwhelming odds. But the Adeptus Astartes rarely began an assault they could not complete, and there were precious few such missions.

The advance continued, not one of the vehicle or squad commanders even contemplating halting unless issued with a direct order to do so. Energy bursts *spanged* from the Predators' frontal armour and hammered into their turrets, then another mine sprang from the ground and exploded directly above an Iron Hands tactical squad further down the line. The explosion sounded like a sonic boom, the rapidly expanding ball of energy casting a luminous blast wave in a wide circle. Three more Space Marines fell, one of them having sustained a fatal wound.

'Lahmas to Sarik,' the voice of the Scythes of the Emperor Devastator sergeant came over the vox-net. 'Enemy spotter located. Engaging.'

The air above the Space Marines was lit by a hail of heavy bolter fire as Lahmas's Devastators hammered the position from which the enemy had been observing the advance. But Sarik was not taking any chances. 'Breaching duty!' he yelled. 'At the double!'

The Predators' engines roared as they lurched forwards at combat speed, the Space Marines behind them increasing their own pace to keep up. Sarik glanced behind him, noting sadly that the broken forms of at least five fallen battle-brothers littered the open ground. He made a silent promise to avenge their sacrifice now, and return for their bodies later.

A sharp explosion halfway up the side of one of the landing pad's supports drew Sarik's attention back to the assault. The entire side of the structure was peppered with ugly black scars, the unmistakable sign of massed heavy bolter fire.

'Spotter neutralised, brother-sergeant,' Lahmas reported curtly. 'Resuming overwatch.'

Sarik's force crossed the remainder of the open ground without incident, weathering the constant hail of fire incoming from the prowling tau flyers. Within minutes, the breaching duty squads had planted dozens of krak grenades on the nearest three energy shield projectors, and the way into the Gel'bryn star port was at last clear.

Sarik dived to the left as a wave of energy bolts screamed in, rolling across the hard white surface of the landing pad and coming up in a kneeling position, boltgun raised. With a flick of his thumb he set his weapon's shot selector to full auto, and squeezed off a rapid-fire burst at the three tau warriors.

The bolts hammered through hard shell armour and detonated in soft flesh. The first tau was blown backwards into the warrior behind by the impact, then exploded as the bolt-rounds detonated inside his chest, showering his companion with purple gore. The second tau took a round to the throat between helmet and chest armour, his hands grasping the wound instinctively. When the round exploded the warrior's head was torn right off, and sent spinning across the hardpan.

The third tau tried to fall back, firing as he went, but the last of Sarik's burst stitched across his shoulder armour and down his right arm, the detonations blowing the limb away in a shower of vaporised blood, and the weapon it had carried clattered to the ground. The warrior turned to run, and two shots to the back took him down for good.

'Hunters!' Sarik called into the vox-net as he glanced upwards at the circling tau flyers. 'Bring them down!'

The Whirlwinds' commanders acknowledged Sarik's order, and two seconds later a wave of a dozen missiles streaked in from below the raised landing pad, their engines bright in the dawn sky. The tau flyers saw the danger and began to turn, but not before the wave of missiles had split into two, each group arrowing in on one of the nearest two targets. The two flyers were struck simultaneously. The first was hit square in the flank, spinning crazily around as its pilot fought for control. Its engines screamed as they fought for lift, and the craft was soon lost to view. The second was hit directly in the cockpit, the entire front of the vessel exploding outwards and showering the landing pad with white-hot debris. What little was left of the airframe appeared suspended in the air as its anti-grav systems remained online a few seconds more, then it simply dropped, like a boulder, straight down as its systems failed. The wreck struck the edge of the landing pad and sheared in two, touching off a secondary explosion before disintegrating.

Only two flyers remained, one circling back and around the opposite end of the landing pad, its chin-mounted cannon sweeping back and forth. Sarik judged it had been ordered to hold back to protect the lander when it finally launched, which Sarik was determined it would never do. The other was moving forwards towards the hatch, its nose dipped as its multiple-barrelled cannon cycled up.

'Ancient Mhadax to Sergeant Sarik,' the mechanical-sounding voice of the Scythes Dreadnought came over the vox. 'Engaging.'

The entire front section of the flyer erupted in pinpoint explosions as the Dreadnought opened up with its assault cannon. So heavy was the fusillade that the craft's forward momentum was arrested, a thousand solid rounds hammering into it in seconds. The armoured nosecone splintered under the relentless assault and was eaten away in an instant. The Dreadnought focussed its fire on the penetrated segment, a hundred more rounds chewing into the flyer's exposed innards.

The flyer disintegrated in mid-air as the assault cannon rounds hollowed it out from within, the rounds now passing straight through its ruined frame. The flyer did not even explode – it literally disappeared before Sarik's eyes, reduced to fragments that scattered wide and fell as hard rain across the entire landing pad.

'Go!' Sarik called to the Space Marines pouring out of the access hatch. Then he was up and running towards the next group of tau backing across the landing pad towards the open rear hatch of the lander. At least thirty tau warriors were at the top of the ramp, keeping up a constant rain of fire intended to suppress the Space Marines and keep them at bay as the last few squads dashed for safety.

Sarik and his squads were halfway across the pad when the four huge, downturned thrusters mounted at each corner of the lander cycled deafeningly to full power. The air rippled as the thrusters powered up and anti-grav projectors thrummed into life with a rolling, sub-acoustic drone.

The Space Marines fired from the hip as they pounded across the hardpan, gunning down the last group of tau left on the pad. The shuttle bounced as the anti-grav cradle took hold, and the thrusters reached full power with a deafening wail.

'Rapid fire!' Sarik bellowed over the howling of the quad thrusters, raising his boltgun to his shoulder and squeezing off a staccato burst right into the gaping rear hatch. Two of the tau warriors were slammed backwards, and the fire of the rest of the Space Marines took down three more and peppered the bulkhead with explosions.

With a tortuous wail, the shuttle wallowed, then began to lift. The last surviving tau flyer banked protectively overhead, its chin-mounted cannon pulsing blue as it opened fire.

The surface of the landing pad was chewed up as burst cannon fire swept in towards Sarik and his warriors.

But Sarik stood his ground. 'No mercy,' he growled, and reached for the melta bomb at his belt. Twisting the plunger, Sarik set the fuse to three seconds, and hurled the charge in an overhead throw that sent it sailing upwards straight towards the lander's open rear hatch. The flyer's fire scythed in towards Sarik, but only when the melta bomb was clear did he dive to one side.

Sarik hit the surface hard, rolling over to look directly upwards as the melta bomb arced through the air and disappeared into the shuttle's hatch.

Time slowed to an impossible crawl as Sarik awaited the melta bomb's detonation. The shuttle laboured upwards, its thrusters at full power as the anti-grav cradle kicked in. The shuttle was twenty metres up and climbing when it suddenly trembled, its progress abruptly arrested. The underbelly swelled grotesquely as nucleonic energies distended the airframe, like a dead thing bloated by corpse gas. Fierce energies raged inside the distended hull, visible through the taut fabric of the distorted armour. The illumination grew, spreading outwards until the entire swollen underside was aglow, the air distorted in a baleful shimmer.

The doomed shuttle shook again, and a mass of flame coughed outwards from the open hatch, followed by a rain of debris and the flailing, flaming bodies of several dozen tau warriors.

Even as blackened body parts slammed down all around, the shuttle exploded. Sarik turned his head away as the sky was turned orange. He screwed his eyes shut, feeling the nuclear wind tearing at his armour and exposed skin. The landing pad shook violently as fragments of the lander hammered downwards and a million red-hot pieces of shrapnel scoured its surface.

Then there was quiet. Sarik rolled over and opened his eyes, the dawn sky lightening overhead. Painfully, he came up onto one knee and scanned the landing pad. Not a single square metre of the surface had been left untouched by the explosion, the pristine white turned to scorched black. Flames licked the hardpan and fragments of debris were scattered all about. Some were just about recognisable as parts of the tau lander, while others, Sarik guessed, belonged to the smaller escort flyer, which must have been caught in the devastation. Most of the debris was so distorted it could have been anything.

A curse sounded from nearby, and what Sarik had at first taken as a mass of debris rose up, revealing itself to be a battle-brother of the Scythes of the Emperor Chapter. The warrior's formerly black and yellow armour was now simply black, its every surface caked in dust and debris. The Scythe reached up and unlocked the catches at his neck, removing his helmet. His face looked startlingly white compared to the condition of his armour.

'Your orders, brother-sergeant?' the brother said dryly.

A burst of laughter rose unbidden to Sarik's throat, and he grinned widely despite himself as he looked around. The rest of the battle-brothers that had charged at his side across the hardpan were slowly regaining their feet, bolters raised as they tracked back and forth across the scene of utter devastation.

'My orders?' said Sarik, wiping a gauntlet across his blackened face. 'Inform crusade command,' he said.

'Operation Hydra primary objective secure.'

When the top of the raised landing platform had been engulfed in flame, Lucian had thought that everything and everyone up there must surely have been slain. Battlegroup Arcadius had been closing on the wrecked bunker line when the dawn sky had been consumed by the destruction of the tau shuttle, and the hot shrapnel had rained down on bodies nowhere near as well protected as a Space Marine's. Three riflemen had been injured by the shrapnel, one severely, and the tanks of the 2nd Armoured, engaging bunkers the Space Marines had bypassed, had been peppered with potentially lethal fragments.

It was only as Lucian was climbing over the ruined fortifications that his vox-bead burst to life, the news not only of Sarik's victory, but of his survival filling every channel. The 2nd Armoured had secured the minefield between the bunkers and the shield projectors, and Lucian had made his way to the landing pad.

'A great victory, my friend,' Lucian said to Sarik as the two stood upon the platform looking out at the aftermath of the destruction. 'A truly great victory.'

'Aye,' Sarik replied, his gaze sweeping outwards past the still-burning hardpan to the city beyond. The sun was rising and the eastern skies were a blaze of luminescent turquoise, their tranquillity marred only by the scores of black, smoking columns rising kilometres into the air. 'I only pray it achieves the desired outcome.'

Lucian glanced upwards into the sky, thinking of the Exterminatus which might rain down upon Dal'yth Prime at any moment. Then he thought of his son, Korvane, who was up there now, on the same vessel as the murderously insane Inquisitor Grand.

'We'll soon find out,' said Lucian. 'Gauge wants a conference, right away.'

'Where?' Sarik said.

'Armak's command vehicle,' said Lucian. 'Coming?'

'Aye, I'm coming,' said Sarik, turning his back on the wreckage-strewn landing pad and the burning city beyond.

Sarik stood aside as Colonel Armak's adjutants and subalterns tramped down the ramp of the Brimlock command Chimera, then ducked inside. The interior was cramped, especially for a Space Marine in full battle plate, and lit solely by the illumination of two-dozen flickering readouts.

Sarik seated himself as best he could, and Lucian and Armak followed him in. The colonel of the Brimlock 2nd Armoured and Gauge's chief officer on the surface hauled a lever on the bulkhead over the rear hatch, and the ramp rose up with a hiss of pneumatics. Only when the hatch had slammed shut and the vehicle's overpressure systems sealed it entirely from the outside did the colonel speak.

'Gentlemen,' said Armak, then he paused as he looked towards Sarik. 'Brother-sergeant, can I get you some water?'

Sarik snorted in amusement, though he appreciated the sentiment. He nodded, and Armak tossed him a half-full canteen. Instead of drinking from the vessel, he sluiced it over his face, ridding himself of just a small portion of the grime and dried blood caking his features.

Sarik set the canteen down on a nearby tacticae-station, and Armak reached across to a command terminal and entered a code into its keyboard. 'I'm opening the most secure link I can, one normally reserved for Codes and Ciphers.' The terminal lit up as reams of data script scrolled across its surface.

Sarik and Lucian exchanged dark glances, the rogue trader raising his eyebrows to indicate he had no idea what Armak was about.

'How secure a link do you need?' asked Sarik. 'And why?'

'You'll see, brother-sergeant,' said Armak. 'One moment, please.'

The terminal droned and chirped for another ten seconds, then it chimed to announce its system had achieved machine communion with another. All of the tacticae-stations in the Chimera's passenger bay burst into life as one. Half of them showed General Gauge seated in a chamber equally as dark as the Chimera's interior, while the other half showed Captain Rumann, standing at the command pulpit of the *Fist of Light*.

The Iron Hands captain was entirely immobile, his augmetic features unreadable. General Gauge appeared gaunt and washed out, though his eyes still shone with the cold, steely light that was so familiar to Sarik and Lucian.

'Veteran Sergeant Sarik,' Gauge said. 'Please accept my congratulations on your victory, and my commiserations on your losses.'

'Both are welcomed,' said Sarik. 'Though neither is necessary.'

Gauge nodded, expecting the response, then addressed Lucian. 'Lord Gerrit. Your rallying of the ground forces in the aftermath of Cardinal Gurney's... withdrawal, contributed greatly to the capture of Gel'bryn, and averted a rout of catastrophic proportions. Your deeds shall be remembered.'

Lucian made a dismissive gesture with his hand, but Sarik knew better. The rogue trader was rightly proud of his actions.

'Colonel Armak?' said Gauge.

'Sir?' Armak replied, as if he had not expected to be addressed by his commanding officer.

'You have been serving as brevet general. That rank is confirmed. Congratulations, General Armak.'

The officer's expression told of his genuine surprise, but Gauge continued before the officer could reply. 'Now, to the real reason I have called this gathering.

'The Damocles Gulf Crusade has reached a critical juncture. We are faced not with one enemy, but two. Though the tau have fallen back from Gel'bryn, a massive war fleet is in orbit already, and Grand might unleash his Exterminatus at any moment.'

Gauge allowed his summary of the strategic situation to sink in, then continued. 'I propose we muster all forces at Gel'bryn star port, and evacuate.'

Sarik took a deep breath, the blood and sacrifice of the last few days flooding his mind. Then, Captain Rumann spoke for the first time, his machine-wrought voice sounding all the more metallic across the clipped and distorted channel.

'No,' Rumann stated coldly.

General Gauge nodded sadly, evidently expecting the captain's reaction. Then Lucian cut in. 'Wait,' the rogue trader said. 'All of you, just wait. Wendall,' Lucian used the general's first name, 'tell us the truth. How bad is it?'

Gauge nodded his thanks towards Lucian. 'When the tau were first encountered, by Lucian and other rogue traders, they were deemed a low-level threat. They were found only in small groups, coreward of the gulf, and usually acting as mercenaries or advisors to planetary governors who had... strayed, to a greater or lesser extent, from the rule of the Imperium. But that was uncovered as a ruse. They were acting as fifth columnists, infiltrating system after system in an effort to expand their sphere of influence. The crusade was raised to put that threat down. Every shred of intelligence and analysis available to us indicated they could hold no more than a handful of worlds. When they were first catalogued, millennia ago, they were no more than over-evolved dromedaries with no technology more advanced than sharp sticks.'

Gauge let that hang for a moment, then continued grimly. 'Yet here they are, in control of an entire star cluster, possessed of a substantial fleet capable of interstellar travel, unheard-of tech, and weaponry that, frankly, outguns most of our own.'

'Sedition,' Captain Rumann said flatly. 'No inferior xenos can stand before us...'

'But that's it!' interjected Lucian. 'Quite clearly, the tau are not inferior, and they *are* standing against us.'

'We've given them a bloody nose,' said General Gauge, smiling wryly at his unintentionally ironic turn of phrase. 'But their reinforcements are here already, and despite previous promises, ours are not. We pull out now, or we spend the rest of our lives as their prisoners.'

'No Astartes will allow that to happen, general,' said Sarik. 'As well you know.'

'We all know you'll never surrender,' said Lucian. 'But is it not true that all your doctrines teach that futile expenditure of life is as great a sin as surrender?'

'Do not presume to preach the *Codex Astartes* to us, rogue trader,' Captain Rumann growled. The captain's anger was expressed as much by distortion and feedback as by any change in his mechanical voice patterns.

Sarik could no longer contain his annoyance. 'Let him speak.'

'What?' said Captain Rumann.

'Lucian is correct,' said Sarik. 'Our doctrine states that a tactical redeployment to muster for further action is preferable to a hollow last stand, if at all possible.'

'You intend, *Sergeant* Sarik, to stand by them in-'

'I do,' growled Sarik, aware that the others appeared uncomfortable to be witnessing the confrontation. He was also aware, painfully aware, how divergent the views of his Chapter and the captain's were. The White Scars' methods of war were born of the noble savages who had made war across the steppes of Chogoris for millennia, masters of the lightning strike that was reflected in the Chapter's very symbol, which he wore proudly on his shoulder. When facing a larger foe, the Chogorans would strike, then pull back, then strike again, until the enemy was bled to death one drop of blood at a time.

Captain Rumann on the other hand was a product of the Iron Hands Chapter. Their determination and resilience was born of their own beliefs about the frailty of the flesh, which they replaced with iron by augmenting their bodies with bionic components. Within each burned a heart as fierce as molten iron. But now, the Iron Hands' legendary determination was, to his mind, in danger of turning into blind stubbornness.

'What sense is there, what *honour* is there, in the crusade overstretching itself and being cut off?' said Sarik. 'I propose that we do as the general says: evacuate, consolidate, and return with a war fleet capable of fulfilling the bold promises made at the outset of the crusade.

'That way,' Sarik concluded, 'will we find honour.'

A tense silence descended, disturbed only by background static churning from the vox-horns. Then Rumann answered. 'I will not order my forces to retreat.'

'Then order them to re-deploy, brother-captain,' said Sarik. 'A great victory may be won here. But not now, not like this.'

Captain Rumann simply nodded.

'Then we are in agreement on this?' said General Gauge.

'We still have the issue of the Exterminatus,' said Lucian. 'If that goes ahead, even after we've evacuated, all of this will have been for nothing.'

'That, gentlemen,' said Gauge, 'is another matter, which forms the basis of the reason for Admiral Jellaqua's absence from this conference.'

'Explain,' said Rumann.

'Right now, I cannot,' said Gauge. 'Not even on this channel.'

'Why can you not...?' said Sarik, but his words trailed off as every pict screen at every station in the Chimera's passenger bay flickered with static, went blank and then returned. The faces of General Gauge and Captain Rumann had been replaced by that of another.

'Because,' said Inquisitor Grand, 'he is a traitor... As are you all.'

In the hours after its capture, Gel'bryn star port came rapidly to resemble a makeshift Imperial Guard muster point. The 2nd Brimlock Armoured quickly established a cordon around the entire complex, their tanks and support vehicles acting as bunkers with their weapons trained on any approach a counter-attack might develop from. The Rakarshan Rifles of Battlegroup Arcadius were the next regiment to move in. Major Subad dispatched the light infantry companies to secure the complex's many buildings, towers and storage facilities, in case the tau had left their carnivore allies as stay-behinds.

The Brimlock regiments poured into the complex after the Rakarshans had spread out, the flat expanse of ground beneath the raised landing platforms soon filling with grumbling armoured vehicles. Hydra flak tanks tracked their quad-barrelled autocannons back and forth across the skies, anticipating a tau air strike at any moment. Thankfully, the sacrifice made by the aircrews of the Imperial Navy at the very outset of Operation Hydra had severely punished the tau flyers, and none appeared.

As the regimental provosts set about marshalling the huge numbers of men and machines flooding into the star port, attached tech-priests invaded the control towers. Ostensibly, the adepts of the Machine-God were tasked with fathoming the operation of the star port's anti-grav cradles, which would speed up the landing and liftoff of the hundreds of troop transports that would soon be in operation immeasurably. It took the tech-priests less than an hour to master the anti-grav generators, and another for them to begin disassembling at least one of the devices for later study.

The mighty god-machines of the Legio Thanataris dispersed to form a wide ring around the star port, their crews vigilant for signs of tau activity. Wherever they trod, the Titans caused as much damage as an Imperial Guard artillery bombardment, and they had soon cleared a rubble-strewn killing ground around the complex, over which they stood silent sentinel with weapon limbs scanning the horizon.

The Space Marines spread out into the surrounding areas too, coordinating their actions with the princeps commanders of the Battle Titans. Sarik ordered his force to ensure that no enemy infantry were lurking in the ruins around the star port, and the squads soon drove off several groups of carnivores that attempted to ambush them amongst the shattered habs. These skirmishes were tiny in comparison to the scale of Operation Hydra, but Sarik ordered the savage aliens hunted down and slaughtered, so vile was their habit of eating the flesh of the fallen.

It was as the first of the troop transports were descending on the star port on boiling pillars of flame, that Lucian, walking towards the Rakarshans' lines to take his leave of the bold mountain fighters, received a transmission from Sergeant Sarik.

'Lucian?' Sarik began, the rogue trader sensing something unusual in the Space Marine's tone. 'What is your present position?'

Lucian halted, looking around for a landmark. Imperial Guard troopers, battered and bloody, trudged past him in long files, many fully laden with what weapons and equipment they could evacuate with them. An entire heavy weapons company was passing through the breach the Space Marines had made in the bunker line, which had been widened and made safe by Munitorum pioneers. 'I'm at phase point nine-zero,' he said, using the term the Tacticae planners had coined for the outer perimeter of the star port. 'Why?'

'I'm five hundred metres north east of your position,' said Sarik, ignoring Lucian's question. 'Get here, now.'

What now, Lucian thought, drawing his plasma pistol and checking the charge. It was down to ten per cent. His power armour was scratched and scored, much of its surface black with carbonisation and soot. He was fatigued and thirsty, and well in need of rest, yet he loosened his power sword in its scabbard as he pushed through the lines of the Imperial Guard troopers flooding in the opposite direction. Many cast him irritated glances as he forced his way on, but many others wore vacant and shell-shocked expressions that spoke of the ferocity of the battle they had just faced.

Clearing the breach in the bunker line, Lucian located the direction Sarik had indicated, and hurried towards it as fast as he could manage. His power armour lent him some strength at least, though not much more than it took to bear its own weight. The suit had served him well, but it would need much attention to restore its war spirit to its full vitality once this was over.

He passed along a wide boulevard, its surface caked with a dried paste made from the blackened remains of the alien carnivores. To one side he saw a pair of Space Marine Apothecaries, one from the Novamarines, the other from the White Scars, recovering the scattered body and armour parts of a slain battle-brother. He could not tell which Chapter the dead warrior was from, for the armour was so encrusted with gore and ash its colours were entirely obscured.

Lucian gave the two medics a wide birth, leaving them to their sad duty out of respect.

After another few minutes crunching through the corpse litter, Lucian saw the white-armoured forms of a group from Sarik's Chapter gathered up ahead. Around twenty White Scars were gathered about a ruined, smoking dome, the rubble of its destruction strewn all about.

As he approached the White Scars, Sarik turned and waved him over.

'Lucian,' said Sarik. 'She'll talk only to you.'

'Who?' said Lucian as the White Scars parted to make way.

The dome had not been ruined by ordnance or the tread of a Battle Titan, but by the impact of a small craft of tau origin. That craft protruded from the cracked eggshell structure, and a figure was sat languidly upon its upper surface, clad in the tattered remains of tau water caste finery.

'I thought you'd never get here, father,' said Brielle.

Lucian approached the downed saviour pod, for that was what he judged the craft to be, in silence. Sarik clapped Lucian on the shoulder as he walked past, then the Space Marine led his warriors away a respectful distance.

As Lucian approached the pod, Brielle pushed herself off and slid down its rounded surface, coming to rest, barefoot, in front of him. Lucian's eyes narrowed as he met his daughter's gaze.

'Well?' he said.

Brielle's lop-sided grin faded, and she cocked her head, her plaited locks a dishevelled mess.

'Well what…?' she muttered petulantly.

'You are dead,' Lucian said flatly. 'You assaulted an agent of the Holy Orders of the Emperor's Inquisition and disappeared.'

'I never *said* I was dead…' she started.

'You never said *anything*!' Lucian bellowed. For some reason he could not begin to fathom, he was not the slightest bit surprised to find his daughter, who he had every reason to believe dead, standing here, in a burning tau city, light years away from where he had last seen her. He fought back the urge to strike her, so maddening was her manner.

'I didn't get the chance,' said Brielle. 'And I'm sorry, father. I'm really sorry.'

'What happened?' said Lucian. 'Why all this?' he gestured to the downed saviour pod, but both knew he meant a whole lot more.

'I'll tell you everything, father,' Brielle stepped closer as she spoke. 'But first, I have to tell you about the tau fleet...'

'The tau fleet in orbit on the far side of this world?' Lucian cut in. 'We're not stupid, Brielle.'

Her expression darkening, Brielle ploughed on. 'The tau intend to demand the crusade's surrender,' she said. 'They wanted me to be their envoy, and that's how I got out. I tricked them, I...'

Lucian raised an eyebrow, well aware that his daughter was only telling him part of the truth, the part that suited her the most.

'...but they have no idea of the crusade's true strengths,' Brielle continued. 'They don't know about the reinforcements.'

Lucian barked out a bitter laugh, and his daughter assumed a crestfallen expression.

'There aren't any reinforcements,' she said, a statement rather than a question.

'We're pulling out,' said Lucian flatly. 'But I imagine you guessed that. If you'd left it any later to enact your cunning plan,' Lucian smirked, 'you'd have had to stay behind.'

'I didn't want to go in the first place,' Brielle said, her pout making Lucian laugh despite himself. 'Grand attacked *me*. I didn't mean to kill him...'

'Well, you can apologise in person,' said Lucian.

Brielle stopped dead in her tracks. 'He's alive?'

'No thanks to you, yes,' said Lucian. 'Though he sustained serious wounds.'

'If he's still alive,' she stammered, 'he'll–'

'Grand has lost it, Brielle,' Lucian interjected. 'He's insane and he'll kill us all if he can.

'You're hardly the top of his list.'

'All will rise!' the convenor bellowed, his metal-shod staff of office striking the deck of the council chamber with a resounding thud. Korvane Gerrit rose from the council seat normally occupied by his father, and the remainder of the gathered councillors rose from theirs.

The chamber seemed empty, with several seats around the circular, black marble table unoccupied. Korvane's father, as well as Veteran Sergeant Sarik, was still on the surface, while Captain Rumann was engaged on the *Fist of Light*. Those not present in person would nonetheless witness the session, by way of the images transmitted by a score of servo skull spy-drones hovering discreetly in the shadows, their multiple lenses whirring and clicking as they tracked the scene. General Gauge had not yet arrived either.

Inquisitor Grand sat across the table from Korvane, his black robes seeming to draw him into the shadows, or perhaps to gather the darkness towards him. What little of the inquisitor's flesh was visible was covered in a chaotic mass of scar tissue, the result of the flamer attack unleashed by Korvane's sister months before. Thinking about Brielle made Korvane's skin crawl, for he too had suffered at her hands. While he could never prove it, he harboured the suspicion that the accident aboard his vessel had been caused by her. Korvane had drawn on the resources of the Clan Arcadius to ensure his wounds were treated, and while they had largely healed, they still pained him greatly.

It appeared to Korvane that the inquisitor wore his wounds proudly and overtly, allowing the scar tissue to enshroud his limbs as nature intended. Perhaps he was making some point about the ascendancy of the human form and the purity of its function, Korvane thought, for the Inquisition was riven with hundreds of different doctrines and philosophies that sometimes set its members violently at odds with one another.

Cardinal Gurney sat to Grand's right, glowering at Korvane. No doubt word of Lucian's rallying of the troops following Gurney's untimely departure had spread. It was now obvious to all gathered that the cardinal had left the surface having been forewarned of Grand's intention to bring forward the Exterminatus, but something had happened to forestall the devastation that hovered over Dal'yth Prime like the executioner's axe.

No one knew why the disbanded council had been reconvened, or why Grand had not overridden the convocation. The atmosphere was tense, and the council chamber noticeably colder than usual.

'Admiral Jellaqua, of the Imperial Navy,' the convenor intoned, 'and...'

Jellaqua leaned in to whisper into the convenor's ear, then the man announced, '...Interrogator Armelle Rayne, of the Holy Ordos of the Emperor's Inquisition.'

The air in the council chamber grew colder still. Another figure appeared at the door behind the admiral and his companion.

'General Gauge,' announced the convenor, striking the deck once more. 'Admiral Jellaqua has the chair. Let the council convene.'

General Gauge took his seat three places to Korvane's right, nodding to him as he did so. The portly Admiral Jellaqua sat himself next to Gauge, gifting Korvane a surreptitious wink as he settled into his chair. The individual who had been introduced as Interrogator Rayne took the seat between Jellaqua and Korvane, and as she sat, she pulled back the hood of her outer robe.

The interrogator was a striking woman, her head bald and her skull subtly elongated, as if nature or augmentation had sculpted her into a new form. Her eyes too were ever so slightly altered and the irises were mirrored. Her features were sharp, almost angular, and her lips full. The side of her bald cranium was tattooed with an intricate tracery of arcane symbols: the aquila, the 'I' of the Inquisition, and many other glyphs worked into dazzling patterns.

Rayne noted Korvane's scrutiny, and turned towards him. She inclined her head in greeting. 'Korvane Gerrit of the Clan Arcadius,' she said, her voice like the purr of a felid. Korvane realised she must have been casting some psyker's glamour to subtly manipulate the councillors' perceptions, and forced his attentions towards the gatherings.

Rayne caught Korvane's eye the instant that thought crossed his mind, the ghost of a wry smile touching her lips.

'Fellow councillors,' said Admiral Jellaqua. 'I have called this extraordinary session of the crusade council...'

'This council is dissolved,' Inquisitor Grand growled, his voice low and threatening. 'By the authority of the Seal.'

Jellaqua's eyes narrowed as he dared meet those of Inquisitor Grand. 'Nonetheless,' the admiral matched Grand's tone, 'there is much to discuss.'

'There is nothing to discuss!' Cardinal Gurney growled as he rose to his feet. Jellaqua smirked slightly at the spectacle of the firebrand preacher performing the role of the inquisitor's attack hound, but otherwise kept his gaze fixed squarely on Inquisitor Grand.

'As I said, there is much to discuss,' said Jellaqua, then inclined his head towards the interrogator at his side. 'I present Mamzel Rayne,' he paused, the air growing colder as he spoke. 'Envoy of Lord Inquisitor Kryptman.'

Korvane's breath formed a cold, billowing cloud as he breathed out. Mere days had passed since the astropathic communication informing the council that Kryptman's envoy would be joining them. None had expected the envoy to arrive so quickly, for the crusade itself had taken long weeks to cross the Damocles Gulf. Korvane had heard the whispered spacer's tales of the archeotech vessels the highest servants of the Inquisition had access to – perhaps they were not mere tales at all.

Interrogator Rayne stood, her black outer robe sliding from her bare shoulder to fall across the chair behind her. She was adorned in a long, flowing, off-the-shoulder gown made of the finest black void-silk Korvane had ever seen. She appeared more a noble of a high court than an agent of one of the most feared institutions in the Imperium.

'My thanks,' Rayne nodded to the admiral, before her gaze swept over the gathered councillors. Gurney was lowering himself back into his seat, his face a mask of righteous, yet impotent fury, while Inquisitor Grand had visibly stiffened in his chair, his spindly body coiled as if ready to strike at any moment. Logistician-General Stempf would clearly rather have been anywhere else than at the council table, and he studiously avoided the interrogator's gaze as it swept over him.

The three new councillors, who Korvane had recruited, seemingly futilely for the council had been disbanded by Grand straight after, met Rayne's gaze confidently. Korvane knew that he had chosen the three well, that they were men of principle who had nothing to hide from the interrogator's scrutiny.

'I come before this council as the emissary of my master, Lord Kryptman. The missive I have to impart comes directly from him, and he has sanctioned me to act in his name, in all things.'

Korvane could not help but feel that the last statement was aimed directly at Inquisitor Grand. The air grew colder still. All of the councillors knew that Inquisitor Grand was the source of the drop in temperature, and several cast wary glances around the table, yet none dared show any overt sign of discomfort or fear.

Interrogator Rayne reached to a pouch at her waist and withdrew a small, circular device with a glassy orb on its upper surface. Activating a command stud, she slid the device across the surface to the centre of the table, and stood back with her arms folded.

The orb flickered to life and then cast a column of harsh white light into the space above it. The shaft danced with motes of energy, which resolved into a figure. It was a stooped, old man, clothed in the robes of an inquisitor, and he was possessed of such power and authority that all in the chamber felt utterly cowed.

Then, the glowing, transparent figure spoke, his rich, low voice filling the chamber.

'I am Inquisitor Lord Kryptman,' the projection began. *'And I come before you with the full authority of the High Lords of Terra themselves. There is scant time for explanations and none for debate, so I will get straight to the point.*

'All commands receiving this message are hereby ordered, by the authority of the Senatorum Imperialis, to cease all military operations and set course for the Macragge system in the Realm of Ultramar. Every possible asset is to be mustered and no resource expended except in the execution of this order.'

The flickering projection of Inquisitor Lord Kryptman paused, as if gathering his thoughts.

'Fellow subjects of the God-Emperor, I shall not lie to you. A threat the likes of which the Imperium has not faced since the dawn of this age is descending upon us. I do not know if this is the beginning or the end, but I tell you this. If we do not defeat it at Macragge, the entire Imperium may fall.

'Heed the words of my envoy as my own, and obey what orders you are given as my own.

'That is all.'

Profound silence descended on the council chamber, only the faint whirring of the servo-skulls' spy-lenses audible as they hovered in the shadows. The projection faded to nothing, and Interrogator Rayne stepped forwards, placing her hands at the table's edge and leaning in hawkishly to address the councillors.

'The Damocles Gulf Crusade,' Rayne began haughtily, 'though a righteous and noble undertaking, is ended.'

A thin skein of ice appeared on the surface of the marble table, spreading outwards from Grand's gnarled hands where they gripped its edge. A sense of primal dread settled on the chamber, and Korvane knew that dread was the inquisitor's ire, made manifest by the agency of his formidable psychic potential. Rayne's glance settled on Inquisitor Grand for a moment, before she continued without comment.

'All available forces are to answer my master's call and muster at Macragge.'

'What threat?' Cardinal Gurney stammered. 'What could possibly–'

The interrogator went from haughty calm to banshee rage in a heartbeat. 'You will be silent!' Rayne screamed, her rage so focussed and sharp it was as if she had drawn a power sword and plunged it directly into the cardinal's heart. 'By the authority vested in me by my master, I *order* you to be silent.'

Cardinal Gurney looked like he had been bodily assaulted, his face draining of its colour as he visibly shrivelled before the interrogator's anger. Korvane knew that the cardinal, as an officer of the Ministorum, could claim to be outside of Kryptman's authority. But then again, the lords of the Inquisition relied not on rulebooks to impose their will, but on influence, and Gurney was well outranked in that regard. Korvane glanced towards Inquisitor Grand, who had remained silent throughout. Grand was rigid, but now a frosting of ice coated his flesh.

Several of the councillors swallowed hard, as much through fear of the inquisitor as dread at the envoy's words. What could possibly threaten such a vast expanse of the mighty Imperium of Mankind? Even the most widespread rebellion, the mightiest ork incursion or the most ferocious crusade of the arch-enemy rarely afflicted more than a sector of Imperial space. To threaten an entire segmentum, an enemy would have to be of a scale not witnessed since the Imperium's darkest days.

'The enemy of which my master speaks is a previously unknown xenos-form, which he has codified *tyranids,'* Rayne continued, satisfied that Gurney's interruption was at an end. 'Already, they are classed *xenos terminus*, but serious consideration is being given to creating a new threat rating, just for them.'

'What are these... tyranids?' said Korvane. 'What is their nature?'

Rayne turned her head to look down at Korvane, before replying, 'They are beasts of nightmare.' Her gaze became distant as she spoke, as if recalling sights she would rather not describe. 'They take a million forms, from gargantuan, world-razing monstrosity to flesh-eating parasite. They are teeth, claw, tentacle and maw.' The interrogator stopped there, and Korvane had little desire to learn more, though he knew he would.

'How were they discovered?' Korvane pressed.

'Initially, when outlying worlds surveyed long ago by the Exploratus, fell silent.'

Korvane nodded, reminded of the misfortunes that had overtaken the Clan Arcadius in recent years, as ancient hereditary trade routes to the galactic east had run dry, seemingly without cause. Worlds that generations of his dynasty had traded with had gone silent, the once ceaseless flow of exotic goods slowing to a mere trickle. The clan's fortunes had suffered so badly that Lucian had pinned all of his hopes on the Damocles Gulf Crusade, aiming to establish exclusive trade deals with the tau once they had been put firmly in their place. Grand's Exterminatus had threatened all of that, but Rayne's news spoke of something far worse than a threat to a single world.

'Having perceived a pattern in reports of worlds once catalogued as sustaining life being reduced to barren rocks, my Lord Kryptman received dispensation to investigate. At the Explorator base at Tyran Primus, he found evidence of a xenos abomination so virile and ravenous its organisms can strip an entire world of its biomass in days.'

'To...' Logistician-General Stempf stammered, '...to what end?'

'That is under investigation,' Rayne answered. 'Certainly to feed, presumably to reproduce, but we do not yet understand why they need so much biomass or to what use they put it. But they descended on Thandros like a swarm of voracious locusts, like a beast rising from the depths of the ocean. Then it was Prandium.'

'And after Prandium,' said Jellaqua, 'comes Macragge, fortress home world of the Ultramarines.'

'Surely,' said Tacticae-Primaris Kilindini, speaking for the first time at council, 'an entire Chapter of Space Marines can hold this species at bay. To assault Macragge is suicide on a racial scale...'

Interrogator Rayne studied the Tacticae for a moment, as if he were a curious morsel on a sample dish laid out before her. 'No,' she said flatly. 'Let me make this quite clear.'

'The tyranids are more than a species. They are a blight, a swarm. They are a storm of teeth and claws and chitin and saliva, and they hunger to consume us all. They are a billion billion ravening organisms bred for one purpose and one purpose alone: to kill. Each organism is but a single cell in a mass that is spread across light years of space. Where that mass travels, its thoughts drown out the light of the Astronomican and cast the warp itself into impassable turbulence. Astropaths caught in that 'shadow in the warp' would rather scratch their brains out than endure the chittering of a trillion voices that all speak as one.'

'So no, Tacticae-Primaris. The Ultramarines alone cannot hold this foe at bay. It will take every Chapter, regiment, Legio and fleet on the Eastern Fringe to afford even the slightest chance of survival, yet alone victory.'

There was a drawn-out pause, before Korvane spoke up. 'How long.'

'In truth,' sighed Rayne, 'we have no way of knowing. Every unit of every arm we can reach is being recalled to Macragge, whatever their status. We may have months, or just days, but should Macragge fall, nowhere will be safe.'

'I have already briefed Interrogator Rayne as to our ground forces' status,' said General Gauge. 'Most of our units are at or closing in on the Gel'bryn star port. The evacuation is already under way.'

Now the temperature in the council chamber was dropping towards sub zero, and Rayne turned her gaze on Inquisitor Grand.

'You have a statement to make, inquisitor?' Rayne said haughtily. 'An objection, perhaps?'

Grand's hold on the side of the marble tightened, his knuckles turning white. Frost crept up the glass drinking vessel in front of Korvane, and he knew that should he touch it his skin would adhere to its surface. Though little of Grand's face was visible beneath his hood, his scarred mouth scowled as he answered.

'The Writ of Exterminatus has been cast upon this place called in the base tongue of the xenos *Dal'yth Prime*,' the inquisitor growled, his disgust at using the tau's name for their world plain to read. 'I have pronounced my sentence upon the xenos of the world below, and that sentence shall be enacted.'

Interrogator Rayne tipped her regal head back and looked down her nose at the inquisitor. For one of her rank to display such open contempt for a superior would ordinarily have provoked the most lethal form of censure. But Rayne was speaking with the authority of an inquisitor lord, and all present in the chamber knew it.

Inquisitor Grand knew it.

'The Writ of Exterminatus is hereby revoked,' said Rayne, her eyes boring into the shadows within Grand's hood. 'By authority of my Lord Inquisitor Kryptman.'

A sharp groaning echoed through the chamber, the sound of metal and wood distorted by the cold.

Something dropped suddenly from the shadows above the conference table, smashing to a thousand shards and causing all except Grand and Rayne to pull back sharply and several to utter curses and exclamations. Korvane's heart thundered as he saw that the icy table surface was now covered in bony splinters. One of the servo skulls had frozen solid and plummeted from the air, shattering on impact with the cold, hard marble.

'To leave an enemy at our backs is–' Grand began.

'Entirely the point,' interjected Rayne, her tone low and as cold as the air in the chamber.

'It is decided,' said General Gauge. 'On Kryptman's authority.' At a nod from the interrogator, Gauge went on. 'If these tyranids are the threat they appear, then the tau are more use to us alive than exterminated.'

'Blasphemy!' Cardinal Gurney spat. Rayne shot him another dark glance, and he looked to the inquisitor at his side, but said no more.

'I think I see it,' Korvane spoke up. 'If the incursion is dire enough to imperil the entire segmentum, then the tau will likely have to face it too. It is not unheard of for humanity to stand side by side with xenos against a mutual foe. Have our forces not taken to the field alongside the eldar, against the arch-enemy?'

'Indeed,' said Rayne. 'And if the tau will not cooperate in this, they will face the tyranid swarm alone. Either way,' she reiterated Gauge's words, 'they are more use to us alive.'

'As a backstop,' said the Tacticae-Primaris, nodding. 'Better the invaders expend their energies against the tau's worlds than against our own.'

Interrogator Rayne looked around the table to each of the councillors, allowing her words to sink in. She ended her sweep on Inquisitor Grand, her gaze lingering on him along with that of every other councillor present.

Slowly, the inquisitor rose to his feet. He turned without a word, and stalked from the council chamber, frost billowing in the air behind him.

Leaning back in the seat in the passenger bay of his Rhino, Sergeant Sarik exhaled slowly. The pict-feed showed the council breaking up. The councillors each had a myriad of tasks to undertake, for the crusade fleet would be disengaging as soon as practicable. Sarik and the rogue trader had watched the proceedings in grim silence, barely able to conceive of the scale of the xenos incursion the interrogator had described. With a flick of a control rune Sarik deactivated the command terminal, the pict screen fading to grainy static.

'Well?' said Lucian.

'Any misgivings I had about evacuating are now entirely assuaged, friend Lucian,' Sarik replied. 'The storm rises, and soon worlds shall burn, of that I am sure. Honour demands the Astartes answer the call to war.'

'And Dal'yth Prime?' pressed Lucian.

'Honour is satisfied,' said Sarik. 'You are troubled?'

Lucian paused before answering, then nodded. 'Sarik, you are a mighty warrior, and a noble man...'

'But?' said Sarik, a hint of amusement glinting in his eye.

Lucian smiled, though his own eyes showed no amusement at all. 'But, your battles are fought in the open, against foes you can see and understand and kill.'

'And yours are not,' said Sarik.

'Aye,' Lucian sighed. 'They are not.'

'How then must you win your own battle?' Sarik said. 'Tell me this, and I offer you what aid I may provide.'

'This is not over,' said Lucian flatly.

'Explain, please,' said Sarik, judging that Lucian referred to something more than the crusade and its battles against the tau.

'Grand won't let it end like this,' said Lucian. 'Since the earliest days of the crusade council's formation, I've suspected that he had something more than conquest in mind. The fact that he concealed his possession of an Exterminatus device suggests to me he never intended to suppress the tau, or to conquer them, or to contain them on this side of the Gulf.'

'Lucian,' sighed Sarik. 'The fact that an inquisitor demands the extermination of a xenos species is hardly outside of his remit.'

'True, but he was prepared to sacrifice the ground forces, including your own, in the execution of his Exterminatus. He's a radical, Sarik, I'm sure of it.'

'The internal politics of the Inquisition are no concern of mine, Lucian,' said Sarik. 'But I believe you are correct. Whatever his agenda, it is clearly a danger to us all. What do you think he will do next?'

'I don't know,' said Lucian, his expression pained. 'But I need to be there, to stop him.'

Sarik nodded slowly, weighing up the consequences, for his Chapter as well as himself, of what he was about to say.

'Then I too must be there,' he said solemnly. 'Your Warrant of Trade is a powerful totem, Lucian, but so too is the Inquisitorial rosette. You will not face Grand alone, on that I swear.'

CHAPTER ELEVEN

Korvane pressed his back against the cold, iron bulkhead, listening intently to the sound of Grand's footsteps receding further down the shadowed, red-lit passageway. The metal of the bulkhead was cold because Grand was exuding billowing clouds of frost in his wake as he prowled further from the council chamber. As Korvane readied himself to move on again, the frost under his hand turned to liquid as normal temperature returned, thin, oily runnels streaking down the walls.

When the inquisitor's footsteps were almost too distant to hear, Korvane pressed on again. His heart pounded with barely suppressed terror as he considered for the hundredth time turning back. This was insane, he told himself. In going after the inquisitor, he was putting himself in mortal danger, for Grand was known to be a powerful psyker and as well an accomplished torturer.

Nonetheless, this had to be done, Korvane thought as he felt the now familiar weight of the ring his father had given him. The gift was far more than an object, far more even than the contents of the stasis tomb it would unlock. It had given Korvane strength and courage, even as it had loaded him with the responsibility of the heir of Clan Arcadius. That was why he was trailing an insane inquisitor through the bowels of an Imperial warship.

Because he had to, because honour and duty demanded nothing less. Korvane had always assumed that being at or near the head of a rogue trader dynasty should remove one from the action, with legions of underlings to get the dirty work done. He now understood that the reverse was true. He could understand exactly why his father had desired to participate in the ground war, and it was nothing so prosaic as ego.

Some things you just had to do yourself.

With the *Blade of Woe* preparing to take thousands of passengers on board and getting ready to make warp, the subsidiary passageways through which Korvane passed were virtually empty. Every available crewman was at his station, attending to the myriad tasks required of him prior to departure. Korvane wished he were back in the command throne of his own vessel, the *Rosetta*, pursuing the fortunes of the Clan Arcadius, not engaged in internecine political wars with parties who should count one another allies against a common foe.

Inquisitor Grand.

Korvane tried to keep his footfalls as silent as possible as he stalked the passageway, knowing that such sounds had a habit of reverberating in odd, unpredictable ways in the bowels of a starship as large and venerable as the *Blade of Woe*. Even with the ever-present throb of plasma conduits and the distant whine of the drive banks cycling to idle, his footsteps might betray him to the inquisitor.

More likely, however, Korvane's own thoughts would betray him. Grand was a psyker of prodigious power, and while Korvane did not know if the inquisitor was an empath, he must assume that he was. He had to keep his distance, in case Inquisitor Grand heard not just his footsteps but his mind.

Korvane realised that the air was getting colder, meaning Grand must have slowed or come to a halt. He glanced around to get his bearings, but the red illumination of ship's night cast the entire scene in stark shadows. He followed a conduit feeding into a purge manifold, and squinted to read the text stencilled on its corroded outer casing. *Sub-deck delta twelve, sector D*.

Korvane processed the coordinates, comparing them to what he knew of the *Blade of Woe* and other vessels of its class. It was hard, for the vessel was ancient and had been added to, renovated, overhauled and rebuilt numerous times over the millennia. The stencil told him that he was amidships, eighty-three decks below the secondary mycoprotein vats that turned the crew's waste solids into edible tack. He should have known that from the low-level stink that permeated the whole deck. Another half a kilometre fore of his position would be the vast cryo-chambers in which slain crewmen awaited reconstitution, and twenty more levels below him was the low deck sump in which entire communities of mutants lived without ever crossing paths with a crewman. Recalling what he could of the *Blade*'s impossibly complex internal arrangement, Korvane realised that there was a tertiary docking bay not far away. Could that be Grand's destination?

Slowing as he approached a junction, Korvane drew his laspistol and loosened his power sword in its scabbard. All men and women of his background were required to master such weapons, but he had rarely had cause to use them in anger.

Coming to the junction, Korvane peered around to the passageways beyond. Grand's trail was unmistakable, the glistening skein of ice on the bulkheads marking his passing towards the hangar Korvane knew lay to the right. Perhaps the inquisitor was planning to escape by lander, Korvane thought, before dismissing the notion. Somehow, he knew that the truth would be far worse.

'Indeed it is…' a rasping voice whispered from the hangar portal. '…much worse.'

'Come, scion of the Arcadius,' said Inquisitor Grand. 'And you shall reap what you have sown.'

Every shred of Korvane's being screamed at him to turn and flee; yet he could not. One leaden step at a time, he passed through the open hangar portal and into the cavernous launch bay. Though only a minor facility compared to the *Blade of Woe*'s main bays, the space was so large it rivalled the interior of a mighty Ecclesiarchy cathedral.

The hangar was cast in the bright, turquoise light reflected from the surface of Dal'yth Prime. The world filled the view through the open hangar, the air held within by an invisible energy shield. Serene seas framed the arid continental masses, the scene so pristine it belied the devastation Inquisitor Grand had sought to work upon it. How quickly the glowing orb would have been transformed into a black, shrivelled wasteland if the inquisitor had not been countermanded by one of the few in the galaxy with the authority to do so…

Korvane felt his legs stop moving as he reached the centre of the hangar. Before him, held firmly in the cantilevered arms of a ceiling-mounted launch cradle, was a matt-black, elongated form five metres in length. It reminded Korvane of an ocean-borne predator, its prow blunt, with numerous angular fins protruding from its length. The object's rear section was a compact plasma drive with a single thruster, ready to power it through the atmosphere on the hell-dive of Exterminatus that would spell its death, and that of every living organism on the world below.

'You are correct, Arcadius,' said Inquisitor Grand as he emerged from behind the torpedo. As he moved, he ran one hand along the torpedo's flank, fingering each sharp fin as his wizened touch passed over it. Where that hand caressed the matt-black skin of the torpedo, the kiss of frost was left in its wake.

Korvane's heart thundered as he forced himself to stand erect before the traitor. He would die, of that he was sure. But he would do so on his feet, with his head held high, like a true son of the Arcadius.

Inquisitor Grand reached his gnarled hands up to his hood, and lowered it, so that his face was visible. His entire head was a single, badly healed wound, with clumps of silver hair poking out between knots of scar tissue. His ears were mere stumps, his eyes lidless slits between folds of wizened, twisted skin. His nostrils were ragged flaps of skin above his mouth, which was all he normally allowed others to see. His lips were formed into a bitter, feral sneer.

'You're going to do it...' said Korvane. 'You're going to defy Lord Kryptman...'

Grand's sneer twisted further as his hand came to the end of the torpedo, his touch lingering on the flared plasma thruster. 'Please accept my apologies, Arcadius,' Grand leered. 'You really aren't worthy of an extended valedictory diatribe. I think I'll just kill you...

'That,' Grand added with a twisted grin, 'will really piss your father off.'

Grand brought his right hand up, the sleeve of his robe falling back to reveal yet more ravaged scar tissue. Korvane's breath came in laboured gulps, and his limbs froze solid as wracking cramp gripped his muscles. Slowly, one gnarled finger bending back at a time, Grand made a fist.

As Grand's little finger folded back, Korvane felt an icy flare of pain in the centre of his chest. As the ring finger curled around, the ice crept into his heart. When the middle finger folded inwards, a dozen icy daggers speared into Korvane's heart.

Grand paused, bringing his thumb and index finger together slowly. Korvane felt his heart falter, his pulse becoming weak. The strength was rapidly draining from his muscles as ice spread through his veins. Blackness pressed in at the edges of his vision, and he tore his eyes from his leering executioner so that the last sight he saw might be that of the serene world for which he had given his life.

His vision swimming, Korvane struggled to focus on the scene beyond the hangar bay portal. The turquoise orb of Dal'yth Prime was suddenly white and angular and entirely out of focus. With the last of his strength, Korvane struggled to resolve the scene, which made no sense to his oxygen starved brain.

Then, the view beyond the hangar portal swam into focus, and Korvane's lips formed into a weak grin.

The serene globe of Dal'yth Prime was all but obscured by the sight of a Thunderhawk gunship rising on flaring manoeuvring jets, veering slightly as its pilot brought it in towards the void-sealed portal.

Inquisitor Grand spun where he stood, turning to face the gunship. The instant his attention was turned elsewhere, Grand's icy hold was relinquished. Korvane dropped to the hardpan, his limbs screaming with the pain of frostbite. Gasping for breath, he rolled onto his side as Inquisitor Grand stalked around to the opposite side of the torpedo, the inquisitor watching calmly as the gunship pierced the void-seal and set down nearby on screaming retros.

With a last burst of gas, the gunship settled on flexing landing struts. Even before it was fully down, the hatch at its blunt prow lowered on hissing hydraulics, and slammed to the deck with a resounding clang. A group of figures tramped down the assault ramp. Korvane's eyes struggled to bring them into focus.

The first of the figures to set foot on the hardpan was a Space Marine, his formerly pristine white power armour scorched black and smeared with gore. A flowing topknot capped the Space Marine's head, and his face was traced with an intricate pattern of honour scars. Veteran Sergeant Sarik of the White Scars.

When Korvane saw the next figure, his heart leaped. It was his father, resplendent in his heirloom power armour that was almost as battered and dirty as Sarik's. Lucian wore his hair in a style not unlike the sergeant's, a hint at the fact that the Clan Arcadius had long-established links to the Chapter's home world of Chogoris. The Space Marine and the rogue trader both drew their blades as one, spreading out as they approached the waiting inquisitor.

As the two parted, a third figure was revealed behind. It was a woman, ragged strips of silver fabric flowing around her body and long, plaited hair streaming madly behind.

'No...' Korvane gasped. 'You bitch...'

A rasping chuckle echoed through the cold air of the hangar, audible even over the sound of the gunship's engines powering down. Korvane realised the sound was coming from inside his own head, and the voice was Grand's.

Korvane's joy at the arrival of his father was dispelled in an instant by the sight of his stepsister, still alive, and at Lucian's side. Bitterness and hatred welled inside his heart, causing stabs of pain far worse than those inflicted by Inquisitor Grand. She had tried to kill him months before, but Korvane had thought her dead, as had everyone else. Now she was back, and it would all start again.

But not if Inquisitor Grand killed her, Korvane thought as he slumped backwards on the deck, allowing the pain of the psychic assault to wash over him, to carry him away on the waves of a bitter, cold ocean of hatred.

Sarik drew his chainsword as he stepped onto the deck of the hangar bay, his gaze settling on the wizened form of Inquisitor Grand. The floor all around the inquisitor was slick with ice, and beyond it lay the barely conscious form of Lucian's son, Korvane.

Behind the traitor, for that was what Grand surely was, waited the unmistakable form of the Exterminatus torpedo, sleek and black and held in place by the claws of its launch cradle.

Sarik moved to the right as Lucian stepped to the left, aiming to encircle the calmly waiting inquisitor. Lucian's daughter came behind, and beyond her at the head of the gunship's assault ramp came Major Subad and Sergeant-Major Havil of the Rakarshan Rifles.

'You named us traitors,' Sarik called out, shouting to be heard over the Thunderhawk's whining jets. 'I name *you* traitor, Inquisitor Grand, and you will face my judgement.'

Inquisitor Grand simply smiled grotesquely, and raised his wiry arms to his sides. The air temperature plummeted and a patina of ice crept across the decking towards Sarik's armoured boots. He gunned his chainsword, but held his ground. Grand was no fighter, Sarik judged, but would be deadly nonetheless.

'It is not within your power to judge me, Astartes,' Grand sneered, his rasping whisper carried over the powering-down jets and directly into the minds of all those present.

'I issue you this one, simple warning,' Grand continued. 'Depart this place now, before I freeze your blood in your veins.' Glancing towards Brielle, Grand added, 'But she shall stay, and face punishment for her assault on my person and her consorting with xenos.'

Sarik growled, a curse forming on his lips. Lucian swore, but before either could intervene, Brielle had stepped forwards and was pointing directly towards the traitor.

'You remember this, gak for brains?' she spat.

Grand froze, staring at Brielle's outstretched hand.

'Yes you do,' Brielle sneered. 'Now shut the hell up.'

A sheet of liquid fuel surged out from the miniature flamer unit disguised as a ring on Brielle's index finger. The jet speared through the cold air and ploughed into Grand's chest, but truly the fates mocked Brielle as the chemical failed to ignite.

The inquisitor grinned cruelly as he took a step towards Brielle, his arms rising to unleash a lethal blast of psionic force.

As Brielle backed away from Grand, terror writ large on her face, Sarik drew his bolt pistol. He fired, the bolt plunging into Grand's form and finally igniting the flamer's fuel.

In an instant, the inquisitor was completely engulfed in flames, the promethium fuel clinging to his body as it burned through his flesh. The robes were seared away, their remains smouldering on the deck at his feet. Grand had become a naked torch, his limbs wreathed in dancing fire, yet somehow, he was still alive.

The human torch spun towards Sarik and threw a flame-licked arm out in a violent gesture. The bolt pistol was struck from Sarik's grip by an invisible force and sent spinning across the deck.

'Abomination!' Sarik cursed, bringing his chainsword up to the guard position. Others moved in around him, Lucian from the inquisitor's rear, Subad and Havil not far behind.

Seeing Lucian drawing his plasma pistol, Sarik bellowed 'No!', but too late; Grand spun the other way and with another gesture sent a piledriver of invisible psyker-force into Lucian's chest. The armour buckled as Lucian was propelled backwards. Bricle dashed towards her father's prone form, and Grand tracked her, girding his flaming, twisted body to leap forwards with supernatural force.

A figure appeared between the inquisitor and Lucian's daughter, a power cutlass raised high. It was Major Subad. He moved with the lightning speed of years of training with his blade. Subad darted in, delivering a vicious slash to Grand's stomach that should have spilled his guts across the deck. By sheer force of will, Grand was defying death even as the raging flames consumed his flesh.

Sarik took advantage of the distraction Major Subad was providing, working his way around behind Inquisitor Grand. Subad dodged aside as Grand lashed out with flaming claws, searing a smoking wound across the Rakarshan's right arm.

Subad tossed the blade to his other hand without breaking stride, and lunged forwards again.

The curved sword scythed towards Grand's head, but the inquisitor moved left, a tail of flame and roiling embers trailing behind him like a ragged cloak. He swept around the torpedo, moving in towards the launch cradle's command terminal hanging down on a sheaf of cables.

Sarik saw what Grand intended and moved in, his chainsword screaming. Rounding the launch cradle, Sarik closed on Grand, and saw that his body was disintegrating in the heart of the conflagration that still engulfed him. Slivers of smoking, charred meat were sloughing from his bones with his every step, yet still, his bitter, indomitable will drove him on well beyond the point of death.

Grand was bent over the command terminal, and as Sarik approached he turned, his charred face a black coal in the heart of a furnace. His eyes, mouth and nostrils were lit from within, the fire so consuming him that he was no more than a hollow skeleton of blackened bone.

The inquisitor brought his flaming, skeletal hand down and punched the command rune. A klaxon wail started up, low at first, but rising to the banshee dirge that announced the death of worlds. The illumination in the hangar suddenly changed to strobing red as the alert lumens flashed into life.

Through the crackling of flames and the howling of sirens, Sarik heard distant, echoing laughter. Grand stumbled backwards, away from the launch cradle, as hydraulics engaged and white gases hissed from purge vents.

Grand lurched, what was left of his body losing form and stability in spite of the staggering power of the mind that sustained it. As the traitor fell, Sarik charged in, his chainsword ready to deliver the killing blow.

An arm looking more like the blackened branch of a lightning-struck tree was raised. The air rippled and an invisible hammer pounded into Sarik's chest, driving the air from his lungs and cracking the plate wide open. He staggered back, fighting to remain standing as the rapidly failing systems in his war-ravaged power armour flooded his body with combat drugs and stimms. He rose on one knee, to see Sergeant-Major Havil appear behind the inquisitor, his massive ceremonial power axe raised in a double-handed grip.

The sirens reached a deafening crescendo, and the torpedo's plasma thruster ignited. The launch cradle lurched violently, and the cantilevered arms depending from above flexed and shivered as the thruster built power.

Havil's blade swept in across the horizontal, as sure and true as the executioner's axe... then melted into splattering lava mere inches from Grand's blazing form, orange gobbets scattering across the deck. Grand struggled to his feet as he turned fully to face the sergeant-major, who was joined a moment later by Major Subad.

Sarik forced himself to his feet as the inquisitor raised both hands towards the two Rakarshans. The air twisted and distorted around him, the fabric of reality sucked into a swirling maelstrom centred on the inquisitor. Havil raised the haft of his ruined weapon before him, while Subad made ready for one final lunge with his curved blade. The air seethed and screamed, as if the universe were drawing breath, then exploded outwards in an unstoppable tsunami that propelled both Rakarshans backwards and out of Sarik's line of sight.

The torpedo's thruster reached full power, and the launch cradle's arms let it go. Instead of dropping, the torpedo hung in the mid-air for a moment. Like a predator scenting its prey, the torpedo blasted forwards, through the void-seal, and began its hell-dive towards Dal'yth Prime.

Sarik was consumed by grief. He had failed.

Grand's back was still turned on the White Scar. Even through the pain and rage threatening to consume him, he saw his opening, and took it.

Sarik drew the chainsword back over his shoulder, then swept it down hard. The whirring teeth shattered Grand's hollow, flaming skull and cleaved downwards through his torso, shattered ribs exploding outwards along with a fireball of foul gas.

The swirling psychic maelstrom still raging in the air exploded outwards, unleashed and unchannelled without the inquisitor's fearsome will to focus its impossible energies. The air twisted around itself, turning reality inside out as dimensions converged and lines of psychic power burned through the aether.

Sarik threw himself clear as the vortex expanded, rolling across the hard metal deck towards Brielle, who was kneeling over the barely conscious form of her father. He rose to his knees as the vortex buckled the deck panels behind him. He grabbed Lucian's armour by its neck collar with one hand, and Brielle's arm with the other and hauled them both backwards towards the inner hatch, the maelstrom chasing them all the way.

At the last, Sarik pounded the hatch release, and the blast door crashed down behind him as the vortex engulfed the hangar. Witch-fire ravaged the bay, bolts of aetheric vomit splashing through the void-seal in a slow-moving fountain of impossible energies.

The maelstrom churned outwards from the portal, spewing across the void in a rapidly expanding aetheric blast wave. The *Blade of Woe* slewed and listed slowly as the energies spat from her midsection, a thousand klaxons sounding as emergency retro thrusters coughed into life to correct the sudden and drastic course deviation. The very void of orbital space rippled and buckled, the globe of Dal'yth Prime appearing like a reflection in rippling water.

Then the leading edge of the maelstrom overtook the Exterminatus device as it plummeted downwards, hungry to consume the cells of every living thing of an entire world. The torpedo quivered, its shark-form length elongating as if caught at the event horizon of a black hole. Black ripples passed along its length, and then it detonated, a million shards of metal streaking through the heavens trailing searing white contrails behind.

A trillion murder-cells died in the furnace of re-entry, seared from existence by the elemental nucleonic fires.

On the surface of Dal'yth Prime, a new sun appeared briefly in the jade skies, then winked out of existence once more, its passing marked by a slowly descending shower of meteors.

EPILOGUE

'Questions?' said Lucian, slowly scanning the crowded council chamber.

The crusade council had convened for one last session, but such a weight of business lay before it that the conference had ground on throughout the night. A million details had to be thrashed out, from the embarkation of thousands of ground troops to the distribution of millions of tons of capital munitions. Several hundred motions had been proposed, debated and passed in an effort to tie up every possible loose end. The treacherous, insane Inquisitor Grand had been replaced on the council by a Munitorum Plenipotentiary Delegatus by the name of Captain Palmatus. Lucian had never met Palmatus before, but found him capable and shrewd, and the council's business had been conducted with a speed and efficiency not seen throughout the entire crusade.

With all of the council seats occupied for the first time in what seemed like months, the chamber had filled with other officials, many of whom had a statement or request to make. Master Karzello, the crusade fleet's senior astropath, came before the council and told of the alien snarls and screeches resounding through the minds of the astropathic choirs, driving some insane and others to take their own lives. Interrogator Rayne confirmed the phenomenon as the gestalt echo of a trillion xenos minds, howling their hunger into the void. Pator Ottavi, the Navigator Korvane had brought into the council, described the shadow that had settled over the warp, even blocking out the light of the sacred

Astronomican which shone from distant Terra and guided the Imperium's vessels through the benighted void.

Others too had spoken. The Ultramarines sergeant Arcan had told of his urgent need to return to his home world, and requested the aid of his brother Chapters. Arcan was scarcely recovered from the wounds inflicted on his body when his Rhino had been struck by fusion blaster fire, and both of his legs had been replaced by heavy augmetics. Despite his injuries, the Ultramarine's words had stirred the hearts of those present, and all who had the authority to do so had pledged their aid in the defence of Ultramar.

Then, the tau had come before the council. Few of those crowded into the council chamber had even laid eyes on their foe; in fact most had never before confronted any type of sentient alien. When Aura and his fire caste honour guard had entered the chamber, utter silence had descended. The Space Marines had watched impassively, not acknowledging the aliens' presence but at least refraining from pumping a magazine full of mass-reactive explosive rounds into their heads. The Adeptus Astartes had far larger concerns than the tau, Sarik had told Lucian before the session, concerns that made these comparatively benign aliens pale into utter insignificance.

The initial discussions had been stilted and difficult, with the tau envoy making all manner of veiled threats. Yet, Lucian had brought into play every ounce of his diplomatic skill, drawing on a lifetime's experience of trading with all manner of societies and races the length and breadth of the Imperium. With Rayne's blessing, Lucian had imparted something of the coming tyranid swarm, though he had twisted the truth to suggest that the tau were actually in more danger than the Imperium. It was hoped that in doing so the tau would allow the Imperium to depart unopposed while they fortified their worlds against the coming storm, and cause them to focus all of their efforts against the tyranids. Whether or not the envoy had entirely believed him, Lucian could not be sure; but regardless, face was saved and honour maintained, and the tau had not only agreed to allow the fleet to disengage, but the seeds of future cooperation had been sown.

Most importantly, from Lucian's own perspective, he had forged a number of highly lucrative, exclusive contact treaties with the tau, securing the fortunes of the Clan Arcadius for decades to come.

His mind had wandered as the council session had dragged on into the early morning, Lucian calculating the profit his dynasty stood to make. Perhaps he would rebuild the family manse in Zealandia Hab on Terra, or purchase a paradisiacal garden world for the same outlay.

When the council had finally come to vote on the ceasefire motion, only Cardinal Gurney had objected. It appeared to all that Gurney's career in politics was as good as over, yet he planned, by all accounts, to accompany the fleet to Macragge, to use his fiery rhetoric to drive the ground troops forward in the glory of the Emperor. Lucian grudgingly accepted that was the best role for the cardinal, but silently hoped he went and got himself eaten by some slavering alien monstrosity.

At the last, Brielle had been summoned to address the council. Lucian's daughter had given a detailed, if somewhat truculent account of her dealings with the tau, in which she had justified her actions by claiming she had sought all along to bring the aliens to the negotiating table for the benefit of all. Lucian had to admit, Brielle had given an impressive performance, playing the innocent victim to Grand's hostility and the selfless servant of the Imperium in her crippling of the enemy's command and control system that had caused the tau armies to lose coherence during their retreat from Gel'bryn. Most of the council had lapped it up. Lucian was nowhere near so gullible, but propriety was maintained, and his daughter returned to his side.

As Brielle sat back down, Lucian repeated, 'Does the council have any questions?'

Most of the councillors appeared too weary to query anything of Brielle's statement. Lucian was about to call for the motion to dismiss his daughter, when Cardinal Gurney stood.

'I call for a motion of censure,' Gurney scowled. 'For the crime of conspiring with xenos.'

Lucian sighed inwardly, though outwardly he maintained his composure. 'And who will second this motion?'

Gurney looked to the Logistician-General to his right. Ordinarily, Stempf would have toed the line of his council faction. But with the demise of Inquisitor Grand and the settlement of the ceasefire, that faction had to all intents and purposes ceased to exist.

Stempf stared at the black marble table in front of him, suddenly very interested in the lines of deep maroon flashed through its polished surface.

'It appears, cardinal,' said Lucian, 'that none here will support your motion.'

Gurney's eyes flashed with impotent rage, and he sat back down, casting a vengeful glance at his former ally by his side.

Brielle was trying hard to disguise a dirty smirk by fiddling with a lock of plaited hair.

'Then if there are no objections,' Lucian announced, 'I propose this final session of the Damocles Gulf Crusade command council is closed.

'Thank you, gentlemen.'

With a curt gesture, Lucian dismissed the crewmen tending to the sensorium terminals of the observation blister high atop the *Oceanid*'s spine. Turning to his son and his daughter, he spread his arms wide. 'Welcome back,' he grinned, 'the pair of you.'

Brielle and Korvane refused to acknowledge one another, addressing only Lucian. Brielle stepped up to one of the arched, leaded ports and stared out at the mass of activity in Dal'yth Prime's orbit. She muttered something, which Lucian could not quite hear.

'Brielle?' said Lucian.

His daughter turned, and Lucian saw an unfamiliar hint of sadness in her eyes. 'I was saying a prayer,' she said. 'For them.'

Lucian followed her gaze, towards a trio of huge troop transports that hung in formation ten kilometres to the *Oceanid*'s starboard. Each carried an entire regiment of ground troops, and Lucian knew that one might be carrying the noble Rakarshans.

'They're all going to die,' Brielle said flatly.

Korvane grimaced, evidently unconvinced by his stepsister's uncharacteristic show of empathy.

'All of them,' she said with grim conviction. 'And billions more.'

Lucian felt a cold shiver pass up and down the length of his spine, as if Brielle's words were somehow prophetic; as if she were gifted some insight denied to others. He suddenly felt the weight of his own mortality, for the span of his life had been extended beyond the normal measure by the application of rejuve treatments few in the Imperium had access to. As he pictured entire sectors stripped to bare rock by a species of ravening alien abominations, the thought struck him; perhaps the ancient and noble line of the Arcadius would end with him. Who then would remember his deeds and honour his name?

At Lucian's side, his son closed his hand around the ring his father had given him, the ring containing the cipher matrix of the stasis-vault on Terra, where rested the most valuable asset in the dynasty's possession: the Arcadius Warrant of Trade.

Sergeant Sarik was knelt in prayer in the *Nomad*'s chapel. Through an armoured portal wrought in the form of the White Scars lightning-bolt Chapter icon he could see the crusade fleet mustering for war, scores of tenders and service vessels swarming around the wallowing capital ships as crews and supplies were ferried back and forth. Most of the ground forces were already embarked, though it appeared that at least one Brimlock unit would be left behind, from the initial deployment at least.

The chapel represented a small part of Sarik's home world, the pelts of huge Chogoran beasts adorning its walls lending it the aspect of the interior of a chieftain's yurt. Mighty curved horns adorned the walls, many inscribed with the names and the deeds of the warriors who had slain them in glorious battle. In the centre of one wall was mounted a massive, reptilian skull, taken from the mica dragon that Sarik and his fellow scouts Qaja and Kholka had slain together on Luther McIntyre when all three were but neophytes. The scent of rockrose hung heavy in air, the dense smoke drifting upwards from an incense bowl set in the centre of the chapel. Upon the altar beneath the lightning-bolt portal was laid a sacred stone tablet bearing ten thousand-year-old script hewn by the hand of the White Scars' primarch himself, the proud and wild Jaghatai Khan.

Sarik was in the chapel to recite aloud the name of every battle-brother that had fallen in the battle for Dal'yth Prime. Each would be honoured later, he knew, according to the customs of each Chapter represented in the crusade force, but Sarik had been their field commander, and he owed them that much. The tally had been great, for the tau had proven a fearsome, yet ultimately honourable adversary. He felt no ire towards the aliens, and accepted the necessity of the re-deployment to Ultramar. Sarik was a warrior of the Adeptus Astartes, a son of Jaghatai Khan, who was himself a son of the Emperor. His duty was to a higher calling.

As Sarik completed his litany, commending the souls of the fallen to the eternal care of their ancestors, a revelation born of his meditation came over him. Where previously he would have raged impotently at the loss of so many brothers, brooding alone for days on end at the injustice of the galaxy, a new clarity and wisdom now settled upon him. It was as if the script inscribed on the stone tablet before him by his primarch had been written just for him, for they spoke words the meaning of which Sarik had never truly understood though he had read them countless times. In the crucible of the battles fought these last few days, Sarik had been re-forged, like a dulled blade returned gleaming from the hand of the master artificer.

Sarik felt renewed purpose and resolve deep in his heart. Though the tyranids represented a dire threat to the very survival of mankind, they were also the agency by which the champions of the Imperium would come together and find honour and glory beyond measure. Even now, garbled reports were coming in of the terrible enormity of the tyranid invasion. Sarik's battle-brothers in his own and many other Chapters were dying, giving their lives to hold at bay the most devastating incursion the Eastern Fringe had ever witnessed.

Sarik swore, to his primarch and to his Chapter, that he would stand at their side come what may. By his savage pride and the honour scars carved into his weather-beaten face, Sarik vowed that the tyranids would know the wrath of the White Scars, and of all of humanity.

ABOUT THE AUTHOR

Andy Hoare is the author of the Space Marine Battles novel *The Hunt for Voldorius,* as well as *Commissar* and a number of Warhammer and Warhammer 40,000 short stories. He spent many years working in the Games Workshop Design Studio and now writes background and rules for Forge World's Imperial Armour and Horus Heresy books.

YOUR NEXT READ

CASTELLAN
by David Annandale

The Grey Knights are tested as never before when a mighty warp storm tears Imperial space apart. Unless Castellan Crowe and his battle-brothers can bring the escaping daemonic tide under control, mankind will be destroyed by Chaos.

Find this title, and many others, on blacklibrary.com

The causeway of flesh burned before Garran Crowe's eyes.

The Stormravens *Purgation's Sword* and the *Harrower* strafed the end where it met the island of Hive Skoria. Washed by the turgid waves of the ocean of sludge, soaked in the effluent of tens of thousands of years of industry, the bodies ignited. The conflagration spread wide. A wall of flame cut Skoria off from the mainland. The fire rose and fell with the waves. Noxious smoke billowed thousands of feet into the air. Skoria was a phantom, the dark mass of the hive appearing and disappearing behind the firestorm. The last hive of Sandava III to be spared the daemonic incursion was unbowed. The channel between it and the mainland was a flaming moat. The towers looked down on the end of a war.

'This is the final stand of the abominations!' Crowe voxed to his strike force. 'We have them at bay!'

This is no victory! the Black Blade of Antwyr snarled in answer. The voice in Castellan Garran Crowe's head lashed out in rage. ***You struggle in futility***, it warned. ***Your hope burns.***

Crowe heard desperation in the sword's raving. He heard impotence. It was Antwyr that had failed on Sandava III. It was Antwyr's hope that burned. It had failed to break Crowe with despair. He was renewed. At the head of two squads of Purifiers, he was closing in on the shore of the mainland, and he was closing in on the end of the war. Antwyr shrieked, and Crowe plunged it into the body of the fiend of Slaanesh that charged him, gabbling its desperation to pummel with its hooves. Its tail stinger struck over his shoulder at his spine. It failed. The iron halo mounted above his power pack generated a gravitic conversion field that turned the blow away. The stinger shattered against artificer armour whose sanctity had been confirmed by a thousand battlefields. Crowe twisted the blade in the thorax of the fiend. The daemon stumbled forward, impaling itself on the indestructible metal, and falling into the terrible light of Crowe's purity. His righteous anger matched the wrath of the blade. Where he walked, the sombre day of Sandava III blazed with harsh, merciless holiness. The daemon's shape tore open from the thorax, peeling back, disintegrating into ash from the inside out. It issued a last, gargling scream, and then Crowe marched through the swirling cloud of its remains, already swinging the sword to decapitate two more fiends that lunged for him, jaws agape.

The squads marched behind him in two close formations. There was a space between him and the two Knights of the Flame at their heads. There was room for daemons to get between the castellan and his battle-brothers, if they were reckless enough to make the attempt. The few who tried did not fight long. The gap was a needed distance. It diminished the voice of the Blade of Antwyr just enough for the other Purifiers to push its taunting and insinuations into the background and focus on the extermination of the daemons. The war on Sandava III had been a hard one, and a long time for the other Grey Knights to be exposed to Crowe's presence. The burden of Antwyr was his to bear, and never set aside. His grip, the surest prison of all, must forever be on the hilt of the corrupt, corrupting, indestructible relic. By the Emperor's will, his being had been shaped for this task. His brothers were strong in faith and sinew, yet the sword was a spiritual poison, its corrosion so powerful it could erode even their defences.

There was another gap between the Purifiers and the strike force from the First Brotherhood. Two Terminator squads had taken part in the salvation of Sandava III. Beside them rumbled the Land Raider Crusader *Malleus Maleficarum*. Heroes beyond taint, a dozen warriors now who had exterminated a world-wide plague of daemons, they still needed to keep their distance from Crowe.

'*You seem renewed, brother castellan*,' said Drake, a Knight of the Flame, the voice of fellowship reaching across the physical distance between his squad and Crowe. He used a private channel, for Crowe's ears alone.

'I am, brother.'

'*That was no simple victory against the daemon prince at Labos, then.*'

'It was not.'

Hive Labos, a thousand miles west on the mainland, had been the centre of the incursion. There Crowe had destroyed Varangallax. The transformed keep had fallen, the guiding hand of the incursion was no more, and the purification of Sandava III had become a matter of time. Crowe's struggle against Varangallax had also been a personal one. 'The enemy sought to make me despair,' he said to Drake. 'It confronted me with the echoes of our losses on Sandava II.'

'*Old ghosts.*'

'Indeed.'

His spirit had been drained by the decades of being besieged by Antwyr. Varangallax, a monster born from the tragedy of Sandava II, had tried to break him down with visions of the futility of all his struggles. It had failed.

'My burden is my honour,' Crowe said. 'I welcome it.' He welcomed Drake's perception, too. It was a reminder of brotherhood that transcended the isolation that was Crowe's lot. It would make easier the return of that isolation, at the end of this battle.

In a final push to taint the world beyond salvation, the daemons were attempting to reach Skoria. From the ruins of Hive Conatum, less than fifty miles south of the narrows between the mainland and the island of Skoria, the abominations had dragged the bodies of millions of slaughtered civilians. They had thrown the bodies into the viscous sea, and so had created shoals of corpses, building flesh upon flesh until the causeway advanced, a finger of damnation, across the waters.

They had not reached the other shore. The Stormravens were destroying the causeway, filling the air over the channel with the clouds of human debris. They strafed back and forth over the flames, knocking the furthest point of the causeway back and back away from Skoria. Crowe brought up the Purifiers and the strike force of warriors from the First Brotherhood behind the final daemonic horde, closing from the south and west. To the north of the corridor from Conatum to Skoria, the land shot up in jagged, heavily mined peaks. To the south-east, a fault line began as a mile-wide canyon before Conatum, and as the land dipped, became a talon-like inlet a hundred miles long. The daemons' advance had stalled, and now they were trapped. Ahead, they faced an impassable ocean of fire. At their backs came something worse. A relentless force of silvered grey cut them down.

This is something more meaningful than victory, Crowe thought. *It is a cleansing.*